Voyage

Elizabeth Walker

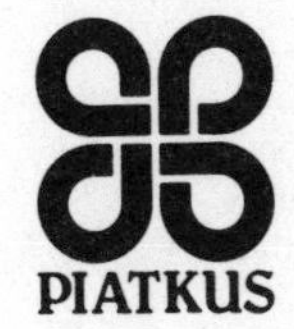

First published in Great Britain in 1987 by
Judy Piatkus (Publishers) Ltd of
5 Windmill Street, London W1

British Library Cataloguing in Publication Data

Walker, Elizabeth
Voyage.
I. Title
823'.914[F] PR6073.A4/

ISBN 0-86188-662-3

Phototypeset in 11/12pt Linotron Times by
Phoenix Photosetting, Chatham
Printed and bound in Great Britain by
Mackays of Chatham Ltd

Voyage

Part One: Harriet

Chapter One

Chandeliers swayed and tinkled as the great ship leaned into the Atlantic swell, parting the waves with calm authority. In the saloon the sound of the engines was no more than an indeterminate hum, easily obscured by the babble of conversation. The motion of the ship could be felt only as a slight pressure against the soles of the feet, countered by a sinking in the stomach that was so far from unpleasant as to be almost enjoyable. This could be anywhere, thought Harriet, wiping a damp palm on her satin skirt. These expensive, confident people could be thronging the floors of any luxury hotel, and in any one of them Harriet would be just as out of place. She should never have come.

Stewards moved between groups, offering drinks and canapés, and as a tray passed her Harriet fielded another drink, adding her empty glass to the pair already behind a potted plant. Someone had stubbed out a cigarette in the plant's dry soil. Its tired leaves needed a drink more than she did, but they weren't going to get it. Harriet gulped icy champagne and wiped her other hand down the side of her dress, staring at the crowds with a fixed and senseless smile.

Everyone seemed to have someone to talk to. They chattered and laughed, tossing their heads and uttering shrill cries and exclamations, the rich, the beautiful, the old. In the midst of all the noise one could distinctly hear the rattle of diamonds on animated wrists and throats, rich old ladies wearing bucketfuls of cash. Occasionally Harriet noticed the odd pop star or daughter of a billionaire, an actor looking more lined or perhaps shorter than he did on celluloid, a gossip column regular scanning the crowd from beneath heavy lids. Charming people, touched by a magic wand and given everything. Useless to wonder why it should be that, born into the same cold world, they were rich and famous while Harriet was nobody.

She shifted from foot to foot in the uncomfortably high-heeled shoes that were too new and too high and too young for her. What was she doing here? Why should she have thought that courage would suddenly come to her, that she would be transformed into the poised and social being that she wished to be? The Harriet who had sat in the corner at the school dance was the same Harriet who cringed against the palm now, watching in trepidation as the officers trawled the room, fishing for just such as her, the social failures. It was like watching skiing, everyone else a downhill racer when she could barely stand on the nursery slope.

'Are you all right, Miss Wyman?'

She jumped. One of the officers, a tall young man with hair already receding from his temples, was gazing down at her anxiously. What had she been doing to single herself out? Why had he noticed her?

'I'm – I'm quite – thank you. Quite all right. Thank you.'

'If you'll forgive my saying so, you look a little flushed.'

'Do I? It is rather hot.' She flushed still more, aware that her foundation, an unsuccessful purchase just before she left home, was caking in lumps around her nose. What must she look like if even he had noticed?

'Shall I introduce you to someone? Mrs. Thorner perhaps, she's from Maryland. A charming lady, very easy to talk to.'

Harriet stared up at him, torn between a desire to escape from her obviously solitary position and a fierce resentment of his pity. For he was pitying her, pitying her gaucheness, her shyness, her ill-fitting dress and streaky make-up.

'I don't want to talk to anyone,' she said, and even to her own ears it sounded childish. 'I mean – I like watching everyone.'

'Do you?' Patent disbelief.

Harriet tipped back her head and gave him a haughty stare, willing him to believe that she was a philosophy lecturer, an artist, perhaps even a wealthy recluse. And besides, was she so desperate that she wanted to join in any of the conversations around her? Just listen to them: 'Hi, Jeannie Goldbloom, from Wyoming. Don't tell me you're American because I simply won't believe you! Australian? Well, how thrilling!' Variations on the theme could be heard all around the room, and if Harriet did meet the charming Mrs. Thorner what could she say? Harriet Wyman, from Manchester. Spinster. No money, no looks, not even an interesting family tree to commend her. She gulped the rest of her champagne.

'I'll get you another drink.' The officer was looking uncomfortable. Perhaps it was catching.

She waited while he summoned a steward with a practised flick of a finger and gestured for Harriet to be offered the tray. She took a drink and sipped it. Champagne was quite nice once you got used to the bubbles. If you drank enough it made embarrassment seem much less painful.

'Do you like doing this?' she asked airily. 'Having to talk to people, I mean. People like me. People you don't really want to talk to?'

'But I do want to talk to them,' said the officer insincerely. 'I want to talk to you – ' His smile was slipping. His eyes slid away to the view over her shoulder.

'What about?'

'Well – about the ship, and New York, all sorts of things. Look, I will introduce you to Mrs. Thorner – '

'No! I mean – I'm all right. Really.'

He cleared his throat. 'Well, I suppose I must circulate. We must talk again.'

He abandoned her, no doubt with relief. She didn't understand small talk, she never had. Yet she would very much like to know what he really thought of this floating circus, with its strange and noisy creatures. The competition winners, for instance, all in tourist class as a reward for victory in some nationwide bingo game. Needless to say they were not invited to the captain's cocktail party but they thronged the corridors and walkways, seemingly always drunk, always sweating, and with an inexhaustible supply of funny hats and double entendres. What did the officers make of them? Were they light relief with their enthusiastic participation in everything from deck games to massage, or were they seen as an unfortunate lowering of the tone? Harriet couldn't herself decide, having that morning been grabbed by a paunchy man with a key down his trousers yelling at her to help him get it out, quick. It was all part of some game or other. Harriet went scarlet but everyone laughed. 'Only a bit of fun, love,' said the man, and afterwards she thought it might have been. She never knew how to cope with things like that somehow, anymore than she could cope with things like this.

Her dress was becoming clammy with sweat and looking round the room she could see that, as she had suspected, fake off-white satin had been a mistake. It had been too tight from the start, but she had been sure she would lose the odd pound or two. She hadn't. And expensive as it had seemed when she bought it, against the silks and laces all around her the dress looked cheap and nasty. The neck didn't seem to fit properly either and she pulled at it, consoling herself with spotting other dresses which although no doubt vastly expensive were every bit as unsuitable. There was a scarlet tulle tent striving to obscure a lady twice as wide as she was high, and a primrose yellow taffeta creation complete with rosebuds that would have looked slightly odd on a six year old let alone the lady unwise enough to wear it with a tiara, two bracelets and a choker.

Harriet began to feel uncomfortable about her own earrings. Did they make her look like a Christmas tree? She was never sure what she looked like, that was the trouble, she could never know if her classic look was only timid, or her adventurous moments ridiculous. Yet she was sure that her dirty-white fake satin too tight dress was a disaster. She would abandon this awful party, go back to her cabin, take it off and cut it up into shreds.

She turned in a rush, staggering on her heels. A steadying hand caught her elbow.

'It's all right, we're not sinking yet.'

Harriet blushed scarlet, as she always did. Despite all her mother had said she had never grown out of it, any more than her puppy fat. 'Excuse me. I must go, I really must.'

The square, stocky man grinned at her, his teeth very white against weatherbeaten skin. He did not let go of her elbow. 'But I've only just got here! And you are the only decent-looking unattached girl under seventy in the room, so don't rush off and leave me. Andrew Jakes.'

Harriet squirmed to release her elbow but he gripped it, past politeness. Perhaps he was drunk. She was certain that she was, hot and cold by turns. 'I've got to go,' she insisted.

'Why?'

'Because – because I'm wearing the wrong things,' she blurted. 'I didn't realise what it would be like. I haven't been on a cruise before and I've got to take my earrings off.'

The man squinted at her earrings. 'They falling apart or something? Look all right to me.'

They were her mother's earrings, old diamonds in a dull setting. 'They don't look right,' she said feebly.

The man gave her a considering look. She blushed again. 'I admit they're not the world's greatest,' he said, 'but I shouldn't think anyone will notice. Not when we can all stare at this lot. I mean, just look at them!'

She gulped but obediently swivelled her head to scan the room. This time it did look different. There was the arty duke of somewhere, known to be homosexual, sporting a green velvet dinner jacket, red and white striped waistcoat across his considerable paunch and a fob watch. Laughing, her mouth four inches wide, was a television actress whose neckline descended to her navel, her undoubtedly scrawny breasts restrained by shoulderstraps.

'Now if you wore that they'd look at you,' said Jakes.

'I couldn't!' said Harriet.

He glanced at her considerable bosom wedged shapelessly into the unflattering dress. 'No, you couldn't, there's far too much of you. Where the hell is the booze around here?' He lifted a hand and yelled 'Oi!' with the result that a steward appeared like the genie of the lamp, proffering glasses. Jakes took four, stacking them behind the plant. 'Someone's been having quite a little party already,' he commented, and grinned at Harriet. His eyes were clear grey, and seemed to be on a slightly lower level than her own. Damn these ridiculous high heels!

She smiled back, cautiously. 'I don't often go to parties,' she confessed.

'I can tell that. Bingo winner are you? Don't worry, I won't have you slung out. I don't suppose tourist class is your scene right now either. They're passing matchboxes from nose to nose – the winner gets to drink a pint in ten seconds – and a fat woman wants to strip but her husband won't let her. I told him he was being small-minded but he wouldn't change his mind. Pity.'

Mortified, Harriet turned away. 'I am not a Bingo winner,' she said stiffly, 'and I will go now. My feet ache.'

'Oh God, don't go. I don't know what's the matter with me tonight, I can't please anyone. Look, I know this cruise is deadly but we real people have got to stick together while the androids cavort. Of course you don't play Bingo, I can tell that from your earrings.'

Harriet felt herself grin. 'How can you tell?'

'Old lady in Bath earrings.'

'They're my mother's actually,' she said.

'Oh, yes? Travelling with you, is she?'

'No. She's – not very well at the moment.' Was she imagining it or was he watching her with an interest that was anything but casual? She wished he wouldn't, it made her skin prickle. Like the motion of the ship, if it went on long enough she might almost enjoy it.

'Worrying when they're ill,' said Jakes. 'Does she have someone to look after her?'

'Oh, yes,' said Harriet quickly. 'I mean, it's a very big house – she'd have to. Full-time nursing care.' She took a large gulp of champagne. Her mind constructed an attractive scene: her mother in a lace peignoir, rapping on the polished floor with an ebony cane. A nurse came running, crisp white cap askew. Harriet looked at the man beside her. Truth had no place here. 'I had to get away for a while,' she confided. 'What with the garden and the dogs – and old people can be so demanding. I wondered where I should go and New York sounded so exciting. Then when the travel agent suggested going by sea, I thought – '

'It would be fun,' finished Jakes for her. 'We all make mistakes. Perhaps it is fun if you're eighty. Your mum would have loved it.'

'What are you doing here?' asked Harriet, suppressing a nervous giggle. Impossible as it had seemed five minutes before she was enjoying herself, and Andrew Jakes seemed to be too. She wished she could take her shoes off and stop looking down at him.

'I'm a sailor,' said Jakes.

'But – you don't sail this! You start it up and point it.'

He nodded. 'Couldn't agree more. Bloody thing's as much use as a vibrator in a nunnery. It's a long story. There's this guy owns a yacht – you've probably seen him, grey-haired bloke with a Rolex and a monster ego – and he wants me to see if I can sort it out for him. New, you see, and built in three different yards. You might as well try to *knit* a decent tub. It's got a lot of problems, and from the sound of it it's rigged wrong. Dog's dinner of a boat. Well, I was in Blighty and he came hot foot to find me. "Jake", he says, "I need you, only you can save me." I was bloody flattered, except that now I realise he'd asked everyone else and they wouldn't touch it with a barge pole. He added this trip as an extra little perk, and like the pillock I am I accepted. Didn't realise I was supposed to chat up his wife and impress all his ancient sailing buddies, not one of whom has been to sea in anything smaller than the *Ark Royal*. My good girl – by the way, what's your name?'

'Harriet. Harriet Wyman.'

'Just call me Jake. Anyway, Harriet, I saw you looking just as miserable as me and I thought, "Let's go talk to Harriet."'

She laughed shrilly and tried to wipe her damp hands on her skirt again. He scowled at her. 'Don't do that, you're ruining it. If you're hot, we'll go and get a breath of air.'

'All right,' said Harriet meekly.

The passageway outside the saloon was blessedly cool, but Jake propelled her up and down stairs, through doors and corridors, until at last they stepped out on a deck. Far below were the waves while above stretched the dark bulk of the superstructure of the ship. The lights shone out over black water, and the moon hung in the sky as if put there to provide the passengers with a view. Tears pricked Harriet's eyes. This was just as she had imagined it, perhaps better. Standing here, looking out, you could feel that the ship was indeed the world's centre. Perhaps life could offer you what you wanted.

'Cool enough for you?' Jake was standing very close behind her.

'Yes, thank you,' murmured Harriet. She looked along the deck. In the shadows stood the actress and a man. He was nuzzling the scrawny breasts while she tossed her head and uttered little cries.

'Hoping to win a bloody Oscar,' said Jake, and squeezed Harriet's plump bottom.

She said breathlessly, 'What are you doing?'

'What do you think? How old are you, Harriet?'

'Twenty-six.'

'Really?' You dress like a hundred and eight. Still, twenty-six is old enough to enjoy having your fanny squeezed.' He pressed himself against her back and she felt something hard. Surely he couldn't – she glanced along the deck. The actress was writhing, her hand at the man's crotch. Jake's hips pushed insistently against Harriet.

'Stop it,' she said, trying to wriggle away. She wasn't so far gone that she couldn't tell when she was being used.

'What?' He pushed again, all the time watching the couple further along. Their groaning and gasping was becoming more and more abandoned. Suddenly a door opened and the deck was flooded with light. A rapid scramble and the couple were gone.

'So that's how she hopes to get on in New York,' said Jake thoughtfully.

'Do you know her?' asked Harriet coldly, trying to squeeze out from between Jake and the rail.

'Met her first night out.'

Harriet felt a pang. He'd tried everyone before he started on her. 'I think I'd like a drink,' she said.

'Good idea. Come down to my cabin, I've got some booze. Gin and something.'

'I don't drink gin.'

'About time you did then. Come on, Harriet. No need to stand there quivering all night.'

At home she had spent many nights lying awake imagining what the ship would be like. One picture that continually repeated itself was that of a cabin, a suave, expert seducer, and Harriet. Usually, though not always, she resisted him, but she was always either sure of herself and in control or swept away on a tide of passion. This seemed very different. She wasn't even sure if Jake meant to seduce her.

'Sit down,' he said, waving airily at the bed. 'Gin and orange, you'll like that.'

'What will you have?'

'Pink. Move up, there's a good girl. Nice clear skin you've got, Harriet. You've been living a clean life, I can tell. Twenty-six years of purity. Where d'you come from?'

'Manchester,' she said on a hiccup. She couldn't get the hiccups, not now.

'Never been to the place. Rains a lot, doesn't it? Look, Harriet, shall I tell you a secret?'

She fought with a rising hiccup and swallowed some more of the sticky drink in her glass. 'Yes, please.'

'Well – it's this. I'm in a bit of a spot. It isn't permanent or anything, it's just for tonight. Seen the games room on board? All green suede and leather chairs, very plush. I was in a game of cards there and I lost a bit more than I intended. You know how it is – well, perhaps you don't. Think of it as another game of draughts with your old mum. It isn't important, but I would like to settle up before morning, and of course the bank's not open at this time of night. Gentlemen don't leave their debts outstanding, gives the foreigners a bad impression. So how about it, Harriet?'

'How about – hic – what?'

'Dishing it up.' She stared at him blankly, still hiccupping, and he ran a hand through his springy dark hair. 'Oh, Christ, you must know what I mean. I'm asking you to lend me some money.'

Harriet stared at him. She knew now exactly why he had bothered with her. 'Did you want a lot?' she asked cautiously.

'No, only a few quid, and only till the morning. Come on, Harriet, live a little. I'll give you a game of quoits in the morning. Tell you what, I'll pay you back over lunch tomorrow, on the Promenade Deck.'

She could wear her blue frock. People would see her having lunch with this man, this exciting, terrifying man. She would be able to remember it for years, lunching on the Promenade Deck with an attractive man, wearing her new blue dress. It wasn't a lot of money, it wasn't important. 'You'll have to come to my cabin,' she said weakly.

Jake blew at the nondescript strands of straight brown hair covering her ear. She could smell him, hot and dangerous. 'What a sweet girl you are,' he purred. 'What a pretty girl you are, Harriet.'

As she walked to her cabin the floor seemed to undulate. 'The ship's in a storm,' she said. 'It'll be too windy on the Promenade Deck.'

'Then we'll go to the Verandah Grill,' said Jake, wildy naming the premier à la carte restaurant on board. He steered her to a straight course and propped her against the wall outside her cabin.

'My blue dress isn't grand enough,' said Harriet.

'Come as you are,' said Jake, fumbling in her bag for her key. He found it and unlocked the cabin. 'In you go, Harriet, this is no time to go to sleep. Where's the money then? What a good girl you are.' She waved vaguely at her dressing case and flopped down on the bed. Jake went to the case and rummaged through it.

The cash was beneath the jumble of bottles and belts. He stood blinking at the two piles of notes in his hands. She must be rich to carry this much money. He'd known the instant he saw her that she was worth a bit. Travelling first class, shy, dowdy, you could tell daddy had left her a mint. Dollars and pounds, and the case wasn't even locked. No doubt the traveller's cheques were with the purser.

He turned to see Harriet sitting on the bed staring owlishly at him. In a moment of joyous gratitude he took her face in his hands and kissed her hard on the mouth. 'You wonderful girl,' he said thickly. 'See you tomorrow.'

The door closed with a click. Still sitting on the bed, Harriet put her hand to her lips.

Chapter Two

Harriet woke feeling sick. She lay still for a few ghastly seconds then flung out of bed into the bathroom. As she hung over the bowl the headache started, piledriving its way through her skull. I'm dying, she thought, soon I shall be dead, but it won't matter because of last night. At last something happened to me.

She staggered back to bed and sank gratefully on to the pillows. Thank God the ship had stopped rolling about. Last night it had been hard to stand up. In a moment, when her head stopped aching, she would think about last night and savour every minute. She lay in an uneasy doze, now and then racked by shivers.

There was a knock on the door. She clutched her sheets nervously and said nothing, but the knock came again. 'Come in,' she croaked, and pulled herself up a little as the stewardess entered with a tray of tea. A divorcee, slightly raddled by life at sea, she cast a practised eye over Harriet.

'Oh, dear me,' she said. 'I'll bring you something. Did you enjoy it, dear, that's the main thing?'

'I think so,' whispered Harriet. 'I met this man – '

The stewardess lifted an eyebrow. She had heard that her charge in 431 had fallen foul of Black Jake and had assembled some words of warning. She tended to the tray first. 'Did you, dear? Sit up and have some tea, you'll feel better.'

'He was called Jake. He was awfully nice – '

The stewardess grunted noncommittally. Surely Harriet had not passed from introduction to seduction in one short evening? She would have said Miss Wyman was far too plain and a great deal too staid, but people often did lose their heads on cruises. 'Bit of a rover that one, I hear,' she said casually. 'He's very well-known in the Caribbean, we saw quite a bit of him when we cruised there last year. You won't believe what they call him – Black Jake the Pirate, of all things.'

Harriet sipped at her tea. It scalded a trail right down to her stomach. 'Why do they call him that? He was nice.'

'Was he? Sit up, dear, I'll plump your pillows. I suppose it's just a name, but he is a drifter. Never has any money and a different girl every week. But they do say he can sail – he was in the Olympic team once but they dropped him. I gather he wouldn't do as he was told.'

A vague worm of disquiet was wriggling in Harriet's brain. Gradually the full picture of last night was coming back to her. 'But he does have some money, doesn't he? Otherwise he wouldn't be here?'

'I don't know how he's here, dear, but I imagine he's bumming a ride with Mr. Derekson, he's in his party.' She shot a sharp look at Harriet. 'You didn't lend him any money, did you, dear? Take it from me, it wouldn't be sensible.'

On a reflex, Harriet shook her head, 'No. No, I didn't.'

'Well, then, no harm done is there? I'll bring you that drink and you'll feel much better in an hour or so. Don't want to spoil your trip now, do we?'

Harriet's wan smile remained fixed till the stewardess was gone. She couldn't really have given him the money. If she got up and looked in her dressing case it would all still be there, safe and sound. She was careful with money, frugal even, husbanding the pennies and the pounds each week to pay the electricity, the gas, the water rates. Harriet Wyman was too old and too sensible to lend money to a man she met at a party, and besides, what did the stewardess know about him?

A great deal more than I do, thought Harriet. She felt cold suddenly, cold and rather frightened. She should have told the stewardess, but she couldn't bear to look such a fool. And besides, he had said he'd pay it back.

It was lunchtime before she had the strength to rouse herself. All morning she had lain waiting for him to come to her cabin, expecting him to send the steward with a message. Eventually she crawled out of bed and went to her dressing case. There sat her passport, in solitary state. So she *had* given him the money. All of it. For a while she sat on the floor, staring at the space where the money should be, but at last it occurred to her that if she did not get up the stewardess would come back and might question her. She couldn't admit to being that much of a fool.

Moving like an automaton, she went through to the bathroom and showered. Her flesh cringed at the assault yet she rubbed its spongy folds as if determined to wash away last night and its stupidities. Then she put on her blue dress, blindly fastening the buttons, dragged a brush through her hair and went to look for Jake.

She couldn't remember which cabin he was in and had to ask, blushing, at the purser's office. 'He borrowed something – I wanted it back,' she confided, realising too late that it would have been far more sensible to make no explanation at all.

'364, madam,' said the purser, smiling with what Harriet interpreted as knowing scorn. She blushed still more, rousing in the purser's bored mind a vision of wild sexuality beneath that unpromising exterior. After all, cruises did have strange effects on people . . .

Harriet found 364 quite easily, but there were people about, talking and making arrangements. She walked past three times, earning herself surprised looks from a group that saw all three attempts, and at last, as they moved off, knocked on the door. There was no reply. She knocked again louder, then much louder, finally hammering on it. 'Let me in! Jake, let me in!' At last, when she was breathless, she heard a long, painful groan from within. Bumps and thumps, and finally the door opened a crack. Jack peered out at her, his grey eyes bleary. 'Oh God, go away.'

'Let me in, I've got to talk to you.'

'Later. Go away, I'm dying.' He made as if to shut the door, but Harriet flung herself desperately against it. Taken by surprise Jake fell backwards and sprawled across the bed while Harriet fell to her knees inside the cabin. She gazed up at him like a praying nun. 'I've got to talk to you,' she said pleadingly.

He rolled back on the bed. He was wearing only his underpants, she saw, and his body was covered in short, black hair, thickening into curls on his lower belly and thighs. She gained an impression of close-coupled strength allied to total disinterest. 'I've got one hell of a hangover and I don't want to talk,' he growled. 'Just bugger off, will you? I'll see you tomorrow.'

'But we get there tomorrow,' moaned Harriet. 'And I must have my money. Do get up, Jake. I'll come with you to the bank. If you don't get up they'll shut, and I've got to have my money.'

The grey eyes scanned her anxious face, then closed. He pillowed his head on his hand. 'Don't know what you're so worried about. Wasn't much.'

'Well – yes, I know it wasn't, but I want it back. You promised.'

'See about it in an hour or so, will that do? Look, I didn't get to bed till half-past five. Do me a favour and piss off.'

'What were you doing till then?' asked Harriet shrilly. She got up and stood over him, almost prepared to hit him.

'Gambling,' said Jake flatly. 'And I lost, so piss off for a bit. I said I'd pay you back.'

Relief made Harriet's face glow. 'You will, won't you? Because I know it isn't a lot of money, not when you see what things cost on board, but to me it's a lot. An awful lot.'

'Oh, hearts and flowers,' said Jake. 'That's the rich for you – hang on to every last farthing, even when they've got millions.'

'But – I haven't got millions,' said Harriet, confused. 'Jake, you will pay me back, won't you? Today?'

'Look, I bloody said I would, didn't I? Now just piss off, woman. Go and lie down or something, you look worse than I feel. Go on, get lost.' He pulled a pillow over his head and ignored her.

Harriet went. At least he had said he would pay her back. She'd come back this afternoon, when he was feeling better. Wandering out into the corridor, she thought of lunch and discarded the idea. She was too tense to be hungry. Instead she walked the passageways of the ship, going this way and that, lost and bewildered. Eventually she came to the games room, her way barred by a heavy door in studded green baize. She had never dared to open it before but now she did, only a crack at first then flinging it wide as she realised there was no-one inside.

The room had no portholes, and was lit entirely by lights swinging low over the baize gaming tables. The walls were floor to ceiling green suede, the furniture studded green leather. It was a small room, and the decor rendered it almost claustrophobic. Dark wood cupboards stood to one side and when she opened them she found unopened packs of cards, a chess set, dice in a leather cup. It was all so formal that she found it hard to believe it was possible to play for money in here. The captain wouldn't allow it, surely. So what had Jake done with her cash?

The door opened behind her and Harriet started guiltily. It was an officer, looking at her enquiringly. 'Can I help you?' he asked accusingly. 'This room is reserved for first-class passengers.'

Harriet pulled at her crumpled skirt, knowing she looked dreadful. Two of her buttons were done up wrong and her hair was a bush. 'I am first class,' she said stiffly. 'I was curious, that's all. Do they really play for money? Someone said they did.'

'They do indeed,' said the officer, unbending. 'Especially on the Atlantic crossing, we have quite a school going. A very great deal of money can be lost in here, I assure you.'

Harriet nodded and made for the door. The officer held it for her and watched as she went out. If she wasn't careful they'd start thinking she was batty. In fact, if they found out what she'd done they'd be sure of it!

She went back to her cabin but couldn't rest. She stood for a while staring at her face in the mirror: brown eyes with nondescript lashes, snub nose with a bend in it, small, jutting chin. Today her skin looked lifeless and blotchy. Her hair, cut short to keep it tidy on the cruise, stuck up unbecomingly. How could she have thought Jake liked her? How could she have been flattered?

At last she went back to his cabin and knocked on the door. There was no reply. She knocked harder, and harder still, but no-one answered. He must be out, he wouldn't lie in there and not say anything. She began to search the ship, discovering obscure bars and discos where people gathered happily. He didn't seem to be in first or second class.

Suddenly she remembered that last night he had joined the Bingo winners in tourist class for a time. He might be there again. Her tired feet flew down the passages, up and down stairs, sometimes racing up steps as the ship went down, sometimes pressed into each flight as the vessel swung up on a wave. Even before she reached the tourist dining-room she could hear the singing:

'Roll me over in the clover,
Roll me over, lay me down and do it again.'

If she wanted to find Jake she'd have to brave the Bingo winners. Desperation drove her on.

Jake sipped at his beer and joined in the chorus. His headache was subsiding into a dull ache, lulled by the thought that in a mere twenty-four hours he would escape this hell on water and get back to the real world. God, what a trip. From the first Derekson had been after him, demanding detailed notes on what he intended to do with his boat. As if Jake could tell before he saw it! Sea trials were sea trials, but when you were faced with some hybrid plastic tea chest incorporating everybody's wilder notions you couldn't tell what might be necessary. He'd been unwise enough to hint that it might be necessary to restep the mast, which hadn't gone down well. From that time on it had been nag, nag, nag. Did he realise how long this boat had been in the making, how much it had cost? Hell, Derekson could afford it, and he could afford to pay Jake while they travelled to New York. Derekson knew he was skint. He knew that was why Jake was prepared to waste time making a seaworthy silk purse out of a leaky pig's ear. Yet he hadn't stumped up, which was why Jake was now being pursued round this gin palace by a dowdy woman who could well afford to lose a bit. Mother lived in a stately home, by the sound of it. She wasn't short.

Jake took another swig of his beer. He would have preferred

scotch, but someone else was buying and he couldn't return the compliment. Why the hell had he joined that game anyway? He could have gone to bed and woken up fresh as a daisy, instead of which he felt like chewed string and had to cower down here hoping Harriet Wyman didn't turn up. Funny creature. He found it hard to believe she hadn't known he couldn't pay it back. She couldn't be that stupid. A vision of her this morning kneeling white-faced on his cabin floor, rose before him. Surely she could have shown a little pride. She'd looked terrible. It was only money, for God's sake.

'And this is number three and she's sitting on my knee,
Roll me over lay me down and do it again. . . .'

The fat lady was dancing again. She'd get her clothes off before the trip was over, he was sure of it, though just at the moment he wasn't convinced his stomach could stand the shock. His head was aching something terrible and if it wasn't for Harriet he'd go back to his cabin and to bed. He gazed longingly towards the door, and standing there, gazing longingly at him, was Harriet.

She came slowly across the floor towards him, almost colliding with the fat lady who was doing the hokey cokey by herself. She looked as if she had been crying.

'Hello,' said Jake. 'Have a seat.'

'Thanks.' She sat down next to him as the song roared to its climax.

'Now this is number ten and we'll do it all again,
Roll me over lay me down and do it again – '

'You don't look too happy,' said Jake. 'I said I'd pay you back.'

'And you're skulking down here. You haven't got it, have you?'

'Oh, look – I will have it. I've just got to do this job. I'm sorry you didn't understand, I didn't force you to give it to me. I'll owe it to you. I always pay back loans in the end.' To men, he added silently. It always seemed rather different with women.

'I need the money now,' said Harriet in a desperate whisper.

'Come off it, you can always cash a few traveller's cheques. Damned dangerous carrying too much cash around anyway, you can fall prey to conmen like me. Give me your address and I'll send it on to you in a few months' time, it's the best I can do.'

Harriet stared at him, licking at dry lips. 'But I haven't got any traveller's cheques. That was all I had, everything. I brought it like that because – well, I came in a rush, and when my father was alive he always said you couldn't beat cash and I'd left it too late at the bank. When I went in to ask they said it would be weeks. I wasn't thinking straight, it was the drink and everything. I can't get home without that money.' She sniffed, fighting tears.

'For Christ's sake, spare me the sob story,' said Jake impatiently. 'You've got your return ticket, surely? Cable the old mum in the stately home. She can flog a Rembrandt or two.'

Harriet blew her nose furiously. 'She isn't in a stately home – or rather she is, but it's for senile old ladies. We don't have any Rembrandts. All I had was what you lost in that beastly little room last night. And I can't get home because I was flying back and they said it would be cheapest if I bought a standby ticket in New York – ' Her voice rose hysterically.

'Shhhh!' hissed Jake. 'Don't tell everyone. Come back to my cabin and drink some gin. I think you need it.'

They plodded silently back through the ship. Every now and then Harriet sobbed into a tattered tissue, until at last Jake gave her his handkerchief. It was covered in brown whisky stains but she took it and used it. When they reached his cabin he poured them both a gin, and they sat side by side on the bed sipping it.

'You are a bloody stupid woman,' he said at last. 'You don't look it but you are. They shouldn't allow you out on your own.'

'I didn't know the world was full of conmen,' sniffed Harriet. 'Or at least, I didn't think I'd meet one at the captain's cocktail party. I thought you were rich.'

'Like I said, you're stupid. Can't you tell a secondhand suit when you see one?'

'Well, can't you tell a cheap dress, for that matter? All you saw was the earrings.'

He brightened. 'There you are, that's it! Flog the earrings.'

Harriet withered him with a look. 'They're worth about fifty quid.'

'Better than a kick in the teeth. Look, it's not my fault you're stupid with money, you can't blame me.'

'Of course I blame you, who else is there? And I'm going to tell the captain. I'm going to tell everyone, even Mr. whatever he's called that's giving you the job. Then they'll all know what sort of a man you are, stealing people's money. You're a thief, a horrible, mean thief, and you don't care what happens to people, you just take all they've got and – oh!'

Jake reached out a foot and pushed her off the bed. Her gin and orange rose up and descended all over the front of her dress.

'Oh, God, I'm sorry,' muttered Jake, reining in his temper. Two tears rolled down Harriet's cheeks. 'Will you stop snivelling!' he snarled. 'And you can tell who you sodding well like, it won't bring back that money. You're going to have to sort yourself out, try the British Embassy or something. Try a home for the congenitally stupid! But for now, just stop being a spaniel and leave me alone!'

He flung himself off the bed and into the bathroom, slamming the door behind him. There was the sound of the shower starting to run. After a while Harriet crawled to her feet, opened the door and went out.

Chapter Three

Afterwards, trying to reconstruct the events of that last day, she could never be sure if she had done things at all or simply imagined them. If an event had taken place, and she was certain that it had, then its time and significance were lost to her. She found herself in a hazy dream, without clear thoughts or any sense of reality, and the dreamlike quality of the hours seemed to be enhanced by the attitudes of others. No-one spoke to her; no-one addressed her with even the most trivial acknowledgment of her presence. She went on drifting about the ship as if invisible, watching the frenetic enjoyment all around. There was a sense of expectancy in the air and in this at least she shared, although others were merely intending to cram as much fun as possible into the last few hours before docking. Harriet was counting the minutes before her execution.

Afterwards, there was an image in her mind of the forward lounge, perched high above the waves. She had gone there and looked out over the sea, mackerel-backed and heaving, towards the dark smudge of land on the horizon. Everything seemed remote and unreal as she stood in the warm, food-scented air and looked across waves topped white with running spray. In that moment, watching the seabirds dip and wheel around the great liner, she felt she was witnessing the truth about her life. She stood enclosed, walled in, and outside was the world.

Desolation come flooding in, welling like blood from somewhere small and painfully tender, deep inside. Suddenly there was nothing she wanted more than to leave it all, escape. But however hard she hammered on these glass windows, however violently she threw herself against fate, she could never break through to that place where others lived and breathed and were happy.

Although beyond hunger she turned up on time for dinner that evening. She wanted to see Jake, because he alone seemed to give her a sense of her own reality. He alone knew what was happening to her. But he wasn't there. Sitting beside his empty place was Derekson, a man with more money than Harriet could imagine, who would spend more on shoes than she had lost. He was tall, plump, old, and had that indefinable air of authority that went with success and riches. All the men in first class had it, with the result that there could never be any queues since everyone was convinced they should be first. No wonder the crew were so excessively unctuous, thought Harriet, picking at some highly coloured but essentially bland creation on her plate.

Her neighbour, Mrs. Benowitz, raised a thin eyebrow. After three days of sustained mealtime proximity she had at last decided to notice Harriet. 'Seasick!' she declared triumphantly. 'I could tell you hadn't the stomach for it. You should have been sailing last fall. I was the only one at breakfast for a week, and even the steward turned green when I asked for bacon.'

Harriet stared glumly at her plate, but Mrs. Benowitz needed no encouragement. 'You need a good, thick stomach lining, and I of course inherited mine from Grandpa Daley who was sailing master of the *Buckskin*. That was the vessel that held the record for the fastest passage from Hawaii to San Francisco, although he lost it a week later. Ill health prevented its recapture. I have inherited his constitution and – ' 'I don't know anything about boats,' said Harriet jerkily. 'I've never been on one before and I shall never go on one again. It – it isn't something I like to do.'

'Land-based ancestors,' said Mrs. Benowitz with a nod of her solid perm. 'You can never hide from it.' She turned haughtily to her other neighbour, an Austrian with a hearing aid that appeared to be impervious to Mrs. Benowitz. He absorbed her monologue with the tranquillity of a man in tune with his food and his thoughts. Harriet stared mournfully across at the Derekson table.

Mr. Derekson seemed to be in a state of irritation, missing no opportunity to snap at his wife. Now and then the other men in his party made some comment with which he sombrely agreed or pointedly ignored. I can't talk to him, thought Harriet. He's annoyed already, and to add to it will achieve nothing at all. He would believe whatever Jake told him before he listened to her, and in none of her imaginings could she see this grim-faced individual restoring her lost cash.

As for his wife, she had given up conversation and was stolidly munching the food. Her face was wrinkle-free and expressionless, like a ping pong ball, Harriet observed, unaware that she was witnessing a bad facelift. The woman could be kindness itself and no-one would know.

All at once the noise of forks on plates, the hum of conversation, began to swell in her head. It came at her in waves, rising to a roar, only to recede to a far-off buzz like a swarm of wasps. Fear seemed to choke her, every breath an effort. Panic-stricken, she sucked air into her lungs and thought she might be sick. That was a humiliation she could not face.

'Excuse me. I must – not well,' she muttered, pushing herself to her feet.

'What did I tell you?' said Mrs. Benowitz triumphantly. 'Hasn't got the stomach for it.'

Harriet stumbled into the comparative quiet of the passage. She felt very sick now, and cold and frightened. But she couldn't stay here, with stewards passing constantly to and fro. She wore last night's shoes, because they were all that she had for evening, and tonight they seemed higher and more uncomfortable than ever. Staggering a little, like a drunk, she went in search of one of the ship's many bars.

The shipboard combing at the door almost brought her down, and in saving herself she cracked the heel of her shoe. She felt stupid, hobbling in on a wobbling shoe, but there was no-one in the bar, not even a waiter. Fortunately it was one of the more intimate drinking dens on board ship, with banquettes arranged in pairs. Feet throbbing, she slid on to the cold leather, at last kicking off her shoes. The pleasure was so intense she could almost taste it. Odd that she should be capable of such elation in one direction when she was sunk in gloom in the other, she thought vaguely. Perhaps a mind could only take so much fear before it seized the chance to register on an unused scale. Clasping her hands violently together she screwed up her face in visible effort, forcing herself to think through the situation she was in. She had no money and no contacts. She wouldn't even be able to settle her drinks bill on board ship, unless they accepted baggage in lieu. They might, of course. But after that, what happened to people arriving destitute in New York? Nothing pleasant, that was certain. The authorities might even send her to some horrible women's prison while they investigated her background. Harriet closed her eyes and shuddered. It was all Jake's fault, and he was going off to his job without any thought at all for what was to happen to her. The worst part, the thing that really enraged her, was that he had somehow contrived to make it seem all her own fault. He even made her feel guilty for bothering him about it.

'Madam?' The waiter, who had been taking the opportunity to have a cigarette behind the scenes, suddenly appeared beside her.

'I'm waiting for someone,' said Harriet hurriedly.

'Of course.' He moved away to another banquette where someone else must be sitting, although they were hidden from view. There was the sound of a man's voice. Then, as she watched, a man's hand with thick squared fingers gestured and then disappeared again. Jake! It had to be Jake. As the waiter retreated behind the bar, Harriet swallowed and rose to her feet.

'Hello.'

He had been making notes on a pad heavily criss-crossed with lines and calculations. As he saw her his teeth came together with an audible click.

'You don't go away, do you?' he said.

'Nowhere to go.' She sat down opposite him and silence fell.

'At least you're not crying,' he said at last.

'I'm saving it for tomorrow. What will they do with me, do you think? Will they send me to prison?'

He looked taken aback. 'Christ, I don't know. Do they send people to prison for being skint?'

'I've no idea. It just seemed they might. I mean, what else can they do with me? I can't even pay my bill on the ship.'

He sighed and ran a hand through coarse, wiry hair. 'There must be someone you can turn to. What the hell were you doing bringing everything on a cruise like this? What were you hoping to get from it?'

Harriet shrugged. 'I think I wanted a taste of life,' she said slowly. 'Only I didn't know it would taste so horrid.'

Jake ignored her philosophy. 'Borrow from someone,' he insisted. 'You must work. What about your boss?'

She shook her head. 'I don't work. I was looking after my mother till she went into the home.'

'You should have joined her, if you ask me. Please, stop looking so bloody miserable. It isn't the disaster you think it is. Everybody's hard up sometime, unless you're Derekson, of course. You'd think he'd be a bit more liberal with it, really.' Harriet hardly seemed to be listening. Jake sighed. 'Look, I'll try and help you out. Get your final account early tomorrow and I'll pass it in to Derekson. I'll swing it somehow. Then at least you can get off the ship.'

'What happens after that?' asked Harriet bleakly. She had a sudden vision of herself standing on the dockside, without even the fare for a taxi. When she contemplated that scene Jake almost looked like a friend. A tentative smile hovered around her mouth.

'You'll have to fend for yourself,' he snapped. His irritation was palpable. He shifted in his seat as if longing to get up and leave and never see her again. To him she was a gullible, wingeing nuisance.

Before she could suppress them, tears welled up in Harriet's eyes again. She mumbled something and got up, blindly encountering the waiter with Jake's drink on a tray. Whisky splashed over the sad white dress, the last, the final straw. The waiter twittered, Jake swore, and Harriet put up her hands in a mad, hysterical gesture. 'I don't believe this is happening to me!' she shrieked. 'I can't stand it, I don't believe it's true!'

'There, there, there,' said Jake impatiently, waving the waiter aside. 'It was a horrible dress anyway.'

'What does that matter? What does anything about me matter to you? All you want is for me to go away and not bother you. I might just as well kill myself! I'd be better off dead, they could bury me at sea. I can't afford a coffin anyway. It would save everyone from having to bother about me.' She scrubbed viciously at the brown marks on her dress, almost tearing the fabric.

'Don't be ridiculous,' said Jake wearily, catching hold of her arm. Without her shoes she was half a head shorter than he was. 'You're starting to be very stupid.'

Harriet glared at him, tears of rage and fright running down her cheeks. 'Oh, no! It was last night I was stupid, now I'm being sensible. I'd be better off dead!' She dragged her arm from his grasp and started to run towards the door, meeting the first of the diners coming in. She blundered into them, not even bothering to apologise.

'Harriet!' yelled Jake and started after her. Was she really going to kill herself? The possibilities on board ship were certainly there: top deck, over the rail, and Bob's your uncle. Killed on impact most likely, and not the first to take that way out.

An old gentleman on two sticks was negotiating the doorway and Jake had to wait vital seconds. When he got out Harriet's bare feet were racing up the companionway. So she was going topsides. 'Harriet!' he bawled. 'Stop that woman! She's going to kill herself.' Heads turned but nobody did anything. Jake took the steps two at a time but Harriet was well ahead, halfway up the next flight. 'Stop!' roared Jake in quarterdeck tones. 'Stop that woman!'

'That sure looks like fun, sonny,' said an aged matron longingly. Oh God, thought Jake, this is a nightmare. I will never, ever borrow money again. 'Stop!' he bellowed again, but Harriet was through a door and on to the deck. He cannoned after her, two strides behind, and pinned her to the rail. He could hear the breath scraping rawly in and out of her lungs.

'I could throw you over myself,' he hissed.

'I wish you would. Go on, do it!'

He looked down at her shuddering figure, eyes tight shut in a grey face. Drops of sweat had formed on her top lip and her lank hair clung damply to her head. She smelled of whisky and misery.

He realised very clearly that he didn't care if she did kill herself, but he did care if she did it because of him. And except for his work there were few things he did care about these days, because he did not need other people's burdens, he did not need the weight of his own guilt. She had put a claim on him, simply by being naive. He gripped her hard, despairingly angry. 'God damn you, Harriet,' he whispered, but she only moaned and shuddered a little more. He sighed. His grip relaxed. 'Let's go back to your cabin,' he said resignedly.

It was still very early, the sounds of laughter and music filtering through to the cabin. Harriet sat on her bed watching Jake search the cupboards for something to drink, but there was only mineral water. 'You might at least get undressed,' he snapped, glaring at her.

Harriet swallowed. 'What for?'

'Because your dress is ruined and in your present state of mind you should be in bed. Don't worry, I'm not going to rape you. You're not my type.'

A spark of fight ignited in Harriet. 'I would be if I was rich enough. All you care about is what you can get out of people.'

'Just get undressed, will you?'

She picked up her nightdress and went through to the bathroom. Her heart was no longer thundering in that irregular, terrifying way; she could open her lungs and breathe. She was almost certain he would look after her, provided she gave him no chance of escape. It would be stupid to trust him, though, in anything he said or did. She cleaned her teeth with her usual thoroughness, put on her pink, high-necked winceyette nightdress and went back into the bedroom.

Jake cast an eye over her. 'Do you pay money for these clothes?' he queried unkindly. 'I mean, they look as if they were left to you by a dead aunt.'

'Don't be so rude.' She got quickly into bed, pulling the covers high up.

'You can go now.'

'No, I can't. You keep threatening to kill yourself.'

She blushed. 'Only once.'

'Twice. Did you mean it?'

She nodded, slowly. 'I did then, yes. I don't know if I would have done it, though.'

Jake threw himself on to the other bed. It was an odd movement, abandoned and yet controlled, as was everything he did. He was not a man you could ever imagine breaking something, thought Harriet, he seemed to be disciplined against clumsiness. 'You needn't think I'll look after you forever,' he said sourly.

'I don't want anyone to look after me. I wouldn't need it if you hadn't taken my money.'

'You gave it to me, you stupid – ! Ye Gods, you're no more fit to be out on your own than a blind kitten. Twenty-six years in this world and not a grain of sense acquired in any one of them. And don't lie there all big-eyed. Go to sleep or read or something.'

'I can't sleep with you here,' said Harriet. 'Besides, it's too early.'

He grunted morosely. She was embarrassingly aware of him: of the rounded curve of muscle pressing against the legs of his trousers, the unidentified bulge at his crotch. It was the first time in her life that she had been this close to an attractive man, alone, in a situation of such intimacy – discounting, of course, their initial encounter. She had been too drunk then for it to register. He shrugged off his jacket, loosened his bow tie and leaned back with his hands behind his head. The lazy, confident movements made Harriet shiver.

'We can't just lie here,' she said in a high-pitched voice.

'Don't tell me I'm making you nervous. Relax. You wouldn't have got yourself into this state if you'd learned that. Except you were pretty relaxed last night, you must have been. How much did you drink?'

'I don't know. It made me feel better somehow.'

'Did it indeed? God, what a mess.' He rolled on his elbow and stared at her, half scowling, the stubble of a black beard just beginning to sprout.

Harriet sat up jerkily. 'I never lie around doing nothing, I can't. Why don't we – why don't we play chess?'

He brightened visibly. 'Do you play chess? Have you a set?'

'It's only a travelling set, magnetic pieces and so on. I used to play it with my father. He was awfully good.'

'Don't worry, I'll give you a two pawn start,' said Jake kindly, sitting up and rubbing his hands. 'Red or white?'

They woke in the morning bleary-eyed. Drugged with sleep, Harriet lay watching him move around the cabin and wondered vaguely who he was. Then she remembered chess till four in the morning, with Jake determined to beat her. She had hung on doggedly for an eventual draw.

'Hurry up and get dressed,' said Jake, wandering in and out of the bathroom as if the cabin was his own. 'I want to introduce you to Derekson.'

Harriet gulped. 'I don't think that would be a good idea.'

'It's the only idea I've got, so we'd better get on with it. But don't suggest chess, his ego might be damaged when he lost.'

'Unlike yours I suppose,' she said drily.

He grinned. 'It's not my ego that hurts, only my faith in my judgment. How can you be so stupid and still be good at chess?'

She swung her legs out of bed and trailed past him into the bathroom. Last night her skill at chess had been allied with grim determination, because beating him was what he deserved for what he thought of her. The shock on his face when she checkmated in five moves had been almost as delicious as being given back her money. Almost. Her stomach resumed its lurching. If only today need not happen; if only she could somehow acquire the cash for a night in a hotel and an instant return flight home. This was life all right, but it was far, far too frightening.

She dressed very carefully, in a tweed suit with a scarf at the neck, trying despite herself to wring a compliment out of Jake.

'Haven't you got anything that isn't stodgy?' he complained when he saw her. He was wearing last night's dinner suit with the shirt open. Black hair on his chest curled into view below a throat with a deep, outdoor tan. He looked infinitely piratical, thought Harriet, fingering her scarf. Did she look stodgy? Perhaps you had to be very much thinner for the County look.

They went into breakfast together, but as Harriet started towards her own table Jake caught her elbow and steered her forcibly to Derekson's.

'Really, Jake, I don't think – ' she muttered in a frantic whisper.

'Shut up,' he hissed. 'Let me do the talking.'

Derekson looked up in surprise as they approached. His wife looked up also, but her face remained expressionless. It was unreal and somehow horrible, thought Harriet, hot with habitual embarrassment.

'Morning all,' said Jake cheerily. 'Anyone mind if Harriet joins us? Sheila, Angus, may I introduce Harriet Wyman. Harriet, Mr. and Mrs. Derekson.'

'How do you do?' whispered Harriet, and sat down hurriedly in the seat Jake held for her.

'And where were you last night?' asked Derekson, taking no notice at all of Harriet.

'I was – otherwise engaged,' said Jake. 'Sorry.'

'I had half the ship searched for you. You knew I wanted to discuss policy yet you deliberately hid yourself away somewhere. What's the meaning of it? Well?'

Jake leaned both elbows on the table and stared at the cloth. This row had to be defused right now, and he wasn't sure how to start. He turned to Derekson's wife. 'How are you feeling this morning, Sheila? You look very well.'

The mask eased stiffly into a smile. 'Fine, thank you, Jake. I'm so glad you could make it for breakfast. We missed you last evening.'

'Did you? That's very kind. I hadn't quite got my thoughts straight on the changes to the boat, I needed some time.' He smiled at Mrs. Derekson, saving his face by making his excuses to her.

She turned her frozen gaze to Harriet. 'Are you enjoying the trip, Miss Wyman? It really has been very smooth.'

'Yes. Very smooth,' squeaked Harriet, thinking to herself that it had seemed one of the roughest passages of her life so far.

Derekson poured himself a second cup of coffee and said, 'This one of your jokes, Jake? One of your try-ons?'

Jake shrugged and met his eye. 'Depends how you look at it. I think we should go over the plans this morning, while we're fresh. I've been giving them a lot of thought.'

Derekson grunted and looked sourly at Harriet. 'I should hope so.'

Without appearing to notice the atmosphere, Jake plunged his nose into the breakfast menu and peremptorily ordered full English breakfast for Harriet and himself. When it came she could hardly eat it, watched as she was by a grumpy millionaire and his expressionless wife.

'What are you going to do in New York?' asked Mrs. Derekson with what might have been kindness, or again might not.

Harriet gulped. 'She hasn't any firm plans,' said Jake easily. 'We thought she might come along to Boston and look at the boat.'

Derekson paused in the act of wiping his mouth with his napkin. 'I think I mistake your meaning,' he said slowly.

Jake took time to finish his mouthful of bacon. 'Just seemed to me that she might enjoy it. She's never been to the States before but she did want to see Boston. I thought it might be an idea if she took up one of the spare seats in the plane.'

'In – my plane?' asked Derekson cautiously.

'Yes. If it's all right with you.' Jake grinned, very widely, somehow conveying that he knew he was being presumptuous but nonetheless, because he was Jake, thought they should accede. There was something raffish yet endearing about that grin, thought Harriet, aware of the flood of conflicting emotions assailing Derekson at that moment. If you didn't know Jake too well you could easily fall victim to his charm.

'Well, I'm sure if Miss Wyman would like to travel separately – ' said Derekson.

'That's just it,' said Jake. 'She doesn't seem to be coping very well on her own. I think Harriet needs to see what American hospitality really means. As I said to her, there is no-one so generous as an

American. We British simply can't compete.'

Derekson looked sharply from Jake to Harriet. For a brief moment she met his gaze, and then cast her eyes down to her plate. He knew he was being taken for a ride and was unsure whether to go along with it or fall out with Jake right now.

'I'm sure Miss Wyman will just love Boston,' said Mrs. Derekson from behind her mask.

Her husband screwed his napkin into a ball. 'Yes, I'm sure she will.'

The ship docked shortly before lunch. Harriet sat with her two bags and waited for Jake to emerge from his consultations with Derekson and collect her. The structure that had been life on board was breaking up before her eyes, falling apart into the strands of which it was made. It was finished, here. If she had felt lost before how much worse would it be out there, beyond the grey customs sheds and cranes? The skyline of New York, familiar from so many television shows, loomed like silver grey pencil stubs. It looked wholly menacing.

After a while Mrs. Derekson appeared, wearing a fur coat and hat, and sat down beside her.

'And what part of England do you come from?' she asked tightly.

'Manchester,' replied Harriet, folding her gloves into a ball.

'Is that a pretty part? I don't know it.'

'It rains,' said Harriet, although she wasn't herself aware that it did, excessively. But it was what people said.

'It rains here, too,' said Mrs. Derekson.

'Oh.'

Suddenly Mrs. Derekson said, 'Do you think my face looks queer?'

Harriet blushed. 'No – no, not at all.'

'I do. It's my third lift and he's made it too darned tight. He says it will relax, but as I said to him, how long do I have to walk around like a goddamned mummy? Does it look odd to you?'

'It doesn't seem odd at all,' lied Harriet.

She grunted. 'Jake says it makes me look inscrutable. He's a nice guy, Jake. You got a thing with him? I wouldn't have said you were his type really. But then, no-one is for long.' She attempted a laugh but the skin restrained her.

'We've got – mutual interests,' said Harriet.

'Honey, the only thing he's interested in is a boat. I've had a funny thought about him. You know men always think boats have souls? Well, I think God made a mistake, and somewhere out there's a yacht that wants a home and family while here we've got Jake, setting sail again. Is he bullying you, honey? Is that it?'

Harriet felt a desperate urge to confide. But when she looked at Sheila Derekson's blank face, and knew that she could tell her anything and it would not change, she simply folded her gloves again and said: 'It's quite all right, thank you. Everyone's been so kind.'

Passengers were at last disembarking. It seemed to take forever as people streamed erratically down the gangways. At last Derekson strode into view, chatting animatedly to Jake, and the conversation barely paused to acknowledge the two women.

'Glad to see you're both ready. What happens if it doesn't take the strain then? If it does crack? Walter said it couldn't happen.'

Jake wrinkled his nose as if at a dead dog. 'Oh, it can happen – delamination. The sandwich gets unmade, if you like. If it's going to happen we want to see signs of it early on, we don't want to be in mid-ocean with a race to win. And if the rigging needs major changes we don't want to bother if the hull's falling apart. So I'll push her. Let's hope for some foul weather.'

Derekson laughed, a brief sparkle that changed him utterly. Suddenly he was a man with an enthusiasm, a surge in his blood that he had thought never to feel again. 'God! I wish I could sail with you. It'd be something else.'

'You can say that again,' said Jake. 'You'd be sick as a dog, everyone is. But I'll give you a taste if you like, try and get away for a day. Just don't expect to be put off halfway through.'

'I won't. Thanks.'

Harriet watched in amazement. It was quite possible to believe that Jake owned the boat and was doing Derekson a favour by letting him set foot on it once in a while.

'Walter's coming on later,' said Sheila Derekson.

'Are we ready then?' asked Jake.

They all were. He led the way shorewards and the rest of them trotted obediently behind.

Chapter Four

New York passed Harriet by. She was there only long enough for bewilderment, swept with the Dereksons into a vast car then an overheated restaurant.

It was difficult to know how to behave. Jake clearly expected that she should be the mouselike governess figure, saying little, eating less, drinking hardly at all, and for the most part she conformed. But inside she was burning, boiling, longing to break out in some totally shocking way. Here, everything seemed permitted, you need only look around you. For instance that immensely tall black girl wearing a peacock feather in her hair, long legs encased in red thigh-high boots. She was talking to a man so impeccably dressed that he might have emerged from an English bank, except that he carried a neat leather purse.

'There's a man with a handbag,' said Harriet.

Sheila Derekson looked across. 'So there is, honey. Drink your martini. If we don't get zonked we'll have to listen to boat talk for the next six hours. You sure you want to come along?'

The question made Harriet blink. She had to come along, but did she want to? It was quite possible, and probably quite sensible, that she should confide in Sheila. The money would be loaned, no doubt, there would only be a little embarrassment. But then – no plane, no Boston, no thrilling uncertainty. Yesterday she had wanted to die. Now, suddenly, she was on the threshold of something. This was the most exciting time of her entire life. 'I should like to come,' she said breathlessly, taking a gulp of martini which made her eyes water. The drink was almost neat gin.

Sheila patted her on the back. 'I can't promise any fun.'

The meal was strange: bits of raw fish in strong sauces, barely cooked vegetables on red-hot plates.

'God, this is horrific,' said Jake, poking at what might have been squid.

'Do you really like this stuff, Angus?'

In all likelihood it was a question which had not occurred to Derekson, who for years had been sated with the world's finest cuisine. He was barely hungry when he came to eat, and the food barely interested him. 'I'll get you a steak if you want,' he offered.

'No, thanks. They probably wouldn't cook it. Don't eat it if you don't want to, Harriet, it's not school.'

'Some of it's all right,' said Harriet, who had indeed been nobly swallowing everything, sending it on its way with another gulp of martini.

'This place is supposed to be really chic,' said Sheila. 'Oh look, there's Senator White. Wave, Angus. With my face like this he'll think we've found out about his taxes.'

'What about his taxes?' asked Harriet.

'No idea, honey, but there's bound to be something, there always is. Have another martini.'

'Don't get drunk, Harriet,' said Jake. 'Have some water.'

'I like martinis,' she said.

'Good,' agreed Sheila. 'So do I.'

When they drove to the airport, both women were three sheets to the wind.

'Look at the view, Harriet,' declared Sheila. 'That's the big apple for you, full of worms.'

They were passing through streets filled with rubbish. An old woman shuffled by with a dirty coat pulled round her. 'That could be me,' said Harriet hazily.

Sheila patted her hand. 'Don't be foolish, honey, that doesn't happen to people like us.'

'But it could,' said Harriet. 'You don't know, but it could.'

Jake turned round from the front seat. 'Harriet, be quiet,' he said firmly. 'Look at the view.'

She felt unreasonably hurt. Why did he treat her so horribly, as if she was a child or a dog or a mental case? It made her look stupid in front of people. She fell to studying the curls of hair over the collar of his shirt, a less than clean, less than new collar. Damn Jake. Damn him.

The men were hammering away about through hull fittings, whatever they were. Jake didn't like whatever it was Derekson had installed in the boat, which was the stance he seemed to take on everything.

'It's what Walter recommends,' declared Derekson in a last ditch stand.

'Say no more,' said Jake and contemptuously abandoned the conversation. The airport signs were upon them and he shot a glance at Harriet, meeting her fulminating gaze. 'What's the matter with you?'

'You,' she snapped. 'You're being horrid to everyone. Why can't you ever be polite?'

Angus Derekson crackled with laughter. 'Good on you, Harriet. You tell him.'

'You really are drunk, aren't you?' said Jake.

'I'd rather be drunk than rude.' The car slid to a halt. Without waiting for the door to be opened Harriet fumbled for the catch and fell out, the cold air meeting her like a wall. Jake was behind her. He caught her arms and steadied her as she swayed. 'I feel ill,' she said sadly.

He grinned, almost ruefully. 'Do you? Oh, Harriet, what am I going to do with you?'

'Give her another martini,' said Sheila, her fur hat askew. 'With you around she needs it.'

The plane was red and white, perched at the edge of the airfield like a fly on a cake, while the huge Jumbos thundering endlessly in and out resembled albatrosses in comparison. There were only six seats. 'I thought Walter was coming,' said Sheila. The Dereksons kept on mentioning Walter, a man about ten years younger than Derekson who had spent the days on the liner vigorously expounding sailing theories.

'He was. He should be here,' said Derekson, looking angrily at his Rolex.

'Probably got tied up,' said Jake. 'We'd better get going or we'll lose our slot.'

'We'll wait a bit longer,' said Derekson, and after a moment Jake shrugged.

'Come and sit by me.' Sheila patted the seat and twitched her skin into a smile at Harriet. Jake, who had wedged her out of harm's way next to the window, scowled and let her out. 'Don't drink,' he said firmly.

'Party pooper,' said Sheila. 'Harriet and I understand each other.' She uncorked a hip flask under cover of the seat, pouring herself and Harriet a nip each of brandy. 'Medicinal,' said Sheila. 'I need it a lot since I had this goddamned lift.'

'Why did you have it?' asked Harriet, watching the pilot, a worryingly youthful individual, twirl handles in the roof.

'Honey, when you've been married as long as I have, and all your husband's friends have women thirty years younger than you are, you have your face lifted. I don't want to be left with just the alimony to keep me warm at night. I wouldn't have anyone to complain to.'

'He won't divorce you because of a few wrinkles, surely?' She touched her own plump cheeks, aware that a few crow's feet had appeared over the last year or so.

'Oh, it isn't the wrinkles,' said Sheila. 'It's seeing your wife old. It tells a man he's old too. And now I've had this go wrong I don't look old but I do look stupid. Yeah, I wouldn't be surprised to see something your age crawling about soon, once he gets tired of the boat. He's bored with good old Sheila.'

There was something flattering about such confidences but again they confirmed Harriet's role as a neutral observer. There was never any suggestion that she might herself engage in living, even if she were the same age as the unknown predator. Other women always knew Harriet was no competition.

The pilot called back to Derekson. 'We shall have to take off in a minute, sir. They won't wait for us.'

'Hell!' Derekson flung himself into a seat and scowled. 'OK, take her up. Walter can come on later.'

'Right sir. Thanks.' The pilot began revving the twin engines. In the confines of the small plane the note became a scream, and then beneath the wing Harriet saw the errant Walter running towards them, his coat flying open and his bag banging his knees.

'Wait, wait, here he is,' she called.

'I wish you'd be quiet, Harriet,' said Jake in an odd voice.

The door was opened and Walter staggered breathlessly into the plane. 'I nearly missed you. Sorry Angus. Jake told me you were going in the morning.' He glared accusingly at Jake who simply smiled, clear grey eyes quite unrepentant.

'Perhaps you misunderstood,' he said with lead in his voice.

Walter wiped his sweating brow and they all rearranged themselves in the plane. Harriet was once again appropriated by Jake and wedged against the window, Sheila stretched out on two seats and Walter and Derekson sat together. The engines resumed their rising scream.

'Why did you want him left behind?' asked Harriet in a whisper.

'Because he's a prat who keeps contradicting what I tell Derekson. I can't work with that fool. He won a good race twenty years ago and has lived on the glory ever since. He doesn't know a damn thing, but Derekson listens to him. Why the hell did you have to shout?'

'I wouldn't if you'd told me,' said Harriet. 'Don't treat me like a fool.'

'Stop acting like one then. You don't have to accept every drink that's offered, Sheila Derekson's been pickling her liver for years.

You keep up with her and you'll be in hospital in two days.'

'Oh, don't go on!'

They subsided into uneasy silence. Harriet felt restless, the booze coursing through her bloodstream and stimulating her to action she could not take. She shifted in the small seat, her thigh against Jake's. Each was as thick as the other, and he was a well-muscled man. She really must lose some weight, she told herself, the same instruction she had been ignoring for ten years. While she was considering this the little plane began to move, slowly and gently, for what seemed like a very long way. Suddenly they swung round and began the take-off run, building speed with frightening rapidity. Harriet let out a small scream and clutched at Jake.

'It's all right. Don't tell me you're scared of flying.'

'I don't know, I've never done any. I want a parachute.'

'You'll have to inflate your knickers instead. Don't look out of the window, even I hate doing that. Wow! We're off. OK, you can look now.'

Harriet released her hold on Jake's arm and stared out of the window. The ground was receding rapidly, but the structure in which she sat, into which she had stepped so unconcernedly, seemed suddenly very flimsy. 'I don't think I'm going to like it,' she said with a gulp.

'Too late, as the actress said to the bishop. Pretend you don't mind. You do this all the time at home, remember? And don't you dare confide in Sheila! I've done this much for you after all.'

'You don't want Walter to see you look a fool,' she said shrewdly.

'Perhaps I don't at that.' He patted her plump hand. 'Be a good girl, eh, Harriet?'

They were to land at a private airfield near Boston. It was by then quite dark, and Harriet looked down at the lights and the black curtain of the ground, re-running in her mind every report there had ever been of a light aircraft crash. The pilot muttered into his radio and stared at a battery of illuminated dials. Jake shifted in his seat beside her.

'I wish it was over,' said Harriet.

'I know. I hate having my fate in someone else's hands.'

'No-one else seems scared,' she whispered.

'No bloody imagination. If we were meant to fly, God would have made rubber mountains. I always do a bit of repenting at this point, I never get around to it otherwise.'

'Repent about my money,' she said sourly.

'Why should I when I've got you as my hair shirt? No, I keep it to promiscuity and rape, that way I can relive the act. My past life flashes before me as a series of porno movies. By the way, what are you going to do in Boston?'

She blinked at him. 'What do you mean?'

'I mean, what are your plans? I've got you here, in some style I might add, so what do you mean to do with yourself?'

Harriet's voice rose more than a little. 'But that's up to you, isn't it? Until you give me my money back. Or shall I tell everyone what's been going on? Let Mr. Derekson see just how trustworthy you are?'

'Shhhh! It was only a thought. It occurred to me that you might have developed some independence. I didn't realise you were making a career out of being a limpet.'

Her foot shot out and kicked him hard on the ankle. 'Do that again and I hit you back,' he hissed. She could see that he meant it.

They touched down featherlight on to the tarmac. A collective sigh went round the plane and Harriet started to gather her things. Her stomach was churning again. Jake had pitched her straight back into anxiety.

'Here's the car,' said Derekson, as a white limousine about half a mile long started across the ground towards them. 'Where can we drop you, Harriet?' She shot a desperate glance at Jake but he showed no inclination to leap to her rescue.

'Er – I really don't know,' she said helplessly.

'Well, I can recommend a few good hotels,' said Derekson.

'Thank you. That's – ' she tailed off miserably.

'Really Angus, Harriet can stay with us,' declared Sheila. 'Walter can show her around. He'll like that, won't you, Walter?'

Walter looked at Harriet for almost the first time. 'I may well be a little busy with the boat – ' he began. 'I daresay I could bring Harriet down to the harbour each day.' He set his jaw, staking his claim to daily visits to the yacht.

'That won't be necessary,' broke in Jake suddenly. 'I'll look after Harriet tonight, there's a hotel near the wharf. Homely, the sort of thing she likes if I'm any judge. A girl like Harriet can't take too much excitement, it's not her style. We'll sort out her itinerary for the visit after she's had a look at the boat. I promised you that, didn't I, Harriet?' He slid his arm round her waist. It felt like iron.

'So you did,' she said tightly. 'Well, if you insist, Jake – '

'I do.' He bent his head a little, took the top of her ear in his teeth and bit, just too untenderly for kindness. She had to blink hard to keep back the tears.

Jake insisted that he and Harriet be dropped by the wharf, their bags clustered around their feet. 'You'll never get the car turned round up here,' he assured them. 'It's only a step. Thank's a lot, Angus, Sheila.'

'Yes. Thank you both very much for everything,' added Harriet. 'It really has been so kind of you – '

'Don't think of it, honey,' said Sheila lazily. 'Look us up soon. What we girls need is a really good talk. We don't know anything about you, Harriet. Bring her over real soon, Jake.'

'I will,' he promised.

They were left with the wind whipping round them as the white car sped away up the road. It seemed very dark and very cold, the looming buildings forbidding, the waters lapping against the quay.

'What time is it?' asked Harriet.

'About two, I think. Come on, pick up your cases.'

She heaved them into her hands. Jake shouldered his own bags, both canvas. Only a few lights showed here and there and she could smell saltwater and seaweed. In the darkness to her left loomed the spikes of masts, and further out beyond them, the lights of boats at anchor. She tripped over a loose cobble. 'How far is this hotel?' she asked.

'Buggered if I know.'

'Well, where are we going?'

'To the boat, of course! God, Harriet, where am I going to get the money for the two of us in a hotel? Derekson hasn't coughed up a dime so far, not in actual bunce.'

'But I don't want to go on a boat. Is it big?'

'Big enough. Here, give me one of those. The real problem is going to be finding it.'

Harriet felt too tired and confused to complain. She staggered along behind Jake, wondering what would happen if they were mugged. Everyone got mugged in America after dark, travel agents virtually put it on the itinerary. 'Tuesday evening – mugging. Do not resist.'

She began to giggle to herself and Jake turned round. 'What on earth is funny?'

'Oh – everything. I can't explain. Oh!' A man was lurching out of an alleyway towards them. Mugging did not seem so funny any more. She shrank behind Jake. The man shuffled across their path, bearded and terrifying.

'Where's the *Real Sheila*?' called Jake unconcernedly. 'We're looking for her.'

'Wassat? Wassat you say?' A wino of many years standing. His fingers, strangely long and slender, clutched his bottle.

'The *Real Sheila*. She's anchored off, I need a boat to her.'

‘I can get you a boat. *Real Sheila*, I can get to her.’

‘Get on with it then, mate.’

The man shuffled off in front of them, Jake and Harriet trudging behind. It was almost surreal, thought Harriet, the dark wharf, a few lights behind curtained windows, ahead the nightmare figure of the man. The cold was making her shiver, the chill spring wind biting through her jacket. She was very tired and felt as if she was thinking in a fog, a blanket of weariness that clogged the channels of her mind. If only she could sleep, then she would be able to cope with all this. In the morning she would know what to do and what to say to Jake. Now he seemed as much a part of the nightmare as the wino. Her ear still hurt where he had bitten her.

‘Here.’ The man had stopped beside an iron ladder descending into the water. At the bottom lay a small boat, its outboard motor swung up.

‘That’ll do,’ said Jake. ‘I’ll steer, you tell me which is the *Real Sheila*.’

The man grunted. He turned, infinitely slowly, and began what seemed a death-defying descent into the abyss, his bottle still clutched in one wavering hand.

‘Just don’t let him fall in the boat,’ said Jake grimly. ‘It would sink.’

‘We can’t go out there in the dark,’ whimpered Harriet. The night was like soot. When the moon went behind a cloud she blundered like a blind woman.

‘I’m not kipping on the dockside, thanks very much,’ said Jake. ‘Throw the bags down in a minute.’ He was off down the ladder like a monkey. Harriet pushed the bags over the edge, leaving her big case until last. ‘The dinghy’s full,’ called Jake softly. ‘Stow that one somewhere, we can come and get it in the morning.’

‘But it’s got most of my things in it!’

‘Put it in here and the boat’ll sink. Stow it! Come on, Harriet.’

All at once she was at the end of her tether. She looked hopelessly about and saw a tarpaulin draped over a small boat upturned on the dockside. She heaved up the heavy oilskin folds and pushed her suitcase underneath, glad only to have the task completed and to be one step nearer sleep. Then to the ladder. She teetered on the first few rungs, clung with sudden fright, and descended with a thump into the dinghy.

‘Come hither, Fairy Tinkerbell. Right, let’s start this thing.’

The wino sat in the prow, his expression serene, as if they were on a trip round the harbour. He took no interest as Jake pulled the engine, but revived when it roared into life, splitting the night like thunder. His long fingers waved royally towards the sea. ‘*Real Sheila*. Real beauty she is, real nice boat.’

'Glad to hear it,' said Jake. 'Untie the painter, Harriet.'

She was too cold, the knot wouldn't undo. At last Jake, cursing, came and did it for her. The little dinghy chugged off.

Jake had no real expectation of being directed straight to the *Real Sheila*, but to begin with he was prepared to follow the wino's directions. The dinghy slapped into the waves. From time to time the gathering breeze whipped spray over the side. Harriet huddled in utter misery, her feet in an increasing puddle in the bottom. She was too cold and weary even for interest in her fate.

Then the wino said: '*Real Sheila*. There you are.' He was pointing towards a slim, streamlined yacht, surprisingly narrow, bucking a little against her mooring. They could hear the crack and whine of the wind lashing the rigging against bare poles.

'Saints be praised,' said Jake in genuine surprise. 'Ahoy there *Real Sheila*! Wake up, you bastards!'

Chapter Five

The dinghy, engine cut, bumped hard against the side of the *Real Sheila*.

'Fend her off, Harriet,' bawled Jake. 'Don't go to sleep!' As if she could with her feet turned to ice and the wind sticking needles into her skin! As the dinghy again swung in she put out tentative hands and pushed, encountering smooth, wet plastic. There was little effort involved. As the dinghy rose on each wave she fended it off rhythmically. A face appeared over the *Real Sheila*'s rail.

'Doctor Bloody Livingstone, I presume. You coming up, Jake, or staying out all night?'

'Put the kettle on, Mac, there's a good chap,' said Jake, throwing up a line. 'But give us the ladder first.'

Grumbling, the man pulled them round to the stern and tossed down a rope ladder. 'Up you go, Harriet,' said Jake cheerily. She looked bleakly at the rungs, bouncing energetically off the side with the force of the wind and waves. She looked at the black water into which she would fall if she missed her footing.

'Cup of tea at the top, Harriet,' said Jake through gritted teeth, and then, as she clutched for the ladder and missed, swore vilely.

'It won't stay still,' wailed Harriet.

'Get up it, will you? I'm not staying here all night while you have the vapours. Just grab it!'

She grabbed. Then, as the ladder stayed still and the boat beneath her feet moved, she gave a strangled shriek and scrabbled for a foothold. One shoe fell off and plopped into the sea; her stockinged toes clung monkeylike to the rope rungs.

'Good girl, Harriet,' said Jake, and from above came an amazed voice: 'I think he's brought his bloody aunt!'

Harriet struggled three rungs higher, then hands reached down and dragged her over the rail. 'I am not related to Jake,' she said furiously. 'And if I was, I'd shoot myself.'

A thin, bearded face peered into her own. 'No need to get yourself all worked up.'

Jake swung on to the deck behind her. 'Bring the bags up, Mac, would you? Is Lewis here yet?'

'Here, Boss,' called a voice. A tall, fair young man carrying a torch emerged from the companionway and came aft towards them. 'Are we having a party or what?'

'Jake's brought his fan club,' said Mac. There was a distinct Scottish burr to his voice. 'She doesn't seem too happy, Jake.'

'Harriet is never happy, are you, Harriet? Meet Mac and Lewis, they're crewing this tub.'

Harriet kicked off her remaining shoe and went silently forward. She climbed into the cockpit and down into the cabin. A warm yellow glow beckoned her in, out of the biting night wind, away from the sea. As the walls closed round her she felt a sense of great security. There was the kettle, popping on the stove, there was a bed, rumpled from the recent presence of its owner. She sat down on the bed, feeling her skirt rough and damp against her legs. Her shoulders slumped in exhaustion.

'How d'you do, Harriet?' Mac nodded towards her. 'You're sitting on my bed.'

'I'll sort out somewhere for her in a minute,' said Jake easily, automatically ducking his head as he entered. Lewis followed on his heels and busied himself with cups and a packet of biscuits. All three men were talking non-stop, taking only a passing interest in Harriet. She didn't mind, content just to rest, out of the wind, safe from the sea. She took a biscuit and a cup of coffee and sat shivering. Her teeth rattled on the biscuit as she tried to bite.

Suddenly Jake noticed her again. 'Christ, will you look at this girl? I don't know what to do with her.' He took away her empty cup and began to peel off her jacket. She didn't resist.

'Who is she?' asked Lewis.

'She's just Harriet. I can't seem to get rid of her, she's like the gypsy's curse.' He began to unbutton her blouse, with noticeable expertise.

'Stop that.' Harriet flailed at him weakly. 'You can get rid of me quite easily if you give me my money. Leave me alone, Jake!' She jerked away as he unfastened her skirt. 'Leave me alone. I just want to go to bed.'

'Which is where I'm putting you,' he said matter-of-factly. 'Stand up and get your skirt off, you're making Mac's bed wet.'

'Stop it!' Blushing and tearful, she hung on to her skirt. Jake ran a hand through his hair. 'Bloody hell. What do I do with you, let you freeze to death? We're not going to rape you, driven out of our minds by the sight of a woman's legs. Look, I'll hold this blanket up. You can take off your clothes, right down to your petticoat, and then you can get into the forward berth, that one through there. And if anyone is seized by uncontrollable passion, I'll fell him with a blow from my mighty fist. Will that do?'

Harriet glared at him. 'I do so hate you, Jake,' she said venomously.

Lewis began to laugh. 'What is this, some kind of sideshow?'

'I wish it was,' said Jake, 'I wish it was.'

Harriet woke from a dream which had been unpleasantly vivid and detailed. She had been talking to her mother, in the living-room that was all of the world her mother ever saw, and they had been discussing Jake.

'I don't know what you are thinking of, Harriet,' said her mother petulantly. 'The man's a rogue. You had the chance to leave. Why don't you ever behave sensibly, Harriet? Really, I always knew you wouldn't be able to manage on your own. It's always the same, you can't be relied on for a minute. My medicine's late, Harriet. You've forgotten my medicine. Harriet – '

'You've had it, mother,' she replied wearily. She was always endlessly weary.

'No, I haven't. You've forgotten it, Harriet. You always forget things.'

'No, mother, it's all right, I haven't forgotten. Look, here's your knitting, why don't you do that?'

'Not when I haven't had my medicine.' The brown eyes, not in the least dimmed by age, suddenly stared fixedly. 'You want my money,' said the old woman. 'Who are you? You want my money. And you haven't given me my medicine.'

'It's Harriet, mother,' intoned her daughter. 'And I've given you the medicine.'

Tears began to roll down the old woman's pale cheeks, so swiftly and silently that it was impossible to know if genuine sadness was the cause or if this was only some weird reflex. The voice went on: 'I don't like this man, Harriet. You never could be trusted. Why won't you give me my medicine?'

She jerked awake and lay in the narrow berth, staring at the ceiling two feet above her head while her heart pumped wildly. Where was she? At least it wasn't home. The dream had been so real that she could still see, as if burned on her brain, her mother's rapidly jerking hands, commanded by a disintegrating brain. Would she always see her like that? As if you had once owned a beautiful limousine, but in retrospect saw only its rusting hulk being crushed at a scrapyard. No memory of the luxurious upholstery, the speed, the wonderful holidays spent touring in the car; it was all rust and twisted metal and disillusion. That was real tragedy: the obliteration of her mother by disease into a nagging, resentful old woman.

Her mental confusion had come almost as a relief, tangible proof of the changes that had been so bewildering when they first appeared. The loving mother, almost too sheltering, turned suddenly unkind. Endlessly critical. That had been all it was in the beginning, a gradual darkening of a once bright spirit. The death of a brain is like turning out the lights in a highrise office block: first a few go erratically, here and there, then a whole floor is dark, then another. Suddenly the entire front of the building is black and unresponsive but here and there lights twinkle on in the darkness. Perhaps there is someone working late. There are still small recognisable pockets of life in what is now an almost deserted building.

She sat up quickly, and cracked her head on the cabintop. She yelped and rubbed at her scalp, looking angrily round at the space Jake deemed suitable for her occupation. There wasn't room to swing a cat, except perhaps a very amenable one that had no objection to lockers and bags and canisters labelled DANGER – HANDLE WITH CARE in three languages. Also it was gloomy, the only light filtering in through a small skylight set high up, and added to that it was cold. Damn Jake! Damn his black heart.

She wrapped a blanket round herself and climbed gingerly out into the main cabin. Mac the Scotsman was there, cutting his toenails. He had large, knobbly toes which sprouted hairs at every joint. They were possibly the least attractive toes Harriet had ever seen.

'Good morning,' she said shyly.

'Morning. Jake said to make sure you ate something when you woke up. The frying pan's over there.'

He seemed unnecessarily morose. Harriet shrugged the blanket more closely about her shoulders, negotiated the cluttered table and approached the cooker. The frying pan had clearly cooked many a meal previously, and resting on the blackened fat was a toenail clipping. A wave of nausea rose in her throat which she fought, a hand over her mouth.

'This place is disgusting,' she whispered when she could speak. 'You could die of some foul disease living like this.'

Mac dusted the clippings on his bed on to the floor. 'We've got a job to do. We're not playing house.'

'I don't think anything excuses not washing,' snapped Harriet. 'Even Jake doesn't smell!'

Mac's narrow head jerked up. 'There's nae need to be rude,' he said stiffly.

'Isn't there? Can you lend me some clothes, please? Mine are still on shore. I shall need some trousers and a jumper. It's going to take hours to clean this mess up.'

'Glad to see you're going to be some use to us,' said Mac, pulling malodorous socks back on to his feet. 'You can borrow my clothes – if you think they're clean enough, that is.'

Harriet looked at him. As always she had said what came into her head, with no thought of the offence it might give. 'I'm sorry,' she said, going rather pink. 'I got out of bed on the wrong side. I didn't mean to be rude. I can see it must be difficult in here.'

Mac allowed himself to be mollified. 'Yes, well, we didn't expect to have to entertain a lady.' It occurred to Harriet that he was as embarrassed by her presence as she was by his. They were mutually uncomfortable, and the knowledge reassured her. When offered a pair of stained canvas trousers, a Guernsey jumper with holes in the elbows and a pair of canvas shoes, she accepted with unusual grace. 'Thank you. These'll do fine.'

'None of my socks are clean, I'm afraid.'

'I'll manage without socks, thank you,' said Harriet hastily, and retreated into the fo'csle to get changed.

She emerged with the jumper pulled well down over trousers that would not do up. Mac's narrow frame in no way resembled Harriet's substantial one, and once again she resolved to lose weight. The cruise had added insult to injury, piling calories before her at every meal. She had always liked her food. Even now, with the toenail clipping to haunt her, she was ravenously hungry.

Mac had thoughtfully boiled the kettle to provide her with hot water for the dishes, and was now preparing to go topsides.

'Where's Jake?'

'He and Lewis have gone ashore,' said Mac. 'They're trying to accuse him of stealing that dinghy you came in last night.'

'Oh, good,' she said. 'Perhaps they'll put him in gaol.'

She pushed the sleeves of her jumper up to the elbows and started on the revolting mass of dishes in the sink. They bore traces of many washes in cold water, and a recognisable history of food for days past, but they were good quality melamine and, looking round the cabin, Harriet could see that this was a yacht furbished in style. Cupboards folded away into the roof, the fridge was hidden neatly to one side and the cooker, on gimbals, would be very smart once cleaned. There was a wooden table that folded and swung to the side when not in use, and set in a corner was a chart table, with a separate light, maps and rulers. Harriet was filled with a determination to have it all as it should be: neat, clean and tidy.

Two hours later, when she had delighted herself with the change from squalor to pleasant homeliness, she bagan to fry herself bacon and eggs. As the smell began to stir her gastric juices, the door to the outside world opened and Jake rattled in, followed by Lewis and Mac.

'Good girl, Harriet,' he said cheerfully. 'Two eggs for me, please.'

'I was just cooking for me,' she said crossly. 'I did the clearing up, I get the food.'

'And I've just saved you from being dragged off to gaol,' said Jake. 'I didn't say a word about you being my accomplice. You are an ungrateful woman.'

'But look what she's done, Jake,' declared Lewis, gesturing at the cabin. 'It's a palace! What a woman you've brought us, she's a real honey. Thanks a lot, Harriet.'

'Thank you.' She went a little pink and busied herself putting rasher after rasher of bacon into the pan.

They ate with real appreciation, and afterwards, drinking coffee, began to chat.

'Derekson's still got that creep Walter in tow,' said Jake. 'He's going to cause trouble.'

'You'd think he'd have learned his lesson by now,' said Mac. 'Boat's like a wildcat in a following sea.'

'Walter doesn't like them beamy,' said Jake, and gave a mirthless smile. 'Let's invite him on board for a gale.'

'Wouldn't come,' said Lewis. 'He knows where it's safe. This boat stinks, Jake. We've only had her out twice and we can't get her to go. She'll broach with a half point wind shift. *Real Sheila* my arse. Real bastard, more likely.'

'Ladies present,' said Mac austerely, and Jake grinned.

'Are you shocked, Harriet? Does our bad language offend your virginal ears?'

'Don't be silly.' She leaned her elbows on the table and sipped her coffee. It was cosy in the cabin, rocking gently with a meal inside her and the men appearing to accept, even to be grateful for, her presence. 'What's going to happen, Jake?' she asked. 'About me and my money.'

He shrugged. 'Dunno. I can pay you back when the job's done. Till then you can be chief galley slave if you want, but you'll have to keep out of Derekson's way, of course.'

She considered. Life on a boat didn't seem too bad, now that she had sorted things out, and Boston was sure to be a fascinating city that she could explore at her leisure. It might be a very good way to spend her holiday. As if reading her thoughts, Jake said, 'People pay thousands to get trips on a boat like this.'

'I hate to remind you, but I have.'

Mac grunted and Lewis hid his face. Jake merely said, 'Don't be bitchy, Harriet. When you go back home you'll be thanking me for giving you such a wonderful time.'

'Where is home?' asked Lewis.

'Manchester,' said Harriet absently. 'It rains. Oh, Jake, you've forgotten my case. Can you fetch it, please?'

He nodded. 'Sure thing. By the way, one of your duties is the washing, Mac'll take you across to the laundrette.'

'Laundromat,' said Lewis. 'You won't find a laundrette in Boston.'

Harriet smiled across the rim of her coffee cup. Against all expectations, things were turning out all right. She had three good chums – except that one of them was Jake – and her days would be spent seeing Boston in the spring, and going on exhilarating trips on the yacht. She didn't mind, of course she didn't mind, helping out with the domestic details that were beyond the men.

Mac took her onshore to do the washing. Boston appeared at the same time very foreign and yet very English, thought Harriet. On the skyline the spikes of tower blocks made their American mark, but here by the harbour there were streets and warehouses, cafés and apartment blocks. It was clear that Bostonians had revamped their deep harbour for industry and put the yachts and their marinas here, where the buildings of a bygone age added charm and atmosphere to the scene. Harriet extracted some coins from Mac and bought herself a guidebook. She wished very much that she had some better clothes to wear, feeling painfully conspicuous in Mac's castoffs.

'I feel like a tramp,' she confided to him. 'Is Jake going to get my clothes?'

He mumbled something unintelligible.

'We could have a look on the way back,' continued Harriet. 'If we don't pick up my case someone might steal it. But I don't know if I can spot the place it was left, I don't know the harbour too well.'

'Best leave it to Jake,' said Mac, staring into the middle distance like an artist contemplating perspective. He was a very unwilling conversationalist, thought Harriet, though they worked well enough together. They were two people used to expecting little.

The spring day was drawing to a chilly close. As they bobbed back in the *Real Sheila's* dinghy, shopping and clean laundry stacked in bags around their feet, Harriet shivered. The thought of the little cabin was reassuring, a haven from storm and new experiences. She had a slight headache. The presence of Mac, and the imminent presence of Jake and Lewis, weighed on her. She wasn't used to so much company, it exhausted her. Solitude was something she had taken for granted for so long that she didn't know how much she needed it.

'Don't you find it hard?' she asked Mac. 'Being with people all the time? In so small a boat, I mean.'

He grunted. His little eyes were screwed against the wind, his beard blew in small, grizzled streamers. 'I've been with Jake a long time. I'm used to him.' The omission of Lewis was significant. Did the clean American find the grubby Scot offensive, or was it something deeper, some seamanlike prejudice?

The sea was broken up and choppy. The dinghy bounced at the foot of the ladder, but this time Harriet knew what was expected and swung up with some credit. Lewis gave her a casual hand over the top rail, then took the bags from Mac. She went down into the cabin. Jake was sitting at the table writing in pencil on a large block of paper. It was very neat script, she noticed, with forceful up and down strokes.

'Jake', she said, 'you've forgotten my case.'

'Hmmm. Tomorrow. Don't worry.'

'But I do worry! It's got my things in it and I need them. Someone might steal them.' She modified the demand with a deprecatory smile, but he barely looked up. She picked up the kettle and filled it, raising the water with a footpump, a task that required a knack. 'Jake,' she said again, on a rising note, hinting at nagging.

He threw down his pencil and looked up. 'I'm sorry, Harriet,' he said. 'I meant to tell you but I didn't want you upset. When I looked this morning the case was gone, someone had taken it. It doesn't matter, you couldn't have worn those things anyway on a yacht. You've got all your papers.' She stared at him blankly. 'But it can't have gone! Not right away, it couldn't. Anyway, if it did we must tell the police.'

He watched her speculatively and then, seeming to feel that all was well, turned back to his writing. 'Not in America, Harriet. If you don't want things stolen here, you don't leave them lying around.'

The fury that rose up in her was so swift and firey that it shocked even her. She stared down at Jake's bent, uncaring head. 'You bastard,' she hissed. 'You knew that last night, yet you made me leave it. How am I going to go around and see Boston without any clothes? I'd be thrown out of every gallery as a tramp if I went like this!' She gestured to her jeans and jumper, but Jake wasn't watching. His disinterest struck a chord. She had seen this evasion before when he was guilty – and of more than he had admitted, she was sure. Jake's canvas jacket was hanging on the row of pegs next to the sliding door concealing the head and washbasin. She crossed to it and went through his pockets with swift, determined fingers.

'What the hell do you think you're doing?'

She turned, brandishing the money, a thin wad of notes that he had somehow acquired since his penniless state of last night. It could have come from Mac or Lewis, but Harriet thought not. She knew, as if she had seen him, what Jake had done. 'You sold my things,' she whispered. Rage made her voice tremble erratically. 'You've taken everything. First my money, now this! I should like to kill you, Jake, because you've done it and you don't care. You horrible, horrible – ' She flung up her arm to punctuate her words with blows, but Jake, at last paying her full attention, caught her wrists. She writhed against him and when his arm came near tried to bite.

'Calm down, will you,' said Jake in irritated tones. 'It wasn't like that. Why don't you listen.'

Mac, descending the companionway, observed the scene and said drily, 'Have you upset the lassie again, Jake?'

'She's got the idea that I sold her clothes.'

'Oh, aye.' Mac allowed a wintry grin to pass across his features. Lewis, also observing the tableau, commented, 'I didn't think she'd like it, Jake.'

'At least one of you has some human decency!' shrieked Harriet, aiming a canvas-clad foot at Jake's shins.

'Will you stop that!' he snapped. 'Pull yourself together, Harriet. We needed some money and the only thing we had was your case. You'll get it all back when I get paid. Anyway, you didn't need those clothes. You don't want to go wandering round Boston, you'll be much too busy on board.'

Harriet, tiring, slumped in his grip. 'I wanted to see the sights,' she said tearfully.

'Well, I'm sure we can arrange something,' said Jake, vaguely soothing. 'Will you behave if I let you go?'

'Yes,' said Harriet meekly. He let go. She waited until he was sure she wasn't going to hit him, then swung back her arm and clouted him hard over the ear. 'Serves you right, you bastard,' she shouted, retreating round the table.

'You hellish bitch,' he said, rubbing his ear. 'I wouldn't put it past you to slit my throat if you got the chance.'

'That's what will happen if you don't pay me back.'

'All right, all right, that's enough,' said Lewis, coming between them.

'And who said you were skipper to be calling order?' demanded Mac, taking his first positive interest. 'You're a bit too free with your orders, laddie.'

'And you're all a bit too free with the insults,' said Jake. 'Stow it, the lot of you. We're all in the same crew – including you, Harriet – and what I say goes. We'll have no more of this. We know where we stand and we leave it like that. Harriet, get on with dinner.'

'You are a bloody pirate,' she said venomously. 'If I don't behave do I get to walk the plank?'

''Course not. We put you on shore in what you stand up in. But if you do as you're told, you'll have a bloody good time and you'll get all your money back, so why not be a good girl and cook dinner?'

She glared at him, her hair tumbling into her eyes. Then she tossed it back with what was possibly the first truly haughty gesture of her life, and went to peel potatoes.

Chapter Six

In the morning a brisk breeze was dancing across the harbour under a smiling sun. Little waves raced by, losing their heads to the wind from time to time and slapping up against hulls like naughty children meeting a parental hand. Harriet, poking a sleep-tousled head out of the companionway, felt happy despite herself. How could she want to see Boston's art when there was this to enjoy, the world set before her at a new and totally charming angle? Still, she would not smile at Jake as he slid an arm around her waist.

'How about if I say sorry?'

'All you want is breakfast.'

'You're right, we've got to get going. Derekson will turn up this morning and I want us to be out to sea.'

Harriet lost her blank indifference in a trice. 'Are we really going out? I mean, should we? Out there? Isn't it awfully dangerous? The wind seems very strong.'

Jake laughed and kept on laughing. He seemed to think she was terribly funny. She gazed up at his sharp white teeth and thought how fierce he was, how frighteningly without restraint. He would do anything if it suited him well enough.

'Go and cook breakfast, love. We've got to get under way.' He sent her off with a pat on the bottom and despite herself she warmed to him. It was so nice to be treated intimately. Only when that chord inside herself vibrated did she know that it was something she missed, perhaps had always missed.

She gave Jake fried bread, which he loved but which Lewis considered barbaric. Lewis was a health food nut, spreading polyunsaturates on wholemeal bread and drinking disgusting decaffeinated coffee. At the other end of the scale was Mac, white bread, white sugar and butter an inch thick, openly contemptuous of what he considered to be Lewis's pansy ways.

'You'll die the same as the rest of us,' he declared, tucking into his food. 'You won't live any longer and you won't have had as much fun.'

'There's no harm in living a healthy life,' said Lewis.

'And I'll thank you not to patronise me,' retorted Mac. 'Who do you think you are with your holier than thou smirking, muttering about animal fats the moment I think about eating pork chops? Who says you're healthier than I am, eh?'

Harriet looked from Lewis's long-limbed strength to Mac's narrow-chested weediness and hid a smile. Lewis, foolishly allowing himself to be drawn, began to tell Mac how his arteries were clogging and his liver packing up. 'And you should listen too, Harriet, you're grossly overweight.'

She went scarlet, halted in the very act of eating a bacon sandwich. 'I do try and slim,' she said helplessly.

'Leave the girlie alone, she's a strapping wench,' announced Mac. Harriet was torn by her desire to appease them both, which could not be achieved by either eating or not eating the sandwich. They both watched her. Blushing, she opened the sandwich, took out the bacon and ate that.

Jake, who had been vaguely listening while studying a chart, chuckled. 'You do amuse me, Harriet, you really do. Come on everyone, let's go. Everything that moves tied down, please, Harriet, and I mean that. There'll be trouble if I come down here and find baked beans scattered all over the shop.'

'Lot of fibre in baked beans,' said Lewis earnestly, and couldn't understand why Harriet and Jake laughed.

They used the motor to draw the *Real Sheila* away from her mooring. Harriet was reassured by the chugging noise, feeling that at least she would not be totally at the mercy of the wind. But, before she could become used to the new motion of the boat, bouncing a little as it met the sea, Jake shouted, the engine cut, there was the sound of feet on the coachroof and the *Real Sheila* heeled dramatically. Harriet's neat world tumbled around her. A cupboard door fell open, hitting her on the head, and tins cascaded on to the floor. An open pack of washing powder threw itself from somewhere and lodged like white sand in the crevices of the nonslip rubber floor. From the fo'clse, which she had forgotten, came ominous crashes.

Jake's head appeared in the companionway. 'What did I tell you, Harriet?'

'You didn't tell me you were going to turn the world upside down,' she shrieked, hanging on to the table edge. Its rubber border, which had at first seemed foolish and impractical, now looked like sense. 'When does it stop?'

'It doesn't. Get cleared up and come on deck. You'll like it.'

He disappeared and Harriet ran a hand through her hair. The place was a shambles. How was she to sort it out when there was nothing and nowhere still and level? It was like a fairground ride when your only thought is that sooner or later it must stop, but according to Jake this was the way things were at sea. 'This is all his fault' she mumbled, chasing tins across the floor. The morning's breakfast was sitting unhappily in her stomach, reminding her of its presence more and more urgently as the minutes passed. She wished the noises would stop too: yells from on deck, the rushing of water, the groaning of what she imagined were spars and rigging, though if anyone was groaning it was probably her. Clearly she could not stay below. She cannoned up the companionway, fell over Mac and collapsed over the rail. The water, once some feet away, was now conveniently positioned an inch from her nose.

'Give Harriet a lifeline,' yelled Jake.

'I don't want a lifeline, I want to die,' she moaned.

'Breathe deeply,' Lewis advised, prising her from the rail and fastening a belt round her. 'Think how much weight you'll lose, Harriet.'

When all that she could cast overboard was long gone, Harriet crawled into the cockpit and slumped behind Jake. He was standing at the wheel, legs braced against the angle of heel, watching compass and sails with total absorption. Suddenly, and for no apparent reason, the stern of the boat swung violently round, booms swung, sails cracked, and Mac and Lewis, on the foredeck, dived for cover. But no-one except Harriet seemed unduly perturbed.

'Told you she was a bitch,' called Lewis, working the mainsheet winch.

'Hmmm. Either the ballast's wrong, and I don't think it's that, or we're taking water. Did she do this when you first had her out?'

Mac slipped into the cockpit, his wiry frame well suited to the apparent clutter of the yacht. 'She wasna so bad, Jake. We were more worried that she didn't come up to the wind.'

Jake nodded. 'It's a leak, probably a fitting that's only submerged at this angle of heel. We'll put her on the other tack. Lewis, you take the wheel while I have a look below.'

As he turned he saw Harriet's huge-eyed, panic-filled face. 'What's the matter with you?'

'Are we going to sink?' she asked breathlessly.

'Don't be so bloody stupid, it's only a little leak. The time to worry is when you see things floating up out of the cabin, and only then if you left your wallet down below. Believe me, Harriet, we will not sink! Even if we did, we've got the radio, and the liferaft, and we can fire off a distress rocket and be saved by two ten-year-old boys in a canoe. We're only a couple of miles offshore. Look, there's America.'

He gestured towards the land, just visible over the looming rail of the yacht.

Harriet, clinging to the seat in order to prevent herself sliding off it, tried to smile. 'So we're quite safe,' she agreed waveringly.

'Absolutely. By the way, put your lifejacket on.'

He disappeared below, leaving Harriet confused and almost angry. You could never trust Jake. He never told you the truth and she doubted that he would recognise it if he did, but the others had faith in him.

She asked Mac for a lifejacket, and while he showed her how to put it on, said: 'Is Jake a good sailor?'

Mac almost smiled. 'You could say so. In heavy weather he's about the best, I'd say. Light airs, perhaps not so good. He gets a bit bored unless there's money on it. And for sorting out a rubbish tip of a boat like this, there isn't anyone can match him.'

'Why doesn't he have any money, then?'

Mac shrugged. 'He can't hold on to money longer than a week, can't Jake. There's always a scheme, or a trip to take, or a girl to impress. Look now, he's going to have to pay you all he earns for this job.'

'He owes it to me,' said Harriet menacingly. 'He can't wriggle out of it.'

Mac grinned. 'Can't he?'

A sudden roaring sounded from below, and in answer to it Mac went down to help Jake. Alone but for Lewis at the helm, Harriet began to relax. The sun was shining, the breeze was blowing right into her, cleaning her out right down to her toes, and her sickness was subsiding to a mere tenderness of gut. She began to wonder what she must look like, without make-up, her hair in need of a wash, a lifejacket adding to her bulk. She must remember to try and make the best of herself. The men barely considered her as a woman at all; she was simply Harriet who did the cooking. The wind was making her eyes water and she wanted to go to the toilet. She ducked down below.

Jake was in the cabin. 'Don't use the loo. That's what's leaking – the water intake isn't fitted right. I told Derekson you couldn't have household plumbing in a racing yacht, but dear Walter knew better. Just a cock would have made all the difference, a single bloody cock. Instead of which, we now have a cock-up.'

Harriet squeezed her thighs together. 'What do I do then?'

'Bucket, my sweet. Don't worry, I won't look. Bet you've got a lovely pink bottom, too, a real handful.'

'You should know, you've squeezed it,' snapped Harriet. 'Do I take it you want something, Jake?'

He looked surprised. 'Not really. Coffee and sandwiches wouldn't come amiss, though.'

She snorted and put the kettle on, watching in terror as it remained straight on the cooker despite the boat's crazy angle. How was she to balance on a bucket in these conditions? It was all right for the men, they casually unzipped and peed over the side, and anyway they had a different attitude to these things. It was prudish to be embarrassed, she knew, but the thought of parading through the boat with her bucket to empty it over the side filled her with horror. Somebody, probably Jake, would be bound to make a rude comment.

Eventually she had to go. While they all munched sandwiches topsides she retreated to the fo'clse with her bucket. When she emerged with it and proffered it tentatively to the waves, Jake said, 'Hang on to it, Harriet, or you'll lose it.'

'Shut up!' she said with unnecessary vehemence, and as he had predicted the sea whipped the bucket out of her hand and sent it bobbing and bouncing away.

'Well done, Harriet,' said Jake.

She sat down with them and tried to eat a sandwich, but it would not go down. The sky was darkening, the brilliant morning was subsiding into a cold and dull afternoon. The motion of the boat was becoming less settled. She seemed to be shuddering at the impact of each wave.

'We'll take a reef,' said Jake. 'I don't like this sail plan at all, it's a real mess. Derekson had better order a new staysail, just for starters.'

'The boat's too bloody narrow,' said Mac angrily. 'That's the real fault.'

'Well, we're stuck with that. My main worry is the hull construction. With so much wrong that you can see, what's that like? We'll have to push her once we get this leak sorted, see if she can stand it.'

'That's the day I look round Boston,' said Harriet determinedly.

'Sure, sure, we agreed that. Right chaps, ready? Prepare to come about.'

The *Real Sheila* bucked her way back to harbour like a badly broken horse, shying away from the wind and sometimes refusing pointblank to put her tail to the seas. Now and then a wave slapped over the cockpit, sending green water down into the cabin before they had time to shut the hatch. Huddled in the cockpit, Harriet watched in terrified misery as the *Sheila's* stern was pushed this way and that, once taking sea right over it. A gout of cold water ran down the neck of her borrowed oilskins but the boat came up, and the water drained neatly away out of the cockpit. She began to realise that the faults Jake railed at were not in themselves dangerous – the boat simply did not meet his rigorous standards. It more than met hers. He wanted performance: she merely hoped that it would go more or less as pointed and stay on top of the water.

Mopping up the cabin, she all at once felt sorry for herself. This wasn't the holiday she had imagined. But it never did to dwell on the might-have-beens, let alone to envy the lives of others. Look at Sheila Derekson, with a tub of a boat named after her, a drink problem and a failed facelift. If Harriet wanted things to be different she must make them so. That was the philosophy that had sent her on that cruise in the first place. And now look. At least things were different.

Almost as soon as they settled to their mooring, a speedboat fizzed away from the shore towards them.

'Derekson,' said Lewis shortly. Glances passed between all three men.

'Leave the talking to me,' said Jake. 'Get forward, Harriet.'

'I won't.'

He turned in surprise. 'What do you mean, you won't? Do as you're told.'

She felt herself becoming belligerent. 'I won't hide like something you're ashamed of. I'm one of the crew, you said so. I'm working, I'm not some sort of floozy.'

Mac nodded. 'She's right, Jake. I mean, no-one could take Harriet for a fancy bit. It's not as though we're having some sort of orgy, he must see that.'

Jake considered. 'Oh, stuff it, I don't suppose it matters. Besides, I've got better things to think about just now. Pipe the bastard aboard, Lewis, will you?'

Derekson had brought Walter with him. The two men clambered up the rope ladder while a white-hatted helmsman stayed with the powerboat. Both wore designer yachting gear: smart white shoes, peaked caps, well-pressed trousers and striped matelot jerseys which were a million miles from the stained trousers and jumpers favoured by Jake and his men. A thin drizzle was falling, and they at once went below.

'I think you remember Harriet. She's cooking for us,' said Jake, taking the bull by the horns.

Derekson stared at Harriet. She ran her hands down the sides of her trousers and smiled weakly, knowing she looked terrible. 'I'm enjoying it a lot,' she lied.

'I don't remember you saying that you intended to sail with the boat. I thought you had other plans, Miss Wyman,' Derekson said with a distinct chill.

'She did,' broke in Jake, 'but I convinced her they could wait. She cooked one meal and we were all so impressed we persuaded her to stay. I'm seeing to her pay, of course.'

Derekson raised a sceptical eyebrow. 'Is that so? But it isn't a matter of money, Jake, we must prioritise here. This is a seagoing boat. If you remember our last conversation, you weren't prepared to let either Walter or myself join, and we are both experienced sailors. If you push the boat as you should then Harriet's going to feel very unhappy aboard the *Real Sheila*. And if you don't push her then I'm going to be unhappy. I think we should understand each other, Jake.'

Jake stared at Derekson for a moment, then dropped his eyes to the cabin sole. It was in no sense a gesture of submission. 'I think you can rely on me to be the best judge of what is right for this boat,' he said tightly. 'Harriet and I have agreed that she will go ashore on days when the weather is such that she will be unlikely to enjoy her sailing. As it happens, she's turning into a very competent crew member. I'm very pleased with her.'

She felt herself blushing from her toes to the roots of her sad tangle of hair. As if to provide visual aids for Jake's description of life aboard ship, she began busily to fill the kettle and make coffee for everyone.

'I see,' said Derekson in a flat voice. There was no way of telling if he was convinced.

Walter, with no interest at all in the exchange, said, 'What's this Lewis means about a leak? Is there a leak? Is it serious?'

'Depends on how you feel about broaching,' said Jake. 'We need a shipwright for a morning, that's all. Send one out, will you, Angus, first thing. I've made a list of all the points we must tackle, some of them more urgent than others. And by the way, we need some new sails.' The men settled themselves round Jake at the table. Harriet could not understand the relief she felt at being allowed to remain where till that moment she had thought she did not want to be.

The discussion mellowed Derekson. Jake's immediate and determined grasp of the *Real Sheila's* problems gave reassurance where before there had been confusion and doubt. The boat had been conceived in enthusiasm, but almost from the first there had been problems, arguments, mishaps. He had not understood that in boats, as in most things, compromises must be made, and he had not known where to make them. Did you sacrifice seaworthiness for speed, weather helm for fine air sensitivity? If this was the best keel and that the best mast, why did they not work when you put them together? If one expert extolled one type of hull, yet it was disparaged by another of equal standing, whom did you believe? The problems had mounted until pleasure was the last thing Derekson could get from his boat. He had even reached the point where his stomach sank when he woke in the morning and thought of it. But he would have had to be desperate to call on Andrew Jakes. It was well-known that Jake hadn't seen a job through in at least two years: losing interest, rowing with the owner, going off on some new and fantastic scheme of his own. Derekson knew he must keep him on a short leash, and knew also that Jake was not a man you could unduly restrain. It was an uncomfortable relationship.

The Harriet problem niggled him. His gut feeling was that she would cause trouble, but when you looked at the podgy, unglamorous reality the thought seemed ridiculous. He disliked women who took no care of themselves, he thought spitefully, but all he said was: 'If you'd like to freshen up at any time you can of course make use of the clubhouse. I have made arrangements for the crew.'

'Thank you. That's very kind. I should like a bath,' said Harriet miserably, correctly assessing his view of her. Derekson was so relentlessly clean and she was so manifestly dirty. It did not make for self-confidence.

Chapter Seven

If a building could have sported gold braid, Harriet felt that the Derekson clubhouse would have done so. She had never seen a place emanate money so conclusively as this, from the whitewashed exterior and holystoned steps to the vast hall with its panelling in limed oak. Shabby and dirty, she followed Jake like a mongrel dog that had somehow strayed into Crufts. 'I'm skipper of the *Real Sheila*,' announced Jake to the uniformed flunkey who accosted them. 'Name of Jakes.'

Suddenly heads started popping out of rooms, all staring, but Jake seemed unaware of them. 'Come on, Harriet,' he said, starting up the stairs. 'Let's get you a wash and brush-up.'

As they went up two elegant ladies went down. Harriet slunk past and whispered to Jake, 'I feel terrible, like a tramp!'

'Nonsense,' he declared. 'We look like people who go on real boats, not cruiseline wallahs. Relax, they'll think you've endured a hurricane. If anyone asks you say that the breeze did seem rather stiff, but you hadn't any worries till you were pooped and the cockpit flooded, soaking your chicken marinade. Then complain about the size of pipes in self-draining cockpits.'

'Conman.'

'Mouse.'

He shut the door of the room firmly behind them and went through to inspect the bathroom. 'You bath, I'll shower,' he declared. 'That should save time.'

She felt herself blushing. 'But you'll be able to see me.'

'Only when I'm out of the shower, and I promise not to look. Don't be such a prude, Harriet.' He went to the shower and turned it on, then began to strip off. Harriet watched in horror and when Jake caught sight of her face he stopped in the very act of removing his underpants. She could see – him. He began to laugh. 'I keep forgetting what an innocent you are, sweetie. Where have you been for the last ten years, in a convent?'

'I've been looking after my mother,' said Harriet confusedly. She felt dizzy. She could smell him, hot and vital, a mixture of sweat and salt and something indefinable. He had thick, well-muscled legs, the hair growing profusely where they merged into his body.

He came and stood very close to her. 'You've never seen a man naked, have you?'

She shook her head. Her unwashed hair brushed his smooth, brown shoulder. 'Shall I tell you something Harriet?' His hands were gently encircling her body. Even through the wool of her jumper, they felt hot.

'What?'

'I find virgins very exciting.'

She lifted her head and met his eyes, clear as water. He pulled her to him and her nipples, taut and stiff, met his chest. 'You think I'm fat,' she said hoarsely.

'Did I say that? You've got such a lovely bottom, Harriet, I could really get hold of that.' His hands clasped the cheeks of her bottom and she felt him hard against her. For a moment it was delicious. He ground against some place infinitely in need of touching. She moaned. Suddenly he pulled up her jumper and dragged one of her breasts free of her bra, fastening his lips to it hard. The sensation tugged at her as he tugged. She closed her eyes and thought she might faint. She gasped as he pulled too hard, and her eyes opened. Harriet looked down and saw a man sucking, almost gorging on her nipple. She dragged violently away.

'Stop it! You revolting man.'

'Don't be stupid, Harriet.' He was reaching for her again, and he was bulging horribly, disgustingly from his underpants. He must be deformed, she thought, nothing that size could be normal.

'Get away from me.' She covered her nipple with her hands. It was wet and throbbing, hardly seemed part of her. He stood legs apart in front of her and touched her bottom again, saying, 'Come on, Harriet. Let me.'

'No!' She spun round and crouched with her back to him. He rubbed eager palms against her buttocks, but did nothing else. Heat began, deep inside her belly. She began to relax, to feel that she should stop this but could not bear to do so. Then, as she lifted her shoulders in submission, he caught her hand. She felt him, hard and thrusting against her palm, and he held her hand there and would not set her free. His hips thrust violently, his face contorted and he convulsed against her fingers, groaning ecstatically.

'You're horrible,' she hissed. 'Perverted!'

'Frustrated is the word,' he said, panting. 'I am sorry, Harriet. I didn't mean to be quite so businesslike. Christ.'

'You only brought me here for that,' said Harriet tearfully. 'You think I'm fat and ugly but you wanted a woman and there wasn't another one about. You didn't even – you couldn't even be bothered – ' She wasn't entirely sure what it was he hadn't done that she wished he had, yet she felt utterly let down.

Jake slumped in a chair and wiped his forehead languidly. 'Look on the bright side – at least you didn't lose your virginity to a bastard like me. And I didn't have it planned, actually. It was thinking about those breasts of yours in the bath that started me off. Say what you like, you have got a fantastic pair. You should show them off a bit.'

She was washing her hands busily at the basin. 'I don't want you to look at me, ever. Don't you ever try that again, and don't you ever mention it to me. I don't have to let you use me.'

He shook his head, looking almost pained. 'Sweetie, don't think of it like that. It isn't true. You don't want to take these things so seriously.'

'Well, I do. Get out, Jake. I want a bath.'

They were quiet afterwards, Jake unable to hide his lazy contentment. Harriet raged at him silently, and he knew she did. He took her for a drink at the bar, acknowledging acquaintances here and there. But he choked off would be conversationalists and instead concentrated on Harriet.

'Drink your martini, you'll feel better.'

She pushed her hair out of her eyes. The cut was growing out, and without proper drying had frizzed into a soft bush round her head. 'This time you've really upset me,' she said flatly.

'I know. I was wrong and I know it, that was no way to treat you. Look, let's go and buy you some clothes, just a few things to get you by. I'd get you more but – I haven't the money Harriet, really.'

She wondered if she felt mollified or not. When he said things like that she instinctively warmed to him, but Jake knew how to charm people. He could be lying now with wads of notes hidden somewhere. Yet she thought not. One thing she was learning about Jake was his inability to hold on to money, and if she did not get her clothes now, while he had a bit, there would be no use bleating in a day or so when his pockets were really to let.

She stared round at the few women in the bar. They wore spring colours, clear blues and lemons, and sat in the floorlength windows looking out across the sea. Harriet knew, she had no doubt, that she could never look like them, elegantly understated and subtly made-up. But even she could look a little less ramshackle. She finished her martini.

She had not expected to go shopping for clothes in a ship's chandlers. Nonetheless Jake assured her that this was the place to find really suitable gear for life on a boat, and as she scanned the oilskins and waterproof trousers, the coarse wool jumpers and ear flap hats, she had to agree that it was suitable. Why had she imagined he would want her to look like the other women occasionally sighted on boats, wearing slim white trousers and crisp blouses?

'Those are for people who don't really sail,' said Jake dismissively when she mentioned it. 'You need something practical. Look, this is the sort of thing.' He held up a jacket that could have stood up alone if required.

'I thought you wanted me to show off my – chest.'

'Not in a Force 7, I don't. This is just what you need, try it on.' It was a very roomy jacket. Harriet thought she looked like the side of a house in it. Jake said that was so you could put jumpers underneath. She didn't want to be miserable with cold, did she? He'd had a jacket just like this once, he'd worn it in a gale off Ushant. But it was warm and it was cheap, reduced several times by the look of it since no-one else had been desperate enough to take a lifeboatman's jacket in a lady's size. As always Harriet's vague ideas of what she wanted were submerged by other forces. She emerged with a selection of clothes that were undoubtedly very warm.

Jake's good humour evaporated as they chugged back across the harbour to the yacht. Moored at its stern was the powerboat, and clearly visible on deck was Walter's peaked cap. 'Oh God,' said Jake. 'Prepare for the gospel according to the *Cutty Sark*.'

'What's the *Cutty Sark*?' asked Harriet, muffled in her jacket.

'Record-holding tea clipper. Vast sail area and huge crew to work it – Walter likes the principle. You wait, you'll see.'

Walter was sniffing round the deck like a trainee bloodhound, watched in silent hostility by Lewis and Mac. When Jake appeared over the side they immediately gravitated towards him.

'Wants the mainsail bigger.'

'Thinks the shrouds need adjusting.'

'Does he now? Hello, Walter, glad to see it's your day for the Spithead Review. Kettle on, Harriet, we need some coffee.'

Her hackles rose but no-one was taking any notice of her. She went below and put on the kettle, while men tramped the deck over her head and pretended to conduct a civilised argument. When at last they came below Walter was red in the face.

'In all my experience I have never heard of a plan like it,' he said vehemently, taking a cup from Harriet as if she were a waitress. 'There isn't a boat afloat that has such a rig.'

'Derekson isn't paying me to copy other boats,' said Jake, surprisingly mildly. 'Sailing is the art of altering sail shape to wind, not making the tub top heavy and expecting it to go. This boat will carry the sail that can be comfortably managed by a racing crew, and I assure you she will move.'

'She isn't the *Cutty Sark*,' said Harriet authoritatively.

'Quite right, Harriet. And she doesn't need a crew of ten either.'

'If she had more men she could be worked far more efficiently,' said Walter. 'I told Angus it was ridiculous to try and work her with only three – '

'But she won't have three when she's racing! God, man, can you imagine what it would be like trying to sort her out with eight men aboard? As it is we can see what needs doing. I admit you get the odd hairy moment when you're sailing shorthanded, and I'll give you leave to complain when she sinks. Now come on, Walter, we can work together on this. You've got a lot of experience, and when we're a bit further on I'd appreciate it if you came out with us for a day. But I want it clear that you leave the decisions to me, OK?'

Walter looked at him with an old man's stubborn dislike, rejecting the olive branch out of hand. 'I'll have you know that Angus isn't at all happy about you sailing with your fancy piece aboard,' he said petulantly.

Mac laughed. 'She's no very fancy,' he declared.

Harriet felt the blood surging into her cheeks and then ebbing, to leave two bright red patches in deadwhite skin. 'Don't be so rude to Harriet,' said Lewis. 'She's got ears.'

'She's got a lot more than ears,' said Jake ambiguously. 'You've no need to worry, Walter, Harriet is here to work. And even if she wasn't, I reserve the right as skipper of this boat to run things as I see fit. Harriet's presence does not affect the running of this boat, and until it does neither you nor Angus has any say in the matter. Now, I wish to catch the tide. Good day to you.'

Walter picked up his cap and left in certain dudgeon. No-one said anything, but began at once to prepare to put to sea. Alone in the cabin, Harriet wondered why Jake had defended her. She thought back to the clubhouse bathroom and shuddered. He had been horrible. In all her life she had never imagined that anyone could be so casual about such a thing. In the darkness of her bed it was possible to imagine people doing unthinkable things, but in broad daylight, standing up – tremors racked her again. Yet she knew she could have stopped him, if she had wanted. Shame bowed her head. All the same, when Jake opened the door and yelled 'Make some sandwiches, Harriet, there's a good girl', she went hot with more than embarrassment.

Somehow a week passed, seven days in which the yacht flogged up and down the coast, seven days in which Harriet toiled below deck. Once they stayed out all night, the wind as fierce as a dog, blowing in sharp gusts that allowed the yacht almost to come up, and then pushing her over again with a sickening sway. Harriet slept little, lying in the cramped berth held in by a strip of canvas lashed across the side. The sound of seas breaking on deck woke her again and again. She was beyond sickness but not beyond fear. Towards morning she got up and found that no-one else was in the cabin. She felt suddenly fearful that they had abandoned ship and left her, running up the steps to fling open the main hatch. A wave slapped her in the face and ran cheerfully down below.

'Shut the hatch, Harriet,' yelled Jake. She did, but with herself on the wrong side of it. The wind tore at her hair, the greyness of sea and sky merging into a world a thousand miles from the damp cabin she had just left. When she looked over the stern, row upon row of waves seemed to pursue them.

'Glad you've got that jacket, eh, Harriet?' said Jake. 'Put on a lifeline, there's a good girl. Lewis, are you sure you know where we are? We should have seen that light half an hour ago.'

Lewis, looking grim, disappeared into the cabin to mutter and draw lines on charts. 'Are we lost?' asked Harriet, keeping her voice determinedly casual.

''Course not. This is the sea, that's the sky, and somewhere out there is a bloody great rock we'd rather not hit. Once we see the light we'll know – '

'Dead ahead, skipper,' yelled Mac suddenly. 'Light dead ahead.'

Jake swung the wheel hard, yelling at Lewis to get back on deck. 'You've nearly sunk us, you navigational incompetent!'

Harriet huddled in a corner of the cockpit, willing herself not to go below where although it seemed safe you would be trapped if the boat sank. She could just see the instructions on the liferaft, but too faintly to fully understand them. The wind raged deafeningly. She was sure that nothing could save them now, for all the desperate winding of winches and heaving on lines.

'Bloody winch has jammed,' yelled Mac, and went for'rd. Harriet couldn't understand why they didn't give up and take to the liferaft. The distress flares were all by her berth, but that couldn't be helped. They must send out an SOS on the radio, they might still be saved.

Jake was muttering on about the winches. 'Useless design. We'll get them changed when we get back. Give Derekson the bill when it's too late to argue.'

What a thing to be considering at a time like this! 'Why don't we just abandon ship?' she wailed, if only for the sake of hearing one sensible voice.

Jake glanced down at her. To her amazement he was laughing. 'Poor old Harriet. Tell you what, when we get back you can have a day looking round Boston. You'll like that, won't you?'

'We won't get back. You're just saying that to stop me having hysterics.'

'Actually I mean it. We should be laid up for a day or so anyway to have everything seen to. Go and make some sandwiches, sweetie. I promise I'll let you know if we're going to sink.'

'I'm not going down there, I'll be trapped!'

'Well, you're not staying up here, so it's either that or over the side. Down below, Harriet. Now.'

'Bully.'

Reluctantly she went below. Despite the damp and the angle of heel the cabin seemed very homely, bathed in warm yellow light. She felt unreasonably tearful and busied herself making sandwiches.

They were heading back to harbour when Derekson called through on the radio. Jake talked to him for some twenty minutes, and though she could only hear one side of the conversation, to Harriet it seemed clear that it was not going well. Derekson had asked about the winches and Jake had told him. It appeared that Derekson himself had chosen the design. They again discussed the new sail plan, and clearly Walter had been doing his bit, convincing Derekson that he was about to be asked to buy a new, untried, and probably disastrous idea. Once again Jake made his points, his frustration clear even over the radio. Eventually the conversation ended. Jake sat slumped.

'What is the use of it?' he whispered. 'What is the bloody use?'

'Won't he do any of it?' asked Harriet.

'I don't know. He might, in about six weeks when I've talked myself hoarse. If I had the money I'd build such a boat . . . Instead I have to waste my life putting up with prats. I can't see any reason to it.'

'Six weeks isn't so long,' said Harriet. 'You shouldn't want everything so quickly. He can't be expected to change everything at once. If he saw that one or two of your ideas worked, then he'd be all right. And if you did make this boat good then everyone would let you do what you liked with their boats, wouldn't they?'

He glared at her. 'Now we've yet another authority on board, I see.

Why don't you go and cook something?'

He sat for some minutes, gloomy and bad-tempered. She thought he was thinking about Derekson, but suddenly he lifted his head. 'It does sound wrong. Don't you think so?'

'What does? I can't hear anything different.'

But he was already prowling around the cabin, unpinning great sheets of plastic that lined the walls so he could peer at the hull and put his ear to the skin to listen to it. Eventually he called Mac and Lewis down to listen. 'Delamination,' he said grimly. 'I'll swear it is.'

'Can't see anything,' said Lewis. 'I don't think Mr. Derekson will believe you, Jake.'

Mac nodded. 'He's right there.'

Jake considered for long minutes. If he went back now and told Derekson his suspicions, the chances were he would not be believed. If he didn't tell him, and they put in train some of the minor, though expensive alterations required, then good money would inevitably be thrown after bad.

'I've got to prove it,' he said. 'Sorry, Harriet, no sightseeing for you. Ready about, there's a good storm force blowing and with any luck we'll have some nice dents to show Angus Derekson in a day or two.'

'But I want to get off!' declared Harriet shrilly. 'I'm not staying, it isn't fair. Jake!'

'There's always the dinghy,' he offered. 'I haven't any choice.' She threw down her tea towel. 'Yes, you have! You can put in and tell Mr. Derekson what you suspect, put me ashore and then go out again. You're just being stubborn, that's all. You're worse than Captain Bligh. We should take a vote on it.'

'You don't take votes on boats, the skipper's word goes. God damn it, Harriet, you can go and look at art galleries any day of the blessed week. Don't be so difficult.' He pushed past her and went quickly on deck. Mac and Lewis followed, neither of them meeting Harriet's furious gaze. She felt betrayed.

The boat was not provisioned for days at sea and they were down to cocoa made with dried milk, and tins of tuna, beans and soup. In her rare sorties on deck, usually carrying food, Harriet could see no other boat anywhere, just the expanse of metal-grey sea heaving all about them. They were carrying too much sail, deliberately stressing the boat, and the cabin quickly became a slum, full of wet clothes, dirty plates and water. Exhausted and aching from the strain of life at an impossible angle, Harriet tried ineffectually to clear up. She was too tired even for anger.

'When are we going back?' she asked Mac tearfully as he came below for a plaster for a gashed finger.

'When the boat starts to fall apart. Dinna fret, you'll annoy Jake.' He returned topsides.

Half an hour later Jake came down. He went at once for'rd and began tossing Harriet's carefully stowed possessions back into the cabin. The pumps had been switched off so that he could listen to the hull, and the water in the bilges rose to lap at the cabin floor. Damp spread inexorably.

'I want to go home. I want to go home,' she whispered to herself.

'Not yet, ducky.' Jake was passing on his way topsides. 'Come up for a bit. We saw an oil tanker a while ago, they wanted to rescue us. I told them we were practising for the Americas Cup.'

'I don't want to be at sea,' muttered Harriet. 'I want to be rescued.'

Jake went happily on his way and Harriet was left looking at the cabin. Gradually she became aware that her clothes were sitting in half an inch of oily water. When she went to look more closely she found that even her few underclothes were soaked.

For a moment rage threatened to choke her. Not only did Jake steal her money, he pressganged her aboard ship, made her do disgusting things, forced her to endure gales, broke his promises to put her ashore, and then – he made her knickers wet. It was enough, and suddenly it was too much. The boat was heeling violently, but she didn't care any more. Deliberately, almost religiously, she went to the sailbag that contained Jake's dry clothes, and resolutely emptied it on to the cabin floor. She remembered as she did so that she had accompanied many of these same clothes to and from the laundromat, but that was unimportant. Her own clothes had soaked up most of the water, so these remained comparatively dry, a situation she determined to remedy. She steadily opened a tin of soup, taking care despite the boat's antics not to spill a drop. Then she emptied the contents all over Jake's clothes. Vegetable soup, she noticed, nice and indelible.

Nobody came down to see. Such was her fury that it occurred to her she might pull the plug out of the boat, if it had one, then they'd have to take notice of her. But they probably didn't have plugs any more, everything was far too high-tech. Instead she opened the cupboards, one after the other, and watched interestedly as crockery poured out on to the floor. The noise was very satisfactory, like a thousand tea trays falling at once. A box of washing powder flew elegantly across the boat, leaving a shower of pale blue grains following its trajectory.

Lewis's head appeared at the top of the companionway. 'Have you gone mad?' he yelled.

'Yes,' replied Harriet, and threw a tin of tuna at him. He ducked back out of sight, and was replaced in a second by Jake.

'God all bloody mighty,' he said, surveying the mess.

'Don't blaspheme.' Harriet looked round for a suitable missile.

'Throw that, and it'll be the last thing you do.'

She took careful aim and despatched a bag of tomatoes in his general direction. They exploded messily against the bulkhead.

'What do you think you are doing?' howled Jake. 'Are we going to have put you in irons?'

'All I want is to go back,' said Harriet. 'All I wanted was a holiday. You promised I could go sightseeing. You've taken all my clothes and now you've ruined all the ones I had left – so I've spoiled yours. And I've made a mess of your horrible, beastly boat. See how you like it.' She dragged open another cupboard door, and was herself amazed when a large calor gas cylinder crashed out on to the floor. Mac and Lewis appeared, like a Greek chorus.

'You'll have to tranquillise her,' said Lewis.

'Don't be so daft, we've only got aspirins,' said Mac.

'Get back and sail the boat,' snapped Jake. 'I'll deal with Harriet.'

He took a menacing step forward, and Harriet retreated behind the table. Suddenly the boat lurched violently, and seemed to hang in the water. The heel, to which they had all become quite accustomed, seemed suddenly acute and dangerous. The boat stayed where she was, motionless, and for a dreadful, endless moment they waited for her to roll over. Then, as she shuddered back towards upright, all three men raced for the deck. Slowly, with a sense of guilty doom, Harriet put on her huge coat and followed them.

She came upon a scene of ghastly confusion. Rope and canvas seemed to be everywhere, but as she tried to see what had happened water slapped her in the face. She clung to the cockpit side, coughing up green sea, and saw that a sail was trailing over the rail. It acted like a giant hand, holding the boat down, while the seas pounded and the mainsail flogged. Jake grabbed her and hauled her to the wheel. 'Hold it there. You let it go and you're really in trouble.'

Harriet hung on to the wheel while the men fought with the sail. She couldn't hold it, and Jake knew that she couldn't, but at least she could keep the boat somehow heading into the wind. It seemed that hours passed. I have wrecked the boat, thought Harriet. I lost my temper and wrecked the boat. All at once the wheel kicked in her hands, lightening as the sail slid over the side. The boat seemed to rear up out of the water in its eagerness to get under way.

'There's a bloody great dent in the bow,' called Mac as Jake grabbed at the wheel.

'Thank you, Harriet,' said Jake.

The afternoon was blending into night when they limped back to their mooring. Nonetheless as they dropped anchor Derekson's powerboat ripped through the whitecaps towards them. Harriet sat in the cabin shaking. It was all her fault.

Derekson stood on the companionway and stared at the cabin.

'It was one hell of a storm,' said Jake cheerfully. 'There's a sail gone and we've cracked a crossmember on the mast, but it was worth it. We've got what we were looking for: delamination.'

'You have deliberately wrecked this boat,' said Derekson slowly. 'Walter had a report from a tanker this morning that said you were carrying all sail. This was deliberate vandalism, simply because I wouldn't accede to your half-baked ideas.'

'I think we agreed that if the hull – '

'I don't care what we agreed,' snapped Derekson. 'I knew there'd be trouble from the moment you took up with this fiddle-faced Susie here. There's been a fight in this cabin. There's hundreds of dollars worth of damage.'

'Make that fifty,' agreed Jake. 'And I don't see why we should blame Harriet when – '

'Why not?' chipped in Mac. 'It was her.'

'When I want your advice, I'll ask for it,' snapped Jake.

'I want her off this boat!' declared Derekson. 'Now!'

There was silence. Everyone waited for someone else to speak. At last Jake said, 'I think we should discuss what is really at issue here, and that is the state of the hull.'

'I won't discuss anything until she's off the boat. You're obsessed with the woman.'

'It's up to me to dismiss the crew,' said Jake.

'She's not crew, she's – '

'Crew,' said Jake. 'If you insist on dismissing her, then I go too. I've done my job anyway, you've got my notes. My advice is to ditch this tub and use what you've learned in the next one.'

'If you leave, it's without pay,' said Derekson.

Jake sighed. 'Now that is unreasonable. I really don't want to lose my temper, Angus.'

'I'll deduct the damage to the cabin.'

'I'm owed a month's pay and I expect to get it.' Jake stared belligerently at Derekson. The older man reached for his chequebook.

'I want you and the girl off within the hour.'

Standing on the dock in the rain, carrying her worldly goods, Harriet had a distinct sense of déjà vu. As if to emphasise it, Jake said, 'You won't believe how many times this has happened to me.'

'Oh, I would,' she said. 'You've got a deathwish.'

'That's your trouble, not mine. I just don't like being pushed around.' He led the way along streets shiny with damp. The paving stones gleamed in the light of street lamps that also lit the drizzle as it fell. Harriet was cold and very weary. At the back of her mind was the fear that Jake was about to abandon her.

'Where are we going?'

'I don't know. Somewhere. There must be a cheap hotel.' They wound their way through the backstreets, past well-painted signs and neat front doors until they reached some steps shabby enough to be affordable. They trudged dispiritedly out of the rain.

Chapter Eight

The room was small and cramped. Anyone opening the door of the single wardrobe was forced by lack of space to kneel on one or other of the lumpy beds. The bathroom was down the hall, a dingy, stained affair that always seemed to be occupied. Nonetheless Harriet managed to bath and wash her hair, and returned to the room in a better temper. Jake was lying on his bed, hands behind his head, staring at the ceiling. The room was chilly but he seemed not to notice. She could see an inch of smooth brown skin above the waistband of his trousers.

'I wish we could have had two rooms,' she said distractedly. She was finding again that she was uncomfortable alone with him, that his calmness was not reflected in her. She hunched her shoulders within her thick wool jersey and sat on her bed, chin in hands.

'You hungry?' He sat up. Harriet wondered if she should deny it, because it was her money they were spending after all. She wondered when to broach the subject and decided it would be best over a meal. 'I am, actually.'

'Right, get your coat on and we'll go and celebrate our liberation. Come on, don't sit there looking peeved.'

Harriet donned her lifeboat jacket and followed him down the stairs. The night was horrible, tailormade for sitting indoors by the fire listening to the rain instead of which they were scuttling through deserted streets. But at least they weren't at sea, thought Harriet gratefully. It took something like her past incarceration below decks to show how wonderfully reassuring cold wet streets could look. Even the wind seemed kindly, because it threatened others and not them.

'Let's run,' said Jake, and caught her hand. They sprinted through the rain, alive and healthy and free. They only stopped when Jake spotted a small bistro down a side street, with bullseye windows misted by the heat within and a blackboard almost washed clean, but still bearing the word 'soup'.

There weren't many people inside. They sat next to the heater and Jake ordered two whiskys. They sipped while they decided what to eat, and in minutes Harriet felt drunk.

'I've never drunk whisky before,' she confided owlishly.

'You've never had any fun at all, Harriet. You'd better have the soup. We'll both have the soup, and then the seafood pancake. You don't want a steak, do you?'

She wouldn't have minded a steak, but she was too tired and too drunk to care. 'You mustn't spend all my money,' she heard herself say.

Jake raised his eyes from the menu to glance at her. 'You never give up, do you? It's only money.'

'It's only my money, you mean. Please, Jake – we agreed.' Somehow she felt in the wrong, as if she was being unduly mercenary. His eyes looked through her coldly. She felt herself blush.

'What would you do with it? Go straight home or what?'

'I – I don't know. I hadn't thought. Have my holiday, I suppose. Wouldn't that be the best thing?'

'If that's what you want. If that's all you want.'

She was confused and pushed at a strand of hair which was falling into her eyes. Jake reached over and brushed the lock gently out of the way. 'You don't have any ambition.'

The whisky was burning a hole in her belly; it was delicious, destructive, divine. She had ambition, if that was the name for unfulfilled, undirected longings for her life to be different. She was not, had never been, resigned to her fate. It was just that over the years, when there was nothing else to do but keep on with what she was doing, she had lost her courage. Or perhaps it was simply that the vision in her head, never clear, had become ever more misty and indistinct. Now she couldn't remember the dream, but that there had been one she remembered very well.

The soup arrived, thick and hot, with great wedges of bread. Harriet spooned it up avidly, aware that over the past days she had barely eaten. 'What will Mac and Lewis do?' she asked. 'I was surprised that they stayed.'

'They won't, for long. They can't stand each other, and once Derekson realises the boat's knackered, and the season's getting underway in the Caribbean, they'll upstakes and move. I'll catch up with Mac sooner or later, I always seem to.'

'He doesn't like me.'

'Doesn't he? I don't think he likes anybody much. That's what happens when you go through life looking after number one. He's got a nice fat bank account. One day he'll retire to Glasgow and live a lonely life in a bedsitter. Not because he can't afford anything else, he'll just have got used to being mean.'

'*I'm* not mean!'

'Yes, you are. And I don't mean money, I mean you. You don't give yourself – your time, your enthusiasm, anything. It's all "Hang on tight, give nothing back". You behave as if you had a bag of jewels and the rest of the world was trying to steal them. People aren't like that, Harriet. Even I'm not like that. If you don't give a little you don't get a thing.'

She sat looking down at her plate and wondered if he was right. She'd never had enough of anything to be generous with: looks, friends, anything. 'You're not that marvellously giving yourself.'

'Maybe not. But I don't make myself miserable the way you do. I do what I want. You see what you want but you can't get to it; you're hedged in by fear and doubt and insecurity. Look at you now. All that money, and despite everything you're going back on to your hamster wheel, back to the things you know and hate. What is it – a typing job in a Manchester office? Harriet, Harriet, live a little.' Somehow he had got hold of her hand, was gripping it in warm, tight fingers. He didn't let go even when the waiter came, it was Harriet who pulled back. Somehow that seemed a gesture of the utmost significance.

The rain had stopped when they walked back to the hotel. It was still cold but stars gleamed high in a blue-black sky. The smell of green things filled the air, budding even in this late spring, putting forth shoots as an act of faith and hope. She wondered if he wanted to make love to her. Would something happen in that dark room? Would there be two people in one lumpy bed, skin against skin, touching, licking, doing things that were hidden by the night? She remembered how big he had been, how strong, how determined. She hadn't known about any of that, they didn't tell you about that. He took her arm and there was heat in the pit of her belly.

When they reached the room she waited, watching him. It was for him to ask and her to give. But he was waiting, too, looking at her with those clear grey eyes, a square man, a stocky man, with a neck as thick as a bull's. Perhaps she should say that it was all right, that she wanted him to – wanted him. But tomorrow, what would happen then, when he knew her need was as great, greater, than his? She mustn't ask, it would be wrong. He threw his coat on the bed, she saw the muscles in his shoulders flex briefly. Would he think she was fat? If the light was out, then she might ask, but not when he could see her.

'I'll get undressed in the bathroom if you like,' he said, watching her.

What did he mean? 'Would that be best – do you think?'

'It depends on how you feel about it.'

Why did he make everything her fault, her decision, didn't he know how hard it was for her? She stood fingering the buttons of her coat, saying nothing, looking nowhere. Jake sighed and went out. Harriet, filled with misery, crawled into bed.

Despite everything she slept well that night, after a restless ten minutes in which she could think of nothing but Jake's breathing, Jake's rustling, Jake's sudden brief snoring. Once she knew he was asleep she relaxed, safe once more, and in a moment she too slept. Food and warmth and a solid bed were effective counters to dreams.

When she woke the next morning Jake wasn't there, and he wasn't in the bathroom either. She felt a familiar, creeping terror. He had left her. He had taken her money, left her with an unpaid bill and gone, all because last night she hadn't wanted – hadn't told him – because she hadn't. It was typical Jake, typically cruel and thoughtless and abrupt. You either went with him totally or he dumped you. Tears welled up and she crouched on the bed, whimpering and stuffing her fists in her mouth, telling herself that it would really be all right. She wasn't so badly off. She had some clothes now, sailing ones, and she could always go to the Embassy, she needn't tell them everything. Someone would help her. But misery rose, despite all her reasoning, and she flung herself on the pillow, hitting and biting it, hurting her fists, chewing at them because she was hurt and angry and alone.

The door opened. Harriet froze on the bed, her face still buried in the pillow.

'What the devil are you doing?'

She rubbed her bitten hands across her face and sat up, trying to look normal. 'I was feeling miserable. And cross.'

'What about? Have you been talking to someone?' He seemed truly bewildered, and Harriet scrubbed at her face again.

'No, no. It was just – I thought you'd left me.'

A grin flitted across his face. 'I don't suppose I should flatter myself it was me you were missing.'

He had brought in a carrier bag full of breakfast, coffee in polystyrene cups and hot, sugary doughnuts. They munched comfortably together while Harriet turned over in her mind various ways of tackling the subject of the money. They did not seem to be able to talk about it without some fundamental clash of view points because Jake seemed to think that whatever he had owed her was now a debt repaid.

'About the money,' he said suddenly.

Harriet jumped, because he had spoken her thoughts. 'Do we have to talk about it now?' she said with airy inconsequence.

'Well, it might be best. I've bought a boat.'

Her mouth opened, and then closed again. She looked down at the floor, up at the ceiling, and then at Jake. He was looking very tense. 'You bastard,' she said slowly.

'I knew you'd say that. It's for the best, Harriet. Now we can go to the Caribbean and get some sun. We can get out of this damned rain and live a bit. You don't want to go back to Manchester.'

'You might have asked me,' she said feebly.

He grinned. 'You'd have said no.'

'Of course I'd have said no! I hate boats. I don't want to go on your horrible boat. Anyway, it'll sink. You couldn't get anything good for that much money.'

Jake considered. 'It is a bit rickety, but I think it'll do. You know, your habits of mind are really beginning to get me down, Harriet. You'd miss the Pearly Gates because you were looking for your handkerchief.'

She put her hands in her hair and tugged it hard. 'I am not small-minded.'

'You're not exactly a free thinker, either. Look, get your things together. Stuff everything in your pockets. We need every penny we've got to buy food; we can't pay the bill as well.'

Harriet's eyes grew wide. 'What happens if we get caught?'

'We won't get caught. All we have to do is look as if we're going out shopping.'

Harriet put on most of her clothes, and stuffed the rest under the lifeboat jacket. Jake put his things in the breakfast carrier, but slung a pair of trainers over his shoulder, tied together by the laces. They went downstairs, Harriet furtive, Jake whistling. The woman at the desk eyed them like a rattlesnake.

'Know anywhere I can get these shoes repaired?' asked Jake cheerily. The woman stared at him, then turned aside to light a cigarette.

'She knew,' hissed Harriet once they were on the pavement.

'I think you're right. You see, there are people in this world who don't think only of money.'

'She's probably calling the police right now,' said Harriet, increasing her pace to a near trot. She couldn't believe how casual Jake was about the whole thing; he took risks and made decisions with almost no thought at all. Throughout her life Harriet had weighed this against that, slept on problems and solutions alike, and his cavalier attitude amazed her. Now she could see why he had borrowed her money in the first place: it had simply seemed like a good idea at the time. That was the thing about Jake: he thought of an idea and did it, whether it got him into a hole or not. If it did, he got himself out of it. She couldn't help but admire his style.

It was one of those mornings when the rain drizzles like badly strained peas, with a watery sun illuminating the scene from time to time. Two boats were moving into the harbour, one a true gin palace with tinted glass and twin motors, the other a schooner that must have seen fifty years at sea. Both Jake and Harriet sighed longingly, each for a different dream.

'Come on,' said Jake as the schooner moored and sent her sails tumbling. 'Let's take a look at our rubber duck.' He led the way past the trim yachting shops and cafés to the repair yards and junkheaps that hang on the coattails of affluence. The best boats, the prime boats, go to prime, expensive yards. It is the not-so-good vessels that gets tarted up in the not-so-good yard, run by a man who knows better but cannot afford it.

Harriet eyed the pock-marked hulls slung up on trestles in the mud. Plastic ones had holes in, wooden ones had rot. They stopped by a wooden one, new planking clearly visible against green slimed originals. It was a very small boat.

'What's it called?' asked Harriet tightly.

Jake looked taken aback. 'That has nothing to do with anything. It doesn't matter.' But Harriet was scrabbling on to a box to peer at the worn lettering on the prow.

'It's called *Dashing Away*,' she shouted. 'That's not bad, is it?'

'We're going to stick her in the briny and step the mast today,' said Jake. 'You'll be OK getting the shopping, won't you, Harriet?' He watched her climbing ineptly up a trestle to peer in at the cabin, her hair a damp bush round her head, her nose shiny and her body square and solid in the coat he had bought her. Was there ever anything so graceless? If he had any sense he'd dump her right now, but he knew he wouldn't. There was something oddly attractive about her sharpness, her vulnerability. There was something exciting too in her soft inexperience, like a rare snail discovered without its shell.

Afterwards Harriet could never believe that she had been led so tamely to such a cockleshell and allowed herself to be set adrift on the ocean. Ignorance seemed no defence when set against all the signs telling her not to go; a liferaft with the instructions on how to inflate it so perished that they were illegible; the smell of decay in the little cabin, that Jake assured her would vanish as soon as they dried it out. Why did she never query how they were to dry it on an ocean passage? Even she could see that rain was dripping in through the edge of the coachroof. She had been mesmerised by Jake, and she knew also what he would say if she complained.

Besides, she had been brought up on tales of single-handed derring-do on the waves, it was an era in which men seemed to circumnavigate the globe with as much ease as a toy boat buzzing round the lake in the park. It had become possible to believe that a bathtub with a sail could round Cape Horn, manned only by a dog singing 'Rule Britannia'. She was a little surprised to discover that *Dashing Away* had no self-steering, though.

'How do you get any sleep?' she asked anxiously. 'Do we stop?'

Jake's mouth twitched. 'Not exactly. Watch and watch about is usually the best method.'

She stared at him. 'You want me to help?'

'You did say you wanted to. You said it looked like fun.' He was doing something seamanlike with a sail that even to Harriet's untutored eye looked well past its best. She sat down next to him on the rough stone of the seawall, dropping her chin into her hands in a characteristic gesture.

'It'll be all right,' said Jake, briefly tousling her already tousled hair. 'The boat's sound enough. Just think, lazing on the deck in the sunshine, sunburn our only worry. The end of this bloody awful weather!'

It was starting to drizzle again and a thin, cold breeze was whipping across the bay. Harriet couldn't wait to get started.

There was a certain charm about *Dashing Away* as they cast her off from her mooring and set sail. She stood out like a period piece in a modern musical and her short, bobbing progress was very like a duck. They passed within a few cables of the *Real Shiela*, moored and with no sign of life aboard.

'I hope they ditch her,' said Jake, bringing the tiller round a little to have a better look. 'That's an unlucky boat and she'll kill someone one of these days.'

'I never thought you'd be superstitious.' Harriet was huddling down in the cockpit to escape the wind. Her knee brushed Jake's thigh and she withdrew it as discreetly as she could. They were living in horribly close proximity.

'All seamen are superstitious. There's so much that's out of your control. You can do everything right, have the best boat in the world, and still if your number's up, down you go to Davy Jones. Mostly you get away with it, but sometimes its close enough to let you know you were bloody lucky. Sometimes – sometimes it's as if someone's teasing you, letting you see how easily you could be killed. Then another time it's quite impersonal. Huge seas, about their own business, and you don't matter at all. The last thing you need's an unlucky boat.'

Harriet swallowed and hunched herself smaller. 'Is this an unlucky boat?'

'Can't be can she, at her age? Don't worry love, we're not going anywhere dangerous.'

Relief made her smile. She looked up at him through her tangle of hair and he grinned back. 'You've got a lovely smile, Harriet. You don't have to keep it just for special occasions.'

The compliment unnerved her. Abruptly she said, 'Can you show me how to steer? I think I'd better have some practice.'

He moved across to let her take the tiller, and as she passed in front of him his thighs pressed against her bottom. 'Everything improves with practice,' he said ambiguously. 'Keep her into the wind, she won't sail close but keep her as close as you can.'

Since they both had to sail the boat they were not often in the cabin together. Harriet told herself that it was a relief. Their bunks were either side of the cabin, and in such a small boat there was no centre table. When the boat was heeled one or other of the bunks was untenable unless they used bunkboards, when it was very like sleeping in a coffin. So they shared a bunk, one vacating it as the other moved in which, as Jake said, ensured it was always warm. 'I dream of you, Harriet,' he said as he turned in and she turned out. He took the graveyard watch in the small hours, she the early morning.

'Just make sure you wake up if I yell,' she said not as yet able to relax at the tiller, even when the breeze was no more than fresh and the sea full of nothing. In fact the emptiness unnerved her if she allowed herself to dwell on it. She developed a technique for steering which involved looking out at the sea for a count of ten, then looking in at the boat for a count of twenty. The boat might not be huge but it was home, and all there was of home. If she looked closely enough she did not have to be aware of the sea at all.

One grey early morning, three days out, she was gazing at the mainsail and counting the fastenings, bottom to top. Suddenly, it seemed to her inexplicably, a wave leaped up over the stern of the boat and fell on her. She shrieked, the cockpit filled with water to her knees, and Jake ricocheted up from below, yelling: 'Get her head to the wind! Quick, or we'll take another one.'

The boat was moving sluggishly as the water sloshed around in the cockpit. It was draining gradually, but Jake helped it on its way with a bucket for a moment or two. Then he took the tiller from Harriet. 'The wind shifted. You didn't notice.'

'But why did the wave come in?' She peered round at the sea, which did not seem to have any waves large enough to come on board.

Jake grinned. 'Watch.' He swung the tiller round, the yacht came broadside to the sea and a wave slapped against them, its head diving neatly into the cockpit. Harriet gasped as the cold water slithered down her neck. 'All right, I see.' She picked up the bucket and bailed for a bit. 'You can go back down now. I won't do it again.'

'No, you go and get dry. Make a cup of something hot, you could do with it.' She went thankfully below.

Jake sat at the tiller, pondering the minor crisis. It was asking a lot of a complete novice to steer the boat while he slept, especially as the glass was dropping and the wind beginning to stiffen. There was a gale blowing up. He thought about running for harbour, but they weren't well placed. They could find themselves on a lee shore very easily, and he'd prefer to have some searoom, especially as the boat wasn't sailing well. The new planking was letting in water, he was pumping the bilges every two hours. He told Harriet it was normal and she, bless her little cotton socks, believed him. Her blind trust in his seamanship amazed and moved him, she never queried anything. And here he was about to put her through a gale, in a leaky old tub with a suspect mast. When she brought up a mug of cocoa, made with dried milk, he suddenly put his arm around her and gave her a hug.

'You're a good girl. Hold the tiller while I take a reef will you, love?'

The gale hit them at about two in the afternoon. They were ready for it, or at least Jake was. The wind was fierce, perhaps a Force 8, but the sea was kind to them, developing a large swell over which *Dashing Away* bobbed bravely. The motion was wearying, so much so that Jake considered heaving to but decided that would be worse. Instead he lashed the tiller, set the storm jib and ran before the wind.

They sat below, side by side on the bunk, their feet wedged against the bunk opposite. 'Tell me again this isn't bad,' said Harriet as another gust hit them, like a dog tearing at a rabbit.

'It's not bad. At least you're not sick, that would be worse.'

'When I'm sick, I want to die. Now I'm scared I might! Aren't you scared, Jake?'

He reached out and put his arm round her, drawing her close. They were both wearing so many clothes that there was no contact they could feel, but it was comforting. 'I get scared,' he admitted. 'But this isn't scary, just bloody uncomfortable. And we're making fantastic time. We're not going in quite the right direction, of course, but you can't have everything.'

'Tell me again what it's going to be like,' said Harriet, half-closing her eyes. Despite everything, this was nice. Very nice.

'Blue seas. Blue skies. You showing some flesh. Brown arms. Brown shoulders. Lovely brown luscious – breasts. Nipples like dark, firm cherries.' His leg was sliding rhythmically against hers, up and down, up and down. Harriet let out her breath in a long sigh. Her world was full of noise, and heat, and Jake's leg moving up – and down.

'The wind's shifted,' he said, and released her. 'I'll go and have a look.' He disappeared topsides and left Harriet to herself. She slid a hand inside her jacket and touched her breast. It was an amorphous lump beneath her jumpers, squashy and unexciting. What would Jake do when the weather got better? What did she want him to do?

The gale abated towards midnight, by which time they were both bruised and exhausted. Cooking had been impossible so they had eaten dried fruit and drunk water, dozing propped against each other on the bunk. There was nothing to do but wait for it to be over, and though Jake from practice quickly lapsed into the somnolent state that was required, Harriet found it harder. Never in her life had she sat and endured; there was always something to do, to eat, to watch, to think about. Now she could not even read, because the print shivered sickeningly before her eyes. Dried fruit did no more than curb the sharpest pangs of hunger and there was nothing to watch but the swaying of the lamp. Yet the time passed, hours and hours of it, almost a lifetime it seemed, until at last Jake roused himself.

'That's it, I think. Let's hope for some sun in the morning. I need a sight, we could be anywhere.'

'I'll cook something,' said Harriet vaguely.

'Don't bother. I'll see to the boat, you get into bed and get some sleep.' Jake pulled open the hatch. At once the night, excluded for so long, rushed in weeping and wailing. When Jake pulled the hatch closed Harriet began to take of her jacket. Even in that brief time spray had soaked the floor, adding to the constant drips that ran down from the roof. The bed felt damp, but it would have to do. She crawled stiffly under the covers.

Jake was worried, extremely worried. The backstay was slack and even without that pointer he could see the movement at the foot of the mast, and this was after a pretty mild blow. Should they put back or battle on and hope for the best? He considered what would happen if the mast went. The hull was leaking, but not terminally. The only casualty was his stamina, since he was forced to pump two-hourly during the day and whenever he woke up at night. Yet Harriet still saw nothing that was outside his control.

But even she realised that he was preoccupied. 'It is all right isn't it?' she asked over lunch, a stew prepared with great care by her and eaten distractedly by Jake.

'Depends what you mean by all right.'

'We're not going to sink.'

'Not sink, no.' He chewed on a lump of potato. There was no point pretending. He put down his fork. 'We're taking water. We can pump it out, but it's tiring, and it might get worse if it starts to blow. And the mast is weak, I knew that when we started. It could go. Now that isn't the end of the world, we can still get to land, but it won't be much fun. For now I'm going to lash a few bits and pieces and try to take the strain a bit. I'm not sure if we should go on or go back, and that's being honest.'

Harriet looked down at her plate, and pushed two pieces of meat into a line, then added a pea and a slice of carrot. One thing always led to another. When she gave up work to look after her mother she had never imagined that the step would be the start of many, leading on and on and on, a spiral staircase turning in on itself. 'Would you turn back if you were by yourself? Or would you go on and risk it?'

Jake's square hand gripped his fork. He had bigger hands than fitted his size really. 'The question doesn't arise. I wouldn't be in this boat on my own, she's not equipped to go singlehanded. But in another boat, with the same problems – yes, I'd go on. For one thing, it should be a damn sight cheaper to get the boat repaired in Nassau, and I could earn the money to do it, too. But you don't have to go by that, Harriet. The boat's leaking, the weather's dirty – if you want to go back, we will.'

She got up and put her plate by the cooker, then she went on deck. The wind was freshening. Already *Dashing Away* looked to be carrying too much sail. It occurred to her that she would never have known that before. Jake wasn't pulling any punches about this trip, not now anyway, and she had a strange feeling about it all. Her chrysalis had remained closed for too long, and emerging from it was cold and lonely. Perhaps she needed danger, a cathartic experience, to force her to slough off the unwanted baggage of her life. She didn't want to go back, not even a little way, she wanted to go on, to the blue sky and blue sea and the sunshine.

She went below. 'I think we should shorten sail.'

Jake blinked. 'Aye aye, master mariner. Ready about?'

'No. You promised it wouldn't sink.'

He laughed, rather ruefully. 'God save me from a trusting woman.'

* * *

In a week Harriet felt that she had been at sea forever. Life had always been wet and cold and achingly wearisome, she ceased even to query that it should be so. As gale followed gale, she came to watch unmoved as waves chased the stern of the little boat, lifting it high and then dropping it endlessly down into the trough. They barely spoke at all, except to mutter about the boat. Jake spent hours each day adjusting the complicated mast support system he had devised. Harriet learned to pump the bilges. On the two occasions when they were forced to heave to, trying to steady the boat's motion with a sea anchor, Harriet spent the time rolling suet into strips and forcing it into the leaking coachroof. It made very little difference to their comfort, but it absorbed her.

Real terror came only once. Jake was working on deck, his swollen hands trying to fasten a new rope lashing on the mast. He had done this four times in three days, for the whip on the mast loosened ropes like knitting wool. Harriet was steering, trying to keep the boat heading smoothly over the confused seas. She saw the wave that brought them to grief, but watched it without real interest. It was big, but so were others. Too late it dawned on her tired brain that it was rushing upon them with the speed of a runaway train.

'Jake!' she yelled at last. He looked up, saw the wave and shouted something. She didn't hear it. One moment he was on deck, the next he was gone. The deck wallowed beneath tons of water, then *Dashing Away* climbed out like a dog after a swim. Harriet felt a sudden desire to rush below and go to bed, for when she woke Jake would be back on board and it would be all right. With an effort of will that left her shaking, she turned round and looked behind. There was Jake, clinging to his lifeline and floundering in the water.

'Jake! Jake!' She waved as if he was in for a swim. He lifted an arm, sluggishly. His face was grey-blue. Abandoning the tiller, she grabbed the lifeline where it was fastened to the rail and heaved, but she couldn't move him. The water clung like glue. Again he waved, twice, and at last she understood. She flung the tiller over, hard. The boat gybed violently, horrible cracks and bangs coming from the sails; another wave crashed over them, filling the cockpit and leaving them wallowing. But Jake was suddenly alongside, hanging on with bloodless, pudgy fingers. He looked half dead, thought Harriet, and then knew he was nearer to it than that. Abandoning the tiller she ran to the rail and grabbed him, trying impossibly to haul him in. He was leaden, his oilskins slipping through her fingers. Another wave, more water, the boat was nearly swamped. Harriet caught her fingers in the lifeline and dragged that aboard at last. She took a turn round a cleat and heaved, another turn, another heave. Jake rolled over the rail and splashed into the cockpit.

In the evening, with the boat almost dry and the wind slackening, they decided he could not have been in the water more than three minutes at the most. At first Harriet couldn't believe it. She would have said it was fifteen or more.

'In fifteen minutes I'd have been dead,' said Jake, still shivering, still without real feeling in his fingers. 'It's cold in there. Thanks, Harriet. You did really well.'

'It was my fault you fell in,' she admitted despondently. 'I saw the wave. I didn't think anything of it.'

Jake shrugged. 'If I take inexperienced crew to sea I should expect trouble, shouldn't I? You can't learn everything overnight. Christ, I'm cold. Break out the brandy, will you?'

They had brought two bottles of brandy and one of whisky, carefully wrapped in towels. Harriet poured them each a small measure, but Jake took the bottle and doubled them both. 'We deserve it,' he said decisively. They drank it, listening to the mast complaining.

Chapter Nine

A storm-driven boat is never dry. There comes a time when there seems neither warmth nor comfort anywhere. Clothes are wet, the bed is damp, the food is never hot and the wind keeps blowing. Harriet passed beyond weariness, even beyond fear. She lodged in a state of dumb misery, going about her tasks like a programmed machine. Once, steering in a world of grey spray, she sat hunched in oilskins that through age and immersion were becoming porous, and watched Jake working. The sight amazed her; she knew she could no more have laboured like that than fly. Sails up, sails down, tie this rope, loosen that, on and on and on. She began to wonder if he was really there, because there were lots of tales of people alone on boats imagining help. Perhaps Jake was dead, she had never got him back on board at all and this figure, labouring endlessly, was his shade. She flexed her stiff fingers on the tiller and hunched further down, seeking the illusion of warmth.

In a while he came and took the tiller, sending her down below to thaw out. Encountering for the first time in her life the essential difference between men and women, that is physical strength, she was unreasonably impressed. Jake seemed to her to be invincible. She steadied herself against his knee. 'Shall I try and make a drink?'

'If you like. Don't bother if it's too difficult. It's easing, you know. What we're getting now is a cross swell, the wind's dropping. And it's getting warmer.'

'Is it?' Harriet's teeth were chattering. He smiled, his teeth startling white against the growth of black beard. He touched her cold cheek. 'Poor old Harriet, what a life. I promise it will get better. In a day or so we'll be so hot we'll be praying for rain. And the old tub's holding out, we've still got a mast – just.' He cast an eye at the forest of ropes above his head and wondered himself how it all stayed together. But perhaps it was more marvellous that Harriet was bearing up, because he knew what this must seem like to a beginner. Understanding nothing, trapped between sea and wild air, everything new and uncomfortable – he admired her courage and her stamina. There weren't many girls would have done as well.

That night he took two watches, letting her sleep on. The sea was calmer now and despite his exhaustion his mind felt very clear. He loved moments like this at sea, when he had been tested and not found wanting. One day the question would be asked and he would have no answer, of that he was quite sure, but so far he had risen to each challenge, taking greater and greater risks and always winning. He enjoyed the unexpected terror that was always there at sea, one moment cruising in style, the next in fear of your life. Good boats and good weather didn't interest him, he supposed that was becoming very obvious. He looked up at the white stars, set at distances more vast than he could comprehend, and wondered what he was doing with his life. Looked at objectively one would think he was working on killing himself.

Harriet sprawled on the deck with her eyes closed tight against the sun's glare. What a pity her sunglasses had been lost along with everything else, she thought sleepily, and despite the warmth felt uncomfortable. Her salt-encrusted trousers rubbed against her legs, her jumper was a hair shirt. If it got any hotter she would have to find cooler clothes, though as she scanned the selection drying on the rigging she could see nothing at all that would do.

Shielding her eyes with her hand, she covertly watched Jake. He was wearing a pair of shorts and nothing else, sitting in the cockpit with his feet up. He embarrassed her. This morning he had unzipped and peed over the side, as if it was natural, as if by now they knew each other so well they didn't have secrets or inhibitions. The sweat ran in slow droplets between her breasts, passing from nerve ending to nerve ending, each one sending shudders of electricity through her. Her bra was waving flagrantly from the washing line.

Jake lashed the tiller and crossed the deck towards her. 'You must be boiling, Harriet. Go and get my other shorts on, they're in the sailbag. You'll probably find a couple of shirts, too.'

He was adjusting his lashings, so he hadn't come to talk to her. Harriet pretended to be dozing. 'I'm not hot,' she said sleepily.

'Nonsense. You're purple in the face. Go below and get changed. I'm not asking you to turn out topless, for God's sake. Or should I ask you? What would you say?'

She sat up and pulled her fingers through her mat of hair. Her breasts, swung, taut nipples chafing against the rough wool of her jumper.

'Don't be disgusting,' she said tightly.

Jake laughed. 'What an old maid you are.'

She scuttled below, furious at him and at herself. She ought to go up there now, topless, and watch his face. Even the thought made her go hot, and she quickly hunted for the shorts. She was sure they wouldn't fit. How embarrassing that would be. Yet when she pulled them on she found that not only did they fit, they were inches too big in the waist. She prodded herself. Without scales and without familiar clothes it was very difficult to know if you had got thinner, but it was possible. She pinched her bottom and her midriff, then peered in the two inch square mirror on the bulkhead to see her cheeks. After all, it would be surprising if she hadn't lost weight, because decent meals had come to feature as occasional events in her life. What a pity that creased canvas shorts were so unflattering.

She pulled on one of Jake's rather tatty shirts, rolling the sleeves to the elbow. Experimentally she knotted the ends underneath her breasts. They sagged voluptuously against the thin material, the darker aureoles clearly outlined. Suppose she went up like that? What would he say? Quickly she unfastened the knot and let the shirt hang baggily outside the shorts.

When she went up on deck Jake was fiddling about with a length of line. He glanced up casually. 'Good girl, that's a lot more sensible. Thread these hooks on here, would you, please? I keep seeing fish and we might be able to catch some with a bit of luck.'

Silently, with her legs tucked neatly under her, Harriet threaded fishhooks.

They sprinkled shredded suet as bait, casting it over one side or the other in the hope that it would encourage lack of caution in the fish. The sun climbed higher in the sky, turning the sea into jewelled blue glass. *Dashing Away* chuckled as she sailed, or so it sounded as the water bubbled past her sides. Harriet lay watching the fishing lines, wondering if Jake was watching her, but whenever she looked he was gazing at the sails, or out to sea, or at the compass.

She looked at her legs, protruding like white stalks from the shorts. They were quite nice legs really, and would be much nicer when they were brown. Perhaps they were a bit short, but then if they were three inches longer she would be taller than he was. Some men liked very tall women, of course. She glanced at Jake. He had such big shoulders, yet they looked nothing in clothes. Was he unnaturally big in other parts? With no experience at all to draw on she didn't know and at the thought of that – it – him – a flood of heat spread through her. It would hurt, they said it always did the first time. She pulled her legs jerkily under her and looked back down at the fishing line.

'Jake! Jake! We've caught two!'

Jake declared that they would have a feast. The boat was sailing herself well on this heading, and at last they were dried out and well rested.

'We'll splice the mainbrace,' he said, extracting a bottle of brandy from its nest and putting it in a position of honour in the cockpit.

'You'll have to gut the fish, said Harriet. 'I always ask the fish-monger to do it.'

'It's a good thing I'm a man of many talents,' he said, sliding a knife expertly down the belly of each fish. Harriet privately agreed. She had never met anyone like Jake. When he gave her the fish she ducked down the hatch, and her bottom brushed his thigh. 'For God's sake don't burn them,' he called.

They ate on deck, watching the sun extinguish itself in the sea. The sky was purple and green and deepest orange, yet the horizon was black-edged. For once Harriet allowed herself to be over-whelmed by a sense of great isolation, conscious that they were indeed just a speck on a huge water-filled saucer where there was nothing and no-one except she and Jake and *Dashing Away*. She sipped again at her brandy, half a tumbler full.

'You're a good cook,' said Jake lazily, his back against the mast.

'No, I'm not. I can only do plain things.'

'I like plain things. But I like pretty things, too.' He grinned to himself, seemingly oblivious of Harriet.

'Jake,' she said suddenly. 'Have you had many women?'

He opened his eyes and looked at her. 'That depends on what you mean by many.'

Harriet sat up. 'How many? How many women have you – ?'

'Fucked? That's the word you want, Harriet. Let's see – oh God, I don't know. One night in Manila I ended up with three and whether I fucked one three times or three of them once I shall never know. I took a week to recover, I know that.' He laughed and took another gulp of brandy.

'I've never done it at all,' said Harriet in a high, tense voice.

Jake raised an eyebrow. 'And I never would have guessed.'

'But I could you know! I'm not – I mean – I could.'

'I know you could, love. Everybody can, it's whether everybody will, isn't it?'

He seemed almost asleep, leaning against the mast, one leg raised, no tell-tale bulge against his shorts. Why didn't he want to do it to her? thought Harriet wildly. He had before.

'Some people don't ever. Do they?' Why didn't he wake up and take notice of her?

'They'll put it on your tombstone, Returned Unopened. All those juices and hormones and nice pink orifices all gone to waste. Dried up, that's what you'll be, Harriet. But at least you won't ever have done anything disgusting.'

Now he was looking at her, staring straight at her in the half light. Sometimes you have to take chances, she thought confusedly; sometimes you have to become vulnerable. Her fingers, stiff and unnaturally slow, began to undo the buttons of her shirt. Jake watched, his eyes fierce and pale. The silence was as thick as a steel bar. At last, Harriet fumbled with the last button. She opened her shirt. Still Jake only watched.

'I'm not dried up yet,' she whispered.

His tongue came out and licked his lips, suddenly she could hear his breathing and it made her bold. She cupped a breast in either hand, kneeling and putting back her shoulders so that her nipples pointed at him. Throatily, in a voice she didn't recognise, she said, 'I thought you liked virgins.'

When he moved it took her by surprise. One moment he was leaning against the mast, the next he was standing over her, pulling her to her feet. He bent his head and kissed her, his tongue searching her mouth but it wasn't what she wanted and she pulled away.

'I'm not dried up,' she said again, fumbling herself at the buttons of her shorts. They fell to her feet and she stood there, naked but for the shirt still hanging from her shoulders. Jake touched her. He moved his hand from her thigh to the forest of her pubic hair and then down. A cry broke from her, almost of pain, as he touched nerves that had been tense for days.

'Oh, Harriet,' said Jake softly. 'And I told myself I wouldn't do this to you.'

'You've done everything else,' she said.

He was mouthing her shoulders. 'Have I?' He touched her again, skilful and flat-fingered. She felt her hips move against the pressure of his hand.

'Will it hurt?' she asked, trying to put all of herself in contact with him, trying to make him touch the spot that needed him, though she didn't know where it was.

'I don't know,' said Jake, suddenly pulling away. He stepped out of his shorts and was there, naked, protruding hugely from a mat of hair.

Harriet laughed, a shrill, incongruous sound. 'It's too big,' she said.

'You don't know what's big.' He pulled a cushion from the cockpit, still slightly damp, and threw it on the deck, Harriet lay on it. He knelt astride her and pulled the cushion down under her hips. Like a sniper setting up a target, she thought. She wished he'd done it when she was against him; this felt so cold and experienced. But then he lowered himself on to her and she felt him, warm, heavy, smelling of sweat. He held her breasts. The sensation overwhelmed her. She lost thought until suddenly, unexpectedly, she felt him pressing against her, hard and unrelenting. Her eyes opened. She put her hands on his shoulders and pulled herself up, starting to cry out. Now his hands were on her legs, pushing them wider so he could thrust. It was hurting and she scratched at him. He withdrew and pressed again, hard. She screamed. Over his shoulder she could see the black night sky and the sail set against it. She was full of him, he filled up her emptiness entirely. This was heaven.

It was very strange, afterwards. She was bleeding and didn't quite know how to behave. Jake handed her a roll of toilet paper and told her to tuck herself up in bed. She lay with the brandy fumes still in her head, not sure of what she felt, unable to imagine what he was feeling. After a while she looked out of the hatch and saw him at the tiller, looking calm and detached. He glanced down and saw her. 'Go to sleep, Harriet,' he said softly.

'I can't sleep.' She came up and sat behind him. The night was moonlit, phosphorescence sparkling on the wavelets, but the wind was gusting fitfully. At one moment the sails filled like pillows, the next they flapped and the boom swung. After a while Jake said, 'Are you all right?'

She thought for a moment. 'I don't know. I can't – I can't understand how I didn't know about it before. They were new feelings but it's as if I've always known them. It's odd.'

'I seem to remember I felt a bit like that. Different for men, though. They're much more driven.'

'Are they?' Harriet didn't know men at all, didn't know Jake at all, she felt. What was for her a major event was for him nothing much, she supposed. 'I'm sorry I didn't know what to do,' she said.

He laughed and half turned towards her. 'I didn't expect you to know! Anyway, sex isn't for achievers, it's for fun. I thought you were smashing, and now we've broken the ice, so to speak, we can really enjoy this trip. We'll get to Nassau in about a week, by which time we should both be brown and you'll be experienced.'

Harriet felt a frisson of excitement springing up from deep within her belly. On an impulse she stood up behind Jake and put her arms round his neck, pressing herself against his back. He laughed again and drew her round in front of him, pulling the blanket aside to fondle her breasts. She put up her mouth to be kissed, stiffly. Jake whispered against her lips: 'Relax. Let it flow, Harriet. You've got to learn to take it slowly and gently and patiently. Otherwise it's over in five minutes and nobody's had any fun. You really are worth exploring, my girl. Lovely soft flesh that's never seen the light of day. You are OK, aren't you? Time of the month, I mean. I'm not into fatherhood.'

'Oh, I'm sure it's all right,' said Harriet, only concerned that he should continue squeezing her nipples. His mouth tasted of sour brandy, she thought she would never again taste anything so exciting.

The days passed, golden yet with a warm, raking breeze that pushed *Dashing Away* briskly along. Filled with an explosion of energy, Harriet sorted out the cabin, washed clothes, darned things, cooked as tastily as she knew how and was always, instantly available should Jake want to make love to her. As for Jake, he couldn't believe his luck. Prickly, difficult Harriet, a good mate but a tart one, had overnight become the ultimate geisha girl. The boat sailed herself most of the time, and normally he would have been bored, were it not for Harriet and her new hobby. Sometimes she almost embarrassed him by her eagerness to please; it was almost like having a slave at his beck and call.

The change in Harriet was almost magical. Now that it was so hot they both went naked and as she tripped about the deck, breasts swinging, bottom swelling in two round handfuls, he tried to remember round-shouldered, dumpy Harriet and failed. Yet he had only to ask and this soft and glossy creature would lie down and open her legs. Even when she was sore and her breasts bruised where he had gripped her, she still did not refuse him, and hard though it was to believe, there were times when he would have preferred to go back to conversation. Harriet no longer talked, she was much too interested in sex.

'Are you trying to make up for lost time?' he asked one evening when they parted for the fourth time that day.

'I thought you liked it,' said Harriet, pushing her hair out of her eyes. She looked anxiously at him. She had known this would happen, that he would become bored with her and cease to find her exciting. She would die if he never came into her again, she would kill herself if he said he didn't want her. 'Shall I rub your back? Shall I cook something?'

Jake sighed. 'I don't want anything.' He scanned the horizon, bored and sated and restless all at the same time. It wasn't a new feeling, easy living always did this to him. 'There's a sail to port,' he said suddenly. 'Long way off, but we're getting there.'

He got up and began to smarten up the boat, coiling ropes and adjusting the mast lashings. Harriet hugged her knees, watching him hopelessly. It was all going to end. The one man who could make her feel complete was tired of her.

She slept fitfully that night while Jake stayed at the tiller, watching for other boats. When she brought him coffee in the morning and kissed him he barely seemed to notice her.

'Look,' he said and she followed his pointing arm. There was a huge yacht, under full sail including a vast striped spinnaker. She was sweeping past a quarter of a mile away when all at once there was activity on deck. 'They're coming about,' said Jake. 'Took them long enough to notice the state we're in. Go and get some clothes on, Harriet, we can't screw now.'

He thought she was insatiable. She went below and pulled on shorts and shirt, fighting tears of humiliation. He didn't want her any more then.

Try as she would the tears fell and when she went back on deck the schooner was hove to, enormous and beautiful, while they bounced shabbily about beneath her rail.

'How you doing, Peter?' yelled Jake. 'Boat looks like a bleeding royal barge.'

A plump man in white shorts and tee shirt lifted a megaphone. 'You rigged her so you should know. She's going well, Jake. What's happened to you?'

'Few gales, that's all. The mast was dicky when we started, we'll get it seen to over here. Be in Nassau by tonight.'

'That's a bit optimistic. Do you need your position?'

Jake's affronted expression must have crossed even the yards between them. Several men on deck collapsed with laughter. 'The day I need you and your bloody satellites to tell me where I am is the day I'll give up and take to my bath chair,' he roared. 'Get away and give me some sea room. Wave bye bye, Harriet. We'll get some sail up somehow and show the bastards.' He stormed forward and began hoisting the flying jib, which they were too strained to carry under normal circumstances, but would now if it sank them. *Dashing Away* began to scurry across the waves like a duck pursued by a swan. Harriet hung on to the tiller, trying to look seamanlike.

'Nice bit of totty,' roared the megaphone, and Jake lifted two fingers in a very British salute.

The wind was getting fierce as the day wore on, though the sun shone brightly out of a glittering halo.

'Best we do make port,' said Jake to an unusually silent Harriet. 'There's a blow on.'

The schooner was lost to them over the horizon, making swift yet stately progress under her vast canopy of sails. All they could carry was the flying jib and the reefed mainsail on the suspect mast. Even so the little boat was complaining, shuddering over the short seas. Towards evening Harriet said, 'I can see land.'

'Great! Dinner in harbour – we could do with it. Might cadge something off Peter if we're lucky, he seems to have forgotten our last little disagreement.' When Harriet still did not reply he glanced at her. She had brooded all day but he had thought she might come round if he ignored it. 'You upset about something?'

She turned too swiftly. 'No, of course I'm not upset.'

'Good. Because if you are there's no point in brooding and not saying anything. If you're upset say so, I'm no mind reader.'

'I'm not upset,' said Harriet again, in tones that clearly indicated she was very upset indeed.

'Right,' said Jake briskly. 'Then I don't have to bother about it then, do I?'

Harriet could have hit him.

Chapter Ten

The harbour was crammed full of masts, hedgehog spikes springing from the water. Despite herself Harriet was impressed, because she had never been anywhere much, and to arrive at a tropical island out of a sunset, and to have spread before her graceful vessels whose owners leaned on the rails to call greetings, seemed to her like paradise. Stark hotel blocks marred the coastline, but above them stretched the rain forests, covering the hills with green. The place smelled exotic, of wine and perfume and ripe fruit from unknown trees that she knew if she saw them would be in green glades where snakes hung from the branches.

She turned to Jake. 'It's wonderful. It's like heaven.'

He wrinkled his nose, glancing down at the water made turgid by a thousand boats. 'Bit of a slop bucket if you ask me, but it's all right if you like lemmings. It'll do for a week or so, then we'll slip off to somewhere a bit less popular. I know islands that will really impress you, absolutely deserted. Real Robinson Crusoe stuff.'

Harriet, looking in amazement at the beautiful, slender people who raised frosted glasses of planter's punch as they passed, did not think she wanted to experience isolation. Her whole life had been spent alone, she did not need peace but excitement! A tall bronzed young man leaned down from a boat and said, 'You look as if you've had a bit of a hard time.'

Blushing fiercely, Harriet called back: 'Nothing we couldn't handle.'

As they drifted slowly past to meet the harbour cutter, Jake chuckled. 'You're a real poser, you know that, Harriet? "Nothing we couldn't handle", my foot! I'll remind you of that next time we're heeled horizontal.'

Mollified by his attention she tossed her head defiantly. 'We did handle it. They all know who you are, don't they? Everyone's coming to look.'

Jake grunted. She looked at him to see if he was in fact conscious of the attention, but he didn't seem to be. But then people always watched Jake, whether they knew him or not, there was something about him that caught interest. Energy, thought Harriet, that and a certain lawlessness. You knew that if you watched long enough you'd see him do something he shouldn't.

They were directed to a mooring far too central for their humble boat, but then Jake was known to the harbourmaster, too. As they tied up rowing boats approached from all sides, manned by black teenagers touting for trade. Did they want to buy pineapples, ice cream, handbags? Trip to the shore, very cheap? Jake took no notice, casually stowing sails and coiling ropes, while Harriet felt so threatened that she retreated below decks. Suddenly the boats scattered, sent flying on the bow wave of a motor launch speeding across the water towards them. Harriet surfaced and looked enquiringly at Jake.

'Dinner,' he said happily. 'That's Peter de Vuiton, he of this morning's schooner. Best bib and tucker, Harriet.'

'I haven't got anything else!' She wailed in a panic, pulling her crumpled shirt down and wriggling her bare toes.

'Haven't you?' He eyed her with a certain surprise that she should look so tatty. 'No, I suppose you haven't. We'll have to go as hardy matelots then, love. We can't pass up real food for lack of a few sequins. Anyway, remember we're one up to start with.'

'What do you mean?' Harriet could see white starched uniforms and caps in the launch, and epaulettes and cleanshaven faces. Jake looked like a true pirate now, complete with beard, but what about her?

'People who sail in smart boats are morally inferior to types like us, who can't afford to' declared Jake confidently. 'They have to admire our grit, but we don't have to admire their bank balances. Money's a bad thing in sailing, it buys you out of the rough stuff.'

Harriet sighed. She didn't want Jake's puritan ethics, she wanted a bath and clean clothes, perhaps even a pair of shoes. The launch chugged up beside them and *Dashing Away* bounced flirtatiously, as if being propositioned.

'Mr. de Vuiton's compliments. Would you care to join him for dinner, sir?'

Jake sprang catlike on to the rail and balanced there, grinning. 'How kind. We'll come at once.' He sprang into the launch then turned and put up his hand for Harriet. 'Come on, Harriet. No time for the false eyelashes. Food!'

* * *

Faces looked down at them as they climbed the ladder, girls with shining eyes and teeth and hair. Shyness enveloped Harriet like concrete. She felt as if her fingers couldn't grip, her lips couldn't move in speech. Yet somehow she followed Jake up and hovered on the edge of the excited group that greeted him.

'Hello, Jake.' This from a brown and slender girl with ash-blonde hair and a sarong in electric blue silk. Jake grinned and nodded to her. 'Donna. Long time no see.'

'I brought you a drink.' She handed him a tall glass full of ice and fruit. Jake took it without thanks, but he smiled at her.

'Jake!' Peter de Vuiton threw his well-laundered arm round Jake's salt-stained shoulders. 'I never thought you'd make it. Do you know there's a hurricane warning out?'

At this time of year? Can't be much of one.'

'Nobody's staying out to judge, everyone's here. You know Donna, and June, and George is in the saloon. Oh, and Natalie's here.'

There was a distinct pause. Even Harriet was aware of tension. She saw a girl with long red hair and freckles, watching Jake with a glittering smile.

'Hi,' said Jake grittily. 'You do get around.'

'You don't get any richer, I see. Who's this you've brought with you? Doesn't she matter enough for you to introduce her?'

Jake turned and saw Harriet, shifting from one bare foot to the other, looking acutely unhappy. Her hair almost obscured her eyes and she hung her head as if wilting with shame. He sighed. 'This is Harriet. Peter, Donna, June, Natalie. George is in the saloon. By the way, Peter, seen anything of Mac or Lewis? I thought they might have flown out.'

He and Peter strolled towards the saloon. Only Natalie took any notice of Harriet, deliberately hanging back to talk to her. 'How do you come to be stuck in that old tub? Do you like sailing?'

'Sometimes.' Harriet tried to smile back but it was a poor attempt. What must they think of her, appearing on their glamorous yacht like some sort of derelict, a floozy too trivial even to be considered by the man who had brought her? She looked in agony at Jake's retreating back.

'That guy is a shit,' said Natalie decisively.

'Who, Jake?'

'Yes, Jake,' said Natalie. 'Don't tell me he hasn't walked all over you. That's his style, he's always the same, and the girls love it. He had a fling with Donna last season and she can't wait to try it again. Have you had enough yet?'

Harriet blushed. 'I – don't know. Look, I'm awfully sorry turning up like this – I mean I haven't any proper clothes or anything. Jake – he didn't – we had to come away in a hurry.'

She gazed longingly at Natalie's green dress, made of floating pleated chiffon hanging from shoestring straps. Tiny sequins sparkled in the folds. It was the most desirable dress Harriet had ever seen.

'He hasn't done you any favours, has he?' said Natalie, and then, as Harriet looked tormented, added, 'You're not in love with the bastard, are you?'

Harriet couldn't reply. She shook her head violently, and Natalie, realising her confusion, caught her arm. 'Look, I know what it's like. You're dirty and you're hungry and you feel a mess. Why don't you come and have a bath? I'm sure I can find you something to wear.'

'Oh, would you, please? I feel so – '

'Yeah,' said Natalie knowingly. 'Two weeks with Jake and I felt like that, too.'

Natalie's cabin was small but beautiful, and so clean that Harriet could have died in it. 'Our boat is full of wet and mould and sails,' she said.

'And Jake loves it!'

'He thinks I do, too. Or at least he doesn't think I mind.' They looked at each other and started to laugh. It was infinitely refreshing to talk to a girl, and one who was not impressed with Jake. Harriet wondered if she were being disloyal, and thought that probably she was. Had Jake and Natalie had an affair? The thought was like ice in the pit of her stomach, and it did not melt even when she sank into the deliciously scented heat of the bath. Natalie was far, far more beautiful than she could ever hope to be.

The door opened and the redhead came in with clean towels. Harriet sank shyly beneath the water. 'You know Jake well, don't you?' she said jerkily.

Natalie made a face. 'I guess you could say that.' She stared at the girl in the bath, her face stiff and belligerent. 'I might as well tell you,' she said suddenly. 'He won't. He never gives a girl another thought once he's through with her. The bastard fucked me stupid, then dumped me in Jamaica. I was a lot younger then and I was really, really hurt. You've got a great tan, Harriet. Do you fancy a white dress, or pink?'

'Er – white,' said Harriet. She felt a great hole somewhere under her heart. 'Why did he do it?'

Natalie tossed her lovely red hair. 'I guess he was bored. We'd done everything so often that sometimes he wouldn't even try and make me come. Is he still giving you thrills, Harriet? It's the only thing you'll get from him.'

She was very embarrassed. Feeling herself blushing, she said, 'What did you do when he left you?'

Natalie grimaced. 'Picked up with a man on a yacht there. Stayed with him about a year actually, and that taught me a lot. If you're going to spread your legs for a guy, you might as well do it for one that gives you diamonds.'

Harriet sat silent in the cooling bathwater. Was he going to dump her? He was bored, she knew that. But the boat was hers, or at least he had bought it with her money, and he was her first, and he knew it. She couldn't believe he would do to her as he had to Natalie. Yet Natalie was beautiful, glossy and sophisticated, while Harriet was plain as bread.

She wrapped a towel round her wet hair, another round her body and came out. Natalie looked at her speculatively. 'Your hair needs cutting. I'll take you to someone tomorrow, OK?'

'I haven't any money,' she said quickly. She felt it best to get that out in the open.

'That doesn't surprise me, no-one has any money if they take up with Jake. That guy sold my mother's ring. My mother's emerald ring and the bastard sold it! No, you leave things to me. I've a score to settle with Jake. It suits him very well to have girls like you around, good little spaniels that need their coats brushing. This time I'll show him.' She advanced like a green-eyed cat, and Harriet instinctively recoiled.

'What are you going to do?'

'Turn you into something,' declared Natalie. 'Let's have a look at you.'

She twitched away the towel. Harriet tried to cover herself with her hands, but Natalie snapped, 'Stand up! I'm not a dyke, for Christ's sake. Hmmm. You've got a great pair on you, and you're not a bad shape. Been losing some weight?' Harriet nodded. 'Try and lose a bit more,' said Natalie discouragingly. 'Let's see your hair.'

A knock came on the door. 'Mr. de Vuiton's compliments,' called a voice. 'He would like to serve dinner as soon as is convenient.'

'Give us twenty minutes,' called back Natalie. She started brushing Harriet's wet hair. 'We've got to get this off your face, no-one can see you. You've got a nice face, and good eyes. Make the most of them, and keep your hair back, otherwise you look mean. Makes your neck look longer, too.'

'Have you known Mr. de Vuiton long?' asked Harriet between brush-strokes.

'About a year. My previous guy turned out to be a pervert – oral sex and handcuffs. I couldn't take that for any money. Put some of this on.' She gave Harriet a pot of cream. 'So I took up with Peter. He wants to marry me,' she added casually, 'but I guess I won't. He's been married three times before. Why did they quit? that's what I ask myself. And he doesn't screw too well, I'd be catting around in no time.' She saw Harriet's face in the mirror and burst into laughter. 'I'm shocking you! Sorry, Harriet. The truth is I screw for money, a lot of money. Marriage doesn't figure, not till I'm old and grey and very, very rich. Hold still, I want to do your eyes. How about you?'

'I'm just on holiday. I'm sort of between things at the moment. Everything was so dull and awful, and since I met Jake it's been really exciting. He's very – he's – '

'Good in bed,' finished Natalie. 'Honey, everybody likes it with Jake but the best thing you can do is try it out with a few other guys, you'll find enough in Nassau. Maybe a rich old sugardaddy will snatch you up and marry you, then you'll see what a bastard Jake is.'

Harriet turned, clutching the back of the chair. 'But he isn't that bad really! He doesn't mean to be unkind.'

Natalie tapped Harriet's nose with a make-up brush. 'Jake is a bastard, Harriet. The only person Jake cares about is Jake, and the sooner you realise that the better. Right now he'll be climbing into Donna's dress, but he'll take you back to that boat and climb into you, too. That's Jake for you. He'll make you work and cook and give him money, and if you're a very good girl he'll make you come. Loyalty isn't in his book.'

Everyone turned impatiently as Natalie and Harriet entered the saloon. Harriet felt her colour come up, although with Natalie's hand in the small of her back she could not do other than match the girl's confident stride. Her high-heeled sandals clacked on the parquet floor, her tight white dress held her thighs together. Her bust was bigger than Natalie's and her breasts swelled from the strapless top like two brown balloons. Her brown hair, held back by diamanté clips, swung to her shoulders. Tomorrow, Natalie assured her, it would be blonde.

'Good God,' said Jake. 'You look like – very nice, Harriet.' He looked affronted. Donna, hanging on his arm, giggled warily.

'I'm sorry we were so long, Peter,' said Natalie, draping a hand round de Vuiton's shoulder and dropping a kiss on his cheek. 'I was telling Harriet all about Jake.'

'All the juicy bits, I guess,' said de Vuiton, and stood up. 'Let's eat then, shall we?'

As they went through to the dining saloon, Jake detached himself from Donna and caught Harriet's elbow. 'You look like a high-class whore. And don't believe what Natalie tells you.'

She stared at him. 'Why not? She seems to know you better than I do.'

'Oh, Christ.' He abandoned her and went to his allotted place next to Donna. Harriet was next to George, a rotund man married to June, who was very pleased to make up to Harriet. She was dumbfounded. Never before in her life had a man like George even noticed her, unless he wanted her to buy a charity flag.

The meal was fresh salmon, veal cutlets with three sorts of vegetable, and delicious frothy sweets. Both Jake and Harriet devoured the vegetables, because it was weeks since they had seen anything green and edible. Donna was leaning against Jake, openly putting her hand in his shirt and caressing his chest hair, and he was flirting with her, leading her on. Her mouth was always open, noticed Harriet. Donna was as available for Jake as if she were lying on the table before him.

Suddenly she felt something on her leg. George was grinning at her, massaging her thigh with a warm hand. Harriet clamped her knees together and trapped it. 'What are you doing?'

'Exploring,' said George. 'Why don't we go on deck?'

Harriet glanced across at June, who was looking bored. 'Stop it.' His hand was wriggling up towards her crotch. Was she supposed to put up with this? Did Natalie? She reached down and caught his wrist, dragging his hand out from between her legs. June saw the movement and shot her husband a glance of intense loathing.

'Let's go into the saloon,' said Peter de Vuiton, and they all stood up. The party rearranged itself, the men gathering together to talk boats, with Donna still draping herself over Jake, and Natalie, June and Harriet drinking coffee.

'I've been telling Harriet she shouldn't screw for nothing,' said Natalie.

'I've been doing it for long enough,' said June. 'Don't worry about George, groping's all he's up to these days. God, when will something exciting happen?'

Harriet watched her with round eyes. How could anyone find this boring? The sheen of money turned even the fruitbowl into something exotic, because it was Waterford crystal filled with pawpaws and mangos and cubes of fresh coconut. Rings of fresh pineapple lay in perfect circles in a dish of liqueur, an array of tiny silver forks beside it. They sat on real suede, Natalie's goblet was of gold. Harriet felt a sudden deep yearning for the perfection of money, for an end to compromise and thrift and making do. With money like this she would never have to pretend to like nylon or hamburgers or tinned peas; she could have caviare and silk and clean fresh everything. She sighed and looked uncomprehendingly at June, the lines of the woman's discontent visible even through her perfect shell of make-up.

'You want to get rid of him,' advised Natalie. 'Where's the point in sticking it out? You don't talk and you don't screw – get out and find a guy that can make you feel alive.' She stretched out one long slim leg with such sensuous confidence that both June and Harriet knew Natalie would never have a moment's trouble finding a man.

June looked away. 'Maybe I will,' she said unconvincingly, because she would drift on and on in her marriage, too idle to make the break, and perhaps too scared.

It was hard on your own, thought Harriet. You couldn't despise anyone who balked at setting out on that stony road.

Jake glanced across at them. As if shedding himself of a snake he peeled Donna off and came over. He squatted down on his haunches next to Harriet, but his eyes were on Natalie.

'You don't change,' he said thoughtfully.

She stretched her leg again and at the same time reached into her bag for a long, slim cigar. She lit it and sent the smoke spiralling. 'And I don't suppose you do, either. Harriet's been telling me such interesting things, and they sound oh, so familiar.' She gave a catlike smile.

Jake's eyebrows rose sardonically. 'Still as bitter, I see. Pity. We had some fun times once.'

'Did we? Funny I can't remember them. But then I don't suppose Harriet will look back with any nostalgia when you chuck her out either. Have you given her a date yet, Jake? You never stay in the same bed long when you're in harbour.' She took a furious drag on her cigar, but Jake said nothing. Harriet moved restlessly at his side, feeling neglected and superflous. The boat seemed to rock but in all probability it was still. The movement was in her own faith and expectations.

Suddenly Jake reached up and took hold of her arm, pulling her to her feet. 'Come on, Harriet, bedtime.' She staggered on her heels and fell against him, her breasts like fenders against his upper arm. He put his arm round her waist in a gesture entirely for the benefit of the others, Harriet thought. They made their farewells.

'I'll send the launch for you tomorrow,' promised Natalie, and Harriet knowing she was a counter in the game between Natalie and Jake, nodded bemusedly. Donna, all petulance and sulks, whispered in de Vuiton's ear.

'Come to lunch tomorrow,' he called.

'No, thanks,' said Jake. 'We've got things to do. We'll be seeing you around. I'll give some thought to your rudder problem.'

'If you would,' said de Vuiton, extending a proprietory arm towards Natalie. She oozed against him, and his hand slid unchecked down the front of her dress. He stood fondling her openly as the launch took Jake and Harriet back to their boat.

They said nothing until they were alone on the stained deck of *Dashing Away* where Jake looked at Harriet consideringly. 'You don't look like anyone I know,' he said at last.

'But you know some very odd people. Have you slept with Donna? Natalie said you had.' She hadn't meant to sound so hurt. She tossed her hair and hugged her bare arms round herself. The night air was cold.

'She's told you an awful lot of things, it seems. Yes, I've screwed Donna, and so have Peter de Vuiton and George. In fact at the moment she's making up a threesome with Peter and Natalie, all very cosy. Did Natalie tell you that?'

Harriet's eyes widened. 'They don't! Altogether? At the same time?'

He shrugged. 'I don't know the choreography, but if you're interested I'm sure we can get Donna to come over and show us. Harriet, my girl, you have tonight been in the company of some very corrupt sophisticates, and you're too innocent by half. Let's go to bed.'

But she remembered earlier in the day, when he had repulsed her. In the half dark of the little cabin he was excited and eager, his fingers fumbling with the zip of her dress. She pushed at him. 'Don't. I don't want to.'

'Don't be stupid, of course you want to. Anyway I do, so lie back and think of England. You shouldn't dress like that if you don't want to play, it gets nice good girls into embarrassing situations. Christ, you smell good.' He put his face into her neck and mouthed her. Harriet realised he was drunk and rather angry, perhaps at her, perhaps at the people on the yacht. Desire for him licked at her like a flame, but even as she turned to offer him her breasts she saw an image of Natalie's face, watching with green eyes and smiling. She pushed Jake back. 'I don't want to. Not tonight.'

'You've behaved all night as if you're selling it on the quay. Don't be coy.' He reached out his hand and inserted it between her legs, probing for the opening into her body. She twisted as his fingers found their mark and found herself pressed against the palm of his hand. She shuddered and leaned against him and then, as he fumbled with his trousers, pulled away. 'I don't want to.' Much as he despised the way she looked he was turned on by it. As Donna turned him on, and Natalie. Harriet went to the bunk and sat on it, her knees hunched and her arms clasping them.

'They really upset you, didn't they?' said Jake. He stood looking down at her, swaying a little, suddenly calm.

Harriet shrugged. 'Perhaps.'

'You shouldn't believe what people tell you. We've got something good going, why let them spoil it?'

'I don't know what we've got.' She looked at him, her eyes shining against smooth skin and a mass of hair. Jake drew in his breath. 'You don't look like Harriet,' he said.

'There's more than one Harriet. I think there's more than one Jake, too, and I'm not sure if I like all of them.'

'A few weeks ago you didn't like any of them,' he said with a grin.

'Didn't I? I didn't feel like this then. Let me go to sleep, Jake.' Harriet rolled on to her side and pulled the blanket over her shoulder. Jake watched her for a moment, then went to the bunk opposite.

She was woken by the roar of a motorlaunch and Natalie's voice carolling: 'Harriet! Harriet!'

She sat up and ran her hands through her hair. Her mouth tasted foul, she had drunk far too much last night. Jake stuck his head in at the hatch. 'The Bitch of Endor has arrived. Shall I say you're ill?'

'No.' Harriet scrambled out of bed. Did Jake really think she would rather stay on a salt-stained, messy little boat than see Nassau? Besides, Natalie had lent her a dress that must be returned. She threw on her shorts and shirt, hurriedly brushed her teeth and went topside, the white dress of the night before clutched in her hand. Jake was sitting on the rail, talking to Natalie. He looked as hard as nails, thought Harriet, whereas Natalie, leaning back against the seating of the launch, was a fragile wand in billowing rose silk. As always Harriet felt scruffy.

'I'm sorry I took so long,' she apologised, scrambling over the rail.

'There's no rush,' said Natalie easily. 'There was no need to return the dress, Harriet! Keep it. You never know when I might need a favour some time.'

Harriet glanced quickly at Jake. His face was a mask. 'You always were generous, Natalie,' he said. 'Everything you have is shared.'

'And everything you have is stolen,' she replied tartly. 'Come on, Harriet, it's time for your hair appointment.'

As the launch buzzed towards the shore, Harriet felt suddenly anxious. 'You shouldn't be doing this for me,' she ventured.

'I owe it,' said Natalie obscurely, and then, as Harriet looked bewildered, added, 'I can't bear to see me in you. He brought me lower than I have ever been, and if I hadn't had a lucky break I'd have ended up walking the streets. I'm your lucky break, Harriet, your ticket to freedom. Why should he have his willing slave?'

'He didn't want to end up with me,' said Harriet bemusedly. Somehow the sequence of events that had brought her here was becoming confused.

'Oh, yeah?' said Natalie in disbelief.

The launch drew up at the harbour steps and she led the way ashore. Harriet, barefoot as a beachcomber, hopped and skipped behind her. There seemed to be hundreds of people, milling aimlessly in the sunshine. The day held a metallic tint, she thought, and knew that despite the sun there was indeed a storm brewing. Sweat gathered at her throat and ran down between her breasts, making the front of her shirt cling. Men gave her second glances and she felt shy.

Natalie swept imperiously down a sidestreet lined with expensive shops. 'Come along, Harriet,' she called as if talking to a dog. Harriet, as though caught on a choke lead, scurried after her. They entered the hairdresser's, an intimate smoked glass cave reeking of wealth.

'This,' declared Natalie, 'is Harriet.' Clearly they knew about her. With cluckings and concerned movements of their hands, three girls descended on her and guided her willynilly to a chair. They twittered and murmured, caressing her hair as if it were wire wool, their own locks uniformly auburn to match their tinted skins. They were half-caste, thought Harriet, with delicious complexions. How she envied their thick, matt skin; her own looked transparent in comparison. A tall man, also coloured, swept into the salon. The girls fell back, still twittering.

'Jules,' purred Natalie and extended a long-fingered hand. 'We want you to do something with Harriet.'

They progressed from the hairdresser to a clothes shop. Two garments only hung in the windows, one a rainbow-coloured sundress, the other a jumpsuit in white canvas. There were no price tags visible. Harriet tossed her mane of streaked and curled hair. She had resisted going absolutely blonde and instead opted for a streak of blonde in the front. Against her natural brown hair and her tan it looked outstanding. She couldn't wait to show Jake. 'We can't go in here,' she said firmly. 'It's too expensive.'

Natalie stopped and stared at her. 'Well, you can't go around looking like that for the rest of your life. Is Jake going to get you any clothes? Well, is he?'

'I don't know.' It occurred to Harriet that it was quite possible for she and Jake to sit down and discuss their financial position, it was not as unlikely an event as Natalie seemed to think. There wasn't much money, they both knew that, but there was some. 'I'm sure he'd get me something,' she said doubtfully.

'Huh.' Natalie headed for the shop. As Harriet tugged at her arm she turned. 'Look, Harriet,' Natalie said, take her hand with sudden kindness. 'Think of it as a loan. You can pay me back when things are better for you. I know it looks like I've got it in for Jake, and I have, but apart from that I'd like to help. We could be friends, you know?'

Harriet felt herself colour. She had so few friends, she had never been one to make them. It had been difficult even at school because her mother hadn't liked her to bring friends home, which somehow restricted real confidences. She had learned to keep her distance, or perhaps had always wanted to because that was the way of her family. Wasn't it time now to cast off the chains of childhood and judge things for herself?

'I should like to be friends,' she said tentatively. To be friends with Natalie did not mean she was disloyal to Jake, after all.

Natalie was as well-known in the shop as in the hairdressers. What Natalie wanted she received, she had only to murmur 'I think white – don't you?' when the bikinis were being paraded to have all other colours removed and white ones substituted. Harriet knew that alone she would have been bludgeoned into having the ill-fitting pink one that no-one else would buy. Instead she found herself embarrassingly outfitted in three well-cut triangles that showed, it seemed to her, more than she had. That such titillation could result from so small a garment amazed her.

'I don't look decent,' she said breathlessly.

'You not supposed to,' said Natalie. 'How about a couple of dresses? That multi-coloured thing in the window for a start.'

Harriet was bemused by gratitude. The dress seemed to her the most beautiful and desirable in the world and when she whirled before the mirror and watched the colours shimmer she couldn't believe that Natalie was being so kind to her. 'I must pay,' she said helplessly, knowing she could not.

'You don't owe me a cent, honey,' said Natalie distractedly, finding a tight blue sheath that she thought would be just the thing. Harriet wasn't sure, because Natalie's image of her seemed curiously old-fashioned and sexy, tight waists, tight skirts, low necklines. But it seemed rude in the extreme to query Natalie's taste, and so she accepted the gifts humbly.

'Does Mr. de Vuiton pay for these things?' she asked bemusedly.

'Hell, no, I do. But I can afford it, honey, don't worry about that. My reward will be to see you leave that no-good bum to cook his own breakfast in his own leaky tub, while you have a good time somewhere else. You're really pretty when you're dressed up Harriet, and Jake doesn't deserve you.'

She felt herself colour. Somehow she seemed to have lost the power of independent choice. She felt torn between Jake and Natalie, each with their own view of how she should live. They walked slowly back towards the harbour, Natalie looking about her with a ranging eye.

'Ah-ha!' she said suddenly. 'There she is.'

'Who?'

'The hausfrau. While the fat cat's away the mice will get up to a thing or two. Quick, back to the launch, Harriet! You see that big yacht out there? The owner's a German and he's been looking interested. I think I'll just pop across and say hello, because his wife's out shopping and he will be – bored!' She licked her lips rapaciously.

Harriet was dumbfounded. She didn't believe it even when she was summarily despatched on the launch, while Natalie hired one of the numerous bumboats that ferried people to and from the yachts. Jake was waiting impatiently when she got back to *Dashing Away*.

'You took your time. I want to pull round to a yard and have them take a look at the mast.'

'Sorry,' said Harriet absently. She gazed out across the water at the German yacht. Sure enough there was Natalie climbing nimbly aboard. She opened her mouth to tell Jake about it, then closed it again. Natalie was her friend and Jake didn't need her confidences. Look at him now, wholly engrossed in getting the boat organised. She clutched her bags and wondered where she could put her things without ruining them. Somehow, even on such familiar territory, she felt rather lost.

Chapter Eleven

The boat's new mooring was in much less auspicious surroundings than before. Shacks huddled on the shoreline and flotsam floated visibly in the murky waters of the bay. Harriet was very quiet, clearly upset about something, but it seemed to Jake best to let her come round of her own accord. He had an inkling of what Natalie might have said, but he had no desire to rake over old coals. Why should he tell tales that should have been left to die the death? It seemed to Jake that everyone behaved badly at some time, and that to have one's mistakes and ineptitudes paraded was unnecessary cruelty. He didn't judge people, he simply detached himself from them, and he didn't understand those who bore deep and lasting grudges. Harriet should take him as she found him, she shouldn't listen to the tales of others. Besides, he was busy trying to find a new mast at a price they could even consider being able to afford. And what did Harriet do? She went shopping. If the truth were told he was every bit as annoyed with Harriet as she was with him.

Towards evening the de Vuiton launch came buzzing expensively into the cluster of shabby boats gathered at their moorings. Jake looked up and cursed. Harriet looked for Natalie and saw only Donna. She ran her hands down the sides of her stained shorts and wondered if she had time to get changed.

'So there you are, Jake,' called Donna, waving extravagantly.

'So here I am,' he said, straightening reluctantly from his examination of the cabin top that seemed to him significantly more strained than when they had set out.

'We're going ashore for a meal,' called Donna, leaning invitingly against the launch's rail. 'Guess who'll be there! Your friend Mac, and some guy called Lewis he says you know. We met them this afternoon and Peter asked them to meet us at Gavroche. Come on, lover boy, live a little.'

Harriet looked wide-eyed at Jake. 'Mac and Lewis! Jake, we've got to go. You don't want to stay here staring at bits of timber all night, do you?'

He sniffed. 'It wouldn't bug me the way it seems to be bugging you. I suppose there isn't much more I can do tonight, anyway. Go and get ready. I'll lash a few things down, the wind's really getting up now.' He stared down at Donna in the bobbing launch. 'You'll have to wait a few minutes,' he called.

She leaned forward in obvious invitation. 'You know me, Jake. As long as I get what I want, I don't mind waiting.'

'We shall have to see what we can do.' He turned and went down into the cabin.

Harriet, half-changed into her rainbow dress, said in a high voice. 'Are you going to sleep with her?'

He looked at her thoughtfully. 'Would it bother you? I thought you liked this sophisticated lifestyle. Everybody in the wrong beds, that's the way it's played.'

'She wants you to. She doesn't mind who knows.'

Jake shrugged. 'That's her problem. And you don't want to at the moment, so why shouldn't I?'

Harriet swallowed. 'So why shouldn't I sleep around? If I wanted to, that is. You've slept with loads of people. I haven't.'

Jake hit his fist against the side of his head, hard. 'Oh, God. You are really determined to engineer something, aren't you? Just don't, Harriet. You're a beginner at this and if you stir up mud it takes a long time to settle. Why don't we just get dressed and go off for a nice evening and a chat with Mac and Lewis? We can talk about morals and ethics and who I have and have not slept with tomorrow, when we've got lots of time and there aren't several pairs of ears flapping outside. 'By the way, I don't think you should let Natalie turn you into her mirror image, you don't need it. You're – ' he struggled with the compliment. 'You're a very pretty girl, in your own right. All this glamour stuff isn't you.'

She turned her back for him to fasten the dress. 'But people look at me now and they didn't before. I'm not quite the bottom of the barrel. I'm not so desperate I couldn't find someone else.'

'You never were the bottom of the barrel,' snapped Jake angrily. If there was one thing he hated it was this sort of conversation, with some woman trying to make him say things he might have said on his own if not pushed – or might not. He pulled on jeans and a shirt that was more or less clean, then waited impatiently while Harriet applied mascara and lipstick. He hardly recognised her. Without her flab and her stodgy clothes she emerged as a small-boned woman with a sweet and gentle face, dressed up to be rather too tarty. She would have looked better with less make-up, he decided, but thought better of saying so. As he had said, she was such a beginner.

She shook out the folds of her skirt and prepared to leave. He delayed for a moment, wanting to say something to her but unsure of what it might be.

'You will behave?' he said abruptly.

She stared at him. 'Of course I shall behave! It's you that can't be trusted, Jake, remember?' She flounced past him to the launch.

Gavroche was an expensive seafood restaurant set on a small rise and commanding a wide view of the bay. As they walked towards it Donna clung to Jake, deliberately ignoring Harriet and trying to exclude her. Jake was curt with her and turned twice to ask Harriet to walk with them, but she refused, preferring instead to stroll in the rear, her heels clacking delightfully, men watching her swinging skirts. Tonight she felt beautiful. If Jake had preferred Donna when Harriet was dowdy and undesirable, let him have Donna now when Harriet was quite different.

A man rose up from a café table and came across to her. 'Like a drink?' he asked. Jake turned, with Donna still plastered to his side, and said in metallic tones: 'She's with me.'

Harriet laughed and sauntered on. The brisk wind ruffled her hair and she felt as if the world was at last lovely and exciting and dangerous.

The de Vuiton party was gathered around a central table, the champagne buckets clustered like a silo of nuclear missiles. Lewis and Mac both rose as they entered, Lewis calling a welcome and Mac merely wrinkling his nose, which for him was a measure of enthusiasm.

'Jake! Good to see you fella!' Lewis advanced with his hands outstretched. Then he stopped and stared. 'What in holy smoke have you done to Harriet? Harriet, my God, you look wonderful, just wonderful.'

'Thank you.' She felt a little dizzy, as if she had already been drinking. She went across to Mac and impulsively bent down and pecked his cheek.

'You've changed,' he said grimly. 'You were better before.'

'Was I?' She tossed her mane of blonded hair and accepted a glass of champagne. Natalie was watching her, like a mother whose daughter looks very well in the party dress she chose. Harriet couldn't believe she had really gone to that German, not nice, friendly Natalie.

'Come and sit down,' said Lewis and pulled Harriet to a chair beside him. 'Tell me about this trip Jake took you on. When I heard, I thought he'd drown you both. And then I'd never have had beautiful, beautiful Harriet to play with.'

She realised he was already very drunk, but somehow she didn't mind. Lewis was so goodlooking, she thought, in a smooth, golden way, a rather unoriginal assemblage of blue eyes, tanned skin and regular features. He was every teenager's dream, she realised mistily, and wondered who she had dreamed about when she was sixteen. She could remember no more than a desperate attachment to Rin Tin Tin because she had always wanted a dog.

On the other side of the table Jake was trying to talk to de Vuiton while Donna leaned on his shoulder and reached her hand under the table. From time to time Jake pushed her aside, but equally every now and then he kissed her neck. He was leading her on, thought Harriet, making Donna more and more desperate to have him. Why was he doing that? A hand touched her own knee. It was Lewis, grinning at her and stroking her inner thigh.

'What a good thing we're such friends,' he said blearily.

'Yes.' She didn't mind Lewis's hand as much as George's. It was quite exciting, especially with Jake sitting across the table with his hand up Donna's dress. She took another drink of champagne and Lewis went still higher. She leaned back a little.

'Why don't you come back to the boat with me? We've got a great little number this time, 'bout a hundred yards long. And it's quite deserted. Come on, Harriet, let's go.'

'Why isn't there anyone on it?' she asked.

'Because the owner and his family don't come out till next week. Mac and I are going to sail it round and round for them, the sort of thing that drives Jake mad. Has he been driving you mad? You're driving me wild, Harriet. Let's go and excite each other.'

His breath was hot on her shoulder while his hand caressed and caressed her crotch. Harriet looked across the table and met Natalie's benign gaze. She nodded encouragingly. So she ought to let Lewis do this to her, because Jake was Jake and he didn't care and couldn't be trusted. Look at him now, letting Donna make a complete fool of herself while he talked sailing. How terrible to be reduced to that.

Harriet pushed her chair back and rose unsteadily to her feet. She had eaten almost nothing; in fact, the service was so slow that so far there had been almost nothing to eat. Without a word to anyone she walked to the door, her heels clacking expressively. She was going to an assignation and afterwards she would have everything in proportion. How could she understand Jake when she knew nothing of other men? No wonder he was bored with her. Inexperience made her boring.

Outside the restaurant she leaned against Lewis and said: 'You must show me things. I want to learn to do it differently.'

'Oh, Harriet, you wait!' He briefly and unobtrusively kneaded the underside of her breast, a little too hard for comfort. She winced and pushed him aside, walking alone back to the harbour. After a few steps Lewis slid his arm round her waist.

He had some trouble finding the dinghy for his yacht, but at last came upon a shiny little number with a huge motor that he seemed to recognise.

'How will Mac get back?' asked Harriet.

'We don't want him to get back. I can't wait to see what's in that dress of yours.'

'Yes.' The wind was cold and aggressive, whipping round her head in great sobering draughts. Harriet looked across at Lewis and wondered what on earth she was doing. She knew him, she liked him, but he was Lewis. He wasn't someone she slept with. But of course it would be different in the warmth and dark of a cabin. Then she would be able to feel desire. At the moment, though, she was realising how very much she would have liked something to eat.

The motor sent them roaring across to a dark hump of a yacht, rearing out of the darkness like a cliff. Spray whipped over the bow and soaked her dress, yet she was sorry when the journey ended. Lewis fumbled with ropes, tying the dinghy as securely as his drunkenness allowed.

'Are you sure you want to do this?' asked Harriet shrilly. 'I mean, we could go back to the restaurant and finish the meal.'

He didn't reply. With skill acquired from practice Harriet ascended the ladder to the deck.

He took her first to the saloon, a huge room now in total darkness. When he switched on the lights Harriet put her hands over her eyes, dazzled by the glare.

'Harriet,' said Lewis, and tried to kiss her. She evaded him, walking across to the huge round table and saying shrilly. 'What about the cabins? Why don't we go there?'

'I thought we'd do it on the table,' said Lewis optimistically. Harriet thought that it was true men were different from women. He was still as hot for it, and had no inkling that her ardour had cooled. If it had been ardour. Was it really the urge to better Jake, with Donna glued to him like a passionate limpet?

'I'd like to look at the cabins,' said Harriet firmly, as if she were inspecting the boat prior to purchase. Lewis shrugged and led the way out of the saloon, switching on lights as he went until it seemed the yacht must look like a Christmas tree, lights everywhere.

'We'll do it here,' said Lewis, and stopped at the main cabin. Harriet went in. There was a huge double bed.

She had a sudden vision of Lewis lying on top of her spreadeagled body, in an act in which she was uninvolved although participating. The thought revolted her. But perhaps it would be better once she got started and besides, she could hardly make him take her all the way out here and then refuse. Harriet was used to doing what was expected of her. 'Undo me,' she said resignedly, and Lewis's fingers wrestled with her zip. Once undone he began to nuzzle her neck and her shoulders, letting the dress fall to the floor.

'Mind the dress,' said Harriet, pushing him away. She picked it up carefully and folded it. She felt rather sick. Lewis seized the moment to rid himself of his own clothes, kicking trousers, pants, shirt and shoes anywhere. He was very excited, Harriet noted with almost clinical interest. And he wasn't as big as Jake.

'Harriet!' His flesh was against hers, warm and different. He didn't smell like Jake, not at all. An urge to repulse him made her brace her hands against his shoulders, but when she did so he bent his head and kissed her. It wasn't the same, but it wasn't unpleasant. She kissed him back, taking note of the shape of his mouth, the pressure of his tongue, letting her hips rotate against him.

'That is enough!'

Harriet screamed and jumped back. She put one arm across her breasts and the other at the top of her legs. She was whimpering with fright. Jake strode past as if she wasn't there, advancing on Lewis. Good looks or no, he looked ridiculous now, wearing nothing but his socks. He held out his hands in an attempt to reason.

'You could have stopped this before if you'd wanted,' he began, backing round the bed. 'There's no need for a fight, Jake. Harriet's her own woman – '

Jake sprang forward, his fist dealing a short and telling blow full in Lewis's mouth. Drops of blood flew in the air to land on the deep cream carpet. Harriet screamed, because Lewis's mouth had mashed into red jelly. She thought wildly that she wanted to die, because she would never forget this and to remember it would always be terrible. Lewis was climbing over the bed, and as he came near Harriet drew away.

'Get some clothes on will you, Harriet,' said Jake thickly.

'You shouldn't be here. It isn't fair.'

'Isn't it? You're making a fool of yourself and you're too stupid to see it. Where's your pride?'

'Bit strong for you to preach morals, Jake,' mumbled Lewis, stepping into his underpants. 'You don't own Harriet.'

'But I am responsible for her,' said Jake, crossing to where she still stood, naked and shivering. He seized the dress and thrust it over her head, dragging her arms up as if she were a doll.

'You aren't responsible,' she said shrilly, fighting both the dress and him. 'And even if you were, you can't be trusted, everybody says so.'

'Oh yeah. Natalie,' said Jake with hard bitterness.

'Not only her,' added Lewis, taking the opportunity for revenge. 'You'll never get another boat now, Jake, the word's out about you. You can sail and that's about it, you're a fool with money and you don't know how to work with people. You with your big ideas about this or that rig – you couldn't persuade a monkey to eat a banana. Everyone knows you can't be trusted. Look at you now, you can't even keep your girl. I guess you don't screw too well nowadays either.'

Jake stared at him, his eyes like ice. 'I knew you resented me,' he said thoughtfully, 'but I didn't know it ran so deep. What a bastard you are, Lewis. And if you're skippering this tub, I've no doubt at all you'll run it aground within a week. But that's up to you and we all have to grow up and put ourselves on the line sometime. I wish you well, sonnyboy, but I don't think wishing's going to be enough. Harriet, get down to the boat.'

She thought about refusing, but she had no wish at all to stay with Lewis and his bloody face and his bile. It seemed that she had been about to make love to a man for whom she felt almost nothing and now, sober, it shocked her. Jake was right to despise her, she had no pride. Hanging her head she picked up her shoes and went barefoot up on deck. The wind was fierce, even in the shelter of the harbour the waves were white-capped. There was a bumboat waiting at the foot of the ladder, its owner sitting impassively at the tiller despite the boat's jiggling. She turned but Jake caught her arms.

'I can't go down there. He'll know.'

'I don't give a shit. Get down that ladder, Harriet, before I throw you.'

She lifted her head and stared at him. 'You haven't got any right! I can do what I like, we're not married or anything. Perhaps I shouldn't have gone with Lewis, but only because of me, not because of you.'

He closed his eyes for a fraction of a second. When he opened them he said quietly, 'Get down the ladder. We'll go back to the boat and discuss it sensibly. I don't think – we'll have to talk.'

She reached up and touched his face, but he pushed her hand away.

What did he want? To use people and yet have them love him, just as Natalie said. She swung herself over the rail and down to the boat, the wind blowing her skirt high and treating the man below to an exhilarating view of Harriet without her knickers.

Dashing Away was jerking at her mooring like an anxious pony. Jake paid off the bumboat while Harriet went below, but he didn't follow her. He sat on deck, the wind was making his eyes water and he wondered if he was crying. He didn't understand himself tonight, behaving like a lover when he didn't think he was in love.

Nassau was a filthy place. It fed on the worst of people soured by money and excess and jaded bodies. Harriet was like fresh meat amongst blowflies yet all she desired was to become as flyblown as the rest. He should get her away, take her away, and if they drowned it would be worth it. Sighing, he got to his feet, pretending to be unaware that his legs were trembling.

Harriet, waiting for him, felt the boat heeling into the wind and realised they were moving. She assumed that they were changing moorings once again, to a more sheltered spot where they could ride out the storm in relative calm. It was a relief not to have Jake in the cabin, simmering with violent rage, because this time she would have fought back. How dare he upbraid her about Lewis and expect her to ignore Donna? How could he expect her trust when no-one even pretended he was trustworthy? She climbed into bed and pulled the covers up to her chin. Suddenly she saw the scene as Jake must have seen it when he burst into the bedroom and her blush flooded her whole body. She pulled the covers over her head.

Even under storm jib alone the little boat flew across the waves. Jake stood on deck, watching the dark hills of the following seas and knew that beyond them was a hard wind growing harder. The night held the promise of wild disaster, with rushing clouds across the moon and the lights of Nassau receding, sometimes seen and sometimes hidden as *Dashing Away* raced into a heaving ocean from which all other boats had long since fled.

After an hour or so Harriet came on deck. 'What's happening? Where are we going?'

'I don't know. Away somewhere.'

She stared out as Jake stared, for the moment safe as the boat rushed across the seas, sometimes diving into troughs, sometimes having her stern impertinently lifted by a hasty crest behind. The noise of the wind was a continuous high screeching. so that any speech was of necessity shouted behind a cupped hand, and even then could hardly be heard.

'Are you going to kill us?' she yelled.

He met her eyes for the first time since he burst in upon her and Lewis. 'I don't know.'

She pulled her blanket more closely about her. There was nothing to be done then, except ride out this storm into which Jake had thrust them. She was too tired and drained to be frightened, in fact it scarcely seemed real. Waves began to slap the foredeck and she went below to make a thermos of something hot, because soon it would be very bad and the stove would be unusable. Down below, amidst reality, she shuddered with the stirring of apprehension, but she went ahead and made Jake's drink, and took his oilskins up to him in the cockpit. He looked at her as he took the cup and smiled. 'This is better. I'd rather have it like this.' She shrugged and went below, curling up on the bunk and trying to doze until dawn.

Morning was cold and dark, and brought no reassurance. Jake came grey-faced into the cabin, trailing moisture, slumped with exhaustion.

'Are we in the hurricane?' asked Harriet.

He shook his head wearily. 'This is only the trailing edge. But she's suffering a bit too much for my taste.'

Words of accusation rose to her lips. If it wasn't for Jake they could both be safe in Nassau harbour. But there was no point in it, there never was in rows. Nothing would change however much she screamed. She sighed and huddled into the damp folds of her jumper. 'We haven't got much food.'

'No. What did Natalie tell you about me?'

Harriet swallowed. 'We don't have to talk about that now, do we?'

'Yes. I want to know, Harriet.'

There was no avoiding it. She forced herself to think about what she would much rather ignore. 'It seems you and she were having an affair. You took her money and everything, just like me. You sold her mother's ring. And then you left her in Jamaica, and she had to – well – she took up with a man, for money. The way she lives is really your fault. At least that's what she says.'

'And you believed her.' He was watching her with clear eyes, his jaw square and black with stubble. She knew him so well, she knew every pore of his skin. How could she believe it was quite like that? How could she believe anything else?

'I don't suppose you meant to do it to her. You don't mean things, do you Jake, they just happen.'

'But it didn't happen like that.' He stared at the cabin sole, that was already slimy and wet. Harriet thought he wasn't going to say any more, but suddenly he began: 'I wasn't always as hard bitten as I am now. She's very pretty. She always was. When I first saw her I fell for her, good and hard. She was with a guy who employed me to skipper his racing yacht, and after about a month I dumped his yacht, took Natalie, and headed off in a borrowed boat. I shouldn't have done any of that of course. The guy was my friend, he employed me, I was ducking out of my contract. But Natalie and I could really make it in bed, and it seemed worth it at the time.

'Then the money began to get a bit thin and I took a job at a yard on one of the islands, because Natalie wanted things, Natalie needed things. I couldn't make enough, I had to sell things off the boat and that wasn't mine. I didn't know what Natalie was doing while I was working – I think now I deliberately didn't ask. One day I noticed she had a ring, an emerald ring, a huge thing with diamonds all round. She hadn't had that before. I asked her about it and she said it was her mother's. No way was I believing that. So one day I didn't go to the yard, I hung around and watched, and sure enough there was Natalie, tripping from one yacht to the next. Three, she managed, and then back to our boat to await the return of the breadwinner. She had more money stashed under the bunk than I could earn in a year, and she was keeping it to herself, I can tell you.

'We had a showdown: tears, apologies, it was all for you, the whole load of shit. So we moved islands. I didn't get a job for a while, we lived off her savings and that galled her I can tell you. Then I got in with a sailmaker and Natalie promised to be a very good girl. She was for about two days, then she hit the sack with the man who ran the bar on the dockside. They did it every afternoon, the word soon got round. It was the way she was, there was nothing I was ever going to be able to do about it. For about half an hour I considered pretending I didn't know, keeping on the move, starting up in a new place every three months, running ahead of the rumours. But when I thought about what I really felt for her it wasn't love any more and I was bitter as hell.

'So I threw all her clothes into the harbour, all the tarty dresses that she's dressing you up in. I hauled her out of bed with the fat barman and made her run naked through the bar – she didn't like that much. And I took the emerald ring off her finger and flogged it to buy myself a new boat and I left Natalie there to sort herself out the best way she could. She did it the easy way, of course. Natalie always does.'

Harriet swallowed. 'No wonder she hates you.'

'Well, I don't hate her any more. I evened the score and it took the sting out of things. I don't blame Natalie because I've screwed up my life, but I suppose I could. Before her I'd been bloody reliable, and I could say she started me on the road to ruin, but it wasn't just her. I don't like doing what I'm told, I don't like doing the same thing every day, and I don't like playing safe.'

'But you expect me to do all those things,' Harriet said flatly.

Jake looked at her. The swinging lantern that was all the light there was in the cabin cast deep shadows under her cheekbones. 'I keep thinking that I'm watching you grow up,' he said slowly. 'Sometimes you're such a woman, you've got real strength, I don't know where you got that. Then, with Lewis, I've got a child on my hands, getting her own back by letting some guy poke her. OK, sleep around if you really want to, but not just to get at me. That was bloody stupid, Harriet.'

She felt rather silly but said defiantly, 'You were doing it with Donna. She was touching you and everything. You kissed her!'

He looked a bit sheepish. 'Well, I have screwed her before. It seemed a bit farcical to fight her off like a frightened virgin when six months ago I stuck myself up every hole she's got. Like Natalie says, I'm not used to staying in the same bed. Sorry, Harriet.'

She sniffed, feeling slightly mollified. The light was swaying rhythmically. Suddenly it lurched and she found herself still sitting on the bunk but almost on her back. Surprise took the place of fear, she couldn't think what had happened.

'Christ!' Jake fought his way to the hatch, his feet crunching on cereal that had somehow ended up on the floor. Water was running in small streams down from the cabin top that must now be partially under the surface. Jake did not open the hatch. 'Come up, baby, come up,' he whispered.

Harriet felt the blood draining completely from her face. Her skin felt like stretched paper. The little boat staggered unhappily, held down by the weight of the great sea on her side. Then, with a lurch, she swung her mast skywards again. Jake swore inappropriately and flung open the hatch, letting water cascade into the cabin.

It was the beginning of what they both believed was the end of the little boat. The hours merged into an endless stretch of misery, day blended unnoticed into night. For the most part they stayed below decks, silent, enduring, until some new catastrophe demanded that Jake go out again to try and help their craft in her struggle with the storm. Twice Harriet went with him, when he was streaming warps. They manhandled fathoms of rope over the stern in a loop, and at once the motion of the boat steadied as the stern held more firmly into the following sea. It was cold, heavy, dangerous work, that took so long you ceased to care whether you lived or died. Just to have it stop, that was all Harriet wanted.

She staggered below in a state of complete exhaustion. Jake held a mug to her lips and she drank the last of the tea, tasting of the old thermos and only lukewarm.

'I'm sorry about this,' he said suddenly.

'It always tastes like that out of the thermos,' said Harriet.

'I meant about doing this to you. I was angry. I didn't care if I did kill us both.'

'So what's new?' murmured Harriet, wincing as the boat shuddered under the onslaught of another giant wave. When you stood on deck and saw them you couldn't believe you had survived even this long. But Jake never really meant to die. He had a conceit that told him he would always be able to handle things, and in her experience he always could. He gave her a weary grin. 'Tell me about you, Harriet. Your life. What you were doing before you came on that trip.'

She opened her eyes in surprise, because it seemed to her that he rarely had an interest in people before he met them; their importance to him began when they became part of what he, Jake, was doing. 'There isn't anything to tell,' she said doubtfully. 'I worked for a bit when I left school, in an insurance company. Then mother's arthritis got bad and I gave up and looked after her. Now she's in a home.'

'Yes, but what was it like? You looked after your mother for years, what was that like?'

Harriet thought back. Her spirits, which she supposed to be at rock bottom, sank a little lower. It had been a terrible time, a time of imprisonment, watching her youth and girlhood rot away. 'I was lonely,' she said at last. 'You don't have anything in common with other people, you see, because there isn't much money and all you can talk about is the doctor or the bath nurse or something. Mother and I got on very well, for years and years. But then she got confused, you see – ' She tailed off. How to tell of days during which your mother never recognised you, when she imagined you were trying to poison her, steal her money?

'Did you mind?' asked Jake.

She turned to him, nodding fiercely, because he didn't understand that it was hardly a question of minding. She had been deprived of love, of life, of freedom, of self-respect. Yet still her mother would clutch at Harriet's cardigan and murmur piteously, 'Harriet! Harriet! Don't put me in a home!'

Suddenly she had to tell it all. The words came bubbling out in a torrent of pain and self-recrimination. Jake couldn't understand at first, couldn't see that she didn't want him to say anything, only to be there and listen. He put an oilskinned arm round her shoulders. The boat heeled almost flat, an ominous crack came from the rigging, but still she talked, telling him endlessly. Then she fell silent. There was only the wind roaring outside.

'So,' said Jake softly, 'what did you do then?'

Harriet wiped her cheeks though she had not known she was crying. 'One day I sold the house. It was easy, I asked less than it was worth. I paid off the mortgage, it was only a couple of thousand, and I paid for mother to go into a home. Quite a nice place really, if you're old and crippled and mad, right in the middle of the country so you can't get out and bother anyone. I didn't go with her, I just put her in the car and she cried. And – and straight away I went to the travel agent's with all the money I had left and I paid for my cruise. And she might be dead now really, I don't know. I often think about it. Is it better for her to be dead? It might be.'

'I don't know.' Jake was very quiet.

'Is your mother dead?' asked Harriet, wondering if she had touched some nerve. Everyone had a mother, even Jake.

'I wouldn't know if she was,' he said flatly. 'I had the most sensible, boring, suburban, small-minded, tedious childhood that any child could possibly have. Clean hands, clean clothes and minds so clean there isn't anything worth thinking in them. They hated me because I wasn't like them. I was sent away to my grandparents in the holidays, they lived in Southampton. I learned to sail there and as soon as I possibly could I left home and got a job with a boatyard and I have never, ever been back. They weren't sorry to see me go, and I've never regretted going.'

Harriet sighed. 'I don't suppose they meant to be unkind.'

Suddenly enraged, Jake yelled: 'Nobody ever does! Did your mother want to ruin your life? Do you think I wanted to help her do it? Things happen because in the end people always put self first.'

Lying there, in the ghastly, ill-lit little cabin with the world gone mad outside, Harriet felt suddenly hopeless. 'Do you always put yourself first?' she asked drearily. 'Don't you ever do things for other people?'

'Only when it costs me nothing,' said Jake. 'My mother cried when I left. I don't know why, she'd ignored me for five years except when she went to church and prayed for my soul. But – she cried. So why didn't I write or go and see her? Because it cost me. You see, Harriet, you were right. I might say "Trust me, rely on me", but you can't. Sooner or later I'll let you down, when what you need and what I want go in different directions. I would never have done as you did, given up half my life, the best half. I wouldn't have considered it.'

'You might have done,' said Harriet, thinking of how inescapable the trap had seemed at the time. 'And anyway, I gave up in the end.'

Jake shrugged, quite fatalistic. 'Even your love for your mother couldn't hold out against self-love. And you are a loving person, Harriet.'

'Well, aren't you?'

He grinned, but only to deflect the comment, not from mirth. 'I don't think I can be. Sometimes I try to be, but over the years I've lost whatever it takes, I think. Would someone who loved you have brought you here? I don't think so somehow.'

Harriet wiped her nose with the back of her hand. She had yet to digest what he was saying to her, to put it in terms she could understand. Perhaps later she would feel hurt, but not yet. Just telling him everything was like dropping a huge burden, an ugly packload of guilt and deceit and memory.

'Let's make love,' said Jake suddenly. 'I want to be close for a bit.'

He thought she was going to refuse but instead she gave him a small, rather shy smile and began to struggle out of her trousers, his trousers, by now far too big for her. He felt a strong surge of desire, stronger than for a long time, as if she was the first and he a very young boy. He didn't understand himself any more. Why should such emotion flood out to surround an act he had performed so many times before? Sharp, salt-tasting ecstasy. When he was spent he lifted a curl of her hair and blew gently into her ear. She put her hand over her eyes for a moment and he realised he had no idea at all what she was thinking.

Chapter Twelve

The mast went while they both slept. Harriet awoke to darkness, a feeling that the world was spinning, that wherever she was it was nowhere she had been before. The crashing, ripping, smashing noise went on and on. There was the sound of water rushing. A death knell sound. She wondered what it would be like to drown and sucked in frantic breaths as if she could husband air to save her in the depths. Truly she didn't want to die.

And then Jake was there, soothing her in the dark, holding her so close that she could feel his heart pounding, hear his dragging breaths. He was soaking wet. 'Are we finished?' she said harshly.

'God knows. The water's a foot deep in the cabin. We're barely afloat and I think the mast's gone.'

She touched his face, realising that they were both so shocked by the suddenness of the calamity that they could not at once decide what to do. Jake said, 'For a minute there I thought we'd had it. God, I was scared.'

'I *am* scared,' said Harriet, and hugged him. After a moment, when still the water rushed but there was no surge of green sea to drown them, she said, 'We're still here.'

'Yes.' He pulled away from her and she could hear him sploshing about in the water. After a while he found a torch and, miraculously, it worked. In the eerie light they saw that the boat was almost on its side. Although the cabin top still leaked the main flood had come from the forward hatch, stoved in and for part of the time under-water. Now and then water ran in through the hole and added to the depth in the cabin.

'Did we go upside down?' asked Harriet. 'It felt like it.'

'It was a knockdown. I don't know quite what happened, but the mast's gone. Better get rid of that first.' He began to move to the companionway, his legs pushing aside the detritus of their lives as it floated about. An open copy of a Boston guidebook, an Admiralty chart, a bucket. Jake picked up the bucket. 'Hang on to that, we'll have to bail in a minute, once I cut the mast free.'

'Let me help,' said Harriet and followed him. She was freezing cold, her teeth already chattering. Together they struggled onto the deck.

The world was lit by sparse moonlight, and there were stars everywhere. All around the sea raged, but less wildly. *Dashing Away* wallowed, her entire rigging over the rail, the rail itself under water.

'It's easing,' shouted Jake. 'The bastard got us with a flick of its tail.'

He found the wire cutters, always tied handy in the cockpit, and went spider-fashion across the raking deck, cutting the shrouds. Suppose he fell in, thought Harriet. This time he wouldn't be saved, and neither would she. After a moment she went on all fours to join him, holding the wires for him to cut. All at once the mast slid away into the oily water that looked like greasy metal, as so often after a blow. The deck swung up, but still the bow hung heavy into the waves. Only another foot down and they would be finished. The warp was gone, fathoms of heavy rope taken as if they were gossamer. She began to whisper prayers to herself, to promise that she would be so different if only she need not die right now, in this most horrible of places. If she was saved now, tomorrow she would be brave.

'Don't pray, bale,' said Jake, pulling her back towards the cockpit. 'We're still alive, so I think we can assume God has his eye on us. Don't stop. We can't get dry so we must keep moving.'

Grimly, Harriet tried to obey. She filled the bucket and emptied it, filled it and emptied it, again and again and again. Her arms began to ache, then went past aching into pain. After that they simply refused to co-operate and hung useless from her shoulders until an immense effort of will drove them to complete another rotation. Jake never stopped. He lashed some spare canvas over the forward hatch and then set to on the bilge pump, although in what seemed like hours of labour the level in the cabin receded only fractionally.

At last Harriet could do no more. She stood in the water, crying with weariness. Jake came and pulled her on to the bunk, stripping off her sodden jumper and trousers, to wrap her in blankets only fractionally less wet. There was one dry thing, a sweater found in a locker, and as Harriet pushed her frozen arms into the sleeves it seemed a wonderful blessing.

She held on to Jake's wet sleeve. 'You lie down, too. We can't go on forever.'

He gave the ghost of an exhausted grin. 'I got you into this, lovey. I think I owe it to you to get you out.'

She watched him for a while, but she was too tired. When she woke it was morning and the sun was shining. Jake's eyes were red dots in a grey face and the cabin was empty of water.

'Have you done it?' she asked wonderingly. He was too tired to reply.

A thought came to her and she began to rummage in a locker for the small bottle of brandy they had left from the trip before. Everything was wet, but the brandy looked fine. She unscrewed the top and held it out to Jake. He didn't take it. She realised he was barely conscious. Eventually she held it to his lips, and kept it there until he spluttered: 'Enough. Let me sleep. Wake me if anything happens.'

She helped him into the bunk she had just vacated and went on deck to survey the scene. The boat looked terrible, a hulk covered in trailing wire, wallowing amidst whitecaps. but it was still there, and the breeze was blowing warm and friendly. Tomorrow was here and she was alive, but where was the relief? Exhaustion blotted out everything. She knew she ought to do something, but what? After a while she thought about drying things, and draped sodden blankets and clothes over a thin length of rope tied from one rail to the other. It was difficult to persuade herself that anything she did would make any difference to the chaos that surrounded her. Vaguely she thought about food and went below to see what there was.

Almost everything was spoiled, except for the tins which had all lost their labels. After some shaking and wondering she found the tin opener and discovered baked beans and sausages, peaches and a tin of peas. None of it appealed, and anyway the stove was soaked. She tried to light it and failed, and then thought how much she would like a cup of tea. Never consciously mechanical, Harriet discovered a new talent in herself as she stripped down the burner and pricked out nozzles and valves with a bent piece of wire. Reassembled the stove burnt, fitfully and with alarming pops. Food and a cup of black tea made with wet teabags made her feel slightly less bewildered.

She stared for long minutes at the sleeping Jake and wondered why it was that whatever awful thing he did to you it was never possible to be as cross with him as he deserved. He was not honest, but neither was he deceitful, which was a strange contradiction. To cheat truthfully, that was his charm. He was just such a rogue. Such an absolute pirate.

Two days later they were hungry and very thirsty. The water supply had been largely ruined by the capsize and they were rationing the food because they had no idea how long it would be before they reached land. Jake had rigged up a small and inefficient sail, and they bobbed along in vaguely the right direction.

'You realise that we could sail between two islands and never see either?' said Jake conversationally. Any remorse for their plight had evaporated as he became engrossed in the challenge of providing a rig from the inadequate materials available to him.

He annoyed Harriet intensely. 'You're supposed to know how to navigate,' she snapped.

'Bit more difficult than it looks actually, especially since I flogged the sextant to pay for the mast. If we'd had the new mast stepped we'd have been OK too, but we'd still have been just as lost. Shows how pointless money really is, doesn't it? We'd give anything for a mast or a sextant now, and all we've got is the cash.'

'Spare me the philosophy,' said Harriet tersely. She felt jumpy and claustrophobic. She approached her food hungrily and then was sickened by it. How she longed for this to be over.

'What are we going to do when we do make land?' she asked.

Jake shrugged. 'Get the boat seen to, bum around in the sun for a bit. I don't know.'

'And just waste time?' said Harriet. It was the waste of precious days that irked her most about sailing, the time taken to reach the place where you might do something, whereas for Jake it was the getting there that was important. He had nothing planned for when he actually arrived.

'Don't be so busy,' said Jake lazily, watching her hang out yet more clothes. It was hot and she was wearing her new bikini. It made him feel randy and he reached out a hand to caress her smooth brown back. 'You look toothsome,' he murmured, but she moved out of reach.

'You've got to start something – a business. You've got to start doing things.'

'I do things already, I do what I like. Anyway, I've started businesses before. They're bloody hard work.'

'What sort of businesses?'

He linked his hands behind his head. 'Sail design. That was pretty successful, but we got to the point where we had to expand or give up, and expanding meant spending all my time behind my own desk or in front of the desks of bank managers. I got up one beautiful day and the sun was beating hell out of the place and the breeze was stirring up to a blow, and all I could look forward to was fourteen hours indoors in a suit. I quit. Mac was wild, I can tell you, he only cared about the money.'

'You could always get someone else to do the desk bit.'

He reached up and caught her wrist, pulling her down beside him. 'To begin with you can't afford it, and by the time you can afford it you've forgotten why you should. No sunny idylls any more when you start pursuing lucre, Harriet, my girl. I love your chin, do you know that? Your best bit used to be those whacking great boobs, but now I think it's your chin.'

'Chins are not an erogenous zone,' she said, trying to wriggle out of his grasp.

'Right now they are, let's rub chins. That's bloody erogenous that is.' He swung expertly on top of her and Harriet felt both annoyed and aroused. He ought to be thinking of the future, talking of what was to happen. They couldn't bum around all their lives. If he wanted her with him then he must have something in mind that he wanted to do, not just sail from here to there. Oh, but she adored what he was doing to her. For the moment she gave herself up to it.

Another two days and the weather began to close in once more. Harriet was visibly frightened, which surprised Jake. He could not understand that before she had not known what it was that should frighten her, whereas now she could picture every awful thing that might occur. Besides, to her each danger they overcame was one more teaspoonful out of their pot of luck, whereas Jake put it all down to experience.

'If we don't drown, we'll starve,' she said petulantly. 'We're hopelessly lost, we never see any other ships.'

'It's a big ocean,' said Jake calmly. 'Don't worry, you can always bump me off and eat me if need be. Cannibalism is an ancient seafaring tradition.'

'I don't mind killing you, it's the eating I shouldn't fancy.' She stared out at the clouds trailing thin skirts across the setting sun. Another night of noise and confusion, halfway between exhaustion and terror. Why was she faced with only two alternatives in life, absolute boredom or absolute fear? Wasn't it possible to find herself a middle course where every day brought small new challenges? Jake was lashing things down and taking in their pathetic bits of sail.

'What a season,' he said with slight irritation. 'This will go down in the record books. We're in for another big one.'

'Ohhhh!' She picked up the bucket of seawater she kept for rinsing dishes and threw it at him. Jake was transfixed with surprise.

Late that night as they lay in the cabin while the sea beat at the boat, a dull booming sound added itself to the noise of the wind. Jake opened his eyes and sat up.

'What is it?' asked Harriet, clutching her blanket. It was the end, she knew it.

'Surf. We're bloody nearly aground somewhere. Shit.'

She couldn't understand why he wasn't pleased. Out of the dark had come land to save them. They could abandon their sinking tub and walk on dry earth. She seized her small bag of respectable clothing and scrambled on deck. In the blackness the white streaks of rollers breaking on a shore were eerie and scarcely believable.

'If that's a reef we're in real trouble,' said Jake, staring out with much less enthusiasm. 'This is a lee shore, Harriet dear, feared by all sensible sailors. If it's a beach we're not much better off. The boat will be pounded to matchsticks.'

'But at least we'll be on land,' said Harriet breathlessly.

'Oh yes. There is that.'

He was unmoved by anything except the possible loss of his boat. Suddenly she didn't want to be with him any more; she wanted to be on the shore, alone, walking until her legs ached. Why didn't he understand that she had never wanted to go to sea in the first place, that like most of her life it had been foisted on her? Nobody ever asked what she wanted. Jake never asked what she wanted.

The breakers were getting nearer, the little boat was being driven gamely on to her fate. Jake began to make ready with the anchor, because if they could only hold their own he might kedge off when the wind slackened. He tried it for depth, but the bottom was nowhere near. The beach must shelve quite steeply then. They had a chance if they could anchor in deep water next to the shelf. Each wave pushed them further on, each ten yards or so Jake swung the anchor.

There was a smell about land Harriet realised, a tree-filled scent that held in it everything she desired. Again Jake swung the anchor, and this time it bit. *Dashing Away* swung her stern flirtatiously as she was gripped by the nose, and Jake went at once to cast a makeshift stern anchor, so that she should be held bow to the oncoming seas and make less of them. They were perhaps a hundred yards from the shore, a dimly seen sand beach and beyond it the black expanse of palm forest. The wind howled in the palm fronds, branches waving like black arms against the sky.

'It's only about four feet deep on the shelf,' said Jake anxiously. 'If we get pushed on to it she'll break up, no messing.'

'But we can wade ashore,' insisted Harriet. 'Let's just leave her and go.'

Jake hardly believed he was hearing right. Their little craft had carried them bravely for weeks past, had seen them through some of the worst weather he had ever thought he would encounter, and totally unsuitable though she was, she had brought them through it. Yet Harriet wanted to abandon her, as if she were nothing.

'Don't be bloody ridiculous. You can't just leave her, not when she could be saved.'

Harriet stamped her foot on the stained deck. 'I don't want to stay! I didn't want to come! She's hardly worth anything Jake, you know that. We can go and get help, then come back and see to her in the morning. Please Jake.'

'By then she'd be smashed and you know it. But go on if you must, you can get some food and stuff, and some fresh water. Don't be long. If the wind moves a few points I'll have to take her off.'

'Well, you mustn't. If I'm not back you must leave her and come ashore, I won't go otherwise. You will, won't you?'

Jake looked at her earnest face, her hair, now grown quite long, streaming out behind her. She wasn't at all the sort of woman he would have chosen to take to sea, yet she suited him. He didn't like to think of her alone on the dark shore. 'Wait till morning,' he advised.

'No!'

She wasn't going to argue. By morning the wind would have shifted and they would be away. She would have to spend weeks and weeks more in the little boat and in all probability never see land again. This was their chance and he couldn't see it. Holding her bag of clothes above her head she evaded Jake's restraining hand and slid over the rail. The water was shockingly cold, she nearly dropped the clothes. It was also deep, four feet in the troughs of the waves and a foot and a half deeper at the crests. She found herself half-swimming, half-walking, and her bag was soon soaked. But the waves that were to be the downfall of *Dashing Away* propelled her shorewards like a giant hand.

'Don't be long!' yelled Jake through the wind.

She waved a long white arm, like the Lady of the Lake he thought, and felt a frisson of mystical fear. He should never have let her go.

Harriet staggered a little as she stepped on the beach. She put on her sandals but they were wet and the sand stuck to them, so after a few steps she took them off and walked barefoot. It seemed much darker on land than on the water, shadowed as she was by trees bending before the fierce wind. The shoreline was littered with debris, presumably detritus from the hurricane since this storm was nowhere near so bad. There were no lights and no houses. Suppose the island was uninhabited? Suppose there was no-one there at all and Jake went away and she was left here forever? She started to run, her feet padding on the sand, her stiff limbs complaining. When she was out of breath she walked briskly, and then ran again. How long had she been away? It was hard to tell without a watch, it could be ten minutes or two hours.

There was a light. Wavering above the trees was the clear yellow glow of a lamp. It was a house, it had to be! She saw that the treeline was split, as if a wide vista had been cut through the forest to the beach. At once she began to run again, each breath raking painfully in her throat.

As she approached the house she slowed and then stopped. There was something dark and threatening about its bulk, about the single light glowing in an upstairs room. The wind was lifting creeper from the old stone walls and slapping it back with a noise like dry bones. Windows were broken and somewhere an iron gate was creaking eerily.

Was the house abandoned then? She stepped on to the flagged terrace, forgetting her bare feet. Huge terracotta pots lay smashed into shards and pain stabbed as she cut her foot. One of Jake's curses rose to her lips. She thought of turning and running back to the boat but the light in the house – someone must be there. Surely no-one would refuse aid to a shipwreck? Crossing to huge French doors, the panes broken, she turned the handle. It was locked but the key was on the inside, and using a piece of the broken pots she smashed more glass and reached in to turn it. Her heart was beating in little jumps and her foot was stinging and she began to cry, because she was so tired and everything was so terribly difficult. As she stepped into the house she felt chill, lifeless air.

Thick turkey carpet, wringing wet, cushioned her feet. Harriet padded across it, calling weakly, 'Is anyone there? Hello? I need help.' Her voice died in the darkness. She crossed to big double doors and wrestled with the massive handles. Everything about the house was huge, she noticed, feeling like Jack after climbing the beanstalk. 'Excuse me? Hello?' she called again into the black cavern behind the door.

'I must warn you that I am holding a gun,' said a voice. 'One more step and I will shoot you.'

'Oh,' said Harriet helplessly, twisting her sodden bag of clothes in her hands. Suddenly the room was flooded with yellow light. She was dazzled and put her hands up to her eyes. She could just see a man in a wheelchair. He held a shotgun pointed waveringly towards her. He was old, she realised, with deep grooves from the sides of an aquiline nose to the corners of a once-strong mouth.

'Please don't,' she said breathlessly. 'I didn't know anyone was here. Our boat's wrecked and I came for help, but there isn't anywhere except here. Do you mind if I sit down?' She didn't wait for a reply but simply flopped down to the floor and put her head between her knees. She felt terrible, sick and shaking.

'Your foot's bleeding,' said the man.

'I cut it on the terrace, all the pots are broken. I'm so sorry to intrude like this. If I could have some food and blankets and things – we'd pay you back, of course. It was the hurricane – and now this.' She began to cry again, rubbing at her cheeks with flat palms.

'You shouldn't come here, I don't want people here.'

'I'm sorry. I didn't mean – are you alone? You can't be.' Such a frail old man could not be here by himself. Yet the house was filled with decay: ancient wallpaper ripped and hanging, curtains detached from their hooks and half-obscuring the windows. She put out a hand and touched a massive mahogany chair.

'Don't touch my things. I know your sort, you've come to steal. Did the cowards tell you I was alone here? Didn't they tell you what I did?'

Dully Harriet said, 'Our boat's wrecked, I told you.'

The old man started to cough, and though at first he could control it in a moment he was fighting for breath. Harriet got up and went to him, prudently detaching the gun from his jerking fingers. 'I'll get you a drink,' she said, spotting a tarnished silver tray on a giant sideboard. There was a decanter full of something brown, and several glasses. She filled one for the old man and held it to his lips. He sipped and his cough subsided. Harriet poured another glass for herself and drank it down, although it tasted like neat spirit.

'You're from the village,' said the old man angrily. 'I know you are.' He lifted something from beneath the blanket that covered his legs and brandished it.

'No,' soothed Harriet, 'I told you. What is that you have?'

Warily he said, 'Don't you know?'

'Is it a bag of something? May I see?'

Hastily he hid what appeared to be a brown leather pouch, embroidered in some way. 'It isn't anything. Well, now you're here you'd better help me.'

'I can't stay,' she said. 'I've got to get back. Have you food, blankets – anything?'

'I don't know what they've left,' he said irritably. 'They attacked the house, you know, last night. My man was away and so they attacked it. They were too frightened to kill me, the cowards. Instead they left me to die alone, of hunger perhaps. They don't know me. Even now they don't know.' The old face settled into harsh lines.

Harriet said, 'What can I do? What do you want?'

Glaring at her he said, 'I refuse to sit in my own ordure any longer. Are you competent? You do not appear to be so, all big eyes and weeping and hair.'

Swallowing, she replied, 'I have had experience. I nursed my mother for many years.'

'Then we'd better get on with it,' said the old man curtly. He reached for the wheels of his chair, and manifestly failed to move them. Harriet leaned on the handles and with an effort pushed the chair towards the door.

'Jerome should be here,' said the old man. 'I should not be without him.'

At his direction Harriet pushed the chair into a suite of rooms clearly designed for a wheelchair occupant. There was very little furniture, merely tables and cupboards at wheelchair height, a raised bath and a firm bed. But the walls were covered in pictures, from floor to ceiling, with barely an inch of clear space between them.

She gestured towards a picture of a girl. 'That's a Matisse.'

'So it is.'

'Is it genuine?'

'I have never knowingly bought a fake.'

Her eyes ranged the walls, seeing Renoirs, Monets, a Sisley, and one that she was sure was a Velasquez. 'You must be very rich,' she whispered.

He snorted. 'Not by my grandfather's standards. He would never have been reduced to one manservant in a crumbling house – he had forty slaves constantly at his beck and call. I have been deserted. I have wealth but the people have deserted me.'

'Oh dear,' said Harriet inadequately. She pushed the wheelchair to the bed and spread out a towel from the bathroom to protect the covers. Then she eased the old man on to it, the technique remembered from years of manhandling her mother. The old man was surprisingly light, his lower limbs hanging wasted and useless.

'I must apologise for my disgusting condition,' he announced as she stripped away his clothing.

'Not at all,' said Harriet grimly. Such a shrivelled, ancient body, his penis like a little yellow worm. Yet he was too proud to pity.

'Do you have children?' she asked in her best district nurse voice while she cleaned and washed and powdered.

'I do. I have a son, Gareth. We dislike each other. There is a daughter, Simone, by my first wife, a Frenchwoman. A French resident, I should say, I barely know the woman. Married to one of those Frenchmen that resemble small dogs, snappy little things. Always after money, of course. Like her mother, grasping.'

'Just the two?' said Harriet.

'There is another girl, Madeline. A disappointment to me. A grave disappointment. She sleeps with black men.'

'Oh,' said Harriet noncommittally.

It occurred to her that she should get in touch with the authorities.

'Is there a 'phone here?' she asked. But if there was one he would have used it. 'Perhaps it's been disconnected. Where is the nearest 'phone?'

He laughed drily. 'I fear you would have to swim to it. We have no 'phones on Corusca, no 'phones, no television, no motorcars. This island, my island, is unpolluted.'

She was impatient with him, her mind on Jake. 'All very well until you need something,' she said curtly.

At last she had him clean and comfortable in bed. 'I am hungry,' he said. 'I can't stay,' said Harriet. 'I have to get back to the boat.'

'I wish you to stay,' said the old man. 'As you can see I am helpless here.'

'I know, but – ' She sighed. 'Look, I'll make you something to eat. Then I'll take a few things, only a few, and I'll go back to the boat. I'll leave a message somewhere, someone will come.'

'No-one will come,' he said flatly. 'They do not dare.'

'What about your man, Jerome, what about him?'

'I imagine that he is in league with them, he's an islander after all. You must do as you see fit, of course, but I wish you to stay.'

The force of his will was like iron bars. Harriet went to find him some food, wandering through the huge, sumptuous, ruined house. Much had been smashed but little apparently taken. One huge mirror on the stairs had been broken by a rock and the wide, sweeping staircase was littered with shards as big as a man. In the kitchen, a high, cold room smelling of bad meat, the flags were covered in smashed bottles of wine. Picking her way across the debris she found a cupboard containing tins and prepared a meagre spread of crackers and meat paste, followed by cold rice pudding.

'You've been a long time,' said the old man as she returned.

'Everything's in a terrible mess. Everything's smashed.'

'The cowards.' He sneered contemptuously. 'Do you mean to stay?'

'It depends,' said Harriet. 'The boat may be sinking. I must go and see.'

'Put my gun by the bed,' he instructed, and Harriet obeyed. Then he nodded curtly. 'My name is Henry Hawksworth. Good night to you.' She was dismissed.

Jake needed everything but there was a limit to what she could carry. In the end she tied knots in the corners of two blankets and filled them with food, a half-bottle of whisky and some rope found in a kitchen cupboard. The time she had wasted pressed on her, she couldn't wait to go, yet when at last she opened the door and stepped out into the night she would have given anything to stay where she was. Her foot hurt as the cut filled with sand. Her arms ached from carrying her load, her head ached from brandy and weariness. Suppose Henry Hawksworth died, because she had not stayed with him? Suppose Jake left her because she hadn't come back? She began to run down the beach, as fast as she possibly could.

Her footprints guided her in a wavering line, almost vanished now as the rain began to fall. She began to look for pieces of wreckage, because she had been away so long and the boat might be smashed. She had come far further than she had expected, a mile, perhaps two. At last the footprints led down to the sea. There was a pale glow on the horizon, of dawn breaking onto a windswept morning. Cold rain fell on her face as she stared out at the waves, rolling endlessly upon the shore. No boat. No Jake. He was gone.

She stood there for a very long time, clutching her bundles of things no longer required. What was she to think? Had he drowned, so close to shore? If the boat had broken up there would be evidence of it, there would be spars and clothing, even the logbook that Jake preserved so religiously in its little waterproof bag. Yet there was nothing, no sign at all that he had ever been here. She retraced her footprints, placing her feet exactly in her tracks. No mistake. This was where she had walked before, this was where Jake should be.

Her hand went to her mouth, forcing back emotions that she did not understand. He had promised, really promised to come ashore if the wind changed; he had promised not to leave her. Or had he? She had asked for the promise certainly, but had he given it? The scene shifted in her memory. It has been so confused and wild, you didn't remember things clearly when there was nothing to tell you it was important that you should.

His face though, she remembered that, oblique and wary. He wouldn't have planned it. The moment would have come when he could get the boat off, and he would have thought of Harriet and realised it was time they parted. He didn't love her, they weren't going anywhere. He knew she was sick of the boat and the life they were leading, and he was annoyed by her nagging at him to do something.

Her eyes hurt, because she had not blinked for long minutes and the rain was stinging them. Now that this moment had come she knew she had been expecting it from the moment they met. It was as if someone had stepped forward and handed her a letter just before she met Jake, and it said: 'This man will take you up for a while, he'll cheat you, lie to you, change you, and in the end he'll dump you. You may now decide if you wish to proceed.' What should she have done?

Gone back to the same old miseries that she knew so well, only for fear of the pain she felt now? There had been so much pleasure, so much excitement. If she was bitter, and she was, it stemmed from the drowning of her dreams, like rosebuds upturned in acid.

Dawn was casting a grey and silver net over the island, and the lights of the house, still burning, looked dirty and unwelcoming. Harriet went in quietly, because Hawksworth might be sleeping and also because she didn't feel able to speak. Perhaps if she could slide into bed in one of the vast upstairs rooms, and wake hours later to a new day, then she might feel more in control. But as she passed Hawksworth's door his old man's voice cried out: 'Who's that?'

She went in. 'It's me. Harriet.'

'What happened? Why are you here?'

She twisted her fingers. To say it would be to admit that it was real, that tomorrow she would have to deal with the aftermath of today. 'My friend has left me. The wind changed and he got the boat off and he left. He said he would and I asked him not to. I didn't think he'd go, but he did.'

The old man nodded, as if he had expected it. 'You must stay with me then. That is what you must do.'

She put her hand up to her face, because she was crying and bewildered. 'Must I?'

'I take care of those who do as I wish. I will take care of you.' He watched her for a moment, his face calm and authoritative. Then he said, 'Go and sleep. You are not fit. I will talk to you when you have recovered.'

Harriet staggered from the room, her heart thundering unevenly. She picked her way up the staircase, sending a piece of glass crashing down as she passed. The old man did not call out. Upstairs the corridor was wide and lined with doors, little seemed to have been touched. She went in room after room, each one dusty, abandoned, the sheets on the bed nibbled by mice. At last there was one room that was clean and tidy, the manservant's room she supposed. Casting off her clothes she slid between the sheets, an alien male scent filling her nostrils.

'Jake, Jake,' she whispered to herself. Still crying, she fell asleep.

Chapter Thirteen

Harriet woke to hear thumping. She lay watching the sunlight making patterns on the wall, aware that her misery had remained even through sleep. Tears trickled from the outside corners of her eyes into her hair. If only that noise would stop. The thumps were punctuated by a crash and she sat up crossly. It came from downstairs. Perhaps the old man had fallen and was calling for help as best he could. She scrambled out of bed and grabbed a white towelling dressing gown that hung on the door. As she pushed her arms into it there was another crash, and again the rhythmic thumping. Quickly, her mind flooded with possibilities, she picked her way through the debris on the stairs and into Hawksworth's suite.

The old man had dragged himself up in the bed. He was beating the floor with the stock of his gun, while periodically laying about him with the barrel and smashing anything within reach. So far he had demolished a carafe of water, a radio set and a vase. He had also plucked a picture from the wall and flung that across the room.

'What on earth are you doing?' gasped Harriet.

He looked up. 'At last. I should not have imagined that I would have to bang for twenty minutes in order to waken you.'

Harriet glared. 'I don't see why you had to bang at all. You knew I was tired. You could have waited.'

She crossed the room and flung back the covers on the bed, revealing the pale, thin, old man's legs. Panting with effort, she managed to lift him first to his wheelchair and then into the bathroom.

'If you hadn't smashed the vase you could have gone in that,' she said snappily.

'I consider that degrading,' retorted Hawksworth.

'Do you indeed?'

Harriet was in no mood to be conciliatory. Besides, she knew only too well the tyranny of age, how easily the helped could come to dominate the helper. Briskly efficient, she assisted Hawksworth to wash and dressed him in clean clothes. Then she pushed him out on to the terrace, the wheels of the chair crunching broken pottery. 'You can stay here while I clean up,' she told him. 'I'll get you a book if you like.'

Hawksworth folded his hands in his lap. 'At least you don't snivel.'

'Of course not.' Yet she was leaving him here so that she could go back into the house and sob.

As she went slowly and wearily back up the stairs she listened to the hushing of waves, and above that the song of many birds. Sunshine was merciless in its exposure of the house, every cobweb and damp patch in a spotlight. Someone had hacked at the wooden banister rail with an axe, leaving four deep indentations. She fingered them wonderingly and saw that there was blood on the stairs. There was a moment's frozen fear and then she realised it was her own blood. Her foot was bleeding again, and throbbing unmercifully. Tears began flooding down her face.

She washed in cold water in a vast and ancient marble bathroom. Nothing in the house had been modernised with the exception of Hawksworth's suite, so presumably he always lived alone. When she looked through wardrobes in the bedrooms she found moth-eaten silk dresses, and in one a sable coat with half the skins split. In only one room did she find something that she could wear, a blue dress with a wide white collar, a slightly Quakerish get-up. There were shoes too, half a size too big but with her foot bandaged they were passable. She dressed, still wondering what was happening to her. Yesterday Jake and reality, today a waking nightmare. Her image looked back at her from a stained and pock-marked mirror. A tall, thin woman with a pallor and a mane of hair that bypassed prettiness and brought her near to beauty. Never had it pleased her less.

'Perhaps he landed somewhere else,' she told herself, and watched the face in the mirror light up. 'Perhaps he'll come and get me soon. I know he wouldn't leave me!'

Relief was exquisite. Suddenly she was quite quite sure that it would be all right. What would he think if he came now and saw her like this? She smiled again, determinedly, and put her head back in a carefree gesture that was as brittle as the dying ivy on the walls of the house.

The day crept silently onward. She stood on the beach in the sunshine and stared out at the endless waves, then turned and gazed up at the house. So old, so contained and containing. The sun beat down cruelly, she could have lain down and died from the blows, but then a breeze came and rustled the lush green leaves in the forest. She lifted her eyes beyond the house, to the hills rising up to a high plateau, thick with trees and creeper. Such luscious beauty, such abundance, seemed almost repellent.

In the swiftly falling twilight the candles glowed like beacons. Harriet had perfunctorily wiped the dust from one of the many small tables in the house, hiding the scratches with a candelabra and an assortment of dishes. It was tinned everything, but Hawksworth had directed her to bring a bottle of wine from the cellar, a claret of considerable stature. He poured it for her himself.

'It is not often that I dine in style,' he said grimly.

'This isn't style.' Harriet's equilibrium was failing her. 'I thought – it seemed likely that Jake might be here.'

She sat down abruptly in a chair opposite Hawksworth. When she picked up her crystal goblet her hand trembled violently.

'That glass is sixteenth-century Spanish,' rapped Hawksworth.

'Is it?' Shakily she put it down.

'What were you hoping for? That he would change his mind and come for you?'

'I thought he might,' said Harriet, brushing a tear from her cheek. 'I didn't think he'd leave me altogether. He's not reliable, I know that, and he doesn't love me. But – ' She shook her head, dumb with misery.

'Are you with child?'

'Harriet's head jerked up. Fierce colour flooded her face and then subsided, leaving her dead white. How could he know? She stared into the old man's eyes, still and black as a snake's. 'I – think I might be.'

'Does he know?'

A swift, decisive shake of the head. Hawksworth snorted. He reached out for his goblet of greenish glass and drained it. 'Women are such fools,' he said contemptuously. 'Why did you let him get a brat on you? Did you think it would change him? Half this island's peopled with Hawksworth bastards, my own manservant's mine by my wife's black maid. They're nothing to me. They're not Hawksworths.'

Harriet didn't believe him. It was amazing how in old age past sexual potency figured so prominently. The fiction of the dirty old man, trying to live out fantasies that he hadn't dared to consider in his youth, was firmly based.

'Didn't your wife mind?' she asked, humouring him. 'About her maid?'

'I never asked her,' said Hawksworth and began to eat his cold tinned fish. 'It was clear to me that she disliked my attentions sexually and was happy for me to satisfy myself elsewhere. I was foolish to do so, of course. I should have taken the precaution of fathering more than one legitimate son.'

'That was – your second wife?'

'Indeed. The first was a much more spirited creature. Something I did upset her shortly after the birth of our daughter. It was remiss of me to permit her so much freedom. She took the child and left.'

'What was it you did?'

He gazed into Harriet's shadowed eyes. 'I can barely remember.'

Harriet did not pursue it. Looking round at the gloomy room she said softly, 'I'll go to town tomorrow. Someone may have heard something and I can fetch help.'

'You will take a message,' said Hawksworth. 'I will give it to you.'

'Of course.' Harriet toyed with her food, forcing herself to eat some of the fish.

'It's a long time since I dined with a beautiful woman.' Hawksworth reached across the table and took hold of her wrist.

Harriet jumped. 'Please let go.'

He did so. 'Drink your wine,' he said. She was embarrassed by his eyes on her.

The following morning did not bring Jake. As soon as Hawksworth was settled and comfortable Harriet prepared for her outing to Corusca. An outside shed yielded an old and rickety bicycle, and before she left Hawksworth pressed an envelope into her hand. 'Give this to the first person you see,' he instructed.

Harriet smiled. 'But who do you want to have it? I can find them, surely?'

'I wish it to go to the first person you see!' snapped Hawksworth. 'There is no-one on the island who does not understand it.'

'Except me,' said Harriet, but he did not explain.

She mounted her bicycle and began to pedal down the sandy road. Even this early it was hot and lizards scuttled out of her way, running in staccato jerks. There were butterflies too, huge and brilliant, drinking the nectar from heavy-headed flowers. I am in paradise, thought Harriet, listening to the birdcalls deep within the trees. This is the Garden of Eden before the fall, vermilion, lotus-eating land. To stay here would be to lose one's misery, to have it leached away by the sun and the surf and the thick, cool trees. Without Jake there could be no pain, and if too she must lose her happiness, here, on Corusca, would it matter? In this place there was no strife and no ambition. She felt very tired. It would be bliss to lie down in the sun-dappled grass and go to sleep.

The town of Corusca, named as the island itself, was a gentle sprawl of low, white buildings, made beautiful by flowers and trees. At first Harriet could not see what was missing, and then she realised. There were no cars at all, only bicycles propped against walls and garden gates. Beneath the trees stood two horses, wearing fringed hats to keep off the sun and hitched to scruffy farm-wagons. A woman was walking down the street, carrying a huge basket on her back. She stopped and stared at Harriet.

'Hello.' Harriet tried to smile, finding it hard in the face of the woman's blank gaze. She remembered the message she was to deliver. Still smiling she held out the sealed envelope Hawksworth had given her. 'Mr. Hawksworth said I was to give this to the first person I met,' she said, laughing. 'I thought it odd myself, but he's not the sort of man you argue with.'

The woman did not take the packet. She backed away, a low moan beginning deep in her throat. 'Please – I'm sorry – ' began Harriet, taking a step towards her. The woman turned and fled, her moaning turning to a long shrill scream.

Harriet followed her down the street, bewildered, pushing her bicycle. As she passed by doors and windows closed on either side of her, children ran away and watched, big-eyed from the shadows. She walked to the end of the street. There was no sign of the woman. Before her spread the harbour, empty but for one or two small dinghies. Beyond was the vast blue sea. Harriet spun round, turning her back on the ocean. She pushed her bike resolutely into the middle of the street.

'Please,' she called out, 'won't someone talk to me? I need help. I'm a stranger here.'

A small sandy dog lifted its leg against a post and trotted past her, intent on its own day's activity. 'Please,' she called again, 'Mr. Hawksworth sent me with a message. I promise I don't mean any harm.'

A sudden sound made her swing quickly round. She choked back a shriek. A tall black man had materialised beside her, dressed in white shirt and cream trousers. The hostility in his face was unmistakable.

'Let me see this message.'

Tentatively Harriet held it out. He took the envelope, feeling the contents with his long, coffee-coloured fingers. 'You can open it,' said Harriet. Instead he handed the packet back to her.

'You.'

She didn't want to. From the way everyone stared at the packet it was sure to be something horrid. But she had to do something. Wrinkling her nose in anticipation of disgust she tore the paper and drew out what seemed to be a small piece of leather. Looking more closely she saw that it was a tiny bag, with feathers stuck on it, quite similar to that which Hawksworth had been holding when first she saw him.

'Is it a curse?' she asked jerkily.

'Not for you,' said the man. 'How are you with him? There was no-one with him before.'

'Our boat was wrecked, I waded ashore. I thought – has anyone else been found? A man?'

A shake of the head. 'No wreck, no man. You tell the truth?'

She nodded. The sun was hot on her uncovered head, she felt sick and ill. The ground rose and fell before her eyes. Suddenly it rose and kept on rising. There was the slap of hard earth against her cheek, the taste of dust on her tongue. It was sweeter than consciousness.

She awoke to a hard couch and the sound of voices. A plump pink face bent over hers and she saw sandy receding hair, sweat beading the upper lip. The man smelled of alcohol. 'Are you feeling better? Do you understand me?'

Harriet struggled to sit up. 'I'm all right. There's nothing wrong.'

'But you fainted. Please – my name is Muller, I am a doctor here.'

She stared at him, seeing that he was nervous of her and of her situation. 'I'm pregnant' she said bleakly. 'That's reason enough to faint.'

A murmur ran round the room and Harriet realised they were not alone. The man she had spoken to in the street came into her field of vision. 'What you doing with him? What does he want?'

'I just happened on him,' she said jerkily. 'He needs looking after, the house is in such a mess. How can people do that to an old man? They took an axe to the stairs, just wood, just a piece of wood. I don't understand it.'

Muller looked up and spoke over Harriet's head. 'I told you and you wouldn't listen. He is still strong, still has the power!'

The other man muttered something and brushed his hand across his brow.

'Are you Jerome?' asked Harriet abruptly. 'Are you his manservant?'

'And if I was?'

'He wants you back. He thought I would get you back. I know he's difficult but old people always are. You can't just leave them – ' She tailed off miserably. Sometimes leaving was all you could do.

Muller shrugged. They were talking between themselves, taking scant notice of Harriet. 'You tried. He won't live forever.'

'That old spider never die.' The black man sounded so bitter.

A collective sigh made Harriet turn her head to see a little group of people standing together, both men and women. The women were weeping openly and she felt amazement and slight contempt. To be so in awe of a frail old man, truly this was a backwater. No doubt these superstitious people thought she had been magically summoned from the seas, when the reality was so much more prosaic, and so much more painful. The tears seemed to be catching.

'I must get back,' she said jerkily. 'Will you come, Jerome?'

He nodded in resignation. Looking at the clearly chiselled nose and wide eyes she wondered if he was indeed Hawksworth's bastard. It was certainly possible.

'You must not go out in the sun,' advised Muller as she walked unsteadily back to her bicycle. 'Will you stay here?'

'I don't know.' She saw the envelope Hawksworth had given her lying in the dust and she bent to pick it up. But when she held it out to Muller he suppressed a shudder. 'Won't anyone take it? What am I to do?'

'Give it back to him,' said Muller thickly. 'Tell him – we understand. There won't be more trouble.'

He stood close by as she mounted and at the last moment caught hold of her arm. His fat lips trembled oddly. 'Please,' he said, 'please – ' But he let her go and turned away. She was glad to ride off.

While she cycled back to the house Jerome walked, a tall, muscled figure forming an exclamation mark in the road every time she looked round. At first she waited for him now and then, but when he reached her he said nothing and she felt weak from the sun. Finally she rode off without stopping, and when she reached the house left the bicycle where it fell. Cool air descended on her like a cloak waiting for her in the hall.

'You've been a long time.' Hawksworth was looking strained and yellow.

'They wouldn't touch your message. They thought it was a curse.'

'The primitive mind.' He held out his hand to her. 'Come, my dear, you look hot. I have found a bottle of beer, we shall share it.'

They were drinking the beer, tart and delicious, when Jerome came in.

'At last. You should know better than to run off like that, boy.'

'Yes, sir.'

'Will it happen again? Honestly now.'

'No, sir.'

Hawksworth triumphant, Jerome sullen. Harriet knew she did not understand what was going on. Understanding seemed to have deserted her, to have been left on a little boat in the night in a storm. 'I've got to go,' she said. 'I can't stay here.'

'And where will you go? Tell me that.' When she said nothing Hawksworth said to Jerome, 'It is time we looked to our housekeeping, boy, for once again we have a lady to command us. You may pass the word in the villages that I expect their services, that I will not live amidst decay. Harriet shall have the Empress Suite. Have it prepared for her at once. She will of course be staying.'

Chapter Fourteen

It was night. She leaned from her window and listened to the forest, letting the sweet air play upon her face. Something moved in the darkness and she choked back a shriek. It was only a pig, one of a small wild breed that roamed the island, inoffensive but for their assaults on gardens. People put up fences and the pigs knocked them down, as they had done for centuries past and would always do. There was a timelessness about the island, a sense that here was a backwater in which nothing ever changed – although much had since she came.

She turned back into her room, her bare feet silent on the polished wood floor. When she slept it would be in a carved four poster bed; when she woke the sight that met her eyes would be gilded cherubs on the ceiling, peeping shyly through the white muslin canopy. It was a beautiful room, and usually it soothed her because it was proof that she was indeed fortunate and cherished.

Yet tonight she felt restless and enclosed. When she first came here she had been so bewildered and ill, she had done no more than accept what was done to and for her. Wearily, in desolation of spirit, she had allowed Hawksworth to treat her as both lady of the house and nursemaid. Every day, as he directed Jerome to have this or that mended or cleaned, he said to her, 'Is it to your taste, my sweet? We are yours to command.' She had humoured him, because she had not the energy to extricate herself from Hawksworth and his plans.

Tonight she had the energy. Why? Her eyes flicked to the untouched drink by the bed that usually she drank in Hawksworth's company. It was an island concoction of rum and spices, delicious and sleep-inducing. In the early days she had been so glad of it, had given in to Hawksworth's insistence quite meekly. Yet this evening some perverse instinct had made her put it to one side. She would drink it later, she told him, after her bath. His lips had folded in on themselves and he had watched her with that steady, snake-bright gaze.

Was she afraid of him, she wondered. There was no doubt that others were. When he commanded he was obeyed with an immediacy that sprang from terror. Once she had seen a man sob in his presence when confessing that he had failed to renew the garden fence because his donkey had escaped and smashed the spars. The man hadn't come again, and someone else had renewed the fence. It was a trivial enough event but one that had strangely disturbed her.

Hawksworth owned Corusca and Hawksworths had always done so, that much she knew. Henry said that his wealth had come from sugar, but it was hard to believe that even in the heyday of cane it could have provided the funds for so much art and opulence. What was it then? Sometimes he boasted of pirate ancestors, even of slavery, but there was no reference to any present-day money-spinner. Were it not for the bales of goods delivered by the monthly supply boat she would think he existed without hard cash, but silver and velvet and cases of champagne were paid for somehow.

The baby inside her twisted and kicked vigorously, although usually it was very quiet at night. Was that the result of the drink? Was the child, like herself, smothering in apathy? Usually she tried not to think of the creature inside her, but now she felt fear. In the morning, first thing, she would go and see Dr. Muller, much as she disliked him. Suddenly, painfully, she longed for Jake, for his cynical level-headedness. Perhaps the child would be a boy, she told herself. That would be a comfort.

Muller was gardening when she rode up on her bicycle. He rummaged in the earth, red-faced and sweating, his straw hat tipped over his face and stained with soil where he pushed it back from time to time. Rosa, his merry, voluptuous mistress, sat by the door, stringing beans and watching the street. She was married to a fisherman, but her position as the doctor's concubine suited everyone. She had access to supplies from the boat, not given to all, and the things she received conferred status. Rosa's husband had the best boat, and his boat had the best light. Rosa herself had fine clothes and a girl to do the cleaning. By Coruscan standards, Harriet was coming to realise, it was a good bargain.

Rosa called out to the doctor and raised a hand to wave. Harriet slipped off her bicycle and leaned it against the fence but by the time she had entered the gate Rosa had gone. As always, thought Harriet wryly. No-one would be seen talking to her, and most would not talk even when they could not be seen.

'A hot day for a ride,' said Muller, taking off his hat. He licked his lips nervously and Harriet noticed that the hairs on the backs of his hands were beaded with sweat. It repelled her. Suddenly she did not want to be examined by him, doctor or no doctor. The baby jiggled and she steeled herself.

'I thought it was time I had a check-up,' she said.

'Do you feel ill? Is there a problem?'

She assured him there was not. When he still stood motionless, she said: 'We can't talk here. We must go inside.' She pushed past him into the house and reluctantly he followed.

They went into his shaded but still hot, front room. Harriet seated herself on the couch, remembering her fainting fit. Months had passed since then, where had the time gone? She had done nothing, thought nothing, she had simply sat and watched and obeyed. Muller bustled about anxiously, calling to Rosa for lemonade and receiving no reply, leafing through papers that patently didn't interest him. At last he said: 'Does he know you are here?'

'Should he?' enquired Harriet innocently.

'If he is not told he will discover it. Always it is best – you do not understand!' He looked desperately at her.

'Then why don't you explain?' said Harriet urgently. 'I don't know anything about this place! An island, a hundred years behind the times, and everyone on it terrified of a sick old man! What are you all afraid of? He can't hurt anyone.'

Muller went to a cupboard and poured himself a drink, downing it in one. He seemed to be wrestling with himself. Suddenly he burst out: 'It is not my fault. I ask you to understand that. I have no choice, we none of us have choice. I would be so different if I had.' His eyes swam with tears that did not fall and Harriet thought, such easy emotion. He'll do nothing but lie to me.

'Are you German?' she asked, swinging her skirt briskly. 'You sound it.' He didn't, as it happened, but Rosa had said something weeks ago and ever since Harriet had wondered. On Corusca, you did.

Muller's face became very still. 'I am Austrian. I have told you before.'

'I still think you're German.'

He strode to the door and flung it wide, taking her quite by surprise. 'I want you to leave,' he said nastily. 'I will come when your time is near, that is all I can do. I have no respect for you, an immoral woman. Go.'

Harriet stopped very close to him, where she could smell the drink on his breath. His face was working involuntarily. 'Why are you here?' she asked softly. 'I wonder who would like to know that you are here, in the sunshine, well cared for, with nothing to fear but a sick old man and – discovery.'

'You know nothing,' whispered Muller. 'And if you knew it all, what difference would it make? You will stay here forever. I do not wish to see you again.'

Harriet remounted her bicycle and rode off, for once rid of the dull headache that so often accompanied her days. Her thoughts fizzed. Muller would have been a young man in the war, too young, one would have thought, to have been responsible for much . . . enough, though, to send him running for cover in faraway places. And besides, what sort of doctor was he?

Everywhere she looked there were thin children with runny eyes, men with cuts covered horribly with suppurating bandages. As for childbirth, one day an old woman had come up to her and whispered: 'When your time come, you call me, missus. I help you. That fat man, he no damn good.'

She pushed that thought away. If her choice of midwife was either Muller or an ignorant and dirty old woman, she would rather die, she told herself, and pedalled faster and faster still. Pregnancy was a one way street and U-turns weren't allowed. Some women said they enjoyed it but Harriet saw it as nothing but a frightening trap, leading inexorably to pain and danger and the shackles of motherhood. Suppose she didn't even like this baby? Suppose it was a boy and it looked like Jake and every day she felt again the rage she felt now, against Jake and the island and Hawksworth and Muller? She stopped the bicycle. Surely somebody would tell her something about this beautiful, hellish place?

On an impulse she looked quickly behind her, but the road was empty. She got off the bicycle and hid it behind some bushes. Then, walking within the trees at the side of the road, she went back to the village.

Rosa again sat on her step, stringing beans, but Muller was nowhere to be seen. Apart from Rosa, the street was deserted. Harriet walked quickly up. 'Hello!' she said brightly.

Rosa's eyes widened. She looked right and left. 'The doctor ain't here.'

'That's all right. I wanted to talk to you. I won't tell anyone, I promise.'

Rosa grinned, revealing strong white teeth. 'There won't be no need of telling. But I'll say you forgot something. Come in, quick.'

The novelty of entertaining seemed to enthrall the girl. She brought the lemonade she had failed to bring before, on a tray, accompanied by an ancient tin of shortbread. Harriet nibbled a piece and it tasted of cardboard. 'Everybody's so nervous,' she said with a laugh.

'Ain't you nervous, living up there with the old spider?' Rosa made her hands into spider shapes and wriggled them graphically. 'He was mean before he was shot, and he's meaner now.'

'I didn't know he'd been shot! Who shot him?'

'His son, Mr. Gareth.' Rosa giggled at the shock on Harriet's face. 'That's why he don't walk. And I won't tell you no more, 'cos he'll know where you got it. I got some rum if you want.'

'No thanks,' said Harriet dazedly. 'Was it an accident? Surely he didn't mean to.'

'I don't know nothing,' said Rosa teasingly.

Harriet changed tack. 'Do you know how he gets his money? He says it's sugar.'

The girl laughed so hard she had to bend over to contain it. 'It sure is sugar!' she gasped through giggles. 'Sugar-sweet! We don't even have cane no more on Corusca. Oh, dear me!'

'Then how does he get it?' demanded Harriet urgently. 'Rosa, I must know!'

She stopped laughing and went to sit down on one of the hard chairs that stood against the wall. She spread out her arms as if crucified and her bosom was outlined against her red cotton dress. 'In the old days they was pirates, the Hawksworths,' she declared, her eyes brilliant. 'They robbed all them things in the big house, all the glasses and silver. Then they bred slaves. Oh, my, the slaves they had! Sold to pick cotton, they were. Can't do that no more. The old man, well, he used to send the men out after big whale but we can't do that no more either.'

'Then what does he do?' demanded Harriet. 'What is it?'

Rosa brought her arms into her body, wrapping them coquettishly round herself. 'We don't have no pretty young girls on Corusca no more,' she said coyly. 'They the only people get away from here, the only ones.' She got up and nodded hard at Harriet. 'True!'

'But where are they sent?' asked Harriet. She didn't believe a word of it.

'Whorehouses. Muller he say them Arab men like fresh little black girls. But he don't do so much nowadays, not since he was shot.'

Harriet swallowed. 'He deals in drugs, doesn't he? He sells drugs to people?'

'That ain't bad, is it?' Rosa looked surprised. 'That ain't a bad thing?'

'Well, outside, in other places – yes.'

'Iffen Hawksworth does it, then it's bad,' said Rosa laughing. 'Hey, you want some bread? I got some good bread.'

Harriet refused. When she said she had to go Rosa made no attempt to stop her. 'You won't let the spider get me, will you?' she asked, suddenly anxious. 'He put curses on people just by thinking!'

'You don't want to believe such rubbish,' said Harriet firmly.

The walk back to her bicycle was draggingly hot, but when she reached the place where she had left it a horse-drawn cart was waiting. Jerome sat impassively holding the reins.

'You had a good talk with Rosa?' he enquired. 'The old man sent me to fetch you.' He helped her up and clucked to the sleepy nag.

'I see why you don't have telephones,' she said waspishly. 'Do you know what we talked about?'

'Nothing that was good for you,' he remarked.

'Is it true he was shot by his son?'

'And shoulda died. But you can't kill the devil, no sir.'

The horse plodded onward. Thinking logically, it was not all that surprising that the Hawksworths had controlled the comings and goings of the islanders so completely. After all, there was only one channel through the reef, to Corusca harbour, and everywhere else was danger. Even the fishermen sometimes misjudged and foundered in their own home waters, so she and Jake had been luckier than they knew. The currents ripped through the shallows like express trains.

She twisted in her seat and gazed up at the high central plateau, clothed in forest like a modest woman.

'You don't want to be looking there,' said Jerome laconically.

'Why not?'

'Because it won't do you no good.'

'Seems to me nothing on this island does anyone any good,' she snapped.

He nodded thoughfully. 'Not while the old man's alive.'

That evening, she and Hawksworth dined at either end of a cherry-wood table, a light repast of chicken and vegetables, followed by the curd cheese they made on the island. 'Drink your wine,' urged Hawksworth gently.

'I don't want it.' She looked at the rich purple liquid in her glass, a strange colour, but it tasted as it should and it might be the old Spanish glass – how to know when you were victim of your imagination?

'Drink,' said Hawksworth, and the gentleness was gone. 'My dear, I know all your thoughts. I know that you wonder about me. I know that you wonder about Corusca. I know also – ' He laughed suddenly.

'Harriet, you look so lovely tonight. Fear is good for you, your eyes are like pools of honey. Drink your wine, I won't poison you.'

She lifted the glass and drank. Why couldn't she say no to him? She did not dare, any more than the others. And gradually, as she sipped, warm, delightful acceptance washed over her. How much easier not to struggle.

There was a commotion outside in the hall. Harriet turned her head, almost sleepily as two men burst into the room, dragging a third between them. She made to rise but Hawksworth rapped: 'Sit down, Harriet! This is something you should see.'

The victim, a thin, undernourished youth fighting to get free, was dragged to the exact centre of the Aubusson rug.

'Why so late?' asked Hawksworth.

'Hiding in the hills, sir. We had to search him out,' said one of the men.

'I see. You should have brought me his family instead. The example would have been instructive. But, since he is here, I suppose I must deal with him.'

'What has he done?' asked Harriet. Even her tongue felt weighted.

Hawksworth turned and smiled at her. All at once he seemed younger, as if red blood coursed in his veins once again. 'My dear, he has transgressed,' he said simply. 'Don't worry, this won't be unpleasant, He will be placed in the garden for a day or two, that's all. Take him away.'

She went to the window and watched as the men tied the youth's hands behind his back, and then extended the rope to tie it to a tree. He was effectively tethered on the lawn, as if he was a goat. 'You can't leave him there,' she said dully. 'It seems – ' She stopped. The boy was staring straight into her eyes, a look of terror and despair. She closed the curtain.

Hawksworth called Jerome to clear the table. While he worked Harriet walked round the room, touching things, putting her fingers on the thick raised paint of the pictures. Jerome breathed smoothly, quietly, but Hawksworth's breath was coming in noisy gasps.

'Don't excite yourself, Henry,' she said automatically.

He laughed. 'My dear, you are so thoughtful. Put me to bed.'

She did as she was told. When he was settled, she leaned across to arrange his pillow and he took her breast in his hand. She gasped, feeling her nipple taut against his palm. Everything here betrayed her, even her own body. 'Please, Henry, don't.'

'I used to have the girls brought to me,' he said, his voice thick. 'I would choose the ones I wanted, then I'd find them waiting for me in the forest when I went riding, "Please, sir, do it to me, I won't tell."

But the myth remains that I took them by force. I always know a willing woman.'

His free hand pushed up between Harriet's thighs. She fell back across his aged and useless legs, the ball of her pregnancy balloonlike between each of his caressing hands. In a moment she'd stop him, in a second she'd restore this to nurse and patient. He rotated her nipple between his fingers and she felt it ooze fluid. His other hand was probing, inexorably creating excitement.

'Stop it,' she moaned and felt his fingers pushing inside her. He had sharp fingernails. Her back arched stiffly and she fell back.

Grey clouds of guilt swept around her. If she hadn't left her mother, if she hadn't left Jake, if only she could command her thoughts for a moment instead of reaching for them like fish swimming in a pond – was she to hate Hawksworth or herself? He was a helpless old man, so who but herself was to blame?

In the night she heard sobbing. It was the boy in the garden and the noise was of unbearable despair at last given voice. Her head ached so much she could hardly think, but she dragged herself to the window and looked out. He was crouched on the ground, his head bent as he wept. Harriet pulled on her robe of finest silk, and went out to him. He seemed not to be aware of her as she crossed her lawn, her bare feet rustling in the dew-soaked grass.

She touched his shoulder. 'Please – ' she said softly. But the sobbing had stopped. When she touched him he fell to one side, stiff and stone dead.

In Hawksworth's room, raging, she screamed: 'What did you do to him? What sort of man are you? What place is this? I won't stay here another minute, I don't know what I'm doing here! This lovely island – it's a nightmare!'

Unmoved, Hawksworth's face remained still. He might almost have been enjoying an interesting play. 'What is it you suspect, my dear?' he asked, as she fell silent, breathing hard.

'Witchcraft,' she said flatly.

He allowed a smile to twitch his mouth. 'You will forgive my amusement,' he murmured. 'It may be that Jerome believes such things, but then he is of a lower race. But you, my dear Harriet, can you really imagine me capable of magic?'

And of course it was ridiculous. Without any conscious effort she thought of her mother, who had lain much as Hawksworth did now, helpless and vulnerable. If only she had stayed and cared for her, if only, if only . . . 'I should not like you to leave,' said Hawksworth, almost pathetic. 'I should be lost without my Harriet.'

She sighed, and moved to go up to her room. Never in her life had she felt so tired and so confused.

In the brief moments of clarity when she woke Harriet forced herself to think. Jake wasn't coming for her, he wouldn't ever come for her. So who was there to help? No-one on Corusca. Was the old man evil or was she deranged? Perhaps both. Natalie had said something once about insanity being the safest haven of them all – Natalie. She would write to Natalie!

Servants were moving around in the corridors as she wrote, and soon there would be the summons from Hawksworth. She wrote hastily, like a child at boarding school begging to be allowed to come home.

> 'Dear Natalie.
> I wonder if perhaps you could help me? I am on an island called Corusca, Jake put me ashore here sometime ago when we were having problems with the boat, and I haven't heard from him since. It is important because I'm expecting a baby soon, and this is rather a backwater. Don't you dare say I told you so! I haven't any money and there doesn't seem to be any way of actually leaving at the moment – I am in a bit of a fix. If you could either run Jake to earth or think of some way of getting me off her I shall be grateful forever! Thanks. Harriet.'

Stating her predicament so baldly brought it home to her. At least I'm doing something, she told herself. She would take the letter down to the harbour that very day, and hand it to the supply boat captain personally.

For a week, while she was reading to Hawksworth, or playing chess with him, or filing his long nails, she would think of her letter, imagining it passing from hand to hand, mailsack to mailsack, perhaps even now arriving at the poste restante in Nassau.

Then, one evening as they sat together in the twilight, the waves hushing on the beach and the scent of orchids heavy on the breeze, Hawksworth held something out to her. 'My dear,' he said sweetly. 'This was brought to me some days ago. I felt I should return it to you.'

It was her letter. She turned it in her fingers, willing herself not to show pain. 'I wondered if there was any point in sending it,' she murmured.

'Very little,' he said. 'But then, one of the things I find most attractive about you is that unquenchable optimism. So misplaced.'

'It isn't unreasonable to wish for freedom,' she said mildly.

Nonetheless his anger flared, frighteningly intense. 'But what do you lack? I do my best to satisfy you in every way. I wonder at myself, at my gullibility. I am such a fool about women. I should learn how fickle they are, how difficult to please. What am I to do if you are unhappy?'

He was working himself up quite deliberately, and Harriet felt the blood draining from her cheeks. She knew beyond a shadow of a doubt that he held her life in the palm of his hand, could crush her with his old man's rage as easily as closing his gnarled fingers.

'When I caress you it is not for my pleasure,' he went on. 'Perhaps you want a younger man? Shall I ring for Jerome and get him to serve you, or one of the louts from the beach? Would that be to your taste, eh?' He turned to ring the bell and from the dark flush under his parchment skin she knew he was determined on something. He was vengeful, past reason, and he would always be obeyed.

'No!' She went to him, her heart thumping wildly. If he turned against her she was as doomed as the boy in the garden. She took hold of his crabbed hand, turning it palm upward. When she unfastened her robe her swollen breast fell free. Like a sacrifice she lowered it into his hand.

'Dear Harriet,' murmured Hawksworth. 'Good Harriet.'

She wanted to leave, she had to get away! There must be a way, and Rosa must tell her of it. She cycled to the village, every depression of the pedals a supreme effort. If only she could be rid of the terrible, dragging weight in her belly, she thought, then she would be set free. Muller's house showed no sign of life, and when she knocked on the door there was no answer. Perhaps Rosa was down by the harbour, but just in case she knocked again. The door opened a scant inch and Rosa's face, the greenish-grey colour that only black skin can become, peeped into view.

'Go away!' she whispered fiercely. 'You mustn't come no more!'

'Are you all right, Rosa?' asked Harriet. 'Are you ill?'

'They knowed you talked to me and I didn't tell,' moaned the girl. 'I been beat so bad. I hate that man! Iffen I get the chance I'll done kill him. He say I'm lucky I ain't got the bag, so go away!'

Harriet put her fingers in the crack of the door, praying that Rosa would not close it. 'Just tell me who will take me away from here,' she begged. 'Would your husband take me on his boat? Please, please, I have to get away!'

'Don't you never learn?' Some of Rosa's old spirit was returning. 'There ain't no way to get free.'

'Rosa!' Muller's shout made Harriet leap back from the door and

Rosa slam it shut in almost the same instant.

'It was my fault,' said Harriet hurriedly. 'She didn't want to talk to me. She didn't talk to me.'

The doctor took off his hat and turned it in his hands. Harriet sensed that he would love to be cruel to her, but did not dare. Her position was too ambiguous, she might be more important than she seemed.

'I do not think you should leave your house when you are so advanced in pregnancy,' he said shortly. 'You will damage the child.'

'Please don't hurt Rosa,' whispered Harriet. 'It wasn't her fault.'

But the doctor elbowed her roughly aside and went into his house.

On the ride home she decided to pretend she hadn't been away. She left the bicycle in a shrubbery in the garden, and wandered about collecting flowers, as if that had been her occupation throughout the morning. A feeling of utter despair welled within her which she could not reason away. She thought now that she would die here, that the child inside her would kill her.

The garden was full of snakes. A man came to trap them, and on any morning you might see one hissing and furious in a cage, down where the white blossoms drifted like a wedding veil, where the stream rippled with a sound like a child's laughter. Harriet wasn't sure if the snakes scared her, or if instead she felt pity. Poisonous they might be, but they were as trapped as she.

She wandered aimlessly round, picking the heavy-headed blooms that wilted so quickly once they were plucked. Her dress was of fine white cotton, her hat wide-brimmed and shady. When she had an armful of flowers she came up towards the terrace, and saw that Hawksworth was there, watching her. She waved and smiled.

A man came up behind the wheelchair, tall, pale, wearing a suit. Her heart hammered. For a split second she thought it was Jake.

'Harriet!' She approached almost unwillingly, unaware of the charming picture she presented, of flowers and burgeoning femininity.

Hawksworth's expression softened. 'Harriet,' he repeated. 'This is my son, Gareth.'

The son who had shot him. Black eyes under straight black brows. His father's proud nose above a strangely fleshy mouth, a boy's mouth in a man's face.

'How do you do?' she said shyly. On Corusca, where one never saw strangers, she had forgotten what it was to be shy. This man reminded her.

'What are you doing here?' he demanded.

A slight smile twitched at Hawksworth's lips. Harriet glanced at him and said stiffly, 'I'm looking after your father. No-one else was doing it.'

Turning to his father Gareth snapped: 'What are you giving her? What's here is mine by right.'

Harriet closed her eyes briefly. Oh God, they thought she was after his money. 'I can assure you – ' she began, but Hawksworth silenced her with a swift gesture, saying grittily, 'What's here is mine until I choose to let it go.'

'You're taking a damned long time letting go, aren't you?' retorted his son, and Hawksworth snapped, 'No thanks to you. Here to finish the job, are you?'

Gareth took half a step forward but his father lifted his hand. 'I should make it clear that I have changed my will. You get nothing unless and until you satisify me as to your way of life. It is in your interest to keep me alive, my boy.' He signalled to Harriet to push his chair, though he knew that in her present condition it was too heavy for her.

Nonetheless she leaned against the handles, moving it with difficulty back into the house. Gareth paced behind.

'What do you mean?' he asked. He had a lilting, slightly islandish way of speaking.

'I mean,' said Hawksworth,' that I want you to visit me. Not for the pleasure of your company. I wish to see that you are running the Corporation effectively. If not, I shall deprive you of it.'

'What's the Corporation?' asked Harriet.

Gareth swung round on her. 'Who the hell is she, Father? And whose is the brat?'

Hawksworth smiled to himself. He was delighted to have annoyed his son so, Harriet realised. 'She is Harriet,' he said silkily. 'I really have no idea who fathered her child and it is without significance. What does concern you is that I intend to marry her.'

Harriet's shock was total. She put her hand to her face.

Gareth hissed: 'What, do you mean you're going to leave it to her, is that it? Have you gone quite mad at last?'

'I think it unlikely,' said Hawksworth. 'Why have you stopped pushing, Harriet? We are going in to lunch.'

Why, oh why, was there no way out of this? He was only saying it to annoy his son, he was setting them against each other for the fun of it. She would not enter the lists; she utterly refused even to pretend to conform.

'You shouldn't make such jokes, Henry,' she said.

'My dear, you know I never joke.'

As they all settled at the polished table and Hawksworth picked up his linen napkin, he said, 'I've been talking to Muller. A stupid man generally, but useful. He feels it would be possible for Harriet to be inseminated by me. She is both fertile and intelligent, which is more than your mother was.'

Harriet's knife and fork clattered on to her plate.

Without appearing to notice, Hawksworth went on: 'Since I would obviously want a boy and I haven't time to waste on trial and error he is investigating the subject of sex determination. Whether I proceed depends very much on you, Gareth. How I wish you had less of your mother in you.'

There was a dreadful silence. Harriet suppressed an incredible urge to break into screams of laughter. Under no circumstances was she going to marry the man, and neither was she letting Muller or anyone else squirt syringes into her. For the first time she seriously wondered if Hawksworth was mad, locked in some senile world of fantasy.

'You hate us all,' hissed Gareth. 'You always have.'

'Correction: I despise you all. Have you visited your sister?'

'No.'

'Your usual concern for her welfare, I see. You must instruct her to come and see me. She must meet Harriet. Go this afternoon.'

Jerome was approaching with the soup. Gareth leaped to his feet and seized the tureen, hurling its contents against the wall. Jerome stood motionless and Harriet shrieked. Green peas ran down the canvasses of two priceless paintings.

'You will never know how much I hate you,' said Gareth.

As he left the room Hawksworth laughed.

Harriet took the linen napkins and began wiping the pictures. One showed a Left Bank café, and a girl, smiling to herself. Harriet longed to be her, in a world of sense and humour.

'How could you leave me here, Jake, you bastard?' she hissed and drove her fingernails into her hands.

'Did you say something, my dear?' enquired Hawksworth.

She turned. 'Yes. You know I won't marry you, don't you? It isn't possible.'

'It is up to me to say what is possible,' said Hawksworth.

'But there isn't any point. We can go on as we are.'

'I want another son.'

He propelled his chair towards her as she knelt over the pictures. One wiry hand reached down and caught her chin. 'You and your child will have all that you can desire. In return you will give me a son.' He let her go as suddenly as he had grabbed her.

In a lighter tone he said, 'Gareth's taking no interest at all in the hotels, he spends all his money on women and cocaine. When I established the Corporation it was for him to command. I should never have done it if I'd known he was so weak. I can even confess to a certain pride when he finally shot me, except that he waited until I had turned my back. And of course he's done nothing since. I can't imagine why he didn't finish me off and take over. That's what a man would have done.'

'He – shot you? Deliberately? It must have been an accident.'

'I sincerely hope not. It was the first time I felt that the boy was truly mine.'

Harriet got up and left the room. She went slowly and wearily upstairs, conscious of a severe ache in her back. It was the cycle ride and pushing the chair and Gareth and Henry and – her womb tightened. She was taken by surprise and stopped, grunting. Please let it not be now, she found herself praying, please let it not be ever. I don't want a baby and I don't want pain. What I want is – Jake.

Reason told her to return downstairs and tell someone she needed help. Instinct drove her to seek isolation, a safe den where she could hide because she was vulnerable and had no-one to protect her. Jerome might be trusted, she thought, but who could tell what went on behind that dark mask of a face? As for Hawksworth, he would inflict Muller on her and she would not, could not endure it. She would lie down and wish it to go away.

The cherubs on her bedroom ceiling smiled coyly at her through the muslin bedhangings. Perhaps Hawksworth children had been born in this bed, in which case she had no wish to bear Jake's son there. Nonetheless she would do so, because among all the things that she had lost, the most obvious was choice.

Pain was building again, a convulsion of her body that she would not have believed could take place without her willing it. This child had invaded her, was making use of her entirely without permission and it was all Jake's fault, all his blasted fault. How could she manage on her own? Women died in childbirth!

Her mind conjured up every film she had ever seen in which a woman lay tortured on a bed, screaming and thrashing in anguish. It wasn't that bad yet, but presumably it soon would be. Suppose the baby got stuck sideways or something, and she died after days of torment? Jake's voice echoed sardonically in her head, saying: 'Christ, Harriet, the old man notices if you're away five minutes! You know damn well there'll be somebody rattling the door when it's time for tea, so get a move on will you?'

'You wouldn't be so damn cocky if it was you,' she muttered back. 'I bet you've got some girl in bed right now. You've probably fathered hundreds of bastards and never set eyes on one of them. And the latest one is – splitting me in two!'

It was a long, undulating contraction, peaking and then peaking again, pushing her on and on into pain. Her fingers gripped the bed, digging down into it while her back arched up, lifting the distended plum of her body in an arc from feet to shoulders. Fluid coursed hot between her legs, soaking the bed. She fell back, almost sobbing. Was that supposed to happen? For a second she thought it was blood, but the dark patches were simply moisture, the liquid itself clear. Moving hurriedly, because she knew that in a moment the monster would grip her again, she stripped the sodden sheets away and threw her clothes on top of them on the floor.

The afternoon was leaden with heat and in the bedroom Harriet lay naked, sweat running down her face, between her breasts, over her huge belly. 'He would hate me if he saw me now,' she whispered. 'I'm a whale, and these are my two harpoons.' She waggled her stick-like legs and laughed hysterically. Another contraction was building, pushing her further and further on towards hell. Reaching up she gripped the bedhead and threw her head back, emitting a tight squeal from between clenched teeth. Let them not come and see her like this, she would die first!

Something dropped inside her. Instead of fading the contraction changed, she was bewildered, she wasn't ready for it. For a second she thought her insides were falling out, there was a lump she could feel pushing against the opening of her body. Oh God, it was huge, she'd never get it out and it was Jake's fault because he'd done it to her and hadn't cared, he'd left her to suffer like this! It felt better when she crouched, her head bent and her hands tangled in her hair. The thing that was Jake's was ripping her in two, pushing its way through her soft flesh like a battering ram. She groaned and pushed, and pushed again, in league with it against her will. 'Just let it get out,' she hissed, 'get out!' She put her hands between her legs to push herself back from the thing and ease the pain.

Her fingers touched someone else's hair. The shock of it ran like electricity from her fingertips to her heart. The thing had hair, fine, wet hair. She stared down at herself, aware of another great surge and welcoming it, because then she would see. Still it wouldn't come, it bulged almost into view and then went back again. Perhaps it would die in there without air. She thought wildly, I've got to get it out! She pushed again, though it wasn't time, and then the muscle spasm caught up with her and joined the effort. Black hair, black as Jake's, and a tiny smeared face, the eyes tight shut and blurred with mucous. Someone was murmuring: 'Oh, oh, oh,' and it was Harriet. Its little mouth was opening and it wasn't even all out yet! She held the head in hands that seemed too big to cradle it, and in a sudden slide the length of the child came out.

Harriet made a sound between laughter and tears. She was overwhelmed by an emotion so intense it could hardly be called love, an urge to protect and cherish that seemed to spring from nothing. The tiny creased face stretched and grey-blue eyes blinked up at her. 'Just like Jake,' whispered Harriet, and now she knew she was crying. 'I knew you'd be like Jake. I just never thought you'd be a girl!'

Chapter Fifteen

Not even the Hawksworths had expected Harriet to give birth alone and unaided. Old Henry himself was delighted, and insisted that Jerome carry him upstairs so that he could see her for himself and congratulate her on her Hawksworth-like fortitude. She received him sitting up in bed, wearing a silk nightgown and a frilly lace cap that matched the lace and silk of her baby's robes. Jerome had found the clothes. The attics of the big house were stuffed with luxuries from generations past.

'You look well, Harriet,' said Hawksworth as Jerome settled him in a gilt armchair. 'And your courage is commendable. You must have everything you need. Jerome, see to it.'

'Yes, sir.' Sometimes Jerome could infuse a hint of mockery into the most trivial reply.

'Let me see the child – yes, yes, a strong infant. She must have a Hawksworth name.'

'Her name is Victoria,' said Harriet flatly. The child's blue-grey eyes blinked up at her from the cradle and she had to fight the urge to pick the baby up and smother her in kisses. Oh, but she was beautiful. She was probably the most beautiful baby that had ever existed.

Hawksworth sniffed. 'I suppose that will do. She is not, after all, of the blood. My son will be another Henry, rising up out of my great age!' He chuckled with the excitement of it and Harriet turned away to hide her expression. 'We will be married as soon as you are recovered,' said Hawksworth, and signalled to Jerome to lift him.

'Then you truly are senile.' Gareth was standing in the doorway, surveying the domestic scene. 'What is she but some slut washed up on the beach? What do you know of her?'

Hawksworth's head swivelled round to him. 'She has courage, more than any of you. When your mother bore you it took her three days of screaming, and then she couldn't feed you. At last I have found a woman to match me!' He made his hand into a fist and brandished it.

Gareth crossed the floor to the bed and stood over the cradle, staring down at the baby. Harriet put one hand on each of the wooden sides. 'Go away,' she said grimly. 'Don't you touch her.'

'Do you mean to marry him?'

She didn't know what to say. Hawksworth was watching her, Jerome stood by. 'I have Victoria to think of,' she said stiffly.

'The child will be taken care of,' said the old man. 'I shall give everything to my bride.'

Gareth ignored him. 'You're making a mistake. He's never given a woman anything in his life, except trouble. In the end he'll leave it all to me.'

'Then why are you worried?' She met his gaze stonily. Naturally he disliked her, but apart from that he was repellent. Perhaps it was the way he was looking at her, trying little boy charm slapped over hatred like butter on mouldy bread. Dislike of Gareth pushed her closer to his father but it was unwise to make enemies. She tried to be conciliatory. 'I don't want to take anything from you.'

'He has nothing anyway,' declared Hawksworth, and Jerome gathered him up. 'I warn you Gareth, do not upset Harriet. If you do, I might very well lose patience with you altogether.'

They watched as he was carried from the room, managing to remain somehow impressive even when transported like a baby, his useless legs dangling. Gareth bit his thumb and stared at Harriet. As if teasing a caged animal he reached out very slowly and took hold of a long strand of her hair. Suddenly he tweaked it and she caught him with a slap, leaving a clear palm print on his face. 'Don't touch me.'

'Stupid cow,' he said viciously. 'You don't know what you're taking on. I should introduce you to my sister Madeline, then you'll see what happens to his women. You think you're so clever. Wait till you see Madeline!'

When he was gone Harriet lifted Victoria from the cradle at her side. The baby began to grizzle and Harriet pulled her nightdress aside to give it her breast. She was shaking. What on earth was she to do? Her only safety lay in Hawksworth's goodwill. If that was withdrawn what might Gareth do to her? He was like a vicious dog that still responded to discipline, but only just. If Jake had been going to come he would have been here long since, there was no use hoping for that way out. He might be dead, which was no more than he deserved for abandoning her! Rage at her situation focussed on Jake. She was trapped and it was all his fault.

If she tried to leave and failed, Hawksworth might well lose patience. Suppose she did marry him? She might as well be married to him now, nothing would change. If they didn't marry, he'd be her enemy. If they did, then Gareth entered the lists. Couldn't she somehow bring him over to her side? After all, she didn't want the money, and even if she did there was enough to keep them all in funds for this life and the next. In her bedroom alone there was a fortune in antique furniture, not counting the Hogarth casually hung in the recess. Hawksworth was a very old man. She might be set free in a matter of months and then she could at last get away. She watched the sunlight playing on the carved ceiling. Her choices were narrowing.

The baby tugged on her nipple and Harriet smiled at her. It was impossible for the outside world to intrude for long. How had she lived all these years and not known this awaited her, perfect, all-consuming love? The baby wanted and needed nothing that she could not provide, and she in turn was eaten up with adoration. There was nothing to lose by loving, she could immerse herself in need and being needed. Smugly she thought to herself that Jake would never know what it was to give everything and have it returned in equal measure. She nibbled at her baby's pink ear and thought herself on a narrow ledge of bliss.

She came downstairs the next day, welcomed by Hawksworth with flowers and fine wines. 'We'll have a nurse,' he told her. 'And you'll want clothes. I'll write to Simone, she can send you all the latest couture. Shall we ask her to visit us, Gareth? Will you like that?'

From Gareth's muttered curse it was clear he would not. He looked flushed and rather unwell. Hawksworth chuckled. 'Taking too much again, I see. Makes you impotent in the end but I don't suppose you care about that. Drugs are only for the strong-minded, to be used to enhance life not to make up for an empty existence! Time you went from here.'

'Get rid of her first,' said Gareth, jerking his head at Harriet.

'Oh, no.' Hawksworth came across and touched Harriet's hair. 'I shall never get rid of Harriet.' His hand dropped to her shoulder and then to her breast. He weighed the milk-heavy flesh in his palm while she sat absolutely still. 'Isn't she beautiful?' Hawksworth taunted his son with his possession.

The house was lovely in the afternoon. Harriet sat in the high, cool drawing room with the soft scent of jasmine wafting through the open windows. She felt bewitched by idleness. Hawksworth was resting, Gareth was elsewhere, she was lost in the illusion of freedom. A butterfly was trapped against the glass of the window, she could hardly stir herself to free it. There were voices in the hall.

'Where is she? I want to see her!'

The door opened. A tall woman came in, wearing ragged denim shorts and a cotton top that revealed her midriff and the lower bulge of her breasts. She was barefoot and her hair was a birdsnest bleached white by the sun. Her steps were uneven, as if she were high on something. When she saw Harriet she put her hand to her face and giggled. 'And there she is! Doesn't she look nice? Did Daddy give her the silk robe, Gareth? What do they do to each other, do they kiss and cuddle?' She turned and embraced her brother, nibbling his lips and pushing herself sensuously against him. He did not repulse her. 'He likes to grope her in front of me. To show that he's still more man than I am.'

Madeline giggled. 'But he doesn't know you, does he? Not like I do.' Her hand slipped unchecked down the front of Gareth's trousers.

'Go away,' said Harriet.

Madeline appeared to remember her. She released her brother and came across. 'I've got a little boy,' she confided. 'He's called Nathan. He can play with your little girl!'

'No thank you,' said Harriet. 'Why did you bring her here, Gareth? And what's the matter with her?' She stood up and went to free the butterfly at the window.

'What is the matter with me?' asked Madeline. She stood in the middle of the floor, stretched out her arms and began to dance, hopping from one foot to the other, humming tunelessly. Then she stopped. 'I want something,' she demanded. 'Give me something.'

'Why don't you have a drink?' asked Harriet nervously, expecting that at any moment the girl would go completely berserk.

'Where's Jerome?' said Madeline. She put back her head and screamed 'Jerome!' at full stretch of her lungs. The chords on her neck bulged.

He appeared in the doorway. 'Deal with her, will you?' said Gareth. The servant's dark face never changed. He crossed to where Madeline still stood, silent now, but with arms outstretched and head thrown back like a crucifixion victim. He faced her and put his hands in the small of her back. As if he had touched a switch she laughed, relaxed and wriggled herself against him, lifting up her top so that her naked breasts jiggled against his shirt. She began to moan erotically. Jerome led her from the room.

'What is the matter with her?' asked Harriet again, white with shock.

Gareth went across to the drinks cabinet and poured two brandies. 'What is the matter with any one of us?' he mused. 'She's had no education, my father saw no point in it. I had a tutor and I taught her to read. The islanders grow cocaine and she uses that. When she got like this her loving father put her in a house on the beach and left her there. Jerome looks after her and the boy.'

'Who fathered the child?' asked Harriet weakly.

Gareth almost smiled. 'It's white,' he said innocently, 'but really we don't know.'

She knew she must talk to Gareth. 'We don't have to be enemies, you know. I don't want the money, I only want to go away from here.'

'Sadly, I cannot believe you.'

'But it's true! I have to do as he says, we all do. There really is no reason to hate me.'

He smiled and for a moment she thought she had won. He came towards her, hands outstretched – and put them around her neck. 'If I didn't know what he can still do, I would strangle you here and now,' he whispered. Then he bent his head and kissed her.

When he had gone she swilled her mouth out with brandy, then rubbed her shoe against the spot on the carpet where the girl had danced. Hawksworth had got rid of two wives and driven his daughter mad; he had a vicious son who had tried to kill him and who terrorised the islanders and Harriet herself – and she was going to have to marry that old man.

Harriet and Hawksworth dined alone that night. 'I hear you met Madeline' he said, spreading his napkin.

'Yes. She's very disturbed, isn't she?'

'Very like her mother. Now, I think we should be married next week. I've instructed a priest to be brought across, we don't have one here normally. You'd want a priest of some kind, I suppose?'

'Well – we haven't really talked about this at all, Henry. I can't help feeling that it would be foolish to upset Gareth too much. There's no need to rush into things.'

'At my age there is every need,' he said. 'My family's wedding dresses are all stored in the attics, find yourself something. The islanders can have a festival afterwards. Madeline will of course be kept right away. We do not want you upset.'

'Don't you think she should see a doctor?'

'She seen Muller. Please don't fret about her, she's quite happy to be like this. Jerome makes sure she doesn't spawn black bastards. You're getting very persistent, Harriet, and I don't like that.'

She took a deep breath. 'Henry – I really think I should go. There's no place for me here, I'm upsetting everything. I should like to leave on the next boat.'

Hawksworth chuckled. She had never seen him so genuinely

amused, his eyes sparkling as if at some wonderful joke. 'Don't be foolish, my dear. I should be upset if I learned you had been trying to leave me.' He cut into a peach, at first slowly and politely, then stabbing it. The juice splashed on to the tablecloth.

The attics were full of trunks and boxes, it was a treasurehouse of times past. Rocking horses rubbed worn shoulders with china dolls, painted screens leaned against flaking ormolu. The wedding dresses were piled one upon the other, white satin flounces turning yellow, lace crushed out of shape. At the bottom of the pile were the silks, purple and red, designed to be worn over crinolines on waists far tinier than Harriet's. There was one dress in blue, cut low on the bust, its puff sleeves no more than a frill on the upper arm. What date would it be, she wondered? It might be as much as two hundred years old. Who was the bride who had chosen this seductive confection?

She took it to her room and tried it on. The waist was held together with laces. If she pulled it tight it just fitted. The flounced skirt brushed her ankles. Glancing at herself in the mirror Harriet gasped. Long burnished hair on white shoulders, bosom swelling against the dress, slender ankles peeping beneath it. She looked wonderful.

On her wedding morning she dressed slowly and carefully. The island cobbler had sewn slippers of blue velvet to go with the dress and she dawdled while putting them on. A stream of people was approaching the house, all in their best clothes, all unnaturally quiet. She sipped again at the glass of spirit she kept by her side almost continually these days. It kept fear at bay. Sometimes she could believe that fear made the whole island blossom, that only unnamed and unknowable terror kept everyone, including Hawksworth, alive. At last it was time to go down.

He greeted her at the foot of the stairs. He was wearing morning dress, and even now, in age, he was striking. Once he would have been very good-looking, tall, muscled, frighteningly imperious. He held out his hand. 'Ah, the pirate silk I see. A good omen. My dear, you look perfect.'

She forced herself to smile at him. As she entered the drawing-room a murmur of appreciation stirred the watching crowd. There might have been two hundred people. Neither Madeline nor Gareth was there. Jerome propelled the wheelchair, she walked beside it.

'Are we ready?' asked the priest.

Suddenly she couldn't bear it. What was she doing here, shackling herself to an old and wicked man? 'I don't think – ' she began in a choked voice.

'Harriet.' Hawksworth almost purred her name. A small wail came from Victoria, cradled in the arms of one of the servants. She swallowed.

'I am quite ready,' she said huskily.

Corusca feasted that night. They lit fires on the hill and in the streets. Harriet watched from the window, and Hawksworth said, 'Take her Jerome. Let her see it.' The drums thumped insistently, pulsing like blood from the heart, exciting and dangerous. When they reached the village Jerome tethered the horse and took Harriet's arm. A crowd of people danced around a bonfire.

'They're holding snakes,' gasped Harriet. 'Look, look!' A man ran up to them, the serpent high above his head, writhing feebly. He danced like a drunk and then ran away to the fire. Jerome took her arm and led her on. He was visibly excited.

Suddenly someone caught hold of her. It was Gareth. He was naked to the waist, smeared with ash and sweat.

'Hello, Mrs. Hawksworth,' he yelled above the drums. 'Do you like your wedding feast?'

'I don't like the snakes. And the women – ' Two or three were staggering about, their legs stiff and their eyes rolled up in their heads. They held up little figurines in arms that had been slashed until they bled.

'You ought to be flattered,' said Gareth. 'Those women are barren. They believe any child conceived tonight will have Hawksworth power. They think he's going to put his seed into you by magic, and there'll be some left over!'

'It's horrible,' whispered Harriet.

A man, stark naked and very drunk, was striding about in the firelight shouting. Harriet tried to turn away, but the men on either side of her held her arms tight. They were menacing, wild. Whatever evil was abroad that night had drifted like a cloud and settled in every heart. 'Let me go!' she screamed at them. 'The old man will know, I'll tell the old man!' They released her and she ran back to the wagon. A few moments later Jerome followed. Without a word he got up on to the seat and drove back to the house.

Chapter Sixteen

Jake leaned against a wall to catch his breath. His leg was giving him hell, he knew he should have taken the crutches. But after all these months he couldn't bear the badge of sickness any longer. He would rather suffer than stump about like Long John Silver. If it got much worse, though, he'd be crawling in on his hands and knees and it galled him enough to be going there at all.

Mac had called at the hospital once or twice, and sat there uncomfortably for half an hour. His conversation, never relaxed, flowed like setting concrete. 'Pinned it, have they?'

'Pins and plates. The first lot didn't take.'

'Lucky not to lose it.'

'So they keep telling me.'

A long silence. Finally: 'Pity about the boat.'

'Yes, but she wasn't up to much.'

'What happened to the lassie?'

Jake's teeth had clicked together. 'Buggered if I know.'

And now here he was staggering into the shipping office where Mac ruled as foully and efficiently as a doctor's receptionist. To beg. It was bitterly humiliating.

He had to wait in line behind an alcoholic deckhand and a man with a cargo of pineapples who'd been let down by his carrier. Mac was equally curt and unhelpful to both, though no doubt both would be accommodated when they had suffered enough. Jake slouched in a chair with his leg throbbing in red-hot hammer-blows.

'We normally require at least three months' notice of shipment,' Mac was saying accusingly.

'Balls,' cut in Jake. 'Get on with it, you bastard. You know the stuff's rotting. Either you can take it or you can't.'

'I think I know my own business, thank you Jake,' said Mac grimly.

'Please – ' the pineapple owner saw his salvation sliding over a cliff.

'I haven't got all day,' snapped Jake, glaring at the pineapple man.

Mac made out the dockets. The pineapple man, bubbling with gratitude, made his exit.

'Right,' said Jake. 'First I need to look at some charts, then I need about five hundred.'

'Is that all?' Mac looked incredulous.

'And a boat. I've got to find Harriet.' He stumped round behind the counter, his leg dragging badly.

'You'll no sail with that.'

'Men go round the Horn in wheelchairs these days. Anyway, I thought you might come.'

Mac sniffed. 'Pay's good here.'

'Bloody well ought to be, it's like working in a graveyard.'

He pulled some charts down from the rack and searched through, looking for the one he wanted. When he found it he pushed Mac's papers aside and spread it on the desk. 'I left her on one of the islands here.'

'She'll no still be there! It's been months!'

'Well, she's no turned up anywhere else, I've been asking. She went ashore on this island to get some supplies. The wind changed and I kedged the boat off. Half an hour later the island was no more than a spot in the distance. Then of course we piled up on that reef, so I never did get to finding out what happened. It must be a bloody small island. It wasn't on any of the maps I could get in the hospital.'

'You've been dreaming,' said Mac. 'She was drowned.'

Jake glanced at him with sudden anxiety. 'I don't think I'm off my head. I – I couldn't bear it if I'd killed her. She was a damned good mate.'

'She was OK,' agreed Mac. 'Better than that bike Natalie.'

Jake bent his head over the chart. He took out a notepad from his pocket and compared lists of directions and depths, a log of his journey as well as he remembered it. He borrowed Mac's instruments and made some measurements. Then he put a cross on the chart.

'I can't be sure,' he said, straightening, 'but I think that's it: Corusca. Know anything about it?'

Mac blinked at him. 'You trying to be funny? I'm not going there! That's the fucking voodoo place!'

It was a fortnight before they could set sail, because Mac was determined to draw his full month's pay. 'If I'm going to die I'll not go without my money,' he said bitterly. For the first time ever they were sailing with a Bible, bought by Mac as a safety precaution.

'So they chop chickens' heads off!' said Jake in amazement. 'I'm not a vegetarian! As long as they haven't chopped Harriet's head off, I won't complain.'

'People disappear,' said Mac fearfully. 'Don't you think it's strange she's no been heard of?'

Jake said nothing. He did indeed think it strange, and had thought so for months. The conviction that she was dead was growing in him. Sometimes he would lie awake in the night, his leg aching like shit, and he would know that she was gone. But even if that was so, he couldn't bear not to be sure, he had to know what had happened to her. And if she was dead, what would he do? He looked out into a fog and couldn't think of it.

The boat was neat and seaworthy, if lacking in refinement. There was always a good trade in old-fashioned craft, though you had to know what you were looking for. One of the problems was that people always revised their opinion of their boat once they knew Jake was interested, assuming that anything he wanted must be better than they thought. So he'd sent Mac in to buy and got it cheap. Lying in the cabin with Mac at the helm and the place smelling of men's feet, he had a sudden wave of longing for Harriet.

Seen in daylight, it was hard to tell if it was the same island. Certainly it was guarded by a reef, but that was by no means unusual. The outstanding central plateau would not have been seen by night, so that did not exclude it. Jake heaved himself on to the foredeck to shorten sail.

'I can do that,' said Mac irritably. 'Stop trying to prove that you're OK.'

Grimly Jake battled on, himself aware of how insecure he was. Would the leg ever heal, or was he stuck with this painful and hampering appendage forever? He lurched back into the cockpit. 'There must be somewhere to land. We'll take her round the other side.'

'It doesna look friendly.'

'Don't tell me the trees are making faces at you.' But he too felt that the island loomed menacingly out of the sea. The welcoming fringe of beach and palm forest dissolved so conclusively into dark foliage, without any apparent sign of habitation.

'There's a house!' Mac pointed excitedly at high grey walls surrounded by luxuriant gardens. 'It's a bloody palace! Someone's having a high old time out here.'

'Let's hope it's Harriet. The chart says the harbour's round the point.'

They made the deep channel through the reef with some difficulty, taking soundings every few feet.

'You'd think they'd send out a pilot,' complained Mac. 'We're no but a chain or two from shore.'

'Don't want visitors,' said Jake, eyeing the blank-faced houses and the figures standing on the quay and pointing. He took the boat right in to the jetty, where did he but know it only the supply boat ever tied up. Stepping off was difficult. He lurched and half fell, unable to take his weight on his bad leg. It was unnaturally quiet. Two or three people stood watching and then went back into the houses.

'Gives me the willies,' said Mac.

Jake stumped off down the jetty, suffering for the days without walking. He marched grim-faced towards a house and hammered on the door. 'Open up there! I want to talk to someone.'

There was no reply, although an upstairs curtain twitched. He picked up a stick and went from door to door, breaking paint with the stick and yelling, 'Show yourselves, damn you! We don't carry the plague!'

A door halfway down the street opened slowly. A plump man with a sweating pink face emerged and said cautiously: 'Er – I wonder if I can help.'

Jake dropped his stick. 'I think you might,' he said angrily. 'I don't like risking my boat in unknown waters because no-one can be bothered to put out a buoy. And I don't like having doors shut against me for no good reason.'

'We are unused to strangers.' The man twisted his hands. 'My name is Muller. I am a doctor.'

'Andrew Jakes. I'm looking for a girl called Harriet. Harriet Wyman.'

The colour drained from Muller's fat cheeks. He attempted a smile. 'I don't think I know anyone of that name – we have so few visitors – ' Beads of sweat ran down his temples.

Jake turned and looked about him. People were peeping from behind curtains and half-closed doors. 'It was just a thought,' he said to Muller. 'Thanks.'

He retraced his steps to where Mac stood, looking belligerently round at the houses. 'She's here,' he said. 'But they don't want to let on.'

'Christ, let's get out of here, Jake. Call the police or something.'

'I'll see Harriet first. Let's buy some food and do some swimming, something's bound to happen.' Stepping almost jauntily he made his way towards boxes of fruit left unattended outside a shop. He began collecting oranges and bananas, piling up more and more until at last the owner burst into view to remonstrate.

'Surprise surprise,' said jake to the agitated lady confronting him.

'Now, tell me about this island. Good for swimming, is it?'

By evening he had discovered that the people lived either in Corusca or in tiny settlements scattered throughout the island. The big house belonged to someone no-one would name. When he asked about a lady every face turned aside. Sitting on the deck of the boat, bobbing gently on the evening swell, he sipped at a whisky and said to Mac: 'It's the big house. Got to be.'

'This place is bloody evil! I wouldna be surprised to know they eat babies.'

'Hmmm. Actually neither would I.'

'May I speak with you?' A sibilant whisper came out of the night.

Mac's hand jerked and his whisky spilled. Jake remained quite still. 'What can you tell us?'

'She wanted to go. They wouldn't let her. That's a nice lady, she don't want to stay here. You take her away from that house, don't you listen to their foolishness. She tell me she so unhappy.'

'Who's he?'

'The old man. He can make his spells, but I got a charm to keep them off and I gonna be safe, I just know it!' Her laughter crackled softly, a wholesome sound. Jake opened his mouth to ask her name, but someone was calling.

'Rosa! Rosa!'

'That you?'

The woman let out her breath. There was the scraping of her feet on the wooden jetty and the shadows swallowed her up.

Mac reached again for the whisky bottle. 'And that was a long-legged beastie. Spells. What did she mean, spells?'

'They kill people with spells sometimes. If someone believes enough, then if you let them know they're cursed they'll up and die. No-one has to lay a finger on them. Don't you remember old man Taylor telling us about it? How his woman died with pains in her belly after someone showed her a bag?'

'I don't want to be shown any bag,' said Mac.

Jake grinned at him, his teeth flashing white in the darkness. His spirits were rising like mercury in a thermometer, because life was tasting good again, rich and thick upon his tongue. 'I could do with a party.' He looked round for some excitement, something to celebrate his unexpected renewal. 'Let's have a bonfire,' he said suddenly. 'Let's show them what we think of their bloody little island.' He seized a box of matches and rattled them in his pocket.

Harriet saw the blaze from her bedroom window and caught her breath. Usually the fires were high on the plateau, heralded for hours beforehand by the soft rhythm of drums. This was on the promontory, at the old look-out point. She went out into the hall. Gareth was there.

'There's a fire,' she began.

'I know. Where's Jerome?'

'Out, I think.' She went and knocked on his door, but there was no reply. Quickly she gathered her robe around her and rustled down the stairs. Hawksworth was sitting up in bed, reading by the light of a shaded lantern.

'Henry, there's a fire on the promontory.'

His gaze snapped up to Gareth. 'What is this? Is it your doing?'

'It must be Jerome.'

'He's with your sister. Get the guns, we don't know what they're planning.' The atmosphere had been tense for days, ever since one of the house servants had taken to her bed and died.

Harriet ran to the door. If they were to be attacked she must look after Victoria. Should she stay in the house or hide out in the garden? The thought of the snakes made her skin crawl. There was a knock at the front door. She put her hand to her mouth and stood as if frozen. The knock came again. 'Who is it?' she called shrilly.

'Muller.'

Normally she hated him to come to the house, but now she ran to push back the bolts. Jerome always used the side door after dark and this massive entrance was barred against allcomers.

'Get out of my way,' said Muller breathily. 'I must see Mr. Hawksworth.'

She followed him to the bedside. Hawksworth scanned Muller's sweating features. 'Thank you, Harriet,' he said dismissively.

'I should like to know what's happening.' She sat herself down on the edge of the bed.

He waved impatiently at Gareth. 'Get her out of here. Why don't they ever know when to keep out of things?'

Gareth grinned triumphantly. 'I told you what she'd be like. Go on, Harriet, get out.'

She was angry and frightened. The two faces looked at her, suddenly so alike. She was only safe if she kept Hawksworth on her side. 'Henry – ' she began, stretching out her hand. 'I only want to take care of you.'

'Get her out Gareth!' snapped Hawksworth.

Gareth seized her wrists and propelled her forcibly to the door. Muller's face swam before her gaze, pink and satisfied. There was no point in fighting and she did not, but all the same Gareth wrenched at her arm and forced her shoulder against its socket. In the hall he hissed, 'Cry, you bitch, cry! Pretty little thing who thought she had it made, go and howl your greedy eyes out.' She went limp in his hands and he discarded her. Huddled on the floor, she heard him laugh.

She crept back as soon as the door closed, leaning close to the panels. What would they do if they found her? It was not a thought to dwell on. Muller was speaking, his tone apologetic and nervous.

'Don't whimper,' snapped Hawksworth.

'I am sure they know she is here,' said Muller, clearly trying to pull himself together.

'Who told them?'

'I think no-one – perhaps she has written – '

'Don't be a fool. It was your woman again.'

There was a silence. Harriet cringed, imagining someone creeping towards the door, about to fling it open and expose her. When Gareth spoke she jumped. 'Only two men, father. Not much of a problem.'

'But who will come after? People send messages these days. I at least don't want people clamouring to know what happened.'

'You never minded before.'

'Things were different before. It used to be years between outcomers. Now one imagines an entire cruiseliner anchoring offshore and sending parties of trippers to visit us! And what use are you, boy? What would you advise?'

'Let her go,' said Gareth silkily.

Hawksworth gave a brittle laugh. 'How you would like that! With Harriet gone you could kill me and take everything. And what use would you be? It would all be lost in a year. Look at the Corporation, neglected from the day I provided you with it. What did the newspaper write: 'This leaderless amalgam of poor hotels and lost causes?' That is your single achievement, reducing the Hawksworth Corporation to a laughing stock. Oh no, I shall not let Harriet go. Not until I've got a son on her. Muller, what are you doing about that?'

'Well, sir, I – I have been studying the papers as you wished, Mr. Hawksworth.'

'Good, good.' Hawksworth was delighting in taunting his son. Then he rapped: 'Let them come here. Harriet will see them. I will speak to her.'

She fled, picking up her skirts and running silently up the stairs, the door opening just as she whisked out of sight. She ran to her room and closed the door. When Gareth entered she was dressing the baby, fighting to control her breath.

'Father wants you.'

'Indeed.' She picked up a sleepy Victoria.

'You can leave the brat.'

'Not with you around.' Still barely awake the baby was waving tiny pink fists. Harriet's own hands were like ice. Please don't let them hurt her, she found herself praying, I'll do anything if they don't hurt my baby.

Muller was sweating with nerves when she went in, but Hawksworth was revitalised. His face was as lean and hard as rock, but his eyes flickered like a bird of prey's. 'Harriet,' he purred, and held out his hand to her.

'Don't, Henry. You can't expect me to hang on your moods.' She sat down some distance from the bed, aware that to pander to Hawksworth was to lose his respect. Her heart pounded uncomfortably.

'As you wish. My, my, but you are a pretty one. I swear she gets prettier every day, don't you, Muller?'

'It is the Coruscan air,' said the doctor, bobbing up and down.

Harriet thought it might be true. On Corusca there was nothing to do but be beautiful, surrounded by servants and silk robes. Each day she looked at her clear skin and shining hair, and thought what a pity it was that only Hawksworth could enjoy her.

'Perhaps I should let Gareth have her,' he said thoughtfully.

She swivelled to face him. 'No!'

He shrugged. 'I don't intend to. But you must behave, Harriet. Muller, take the child.'

The doctor grabbed for the baby. Harriet hung on, screaming at him. Victoria was shrieking in terror but Harriet was going to die rather than let go. The door opened, she knew it was Gareth. When he held her from behind she was helpless; Muller scuttled across the room with his prize. Harriet turned and sank her teeth into Gareth's cheek, tasting blood, hot and sour. As he flung her away she heard Hawksworth laughing.

'Harriet, Harriet my dear!'

'I'll kill you! If you hurt her, I'll kill you all!'

'Of course. But she isn't going to be hurt. Be quiet, Harriet, and listen.'

She crouched on the floor, her fingers clawed. She'd have Muller's eyes if he hurt her child. They'd torn her robe. She saw Gareth and Muller staring at her exposed breast and pulled the cloth across.

'Some people have come to find you,' said Hawksworth, as if talking to an idiot. 'I want them to go away again. You must send them away. To make sure that you do so I will keep the child while you tell them how happy you are here.'

'Who are they?'

'That is hardly of interest. If you do not send them away then clearly there would be – consequences. We would all regret that, I am sure.'

To her shame tears coursed down Harriet's cheeks. She found

herself crawling, actually crawling to Hawksworth's side, her robe wide open. Muller began clucking excitedly. 'Please let me have her,' sobbed Harriet, clinging to Hawksworth's hands. 'I'll do what you say. I am happy here. You don't have to take her from me.'

Hawksworth passed his hands over her flesh thoughtfully. She leaned towards him, offering herself in return for her child. A few drops of milk oozed from her nipples on to the bed. Hawksworth looked at his son.

'Go and fetch them. This shouldn't go on unnecessarily.'

Disbelievingly, Gareth said, 'I can get you a dozen women! You don't need her.'

'Go and fetch the men,' said Hawksworth. 'Muller, take the child upstairs. I shall call you when I need you.'

The door closed. Harriet stared wide-eyed at her husband. 'Now, my dear,' he said softly. 'Slip out of that rag and come here.'

Jake and Mac were noisy and defiant as they returned to the boat. The embers of their blaze still glowed clear across the bay, in stark contrast to the island's gloom.

'Did you see those shacks we passed?' said Jake. 'The people here are a hundred years behind. I'll swear that kid had rickets.'

'Aye,' said Mac gloomily. He had seen rickets enough as a child. 'They eat that porridge stuff.'

'You'd think they'd have fish even if they can't get meat. What the devil is Harriet doing here, that's what I keep asking myself.'

The euphoria of the early evening had been dispelled by his bonfire. Now his leg was aching and he felt tired and disorientated. The world was full of nightmare. As he bend down to lever himself on to the boat a figure rose up in the cockpit.

'Bloody hell! What do you mean sneaking about our boat at night?'

'He'll have been up to something,' said Mac angrily. 'Mark my words, he'll have fiddled with the cocks.' He switched on a lantern. In the flood of yellow light they saw a tall man, his mouth twitching nervously. Under Jake's stare he started to chew his thumbnail.

'My name's Hawksworth,' he said.

'Bully for you. What do you want?'

'I've come – my father – he wants to see you. You're to come to the big house.'

'Sorry, mate, I'm not going anywhere at this time of night. Come back in the morning.'

The man laughed shrilly. 'You don't understand. Harriet wants you to come. I've brought the carriage, you don't have to walk. I can see you're a cripple.'

'Not half as crippled as you're going to be in a minute,' said Jake thinly.

'Why can't this wait till morning?'

The pale hands waved, a vague and slightly feminine gesture. 'Old men wake up at night. I do advise you to come, Harriet wanted to see you today but my father wouldn't permit it.'

'Why can't she do as she likes?' snapped Jake.

'People don't – on Corusca.'

The sea was lapping softly against the boat. All Jake's antennae told him that the night was full of trouble. 'You game?' he asked Mac.

'I guess so.'

Jake grinned. Sometimes he wondered why he tolerated Mac's dour pessimism, now he knew. When it came to it, Mac was bedrock hard. He mentally checked his pockets for torch, matches, knife. Damn this leg! Simply enduring it sapped strength, mental as well as physical.

'Let's go then,' Jake said to the visitor. He walked ahead of them, narrow-shouldered and wavering, every movement inspiring distrust.

The sense of strangeness persisted as they drove towards the big house. 'It's like a daytrip round Killarney,' said Mac, watching the horse's rump swaying in front of them.

'We don't have cars,' said Gareth. 'Or tractors.'

'Who needs them when you can have starvation?' said Jake.

Moths fluttered around the carriage lights, huge feathery things like ghosts. Ahead loomed the big house. It was quite dark and quite silent.

'Here we are,' said Gareth on a rising note. He pulled up the horse and climbed down. The others followed slowly. The scent of flowers was heavy on the night air, so thick you could touch it.

'I don't like this,' said Mac as they approached the open front door.

Ahead was a faint gleam of light, reflecting on polished wood. Again the scent of flowers, more cloying than hyacinths. In the gloom they made out the sweep of a staircase ascending into space, and many doors.

'This way,' said Gareth and led them down the hall towards the light. He stood aside as he came to the lighted room. Standing stockstill in the centre of the carpet was a woman in a floorlength robe of dark apricot silk. Her hair hung loose on her shoulders and her hands were clasped in front of her. It was Harriet.

Dreamily, she watched them approach. The real Harriet was somewhere high up, looking down on the automaton who walked, spoke and smiled. Jake had hurt his leg, he was limping badly. He looked tired and drawn, but the same Jake, the same as always. Her world, tilted crazily for so long, swung back towards its axis.

'Oh, Harriet,' said Jake thickly. 'You don't know how glad I am to see you. Christ, I was so worried!' He reached out his hands to her, but she stood quite still, saying nothing. Her eyes shone with unnatural brilliance and Jake stopped, staring at her.

'You all right, lassie?' said Mac. 'Looks like a grand place you got here.'

'If you like slave mansions,' added Jake. He tried again to take Harriet's hands, saying softly, 'It's all right, lovey, I'm here now. You can tell me what's the matter.'

Slowly, her hands unclasped themselves, resting in his like cold marble. 'There isn't anything the matter' she said tightly. 'How nice to see you both. Have you hurt your leg, Jake?'

'Broke it. I've come to take you home, sweet, you can't stay here. Didn't I tell you to stay on the boat?'

That inflamed her. 'You! It's all your fault, you abandoned me! I've been here so long – why was it so long?'

'Believe me, it wasn't intentional. And I'm here now. Time to go, lovey, so go and get your things.'

Her movements marked by slight unco-ordination, she walked slowly and casually to a chair and sat down, swinging her legs one over the other. 'I'm not going anywhere. I think I should tell you that I'm married. I am Mrs. Hawksworth.'

Mac was the first to speak. 'You've never married that sly-faced nancy boy, have you?'

'Gareth? No – no, I haven't. His father.'

'You've married his father?' yelled Jake. 'How old is he, for Christ's sake?'

She swallowed visibly. 'Very old. He's in a wheelchair. I – take care of him.'

'You stupid cow,' said Jake softly. 'I can't leave you alone for a minute. Well there's no help for it, you'll just have to get a divorce. Go and tell him – no, I'd better explain to the poor old duffer.' He half turned to the door.

'No!' Harriet got up, feeling as if she was fighting her way through mist. Why couldn't he understand, why couldn't he make it better? She forced herself to wakefulness. 'I'm not coming with you. I'm staying here with Henry because I want to stay here. I – like it. I've got servants and lots and lots of money, I can have absolutely anything I want. I don't want to go. Just imagine, a smelly little boat when I could have this!' She spread her arms wide to encompass the room, the paintings, the heavy curtains, the silver-gilt candlesticks upon the table. Her smile was as brittle as spun sugar.

Jake limped heavily across to her. 'Poor Harriet.'

Tears welled in her eyes and she turned aside. 'Not poor Harriet at all, lucky Harriet. Better an old man's darling than a young man's slave, isn't that it? I'm very lucky. Give me your address and I'll come and visit you sometime.'

His breath was warm on her ear. 'People don't seem to leave here very often, so I've heard.'

'I don't suppose many can afford it. I mean to get involved in charity work, you know. Perhaps a baby clinic – ' Her voice broke on a sob. She swallowed and tried to laugh.

'Harriet.' His hands were heavy on her waist. She jerked aside and walked quickly to the window, lifting the curtain and gazing out into the night. 'You've no idea how lovely the island is. If you were staying longer you could see it.'

'We are staying longer. Quite a while actually.'

She stared at him, her eyes wide and unblinking. 'Please don't. I shouldn't like that. I want you to go on the morning tide.'

'That's bloody unfriendly,' said Mac. 'We gave you a better deal when you were down and out. Not even a dram or a bite to eat.'

'My husband doesn't like his routine disturbed,' she said vaguely. 'Please, Jake, morning tide. I won't ever – I mean, please.'

He was watching her very closely. 'If that's what you want, love.'

'Yes.' She was clasping her hands again, the knuckles white.

Suddenly he said huskily, 'I've missed you so much. I didn't know how much till now.'

She swallowed down her pain. 'Strange, the things you miss.' Abruptly she walked to the door and called 'Gareth!' He appeared out of the darkness. He and who else had been listening? 'They'll be going now. Drive them back, please.'

'Of course, Harriet.' He gripped her arm, smiling. Jake and Mac passed out into the hall. At the last moment Jake looked back to see her standing in the doorway, straight and silent. He lifted his hand but she might have been made of stone.

Back on the boat Mac said, 'And that was a rum do! Who'd have thought it? Harriet!'

'Best get some sleep if we're sailing in the morning,' said Jake.

'You'll never just up and go? Man, you're mad!'

'Very likely. But if Harriet wants us to go, then go we must. Looked well, didn't she?'

'Didn't look like Harriet, if that's what you mean.'

Chapter Seventeen

Harriet sat in her room, waiting for the morning tide. Her nerves were like shards of glass, cutting her with every breath. Far away down the long corridors of the house she could hear Victoria crying, wailing for her mother and food. Twice she had gone and asked to be allowed to feed her, twice they had refused. If only Jake would go! If only he would see that what she asked was what she truly wanted him to do. And yet, and yet – to see the two of them standing there was like watching real people step into your dream. The Hawksworths were smooth as snakes, while Jake and Mac were as craggy and unshaven as the goats that lived in bad-tempered isolation on the Coruscan hills. She was becoming very fond of the goats that watched Hawksworth power and influence with such scornful yellow eyes. She admired anyone that stood against them.

The crying was becoming weaker, degenerating into hopeless, sobbing hiccups. Again Harriet fingered her knife, filched from the table on a day when such tactics seemed ludicrous. Jerome knew she had it, she had seen him watching her. He wasn't on her side, but then neither was he on Hawksworth's. Each of them fought only for themselves.

Footsteps in the hall. She hid her knife in her sleeve and watched the door. Gareth stood there. 'You can come for her. They've gone.'

The relief was like a flood of pure gold. Quickly she turned and slid the knife into her pocket, then ran with rapid steps past Gareth to her child.

Muller was sitting by the cradle, pretending to apologise. 'You understand – I had to.'

She withered him with a look. He was her enemy now and forever, he had hurt her baby.

Victoria smelled of wet and misery. Harriet gathered her up and put her lips to the damp head, murmuring meaningless sounds of comfort. But she wouldn't feed her here. She went quickly back to her room, her breasts aching with unshed milk. As the baby sucked with desperate intent she murmured: 'I won't ever let this happen to you again. I won't ever let them hurt you, darling. Trust me, trust Mummy. Never, ever again.'

Thought began again now she had the baby with her. Besides, whatever it was they gave her never lasted right until morning. Jake had hurt his leg, he could hardly stand on it. Poor Jake, how he would hate to be restrained like that. Dear Jake. He had come for her, months too late but he had come. She shed tears of gratification. What had he thought of her? Had he thought she looked well, had he thought her beautiful? Had he truly missed her?

She wondered what he was doing. Looking for somewhere else to land in all probability, it was quite unlike Jake to give in tamely to any request of hers. But there weren't any other harbours. He could, of course, anchor off and swim ashore as she had done, but she now knew how lucky she had been to survive, how lucky the boat had been to avoid destruction. The storm had confused the currents which for most of the year swirled in the shallows, each season drowning some unwary swimmer, and the reef always took a toll of fishing boats.

There was a knock at the door. 'Who is it?'

'Jerome.' It was almost a whisper. Harriet let him in and sat, holding her baby, watching him. They were like prisoners meeting illicitly, each suspecting the other of treachery.

Jerome spoke first. 'We gotta get rid of the old man.'

Harriet flinched. 'I can't – I wouldn't know how – '

'I don't mean like that! Don't think it would do for him anyways. Mr. Gareth, he shot him, but he don't die. A boy upcountry he swear he hit him when the place was raided, but that boy he dead and Mr. Hawksworth ain't. We gotta use magic!'

'Don't be silly!'

But she didn't think him silly. When you lived on Corusca you came to believe in things, in the fires and the drums and the unexplained silences. People lived and died by strange rhythms on this island. A man could be killed by words alone. She knew, she had seen it!

'I don't want to kill him' she whispered. 'Couldn't we just – he has such strength, still, at his age. Couldn't we just weaken him?'

Jerome came close to her chair and knelt down beside her. The shape of his face was so like Hawksworth's it made her shiver.

'You come with me tonight. We make magic, you, me and Madeline. Together we take his strength away.'

'What about Gareth?'

'He won't do nothing. 'Sides, he thinks it his island. Me, I think it mine, all mine. I'm gonna take it and he doesn't even know.'

'I can't leave Victoria.'

'Put her in a basket, she won't take harm. But you must bring the old man's grit. You know what to bring?' She shook her head, wide-eyed. He sighed at her ignorance and whispered: 'Something with his blood on it. A piece of his hair, a clip of his nail. And a handkerchief soaked in his piss. That makes a strong magic.'

'I can't get those things! But if I could – it won't kill him, will it? I just want people to think he's lost his power, that's all it needs. If he was dead, Gareth would get me, you know he would.'

'Iffen he die then Gareth won't get no-one,' said Jerome contemptuously. 'You get the grit? He mustn't know.'

'I'll get it.' She looked full into Jerome's face and saw there only stone. He was just like Hawksworth, she thought. He was Hawksworth again in a black skin. It was God playing a practical joke against an old man's prejudice.

'Don't you tell him, now. I can point you, easy.'

'I won't tell him.'

She put the baby down to sleep and went slowly downstairs. Hawksworth never let anyone cut his nails but did it himself, slowly and laboriously. Now she knew why. Likewise his thin remnants of hair were allowed to grow until he could trim them himself with nail scissors. His urine was easy, she helped him several times a day, but the blood – she would have to be devious.

He smiled at her as she entered his room. 'You look rested, Harriet. Come and look at this catalogue. Shall we bid for something? There's a Renoir, not of the first quality but quite pleasing. Something light and gay, that's what we need.'

She crossed to his bedside and pretended to study the catalogue. He smelled stale, he had missed his daily bath. 'You're in a mess, Henry,' she commented. 'Let me clean you up, I can give you a wash down in bed.'

He glanced at her irritably. 'Must you? Oh, very well.'

As she sponged him he commented upon Jake and Mac. 'Two drifters led by the phallus. I've seen the type, they come to the sun because living is so cheap, yet they lack the will to make anything of themselves except prize studs. No wonder you came to me. Men like that can give you nothing. One might as well put one's faith in a bull.' His contempt for their potency was, she knew, a product of his own impotence.

'You give me everything, I need, Henry,' she said softly.

He grunted and allowed her to roll him on to his side. 'Oh dear,' she said suddenly. 'This doesn't look good.'

'What is it?'

'Your toenail. No, don't try to move, I've got you balanced. This nail is ingrowing quite badly. You can't feel it of, course, but I do believe it's beginning to become gangrenous. I'm sorry, Henry, but I must do something about it.'

'Call Muller,' he said impatiently.

'I will not have that man in the house!' snapped Harriet. 'Besides, I can treat it. I just have to clip the nail and dig out the dead flesh, I can do it with scissors. It's not as if it will even hurt.'

'You are making an unnecessary fuss.'

'Will you say that when Muller chops your foot off? Stay still, Henry.'

She fetched the scissors and neatly clipped two pieces of nail. Then, her stomach tight with loathing, she dug the point of the blade deep into his toe. Blood spurted on to a handkerchief. She realised she could have chopped off his toe and still he wouldn't have known. It was a nauseating thought.

'Give me the clippings,' said Hawksworth.

'Really!' She handed over one piece of nail.

'Is that all?'

'Yes. There's quite a hole in your toe though, so don't look. I'll just put on a dressing.'

When he was safely in his wheelchair on the terrace she went back to the bedroom and carefully picked three long hairs off the pillow. All she could think of was the night.

The drums were beating as they climbed up through the forest. Jerome carried Victoria in a basket so that Harriet could use both hands to cling on to roots and tussocks of grass. Suppose in the dark she clutched at a snake? She put the thought from her mind as she struggled upward, towards the fires and the dark, throbbing drums.

Jerome strode ahead tirelessly. Soft from lack of exercise, Harriet's own heart pumped wildly but it was almost a pleasure to feel her body suffer. Madness bred in sloth and inaction, to struggle was to approach sanity.

At the top Jerome handed her the baby basket. 'Don't speak, don't do nothing. Just follow me and do as I say.'

She nodded, mesmerized by the fire reflected in his dark eyes. He seemed taller, thinner, his mantle of subservience shed like a coat. At the edges of the light many people gathered, and beyond the fires was a dark mass of stone. An undercurrent of wailing ran through the air, a low, insistent note like the deep bass of an organ. To the side of the path a woman lay moaning, tearing at tight curls of hair in a trance that took her beyond everything. Harriet padded behind Jerome, watching the heads bow as he passed, noting the silence that spread around him. He had the power, no doubt about that, yet still Hawksworth ruled him.

Suddenly she saw Madeline, reeling towards them. She wore a long white robe, dark-stained down the front. Instinctively Harriet recoiled. The girl smelled sweet, like rotting fruit. She was beautiful tonight, and yet she was repellent. It was as if Madeline herself encompassed all that had once been good and innocent and now was spoiled and rotten and corrupted. Once upon a time she would have been a beautiful child. The girl stopped before Jerome and executed an elaborate, swaying curtsey. Harriet almost laughed. Jerome turned and stared at her. 'Go with her. Stay by her all the time.'

Harriet took tight hold of her basket and stepped after Madeline. They knelt side by side at the edge of the central pool of light, to the left of the great stone. Disjointed dancing was beginning, the women standing and stamping, quite independently, then two joining together. They were naked to the waist. Their breasts swayed and jerked in the rhythm of the dance.

A cup was passed round and Harriet drank some spirit or other. It seemed to have little effect, but she was a hardened drinker these days, used to beginning the day with a tot and ending it on an empty bottle. Smoke drifted across the dance floor. She could barely see what was happening. Many more people were dancing, the noise of chanting and drumming was enough to fill her head. Next to her Madeline swayed and she swayed also. The girl put her lips to her ear and said: 'Do you see Jerome? Do you see him?'

Harriet peered through the wreathing smoke. A man, naked but for a thong belt, his genitals as heavy as giant plums, strode into the ring. He was a beautiful man, oiled and thick muscled. Another man approached him, wearing feathers round his neck. As the women stamped and wailed the feathered man inserted thorns into the flesh of Jerome's chest, pushing them in one side and out the other with obvious effort. Jerome never moved but Madeline, his alter ego, moaned and sobbed.

A laugh attracted Harriet's attention. Standing at Madeline's elbow was a small, blonde child, aged perhaps six years old. He stood and watched in fascination, laughing each time the thorns pushed into flesh.

'Nathan?' asked Harriet. Her voice sounded slow and drugged.

'Hello,' he said cheerfully.

'Run along now,' said Harriet thickly. 'It must be past your bedtime.'

The child grinned at her and scampered away, perhaps to bed, perhaps not. Harriet felt sobered. No longer did the night's passion engulf her. She felt her eyes watering from the smoke.

The ritual skewering went on and on. Man after man cut himself or stabbed himself with nails. Some bled, a mark of failure, others did not and were rewarded with an uprush of chanting. The cup was passed again and this time Harriet put it to her lips but did not drink. Beside her Madeline seemed almost comatose, watching the proceedings with her head sunk on to her chest.

A thin sound trilled on the air, high like a baby's cry. For a moment Harriet's heart stopped. But of course it was a goat. A dark little thing wriggling in the man's arms, a man she did not recognise. She blinked, because it was Jerome, whom she knew, and that – it must be a goat! A cry rose in her throat. She tried to struggle to her feet, fighting against dreadful lethargy. All around people knelt and swayed, their eyes senseless and blind. The ground beneath her feet oozed moisture.

'No! No! It isn't worth that!'

He stared at her, the man she knew and did not know. Thank God, if there was a God, for it was only a goat. Dark blood ran down the stone.

The people were like figures in a mist. A girl was dancing, white skin naked in the firelight. Harriet felt herself to be a ghost, unseen by anyone. Wherever she went, no one saw her. She stood at the rock and watched the girl lie down on the blood. The men covered her, one after the other, first Jerome and then nameless, faceless men. The girl lay, wide-eyed, without moving.

The people were becoming more and more frenzied. Men and women whirled in the circle of light. A high ululation began, spreading out and out until it filled all the air. Harriet put her hands over her ears, she could not bear it. A tall black man stood before her, his penis erect, his eyes quite empty. She felt a sudden, terrible desire to lie down and let him enter her, it seemed as if there was nothing else she could do. A man, a real man, at last, to fill her aching body with strong seed.

As she reached for him she heard her baby cry. Sanity rushed into her head like clear water. 'Oh, my God, no!' She turned and fled, seizing her precious basket as she ran. On the rock Madeline lay motionless as the men copulated with her. All around people whirled in frenzy or lay writhing upon the ground. Harriet crept into the forest, making her way down, down, down to the sea.

Jake wasted no time in leaving Corusca behind him. As soon as the tide began to run he made sail for the horizon, briskly efficient.

'We shouldna leave her,' muttered Mac.

'Getting soft in your old age? Cast off will you.'

It was a day like any other, the sun hanging like a perpetual brazier in a hot, white sky. The sea's glare dazzled. If you sat out on deck too long the very flesh on your bones would burn to nothing. At around twelve Jake said: 'This should do. I'm heaving to.'

Mac's lip curled. 'If we sneak back after dark we'll hole the boat. We had one chance and that was last night.'

'They were threatening her.'

'So we tell the authorities. We've no got to rush in like the bleeding cavalry.' But even as he spoke he was taking in sail.

Jake grinned and got out a sketch pad on which he had made some drawings. 'Look at this,' he called to Mac.

The other man came across, wiping his hands on the hairs of his thin thighs. 'Oh, aye. Which beach is that?'

'The one below the house. I had a little chat with our friend Rosa this morning, while I was getting the water. At high tide here you can take a boat in over the reef.'

'How big a boat?'

'A fishing boat.'

Mac snorted. 'And they've no draught at all! We'll be high and dry as a whore with the clap.'

'She says they clear it by about eighteen inches. We're two feet deeper, so we've got to get rid of six inches. Lighten ship, that's all.'

Mac continued to grumble, but half-heartedly. The thought of a raid excited them both. To go on the offensive against that closed and inhospitable island seemed far more tempting than a meek withdrawal to tell tales. They jettisoned most of the water and much of the food. They kept the spare sails as too valuable to lose before they were quite sure it was necessary. The heavy cabin table went over the side as well, and bobbed about upside down.

The anxiety he had suppressed so far was nagging at Jake. Christ, but Harriet had looked strange. Tense, scared, and yet somehow luminous, eerily lovely. He had smelled drink on her but she had not been drunk, and though she was probably drugged that had not been the whole of it. Whatever the threat that hung over her, it had terrified her utterly.

They set sail just as it was getting dark. The tropical night falls with surprising suddenness, dense as black velvet until the moon gets up. The little boat gathered way with a chuckle, setting to her task with workmanlike efficiency. Jake pulled on dark trousers and a dark poloneck jumper. Mac fastened his grey windcheater up to his neck.

'We ought to black up,' said Jake. 'But once you do that there's no way you can claim you're birdwatching, it's like carrying a bag marked swag.'

'I'm no wearing a hat covered in seaweed either.' What Mac meant was that he wouldn't have minded at all dressing up like commandos, but felt foolish suggesting it. Jake grinned to himself and tried not to think of the pain in his leg. It was just nerves, nothing more.

The island showed up as a dark hump against the moonlit sky, bordered with white where the waves hushed upon the beach. It was difficult to pinpoint exactly where they were.

'What's that?'

High on the hills fires burned. Faint as a whisper could be heard the sound of drums.

'I should never have left Glasgow,' whispered Mac.

Jake felt the hairs rise on the back of his neck. 'Right nelly you are,' he said.

They could just make out the shape of the beaches, and occasionally the square blotch of a building. Jake began to wonder if they had missed the big house, if perhaps it was set further back in the trees than he had thought. But as they rounded a point he saw it again, as he remembered it: tall, square, without a single light glowing.

'Early to bed,' he said conversationally. 'Right, I'm taking her in.'

Mac cursed vilely and went to shorten sail. It seemed that the boat must be horribly visible, although they knew from experience how difficult it was to see a yacht at night, one of their greatest hazards was being run down in shipping lanes. The wind was very light. The boat drifted forward, almost under bare poles. Jake hung over the side, peering down into the murk. 'Call the depth,' he said to Mac and straightened up.

Mac trailed a weighted line, softly calling, 'Six feet. Five. Three feet. Two. Christ, there's a bloody great spur, hard a port.'

The boat swung broadside and wallowed. Coral scraped noisily along the side.

'That's a paint job' said Jake. 'The channel's to the west of that spur, so Rosa says.'

'Now you tell me.' Mac sounded shaken. But as they approached again he called depth as before. 'Five – Five – Five – Four – Two and getting shallower.'

'I think this is it,' said Jake.

Both men were silent. The boat drifted noiselessly forward. 'Two fucking inches' whispered Mac. 'I can touch the fucking stuff.'

'Get ready to dump the sails,' hissed Jake. A gentle shudder ran through the boat. The reef rumbled against the keel like a bad digestion. There was a thump as the rudder took a bash, and then they were through. The boat floated in the calm waters of the lagoon.

Nothing moved on shore, all was calm but for the fires on the hill and the drumming. Jake anchored close inshore. 'Let's go.' He and Mac slid over the side and swam ten yards to the shelf of beach. The cold water bit into the pain in his leg, he wondered what all those lumps of metal did when the cold hit them. He was probably half an inch shorter than during the day.

Numbness persisted as they crept up the beach. Mac had his knife in his teeth. Like bloody Errol Flynn, thought Jake, and felt a laugh swelling his chest. This was really something! Most of the time you engineered excitement, creating the tests and challenges that spiced the days, but occasionally, very occasionally, they came of their own accord. Like wild goose, the taste was altogether different.

They circled the terrace and crept into the gardens. Heavy foliage brushed their faces. Jake was looking for a side door or a convenient window, anything that would admit them given a little effort. Suddenly he stopped.

'Don't move' he muttered. 'Look about. Do you see anyone?'

They both scanned the shadows. Everything seemed still. 'Nothing,' hissed Mac.

'Then look at that.' He moved aside. A spear was sunk shaft down into the ground. The metal point was aimed at the cool moon. Between shaft and tip was the body of a woman, pierced just above the waist. Her feet rested on the floor, her head and hands hung down. A necklace swung like a pendulum, this way and that, two clasped gold hands suspended on a long gold chain. There was a stain on the shaft of the spear where the weight of her body was gradually dragging her to the ground.

'It's no Harriet.'

'No.' Jake's voice was husky. 'It's Rosa. I recognise the necklace.'

'They must know we're coming.'

'She might not have told them. It could be because we talked. I'm not leaving now anyway.'

He skirted the corpse, trying not to see the look of fixed terror on a once lovely face. He had killed Rosa, he had sought her out and brought about her death. The windows of the house looked blankly back at him. He would have to break glass. He heard a thin wail. A baby was crying. As he watched a light clicked on in an upstairs room and the figure of a woman was outlined, long hair falling onto lace clad shoulders. His heart leaped. It was Harriet.

He scrabbled in the earth for a pebble and then flung it with seamanlike accuracy against the glass. There was a gunshot crack as it hit the pane. Harriet stopped, turned and then cautiously opened the window.

'Who's there?' Low, wary tones.

'Me. Let us in, quick.'

'Oh!' Her hand went to her mouth. Then she turned and went swiftly back into the room. They could clearly hear the baby crying. Less than a minute passed. A window slid up to admit them.

Quickly, Jake caught her up and hugged her, fiercely tight. She was shaking uncontrollably.

'It's all right, love, it's all right. Do you know there's a body in your garden?'

A momentary stillness settled over her. 'Who is it, Rosa?'

'Yes. How did you know?'

'She'd upset Henry. I knew he and Gareth were plotting something, but I thought she'd know – ' She pulled away from him and stood, her hands either side of her head. 'I must go upstairs.'

Jake grabbed her arm. 'No time, we have to catch the tide.'

'There's the baby.' Dragging herself away she ran to the door.

Mac cursed under his breath. 'Lassie took the body calmly. How many bodies do they have round here?'

Jake looked round the room. It was a library, walls lined with books, the circular antique table bearing a huge bowl of flowers. Which baby? Whose baby? He went out into the hall and turned to follow Harriet up the stairs. He heard voices: Harriet talking to Gareth Hawksworth.

He crept over the wide treads, his bad leg noisy despite his efforts to be quiet. 'Where have you been?' Gareth was asking. 'You've been out half the night.'

'Don't be silly. I've been here, in my room.'

'You're lying. I wanted to see you tonight, and you weren't here.'

'Yes, I was. I heard you knocking, I didn't reply, that's all.'

'I did more than knock. I have a key.'

She sounded unconcerned. 'If that's true, I must get the lock changed. What did you want Gareth?'

Jake peered round the doorframe just as Gareth put out his hands and took hold of Harriet's throat. She stood, quite still, staring into his face with those brilliant eyes. 'You've been on the hill,' said Gareth. 'I can always tell. Did Jerome take you?'

'Yes. And you daren't hurt me – I'm not Rosa.' Gareth tightened his grip but she moved not at all though her breath was dragging audibly.

'Was Madeline there?'

'Yes.'

'She always did like it. Never could stop her going to the hill.' Almost gently he drew Harriet to him, pushing his thumbs up under her chin to block off her windpipe. She choked and put up her hands. The baby's crying filled the air. Jake flung himself across the room, seizing Gareth's hands and wrenching them back. He gave a hoarse shriek of pain. Harriet staggered and clung to the post of her bed.

'I'll thank you not to maul Harriet,' said Jake, failing to put his knee in Gareth's spine. It hurt too much. Instead he pulled the man's right arm higher until it cracked. Gareth howled and Jake let him fall to the floor.

'Harriet, you come right now. Get down those stairs.'

'The baby – ' Dreamily, she turned.

'To hell with the baby, get going!'

He grabbed her and she fought him, suddenly vicious. 'That's my baby, it's mine! I won't let you hurt her!'

Jake let her go, his expression unreadable. Harriet ran into the dressing room and could be heard soothing a child. Gareth lay on the floor, his arm twisted at an unnatural angle. He was whimpering like a dog. As Jake watched him he looked up.

'I won't forget you,' he hissed. 'And I'll get her, I promise you that. She's a scheming bitch trying to murder the old man she married, a drunken slut. When she's had enough she'll lie down with anyone, her. She's worth nothing!'

Jake kicked him, with his bad leg. The pain hit the top of his head, but the pleasure of seeing Gareth's mouth mash into his nose was worth all of it.

Harriet stood in the doorway, watching vacantly. She held a baby basket and in it was a small pink child. But Harriet hadn't changed, she was still wearing her floor-length lace nightgown. The dark aureoles of her nipples showed through clearly.

'Jesus wept!' Jake grabbed her free hand and dragged her towards the stairs. Awareness seemed to come and go in her. She said suddenly, 'I must change.'

'Too late, we'll miss the tide.' He stumped his way downstairs, thinking that this was a night he never wanted to relive, and yet would, endlessly, in dreams.

Mac was standing in the hall. He gestured towards an open door. 'Seems we've woken this old duffer.'

Hawksworth sat up in bed, his head erect, his long-fingered hands folded on the bedclothes. 'I see you are stealing my wife,' he said conversationally.

'So it would seem.'

Harriet stood holding the baby basket, watching the old man. 'Goodbye, Henry,' she said clearly.

'Have you done for me?' he asked.

'I don't know,' she said. 'I don't know what will happen.'

He gave a low chuckle. 'The bag was beneath my pillow when I woke. We shall indeed have to see. I always felt you'd be the one, none of the others have quite your steel. Not even Jerome. He's known me too long, perhaps. I should have killed you after you sent these men away, I felt it my bones. But one grows weary – destiny is, after all, just that.'

'We're going,' said Jake. 'Leave him.'

But Harriet hung back, staring at Hawksworth, until Jake took her free arm and dragged her from the house.

The tide was ebbing as they splashed towards the boat. Harriet clung to her baby and was hauled aboard gasping, her gown transparent in the early morning light. 'About time you sobered up,' said Jake grimly. 'Get below and sleep it off.'

As they lifted the anchor he could hear her crooning to her baby, although she had barely acknowledged Jake himself. He ducked his head into the cabin and was rewarded by the sight of Harriet, naked, sitting on the bed while her baby suckled. His stomach fell away.

They skated over the reef by dint of jettisoning spare sails. The sun beckoned them, flooding the horizon with promise. Flying fish made silver arcs in the air, running from the shark that slipped silently through the yacht's wake. Dark things beneath the surface, dark thoughts that were never admitted. Who can know what another person is thinking? Jake sat at the tiller and faced the sunrise, finding no joy in that golden morning.

They left her all the day. Towards evening, when she was again feeding the baby, Jake sighed. 'I've got to talk to her,' he said.

'Aye.' Mac took the tiller and sat gazing impassively out to sea. At that moment Jake would have given anything not to be going below but there was no help for it, and besides, he couldn't have borne not to know. Harriet looked up as he ducked into the cabin. There were huge blue shadows under her eyes, her hair was a nest of tangles. She hasn't once said thank you, he thought.

'What were you on last night?' asked Jake. He hated to see the baby sucking so proprietorially, as if Harriet and the child were a mutually exclusive pairing. There were pale blue veins in her breasts. They aroused him embarrassingly.

'They gave me something,' she said dully. 'I was quite sober compared to the rest of them.'

'The rest of who?'

'The islanders. It was a – party.'

'Bloody voodoo orgy, if you ask me.'

Harriet turned her face away.

After a while he said stiffly, 'Well, then. Who's the father?'

Her head snapped up. Her free hand went to her mouth and she started to laugh. 'Don't you know? Can't you guess?'

'I can make quite a few guesses but I don't suppose I'd get it right. The most obvious person is that slimy queer who tried to strangle you last night. You were too stoned to notice.'

'What a horrid thing to say.' She bent her head and touched her lips to the baby's dark hair. 'Her name's Victoria.'

'Very pretty. She can't be the old man's.'

She inclined her head. 'She could have been. In a manner of speaking.'

'Bloody hell!' He turned and fought his way back up to the deck. His leg was killing him, fuelling his rage with real physical pain. 'The bitch says it's the old man's! She actually lay down with someone old enough to be her fucking grandfather!'

Mac looked incredulous. 'She didna say that!' From below they could hear Harriet's wild laughter.

'She's bloody insane!' Jake struck his fist hard against the side of the boat. His knuckles began to bleed.

'You stupid bastard,' said Mac dispassionately. 'The bairn's the spitting image of you.'

Jake was quite still. He swallowed audibly. Then he made his way slowly and carefully back into the cabin. Harriet's giggles died away, but her lips still trembled. Leaning carefully across, Jake looked for the first time into the baby's face. His own clear grey eyes looked back at him. His own jet black hair on a baby's rumpled brow.

'Oh, Christ.'

'I'm sorry,' said Harriet in a voice loaded with tears. 'I didn't mean to have her. But she's so beautiful, isn't she?'

'Did you know,' he said thickly 'when you got off the boat?'

'I – suspected. Don't worry, I won't hold you to anything. It wasn't your fault.'

'That's bloody magnanimous of you.' He sounded doubtful.

Harriet shrugged. 'I know I can't expect anything from you. It isn't in you to be dependable somehow, there's no point in trying to turn a camel into a horse. I can look after Victoria.' She brushed the baby's hair with her lips.

Suddenly Jake was furious. 'If it hadn't been for me you'd have been stuck forever on that place. My daughter would have been brought up amidst God knows what perversions, if she wasn't sacrificed before she was two!'

Harriet flinched. 'Don't talk about things you don't understand. I wouldn't have been there at all if it hadn't been for you, I never wanted to go to sea. I was going for a holiday in New York!'

'Well, if that's what you want, why don't you have it? I'll have the kid and you can go and holiday in fucking New York and pick up where you left off, legs crossed against allcomers.'

'I'd never let you have her!' She threw back her head and glared at him. She wanted to hit him, hit him and hit him again. 'Just think of the life you lead – different woman every night. Two together sometimes, wasn't it? How many since you dumped me, may I ask?'

'None.' He gestured to his leg. 'The boat was wrecked. I've spent the time in hospital having the leg pinned.'

She sniffed and turned her head aside. The baby gave a burp. Harriet absently wiped away the dribble of milk and laid the child in her basket on the opposite bunk, folding her into the covers as if she were the most precious thing in the world.

'What was it like? Having her?'

She sighed. That was a bad memory, and might always be. 'It was – lonely.' She reached out and put her hand on his thigh feeling the long slash of the scar beneath his trousers. 'It isn't right, is it?'

'Dunno. It certainly isn't good. My God, Harriet, I don't seem to get over you somehow.' There was no hope of disguising his erection. It bulged against his clothing like a growth. When he unfastened his zip it rose up like a huge, thick fungus, so distended it seemed it must hurt.

She reached out a finger and touched the tip, feeling a bead of moisture. 'Who would think this would make a baby?'

'Lie down girl. You owe me this.'

She lay on the bunk, wide-legged. He slipped inside her like a piston into a cylinder, gave three thrusts, and climaxed. Filled up and yet unfulfilled, Harriet writhed beneath him. He pulled away and she felt hot semen on her legs. 'Bastard.'

His thumb prodded at her, skilfully stroking. She folded her arms over her face because she needed this and couldn't bear him to know it. On and on, she couldn't come and she couldn't let him stop. Perhaps if she was drunk, she thought wildly. God, she could do with a drink. He was climbing on top of her again. She arched her back and pressed herself against him, feeling him go in and out endlessly but unable to leave the ledge she was on. This was utter, utter torture. Again he climaxed, and lay there panting. She let out a sob. Then she felt his hair on her thighs. Her fingers twined murderously in his hair – and relaxed.

They were short of food, water and ballast. The boat bobbed about on top of the sea like a cork, a restless, difficult motion. Perhaps it was that, perhaps just the aftermath of tension, but Harriet's spirits were at rockbottom. One day she heated some soup and it boiled over on the stove.

'Right mess that is,' said Jake, and at once her tears overflowed. Again in the night when Mac was asleep and Jake on watch she found herself lying wide-eyed with the tears trickling into her hair. Jake came down into the cabin. 'Come up and talk.'

'No! I'm all right.'

'Your crying and Mac's snores are driving me mad. Come on.'

Reluctantly she pulled a blanket round her and went topsides. 'So what's the matter?' asked Jake, stretching his bad leg.

'Nothing.' But she was crying again. Why, oh why, was she crying?

'Is it me? Is it the baby?'

She shook her head. 'I don't know. I don't like any of this!'

'I wasn't planning on take you on a cruise! We'll be in harbour in a couple of days.'

'And then what?'

Jake sighed. 'What indeed? I owe Mac for this boat, and a few other people besides. And with this leg the way it is, I can't get a job sailing.'

'What would you do if you had some money?' Harriet pushed wet hair back from her face.

Jake laughed bitterly. 'That's easy. I'd take you and Victoria and I'd go back to England – South Coast, Isle of Wight, somewhere like that. And I'd build boats.'

'You don't mean that! You hate being tied down, you said so.'

'I think I hate – oh God, what is it really? – being doubted. I hate the way you write me off all the time. Of course I'm going to take care of you and the kid! The trouble with you is you don't expect anything of anybody, you always think everyone's bound to let you down.'

'You *do* let everyone down.'

Angrily, he eased his leg, wincing at the self-induced pain. 'Perhaps I've learned a thing or two. Perhaps I'm prepared to pay for what I want. It's time you and I settled down, Harriet.'

She leaned her chin on her hands, staring at him. 'I don't think you know me any more. I'm so hard now I can scare myself.'

'Not so hard you can't cry. Cheer up, I could make a fortune pearl-diving.'

'We've got a fortune. Or at least, part of one.' She slipped back down to the cabin and rummaged down the side of the baby basket. When she emerged she was holding a small painting.

'What the hell is that?' There was no disguising the excitement in his voice.

'It's a Hogarth, quite genuine. It hung in my room. Of course we won't be able to get market price because it's stolen, but we should get quite a bit. How much do you need?'

'About a hundred thousand. Minimum.'

'It should fetch that.'

All at once tears welled up again and she put her face down and sobbed. This time he left the tiller and put his arms around her. 'What is it? Just tell me, you can tell me anything.'

'I would if I knew,' she wept. 'But I don't.'

Chapter Eighteen

They made for Nassau, that humming, buzzing port set full in the mainstream of civilised life. There could be no greater contrast with Corusca where time seemed to crawl, held back by the island itself as if enshrouded with vines and creepers. That first morning Harriet wandered the streets, weary and cold, while Jake and Mac saw to the boat. She was wearing Mac's spare shirt and trousers. When she saw her reflection in a window for a moment she wondered whose it was.

After a while she went into a café and ate something, she wasn't sure what, only realising afterwards that she couldn't pay. All the money was in Jake's pocket. The café-owner scratched at the hairs on his chest, then picked up a flyswat and demolished a few mosquitoes. They made bloody imprints on the tables and walls, the marks of their passing spattering the labels of the bottles behind the bar. A cat sat washing itself in the sunlight by the door and from somewhere came the sound of a radio playing dance music. Harriet started to cry.

'What's the matter, love?' asked the café-owner's wife. 'Nothing so bad it can't be mended.'

'I can't pay. I forgot.'

'That a beautiful baby.'

'Yes.' A broad, black hand patted her shoulder gently.

'You got a man?'

'Yes.'

'He good to you?'

Harriet wondered. 'I think so. But I keep crying.'

The black woman patted her again, calm and reassuring. 'Well now, that ain't so strange. You thank God for your good man and your baby. Run along now.'

As she walked away the eyes of the café-owner followed her. She could hear him quarrelling with his wife. Everything seemed so strange and distant. It made no sense that she was really here at all.

After Corusca's isolation the bustle bewildered her. People everywhere, passing, jostling, making her adjust her stride to accommodate them when she was used to just walking. She sat down on a wall to look about her, at the dresses and the hair, the way everyone seemed so confident of themselves and where they were going.

A man and a woman approached. The woman was lovely but too thin, and her heels were too high. The man hustled her along, almost brutally, although he was short and fat with little to recommend him to this long-legged beauty.

'Natalie.' Harriet stood up and blocked their way. 'Natalie. It's me, Harriet.'

'Oh, my God. Harriet!'

They embraced, Natalie bent to admire the baby. Her escort said loudly: 'We gonna spend all day fawning on your goddamned friends?'

'Please, Carl, I haven't seen Harriet in ages,' said Natalie anxiously.

'We got a goddamned meal waiting for us! But if you want to visit with your two-bit friends then – '

'I'm so sorry.' Harriet swung on her heel and looked at him. Her tone was icy. Tear-stained and bedraggled though she was, she exuded chill authority. 'I am always glad to meet Natalie's friends,' said Harriet and extended her hand.

Carl shook it awkwardly. 'I don't mean to be hasty but we've got a meal waiting – '

'Are you very fond of food? How interesting for you.'

Carl grinned uncomfortably, unsure what to make of this.

Natalie said shrilly, 'Carl's busy tonight, why don't I come and see you? Where you staying?'

'Our boat's in. Let's meet for a drink.' They made the arrangements and parted. As the pair walked away up the street Harriet heard Carl say, 'Who is that broad? Looks like a tramp but makes like the fucking Queen of Sheba.'

Jake and Mac had in one short morning put the boat up for sale and made enquiries about selling the picture. 'Going to be bloody hard,' Jake told Harriet. 'Everyone's suspicious.'

'Then I'll take it in.' She picked at a corned beef sandwich. 'I am Mrs. Hawksworth. I'm entitled to sell it.'

Jake was unsure if he liked Harriet seizing the initiative. 'I suppose you could – '

'Yes. By the way, we're meeting Natalie for a drink tonight. I saw her in town.'

He grunted. 'Who with this time?'

'Someone called Carl. He was horrible.'

'I'll babysit,' said Mac. 'Natalie and me don't get on.'

'She doesn't get on with me either! Go on your own, Harriet.'

But Jake was there, under protest, when Natalie strolled into the bar that evening. She wore a white silk dress that clung as she moved, and between her tight breasts was a heavy pendant, indenting the cloth suggestively. But even she was upstaged by Harriet who was wearing her lace nightgown over a flimsy white bra and pants. There was an air of elegance and restraint about her which counterbalanced her clothes, and her hair tumbled on to her shoulders gloriously.

'What have you got on? That's antique lace!' Natalie stared lustfully at the nightgown.

'I suppose it might be. Look, I've brought Jake.'

He did not get up, posing his leg as an excuse. Natalie ignored him and sat opposite Harriet, regaling her with a detailed account of her life since last they met. 'But you've been busier than me,' she finished. 'Trust Jake to get you into trouble.' She directed a venomous look at him.

'What happened to Peter de Vuiton?' asked Harriet.

Natalie made a face. 'He got very possessive. Sad, really, because we got on real well most of the time. I don't know what he expected? When he got drunk he got impotent. I had to have something to do.'

'Don't you mean someone?' asked Jake.

'And you can shut up.'

They glared at each other, and then Jake laughed. 'Can't we forget all that? Me and Harriet are setting up house, I'm starting a boat-building business in England. Think of us while you're getting a tan.'

'Yeah.' Natalie sipped at her drink. Her hand was trembling slightly and the whites of her eyes were stained yellow.

'You can do better than Carl,' said Harriet suddenly. She too was revived by alcohol.

'You'd be surprised.' Suddenly she looked vulnerable, the crows' feet at the corners of her eyes showing through the make-up.

'Get out and settle somewhere. Didn't you always want one of the big houses on the hill? Must be some sucker prepared to buy it for you.' Jake flicked her shoulder with a finger, but her mask was back in place. She grimaced drolly.

'Don't see myself making it in a full-size bed! But maybe I'll start looking. Trouble is these days most suckers have wives keeping an eye on the funds. Will you let me know how you get on? I was sorry about your leg, Jake.'

'Me too. Look us up if you find yourself stuck. I mean that.'

He stood to go, and Natalie leaned back to look at him. 'You're still a bastard. And more lucky than you deserve. You've got a queen and a little princess.'

'I just know when to quit.' He reached down for Harriet's hand. He was surprised to notice she was still wearing Hawksworth's heavy carved gold wedding band.

Harriet took a lamp off the boat and sold it to a chandler. Then she walked the streets until she found a shop that hired out clothes 'For evenings, special occasions and theatricals'.

'It's a special occasion,' she said as she entered.

'Wedding?' The man was already reaching for his standard blue and white outfit with the white straw hat, sizes small, medium, large and gargantuan.

'No. More a sort of race day.'

'It either is or it isn't.' He put his hand on his hip and looked at her quizzically.

'Then it isn't.' She met his gaze blandly and passed along the rail, scanning the clothes. 'I've got to look rich and elegant.'

'Black's a very good colour,' he said elbowing her aside and twitching a dusty black dress and jacket from the rail.

'The jacket might do. The dress is past it.'

'A lady who knows the best, even if she can't afford it.'

'Quite right.'

She looked again at the wedding finery, mostly overdone nylon. There was one dress in fuchsia, hanging limply at the back. A spray of flowers was pinned ineffectually at the neck, almost a cry for help. 'I'll try that dress and the jacket,' said Harriet.

'Madam knows best,' said the man waspishly. 'Don't blame me if it's vile.'

But it was far from vile. Harriet's eye had lighted on the one pure silk dress in the shop, its dejected appearance on the hanger no indicator of how it would look when worn. She detached the flowers carefully, smoothing the pinholes with her fingers. It was delicious to be in good clothes again. Just to feel silk against her skin was to be transported back to Coruscan luxury. It hadn't all been bad. She slipped the black jacket over her shoulders and studied her reflection in the tarnished mirror before poking her head round the curtain.

'Do you hire out shoes?'

'Take your pick.' He waved a hand at several rows of footwear. As Harriet hunted for something her size he said, 'My, my, but we do look grand. I admire your taste. Let's see about some jewels, shall we?' He went to a box and cast handfuls of earrings, necklaces and bracelets on to the counter. They sparkled as if worth millions, and every single gem was glass. 'Koh-i-Noor or Star of India?' He held up twin giant diamonds to his chest like tiny nipples.

'Emeralds,' said Harriet, tripping across in black high heels half a size too small. They hurt terribly but were all she could find. From the jewelstore she selected a thin silver chain and a pair of massive emerald earrings.

'If I say it myself you look a real show-stopper. When do you want them for, if that's not a state secret too?'

'I'll take them now,' said Harriet. 'Just let me put on some make-up.' Going back into the changing room she carefully applied the mascara and lipstick she had bought from a drugstore that morning. Her tan was a gentle gold, but her hair was losing the red of the flower-petal rinse she had used on Corusca. Still, it would have to do.

'Perfume,' declared the man as she emerged, and aimed a spray at her. 'Don't worry, it's Joy. I use it myself.'

'Suits you,' said Harriet. 'Thanks. I'll be back before you close.'

'Have a nice time,' he called, waving limply.

As of that morning the Hogarth was carefully wrapped in tissue paper, to give the impression that she had just stepped from some luxury hotel. Old newspaper wouldn't do, she told Jake firmly. He hadn't understood any of this and she had hardly tried to explain. He wanted an end to her Hawksworth connection, an absolute eradication of everything Hawksworth, from her ring to her name to her memories. 'You'll get a divorce,' he had said last night, in a tone that forbade discussion. She had murmured noncommittally but it was as Mrs. Hawksworth that she approached her art dealer; it was Mrs. Hawksworth's eye that scanned the single valuable painting displayed in a velvet-lined window, and put her elegant foot on to the discreet alarm matting inside the door.

'Can I help you?' asked a soft, plump man with a bald patch over which he draped strands of hair.

'Are you Mr. Collins? I was told to ask for him.' In fact she had taken the name off the tasteful shopsign.

'I am he.'

'My name is Mrs. Hawksworth. I have an extremely valuable painting that I wish to sell.'

He beckoned her through to his office, blue-carpeted and lined with pictures. Harriet seated herself on the slim gilt chair before his desk and reverently deposited her parcel. 'Perhaps I should explain,' she said diffidently. 'No doubt you have heard of my husband – Henry Hawksworth of Corusca.'

Mr. Collins swallowed. 'One of our most – interesting collectors.'

'Certainly one of the most discriminating. He is very old and has become somewhat confused. I felt it better – it seemed wisest – to spend some time in Nassau.' She raised her eyes to her host and said in clipped, making-the-best-of-it tones: 'My husband is convinced I am trying to poison him, Mr. Collins. He hasn't long to live. Just at the moment he seems happiest alone with his manservant, I seem only to make him unhappy. One of the cruelties of old age is that it destroys people, even in the memories of those that love them. I want to remember my husband as he was when he was in his right mind.'

Suddenly she saw Hawksworth as he had been that night, with courage that forced admiration despite everything. She found she was fighting back genuine tears. 'I am – protected under the will but at present I am short of funds, for the indefinite length of time that I am to be away. Which is why I bring you this.' Delicately, reverently, the tissue paper was unfolded. 'An original Hogarth.'

Mr. Collins almost choked. He took hold of the picture with the tips of his fingers and crossed to the window. 'Beautiful, beautiful,' he crooned.

Harriet suppressed a smile, remembering Jake's comment. 'Bloody awful thing. Best we do get it sold, I'm not having that in my living room, grinning at me.' But then his taste always ran to seascapes and meticulous drawings of yachts, although even then he criticised details, they'd got the wrong angle of heel or somesuch.

'It will have to be auctioned,' said Collins.

'I don't think so.' Harriet folded her hands, somehow conveying an air of steely intent. 'I don't want my husband to know I've sold it. In all probability he wouldn't find out, but on his lucid days he does take notice of things and I should hate him to feel that I was selling his collection even before he was dead. It must be a private sale, although I will of course give you a letter of provenance.'

'It could take a very long time,' said Mr. Collins doubtfully. 'The private contacts, the need for discretion – it wouldn't be easy. A picture such as this – we're talking of a very great deal of money.'

'I am aware of that. If you give me a hundred thousand now I will consider the picture sold.'

'But it's worth far more than that!' He was gaping like a fish.

'I know. But that is all I require at present. No doubt you are aware of the extent of my husband's collection? It is willed to me.'

Mr. Collins sat down as if his legs were too weak to hold him. 'Wills can change,' he said feebly.

'My husband is no longer of sound mind,' said Harriet in a voice like ground glass. 'Now, I've said all I want to say and I want this finished. A banker's draft would be the most convenient method of payment.'

Collins went again to look at the painting. It was second nature to him to doubt its authenticity, although every instinct told him it was genuine. He had seen too many second-rate pictures, too many poor copies, not to know perfection when it lay in his hands. He found he was hyperventilating and forced himself to control his breathing. Quite apart from the turn he would make on the deal, to be offered such a masterpiece was in itself an accolade. This was a pinnacle from which he could strive for the mountain-top. 'I shall remember this day for the rest of my life,' he said slowly. The woman across the desk, calm, poised, and somehow distant, allowed a slight smile to cross her face.

They celebrated with champagne, Jake and Mac uproarious, Harriet quiet until she had drunk enough. Thank God the booze cheered her up, she thought desperately. Why was it that she felt like this? She was with Jake and Victoria, even Mac had a pleasing familiarity about him, and she was heading for a new life, a life she had longed for once. None of it seemed to matter very much in the context of her all-pervading gloom. Life had suddenly become a joyless procession of days, through which she plodded, dealing with tasks with relentless efficiency. Perhaps it was Jake, she thought in terror, perhaps she didn't love him any more. She leaned against him, trying to force herself to feel something, and he put his arm round her shoulders and refilled her glass.

'It is so good to have you back,' he murmured, and nuzzled her ear. 'I missed you like shit.'

There seemed to be nothing to say. She felt nothing, and if he tried to make love to her tonight, sending Mac out for a midnight stroll, she would feel nothing then either. Only the drink helped, blotting out her mood like a giant paintbrush loaded with whitewash.

Chapter Nineteen

The air smelled of mud and seaweed. Harriet stared down at the murky grey water of the Solent and wondered if this could possibly be the same stuff that chuckled in warm, luminous blue abundance in the Caribbean. Could this even be the same sun, providing no more than grey daylight, peering sulkily through rain-filled cloud. She was very cold.

Fumes from the engines of the ferry made her eyes water. Jake was resting his leg in the shelter of the funnel, so she handed Victoria to him and went down to make herself presentable in the cracked washroom mirror. At least she still had a tan, tinged now with blue since all her clothes were too thin. They were husbanding their money and had bought only the most basic necessities. She thought longingly of that jacket Jake had bought her once, whose practicalities she had despised. What she wouldn't have given for it now.

It was raining as she climbed the companionway once again, thin slashes of wet against her face. Where was the spring? she asked herself. Where the blue skies and lush green lawns of her memories? In England in May it was still all fires and buttered crumpets, and they had no fire to sit before, let alone any crumpets.

'We're coming in.' Jake limped towards her and she took the child, adorable in a fluffy pink suit. Two similar faces, but one drawn with pain and cold, the other quite content.

'Leg bad again?'

'I'm all right. We'll try and get a bus or a taxi or something.' He lurched down the gangway before they had quite finished tying up, and the deckhand on the rope yelled at him.

'You always were a bossy bastard, Pete Hughes,' said Jake, and kept on going.

'Bloody hell, Jake! Damn your black heart!' The deckie flung his coil expertly on to the dockside and came across. 'What the hell are you doing here?'

The two men shook hands. 'Done my leg in,' explained Jake, gesturing at the offending limb. 'I've quit sailing for a bit. Taking up boat building, with Harriet and our little girl. Tell you what, got any idea how I get to some place called The Sluice? River frontage, with a couple of decent big sheds, according to the agent.'

'Bus at the end.'

Harriet came down the gangway towards them. 'Harriet, meet Peter Hughes. He and I got arrested once for sailing a rowing boat without lights in a shipping lane, Pete, this is Harriet.'

'Pleased to meet you,' said Pete. 'He got me in so much trouble me mum used to send me off every morning with a packed lunch and a warning not to get mixed up with that Andrew Jakes. Never did no good, though. He even used to eat me lunch!'

'She gave you enough for ten,' said Jake. 'Remember that old cutter we did up? Nearly ended up in France first time we took it out.'

'Still sailing that is. What you going to build then? Cruisers?'

Jake shook his head. 'Big fish. I've been ironing out problems on them for years. It's about time someone started building them right to start with.'

Harriet moved restlessly. She was freezing and the baby was weighing heavy in her arms. Jake glanced at her and grinned. 'Harriet's turning blue. If we take this place you can come and look us up, about time we had a beer or two.'

'Or five or six if I remember right,' laughed Pete. 'Oh, Christ, the captain's looking. You'll know him, Geoff Bates.'

Jake turned and looked up. The man on the bridge leaned down and yelled: 'Andrew bloody Jakes! No wonder I can't get docked, God help us all!'

After what seemed aeons, Harriet and Jake sat on the bus taking them out to view The Sluice. Despite the whisky pressed upon her by Captain Bates Harriet was dazed with tiredness. Also, no-one seemed to have anything decent to say about this house they were visiting, except that the best way to get to it without a car was across the field from the road. The countryside looked flat and wet. She noticed a small white cottage completely dwarfed by two vast modern sheds huddled on the edge of the sliding water of the river, an unpleasant blending of industry and charm.

'The Sluice,' yelled the driver. 'Let's be having you.'

'That's it,' said Jake. 'Doesn't look too bad, does it?'

'Pity they put the sheds so close to the house.'

'Not if you want to use them, it isn't.'

They slipped and slithered over the field. Halfway across Harriet's shoe came off and she hopped about squeaking while Jake laughed at her. She laughed too, not because it was funny but in admiration at his grit. His skin was transparent. He retrieved the shoe for her and she took one handle of the bag, to save his leg a little. Ahead the gate to the cottage swung creaking in the wind.

The garden was quite overgrown. While Jake hunted in the gutter for the key, Harriet peered through the window. Dirty plates on an old oak table, a wood stove surrounded by ash. A calor gas cooker sat in a corner, encrusted with someone else's grease.

'It can't be empty,' she said.

Jake was fitting the key into the lock. 'Last lot were evicted. I gather they left it in a bit of a state.'

The plates on the table were growing mould. Upstairs there were grimy sheets on beds that sagged and smelled of strange bodies.

'Just needs a bit of cleaning up,' said Jake. 'It's got everything we need.'

'Including dry rot,' said Harriet, kicking at a disintegrating floorboard.

'Well, it is dirt cheap. We're just renting it, love, it's not as if we have to love it.'

'No.'

They went out to look at the sheds. They had been erected two years before for some fly by night venture that never got off the ground. Huge, cold and empty they stood like twin monoliths, dominating the cottage and even the greasy river. 'Christ. They're so right I can't believe it.'

'Are you sure? They're just sheds.'

He turned on her, saying excitedly, 'That's all you need! We've got the cash to fill them just as we like. I didn't tell you before but I've had an enquiry for a design, bloke I know quite well. He and I have talked a few times, tossed ideas around. All I needed was a bit of money and a base. This is it, love. Right place, right facilities.'

'I don't like the house much.' She watched his face. 'But I expect it's only dirt.'

Jake rumaged about looking at things for a while, then sat on the fence in the wind, resting his leg and admiring his new empire.

'Don't you think you ought to get your leg seen to before you take this on?' It was not the first time she had suggested it.

'I'm OK,' he said flatly. 'If I waste six months in hospital there won't be any commission, there won't be any house. I'll get the leg seen to when I've got this going.'

'You don't even know what's wrong with it! Suppose it's serious?'

He shrugged. 'It'll just have to wait.' He was silent for a moment then he turned. 'I'm doing this for you, love, you and the kid. I want to give you what you want. It may be a crummy cottage now but it won't always be.'

Harriet touched his arm. The wind was making her eyes water. 'We wouldn't mind waiting six months and having your leg right.'

'But I would.' He levered himself up. 'Let's get back into town and book in at the pub. If I 'phone the agent before five we might be able to get started tomorrow.'

Over dinner that night, chicken and chips at the bar, continually interrupted by Jake's cronies, he said: 'I'll give Mac a call.'

'How do you know he'll come?'

Jake shrugged. 'He always does. He can lodge here for a bit.'

'He'll want to stay in the house.'

Glancing at her, Jake grinned. 'He can want all he likes. I'm keeping my little family to myself for a bit.' He took hold of her fingers.

'Can I have another whisky?' asked Harriet. 'I can't get warm somehow.'

They moved in the very next day. Harriet struggled with things, finding a dead rat behind the cooker, and ratholes in the cupboard under the stairs. Somehow, in England, there was never anyone to help you, she reflected angrily. Everybody did everything for themselves, whether they were good at it or not, whether they had the strength for it or not. There was no tradition of service, or at any rate none that she could afford. On Corusca she only had to ask, while here she could request all she wanted but still there was no-one to burn the sheets and scrub the floors, no one but her.

The baby made things difficult, cooped up for too long on planes and boats. Now she yelled for attention and was contrary when she got it, sleeping late and little, chewing on the nipple when she fed. But Harriet was determined to conquer both the house and her own mood. On the first night she and Jake sat before the little stove, that she found so difficult to light, and basked in its rare warmth.

'Let's put wallpaper in here,' she suggested, looking at the cracked and yellowed walls. 'Something light and pretty.'

'Not worth it, love,' said Jake. 'The place isn't ours. Besides, we're going to be bloody hard up for a good few months, I'm afraid. Wallpaper is out.'

'We've got a hundred thousand! A few rolls of wallpaper wouldn't cost anything, and I'd put it up!'

He sighed and tried to explain. 'Harriet – all the money's spent. I'm putting that hundred thousand into the business, and the bank's matching it. We live on overdrafts and hope for a bit, till I get the boat finished. I've got to pay wages, rates, rent, telephone, electricity, food, transport – that blasted baby buggy cost nearly a hundred quid.'

She twisted her hands and said softly: 'I didn't realise. And I could have got far more for the picture if I'd waited.'

'We couldn't wait. We had no real claim to it.'

'I was his wife, of course I had a claim!' She sat up and flared at him.

'Don't look like that,' snapped Jake. 'I hate your bloody Mrs. Hawksworth act.'

'You'd rather have me meek little Harriet, I suppose?' She got up and flung across the room. How horrible it was to be without money, how powerless she felt. Her destiny was in hands other than her own. It wasn't really in Jake's hands either but at the mercy of faceless men with contracts and loans and business priorities to consider.

'We've just got to be patient,' said Jake.

'Victoria and I need clothes,' she said hysterically. 'How can we buy anything?'

'We're not destitute, damn it!' He stumped across to her. 'We just have to be careful.'

He never knew that he was asking Harriet to undertake something of which she could never have been capable. She either had money and spent it, or she had none and spent none. Anxiety about funds was to dog her through her days, making each trip to the supermarket a duel with their meagre mortgaged funds on one side, and temptation and rising prices on the other. Jake often said he didn't know how she managed as she did, never knowing that she did it by self-denial and misery. Sometimes, when she couldn't stand the strain, she bought herself a bottle of something, cheap sherry or cider, and soothed herself in the long afternoons, sitting in front of the stove and watching fifteen-pounds-a-load wood burn away.

By the summer they had six workmen, a pick-up truck and a half-built yacht. The only telephone was in the sheds and it rang all day, never for Harriet. She was beginning to feel very out of things, although she helped all she could with the business, addressing envelopes and filing bills and so on. She did it alone, as she did most things, because Jake was always in the shed with the boat and that was no place for a baby just starting to crawl. Sometimes she borrowed the pick-up to go into Cowes or round the coast. The island was full of holidaymakers and the harbour full of yachtsmen, many of whom wanted to waste time chatting to Jake until he put a notice up saying in bright red letters: 'No hawkers, no circulars, and no bloody friends wasting my time. Try the local on Sunday nights, you idle bastards.'

And that was another of Harriet's diversions gone. She had liked chatting to the strange people who drifted to the cottage, seeking Jake's advice about sails or hull design or simply wanting to talk about boats. So she decided to make friends of her own, and joined the Women's Institute and a mother and baby club. They seemed to be on bad days somehow, when the pick-up was in use to collect something vital on the ferry and the bus broke down and never came. Going out at a set time on a set day began to seem impossible, with the baby to feed and the men wanting tea all the time and it starting to rain just as she had dressed Victoria in a thin dress.

Everybody called her Mrs. Jakes, and Jake casually referred to her as his wife too. It annoyed her somehow, as if she had been appropriated without being asked. But she couldn't talk to him about it, because all he ever thought of was his boat, a strange vessel if ever there was one. He had gone steps further than finned keels. The underside of the hull looked like a bizarre submarine, bulbous and distended at one end and tapering to moderate width at the other. No unauthorised persons were allowed in the sheds and periodically Jake made unlikely threats to his workmen if they so much as whispered about the keel. Sometimes his leg hurt so much that the pain glittered in his eyes, eating through restraint and good humour. He would spend all day holding on to his temper, then step into the cottage late at night and yell at Harriet for leaving a baby rattle on his chair. 'You've got nothing else to bloody do, can't you at least keep the place tidy?'

Absolutely silent, she served him his dinner. After a while he said, 'Sorry about that. I must be tired.'

She wanted to hit him and scream at him, tell him all the miserable irritations of her life, but he was indeed tired, and his leg hurt, and he didn't need problems when he had a boat to build.

Then a heatwave rolled across the island, like a glorious fanfare of trumpets. Jake found her a little rowing boat and in the baking, shimmering afternoons she rowed up and down the river, clinging to the shoreline amongst the reeds, exhausting herself. Lying at the bottom of the boat, letting the sun beat on her closed eyelids, sometimes she forgot where she was and when she woke would row furiously to bring herself back to reality.

'You never come,' she chided him. 'You never spend any time with Victoria.' Once or twice he did come, and instead of a solitary vigil the outing was an adventure, rowing where no man had rowed before, eating a picnic of paste sandwiches and scotch eggs and catching minnows for Victoria in a jamjar. When the baby slept they made love amidst the reeds. She remembered that very well because it was the first time she didn't feel anything at all. She lay on the ground underneath him, as unfeeling as if she was dead, as if she wasn't in her body but watching from outside. It was weeks since she had come for him, she had taken to pretending. But now she was as cold and heavy as stone.

'Oh, my love. Oh, my darling girl.' He mouthed her breasts in an ecstasy of passion and she thought, I wish he wouldn't. He's making me wet all over.

She wiped herself, dipping his handkerchief in the river. 'Are you all right, Harriet?' he asked.

'Of course I'm all right. Isn't it a lovely day?' If she smiled brightly enough he need not see the tears.

Once or twice she went to the shed and asked him to come out again, but he ran his hands through his hair and said yes love, he would, but not today, hey? When the boat was finished, they'd have a holiday or something, and don't sit there that's the prototype for a whatsit.

I'm always alone said a small voice of ice. Why am I always alone.

The same thoughts seemed to go round and round in her head, never resolving themselves, always repeated. She dreamed of her mother, seeing again the grey, shrunken figure sitting unquietly in a chair, mumbling, complaining, fidgeting. She's dead, Harriet told herself, she's dead and it's because of me. Yet somehow she could not bring herself to pick up the 'phone and see if it were true. Suppose she wasn't dead and when Harriet visited, as she must, an aged hand plucked at her sleeve and an old, thin voice said: 'Take me home, Harriet. Don't leave me here!' What would Jake say to that?

At last, inevitably, she telephoned the home. To begin with no-one seemed to recognise the name, but at last the matron was found. How kind to call. Yes, of course they remembered Mrs. Wyman. Such a pity the lady had been with them such a short time. Hadn't she been informed? Mrs. Wyman had passed away within three months of arriving at the home. If it was the effects that concerned her then of course whatever still remained could be forwarded . . .

Harriet mumbled something and rang off. Only three months. If she had stayed three more months she would have been spared so much guilt. But of course her mother wouldn't have died if Harriet had stayed to care for her, so really Harriet had killed her own mother. It was ridiculous and Harriet knew it, but somehow she could not stop that thought adding itself to the tumult in her head. She had mourned her mother when she put her in the home, and now must mourn her again, it seemed. There was no sharing what she felt because no-one would understand, least of all Jake who had abandoned his own mother without a qualm. He seemed to notice nothing, and the distance between them, unadmitted, grew.

But gradually they began to acquire a social life. Yachting people invited them to dinner, either informally on their boats or in Cowes. They left Mac babysitting and Harriet wore her lace nightgown, over and over again, while Jake put on his usual patched sports jacket and yacht club tie. He had a selection of club ties, all very prestigious though he could identify none with any certainty. 'People give them to me,' he said vaguely, as if it were some unfortunate and rather tedious habit, although presumably each commemorated some remarkable achievement.

'We'll have to have them back,' he said one night, when they had dined for the third time with some yachting dignitary who ran Cowes Week.

'We can't. The house is dreadful and we can't afford the food.'

'Sod the house,' said Jake. 'They can take us as we are, and as for food I'll cadge some lobsters off the lads.'

'I'm not torturing lobsters for the sake of that stuffed shirt,' snapped Harriet. She felt distraught and jumpy tonight. There hadn't been enough to drink. 'He hates me, you know he does!'

Jake snorted. 'He's frightened to death of you. You behave as if he's just crawled out from under some barnacle-encrusted hull. You show you're bored when he talks about sailing and wither him if he doesn't.'

'All he knows about is sailing!' It wasn't true. He was a nice man who played the violin badly and bred poodles and didn't know how to talk to women. 'Let's have stuffed sole,' she said, pulling the pins out of her hair and letting it tumble.

'Stuff you any time.' Alcohol eased Jake's leg and the absence of pain made him randy. He tried to take hold of Harriet but she evaded him.

'You must be tired. It's five weeks since you had a day off.'

'I still fancy a poke. You're the one who's always too tired, remember?'

He reached out and grabbed her, pulling her close with unnecessary force. She pushed at him and he caught her dress, dragging it down so that one breast swung free. The delicate lace parted. Harriet screamed: 'You've ruined my dress! My only dress!'

'Oh hell, it'll mend. Come on, Harriet.'

'No. It's the wrong time of the month.' 'She stood there tempting him, one full breast swinging, her hair tumbling down, this woman that he slaved for night and day, and she denied him. His erection was like iron. For a split second he actually considered dragging her down and forcing her. There was a pulse beating in her throat, her eye make-up was smudged. He went across to stand behind her, and nuzzled her neck, pressing himself into her because he couldn't resist. 'Please,' he whispered. 'I'll make it quick.'

'No!' She turned and pushed him, quite forgetting his bad leg. Pain knifed through Jake from heel to scalp.

'You bitch!' His hand went out and caught her viciously on the side of her head.

They made it up because they had to, and after a week Harriet's black eye was hardly noticeable. Jake was very distant, or it might have been that she was still so cold. Sometimes she willed herself to go across and touch him, to tell him that she felt so very strange, but the words were never said, her hands remained at her sides. Drink helped of course. If she had drunk enough she could pretend to enjoy things, even the dinner party. They had candles everywhere to hide the stained walls and they borrowed glasses from the pub. Jake tried to help and got in her way all the time, and Victoria cried as the main course was served. Jake brought her down to be admired and the Commander said, 'You really are amazing, Harriet.'

'She can do anything if she sets her mind to it,' said Jake. 'A very gutsy lady.' And he told the story of one of their storms and how she had said, though she couldn't remember it, 'Really, Jake, do keep out of my way when I'm baling. You're spoiling my rhythm,' when he was trying to plug the hole that was sinking them.

'You're making it up,' she said, blushing. 'And you never admitted we might sink. I'd have died of fright.'

'I don't know how you dared sail with him at all,' said the Commander. 'Even hardened seamen go pale at the thought.'

Harriet studied her wineglass. 'Then they don't know him very well,' she said softly. 'He always looks after people.'

'Madam, you flatter me.' He toasted her.

But he was spending a great deal of time away, sorting out the winches and sails and electronics he wanted for the boat. His men kept things going in his absence, a team of temperamental experts who blossomed under Jake's seemingly ramshackle approach. He let them get on with it while they could, and kicked them if they made a balls of it instead of asking for help. They had his unlimited attention, while Harriet, so unresponsive, had less and less.

Chapter Twenty

A letter came from Natalie during one of his trips away.

> 'Dear both,
> 'I'm at a bit of a loose end at the moment what with one thing and another (no comments please, Jake!) and I wondered if I might take you up on your kind offer and come and stay for a while? Don't worry, I'm not going to be a permanent fixture! It's just till I sort myself out.
> 'As you can probably guess Carl and I discovered we weren't made for each other (the woman made for him has poison fangs) and I feel in need of a bolthole just now. Also I'm just longing to see Victoria again! What a sweet little kid. If I don't hear that you've all gone down with plague I shall be with you on the 21st. Love and kisses, Natalie.'

Harriet blenched. The 21st was two days away. What would luxury-loving Natalie think of their tumbledown home with damp making scenic patterns in the spare room? What would Jake say, and Mac, who hated the pub and would love to move in with them? She went and looked at herself in the little mirror above the sink. Lank, dull brown hair unrelieved by any hairdresser, unmade-up face, lines, broken nails. Panicked, she rushed out to the shops, buying a cheap home hair colour and an even cheaper nylon T-shirt that she imagined would rejuvenate her wardrobe. The colourant turned her hair red, the T-shirt was see-through and too short. Jake would say she looked like a whore, she thought dismally, and not even an expensive one. She gulped. Prostitution was not something which one discussed, even metaphorically, in Natalie's presence even though she herself was honest enough about it. Except when she was blaming Jake.

He returned two hours before Natalie. 'Hair looks – nice,' he said feebly, because he knew she would cry if he told the truth.

'Don't pretend. Natalie's coming.'

'Oh, Christ, she isn't! Why couldn't you put her off?'

'Because she only gave me two days' notice, and no address. I'm not too good at smoke signals.'

Weary from travelling and desperate for some comfort, Jake strove for patience. 'All right, all right. Any chance of a cup of tea?'

'What? Oh, I'll put the kettle on.' But she flapped past it, taking some flowers up to the spare room, so Jake hauled himself to his feet and did it himself. Victoria was in her chair, gurgling at him, and for a while he gurgled back. He really should spend more time with her, he thought.

Harriet rushed back in. 'There are a dozen messages for you. Mac says there's a research paper come in about the new material for masts, hinting at deterioration under stress. Apparently you can tell there's something wrong when the sails fall down. He's twitching.'

'I'll bet he is, I read that paper weeks ago. I've rigged it to keep the stress manageable, but I think we have to accept new masts before the old one looks any the worse for wear, especially for Southern Ocean stuff. The owner won't like it, of course. I'll have thought of something better for the next boat.' He sat back in his chair and closed his eyes, rubbing at the almost permanent creases above his nose.

'I need some more money,' said Harriet tensely. 'I can't manage with Natalie coming.'

'Then go and draw it out! You don't have to ask me before you buy loo cleaner.'

'No.' The kettle was boiling and she made the tea. She felt panicky and sick; her heart raced and her skin was damp and she didn't know why. Trying to slow her breathing she handed Jake his mug and sipped feverishly at her own.

Natalie arrived in a taxi, awash with presents and admiration. 'What a simply cute little place you have here! All this olde worlde charm, just look at that rickety old door. Harriet, you don't cook on that thing, do you? I'd be just terrified! Well, Jake, are you going to let me take a peek at your boat or is it so, so secret?'

He eyed her tall, relentlessly slender body. 'You're thinner.'

She grimaced. 'Don't worry, I intend to put some on. Carl put me off my food. Kept throwing up all over me, much better than a diet.'

'I'm sorry I didn't meet him, he sounds a ball of fun,' said Jake. 'Hang on, I'll take your bags up.'

Natalie put a long hand on his shoulder. 'Honey, I never let the disabled carry bags for me. Are you stupid or what, putting up with that leg? It's far worse than before, can't they do something?'

'He won't ask,' said Harriet. 'Says he hasn't the time.'

'And I haven't so you can both give up nagging,' said Jake, and determinedly picked up Natalie's bags, making it up the narrow stairs by willpower alone.

Natalie raised her eyebrows at Harriet. 'Sheesh. He sure is stubborn. You OK, sweetheart? You don't look well either.'

Harriet tried to smile but it slipped. 'It's just the weather. And Jake's leg, and him working so hard.'

'It isn't any of that, is it?' said Natalie.

'Of course it is. We're all right.' She started to clatter dishes, talking rubbish in a high, unnatural voice.

For the first week Natalie's presence was an unbearable strain. Jake was at the shed most of the time, and Harriet was left maintaining an image of happiness and good humour on inadequate resources. There was far too much time to talk, and whereas hours could be spent listening to Natalie's hilarious accounts of Carl's perversions, that still left many hours in which she could ask questions of Harriet. The weather was still very warm, and one afternoon Natalie decided she, Harriet and Victoria would go on a picnic, through a field of cows to a recently cut hay meadow. She dressed for it in skimpy cheesecloth and a wide straw hat, while Harriet wore her old skirt and the nylon T-shirt.

'Why do you buy Victoria such nice things when you won't buy anything for yourself?' asked Natalie, tying the ribbons of Victoria's sunbonnet, that matched her printed dress so sweetly.

'We can't afford it yet.'

'I bet you could. I heard Jake tell you to buy what you need.'

'I never go anywhere, I don't need clothes.'

Natalie shrugged.

They set out on the picnic rather grimly, as something that should be enjoyable but seemed likely to fall short of pleasure. But it soothed Harriet to walk through the fields, listening to the cows tearing damp grass, and to a snipe warbling, and to Victoria whispering 'moo, moo' to herself. The buggy kept getting stuck and they struggled with it, finally abandoning it in the hedge and carrying Victoria into the hayfield without her personal transport. Both women were hot and sticky. They spread out a blanket and sat down to open a bottle of wine.

'Now,' said Natalie contentedly, 'there isn't anything we need do but talk.'

'Hmmmm.' Harriet gazed nervously across the fields. 'We could see what's over there.'

'Drink your wine. You're not happy, are you? Not at all?'

Huge, rather frightened eyes met hers. 'Of course I am. I've got Jake and Victoria. Of course I'm happy.'

'Except Jake's always busy. And you don't like it when he touches you.'

Harriet gripped her glass and said grittily, 'Of course I like it. I love Jake, I love him very much. It isn't him – I don't know what it is! Oh, Natalie, sometimes I think I want to kill myself!' Despite the warmth of the day she was cold; despite the peace around them she was panic-stricken. 'I'm going mad,' she whispered, clutching at her hair. 'I'm going to go mad and then they'll put me away and Victoria won't have her mummy and Jake will find someone else and – '

'And I think it's time you saw a doctor,' said Natalie. 'You've got post-natal depression, clearest case I ever saw. Came on after the baby, didn't it? Everything going for you, nothing right. What's the sex really like? Jake was always one hell of a lover.'

Harriet sobbed. These days she dreaded him touching her. 'It doesn't matter what he does, I don't feel anything.'

'And he's getting browned off because the leg's hurting and he's not getting it and you're always down in the dumps. Honey, count yourself lucky Auntie Natalie is here to help you. By the way, you're drinking too much. You even drink more than me.'

Harriet cuddled her wineglass protectively. If it wasn't for the drink she would have killed herself. 'No, I don't. It's only mild things anyway.'

'Mild it may be, a lot it certainly is. Now, let's enjoy this picnic. I'll tell you what Carl used to do with a cucumber, you'll curl up I promise! Then we'll go back and trot down to see the doctor. And tomorrow we'll buy you a few things and in a few weeks' time you'll be your old self again, as single-minded as an express train.'

'I'm not single-minded. Where did you get that idea?' She was weeping quietly, and the relief in tears was exquisite.

'You ask Jake. You set your mind to something, you do it. Like boats, or sorting out the house, or being a good mom. Now you're so taken up with what's inside your head you haven't got time for any of it. You and Jake are both as lonely as shit, you know that?'

Of course Harriet knew, she had known it for months, but walled up inside herself there had been nothing she could do. And suddenly there was Natalie to take charge and tell her what to do and how to do it. They walked back to the cottage, Harriet crying quietly, Natalie exuberant on good deeds and psychoanalysis.

While Harriet went to wash her face she took Victoria and barged into the shed.

'Get out of here, woman!' Mac was poring over a drawing. Behind him loomed the hull of the boat, vast and strange.

'Someone's got to mind the kid, I'm taking Harriet to the doctor.'

'What for?' Jake leaned down from the deck, his face wary, 'Is she ill?'

''Course she's ill, depressed as hell. Who's going to look after this little treasure?' She bounced the baby and the child crowed. Natalie grinned, vibrant, beautiful, tossing her hair and laughing up at Jake like a witch, he thought.

He climbed down awkwardly. 'Give her to me. I'd better come and talk to Harriet.'

'Oh, no you don't. She's made herself worse trying to kid you she's OK, let her cry it out. I'll tell you what the doc says later.'

Jake took the child and watched as Natalie ran lightly to the door. 'See you,' she called.

'Yes. Thanks.' He caught Mac's eye and tried to grin. 'Harriet's been so bloody odd recently – '

'I wondered what was getting to you. That why you won't get the leg done?'

Jake grimaced. 'Partly. Couldn't leave her that long, not in the state she's been in. I thought she'd come out of it but it's got worse if anything. Did I tell you they said if the pins didn't take they'd have to cut it off?' He made a chopping gesture across his thigh.

'Aye. Well. Stands to reason you'll put up with it, doesn't it?' Mac shook his head as if trying to shake the thought out.

Suddenly Jake laughed. 'No it doesn't, it's just bloody cowardice. I'll go and see about it, there may be something they can do.'

'I don't trust the buggers, they're too free with the knife!'

'Well, you can stand guard over me and make sure they don't chop off anything they shouldn't.'

Mac was a delicate shade of green. He never could stand anything to do with doctors or blood. He was known to faint during injections, even beforehand if he watched them filling the syringe. Jake occupied himself with fruitless speculation. Suppose Harriet's real problem was him? Suppose she was only putting up with him because of Victoria? His eyes smarted suddenly and he held the baby tight. She smacked a pudgy hand into his face. 'Bruiser. Come on, let's find you something to play with.'

He was waiting in the cottage when the girls came back. Harriet barely met his eye. 'Has she been good?'

'Yes, super. She's asleep. What did the doctor say?'

'She should have gone months ago,' declared Natalie. 'He was real cross with her. She's got some vitamins and a hormone pill of some kind, and a sedative. He says she'll sleep for three days and wake up hunkydory!'

Harriet sat dripping tears, like some figure in a tragedy. 'I won't take the sedative, I don't need sleep. I'm better getting on.'

'If he gave it to you, then you take it,' said Jake gently. 'We can look after Victoria. We just want you well, love.'

'And if this doesn't work she's got to go into hospital,' said Natalie flatly. 'So she takes it.'

Harriet moaned and twisted her fingers in her hair. When Jake tried to put his arm round her, she pulled away.

Jake and Natalie sat in the kitchen. Harriet was asleep upstairs, the dead sleep of the drugged. Moths tapped on the window, lured from the summer night by the lamps inside.

'I want to thank you,' said Jake. 'It was really kind. You see how she is with me, I can't get to her.'

'She doesn't mean to hurt you. She's real fond of you.' Natalie leaned back in her chair, her cheesecloth dress falling like gossamer from her extended legs.

'I try so hard to do my best for her. And she never – she never seems to forgive me. I left her on that island and I know she still resents it. I work my rocks off for her and she hardly seems to notice. I don't know what else I can do.' He took a gulp of his whisky, wondering why on earth he was saying this to Natalie.

'She's ill. She doesn't mean it.' Somehow her hand had reached towards him and was stroking his arm, up and down, so gently and softly.

'We don't even make love any more. I can't bear her lying there waiting for it to be over, I can't bear asking her to do something she doesn't want to do because I need the satisfaction. And I do need it. I need it a lot.'

'That makes two of us.'

In a gesture almost of desperation he reached out and put his hand hard on her thigh. Natalie chuckled deep in her throat. 'I know what you need and Harriet won't know, so there's no harm done. I'll fuck you, lover boy, like you've never been fucked before. You can stick that great big thing of yours right where you like, because I need you too.' She lifted her skirt. She was naked beneath it, her long thin thighs already shining with moisture. She touched herself, extending her damp fingers to his lips.

He heaved himself up on his good leg, wrenching at the zip of his jeans. Natalie stood there, laughing. She kept on laughing as he rammed himself against her, into her. She laughed until her laughter tangled itself into a scream then, like a wilting flower, she drooped against his shoulder.

'Oh God,' said Jake harshly. 'Don't tell Harriet.'

'She won't ever know,' said Natalie. When he withdrew from her she lay on the sofa and waited. 'Does she still turn you on,' she asked lazily. 'Do you make her bounce on top of you, swinging those great tits?'

'Harriet's been ill, I don't want to discuss her. You got what you wanted.' He picked up some papers and started studying them. To make love with Natalie and talk about Harriet left a foul taste in his mouth.

Natalie got up and stood in front of him. 'Jake,' she said pleadingly. 'You know me, Jake, once is never enough. You know what I like.' She stood astride his knees, her skirt lifted, pubic hair an inch from his face. He took hold of her narrow bottom, feeling her trembled with arrant desire.

'You're getting worse,' he said thoughtfully.

'I know, I know! Just do it to me, will you? I haven't had enough in three months, and Harriet's asleep and we won't ever tell her.'

He said viciously: 'Will you stop talking about Harriet? If you'll shut up about her then I'll be very, very glad you came to stay.' He leaned half an inch forward and took her soft folds in his mouth, brushing the firm tip of her with his tongue. She came at once, violently, bucking against his hands, and he nipped her in annoyance.

'Don't Jake!' She writhed, suddenly pathetic. 'I'm sorry. Go on, sit back and let me.' He released her and she knelt before him, starting to suck his already erect penis. He watched her dispassionately, wondering why he was doing this, why he should be betraying Harriet, when she was sick, for a transitory pleasure. Oh, but Natalie was a technician, no doubt about that, prolonging this expertly. It was exquisite. How long was it since he'd felt this much release, without the worry and the guilt that went with loving Harriet? He would never hurt Harriet, he told himself, feeling pressure swelling within him. but he had to have this!

In the three days that Harriet remained upstairs, either asleep or barely awake, Jake and Natalie sated themselves. There was little affection just a single-minded determination from each that the other should give them what they wanted. If I do this to you, you must do this to me, they bargained, and between bouts were as casual and detached as ever. Jake sat with Harriet for hours in the evenings, and when she woke, as she did sometimes, briefly, he would say: 'Hi. You OK?'

She sighed. 'Oh, yes. Better. Are you all managing?'

'Yes. I miss you. Get better, lovey.'

Then he would go downstairs, drink some cocoa and screw Natalie over the kitchen table. After Harriet's last pill she said to him, 'We'll have to be careful tomorrow.'

'This is the end. My last fling before I settle down to being faithful. Start looking for somewhere else, will you?'

She scratched the back of her neck. Her mouth went slack when she wanted sex, he noticed. In public she hid it with a smile. 'You don't mean that.'

'Sorry, love. I do.'

Natalie stamped and turned her back. 'Shit, shit, shit.' She was in tears, he realised suddenly.

'Oh, come on,' he complained. 'You can't pretend we had anything going.'

'I don't.' She sniffed stoically. 'But it keeps happening to me, you see. I get too much for a man, even when I go freelance while he's away. After a while stuffing Natalie's a real chore, they can't wait to get back to their wives and their slippers. And I'm left – high and dry. A little older, a little sadder, a lot more miles on the clock. Some kid the other day insisted he wore a condom in case he caught something! What am I going to do, Jake? I take them poorer, I take them rougher, sometimes I even get beat up. So where do I go from here?'

'Give it up. Take it in normal doses, like the rest of us.'

'Like you, eh? You and abstinence have fallen out, my friend. What I need is some cash, then I can buy a house or something. You going to lend it me?'

'Haven't got it. I'll think of you if I'm ever flush, though.' He gave her narrow bottom a pat, his mind already on the papers he had to study that evening. Sex always did refresh him.'

'Jesus, the money I've got through in my time.' She watched the back of his head. He was clearly paying her no attention. She sighed.

Chapter Twenty-One

Harriet felt so much better. She lay in bed, staring at the stained ceiling and in place of the grey fog that had lodged in her mind for so long there was a gentle pink cloud. Nothing seemed bleak any more, when before everything had. She had Jake and he loved her, she had Victoria and she was perfect, the most perfect baby that ever was. There was money, not a lot but enough, and even a good friend in Natalie. I shall get a dog, she thought. That will be fun.

Stretching her arms above her head she studied them. Really she was in better shape than Natalie nowadays. Naturally plump women who managed to keep within bounds never became gaunt and scrawny. Not that Natalie was – yet. But she was getting there. Harriet allowed herself a small feeling of triumph. Today she would wash her hair four times and reduce the red to an acceptable tawny. Why was it she made such mistakes with her hair? How good it would be to put herself in the hands of an expensive hairdresser and have someone else tackle the problem. As it was she would do what she could, and at least buy some decent jeans and a couple of cotton tops. After that she would cook something delicious for dear, dear Jake who had put up with so much, and she would scrub the kitchen floor.

What a pity she couldn't go out and spend a fortune on clothes, she thought regretfully. She had always felt somehow that she had the capacity for great style, but had been thwarted from displaying it. Sometimes she could look stunning; too often she did not. In future she would patronise jumble sales or something, and look good on no money.

Jake came in, looking grim. When he saw her his face relaxed into his rare, expansive smile. 'Oh my, you do look different. You look like my Harriet.'

'I feel like her again, too. I must get up!' She began to swing her legs out of bed but he caught her.

'No, you don't, you take it easy. I'm not having you ill again.'

'But I really am better. Hungry, though.'

'Not surprised, you've only had the odd bowl of soup.' He sat on the bed, looking at her.

She reached up and touched his lips with her fingers. 'You're so good to me,' she said softly. His face crumpled and he put his hand over his eyes. 'Don't, don't!' She tried to hold his shoulders, where the muscle rolled in a wide band, but she couldn't reach. He had the shoulders of a man many inches taller.

'I'm so sorry for what I've done to you,' he said thickly.

She laughed, such a gentle, happy sound. 'You haven't done anything.'

The roses in the garden were tangled into a hedge, and the blooms hung heavily amidst the brambles. Harriet cut several, noting that already petals were starting to fall, the grass was losing its freshness, the leaves on the trees looking weary and dull. Late summer, she thought, and picked an early blackberry, still tart but hinting at ripeness.

The baby was playing on the small patch of grass they had cut, a weedy lump of turf in all truth. Next year they would have a paddling pool and a sandpit and a smooth green lawn, Harriet determined, and the year after that a climbing frame and perhaps – one day – another baby. The days stretched ahead, no longer menacing but full of promise of things to come.

Dinner was almost ready, a chicken casserole with new potatoes and sugar peas. Jake was over at the shed, though everyone else had gone home, and Natalie – where was Natalie? Harriet picked up Victoria, who was at last sleepy, and went upstairs to put her in her cot. For once the child settled down, although usually she grizzled for ten minutes. Harriet seized her chance and crept downstairs, out into the garden and across to the shed.

It was very quiet. The door slid open with its usual oiled stealth, so Jake was still inside. He always locked up carefully at night. Above her loomed the hull, so much larger than it would seem when afloat. Another month and they would be finished in here, and would be launching and doing work on the rigging and inside. Money in their pockets, the end of scrimping and scraping, with more orders pending and Jake getting choosy about the ones he would accept, all even before the boat had shown her paces. How good it would be to have something to spend for once, not to worry about the price of biscuits and whether they could afford beef. She heard voices muffled by the hull, and stepped carefully round the supports and wires and struts towards them. Jake and Natalie. She opened her mouth to call – and then closed it again.

'Come on, lover boy,' Natalie was saying in a low, passionate voice. 'You know you want to do it, unless that's a baseball bat in your pants. She won't know. You owe me, you bastard.'

'Just leave it, will you?' Jake said harshly. 'She's better now and I want no more of this. I won't say I didn't enjoy it but it's over.'

'You getting it from her?' She was panting rhythmically.

'You know I won't rush her.'

'Well then – if you want to take it gently – you'd better take it rougher somewhere else.'

Fiery rage and icy pain met in Harriet's gut. But Jake would stop her, she knew he would. He couldn't, he wouldn't – had he?

'Oh, to hell with it,' he said, laughing. 'Bend over the trestle, you hot bitch.'

Leaning cautiously round the hull, she saw them. Natalie naked but for an open blouse, her skirt a circle on the floor, leaning over a trestle while Jake pierced her from behind. His penis was huge and dark. He held Natalie's thighs and stood straight up while he did it. He was grinning. Natalie's pants and groans quickened. Suddenly she threw back her head, arched her back down and convulsed. Businesslike, Jake thrust twice more and came also. He withdrew, wiping his hands on his trousers.

'Right, I'll just finish up here then I'll be in. Tell Harriet I'll be ten minutes.'

'OK. You ought to get some heat in this place, it's real cold.'

Heart pounding, Harriet picked her way back to the door. She couldn't bear them to know she had seen. The humiliation would then have been total. How could they, how could they – pretending on the one hand to care about her, and then doing that? They were both so terribly casual. Was it she who attached too much importance to it? Jake would probably say it was her fault for getting ill. How dare he? Just – how dare he? She was consumed by cold, murderous rage.

But when they came in, first Natalie then Jake, neither giving any indication that they felt the least trace of guilt, she met them with a smile. 'You two must be tired. Have some dinner.'

'Thanks, love. It smells fantastic.' He put his hand on her waist and kissed her neck. It was all she could do not to stick him with her knife.

'And you, Natalie. What have you been doing this afternoon?'

'Oh, this and that. I saw the breadman. He's going to leave the extra loaf tomorrow. How's about we go shopping in the morning?'

'Rain's forecast actually. Let's see, shall we?'

Natalie and Jake glanced at one another. She was very brittle and she smiled too much. Was she about to suffer a relapse?

'Why don't we go out for a drink later?' said Jake. 'Natalie can babysit.'

'No thanks' said Harriet, wide-eyed and breathy. 'I think I'll have an early night.'

While Jake slept restlessly beside her, his leg hurting, as he deserved, Harriet lay wide awake and plotted. She would have her revenge on him, by God she would. Never had she had more cause. She had sold her picture to give him his yard, she had used her body to give him his baby. Let him manage without her then, let him see how it was without her, and if he put that bitch Natalie in her place she'd come back and stab her through the heart! The palms of her hands were hurting. She glanced down and saw that she was driving her nails deep into the flesh.

In the morning Harriet was heavy-eyed. 'Have an easy day, love,' said Jake. 'Don't cook, I'll get fish and chips tonight.'

'All right,' she said meekly.

He touched his lips to her forehead. 'I hate to see you down. What can I do to make you happy?'

'Nothing,' she said, with utter truth, and pulled away. Jake followed her with his eyes. That was the first genuine comment of the morning, and it had seared. Surely she couldn't know? Not for the first time, he cursed himself, for the desire that drove him, for the ease with which he gave in to it. At the time he would die rather than go without something for which a moment later he wouldn't stretch out his hand.

'I'm going to ask Natalie to go today,' he said.

Harriet turned and gave him a withering stare.

When Jake had gone to the shed and still before Natalie was up, Harriet put together her own things and Victoria's, cramming them into one big holdall. Then she took the joint account cheque book and slid it into the pocket of her anorak, mentally reviewing the times of the ferries as she did so. She wanted to be well gone before lunch. Moving automatically she put out toast crumbs on the windowsill for the blackbirds that came every day, spread out the teatowel to dry, swept the leaves and grass off the flagged floor. They would think she had just gone shopping.

A wall of grief rose up in front of her as she pulled the front door shut. It hung in the air, threatening to fall, and she stood taking deep, calming breaths. This house had never been her own, she had never liked it. She was not to grieve for happiness that had never been, nor even for what might have been. She would remember the wrong done her, she would never let herself forget. Pushing the baby buggy decisively, the holdall balanced on the handles, she marched off across the field.

The man at the bank was clearly bewildered. 'You want to withdraw ten thousand pounds? Mrs. Jakes, that will take the account right to the limit of your husband's credit. I'm not sure I think this is wise.'

'I want all of it. Every penny.'

'We do usually expect notice of large withdrawals – '

'I'm sure you've got that much.'

'Yes. Well. If you would just wait a few moments.' He disappeared into another room. Harriet's heart began to thud. Suppose he rang Jake? But it was her money, it had always been hers, she was owed it and she would have it!

At the shed, Jake answered the telephone with his usual snapped 'Yes?' As he listened his face grew very still. The colour drained away to leave a mask of deadwhite skin. 'I understand,' he said huskily after a time. 'That is quite in order. Yes, I want you to give her the money. I know, I know. I'm not quite that much of a fool! I can't talk about it now. You can do what you like with the bloody loan, but give her the money, damn you!' He rammed the phone down and stood, staring at nothing.

'What the hell's the matter with you?' complained Mac, trying to get round him to pick up a file.

'I've got to go out,' said Jake in the same husky voice. 'Something's happened – God help me for a bloody fool!' He went out, hitting his shoulder on the doorpost, stumbling like a man drunk or sick or dying.

She sat in the open air, watching the ferry steaming across the water towards her. In half an hour she would be gone, and it was leaving that mattered, not where she was headed. The money was a thick wad in the pocket of her coat. Strangely, she didn't even care if it was stolen, all that mattered was that Jake should know how angry she was. Someone came and sat beside her, she didn't look at them. 'Dad, Dad,' said Victoria.

'You were in the shed last night,' he said.

'Yes.'

'I've already told her to go.'

'Bit late, if you ask me. Did the bank ring you?'

'Yes. The money's yours, you can do what you like with it. But I wanted to explain. And to apologise.'

She turned and stared at him. 'I don't think saying sorry's going to help. You were doing it all the time I was sick, weren't you?'

'Yes. As often as we could manage it. And the thing that makes me most ashamed is that I don't give a shit about Natalie, and I do about you. I wanted you to know that.'

'Funny way of showing it.' Now she was crying, and she had wanted most of all to avoid that. She dashed at the tears furiously. 'Why did you do it?' she wailed. 'You didn't have to!'

Wretched, he verged on anger. 'But I did! You don't know, you just don't know – try and see it from my side, love. Building a boat is OK, I don't mind it. When you've done up your leg and you've got a wife and kid to support, it's a good way to earn a living. But every day's pretty much the same, the biggest excitement is when someone reads the plan wrong. It's bloody tame, Harriet! And I thought – and I think – I'm going to lose this leg.' He sighed. It sounded so pitiable, so unworthy. 'It was a fling. Before I get old, before I get crippled, before I'm so tired and grey I can't get it up any more. It won't happen again. If I've got you in my bed, I don't need Natalie.'

'You won't have me in your bed,' said Harriet flatly. 'I couldn't bear it, not after I'd seen you inside her. I'll never get it out of my head.'

'Of course you will!' He put his hand on her arm and she struck it off, hard. 'Don't touch me! Go and paw Natalie, get your thrills there. I'm just dull, plain Harriet who'll put up with anything. You don't mind having me and Victoria around, but you don't want us! You just hate losing things. We're like that sodding boat, *Dashing Away*. You'd rather have saved that hulk then stay with me. You put everything before me, everything!'

'I knew you hadn't forgotten that. However often I say I didn't mean to go, you'll always think I did. You used to think about that when we were making love. Didn't you?'

She licked stiff lips. 'Yes. And about being alone when I had your baby. And about – things the old man did to me. I want to get my own back!'

'Oh, God.' Jake screwed his eyes up against tears. The ferry was docking, the air filled with a cacophony of car engines and winches. 'You're going to lose out, too,' he said thickly, fighting for control. 'You're going to be so bloody miserable.'

'It's better than staying and feeling so second-rate.'

'You, second-rate? When I first saw you I thought you were the daughter of a millionaire! You've got more looks and more guts than any woman deserves, but you're so fucking stubborn! Why not lose a bit of pride – and win a lot of love?'

She stood up, putting Victoria on her hip. 'Because I don't think your love is worth very much. Do you want the money back? I don't need a lot.' She folded the pushchair expertly.

'Of course I don't want it! You can have everything. I'll put it all in your name, I'll start with nothing, but please – Harriet. Don't – I can't face it without you.' His hands were clenched in his pockets, his face averted. She thought, All his friends can see him, they will all see his pain. How easy it would be to go home now, to the tidy kitchen and the blackbirds and the roses in need of pruning. And the room smelling of Natalie. She saw him again, grinning above another woman's writhing body.

'I've got to go,' she said in a tight, choked voice. 'Say goodbye to Victoria.'

'Just tell me where you're going. I'll come and see you, I won't – Harriet, please! On that island, *you* left me then. I told you I couldn't hold the boat there. Just tell me – write and say.'

She stood a yard away, staring at him, her hair a tangled cloud round a dead white face. He knew her so well, knew the rage that held her up. There was no more to be said. His hands unclenched. He was suddenly aware of his leg again.

'Goodbye, Jake.' He watched her struggling on to the boat, rejecting an offer of help as if it were an insult. What would happen to her when the anger ebbed and she found herself, alone, in a strange and hostile place? Why did she always need to hurt herself? She was on the deck, watching him far below. The baby lifted a pudgy hand and waved, calling 'bye bye' into the air. He couldn't bear another minute. Choking back sobs he staggered to the pick-up.

Mac heard the crash as the pick-up returned. A spasm crossed his face.

'Harriet's cloche?' he said matter-of-factly as Jake stormed in.

'No. The fucking front door. And I'll see the end of this little lot, too.'

Under the amazed gaze of Mac and two workmen, he seized a lump of iron and hammered it against the side of the hull. Built to withstand enormous pressure, it resolutely failed to do more than dent slightly. 'Shit,' said Jake, and proceeded to knock the supports away.

'What are you doing, man?' asked Mac, his voice shaking. 'Are you out of your head?'

'If I am it's where I'm staying. This useless barge is going to end its days right here. I'll not see it launched, it's a hell-ship!' He clouted one of the trestles and the whole hull lurched. The men gathered, not sure he could mean it, waiting to see the joke.

'Jake – think a little. Is it Harriet? The wee girlie?' Mac skirted out of range of the whirling piece of iron, knowing too well that Jake in a rage was capable of anything. And this was more than rage. It was grief and pain and self-loathing.

'Don't do it, guv. I spent hours on that boat,' ventured one of the youngsters, who went to sleep at night imagining her beating through hurricanes.

Jake turned on him, brandishing his weapon. 'Hours. *You* spent hours. I've been heading here all my life. I've put everything I ever knew into this boat, and there it sits, all that I'm worth, waiting to prove itself. I'll not leave here till it's matchwood.'

The youngster stepped back, Mac edged forward. 'We'll not let you. It's our boat, too.'

'Like hell it is! You going to make with the readies when the bank calls in the loan? Someone's going to have to.'

'Boat's damn nigh finished, we get paid in four weeks. Leave it, Jakey. Smashing it won't cure anything. Let's talk to Harriet.'

Jake swung round on him. 'Harriet has left me. Get out of my way.'

'Grab him, boys,' said Mac urgently, but Jake shook off tentative hands and swung again at the trestles, this time dislodging one. The great hull lurched downwards.

'It'll come down on you, man!' Mac retreated in sudden fear. The hull was swaying horribly.

'I bloody hope so,' said Jake. Another blow and the boat was teetering, barely balanced. The men started to shout, 'Get out of it, guv, she'll kill you!' Jake laughed and stood still, looking up at his creation as it rocked above him. 'Come on, baby,' he coaxed, and with that the vessel fell. He had a moment in which he felt exquisite relief because unbearable pain was to be crushed out of him.

In that second of inattention, Mac's hand closed on his collar, heaving him backwards with a strength born of terror. The boat did not have far to fall. It lay on its side, a jumble of equipment clattering down around it, two men sprawled amidst ropes. A gas cylinder had fallen from inside the boat and was rolling to and fro next to them.

'Bloody idiot,' said Jake. 'You always think you know bloody best.'

'I know when you've gone barmy. We'll have to get a crane in here to get her up again.' Mac was brushing dust out of his hair. The men were standing together, muttering and staring at them. A brief surge of irritation rose up in Mac. 'Why can't you ever see a thing through? Why do you always smash it?'

Still lying on the shed floor, Jake rolled his cheek in the mixture of paint and grease that coated it. 'I'd do it different if I could.'

'Oh, aye. It's your own fault she's gone. All that trouble to get hold of her, a girl like that, a clever girl, a beauty. I thought you'd got some sense for once. But I don't even have to guess what happened, because it's always the bloody same. Harriet's lucky to be rid of you.'

'Do you think I don't know that?'

Again his cheek rolled, and Mac snapped, 'You can get up, can't you?'

Speaking in tones of controlled agony, Jake said, 'Not really, no. As a matter of fact there's a bit of bone and a lump of metal sticking out of my thigh.'

Chapter Twenty-Two

The market town of Markham is set at the foot of the downs, some few miles from the coast. It boasts a market square and many listed buildings, nowadays housing craft or antique shops catering for summer visitors. To the north is the new part of the town, damaged by bombs in the war and rebuilt to a uniform ugliness, but to the west are ranks of Edwardian terraces. It was here that Harriet trudged, looking for a flat or a room. Nobody wanted children.

The day was growing chill. Everywhere people were headed homeward, lamps were being lit, food cooked. From one house ran two little girls in Brownie uniform. Never in her life had Harriet felt so excluded. The small hotel where she had passed the previous two nights was neither cheap nor particularly welcoming, accommodating Victoria by dint of giving them the worst room on the top floor, the table without a view in the dining room, the tablecloth with holes in. The room was airless yet if she opened the window Victoria was in danger of falling out. She dared not plug in the electric kettle that was the only concession to comfort because it was perched precariously on the dressing table, a scant two inches above Victoria's head. Nights there depressed her spirits so acutely that she pursued a place of her own with single-minded zeal.

She was tired now and close to the river, sliding quietly past in the dusk. She sat on a seat for a moment, watching the ducks float rapidly downstream with the tide, quacking occasionally. Soon they would beat back to safer waters where they would live in peaceful domesticity far from the vagaries of the ocean. Some people were ducks and some weren't, she supposed. It was as well to know where you stood.

Now that she was calmer, she wondered at her own stupidity. Jake wasn't a man who could live without excitement, and she had been very unexciting. She thought about Natalie. It was hard to know whether you could attach blame to someone who acted as they always did, as you should have known that they would. Natalie's kindness disarmed suspicion and made you assume what you knew to be untrue. Her sexual needs were never other than paramount. Strange the way everybody expected fidelity in their partner, but not in themselves. What I do is understandable, what you do is unforgivable. Suddenly Harriet was glad to be out of it. She was finished with sex, she wouldn't swim in those waters again. If she denied the appetite it would wither away, and then she could be happy, on her own, with Victoria.

She got to her feet, resolving to visit her two last addresses before going back to the dubious welcome of the hotel. 6 Lincoln Villas was the next. The man at the tourist office had said it was usually a student rooming house but she might strike lucky. Spurred on by the chill of an English summer's evening, she bustled through the streets.

Her knock was answered by a large grey-haired lady wearing orange trousers and beads. 'Enter, enter, what a charming child! Do say you want a room. I can tell from your face, that tragic courage. All that we ask is that you pay, pay, and pay again. Twenty-five pounds a week, OK?'

'I wonder if I could have a look at it?' Harriet was wrong-footed by the welcome. Everyone else had been so dubious, so regretful, so many light years beyond persuasion. They had seen them come and seen them go and they hated tenants, especially single girls with children.

'Call me Iris,' declared the grey-haired lady. 'Dodie! Dodie! Where's the key to upstairs?' She flung the door to behind Harriet and disappeared into her own room, carolling for the unknown Dodie.

Harriet surveyed the hall. It was in dire need of decoration, but there were bunches of dried flowers here and there and wind bells hung over the stairs, just where they would hit you in the face. A young man with acne bounded down and avoided the bells with practised ease. 'Hi.' He lounged off into the street, leaving Harriet to close the door.

Iris reappeared, followed by Dodie, smaller, plumper, also wearing beads but holding a key. 'We do so love babies!' she declared. 'Don't we, Iris?'

'Each and every one,' Iris declared. 'Sometimes we go and drool at the mother and baby clinic. There is a little black one in a pink bonnet that would make an angel weep. What a treasure this one is.' She plucked Victoria out of her pushchair and bore her up the stairs. Harriet followed, aware of a feeling of slight panic. Was she in the clutches of babysnatchers?

They passed up four flights of increasingly dingy stairs. There was a smell of damp and something indefinable, as in the cottage but sweeter. But the room was huge, an amalgam of several boxrooms by the look of it. A double bed, a junkshop wardrobe, several sagging armchairs and a table still left ample space.

'We have a cot that can go in the alcove,' tempted Dodie.

'You have your own gas ring. The bathroom is on the next floor, but that does mean a certain amount of privacy – no-one else up here, you see.'

'Yes. Yes.' Harriet gathered her courage. 'It looks very nice. I'll take it.'

'Thank goodness!' said Dodie, beaming.

'The tea leaves said it would be a good day,' declared Iris. 'You can pay can't you? One hates to be mercenary, of course.'

'Shall I give you a week in advance?'

They made only the most token resistance.

Harriet moved in first thing the next day, bustling around buying bits of food and a few posters to cover patches on the wallpaper. She was determined not to squander her money, since there was no way of knowing where more might come from. All at once she felt very tired. Iris and Dodie were minding Victoria while she got organised, and she slumped on the bed, letting exhaustion wash over her. A few tears trickled from beneath closed eyelids. If Jake were here this would be an adventure, she thought. He could make anything better, just by being there. How she missed him, a stinging sore once again doused in saltwater, first on Corusca, now here. The feeling was the same, only the place was different.

She summoned up all the things that enraged her about him: his short temper, his pig-headedness, his assumption that what he wanted for you was what you must want for yourself. Most of all she pictured again his infidelity. But he was Jake, and that was all one need say. She knew suddenly with utter certitude, that she could never have lived the life they had planned, because he was a flame that scorched whoever came too close. If you could not shine as brightly, you must be consumed. In his life there was Jake, first and always, and although he would love you, in the end there would be nothing much to love. Oddly enough she was sure he did love her, but what he loved in her was what he was steadily eradicating.

The tears dried to salt stains: her eyes were dry and wide and unblinking. In a moment she would go and fetch Victoria. Tomorrow she would think about what she must do to earn her living. It would be a long time before she wrote to Jake.

* * *

In their youth Iris and Dodie had been dashing and capable, living as lesbians at a time when such things were very daring, championing whales and CND long before causes were fashionable. Times changed and the world fell in step with them for a while, eating brown bread and muesli on the Aldermaston march, singing for peace and plenty and love. A few more whirls in space and the world moved on, to capitalism and growth and a free market economy, to dole queues and riots and black families living in fear on crumbling council estates. Iris and Dodie were left behind. They couldn't hustle in the brash new style; in fact, hustle was one of the words they didn't use. Locked in the slang of a bygone age, trapped by standards that no longer applied, they increasingly found they couldn't cope, they who had always coped. Dodie leant on Iris, and Iris knew what to do. That was as it had always been. Bewilderment didn't fit with their image of themselves and the façade of capability lived on long after its substance was eaten away.

On Harriet's first morning, with the baby grizzling and depression nudging at her elbow, Dodie knocked on the door. 'I brought a few things for Victoria. One can hardly expect to be organised on one's first morning.'

She placed her offerings of muesli and nutlike rolls of bread on the table, then settled herself down in one of the ancient chairs, folding her hands in a strangely nunlike gesture. Harriet smiled uncomfortably. She felt in no state to receive visitors.

'We are so glad you've come,' said Dodie, nodding. 'We've had such unpleasant people recently – the last one was a glue-sniffer, Iris says. One can tolerate the noise, or at least one learns to, but there are other things – ' she shuddered expressively – 'and of course he didn't pay.'

'I suppose you get a lot of that,' said Harriet huskily. Her head ached and she wondered if she was getting a cold.

'I'm afraid we do. Never the people one expects, I might say. Of course, students haven't any money at all nowadays, and one can hardly throw them out on the street when they've got in a muddle, can one? Which is why we're a little tired of students just now.' She patted her hair distractedly.

'Are you in a lot of trouble?' asked Harriet abruptly, unable to prevaricate this morning.

Dropping her voice to a whisper Dodie said, 'I'm afraid we are, dear. Iris says we shall have to sell. We can't keep up the payments and now we're so far behind Mr. Briggs at the bank seems to feel we have no choice. Iris did think about burning the place down, because of course no-one's interested in it, but, my dear, in a terrace? Mr. and

Mrs. Singh live next door. Arson simply isn't on!' She looked to Harriet for confirmation of her view.

'I don't think you should,' she said quickly. 'Anyway, they'd be bound to suspect.'

'Would they? One wonders how. We'd put up a board saying we're selling, but that would mean no new tenants, and besides, everybody wants a survey. My dear, you look a little peaky. Tell me about yourself.'

Harriet gave Victoria one of the rolls and the child gnawed on it thoughtfully. What was she to say? 'I've separated from my husband,' she said finally. 'He gave me some money, so you don't have to worry about the rent. But I must get a job of some sort, because it won't last forever, and I shall go mad if I sit around all day thinking about things – ' She tailed off and stood, hands twirling indecisively.

'If you'd like us to look after Victoria,' said Dodie eagerly, 'we would be so pleased! After all, if you were working and earning then perhaps – one hates to think of money when of course she is treasure in herself – but perhaps – '

Harriet swallowed. 'I'll think about it,' she said stiffly. 'Anyway, won't you want to talk to Iris about it?'

'But we have talked,' said Dodie, rising to her feet. 'We were so lucky to find one another all those years ago, one can never achieve real understanding with a man. They have different priorities in life, one feels. In fact, I have never met a man capable of true unselfishness, whereas it is commonplace amongst women. Do ask if you would like some more muesli, Harriet dear, we make it ourselves. I gather the packets even contain bleach, which is an absolute scandal. Iris and I are very worried about it.'

'I can imagine,' she said wearily.

Dodie was going at last. Harriet sank into the chair her visitor had vacated and pressed her fingers against her forehead. Nothing would happen until she found a job, it was now her most pressing need. If Dodie and Iris were willing to childmind it meant she could look for a day job, instead of being a barmaid or something and paying babysitters. She considered Victoria, staring at her so fixedly that the child began to whimper. Harriet gathered her up, relishing the feel of wispy hair against her cheek, a chubby bottom heavy on her lap. She was never going to be completely alone, this one love would be hers forever.

'You don't need him and neither do I,' she muttered defiantly. 'He didn't need us. If he had, he'd have been different.'

In a small town like Markham jobs were hard to come by. She registered as a typist but failed the test, because it was years since she had typed and she had never been good. That left waitress or barmaid, but the man in the café wanted experience and the man in the pub put his hand on her breast. For a fortnight she became a shop assistant, standing in splendid isolation behind the counter of an old-fashioned haberdasher's that closed after the fortnight having sold up to a do it yourself chain.

'You might have told me,' complained Harriet. 'You could have said it wasn't permanent.'

'You were very good,' said the owner, by way of an apology. But she hadn't been good, she had been bored rigid, so much so that it had been an effort to do even the little that was required of her, and she had skimped the dusting and failed to balance the till.

Next time I will do something interesting, she vowed, and wondered what interested her these days. First her illness and then her parting from Jake had filled up her life to the exclusion of all else. What was it she liked doing? 'Looking at pictures,' she murmured ruefully, because she had always been content in galleries; one of the few pleasures of Corusca had been the superb paintings and nowadays she was something of a judge. On Corusca she had looked at the best and had learned from it, adding experience to the several layers of knowledge she had acquired, through interest, over the years. In the past she had taken her mother round galleries on hot afternoons, and spent the evenings reading about what she had seen. There must be some use for that knowledge, she reasoned. Few people could have lived with as many priceless pictures as she had.

Taking her courage in her hands, she opened the door of Markham's premier art gallery, a tasteful shop in brown and cream full of expensive country scenes and studies of dogs.

'Can I help you?' A rather supercilious enquiry because she was wearing her shopgirl's uniform of navy skirt, white blouse and low heels. The proprietor was in a good tweed jacket enlivened by a purple handkerchief in the top pocket, to show he was an art dealer. He looked middle-aged, bored, contemptuous of those not rich enough to buy his pictures.

Harriet lifted her chin. In her mind the Hawksworth mantle descended on her shoulders. In precise tones she said, 'I am looking for a job. I know a fair amount about art and I should like something a little more challenging than minding a shop. I wondered if you needed anyone, or if you know of anyone who does.'

'Sorry,' said the man flatly. Harriet felt the first burn of irritation.

'I wish you were. I assure you I do know what I'm talking about.'

The man sighed, because she was going to stand her ground and his cup of tea was going cold. 'Which is the fake in this room?' he snapped. 'Point it out to me.'

Harriet glanced around. Her nose wrinkled slightly at the sugary canvases. 'I take it you don't mean those horrible Turner copies? Why do you have them?'

'They sell,' said the man disdainfully, but was no match for Harriet's scorn.

'Oh, yes. There is that, I suppose.'

She went to a misty sailing scene set on a trestle, post-impressionist in feel and execution. It was done in the Pointillist style, dots of colour conveying water, skin, a lighthouse; the beginnings of abstraction without its subsequent loss of purpose. There was something a little heavy about it.

'A good attempt at Signac,' she said crisply. 'Not recent.'

The proprietor raised his eyebrows. 'I congratulate you. The dealer who sold it to me thought it was genuine.'

Harriet gripped the handle of her bag with both hands. 'Is there an opening? I do have to find something quickly.'

The man looked annoyed for a moment, but not at her. 'I do so hate taking people on,' he said crossly. 'They won't go away again when you don't need them.'

'I would,' Harriet assured him. 'I don't really want anything permanent, not that permanent anyway – we could see how it worked out. Couldn't we?' Assurance had flown at the prospect of work. She needed the security of routine. If she hadn't that to cling to then what would there be to keep her sane?

'I'll have to think about it,' said the man cautiously. 'Why don't you come back tomorrow?'

Was this a sly rejection? She looked at him out of the corners of her eyes, a glittering, assessing stare. He straightened his tie and felt a little threatened. 'I assure you I will give it the utmost consideration.'

'I'll come back at ten,' said Harriet, almost challenging him. 'We can talk about it then.'

'By all means.'

He held the door for her, smiling with more warmth than at any time during the interview. As he closed it he resolved to be out at ten tomorrow and let his assistant tell her no. If she hadn't looked at him like that – but still, he wouldn't have taken her on. He knew nothing about her, and as with the Turner copies and the syrupy landscapes that always sold, his habit was playing safe.

Harriet spent the evening convincing herself that it would be all right. He had been impressed with her knowledge, and it was surely no coincidence that he should have shown her a Signac fake, when she had dined opposite the real thing every day on Corusca. In the morning she put on her smartest outfit, a cheap unlined suit bought from a chainstore. Pale blue and without impact, it would lose its body after very few wearings, but if kept for now and then was all right. A nylon blouse and fake gilt earrings went with it, and though she looked very well she had not donned confidence, as she did in expensive clothes. The Harriet that could cope with art dealers and rich men was not a woman that wore nylon blouses.

At ten precisely she opened the door of the shop and stepped inside. During her walk there she had swung from optimism to pessimism and all points in between and was shivering with nerves. Suppose he said no? She had to earn some money. Without an income her ten thousand pounds would melt like snow in summer. The shop was very quiet. After an interval the door from the office opened and a young man came out.

'Oh – yes – are you the lady – ?'

His nerves banished hers. 'I take it the answer is no,' she said tartly. 'Except he hadn't the guts to tell me himself.'

'Er – it was an unavoidable appointment.'

'That he didn't have yesterday. Thank you. His manners are matched only by his professionalism. By the way, I think you should tell him that the exceptionally ghastly Matthew Maris you have over there is quite definitely forged. My husband owns the original. Good day to you.'

She swung on her heel and went out, slamming the door hard. All that trouble and anxiety, and the man couldn't even face her! She was hot with rage, like a steam boiler with no safety valve, and in a moment she would explode. She hoped he would believe her about the Maris, though she had lied. Walking swiftly, her heels rattling on the pavements like gunfire, she took no notice of where she was going. How dare he, how dare they all? How tired she was of being on the receiving end of life's little jokes, of working so hard and getting nothing at the end of it.

She found herself lost, standing in front of a church. Well, she thought, I am without Jake and I haven't got a job and though I'm not starving now I soon will be, so let's see what God has to say about it.

The church was cold. A few tourists wandered about looking at the stained glass. Alone with her anger, Harriet felt the beginnings of desolation, where there should have been peace. She sat in a pew and tried to calm herself, to make sense of her turbulent thoughts. If only things were different. If only she could go home now and tell Jake all about it.

But you're not poor, part of her shouted. You have ten thousand pounds! There must be something you can do with that much money, something that will earn you a living. Yet she knew that however much it was, for almost everything it was too little. Raising her head she watched the pale sunlight making jewelled patterns through the windows on the flagged floor. What should she do? Which way would lead out of the maze and not once again back in upon itself? The flags, solid and dependable when so much was crumbling, struck cool beneath her feet.

Victoria chortled when her mother returned to Lincoln Villas, putting up her arms to be carried. Harriet lifted her, finding balm in the soft head against her cheek.

'No luck,' said Iris shrewdly. 'Oh, well, can't be helped. Have some tea.'

Harriet sipped at the thin and tasteless brew, some wholefood brand they insisted upon. 'I've been thinking,' she began, 'I wondered if I ought to buy a guesthouse.'

Dodie fluttered her hands and Iris snorted. 'Thought this would have put you off. Dry rot, wet rot, rewiring, tenants that flit, fire insurance, decorating – it never stops.'

'It's the rot that's the worst,' said Dodie dismally. 'That never goes away.'

'We can't afford to do it all, you see,' said Iris, anxiety gleaming in her eyes like mercury. 'And it gobbles up the new pieces, simply eats them away. We've spent so much and we might just as well have thrown our money into the canal.'

'Not the canal, dear,' said Dodie. 'So smelly at this time of year.'

Iris looked at her scornfully. 'Don't be ridiculous, Dodie.'

'Is that why it won't sell?' asked Harriet.

'People won't even look at it. And we can't afford to modernise so we can't charge decent rents, and that man Briggs at the bank expects us to sell at any price.'

'And then where would we live?' said Dodie, and wrung her little hands. Harriet sipped her tea thoughtfully.

Mr. Briggs had lived in Markham all his life, a round, cheery man who hated upsetting people. Until the dry rot he had been used to raising his hat to Iris and Dodie in the street, but now he slunk past like a convicted rapist while they stood, outraged and silent, staring at him. Harriet found his manner rather strained until he established that she wasn't about to berate him for cruelty to two old ladies.

'How much is the house worth?' she asked him bluntly.

He put his fingers together in an arch, one of his several affectations. 'Now it's about twelve thousand. If it was in a good state of repair I'd say thirty-five, and that should give you some idea of how big a problem there is. Not something to be considered lightly, I'm afraid.'

'No, but I could borrow to do the repairs couldn't I?'

'Of course, depending on the extent of your contribution. The ladies have borrowed extensively themselves over the years.' And their overdraft was giving him sleepless nights, he might add. He couldn't wait to retire and devote himself to being treasurer of the amateur dramatics group.

Typically, Harriet was tired of being vague. Directness in business was natural to her and usually stood her in good stead. 'I want to pay ten thousand and let the ladies stay in their flat,' she announced. 'Then I'll borrow ten thousand and repair the house.'

He blinked at her. 'Can you do it for ten thousand?'

'I'm sure I can. If I hire the workmen myself instead of using a building firm I might even get it done for less.' She gazed at him with supreme confidence. She had in fact no idea at all of what needed doing or how much it would cost, and the idea of using self-employed workmen only occurred because Jake did it. That he knew what he was about and she did not seemed a mere trifle.

In his mind's eye Mr. Briggs saw a wonderful vision. He'd once again be able to enter the library without cringeing in case he met the ladies; his wife wouldn't be cut dead by their friends at the Townswomen's Guild. 'If you could bring me some figures,' he said hopefully, 'I'm sure we can sort something out.'

That night there was a celebration in Lincoln Villas. Harriet, Iris and Dodie drank Italian wine by the giant bottle, and jotted down notes about what needed doing.

'Joists,' declared Iris, waving an inebriated hand. 'Joists and roof timbers.'

'Not all the roof, dear,' said Dodie. 'Only a piece or two.'

'And floors.' Iris was wandering about now, waxing expansive. 'Floors need a lot of attention. We've had to put Mark's bed over the hole so he doesn't fall through in the mornings. One day the whole bed'll go.'

Harriet jotted down three thousand for the roof and three for the floors, wondering if she would be able to spend the rest of the money on carpets and new bathrooms. She felt rich! In the morning she would write it all out carefully for Mr. Briggs and go and see the solicitor. It should all be done and dusted by the end of the month.

Chapter Twenty-Three

In the balmy days of summer Lincoln Villas had been bright and warm. Now, three weeks before Christmas, it was deathly cold. The grey light of a winter's afternoon illumined only damp patches and torn-up floors; the only comfort was the sparse warmth of Iris and Dodie's gas fire. Victoria played down there almost all the time now, because Harriet's own rooms had long since had the gas turned off. Every now and then the water was turned off too, when yet another rotten beam was discovered and removed. The habits of dry rot were known to her now, she could spot it at thirty paces blindfold, merely by smelling it. Although she would soon lose her sense of smell, she reflected, coming up for air from behind her mask. Long since realising she could not pay for thorough treatment, she was doing the spraying herself.

But, however frugal she tried to be, she was near to the day of reckoning. Wood cost the earth, workmen took forever. Assuming that only the best would happen she would end up with the roof and top floor done and no money to replace the stairs. She had forgotten that stairs were made of wood. The worst case would be everything ripped out and only the roof mended, ten thousand pounds gone in a blink. How would she sell it then, she thought dismally. And it was nearly Christmas.

The doorbell rang. Harriet took off her mask and yelled 'Dodie!' at the top of her voice, but the television was on for Playschool and no-one answered. Muttering crossly she carefully clambered back across the beams, for which training on rope ladders had been invaluable, and went down the doomed staircase. When she opened the door the wind blew in sleet rain and a tall, elegant woman in a fur coat.

'Please – may I come in? It is so cold.'

'It's not much warmer in here.' From the accent she knew the visitor was French. In the light of the bare hall bulb Harriet registered a thin, somehow familiar face, age more than her own, a beaky nose, and beyond the smell of dry rot spray, wonderful perfume. She put her head on one side.

'You're not – ? I'm sorry, for a moment I thought I knew you.'

The woman gave a Gallic shrug. 'Perhaps you do. I think you must be Harriet. I am Simone.'

Harriet's teeth shut with a click. 'I did think I knew you,' she said thinly. 'How do you do.'

'I do most well. May we talk, Harriet? I have travelled a long way today.'

Tilting her head to survey her visitor more closely, Harriet paused. 'Is Gareth with you?'

'And if he was?'

'You wouldn't be welcome.'

'Well then – he is not. I promise he does not know where you are. I felt it better that he should not. So, you see, we are of one mind, you and I.'

'If not of one blood,' said Harriet. 'There are people downstairs, I'm afraid we shall have to talk in my room. It isn't very comfortable.'

As Simone ascended through the house she exclaimed at the devastation. 'But what is to happen here? It is all so terrible.'

'We're renovating it,' said Harriet casually. 'It will look lovely by the spring.'

'All English houses should have proper heating,' said Simone with feeling. Harriet said nothing. Heating was one of the other things she couldn't afford.

Harriet's room still boasted a sofa, balanced on a slice of floor-boarding. Simone sat on it, Harriet on the other side of the divide, on the bed. 'Well,' said Simone and smiled, too brightly. 'How good it is to meet you after all this time.'

'Indeed.'

'Such an interesting house – '

'Simone,' interrupted Harriet, 'what have you come here for? It must have taken you a lot of trouble to find me. Why? What has happened?'

Simone loosed one of the huge buttons on her coat. Beneath it she wore a plum-coloured wool dress, graced with a single diamond brooch. For some reason Harriet was convinced the brooch was fake. 'I have some news,' she said. 'About my father. Your – husband. He is dead.'

Harriet let out her breath in a long sigh. 'I wondered,' she said slowly. 'I knew he hadn't long.'

'They say it was a spell. He said it. I have a letter here that he wrote before he died. It is to you.'

She held out a long envelope. Harriet did not reach for it. 'Read it to me. I don't want to touch it.'

A quizzical smile. 'So you believe.'

'I lived there. I – believe enough to be cautious.'

Another shrug. The envelope was opened with long fingers and two crisp pages spread out. Simone read them aloud.

'My dear Harriet,

'Thanks to you and your schemes I am about to die. I don't grieve for it, and for that you may be grateful. The years weary me. Since you left the days have not been pleasant, and you know I am not a sentimental man.

'Your arrival here I hold to be fortuitous. So often a man of power cannot pass on what he has to those to come. My son, my legitimate son, is ruled by his passions; my other son is black. What can one make of such poor stuff? Nothing of substance, I fear.

'And so I leave all that I have to you. Harriet, my dear, you are strong and you have courage. I know how much you will give to hold what is yours, I have tested you and found true metal. Did you hesitate to kill me? No, you did not. As you did not hesitate to pleasure me when the need was there. Yours is a body yet to know itself fully. Would that I were young enough to awaken it!

'So, it is yours. The Island, the Corporation, the pictures – especially the pictures. The loss of my Hogarth did not escape me. An excellent choice, as I would have expected, a small, little-known piece of much value. If you took less than a hundred thousand you were foolish, although to make things a little difficult I did report it stolen. Are you even now in custody, I wonder? That would amuse me somewhat.

'Much of this amuses me. I shall regret being absent while events unfold because, of course, I do not expect you to keep what you have. My sons will lay claim to it – let them! My daughters will wail for it – close your ears! Hold on to it, Harriet, if you can, if you dare. Only a strong man can defeat a strong woman. If my sons are strong enough, defeat is your portion. Pick up your spoon and eat from the golden bowl, Harriet Hawksworth.

'I remain, in death, Henry Samuel Hawksworth.'

Simone's breath was forming clouds in the December air. Even through the thick accent Harriet could hear Hawksworth's tones in the words she spoke; he seemed to be present there with them, a ghostly third at a very strange party.

'I didn't kill him, protested Harriet. 'And it can't possibly be legal.'

'He made Dr. Muller draw up a new will, and he sent it to his lawyers. It is legal.'

'But what about Gareth? And Madeline and you?'

Simone's small brown eyes watched her. 'Nothing.'

Silence hung between them. Harriet looked again at the diamond brooch, so perfect it could not be real. 'So what is Gareth doing?'

Simone huddled back into her coat. 'He is contesting the will. And he has so far retained control of the Corporation, because you could not be found.'

'That's the hotels? He took no interest in them before.'

'He did not need to before.'

Harriet pulled up the quilt from the bed and wrapped it around her shoulders. A memory of her wedding day came to her, she could smell the flowers as if they were present in this cold, broken room. This was something she had never once considered, not even then.

'Why did you come to find me?'

'Because if this will is set aside because of my father's state of mind, the previous will must stand. Under it I get nothing. This way – I can appeal to your generosity.' Simone sat quite still, then nervously extracted a packet of Gauloises from her bag and lit one with shaking fingers.

'You need money very badly, don't you?'

Smoke was sent spiralling into the air. 'My husband is a couturier. We had a bad season. We have lived on the expectation of something, because the old man always promised me a share. Now we have debts. And he was my father – and you were a wife in name only.'

'Is Gareth going to throw that in as well?'

'My dear, Gareth will stop at nothing to get what he wants. Surely you know that.'

Harriet nodded slowly. 'Let's go downstairs.'

They made their way down to Dodie and Iris's flat, for thin tea and lumpy scones and Iris holding forth about the French nuclear power stations across the Channel. After a while Simone gathered up her gloves and bag.

'Who do I get in touch with?' asked Harriet.

Simone gave her a card. 'This is the English solicitor who is in touch with the Florida lawyers. No doubt he can arrange an advance, but of course you must return to the States. Harriet – I wonder if I may rely on you?'

She tilted her head and looked at Simone once again. Would it be wise to trust her? She doubted if she would ever completely trust anyone again but expediency was a master she was learning to serve. 'I will not let you down,' she said gently. 'You and I must stand together against Gareth. If you help me I won't fail you.'

When the murky winter's evening had swallowed Simone, Harriet went back to the fire. 'Who was that?' asked Iris. 'Do these Frenchwomen bath in perfume or what?'

'She was my – stepdaughter,' said Harriet with a smile. 'She came to bring me some news. Perhaps we can have central heating after all.'

It was days before she came to believe that it might be true. She visited the solicitor and showed him her birth and marriage certificates, then joined Simone for tea at her hotel. When she got home the 'phone was ringing. It was the solicitor advising her that the American lawyers were authorising the deposit of one hundred thousand dollars in her account, to enable her to make arrangements to travel.

Perhaps they think I need my own aeroplane, thought Harriet. Long after the solicitor had rung off she sat hugging the telephone. Money. The power to create beauty, the freedom to spend your days as you wished. No more dry rot spraying, no more anxious nights studying bank statements. This year they would have the most wonderful Christmas ever!

Victoria was as usual playing Dodie up and refusing to eat her tea. Harriet picked up the spoon and efficiently posted soya bean mush into the child's mouth. What a pity they would be here for Christmas, when Iris and Dodie resolutely refused to have turkey and ate nut roast instead.

Money. Plump pink turkey with chestnut stuffing, oranges and dates piled high in silver bowls, beautiful presents in red and gold paper: fur muffs, real leather, cashmere scarves. Suddenly, quite unexpectedly, she longed for Jake. When she was with him it always seemed a proper celebration, and besides, he ought to see his daughter at Christmas. You couldn't rub out the past, it was wrong for all of them. There was no harm surely in Christmas?

The sun was shining as the ferry steamed into Cowes. Muffled in a bright blue suit, her nose cherry red within her balaclava, Victoria clapped her hands and shouted at the seagulls. Harriet dragged her own hair out of her eyes and tried to see them also. The wind was so cold it hurt to breathe it directly, and she sank her chin into the lambswool collar of her jacket. She had dressed very carefully in new green cord trousers, knee high fur boots, brown woolly lined suede jacket and underneath a cream silk blouse. But her beautifully curled and streaked hair would inevitably be a birdsnest by the time they landed since she couldn't stay in the cabin. She felt very sick.

The gangway was being put out. Harriet blinked through her hair at the deckie and saw it was Pete. Her heart was thundering. 'Hi, Pete.'

'Well I'll be . . . Harriet!'

'You're looking well. Is Jake – is he at the cottage?'

'Er – I don't rightly know. Could be out. Have a cuppa at the caff, I'll check for you.'

'That's OK, I'll get the bus.' She picked up her holdall and Victoria and stepped on shore. Pete's appalled face looked after her. Abandoning his post he raced up to the bridge.

'Captain! Sir! That was Harriet. Jake's Harriet!'

'Bloody hell! Well, I suppose he might be sober. Right sailor, on your bike. Whatever you do, make sure the girls are out of there.'

'Aye, aye, sir.' Pete scuttled off the ship so fast it might have been sinking.

Jake was in bed with the barmaid from the Rose. He was also in bed with her friend who'd come for Christmas, and was lazily pumping at her while the girl from the Rose complained. 'It was my turn. If you don't stop that I won't visit you no more and I won't do your washing neither! Leave off, Jake!'

'You don't do the washing, you only talk about it,' he said.

The bedroom door burst open. 'Jake! Get out of there!'

'Not you as well,' complained Jake. 'You deal with Margaret here, I'm busy.'

'I'm not doing it with Pete,' said Margaret rebelliously, although she wasn't usually in the least discriminating.

'You won't half catch it. Harriet's on the bus.'

'Harriet!' Jake flung himself away from the girl. 'Is this some kind of joke?'

'Nope. She was on the ferry. I overtook the bus on the road, she's got the little girl with her. You all right, Jakey?'

He had gone a sickly grey colour. 'Yes, I'm OK. Right, girls, out of here fast.'

Margaret obliged, grumbling, but Hazel lay back and writhed petulantly. Jake seized her arm and flung her on to the floor. 'I said out.'

'Bastard.' Hazel began to scrabble for her clothes.

Jake went into the bathroom and scrubbed himself harshly, using cold water and a lot of soap. It couldn't be Harriet. Not after all this time, Pete had got it wrong. If he believed it was Harriet and it turned out not to be he would burst into tears. Christ, but his mouth tasted foul. He ladled toothpaste on to the brush and wished he could so easily clean away the memory of the night. Definitely one party too many.

He'd been out of hospital a month and in that time he had never gone to bed sober, and rarely alone. In the limbo of hospital, his pain soothed by morphine and his sleep secured with pills, it had been possible to forget. But when he got back to the cottage it hit him very much harder than he expected. She wasn't there. Her absence impressed itself upon him more than her presence, it seemed to him then. He who had always been self-sufficient was all at once dependent upon a table set in this way, the washing stacked in that, a face at the window as he came in from the shed. And since she hadn't written and hadn't 'phoned there had been nothing to do but get on with it, every day promising Mac he would sort through the letters asking him to build this boat or that, and every day not bothering. His first boat was breaking records, and whereas once he had seen that as a mere beginning, now he thought it as much as he could do. He didn't want to build a damn thing, let alone a better boat. Once again he had a good leg, once again he had a good business. As usual he didn't give a shit.

The bedroom smelled of sex and dirty sheets. He bundled the sheets up and shoved them in a corner, he couldn't remember when they were last changed. In the kitchen the old, half-blind dog he had acquired from somewhere had made a mess on the flags and was apologising with a leer and wagging tail.

'Filthy mutt,' said Jake, scraping it up with newspaper. But it wasn't the dog's fault, no-one had let him out. Oh God. Harriet. Please, he prayed, let it be Harriet.

As he dumped the paper in the bin, already overflowing with last week's bottles and cans, he saw the bus draw up on the road. A figure alighted, two figures, a woman and child. Suddenly he couldn't see them clearly. He blinked furiously in the thin winter sunshine, his throat as tight as if he were being strangled. The old dog, who had some hound in him, began to bay.

He waved. She hadn't a free hand, but she put down her bag and waved back cheerfully. He put all his hope into that wave, he saw nothing in it but what he wished to see. Vaulting the wall he ran across the tussocks towards her. As he approached he saw her pause, draw in upon herself. He stopped a yard away. 'Pete said it was you.'

'Your leg! Jake, your leg's better.'

'Got out of hospital last month. They're good at these things in England.'

'I'm so glad.'

'Are you?' He shook his head, threatened by tears, a sensation so unusual he couldn't cope with it. He had cried when she left, but never since. He put out his arms, wordless, and because of his pain she went into them, still holding the child. He clutched them both, burying his face in her hair, pressing kisses on the baby's soft cheek. 'I never thought you'd come back,' he whispered, 'I never thought it.'

'Didn't you? Oh, Jake, you smell so good.' She breathed against him, absorbing the male sweat, so notably absent from her life, so much something that now she smelled it, she knew she had missed. Weakness threatened her. She leaned against him and let his strength support them both.

They went into the cottage, past the baying dog with his head held low as he tried to see them, into the low-ceilinged room that had appalled Harriet when first she set foot in it. There was an arrangement of dried flowers on a shelf, her own work, and it was thick with cobwebs. Nothing else of her remained. All around was squalor: beer cans, whisky bottles, ash, mud and empty takeaway food cartons. The place smelled disgusting.

'Some blokes came in last night,' said Jake. She picked up a carton, growing inch-high white mould. 'They come in quite often,' he added. 'I'll clear it up, don't worry.'

She went upstairs, wrinkling her nose at the smell in the bedroom, turning quickly from the bathroom where a packet of contraceptive pills stared her in the face. Without a second's thought she resolved to let Jake find and conceal them, it was nothing to do with her. Victoria was hungry and tired. She began to grizzle. Harriet felt like joining her.

'I thought – it's nearly Christmas,' she said feebly. The enormity of the task wearied her before she began, and she was already weary, from weeks and weeks of drudgery at Lincoln Villas. Why did she have to come here and start all over again? 'You could at least have kept it halfway decent,' she flared.

'What the hell for? There was no-one in it but me.'

'Well, I can't do it. I just can't.'

'I said I would. If you'd given me some notice the place would have been immaculate.' He went across to Victoria and picked her up. She grinned and hit him in the face. 'Just like your bloody mother,' he said, and laughed. 'Take her out for half an hour, I'll get this lot shipshape.'

Harriet fished a biscuit from her bag and gave it to Victoria. 'I'll do upstairs,' she said, and waited.

'Er – I'll start there. You shove the rubbish into a sack or something down here.' He went up the stairs two at a time. Guilt at last, thought Harriet triumphantly, and began to clear up.

That evening they sat before the fire eating Jake's first decent meal since leaving hospital. Conversation was stilted.

'You said you'd write,' said Jake at last.

'No, I didn't. I've bought a guest house in Markham.'

'Good God. Is it making any money?'

'Not a bean, the dry rot's eating it. But I'm getting the rot seen to. I think I'm going to run out of money before it's finished, though. At least, I thought I was.'

'What's changed?'

'Oh – things. What would you do if you couldn't finish the house? It's for students and people mostly, I'm having to gut it.'

Jake chewed thoughtfully. 'How far have you got?'

'I've done the roof and I should have enough money to do the top floor. I can't afford the stairs or the lower floors. I can do the rot, I just can't afford to put it back together again.'

'Get quotes, did you?'

'No.'

'Then you bloody deserve to be in a mess. Answer's obvious.'

She waited, but he didn't say anything else. Sipping her wine she stared at him balefully. 'What do I have to give you?'

'Well – how about a welcome in bed.'

'I think you've had enough of those, judging by the pills in the bathroom.' She hadn't intended to say that. Sometimes she wondered if she had any control over her tongue at all.

Jake cleared his throat. 'Like I said, you should have let me know. It was just the barmaid. Oh shit, it was two of them. Some men are monks. I don't seem to be.'

'No.' Her voice was icy cold. She thought of Christmas in two days' time and swallowed hard. 'I'll forget it if you tell me about my house.'

He leaned across and took her hand, turning it and kissing the palm. 'You can have that for free. It's all yours, love. Anyway, like I said, it's obvious. Turn it into flats. Do the roof and the bottom two floors, flog them, use the money to fit out the rest. Sell those, buy next rooming house, in ten years retire to the Caribbean. Except you've done that, it'll have to be Bournemouth.'

She put her hand to her mouth, laughing. 'Oh. Oh, yes. How silly.'

He gathered up the plates and ostentatiously washed them. It was the first time she had ever felt she had the upper hand in their relationship and it was passing strange. She said, 'What do you think about when you're making love to different people? Natalie, and the girl from the Rose? Do you think about me?'

He considered. 'Sometimes, yes. Mostly I don't think. That's what you use sex for, to stop thinking. What do you think about?'

'When I was so depressed I used to write out the shopping list in my head. Before that I can't remember.'

He leaned his back against the sink and stared at her. She felt herself flushing under his lingering, considering gaze. Her nipples rasped against her blouse, telling tales of months of self-denial, of dark and turgid heat between her legs. She, who had intended never to have sex again, was tempted to lie down with a man who did it to women with as much thought as he gave to eating sandwiches. But she was special to him, she had to be.

She got up and went across to him, putting her arms round his neck and leaning her head on his shoulder. 'Don't do anything,' she pleaded, feeling his arms tighten round her. 'For tonight, let's just be close.'

He sighed into her hair. 'I revolted you sometimes, didn't I?' he whispered. 'When I made love to you.'

Without lifting her head she said, 'Only when I was ill. I almost hated you for leaving me on that island.' Her breasts were moving against him, she could feel his erection pressing into her belly, creating heat. Where had all the icy anger gone? She didn't need it.

Chapter Twenty-Four

Harriet sat in the firelight, listening to the wood crackle and spit. It was the last load and Jake was outside chopping more, his axe ringing in cold air, beneath crystalline stars and a thin moon. From the presents that morning, through the feast and on into the aftermath of night and repentance of gluttony, he had radiated delight. Victoria had received a train set, too old for her, of course, but had satisfied her father by cooing and clapping when he made it work. He had bought Harriet an anorak, because he thought her jacket too smart, and she had given him a new pair of trousers, accepted warily because he liked his clothes well worn. So much expected of this day, so much received, yet even before it ended she was thinking of tomorrow. Jake thought, she had allowed him to think, that she would stay.

The door banged open and the fire flared. Jake set down his load in a cascade of twigs and dust. 'You could chop all night and still only have enough for a day and a half. This stove eats wood.' He felt Harriet watching him and turned, seeing her eyes shining in the firelight, her hair lit to flame. 'I love you,' he said unexpectedly.

She looked away and again stirred the end of the burning log. 'What are you doing in the business now? I thought Mac seemed a bit impatient.'

They had wandered down to the pub to see him while the turkey cooked. He had been taciturn, slightly offhand, only unbending when the old dog nagged him for a slurp of his beer.

'Wants me to start another boat. I've got a lot of people asking.'

'What will you do?'

He squatted in front of her, white teeth gleaming in his weathered face. 'Build one. I started for you, for Victoria. When you left there didn't seem a lot of point in going on with it. Mac sorted out the money and finished the contract. I tried – I wasn't interested. These last weeks I haven't had anything much in mind, really.'

'What did Mac mean when he said you ought to tell me about court? Have you been in trouble?'

He grimaced. He had been angry when Mac had made the comment, had deliberately turned the conversation. 'It wasn't anything. Some of the blokes got a bit pissed one night and bet me I couldn't get the old dog to sail the dinghy across the river. He goes left and right on command, so I tied him to the tiller and the sheet and set him off. He didn't mind, just sat there barking and tacking nicely till he got out of earshot. Looked like he was going to end up in the Solent so we hauled Pat Jameson out of bed and raced after him in the launch. I caught him quite easily and took him for a little sail, he likes sailing. But what with one thing and another – well, it was a bit of bad luck really.'

'What happened?'

He grinned. 'We got tangled up with a bloody great cruiser, lit up like Blackpool illuminations. We sailed past, no lights, and they reported us.'

'And that's it? No lights?'

His face became thoughtful. Should he tell her, or should he just pray she never found out? 'It was just one of those times when you have too much to drink and do a few stupid things. I'm not saying any more than that.'

'Who else was in the boat?'

He met her eye angrily. 'Look, do you want a blow by blow account? You weren't here, remember. You were the one who walked out. I was the one left with no money, a half-finished boat and a gammy leg.'

'Amazing how you always seem to land on your feet. Although you don't often do it that way up, do you?'

'Not if I can help it,' he snapped.

At last, a squabble. She could never have told him in the middle of good cheer, it would have been more than she could bear. 'I'll be going after tomorrow,' she said stiffly.

'What? Just because of a lark in a boat? Come off it, Harriet!'

'It isn't that, honestly. But that's the sort of thing you do, whether I'm here or not. You don't know how to be like other people.'

'I don't know how to make you happy, that's for sure. Last night, suppose I made you pregnant? Have you thought of that?'

'Then I'll have two children to look after.'

He swung his arm back to hit her, and she cringed. There was a crash. He had struck the arm of the ancient armchair, knocking it into the hearth. He was on his feet, moving blindly about the room, hitting things.

Harriet leaped up and put her arms around him. 'It isn't you, can't you see that? It's me as well. I can't live this life, waiting for you, always waiting, never doing anything for myself! I don't want to be that sort of person any more, I want to see what *I* can be. Jake – please don't think I don't love you!'

He took hold of her hair and shook her head, menacingly gentle. 'When you love people you stay with them. You don't steal their children away, you don't rob them of hope, you don't kick their dreams into the dust.'

'You're kicking my dreams,' she whispered. 'I've got a dream too.'

He released her and strode across the room, turning to lean against the wall, arms folded. 'All right. Tell me about this wonderful dream that can only be fulfilled by Harriet on her own, coming back occasionally for a quick screw and another baby. Tell me how your problems can't be solved by a cleaner and a dishwasher.'

'You could come too if you wanted,' she said softly. 'I just don't think you will.'

'Try me.'

She stood in the centre of the room and told him, twisting her hands all the time. That she was rich, or soon would be, that she was reaching her hands out for a fortune. 'I might not keep it,' she said breathlessly. 'Gareth's bound to fight, he'll say the marriage wasn't consummated and the old man was mad.'

Jake put up his hand and wiped his mouth. 'So why are you here?'

She looked tortured. 'It was only for Christmas! I thought we could be friends. Look, Jake, I know you better than you know yourself. If we went back to the way it was, we wouldn't be happy. You'd be so bored, sooner or later you'd cheat on me, or throw everything up and make us all go and live on a boat somewhere. I don't want that sort of life for us. Why don't we just admit that we can't live together? We don't have to be enemies, we can still care.'

'You want that money more than anything.'

She tipped back her head. Her bosom swelled against her blouse. She looked more desirable and desiring than he had ever seen her. 'No, I don't. I want you more than anything, but you're not on offer.'

'Harriet, I am giving myself to you, lock, stock and bloody offspring!'

'You only ever hand over a piece. The rest isn't anyone's but yours.'

He went out into the night, just as he was, in his shirtsleeves. He walked about for hours, viciously angry. Never in any relationship had he felt anything other than in control, and now, with Harriet, he was losing it. Like a fledgling bird, she had spread her wings under his hand, like a swallow in first flight she had soared and glided. Did he now have to admit that the bird he had loved and protected must be set free? He was the one with the freedom; he the lost, never the loser. Even now the love he felt for Harriet constrained him, forced him to behave in ways that did not suit him. He stood on the bank of the river and watched grey dawn lighten the sky. Harriet came towards him across the mud.

'I brought your coat.'

'Very bloody considerate of you. What about Victoria?'

'She's asleep. Don't hate me, I can't bear it.'

'If I hated you we wouldn't even be talking.'

'Well then – just think, Jake, you'll be able to do what you like. You won't have to make money to feed us all, and when we really need each other we'll be there. I do love you, Jake. The way you are, not the way you'd have to be for us to be happy together.'

'You put so much faith in money. It's wrong, such a mistake.' He pulled her close and put cold hands inside her blouse, painfully kneading her warm breasts. He excited her, a wild man, beyond restraint. They made love standing in the mud and her orgasm made her cry out. Jake said furiously, 'Why couldn't you come before? That was a weapon, lying there like stone. Wasn't it?'

'I blamed you.' She hit his shoulder with her closed fist. 'Anyway, it's all your fault. I wouldn't even be Mrs. Hawksworth but for you!' Anger united them, even while it kept them apart.

Chapter Twenty-Five

Welman and Bradley had their offices in Miami. It was a place Harriet disliked on sight, a city that had been processed by wealth and yet remained slimy at the edges. Tower blocks pushed into the blue sky like cigarette ends and round their filter-tip bases the people milled in a white glare of light. Too much sun had withered too many skins, had burned the character out of the place. Nothing great or innovative was ever achieved in Miami, one felt, it was a playground, a place for wasting time. Harriet itched to be gone from it.

The lawyers lived in a sumptuous apartment with a profusion of greenery in the hall and a brittle receptionist. She was cool and slightly unfriendly, giving the impression that Harriet's appointment did not really exist and that soon she would ask her to leave. Seating herself in a very low-slung chair, Harriet crossed her legs defiantly. She was in no mood to be pushed around just because she hadn't found the time to buy any clothes suitable for the heat. Inappropriately dressed in wool, she felt hot and out of place but remained unintimidated. If she could stand up to Jake when he was raging, this girl was nothing.

There was the sound of a door opening some distance down the corridor. Incredibly, Mr. Younger was coming himself to welcome his ten-thirty appointment. The receptionist looked a little harder at Harriet, seeing a woman in dull, too-hot clothes but with a striking face. If she made more of herself she could be lovely, thought the receptionist, admiring her own tailored skirt.

'Mrs. Hawksworth! How good of you to come!' Mr. Younger, tall and well-upholstered, stretched out his hand.

Harriet rose to greet him, lightly clasping his fingers. 'You are expecting me? I was given to understand that might not be the case.'

'But of course you're expected. Shirley, bring coffee at once. The Crown Derby.'

'Yes, Mr. Younger.' The receptionist watched Harriet's ugly shoes walk down the corridor. If the woman was as rich as Mr. Younger's welcome implied then she could afford to wear what she liked.

The lawyer's office was big enough to dance in, synthetically rose-scented and commanding a wide view of the bay. Harriet bridled warily, smelling not only roses but high fees and self-interest. Welman and Bradley only backed winners on a percentage.

'I gather you saw Madame Lalange yesterday?' It had been Simone who welcomed her at the airport, took her to the hotel and was today minding Victoria. Harriet seated herself not in the cosy togetherness of the low sofa and coffee table arrangement, but in the businesslike upright chair before the desk.

Younger stood for a moment, nonplussed, then went to sit behind his desk. It made everything unpleasantly formal, which he had been at pains to avoid. 'I did spend some time with her, yes. I couldn't tell her much that was to her liking, I'm afraid.'

'So she won't benefit, whichever Will stands?'

'I'm afraid not. Whereas I'm sure that in the unlikely event of the latest Will being set aside, I have no doubt there would be a settlement in your favour. Perhaps even a substantial settlement.'

'Do you have any dealings with Mr. Hawksworth? Mr. Gareth Hawksworth?'

'Well – naturally we have had some contact. Mr. Hawksworth stands to lose a great deal.'

Harriet took a long breath through her nose. She tapped her fingers on the desk. 'Mr. Younger, if you are to represent me I must ask that you have no dealings whatsoever with Mr. Hawksworth. I got to know him well while I lived on Corusca and I found him a difficult and frightening person. If your firm undertakes any work at all for him then I must ask that you send all the papers relevant to my claim to Blumfont, Harding and Wiles.' She named the second most powerful law firm in town, that at present could not touch Welman's prestige. But with the Hawksworth account – money was to be made on this dispute.

'It is sometimes best to settle these matters out of court, Mrs. Hawksworth. Contact between the parties isn't necessarily a bad thing.'

'Gareth won't settle. I'm quite sure he will fight me tooth and nail, he won't rest till he's got everything. If I'm going to talk plainly I must be sure that Gareth can't find out what I say.'

'If you doubt my discretion – '

'Of course I don't! But there is a clear conflict of interest.' She put her hand on the desk and looked full into his face. He swallowed. She was so very direct. 'I'll – see what can be done.'

They settled down to discuss the issues at hand. The estate was in three parts. First there was the Hawksworth Corporation, in essence a failing hotel chain spanning America. It had lacked sparkle when Hawksworth bought it and since then had deteriorated further. 'The hotels are all on prime sites,' said Younger. 'They remain a substantial asset.'

The clams eaten the night before in the hotel restaurant rose sourly in Harriet's throat. The Florida Hawksworth was dusty, out of date and inefficient. The air conditioning roared all night, the 'phones didn't work and she had been forced to ask at the desk for a cockroach to be removed from her bathroom. The bellboy was sent and came out to ask: 'Which one?'

'I shall have to do something about the hotels,' she said thoughtfully.

Next in value came the art collection, upon which no-one could put a realistic figure because no-one knew quite what was in it. Hawksworth art treasures were legendary. It was even suspected that a number of works stolen from private homes and museums had ended their days on Hawksworth walls.

'Gareth hasn't as yet agreed to let the collection be catalogued,' said Younger tonelessly.

'I'll bet he hasn't! By the time you get to catalogue it, half will be gone. We must take steps to have it assessed right now!' She banged her hand on the desk.

'It's a little difficult. Gareth is still in residence on Corusca. The island itself is a Hawksworth possession, of indeterminate value.'

'Yes.' She looked thoughtful. Her eyes, rather large in her face, blinked sleepily.

'Put an offer to him,' she said softly. 'He can keep Corusca and the collection if he gives me undisputed title to the Corporation. That would be fair.'

'More than fair,' said Mr. Younger, blinking in his turn. He was used to divorce settlements in which fairness was never considered.

'Madame Lalange would support that, I think. Gareth would have to see to Madeline out of his share, I'd look after Simone.'

'There isn't any obligation on your part to see to the children,' said Mr. Younger quickly.

'I think there is. I was a very late arrival on the scene, Mr. Younger. The children have lived all their lives expecting riches, they ought to have something. My – husband – wasn't an easy man.'

Younger sat silent, his curiosity writ large on his face. What had Hawksworth been like? In all the years in which they had represented him, they had never once seen him in the flesh. Legends abounded, tales of death and magic, his perverse attraction for women. Why had he married this girl? Harriet smiled at him, and she was beautiful. 'Old men soften' she said gently.

On her way back to the hotel she stopped at a café and ordered coffee. Her mind was made up. She hadn't dared tell Younger but it was her intention to write direct to Gareth and try to placate him. There was no future in making enemies she told herself, staring at the blank sheet of her notepad. He was bound to be vindictive, but she could be magnanimous at least at long range. Quickly she wrote:

'Dear Gareth,
I know you will be surprised to receive a letter from me, but I felt I should write to you before you hear from my lawyers. I have discussed a compromise settlement with them, and this will be put to you in the near future. I do hope we can agree to settle, for everyone's sake. Your father was in no sense an easy man, and you have had much to bear, but surely we need not be enemies? Under the settlement I would take over the Corporation, while you would have the island. It seems fair, and as I feel that this should take place as soon as possible I should be grateful for your agreement. With best wishes, Harriet.'

In all probability she thought, sealing the envelope, that is a letter I should not have written. But it was one she had to write. Gareth's claim was one of birth, he had a right to be aggrieved. Hers was one of opportunity, and though she did not intend ever to give it up, she yearned for goodwill. As she went to the mailbox she stopped, and tapped the letter against her lips. What did Gareth look like? Suddenly she could not remember.

Simone sat on the bed, smoking irritably. Victoria, belligerent, tore up tissues and glared at her. When Harriet came in both faces lit with relief.

'Mummy! Mummy!'

'Harriet, I have never endured so difficult a morning. My head, it is cracking.'

Gathering up her offspring, Harriet kissed Victoria's firm, hot cheek. 'Poor you,' she said vaguely. 'I'll have to get a nurse of some sort.'

'At once. How can we do what we must with this infant so demanding? Though she is of course beautiful,' she added dutifully. To think she had once been dismayed because she couldn't have children.

'What must we do? We have to wait for the lawyers to chew things over don't we?' Simone touched the bridge of her nose with strong, elegant fingers. As if to aggravate her headache Victoria let out a yell and Simone winced. 'Let's lunch,' said Harriet quickly. She longed to be out of the musty room, in which everything was plastic and wore as badly as plastic always does. Wood achieves faded elegance, plastic becomes merely tatty, she reflected.

Over pizza and salad in a pavement café, accompanied by a carafe of red wine, Simone began to revive. 'You must have clothes,' she said decisively. 'You have no style, Harriet.'

'I never have any money,' she retaliated.

'It has nothing to do with money. Chic is without price.'

'I still can't afford it.'

'You can afford now. A woman should always look her best. If she does not it is – it is as if a man went to war without his weapons. He may not need them, but they must always be there. A woman who does not look good will be thought little of, people will take no notice of her. A woman who looks ravissant, she is always considered.'

Harriet sighed. 'I never know what suits me,' she confessed. Victoria put a sauce-encrusted hand on her sleeve. Simone hissed through her teeth.

'We must find a nurse,' she said hysterically.

They found Leah, a coffee-coloured girl with a bright smile and experience of several brothers and sisters. She was capable and seemed likely to work hard, trained to domestic standards rather higher than either Harriet's or Simone's. As soon as she entered the drab hotel room she began to fold clothes and pick up toys, as if by automatic reflex.

'You won't let her get too much sun?' twittered Harriet.

'No, ma'am. But these fine days she'll want to be out. I'll let her play in the shade till she gets used to it. Maybe she could have a sunhat, ma'am?'

'Of course. Anything.' Harriet ladled money out of her handbag.

Simone relaxed visibly as she and Harriet walked away without the burden of a child. Harriet was anxious and subdued. 'Suppose the references were forged?'

'She is on trial, Harriet. You telephoned the lady in California, she and her children loved the girl.'

'It might be a trick. She knows these people in California and she paid them to say she worked for them when they lived here. It wouldn't be hard.'

Simone stopped. 'If you are so worried we will go back and see what she is doing. What will it be? Spending that ridiculous amount of money you gave her on candy, I doubt it not.'

'She'll rot her teeth!' Harriet covered her face with her hands.

'Zut alors!' muttered Simone. 'Command yourself, Harriet!'

In a moment Harriet walked on. If she wasn't to look after Victoria herself there was no point in agonising over what was happening in her absence. Hadn't she left her to Dodie and Iris quite happily? But somehow that had been different, two old ladies in her own land, where she understood the rules by which people lived. Here, although the language was her own, the lifestyle was more unfamiliar than she would have believed. Huge cars, vast houses, gigantic meals, extravagant greetings, everything and everyone on a scale far larger than at home.

Simone seemed secure in it, spending with the freedom of one who has always had money, and still feels rich, despite her empty bank account. Harriet, who had a full one, dreaded her own extravagance. Like an anorexic shunning food because to eat at all was to become gross, she feared spending because she knew once started she would never stop. But there was nothing for it. Simone was determined, and if Harriet was honest with herself, she had longed for someone like this all her life, who would take her in hand and dress her. How lovely Simone looked now, in a sleeveless lemon dress and white sandals, gold ear-rings, a thin gold chain round her neck, her hair caught up in a lemon and brown bandeau that should have struck a false note but did not. Harriet recognised chic, understood it in others, but could rarely achieve it for herself.

They entered a quiet, discreet shop in an expensive sidestreet. Without glancing at the clothes Simone propelled Harriet into a large changing room. 'Take off your clothes,' she commanded. 'I wish to look at you.' Harriet complied, stripping nervously down to bra and pants. Simone stood back and stared critically. 'You need more support from your brassiere, you have very heavy breasts. I see too you are short-waisted, all your length is in your leg. That is the clue to your style, Harriet, remember that short waist. You are swelling here.' She rested a finger on Harriet's belly.

'The food's a little heavy. I'm cutting down,' lied Harriet. She felt a flicker of excitement. Two weeks late, and a gentle bulge could surely mean only one thing.

Simone swept out into the shop and spoke rapidly to the manageress. They were two professionals speaking together, facing their challenge as businesswomen and experts. 'We shall avoid all fuss,' said Simone, wrinkling her nose at a beribboned and furbellowed creation. 'The line must be long, always long. This suit and that blouse, also the cocktail dress, in green, please. Try them, Harriet.'

The colours sang, even in the light of the changing room. Harriet slipped into the heavy cream silk blouse and grimaced a little at the low tie of the neck, which left an inch of cleavage exposed. It would look strange she felt, under the apricot suit, slubbed Shantung with a pencil skirt and long, over-large jacket. Her reflection looked back from the pier glass, undeniably correct, undeniably sexy.

'You must wear your hair in different ways,' said Simone, adjusting the fall of the skirt. 'Sometimes combs, sometimes a bandeau, sometimes up in a bun. You are too predictable, my dear, too conservative. With this I think pearl clusters in the ears, and whatever else you like. On your feet, little pumps for a casual touch, high heels for formality. You make not enough use of your clothes. Now, the cocktail.'

Harriet allowed herself to be bullied into the cocktail dress. It was ruched at the waist, she noticed doubtfully, but the neck was pretty. Left to herself she would have had it, but Simone almost ripped it off her. 'The short waist, the short waist! Something more direct, madame, vite!'

The manageress returned with a dress in dark red lace. It was high at the neck, but the back plunged in a deep vee to just above the crease of Harriet's bottom. Sheer lined, everything was covered but nothing concealed, it was a triumph of subtle provocation. Simone purred to herself.

'I shall bring one or two things from my collection. You lend yourself to brilliance, my dear, you light up for excellence. The dress is wonderful, so respectable and yet so alluring. Very high heels for this, Harriet, and ear-rings only. No other jewels, you understand?'

Harriet tossed her hair at her reflection and Simone and the manageress exchanged a sly smile. This was what they liked, a woman who came alive inside their clothes, like an actress in her part.

Bludgeoned into compliance, Harriet was propelled from shop to shop. Simone did not hesitate to buy armfuls of white blouses, three cotton skirts all very full and very expensive, a selection of leather belts in different colours. Harriet held out for a sporty track suit in vivid green, a look that Simone despised. 'I can't look elegant all the time,' complained Harriet.

'Why not?' was the uncompromising reply.

Back then to the depressing confines of the hotel. The room was tidy for once, and Victoria sat on the floor with Leah playing with toy bricks. 'I brought these for her, ma'am. I hope you don't mind.'

'No. No, not at all.' Weariness enveloped her like a heavy coat. She felt very tired, as she had before in early pregnancy. What would Jake say if he knew? she thought suddenly. It would be best if he did not know.

They had parted in a strange sort of acrimony, he had almost been glad to see her go. What had he said? 'You get in my way.' And so she did, because he was two people, and the man who could live with her was not the man who went to sea, and that wild, singleminded Jake would not stay out in the cold. He came in and wrecked everything, like waves breaching a seawall. It wasn't all her fault, nor was it his, and he knew it as much as she.

Besides he might not even be at the cottage. When they'd parted the conversation had been spiked with danger. She hadn't pressed him on what he would do. As always when she was tired, she began to doubt herself. Perhaps she should go back, give up independence and hitch her star to Jake's, for what it might bring them. It might not be right, but at least it would be familiar.

The telephone rang. Simone picked it up, her eyes half closed against the smoke of a reviving cigarette. 'For you, Harriet.'

It was Mr. Younger. 'Mrs. Hawksworth, I was contacted this morning by the head office of the Hawksworth Corporation in New York. It appears there's a crisis of some sort, they're very anxious for guidance. I should say – I did try to get in touch with Mr. Hawksworth, but he is on Corusca and not available. I felt it best to inform you of the situation.'

Harriet's teeth clicked together. When she parted them she said icily, 'You are late, Mr. Younger. I thought I told you there was to be absolutely no contact with Gareth. I tell you this: if I find again that you have delayed in informing me of a development such as this, it will be the last time we speak together. Do I make myself understood?'

'I did feel that Mr. Hawksworth was probably the proper person to deal with any problems in the Corporation, Mrs. Hawksworth.'

'Disabuse yourself of such notions immediately. I shall fly to New York tonight. Good day to you.' She replaced the receiver, aware of consuming anger yet unsure of its cause. Wounded pride, perhaps. He didn't think she could cope.

Simone was watching her, an interested expression on her face as if she was seeing something she had not believed possible. 'And why should we fly to New York?'

'We aren't, I am. Leah can bring Victoria. I know you must have business of your own to attend to, Simone dear.' It was an effective dismissal.

Simone lifted her eyebrows in acknowledgment. 'I have been from home for some time now. But – you remember our bargain?'

Harriet glanced up at her, taken by surprise. She laughed. 'I don't think you know me very well. I don't go back on my word, I never have. And I'm always shocked when other people do.'

'How very naive.'

'No, I just trust people until I find that I shouldn't. And then I find it very hard to forget.' She swallowed and Simone wondered what she was remembering.

'Some people can be trusted in one thing and not in another.'

'Hmmm. The trouble is, you can't tell what's what then, can you? You never know what to expect.'

Simone chuckled. 'I feel that is life's charm, my dear. If it was all as we expected it would be oh, so dull.'

Chapter Twenty-Six

The plane was full. It took forever to get a drink, still longer for food. Leah was in the window seat, Victoria sat in the middle and Harriet was next to the aisle. It was less than convenient, she was trying to make sense of her first balance sheet with an elbow constantly jolted either by people passing or by her daughter. At last she asked Leah to change places with Victoria and attained some measure of peace. The figures swam before her eyes.

It was no use, she didn't know what she was looking at. She folded the paper away and tried to sort out her thoughts and impressions of the Hawksworth Corporation. At first sight it was a Leviathan, striding across America, impressive in its scope. How was it possible for one hotel chain to span the diversities of such a vast country? Of course it did not. The Hawksworth answer was boring, bland uniformity, the same style, the same room plans, doubtless the same poor food and inefficiency. The one sure thing she had learned from the balance sheet was that Hawksworth Inc. was making a loss.

She pondered the question of hotels, wondering what it was people wanted from them. Different people, different things – or perhaps always the same thing. Comfort, sufficient friendliness, sufficient anonymity. Nobody wanted to be forced to listen to the chambermaid's chitchat when they were on an illicit weekend, but neither did a weary businessman wish to have it impressed upon him that he was of no more interest than his credit card number.

'Please, ma'am, Victoria needs the bathroom.'

She stood to let them past, pressing against the seat opposite. The man who occupied it touched her bottom and she jumped. 'I'm so sorry,' he said, clearly not sorry at all. 'Can I get you a drink?'

'No, thank you,' she said primly and sat back down. Why did she always repulse people? she thought. There wasn't any need. It wasn't as if Jake owned her or anything. If he was free, so should she be.

Except that she wasn't. She made notes on a businesslike pad, suddenly aware that the blouses Simone had purchased were ever so slightly see-through.

New York was bitter cold. The first thing she did was buy herself a calf-length coat in plum-coloured wool, with a matching hat and boots in light tan. Before Simone she would have bought black boots, but the lighter touch fitted, she felt. Everyone in New York was wearing tan boots that year, she realised afterwards. How did you know when, in not being predictable, you were being predictably unpredictable? Only by being French no doubt.

Two days and she had not called on the Corporation, due entirely to cowardice, though she told herself that at first she had been tired, and then of course there was shopping, and Victoria had to be settled – valid reasons none of them. On her third day there was nothing to delay her, not an earthquake, an outbreak of measles or even a broken fingernail. She felt very sick, perhaps from pregnancy but most probably fear. Yawns kept overtaking her, like a nervous hippo. She put on her apricot suit, then enveloped herself in coat and boots. She wanted to take shoes with her for later, but hesitated to appear clutching a plastic bag with her shoes inside. Boots it would have to be. She hugged Victoria, muttered incoherently to a solicitous Leah, and went to ask the hall porter to call her a taxi.

The Hawksworth building was a vast silver tower pointing high into the sky. It seemed as impregnable as any medieval fortress, armoured and buttressed with money. But prosperity was an illusion the Corporation could ill afford, reflected Harriet. But who was she to know? She hadn't even been able to renovate a guesthouse properly. She was so stupid she believed people when they told her things.

She felt really sick and thought she might faint. That was an excuse to retreat, wasn't it? Half a step backwards and she thought of Gareth. He knew she intended to take over the Corporation, that she had decided on it. What had possessed her to think she could do it? How he would laugh when she went back cap in hand to Mr. Younger and said she must think again, how he would chortle to himself. So, there was nothing for it but to go in and if she made a mess of it, so be it. She would know better next time. Almost tearful with fright, she walked up the steps.

At ten-thirty in the morning the foyer was quiet. Harriet's heels clacked on the marble floor as she crossed to the desk. The girl looked up, saw an elegant, rather pale lady twisting her gloves. 'My name is Mrs. Hawksworth. I wish to see Mr. Somers.' She named the chief executive.

'I'm sorry, ma'am, Mr. Somers left yesterday,' said the girl.
'You mean he's on a trip?'
'No, ma'am, he's left the company.'
'Then who is in charge?' She felt rattled by this first obstacle, unable to think what to do.
'There isn't anyone at the present. Shall I get Mr. Thomas for you? He's the financial director,' she explained as the lady before her looked confused.
Harriet waited, walking up and down. The building was desperately quiet for a weekday morning, it was more like a funeral parlour than the hub of a busy firm. The lift swished down and a man stepped out, thin, greying, nearing sixty she guessed. He was looking irritated.
'Mrs. Hawksworth? I am Claud Thomas.'
'How do you do. I'm sorry, have I come at a bad time?' He was almost instinctively ushering her towards the street.
'We have something of a problem at the moment, yes. I'd be pleased to meet with you at some other time, of course – '
'It's your problem I've come to see about,' said Harriet, firmly planting her feet and refusing to be pushed further. 'This isn't a social call, Mr. Thomas.'
He paused visibly restraining himself. 'Perhaps you'd like to come upstairs.'
In contrast to the tranquillity below, on the executive floor chaos reigned. Two men in suits were arguing, a secretary stood in the centre of the floor with a telephone in either hand, and a third 'phone was ringing, without apparently anyone to answer it. Claud Thomas went across and joined in the argument, the 'phone continued to ring.
Harriet picked it up. 'Hello? Forgive me, we're a little busy just now. We'll get back to you. Thanks.' She replaced the receiver, then took the 'phones from the secretary and replaced those also. 'Could you please make coffee?' she asked gently, and advanced on the squabbling triumvirate of suited men. Clapping her hands loudly, she waited for them to turn to her.
'Gentlemen,' she said as she gained their attention, 'my name is Harriet Hawksworth. As from today I am in charge of the Corporation. I would like you all please to come into this office and explain what is going on.'

It was evening. Light snow spattered the glass and far below was the sound of commuter traffic heading homeward. Harriet sat in the chief executive's office of the Hawksworth Corporation and reflected that he had served himself well, had Mr. Somers. His desk was antique oak, vast and leather-topped, the walls were hung in gold damask, the curtains braided in green and gold. There were spaces on shelves where, until yesterday, ornaments had stood. Yesterday Mr. Somers had left, suspected of embezzling many hundreds of thousands of dollars. His departure had been precipitated by the bank calling in its massive Hawksworth loan. In effect, the inheritance by which Harriet had placed so much store was as of today an empty coffer.

All day Harriet had sat with Thomas and Waldenheim and Brunstein, ostensibly enquiring into the disaster, in truth trying to discover if they too had had their hands in the till. Thomas, she felt sure, was clear; he had been excluded from Somers' confidence for months past, had a personal sense of grievance that his life had been made a misery by a crook. Brunstein was the doubtful one, hired not too long ago and perhaps abandoned by his mentor. He was outside now, they all were, waiting. They thought she was going to tell them what to do.

Going over to the window she looked out into the snow. This crisis was her fault, she was sure of it. Naive, innocent, stupid, she had written to Gareth and told him that she intended to take away his toy, and he had taken the trouble to ensure that it was broken when she got it. Mr. Younger had found him 'unavailable' had he? Gareth had decided it was time she learned how little she knew.

The snow was thicker now. Miserable to think that tonight she must return again to the dubious comfort of the New York Hawksworth, draughty and impersonal. If she could she would transform that hotel, and all the others, lead the way in providing comfort and style for travellers. Or, she could sell up, splitting the chain and taking what she could for each part of it. She'd get out with half a million or so. If she turned the chain into a going concern once more and sold that, she'd have ten times as much.

Turning back to the desk she pressed the buzzer on the telephone. 'Would you come in please, Claud?'

He looked tired, she noticed, as if he hadn't slept properly in weeks. 'Somers gave you a hard time, didn't he?' she said.

He was too wary to agree, not yet trusting her. He sat before the desk, clenching and unclenching his fingers.

'Now,' began Harriet. 'We have two choices. We can sell up. Everyone out of a job, all the hotels shut down, the end of the Hawksworth Corporation. You might think it no great loss, it hasn't been going all that long. I don't know.'

'I'm – a little too old to get another job easily,' said Thomas stiffly.

Harriet inclined her head. 'And so are a great many other people we employ, I don't doubt. The alternative is to refinance the loan, and we must do that fast before the bank liquidates. After that we need enough money to put the hotels back on their feet, earning again. I suggest that as a first priority we sell this building, it's a luxury the Corporation can't afford. And we should consider selling the New York Hawksworth.'

'That's the flagship hotel!' burst out Thomas.

'And it's sinking.' She looked at him fiercely, and he shifted under the weight of her gaze. 'Can we get another loan?' she demanded.

Spreading his hands he said, 'We can try.'

'Then we must try, Claud. I want you to understand that the only way you're going to keep your job and earn enough to enjoy your retirement is by working wholeheartedly for me now. I don't understand figures, I won't pretend I do. If you're prepared to stay here tonight and work, then I'll stay and work with you and so will the others. At least – I'm going to sack Brunstein.'

Claud Thomas's head jerked in surprise. 'Are you sure?'

Harriet pressed the buzzer again, summoning Brunstein into the room. She wasn't sure, but with her back to the wall like this she wasn't waiting till she was. Right up until she faced Brunstein she didn't know what she was going to say to him, but when she faced him and saw his too bright smile, she knew. She extended her hand. 'I'm so sorry,' she said gently. 'I think you understand the position the Corporation is in.'

'You don't mean I'm fired?'

'I'm not in a position to fire people. The job simply isn't there any more, I'm afraid. I expect the liquidators tomorrow. The best thing might be for you to clear your desk right away, before everything gets tied up.'

He looked tormented. 'I only ever followed Mr. Somers instructions,' he burst out. 'I'd be happy to refund – '

'Yes,' said Harriet kindly, but underneath there was ice. 'Perhaps you'd better.'

She waited until his footsteps had passed unsteadily to the lift, and then called in Waldenheim. He came like a man expecting execution. 'I'm afraid you're going to be here quite a while,' said Harriet briskly. 'You'd better telephone your wife.' When he still looked blank she folded her hands and laughed at him. 'Do sit down. We three have about twelve hours to work out how to keep jobs for all of us.'

At the weekend Harriet gave Leah the day off and took Victoria to the park herself. People were roller-skating on the cleared paths, and jogging and walking dogs. She felt drained. The past three days had been spent in meeting after meeting, with this bank, that bank, this that or the other finance house. The Hawksworth Corporation balance sheet was now as familiar to her as the palm of her own hand. She knew that the bland columns of figures hid as much as they revealed. There had been massive fraud, not only by the chief executive but by those who found themselves unsupervised in the sprawl of the hotels. The bar staff were fiddling, the chefs were selling food, the chambermaids were taking towels and giving them to relatives. She had been withered by the gimlet eye of one financier. 'They are crummy hotels,' he said succinctly.

Even now, as she walked in the park with her daughter, that same financier was poring over the rescue package she, Waldenheim and Thomas had put together. Damn Mark Benjamin! He was now sitting in his warm family home passing judgment on thousands of other families. Did he even realise what he was doing?

'Better to finish it now than limp on and come out with less,' he had told her flatly.

'I'm sure we can turn it round.'

'What if you don't?'

That was what haunted her now. She was scared of refusal, and even more scared of being asked to do what she had promised. To show what she was made of she had already put the Corporation building up for sale, and had made clear her intention of selling Hawksworth New York if need be. They wanted to see her commitment. 'I couldn't be much more committed,' she told Benjamin. 'All my money's in that firm.' Now she fought the temptation to ring Florida and tell Mr. Younger that she withdrew her offer to Gareth. But it wouldn't be fair. Harriet believed in her luck, and she was quite sure that if she didn't play fair it would fly right out of the window.

'Ice cream,' declared Victoria. Harriet bought her a hot dog instead and the child threw it on the floor, so rather than squabble on this one day she bought an ice cream. She watched herself being weak, justifying it by reflecting that for days she had been strong. It was hard to relax when things were unfinished, like Jake when the boat was half-done and he was twitching. He'd hate this, she thought to herself, this playing with figures and schemes, nothing tangible coming out of it.

When she got back to her hotel room the 'phone rang. It was Mark Benjamin. 'I'd like to meet and talk,' he said crisply. 'Take you to dinner this evening.'

'Oh – thank you. Won't your wife mind? It's Saturday.'

'I work all hours. Pick you up at seven.'

She didn't know what to make of it. The cocktail dress Simone had bought her seemed way over the top, so she tried on a grey silk suit and dithered over what to wear with it. Eventually she rushed out and bought an apricot camisole from a bad-tempered shopgirl who wanted to go home, because, though this was of course business as Simone said, there was no need to look a fright whatever the circumstance. She hadn't liked Benjamin. He had been too quick to see through her thinly veiled evasions, too inclined to dismiss her assurances.

Spraying perfume on her wrists she pictured him, a goodlooking man going over the hill, hair just beginning to recede, his body shape starting to defy him. Of an age when he needed his ego boosting, she judged, and took her hair down from its neat bun to fall in a cascade over her shoulders.

He was absolutely prompt, a small slap in the face for Harriet who was habitually ten minutes late for everything. What's more he was in a cab, surprising for a man who had a chauffeur-driven limousine at his beck and call twenty-four hours a day.

'Where are we going?' asked Harriet, crossing her legs. It was good to be going out into the New York night, watching the glitter and the lights and the tramps warming their hands at heating outlets.

'Small place I know. We can talk there.' He was watching her as she leaned forward to see out of the cab. She stretched a little to emphasise the line of chin, throat and swelling breast. She heard the slight catch in his breath and felt a shiver run down her spine, of excitement, fear, anticipation. What was going to happen tonight? What did she want to happen?

The restaurant might have been small but it was very discreet, the entrance lit by a shaded lantern, the door guarded by a large, attentive man in a dark suit. There was a cocktail area in which one other couple sat and talked, and through an arch guarded by two full-size Moorish statues were the few tables grouped around a tiny dance-floor. The pianist, almost obscured behind greenery, played gentle music and munched cheese straws without ever missing a note. Harriet's eyes took it all in greedily, the leather chairs, the heavy glasses, the technique that had created opulence. Could it be recreated on a larger scale? She wasn't sure.

'Tell me about yourself, Harriet.' Benjamin was watching her.

'No.' She smiled at him provocatively. 'You'd only imagine things about me that aren't true.'

'But how did you end up married to Hawksworth? Nobody saw the old boy from one year's end to the next. He was holed up on that island and no-one ever went near him. I know his son of course.'

'Do you?' Harriet's antennae twitched with alarm.

'I don't like him,' said Benjamin, smiling. Harriet relaxed. He wasn't a stupid man and she should remember that.

They dined on sole dressed with caviare, and Harriet had a swan-shaped meringue more impressive to look at than to eat. As she put down her spoon she said, 'Are you going to give us the loan then?'

'That depends.' He let his eyes scan her, a leisurely, determined stare. She laughed. 'I don't believe it. Not on that, not you.'

'Why not me? I admit I don't usually add the condition. I'm a happily married man, but – '

'Life gets a little dull,' said Harriet flatly. Wasn't that what Jake had said? 'Let's dance.'

Benjamin was clumsy on the dancefloor, and would probably be clumsy in bed. She wondered what he would look like naked. Would he suck in his stomach and watch to see if she noticed? 'There must be lots of other women you could sleep with,' she murmured. He was holding her close enough for her to feel his erection against her stomach.

'I don't want to lay my secretary. I like my women right up there with me, I want someone equal.'

'New York's full of brilliant women. I'm a beginner.'

He ground himself into her. 'That's what I like. You're still soft. I don't want to lay a man that looks like a woman. There's a room back of here I can hire, let's go there. I'll show you a good time.' In the dim light of the dancefloor he cupped her breast, sliding the silk of the camisole against her skin.

She looked up into his face and wondered why she felt so detached. Was this what business was all about, selling yourself for what you wanted? She pulled away and went back to the table. Benjamin followed. 'Shall I get the room?'

'No.' She picked up her bag and faced him. 'I don't know you very well. You don't sleep around usually, do you?'

'My wife won't find out, if that's what's worrying you.' It was the wrong thing to say, and he realised it at once. Harriet tensed her shoulders as if warding off a dirty coat, her mouth twisted bitterly. Speaking in a low, passionate voice she said, 'If you think I should have the loan then give it to me, don't make me pay for it in bed. If New York women are hard then New York men make them that way, by using them, using up all the softness. I don't want my business to succeed if I end up hating myself.'

Mark Benjamin watched her face. The pain was clear to see and all at once he felt real emotion. Here was a woman doomed to disappointment because she did not know how to compromise, and he admired it while at the same time recognising her foolhardiness. 'I'll take you home,' he said gently.

In the cab he kissed her, almost losing control as she let his tongue roam her mouth. 'I could love you,' he whispered wildly.

She pushed him away. 'I don't want to be loved. Men don't know how to love properly.'

She sat up in her drab hotel room long into the night. Leah was murmuring in her sleep next door, homesick and cold. So was Harriet. If the loan wasn't to be then she had only to preside at the funeral of her company, slicing up the corpse to see what was left after the vultures had preyed on it. Eventually she crawled into the lumpy bed and slept.

Chapter Twenty-Seven

Wet Mondays in New York rank high in the list of unpleasantnesses. Harriet went in late, stepping cautiously over the litter swirling in the cold brown rivers that filled the gutters. She felt tired and unequal to the day, registering the bustle in the lobby of the Hawksworth building only slowly.

'Good morning, Mrs. Hawksworth.' The greeting was repeated, people stood back as she passed, employees that she did not know. How cheerful would they look when she sacked them? she wondered.

The elevator door was held open for her by a grey-haired man she had seen before. He inhabited an office on the third floor and did something or other. He half bowed and said respectfully, 'I should like you to know, ma'am, how grateful we are for all your efforts on our behalf. We do appreciate it.'

Slow colour flooded her cheeks. Words failed her, there was nothing she could say. After an embarrassed silence the door closed and she went up in the elevator. Claud Thomas was hovering, waiting for her. 'My dear Mrs. Hawksworth! Congratulations!'

She pushed past him, saying briskly, 'I don't know where everyone's got the idea that we're out of the wood.'

'Well, naturally, there's a long way to go but as you said yourself, with the loan refinanced – '

'It hasn't been refinanced! I – I spoke to Mr. Benjamin on Saturday.'

'And his office worked on it Sunday. I'm sorry, Mrs. Hawksworth, I thought you'd been told. The papers were delivered by hand this morning and under the circumstances – '

She stared at him. After a moment she went to sit at the desk which till a week ago had belonged to someone else, and slowly read through the papers before her. The she opened a drawer and took out a plain piece of paper, scrawled on it and placed it in an envelope.

'Have this sent round to Mr. Benjamin at once, please,' she said softly. 'Claud, we must have a heads of department meeting in half an hour.'

Mark Benjamin, pushing paper and answering calls in his office across town, ripped open the Hawksworth envelope himself. Inside, unsigned, the note read: 'Mark Benjamin, you are what I call a gentleman.' Beneath it were three scrawled kisses.

The revitalising of Hawksworth came at a time when not much was happening in the business world and political and domestic news ranged from the predictable to downright gloomy. So the papers covered it, the boardrooms hummed with it, even the glossy magazines got in on the act, featuring any picture they could get of Harriet Hawksworth. 'Who is this woman?' they thundered. 'Beautiful, cool, sophisticated, she has taken New York by storm. Where did she acquire the taste and skill to turn the Hawksworth hotel chain into a model of modern style? She's not saying, any more than she'll tell us who fathered her adorable little girl. A mystery lady, spending her nights home by the fireside. Can it be that Harriet Hawksworth is nursing a broken heart?'

Harriet threw the magazine across the room. The photograph of her was wonderful, showing her stepping out of the company limousine. Her leg was revealed halfway up her thigh, she looked both sexy and rather proper. But it was horrible of them to hint that she cried herself to sleep at night, everyone would believe it when the truth was so much more mundane. Nobody ever asked her anywhere. At the end of a long, exhausting day, trying to organise a project that was going nowhere near as well as people thought, she went home because there wasn't anywhere else to go. What wouldn't she give for a night on the tiles, she thought wistfully, looking at the worn copy of *Little Red Riding Hood* that she had read to Victoria for the umpteenth time that night. In another four weeks her pregnancy would be unmistakable and that would certainly clip her wings, yet the only invitation she had received at all was to a grand reception a P.R. company was holding the following evening.

The next day she asked Claud about it. 'I wouldn't be out of place, would I?' she asked nervously.

'I don't think so, Mrs. Hawksworth. Do you think we need a new P.R. firm?'

It was something she hadn't considered but she said quickly, 'I don't know, we might. I'd better go anyway.' She returned to reading the reports on the hotels. As usual it was depressing. Everything cost more than she thought it should, staff resented change, with all the publicity guests couldn't understand why everything was still so dreadful. With hindsight she realised she should have kept it all under wraps until the refurbishment was almost finished, and what's more she should have written to each of the managers personally explaining what was happening. Now, belatedly, that must be her task. She struggled with what insisted on sounding like the Queen's Speech to the Commonwealth.

'I appeal to you – I cannot face this challenge alone – co-operation, confidence, achievement!' The words, all of them meaningless, stared at her from the page.

'Sod it,' she snapped, and got up to go. She would put on her glad rags and have fun, and perhaps get some ideas on how to inspire the troops as well.

The hotel hosting the reception seemed at first glance to be every bit as glossy and impressive as she wished the Hawksworth to become. It was in fact rather ordinary but when she was nervous Harriet was apt to feel inferior and amateurish. She used to think Jake had cured her of it, but at moments like this she was sixteen again and too scared to go to the school dance. Summoning her courage she glanced down at her dress and shoes, the lace cocktail number with matching spiky stilletos, and prepared to step from the company limousine. Her chauffeur whispered out of the corner of his mouth: 'Jeeesus, look at all them cameras. You look like a million dollars, baby.'

That made her laugh, and so the picture that appeared in every newspaper the next day was of Harriet Hawksworth smiling as if the world was at her feet.

The head of the PR firm, hearing the buzz of interest, saw her enter. He crossed the room at once, leaving the earnest gentleman to whom he had been speaking in mid sentence. 'Mrs. Hawksworth! I'm so glad you could come, can I get you some champagne?' He steered her in the direction of a photographer who would record them talking together. The Hawksworth Corporation showed every sign of blossoming into one of those marvellous businesses that attracted publicity like iron filings to a magnet. He hadn't expected her to come, and after the pictures tried to guide her into a side room.

'But I wanted to see the presentation,' complained Harriet, like a child at a party denied the ice cream.

'Well, most certainly.' He flashed alarm messages to his aides who whisked ahead of him into the conference chamber. Harriet wondered if they were showing dirty films.

If the aides had not been trying to get him out, Harriet would not have met him going in. As it was there was no avoiding him. Invited last year he was invited this, an oversight for which heads would roll afterwards. Shock made Harriet stop dead in the doorway. He rubbed his hands together and smiled in that lifeless almost sly way he had. She remembered that once he had tried to kill her.

'My dear Harriet.' He extended his hand to her, and in surprise she took it.

'Gareth. I thought you were on Corusca.'

'Business with the lawyers. After that sweet letter you wrote me I've been very busy. We really ought to see more of each other, my dear. We can talk about – old times.'

With an effort, she disengaged her hand. 'Perhaps not, Gareth. How's Madeline?'

'I brought her with me this trip. Corusca's a little different from when you were there last. We're having some trouble with Jerome.'

'What sort of trouble?'

Gareth grimaced. 'He seems to think he's the new Henry Hawksworth. Dear me, these people behave as if we were about to kill each other. Let me show you round, Harriet. The display's the same every year, they never change it.'

She tried to shake him off. 'I have an escort, thank you.'

'Don't make a scene, dear, don't make a scene,' he muttered in her ear and took a firm grip on her elbow. 'Anyway I wanted to talk to you about your interesting offer. I really can't let you have the entire Corporation, that would be ridiculous.'

'I don't want to talk now.' She wrenched herself free and stood apart from him.

'Now, now.' He raised a finger, a gesture as menacing as it was slight.

'You've had enough out of the Corporation already,' snapped Harriet, aware that she was letting her temper get the better of her. And suddenly he too was furious, far more angry than the occasion warranted.

'You slut,' he said loudly, and wiped his lips with the back of his hand, as if she had struck him there. Some people later said she had. 'You seduced my poor old father and drove him to his grave. Couldn't even wait for him to die, could you? Went off with your fancy man knowing he was too weak to change the will, and now look at you, queening it over my inheritance. What is there for my sisters and me? Just the crumbs!'

'Pretty rich crumbs,' snapped Harriet. 'The island and the collection. I'm left with an ailing business that *you* brought to its knees, and I'm looking after Simone. I advise you to settle, Gareth.'

'Oh, you would advise me. You, pretending you're somebody

now, using Hawksworth money, when my father took you up you were pregnant and you hadn't got a penny! He gave your bastard a home and what did you give him?'

'Loving care,' said Harriet tightly. 'You put him in that wheelchair, remember. I don't want to talk to you. Get out of my way.' She tried to walk past, but he caught her hair and dragged her close to him. She let out an involuntary shriek. His breath was hot on her face. He smelled of whisky and his pupils were wide and black.

'I'll take it all from you,' he whispered. 'I won't let you have even as much as you started with.'

'You're stoned,' said Harriet. She jabbed her heel into his shin and with a hiss he released her.

They hustled him out and lavished care upon her, agog with the excitement of the row. Despite herself she felt shaky, she always did when she fought someone. Jake never seemed to feel like that, she reflected. Perhaps men in general took combat more in their stride. For her it seemed to undermine her very existence. Once the rage was gone she couldn't forget her enemy.

She left early and went home. The hotel was quiet, there were few people about. One of the lifts had broken and she had to take one that delivered her some corridors away from her room. She walked wearily along, thinking what an unpleasant hotel it was and how they really ought to sell it, perhaps to someone who would pull it down and build something beautiful.

Suddenly someone grabbed her from behind. She sucked in her breath to scream but before any sound issued she was propelled through a door into a bedroom, sprawling face down across the bed. She knew without looking who it was, knew she should have expected this. Her hands grasped the bedspread, the coverlet they used when a room wasn't let. At least half the hotel was empty.

Despair of rescue goaded her on. She rolled over to face him. 'Don't you dare touch me!' She was at a disadvantage, her skirt high above her knees, high heels scrabbling on the floor.

'Nobody will hear a thing,' said Gareth and took off his jacket.

'You daren't. Not here, not in New York. Everyone would know.'

'They will only know if you tell them. And you won't. You know what I'd do to you, or to that little girl.' He was laughing at her.

A mewing sound rose in her throat and she suppressed it, trying to swallow. It wasn't murder he intended.

He had a thin length of cord in his hands. She tried to get across the bed away from him. As she gained the other side he lunged and caught her. She hit him hard in the face, he caught her wrist and held it while he tied her to the bed.

'Don't. Please don't, I'll give you anything.'

'I'm going to have it all anyway, your case is rubbish. This I count as punishment.' When he caught the other wrist she clawed at him, kicking her foot in its spiked heel at him until he wrenched the shoe from her and stood, threatening her face with the steel point. 'I could blind you,' he whispered, and she believed him.

He took off his trousers and she saw he was still semi flaccid. She prayed he would be incapable and then wondered what he would do if he was. But her fear seemed to excite him. When he came close to her and she turned her face away. almost gagging, he laughed. It occurred to her that he might indeed strangle her, driven beyond caution by excitement.

His hands ripped her dress, pulling out her breasts like ripe fruit. He began to slobber on her and she was crying. Twice he bit fiercely into her flesh. Then he reached up between her legs and tore her clothes, thrusting himself with sudden urgency down on her.

Soon it will be over, she told herself, I have only to wait a few minutes and I can wash and be clean. It seemed to go on and on, her body tight with revulsion, the man wheezing and labouring on top of her. Suddenly he pulled away. For a blessed minute she thought it was over, that he was even untying her.

But it wasn't the end. As she sat up, whimpering, he pushed her on to her face, making her lie on her front half on, half off the bed. He came at her from behind. In an awkward position, every thrust hurt her. She cried out and he laughed and hit her in the belly, driving harder into her until she was clenching her teeth against pain. Long-nailed fingers gripped her between the legs. Her pain was visible in red and black flashes. Then he groaned and the weight on her back lifted.

'Let that be a lesson to you,' he said in a slurred, sated voice. 'That's what a woman like you deserves.'

She heard the door close. Her eyes were tight shut, blotting out what had happened. This isn't real, she told herself. An hour ago it hadn't happened. If I don't open my eyes, if I don't think about it, I can be back where I was an hour ago. I can be safe.

At last the ache in her belly drove her to move. She brought her knees up, gasping with the pain. There was something wrong, something inside her. The marks of his teeth on her breasts and belly made her shudder. It was as if she had been branded. The urge to go home, back to her own things, her own place, was almost unbearable. She wrapped the cover from the bed around herself and picked up all that was hers, shoes, torn clothing, handbag. Then she crept down the corridor to her room.

All she could think of was to wash, to force water up inside herself to banish the foul essence of the man from every crevice, every pore of her body. When she was clean, scoured clean, she would get into bed and pull the covers over her head and never, never get out again.

Faces loomed and went away, piercing her dreams. Sometimes she thought she spoke to them, but no-one ever responded so perhaps she had said nothing at all. Reality was in her head, not outside it.

'Who shall we call, Mrs. Hawksworth? Who do you want to come?'

They had asked her that before, they kept on asking, and each time she said 'Jake'. But perhaps that reply was in her head too, perhaps she didn't say it. How good it would be to have him here. She would know then where she stood, which side of the grave at least. So she tried again, and the doctor put his ear close to the bloodless lips and heard her whisper.

The nurse went through the address book and could find no Jake, although in fact there were very few addresses in it. She showed the entry for Andrew Jakes to the doctor and they discussed if he might be the one. It was left to the nurse to telephone, because it was a difficult call and might have repercussions. So it did, but not in the way any of them imagined.

Chapter Twenty-Eight

There was grit underneath his eyelids, scouring the dry surface of his cornea every time he blinked. The drinks on the flight had soured his mouth but done nothing to lighten his mood. Jake was furious.

He walked grimly down the corridor after the swinging rump of the nurse. Just let Harriet say one word out of place and he'd not stop shouting for a week. He didn't know when he had been so angry. It was the only thing keeping him awake. The nurse stopped. 'We have a gown and mask for you over here, sir.'

'Going a bit far, aren't you?'

'It is standard practice in this unit, sir.'

So he let them put him in a white gown, cap, mask, gumboots, the whole paraphernalia, and then steer him forward like a child in a fancy dress competition, who has no say in what he looks like or where he goes. They took him to a line of perspex cubicles, each one occupied by a prone body sustained by tubes and wires. He caught hold of the nurse. 'This can't be right. She's had a miscarriage, that's all. Harriet Hawksworth.' He used her married name with distaste.

'She's right here, sir. Hasn't anyone explained to you? Mrs. Hawksworth is very seriously ill.'

He felt a sudden chill, as if someone had opened a window on to the cold night. 'How serious? Are you trying – is she going to die?'

Her eyes above the mask looked back with an unreadable expression. 'We hope not, sir.'

This is not happening, he told himself. There must be two Harriet Hawksworths. And for a moment, when he saw the woman in the bed, he felt relief. It wasn't Harriet, it couldn't be. Then he saw her hand, in full view because of the drip that pierced it, and he could never have forgotten her fingers. Long slim fingers on an incongruously square palm. He had always loved her fingers.

The nurse gave him a chair and he sat down. That the body before him was alive was apparent only through the bleeps and flashes of the equipment connected to it. For a minute he wished himself anywhere but here. He wanted to leave, to sleep, to come to terms with it all. Why did the important moments in life always come when you were least prepared? he thought angrily. A decent night's sleep and he'd know what to do.

'Damn you, Harriet,' he said harshly. 'Do you know how long it takes to get here? And it's raining outside. Look, I've got this to say to you: I don't mind you doing your own thing. If that's the way you want it then I'm not going to hang around bleating, but this is bloody ridiculous! If you won't live with me then why do you want me around when you die? You always were keen on drama, only you could turn a miscarriage into a deathbed.'

The head on the flat, comfortless pillow turned slightly towards him. There was a gleam beneath the eyelids. He said wildly, 'If you'd stayed in England you could have had this on the National Health, but you needn't worry – I'll see to the money. Was that why you wanted me here? Christ, but you use people. And keep still, will you, there's a tube up your nose.' He put his hand on her white cap and held it there. A little sigh escaped her lips. The eyes drifted shut.

He found himself stroking her cheek in time with the rhythmic bleeping of the machines. He had trailed half across the world to yell at her and she had managed to upstage him. Trust Harriet. You could always – trust Harriet. If he wasn't so tired he might cry. Jake put his head down on the bed next to her and slept.

Over the next days he found out a lot about Harriet. Between spells at the hospital he went to the hotel to see Victoria and meet Leah. Neither seemed to know what to make of him.

'Will Mrs. Hawksworth be coming home soon?' asked Leah anxiously. She lay awake at night wondering what would happen to Victoria if her mother died, wondering what she ought to do.

Jake looked round at the dismal, overcrowded rooms in which Harriet and her daughter passed their days. Whatever it was, it wasn't homely. 'She's still with us, anyway,' he said bleakly. 'Never was a quitter.'

From there, because he didn't want to go back to the tension of the hospital, he went to the Hawksworth building and saw Claud Thomas. After initial caution Jake was given a twenty minute panic-stricken monologue, detailing all the disasters that threatened due to Mrs. Hawksworth's illness.

'We have even had Mr. Hawksworth, Mr. Gareth Hawksworth, trying to get in here. I'll be honest with you, I've never liked him. It was on his recommendation that Somers was appointed. Where did those funds go, that's what I'd like to know, into whose pocket? But nothing's settled, you see, there's no-one at the helm. And of course the refurbishment is way over budget, and Mrs. Hawksworth is the only one who knows exactly what is happening on that – '

'What makes you think she knows?' said Jake sardonically. 'You have a touching faith, Mr. Thomas, but I know Harriet rather well. Good on ideas, not so good on the follow-through.'

Without asking he picked up the folder of figures that Claud Thomas had placed on the desk by which they stood, and leafed through them. He paused at the current costings for the refurbishment. 'She's certainly getting bloody extravagant. The only thing more expensive than this is satellite research, or possibly boat-building. Look, I'd better take these to the hospital.'

'If she could just consider them,' said Thomas, his relief re-inflating him like air in a balloon. 'She did say something about selling Hawksworth New York, but with nothing on paper one hesitates – '

But Jake was gone. With him these days all roads led back to that one quiet bedside where the oxygen hushed and the monitors bleeped and sometimes, just sometimes, Harriet looked at him.

He talked to her a lot, about the work he was doing on a new hull design for a boat to be built in Australia. 'You realise I should be out there now?' he told her irritably. 'Another two days and I wouldn't have been at the cottage at all. And I had to go down on my knees to get into this blasted country. They don't give you a visa if you've got an unpaid parking ticket. Which reminds me, you won't be able to pay your parking tickets if you go on like this. I'm authorising Thomas to sell Hawksworth New York – the command comes from you, of course. That OK? Good girl, knew you'd see reason. There's a buyer for your head office as well. Doesn't want to pay the price but you can't afford to play hard-to-get so you've agreed. I'm sending Waldenheim out today to find somewhere small, cheap, yet prestigious. He thinks you're being impossible because of your illness. I told him that's how you always are.' He stopped talking and stared at her. The skin on her face was almost transparent. She might have been very old or very young.

Yesterday the doctor had talked to him. 'She has an infection which is proving difficult to treat. The blood loss was substantial and in a weakened condition these things can take hold. It isn't normally fatal.'

'It's been a week now, and she's still barely conscious.'

The doctor had swallowed unhappily. 'That is causing us some concern.'

Jake reached under the thin cover for her free hand, the one without the drip. He gripped it and then took each finger in turn and wrapped it around his own scarred and hairy hand, marked by rope burns and wind galls, one of the nails permanently twisted from an accident racing once.

'With a bit more experience you'll be a bloody good business-woman,' he said, his voice suddenly harsh. 'I didn't think you could do it, you know? I thought you were fooling yourself, hoping for money for nothing. I expected you back, with your fingers burned. Did I tell you I bought the cottage? Not that I'm in it much these days.' He wondered if he should tell her about the girl in the village he slept with off and on, a nice girl, a kind girl, who wanted to marry him. One of those doormat women you felt bad about but trod on just the same. She wouldn't like it when he upped and went to Australia for a year, but he would.

He stroked Harriet's fingers, each in turn. 'I used to think I wouldn't mind if you died,' he whispered. 'But I would, you know. There is absolutely no-one who annoys me as much as you bloody do. When there's nothing in the world to care about any more, at least I can get mad at you. Oh, Harriet.'

The fingers, until that moment seemingly lifeless, tightened with sudden strength. Glancing at her face he saw her eyes flutter open, the lashes seemingly too heavy for her weary lids. But they stayed open, watching him with absolute recognition. Although he had sat by her for days, talked for hours, he felt suddenly embarrassed.

'Hello, there,' he said awkwardly. 'Like a drink or something?' An imperceptible shake of the head. She lay there, looking at him, and as he watched a tear gathered in the corner of her eye and trickled down her face.

Too weak for anything except the dullest platitudes, Harriet lay exhausted in her bed and vaguely absorbed what Jake said to her. His presence comforted her immeasurably, a constant in a world that was frightening, hostile, full of demons. He gave her bulletins on the business, or rather he told her what he thought she should know. It was his voice she listened to, not the actual words. Nothing of the outside world interested her, it had no relevance at all.

The myth that Harriet was in control continued outside the walls of the Hawksworth building, but inside it they deferred to Jake. It wasn't a task he enjoyed, and it showed in the way he handled day to day affairs. Claud Thomas found him brusque to the point of rudeness, Waldenheim thought him unreasonable, Harriet's secretary hated him and wondered if she should give in straight away if he made a pass at her. Mark Benjamin, who had been steeling himself against the erratic handling of the Hawksworth account, was amazed at the ruthlessness Harriet displayed from her sickbed, taking difficult decisions to cut off parts of the company as if she were slicing cheese. He called the hospital twice a week, and each time was told 'no visitors'. So he sent flowers instead, and Harriet's room began to look like a flowershop. Jake came to hate the scent-laden air of the place.

In fact, the longer he stayed in New York the less he liked it. He passed from one over-heated room to another, harassed by secretaries and heads of department when he went to the office, medical staff and ward orderlies when at the hospital. Although the days exhausted him, at night he couldn't sleep and started each morning with a dull headache and a foul taste in his mouth. Stamping into the office one morning more than usually bad-tempered, he snarled at Harriet's secretary: 'Don't you dare let anyone in to see me. I'm just not in the mood.'

'Yes, Mr. Jakes,' she gulped, failing to conceal her surprise at his appearance. He was wearing jeans, trainers and an old jumper, as well as last night's beard, because they always made him shave again at the hospital and for once he was damned if he'd shave twice in four hours.

But, no sooner had he settled at his desk for another scintillating round of balance sheets and reports than the 'phone buzzed. 'Mr. Gareth Hawksworth here to see you, sir,' squeaked the secretary.

'For Christ's sake, Maud, I said no visitors!' roared Jake. 'Tell him to fuck off.'

He flung the 'phone down, wincing at the crash. A second later the door opened and in came Gareth.

The two men stared at each other: Jake heavy-eyed and unkempt, Gareth like a contender for a best-dressed award, in dark suit, cream shirt and spotted tie. He grinned and made to sit down opposite the desk.

'Get out,' said Jake flatly.

Gareth took no notice and settled himself into the chair. 'My my, but you do look rough. It must be anxiety about dear Harriet. I can't tell you how worried I've been.'

The mockery touched raw nerves. 'It wouldn't take much for me to break your arm again,' said Jake menacingly. 'Or your face, for that matter. What have you come for?'

'I should have thought that was obvious. When I go to see my lawyers later today I shall be able to tell them that Harriet has left the Corporation in the hands of her hobo lover who is seizing the opportunity to sell off valuable assets without any authority whatsoever.

Under the circumstances I intend to take over.'

Jake laughed at him. 'Just you try it, sunbeam. I ought to tell you that I have had a report drawn up detailing just what disappeared from where while you were supposed to be running this show. I've sub-titled it *Book Cooking for Beginners*, or *Fingers in the Till*. You might have invested in a decent accountant. You left a trail a mile wide.'

A muscle twitched in Gareth's cheek. 'I don't believe you.'

'Try me.' Jake leaned forward across the desk, his big hands resting loosely on the jumble of paper before him.

Suddenly, Gareth got to his feet. He stood over Jake, hissing, 'I'm not giving up. The bitch can do what she likes, my lawyers will fight her all the way. You don't know what she is. You should have seen her with my father, letting the old man paw her so he'd leave her the money. Bloody little gold-digger!'

Jake lunged for him across the desk but Gareth leaped back, striking out with the flat of his hand as if slapping a woman. He missed, staggered, and Jake grabbed his wrist, throwing him backwards in a move learned in a dozen dockside brawls. They went down together and Gareth grunted in pain.

'Oh, my God! What is this, what are you doing?'

Jake glanced up, startled. A very tall, very elegant woman stood in the doorway, staring down at them. He realised how it must look, the immaculate Gareth being beaten up by an unshaven lout. If he wasn't careful it would make the papers.

'Er – hello,' he said cautiously.

Gareth rolled away across the carpet and the woman helped him up. 'Thank God you're here, Simone,' he said urgently. 'He just attacked me. You know he's selling off assets? By the time Harriet gets out of hospital there won't be any Corporation.'

Simone put her hands to her face. 'It can't be true! Surely he has no authority?'

'I have all the authority I need,' broke in Jake. 'I take it you are the French sister? Where's the other one – isn't she on drugs or something?'

'Madeline is not concerned in this,' said Simone stiffly. 'We have no wish to discuss our family problems with you.'

'And I have no wish to discuss the Corporation's problems with you,' retorted Jake. 'Piss off both of you.'

Gareth laughed, stretching a long arm briefly round Simone's shoulders. 'Now you see what he's like! A stupid, vulgar brute and Harriet does just what he tells her.'

Jake snorted. 'Score nil for character assessment. Are you going or am I going to have to kick you out?'

'As it happens I am ready to go,' said Gareth, sauntering out into the hall. 'I've seen enough. What about you, Simone, are you coming?'

'Not yet.'

She waited until Gareth entered the lift, then closed the door and came fully into the room. Jake waited, his eyes like glass. Whatever this French piece thought she would extract from him while Harriet was ill, she wasn't going to get it.

'Harriet promised me money,' said Simone stiffly. 'As I'm sure you are aware, I agreed to support her case in return for some financial assistance. Obviously I do not want to talk about this in front of Gareth – '

'What, a united family like you?' Jake was scathing. He didn't believe that Simone would back Harriet. It was a plot cooked up between her and Gareth.

His antagonism shook Simone. 'I assure you that it was agreed! I need thirty thousand dollars for my husband's firm. Gareth is not involved at all, I swear it.'

'What about the other one, Madeline? Why doesn't she get a bite?'

Simone pulled her fur coat tight to her throat. Her mouth was a gash of red in her white face. 'She is in a clinic here, she is not well. Must you behave as if I am begging when it was all agreed, a business transaction?'

Jake stared at her. 'OK,' he said suddenly. 'I'll pay up. Twenty thousand, against shares in your husband's firm. Take it or leave it.'

'This is preposterous! I must speak to Harriet!'

'Nobody talks to Harriet but me.' He went across to the 'phone and rang down to Claud Thomas. 'Twenty thousand dollars to Simone – what's your other name? – Lalange. Conditional on receipt of shares. I want an agreement drawn up. Make sure it's watertight, I don't want any problems. Thanks.' He replaced the receiver and nodded to Simone, dismissing her.

'I have never been so insulted,' she said harshly. 'It is outrageous!'

'I dare say. Seems to me you Hawksworths deserve a bit of your own medicine once in a while. Might do you some good.'

She turned on her heel and stormed out, leaving the door swinging wide. Jake breathed in deeply through his nose. God, but he was angry. They were all tarred with the same brush those Hawksworths, grasping and murderous every one of them. His secretary came in and stood trembling, waiting to be fired.

'We've got to improve security,' said Jake vaguely. 'Gareth Hawksworth knows too much about what's happening here, someone's telling him. And I need a report on how he ran the firm, and I need it double-quick. I've told Hawksworth we have it already, so get Waldenheim up right away.'

'Yes, sir.' Maud scuttled out before he remembered her sins.

Jake went over to the cocktail cabinet and poured himself a vodka. It was all bluff and double-bluff, there was nothing solid anywhere in this house of cards. He glanced at the clock. An hour, and then at last he could see Harriet.

At last there came a morning when Harriet awoke and felt a spark of interest in the day ahead. As usual Jake was coming to see her, and he had promised to bring Victoria. The easy tears of illness threatened to choke her for no reason at all.

Because it was a special day, the nurse came in to wash her hair. But before she started she sat down for a moment, watching Harriet with calm, experienced eyes. 'I have to talk to you, Mrs. Hawksworth,' she began. Harriet's hands closed on the sheet.

'What about?'

'I think you know. Do you remember when you were admitted? Do you remember talking then?'

'No. No, I don't.' But it was a feeble lie and they both knew it. The nurse continued. 'If you were attacked it isn't right for you to pretend. You can't ignore it, Mrs. Hawksworth. You have to face it, come to terms with it. People can't just go on with their lives as if it hasn't happened. Nobody's that strong.'

Harriet's voice became shrill. 'I keep telling you, nothing happened. It was a miscarriage, that's all. I'm bound to be upset, but I'll have another baby – won't I?'

There was a silence. The nurse patted her hand, where it clutched and tore at the sheet. 'You have a lovely little girl, I understand. That should be enough for most women. Won't it be enough for you?'

In the space that followed Harriet saw her life stretching before her, devoid of fertility, devoid of youth. Her soul died a small, controlled death.

'Well.' Harriet smiled with false brightness. 'It seems she will have to be. I don't think I'll have my hair washed right now, if you don't mind. Please make sure nobody tells Mr. Jakes about any of this, I don't think he should know. I'll lie down now. I'm rather tired.'

The nurse moved to put her arms around her, but Harriet shook her off. She wanted to be alone, quite alone, to cry and cry and then – to face them all as if none of it mattered. None of it had ever happened.

In the afternoon she sat up, bright and smiling, waiting for Jake and Victoria. Delightful in drifts of lace, Victoria flung herself at her mother. 'Daddy gave me this,' she announced, showing off a locket. Harriet, who disliked children wearing jewellery, grimaced. But it was Daddy this and Daddy that, Leah only occasionally, and Jake leaned by the window listening with an indulgent smile on his face. Harriet felt her nerves fraying. What part did she play in all this?

Victoria prattled on, telling some tale. 'Daddy and me was going to the park,' she began, and Harriet snapped 'Daddy and *I were*! Really, Jake, hasn't anyone been correcting her grammar? She sounds like a slum child.'

Victoria's face froze in shock, and suddenly Harriet was clutching her, sobbing with great dry gasps. 'All right, all right,' said Jake, and came to take the child who was whimpering with fright. He carried her quickly out into the corridor and signalled to Leah. 'Mummy needs a sleep, sweetheart,' he told the little girl. 'You go home now and I'll come along later and bring you something. What would you like?'

'A dolly,' said Victoria, brightening.

Leah's face was unreadable. This is one very spoiled child, she was thinking, but with Mrs. Hawksworth so ill and Mr. Jakes so determined, she didn't know what she should do. Neither she nor the child was ever told what was going on.

Harriet was blowing her nose when Jake went back to her. 'Want a drink?' he asked.

'Only if it's alcohol,' she sniffed.

'Barley water. What was that all about?'

'Nothing. I don't know. I'm losing my grip on everything – even my daughter's going to hell because I'm not there to look after her. I was going to enrol her in a nursery, so she could meet some nice children, but I can't do anything stuck in here.'

'I can enrol her in a nursery! You don't have to pass a sex test, do you?' She tried to laugh. 'No. I think it's fashionable to have men do it, actually. But I wanted to. I wanted to look at them, and take her and everything.'

It was a good enough excuse, too good, because Jake believed it. Harriet hid behind a wall of plausible lies and let everyone think that she was fine, that she was coping, that really there was no lasting damage. At night she swallowed sleeping pills because the hospital was too light and too noisy. During the day she stared unseeing at the television, and waited for Jake to come. She felt safe when he was there.

One day when he came he said, 'They're talking about letting you go home in a day or so.'

'Are they?' She smiled as if pleased, but in reality she was terrified.

What would she do out there, in the dangerous, threatening world?

'So I thought we'd have a talk. About us.'

'Let's not.'

He sighed, already angry, and flung himself down in the thinly upholstered armchair provided for his comfort. 'Look, Harriet, I haven't the time to spend pandering to you. I should be in Australia right now. All the time I spend here looking after you is time I pay for there, because the job's got to be done and the deadline's not moving. You got yourself into this mess but you want me to spend months getting you out of it. You are coming out of hospital, and we have to talk about what happens then. Right?'

She moved her head restlessly. 'Let's talk tomorrow. I'm tired.'

He leaned back in the chair and said loudly, 'I won't have my daughter brought up in that hotel.'

Harriet picked up her water glass and flung it at him, hitting the far wall and sending a shower of splinters into the air. 'You're not having her,' she hissed. 'She's all I've got.'

'Bloody hell, Harriet! All I was going to say is that I've found you an apartment. Leah and Victoria move in tomorrow, you join them at the end of the week. I have never even once thought that I should take her!'

Harriet began to sob. 'Well, you will. I know you will, and then I won't have anything.'

The urge to rant and rave at her was overwhelming. 'What do you want me to do?' Jake asked grimly. 'What do you want me to say?'

She said wildly 'I don't want you to leave me alone. You mustn't. You must stay with me. Please, Jake.'

'What for? So you can storm out again? I've had enough of that, sweetheart. You've done it once too often. Will you stop crying and listen, please?' He crossed to the bed and crouched down so that he could look into her face. She was a wreck, her nose running and her eyes swollen, and he wanted to kiss her.

'You don't want me any more,' she said miserably.

'It seems to me I've got you whether I want you or not! I'll come and see you, I'll come often, and you can come to me. But – you said it first, and I didn't believe you, but it's true. We make holes in each other's lives. And look what you've got here, a thriving empire all your own. You don't want me running it.'

'Don't I?'

Jake picked up a folder he had brought with him, brushed off the broken glass and gave it to her. 'This is where you're at. There's a dozen people wanting to visit and tell you all the awful things I've done, and that prat Hawksworth has issued a writ against the Corporation. We've asked that it should be set aside so the whole thing can get to court. The split will be agreed, it's more than generous.'

Harriet pushed her hair out of her eyes. 'I'm not settling. I can't afford to.'

'How much do you need, for Christ's sake? You're doing OK.'

'I've decided,' said Harriet thinly. 'I want what I was left. I want all of it. I am going to leave that bastard Gareth without a single penny!'

Chapter Twenty-Nine

The apartment was passable, large enough, quiet enough, but not grand enough for Harriet. To Jake rooms were rooms, to Harriet they were outward signs of her inward stature. Suddenly she needed things as never before, houses, cars, masses and masses of clothes. She burned to have things. Every inch of wall space without a picture was a reproach for what she did not have but Gareth did.

She wasn't well enough to go out so she ordered things by 'phone, toys for Victoria, shoes for herself in the wrong size that she didn't return. It infuriated Jake.

'How can I leave you when you behave like a fool?' he stormed, shoving goods back in packages like a man possessed. 'Do you want me to take the 'phone out? Is that what I have to do?'

'No.' Harriet got up and wandered about the room, holding her arms across her body. Slim, her skin smooth, her hair shining, she looked elegant and infinitely desirable. He went to her and nuzzled her neck, feeling her tense. 'Don't be silly,' he said softly, and turned her to face him.

'Jake,' she leaned back and stared at him, 'why are you selling the land in Florida?'

Momentarily diverted he said, 'Florida? Of course we've got to sell it. The land's worthless, nothing but swamp. That fool Gareth bought it, which leads me to believe there was some fiddle on the purchase price. Let's talk about it later.'

He bent his head to her mouth, but as he breathed against her skin she said, 'I'm going to develop it.'

That stopped him. He let her go, stood back and said, 'Have you gone stark raving mad? You spend as if you own half the country, not just a few crummy hotels. You start out on lawsuits that could take every penny you've got left, and as if that isn't enough you decide to fritter the remaining shekels away trying to build in a swamp! Are you trying to convince me you can't manage without Big Daddy to look after you? Is that it?'

She sat on the sofa, a dull workaday thing Jake had chosen. 'Only partly. It just seems to me we have too many business hotels, we don't have anything for holidaymakers and naturalists. The Florida market's enormous. Not everyone wants to sit on some beach and get brown. We can offer something different.'

'It'll be different all right – flies, alligators and rising damp.'

He went and poured himself a drink, making her a gin and tonic without asking if she wanted it. 'I'm going tomorrow,' he said softly.

Her face cracked, like glued porcelain coming apart. 'You can't,' she wailed. 'I'm not ready! You just can't.'

'If I don't go now you'll never be ready, you'll let me do it all. I don't want it, Harriet. This isn't my dream.'

'It could be.' She put her fingers in her drink and flicked drops on to the floor. She was being a little girl, helpless, dependant but naughty. He had never known her like this and it confused him. She came and cuddled against him, suddenly willing to give him anything. 'Look after me,' she whispered. 'Don't leave me alone.'

The night stretched ahead of him, an expanse of time that would be filled with Harriet's pleadings. She moved against him, trying to trap him with what she knew he could never resist. Rising passion fought against sense. When he'd had her, would she cry and plead and beg him not to go? Of course she would. 'I've got to go,' he said thickly. 'I've got to go now.' He pushed her away, hard.

Harriet raged at him as he packed, flinging every insult, betrayal and moment of inattention at him. 'You always let me down,' she shrieked, encapsulating everything.

'I came, didn't I?'

'And it isn't enough! You've got to stay and help me, I can't manage on my own!'

He zipped his bag and stood up. 'I've said that to you a few times. Didn't stop you though.'

'That wasn't the same.' Her throat was raw from shouting. She knew that Leah must have heard, that Victoria was probably awake. None of it had been any use. He was going, she knew him well enough to know that. In a dull, level voice she said, 'Why don't you ask me to go with you?'

He stopped on his way to the door. 'OK. Come on then, lovey, get packed. But you leave it all – and I mean all – behind.'

Harriet didn't move. He nodded, almost pleased with himself for knowing her so well. Suddenly she flung herself at him, clinging and holding with something akin to desperation. 'If I was ill again you'd come? You won't forget me?'

His heart seemed to lurch inside him. Harriet stirred up emotions he thought he didn't have. 'I won't forget,' he said thickly. 'Look after Victoria for me.' He pressed his face into her hair, taking deep breaths as if the smell of it could go with him. Then he was gone.

For a day or so afterwards she cried and blamed Jake for it all, and then, since there was nothing else to do, she had her hair done and went back to work. There was something reassuring about her own office, her own desk, the familiar faces of those around her who, in so short a space of time, had come to seem like family. They welcomed her back as if she were truly vital to the Corporation, when she had feared that Jake had displaced her forever.

'Mr. Jakes was very able, of course,' explained Claud Thomas, 'but he doesn't have your grasp, Mrs. Hawksworth. Hotels aren't just about money. He wasn't – he didn't – ' He took a deep breath. 'He upset a lot of people, I'm afraid.'

'Oh dear,' said Harriet, casting an amused glance at her secretary, Maud. It wasn't returned.

'We're all so glad you're back Mrs. Hawksworth,' she said with undisguised fervour. 'It was like working with Captain Bligh.'

'Weevils in the biscuits and floggings twice a day,' said Harriet, sorting the papers on her desk into piles. Their acknowledgement of her importance made her feel important; their trust in her leadership made her want to lead. It was such a relief after the days of helpless panic. On the spur of the moment, abandoning the caution she knew would have been wiser, she decided to mark her return with a significant event. 'I need an architect, Claud,' she said decisively. 'We're going to build a brand new hotel – the Florida Lake.'

One of the things that enthralled Harriet about business was the way in which an idea, once expressed, gathered momentum all of its own accord. From her vague desire to use a marginal piece of land burgeoned a full-scale project, the largest and most exciting the Hawksworth Corporation had ever known. Architects flooded her with presentations; contractors made tentative approaches, like predators smelling blood. Before the first pile was driven into the swampy subsoil, Harriet's office was daily receiving literature on everything from interior design consultants to bedlinen.

Days which began at eight-thirty ended after nine at night. She knew she was tackling too many things at once, but that was how she wanted it, no time to breathe let alone think. Welman and Bradley were engaged in a tooth and nail fight to have the collection catalogued, and on Harriet's instructions moved to prevent sales of items she knew belonged to it. Once a month, regular as clockwork, up would pop a significant work in a sale. Here a Rembrandt, there a Gauguin sketch, once a Manguin that somehow appeared in a Christie's catalogue. Ownership was always vague, and each time she succeeded in having the items withdrawn. It all helped to blacken Gareth and to add to her case.

Then there was Simone. If Maud had been rude about Jake, Simone raged, alight with fury and injustice. 'He treated me like a criminal!' she shrieked, parading across Harriet's office like a stylish giraffe.

'But what did he say?' asked Harriet, who knew Jake could be difficult – but not that difficult.

'The man is a monster,' declared Simone, and would say no more.

To Jake's credit, Simone had managed on the reduced sum given her but Harriet knew she must at all costs keep her sweet. Doubtfully, unsure if this was the right thing to do, she offered her the post of decorative consultant to the Hawksworth Hotels.

'Obviously we can call on outside firms,' she explained to Simone, wondering if she would regret this moment forever. 'But you are European, you know the feel I want. I'm after a feeling of age, good taste, discrimination. But I also want colour, and comfort, and everything must be hard-wearing, or at least look all right when it is worn. Rugs can fade but they must not wear through. Absolutely no plastic tables. The china must be good, a pleasure to eat from. At the moment no-one understands. I have to look at everything. I want you to look at it for me.'

Simone stared at her unblinking for long moments. Harriet cringed inside, waiting for the cries of insult or the wrong sort of enthusiasm. Did anyone but Harriet herself know what was wanted?

'Oriental carpets,' said Simone suddenly. 'We must find an importer. And lights, we must have beautiful lights.'

'I'll pay you a salary, of course,' said Harriet hastily.

Simone came briefly back to earth. 'What? Of course. The restaurants will be so, so difficult. Those huge rooms and tables, tables, tables. They must be made personal. How can we ask people to eat at the hotel if it has no ambience?'

'How indeed?' said Harriet, feeling tiredness wash over her. Perhaps it was going to be all right after all. Perhaps, in the end, if you worked long enough and hard enough, fine boasts and fine publicity could turn into real achievement.

Summer brought a slowing of the pace. Holidays disrupted work for everyone except Harriet, who could think of nothing worse than weeks with nothing to do. At night she drank to send herself to sleep; at weekends she took Victoria to films or on trips, anything rather than be alone with her thoughts. She had nightmares, a recurring dream in which a monster, a giant and horrible man, ate her up. When he finished her he was going to start on Victoria, she knew that with absolute certainty. After a night in which she had dreamed that dream, she couldn't bear even Claud Thomas closer to her than the width of her desk. Oddly, as time passed, she was becoming more and not less disturbed by men. When a man in the street, a crowded street in broad daylight, caught her arm to tell her she had dropped her glove and she screamed, she knew she had to do something.

She went back to the apartment, carrying the inevitable packages. Somehow, even in her busy life she found time to shop, for herself, for Victoria, for Leah, and if for none of them then for the apartment itself, buying lamps, rugs, even chairs and sofas, so that the original serviceable stuff had to be sent to junk shops. When Victoria put dirty feet on cream damask covers or threw a ball at a spun glass lampshade, Harriet knew such luxury wasn't wise but it was important to her. She couldn't do without it.

The night loomed ahead, with sleep her greatest threat. She poured herself a drink, listening to the faint sound of the television coming from Leah's room. They should move, so that Leah could have more space and Harriet could have more privacy. But tonight it wasn't privacy she wanted. It was release.

She picked up the telephone and punched out Mark Benjamin's home number. A woman answered. 'Could I speak to Mr. Benjamin please?' Harriet asked crisply. 'It's business. The Hawksworth Corporation. I am Mrs. Hawksworth.'

A moment later Benjamin came on, his voice low and warm. 'Harriet! Good to hear you at last. How can I help?'

'I'm a little lonely tonight. I wondered if you were free? I haven't eaten. I know how busy you are – '

'Never too busy to talk to my important clients,' he said matter-of-factly but there was an undercurrent of excitement in his voice. 'Do you think our last venue might be suitable? It has – facilities.'

Harriet swallowed. She felt a sudden charge of sexuality. 'Yes. Perhaps that would be best. Will you call for me?'

'Twenty minutes.'

She put on a clinging tube of a dress, cream, sleeveless, but tight to the neck. Since her spell in hospital she had been thinner than ever in her life, and the dress marked only breasts, hip-bones, pubic mound. Quickly she made herself another drink and downed it, spraying her mouth with freshener afterwards. She knocked on Leah's door. 'I'm going out, Leah. I may be late.'

'Very well, Mrs. Hawksworth. Have a nice time.'

The buzzer went downstairs and Harriet picked up her bag and left. It was all so easy. It must be meant to happen.

He touched her in the car, putting his hand on the inside of her thigh. Do I mind this? she thought. Does it remind me? But that room, that torture had nothing at all to do with a gentle, generous man who didn't want to hurt anyone. Relief made her spread her legs for him and he laughed, unbelieving. 'Hot summer nights take some beating.' He caressed her and she moaned.

They were on fire from the moment they entered the restaurant, and throughout the meal they burned. They ate cold soup and game pie, drinking champagne throughout, and then they danced. Benjamin put his lips a breath from Harriet's ear and whispered, 'I'm so hot I could put it up you here and now.'

She rubbed herself against him. 'Why don't you?'

In an instant he had signed to a waiter. They were discreetly ushered through a curtain, up some stairs, and into a room.

With the door shut not even the dance music filtered through. It was the quietest, most heavily curtained room Harriet had ever seen. There was a bed, a chair, and a small bathroom leading off. Slowly, deliberately, Harriet took hold of the hem of her dress and peeled it upwards. Benjamin was flinging off his clothes, desperate to get at her. She let him unfasten her bra and momentarily hold her breasts. Then she stepped out of her panties. 'I want to be on top,' she said suddenly.

'OK, OK. Anything you want. Just don't ask too much of me, I'm a mite keen tonight. Jeez, but you're beautiful.'

He lay prostrate on the bed, his erection pointing at her. This man didn't have a limp worm, he didn't need to hurt to please himself. Gently, carefully, she lowered herself on to him. Instead of pain, or fear, or revulsion, all she felt was the absolute rightness of it, the way the hole in her was quite filled up. She groaned and began to move on him, this way and that, making him close his eyes as he struggled to prolong it, and she knelt on the bed the better to dip and plunge. The man beneath her convulsed, she was the victor. Subsiding on to him, she let herself come.

Later, in bed together, she said, 'How do you do it with your wife?'

He reached across and pulled her close to him, an intimacy she didn't really like. 'Just the usual. She doesn't like it much. Sometimes I think we know each other too well.'

'I know what you mean.' Matching wild, night-time sexuality with day-time, proper behaviour was not easy. Sometimes it was easier to have fun with someone you didn't have to consider.

Benjamin said, 'How's about we do this once a week? Not here, it's too public. I'll rent an apartment somewhere. We can try a few things.'

She laughed. 'Like what?'

'Like – in the shower. Like – me putting on rubber things that tickle up inside you.' He took hold of her nipple and rubbed it between his fingers.

'We ought to have a better rate on our loan,' said Harriet, pushing herself against his plump but still muscled thigh.

'Thought you didn't want to mix business with pleasure.'

She reached down to hold him. 'We can all do with a few favours,' she said sweetly.

Chapter Thirty

The paper ran a banner headline: HAWKSWORTH HUSTLE. Below was a huge picture of Harriet, encased in tight grey silk fanning into a skirt from the knee. At her side, touching her gloved elbow, was Mark Benjamin.

There was nothing of any particular substance in the article, but many insinuations. The relationship was 'friendly after hours', he was escorting her to the professional dinner 'while his charming wife Patti stays home and minds the kids'. It finished with the coy tag: 'But we're sure the upright Mr. Benjamin wouldn't do anything to sully his impeccable reputation!'

'What a scandal sheet.' Harriet tossed it across to Mark. 'What does your wife think?'

He shrugged. 'I told her it was rubbish. She says she believes me.'

'And does she?'

He looked her full in the face. 'She knows something's wrong. I've had flings before, but nothing – she knows this time it's different.'

Harriet swallowed. This was something she hadn't expected. She was the beginner, he the experienced flirt, surely she was the one likely to get caught? The affection, the presents, the laughs they had together, she had thought were standard. She had not known he thought them special. 'Well then,' she said jerkily, 'it's just as well I'll be in Florida for a while. The hotel is running into a few problems, and someone's got to see to them.'

He stroked her arm. 'But it needn't be you.'

Meeting his gaze she said gently, 'Oh, yes, I think it definitely needs to be me. We need a break, Mark, to think things through. Your wife – she's a nice lady.'

'How do you know? Have you met her?'

She grinned. 'No, but you'd choose someone nice. You ought to take her out more.'

He got up and wandered round the room. Harriet noticed his paunch was a little heavier, his gait a little less light. 'You trying to tell me we're washed up?'

'Of course not! I just think we're getting into deep water, and I'm not sure I want to swim. I'm not sure you do either, not really. I'll go to Florida, Mark.'

He sighed, a depressed, disillusioned sound. 'I didn't bargain for getting hung up on you,' he said wearily.

Looking at him, knowing she should have been flattered, Harriet wondered what he saw in her. A second chance perhaps? A younger, more glamorous woman with whom he could ride the wave of success and achievement? There was no way of knowing.

Heat bit into her skin, even through the silk of her dress. A car waited at the fringe of the private strip, but it did not drive towards her. She teetered on spiked heels towards it, angry before she began. The project was taking too long and costing too much, and they couldn't even be bothered to start up a car for her. As she approached a tall, brown man in a light suit extricated himself from behind the wheel.

'Mrs. Hawksworth?'

'No, Doctor bloody Livingstone. Is this thing broken or what?'

'Why no, ma'am.' He had been half asleep, and this was indeed a rude awakening.

'Go and fetch the bags,' said Harriet, with more ice in her voice than in any of her hotels.

The air-conditioning inside the car soothed her nerves. As they drove from the coast they entered lush, verdant country, the air filled with birdcalls. Humidity was high, the heat draining. The idea of the hotel had seemed brilliant in New York, now she wasn't nearly so sure. After a while the road widened into an area of gravel and limestone, with heavy plant parked here and there upon it and an old bus set up as a cafeteria. The debris had a feeling of utter permanence.

'Where's the hotel?' she asked nervously.

Her escort, McIntyre, swivelled his head towards a narrow, rutted track. 'About half a mile down there.'

'Why so far from the machinery? That's not very efficient, surely.'

He raised an eyebrow, a fraction away from insolence. 'It's a swamp, ma'am. You're building a hotel in a swamp.'

She got out and walked over to the bus cum cafeteria. Sweat was pasting her dress to her. She knew she looked wrong, too smart and too feminine. Inside the bus were some twenty men, talking and playing cards.

'Hi,' said Harriet.

They all turned and stared at her. Someone whistled.

'My name's Harriet Hawksworth. I own this hotel.'

A large grizzled man in a checked shirt got up and waggled his head. 'Well, one up to you, Harriet Hawksworth! Bet a pretty piece like you knows how to get her hands on things!'

She swallowed hot irritation. 'And who are you?' she asked pointedly.

'I guess I'm the foreman around here. Big Tom.'

'And why aren't you working, Big Tom?' She endowed the name with mockery.

Returning the compliment he said, 'Because it's too darned hot, little lady.'

Harriet's temper snapped. 'I don't care if it's two hundred in the shade, get out there and work! As from today anyone who takes an unauthorised break is fired.'

She turned on her heel and stalked out of the bus. Flies buzzed in her ears as she marched, fiercely upright, towards the track leading to the hotel. A mosquito bit her on the eyebrow. Whose damn fool idea had it been to build a hotel here anyway? Was she mad? Mud sucked at her shoes and she heard McIntyre cursing as he trudged behind. She swung round to face him. 'Why is this road in such bad condition?'

'In this weather, ma'am – '

'You get the road made good and the refreshment bus parked by the hotel. Then perhaps there can be proper site supervision.'

Sliding and slithering she finally made it to the hotel. Desultory clangings came from somewhere out of sight. A flock of birds flew up when she called out, but the clanging did not stop. She stood on a cracked block of concrete and stared at what was before her.

The hotel had four wings, like spokes radiating from a central building. That building was to contain the reception and administration facilities, while two of the spokes housed dining room and lounges, the other two the bedrooms. All the wings protruded into the water, supported on floating pontoons. Each was still at the stage of a concrete raft, rusting metal already eating its way through the slabs.

'There should be two wings finished,' said Harriet shrilly. 'That's in the report I received.'

'That was the architect's report, ma'am,' said McIntyre.

'That has nothing to do with it! Are you working for me? Who are you anyway?'

'I'm the co-ordination manager,' he said lamely.

'Well, bully for you,' she said.

* * *

Harriet had not realised how much she had come to depend on the insulated comfort of luxury. When she arrived at the Florida Hawksworth, mud-splattered and sweating, to be received with something bordering on awe, she felt herself calming. The manager was dying to parade the staff for inspection, but Harriet took the time to bathe and change.

How different the place was since her last visit! Thick towels, deep carpets, clean windows and a fresh, clever emphasis on ceramics that suited the climate perfectly. Simone's hand was to be seen everywhere, particularly in the cool blue and silver of the lobby. The silver came from mirrors reflecting greenery, an ornamental pool, an entrancing interior summerhouse that managed to look Victorian in feel but modern in concept. When she looked at this, Harriet could forget the muddy nightmare out in the swamp.

Refreshed by her bath, she dressed in pale green linen that the maid pressed for her. She brushed her hair till it gleamed like copper, a new shade that had seemed a bit garish in New York but was right for Florida, then she telephoned the manager to ask him to introduce her to the staff. They walked through corridors lined with chambermaids, kitchens where the chefs paraded in spotless aprons and tall hats, their equipment laid out in dazzling rows. She spoke to bar staff, sipped a new cocktail, judged the new tablelinen in the dining room to be a very wise choice. It was so much like a royal progress that she began unconsciously to copy the Queen, smiling and nodding as she walked along rows of people, singling out the tallest, the shortest, the blackest or the whitest for a brief chat, occasionally stopping at someone of such mediocrity that in this alone they were outstanding. At the finish, when she had even stood and admired the interior of the cold stores and striven for something pertinent to say – 'Good heavens, isn't it cold?' did not seem all that original – she tactfully refused the manager's suggestion of dinner and asked that she should eat in her room.

'I have a great deal of business to attend to but I wonder if you and one or two of your colleagues, and your wives of course, would like to join me in the restaurant for dinner tomorrow? I should really like to see some of this lovely food I've heard about, and I can't possibly order it all for myself!'

It was the right thing to say. Lieben, the manager, clearly feeling that things were going well, rushed off to have the chefs put on red alert for the following evening, before 'phoning his wife to tell her to mortgage the house and buy something stunning to wear. Alone in her room, Harriet sat on the bed and began to laugh. Was this what she was to expect everywhere from now on? It was difficult to know if she should visit more often, so that they became used to her, or retain her rarity value. On reflection she felt it would be best if she left it to Simone to undertake the routine supervision. When Harriet herself came it would be special.

She gave a few moments' thought to Simone. The woman had seemed strained lately and Harriet had put it down to the long separation from her husband, but even before Harriet gave her the new job, she had been in the habit of spending months away from France, flying back home as and when the mood took her. What sort of man tolerated that sort of life? wondered Harriet. Was it a marriage still, or simply a convenience?

A knock on the door signalled the arrival of her meal, her request for a fish dish simply gratified by the provision of an entire salmon. If she had asked for Lieben's head on a platter she would have received it, of that she had no doubt. 'Thank you – thank you – thank you,' she repeated, as the half dozen or so flunkies arranged tables and napkins and champagne buckets. Suddenly she could stand no more. 'Good God, is one of you going to stand next to me and spoon the stuff into my mouth? Go away do, I can manage. Yes, it's lovely, but I can manage!' She flapped them out of the door and closed it firmly. Then she spooned a bit of this and a bit of that on to a plate, and lay on the bed, alternately eating and reading the report on the Florida Lake.

One thing was very clear to her. Somebody was making a lot of money out of that hotel, and it wasn't her. Half the materials seemed to have mysteriously disappeared; there were men on the payroll who in all probability didn't exist at all. The first sacking would be the firm of architects, and hard on that would come a lawsuit for negligence. But vengeance wouldn't get the hotel built.

She put her chin in her hands and thought hard, trying to put personal pride to one side for the time being. Should she abandon the project, cut her losses and get out? Was it a stupid idea? There was no way she could find out surrounded by slaves in the Florida Hawksworth, that was evident. Picking up the 'phone she made a call then she began to hurry. She went over to the wardrobe where her clothes hung in symmetrical rows, courtesy of the maid. She pulled out a pair of designer jeans, which were the scruffiest things she had, some sneakers and a loose cotton blouse. When she was dressed she tied her hair up in a ribbon, picked up a jumper and crept out of the room, scuttling into a lift just as a phalanx of staff took up station in the hallway, ready to respond to hers lightest request.

Ed McIntyre was waiting for her on the corner of the street. 'This isn't so good an idea,' he said unhappily.

'So what? It's my idea, not yours,' snapped Harriet, getting into the car next to him. 'Let's get one of those boat things. I want to see this swamp.'

'Oh, Jesus.' He looked ruefully down at his neat cream shoes. Harriet tried not to sneer.

It took a while to find someone prepared to take them out in the dark. Harriet sat on the side of a creek while McIntyre tried to negotiate and the flies buzzed and out in the darkness unknown creatures splashed. At last, tired of waiting, she went into the wooden hut and heard for herself McIntyre's feeble efforts at persuasion. Harriet glanced at the bored man across the counter, who didn't want to go and was just too polite to tell McIntyre to go take a running jump at himself.

'Look,' she said, leaning on the counter, 'the man doesn't want to take us, Ed. The best thing is if we buy one of those little rowing boats off him and take ourselves.'

The man laughed. 'I wouldn't do that, ma'am. People have been lost out there. Do you want to meet snakes and alligators?'

'Yes, definitely. Give him some money, Ed.'

'But I ain't selling!' complained the man. 'Besides, a lady like you don't understand boats.'

'Want a bet?' said Harriet, grinning. 'All right then, you'd better come. Give him the money anyway, Ed. We're making him come out when he could be at home with his feet up. Which boat shall we take?'

Somehow the man found himself inveigled into rowing the creek at night. He muttered and cursed, and told them of the diseases they would catch from the night-time miasma, and sometimes he would stop rowing, listen, and switch on the big light he had brought with him. Its eerie beam revealed a strange and ghostly world. An alligator gaped at them from a mud bank then slithered away into the water. The trees hung silver fronds down over the creek, as if in perpetual mourning, and were the creepers snakes, or only creepers?

'Big one there,' said the man suddenly, and they stared at a long trail in the water, so long a trail that they shuddered to think of what swam beneath. Ed McIntyre lifted his feet out of the slime in the bottom of the boat, and slapped his neck where the mosquitoes were biting. Harriet hugged herself in delight.

She slept late the next day, waking to brilliant sunshine and a muddy stench from her shoes. They had dripped on the carpet, and Harriet had to apologise to the maid when she came in to clean. The maid looked most surprised.

It was a good morning to be alive, Harriet decided. For once her thoughts were clear and reasoned. McIntyre could be useful while she was here, but when she left she would sack him. He was ineffectual and disinterested. It occurred to her that once she would have agonised before making such a decision, but that was before Gareth. Survival hadn't been easy after that but she had survived, and to do it she had changed. Today's Harriet existed beneath a tough carapace, and the blow that shattered it would be hard indeed.

Strict site control was obviously going to be essential if the building was ever to be finished. Goods delivered there must be the goods ordered, and they must end up in the hotel. Someone had to stand there and make sure that it happened, but who? There were the architects, of course, a new firm had been recommended before she left New York, but she was cautious. Until they had proved themselves she wasn't putting her faith in them. Which left Harriet herself. And indeed, who else was there who realised that unless this gaping wound in the Corporation's finances was plugged, and quickly, they would all bleed to death? Who else was there who wouldn't take backhanders, sit in the shade when they should burn in the sun, pass a load through because at first glance it looked all right? New York would get by without her for a while, and as for Victoria, she could come out for a week or so later on. Yes, this hotel was going to be built under Harriet's eye or not at all.

Next morning she left, elegantly dressed, waving farewell to the entire staff of the hotel gathered on the front step. Passers-by stared and took photographs, thinking that although they didn't know who she was now, they would soon find out because she sure must be important. Later that afternoon Harriet, in jeans and boots, took delivery of a vast caravan that was winched, inch by inch, on to the dubious ground next to the hotel. It was her new home.

Every morning she woke wondering how she would summon the strength to get out of bed, and every evening she crawled back into it to sleep like the dead. In between she wore hard hat and boots, ate out of the cafeteria and yelled at people.

Big Tom was her personal enemy. A powerful ganger, if he told the men to jump to it they did. If he didn't they didn't. Harriet's attempts to motivate Tom were legion. She tried persuasion, she tried threats, she tried bonuses and pay-cuts, the last of which occasioned a two-day walk out. Finally, exasperated beyond reason, she stormed into a coffee break that was extending to an hour and belted Tom over the head with the lump of wood she happened to be carrying. Blood spurted upwards. Harriet stared at it in horror, convinced that somehow she had just committed murder. So shocked was she that she didn't even cry, simply turned and went to her caravan, sitting there shaking and waiting to be arrested. Nothing happened. When she finally went out she was met with the amazing sight of men working, Big Tom amongst them, wearing a huge white bandage. It was the end of her labour problems.

Not so the architectural ones. The hotel concept was good, the design itself faulty. Pontoons that were supposed to float didn't, watertight seals let in water all the time. She called in an expert on floating bridges, discovered a watertight seal used on oil rigs, and then fell foul of conservationists who wanted the original permission for the hotel revoked. They maintained, rightly, that the construction traffic was playing havoc with the ecology of the surrounding area. Harriet was forced to suspend work on the hotel for a month while a certain variety of toad hopped interminably to spawning grounds, one of which was right next to the hotel. She took it bravely, commissioning one of the naturalists to produce a toad sculpture, to be exhibited in the finished hotel. The opposition simmered on hold.

'Will this never end?' she hissed to herself one day, slamming the door of her caravan. She was becoming very tired of her new home, luxurious though it was. So she read a lot, art books mostly, lingering over the paintings that most took her fancy, committing to memory the details that would mark them out if ever she saw them. Hers wasn't the only caravan on site, but since the lay-off it was the only one occupied. The night was unusually silent. No blaring televisions, no records playing, just the waterland sounds of the swamp. She thought she ought to go back to New York for a while, or get Victoria out here for a holiday, but New York was cold and Leah telephoned every few days with news of Victoria's friends and parties. She was doing fine, there was no need to disturb her.

It was pleasantly warm outside, a moonlit, starlit night. Taking a torch Harriet pulled on her boots and went for a stroll, ignoring the hotel, looking at the wetlands that surrounded it. Solitude was sometimes delicious.

An engine sounded in the darkness, but quickly died. Harriet's scalp prickled. Unexplained noises in the night were always frightening. She turned to go back to the caravan, to see who was coming, but then she thought, I'm alone here, it could be anyone. Her torch clicked off. Feeling foolish she crouched down against some reeds, hearing something slither away into the water. Whatever that was it didn't frighten her nearly so much as the tall, dark figure looming up against the lighted caravan. Who was it? What had they come for?

'Mrs. Hawksworth!' The shout froze her thoughts. Suddenly she was back on the island, on Corusca, and in a black, black night on a mountain. Instead of the fire the caravan light blazed behind him. She remembered terror, remembered too bewitching guile.

'Mrs. Hawksworth! Harriet!'

'What do you want, Jerome?' She didn't move. He wouldn't see her in the dark, dazzled as he was by the lights.

'Time we talk, Harriet,' he called back. 'You safe with me.'

'Oh, yes?' She stood up and walked slowly towards him. His size alone intimidated her, his shoulders twice the width of hers, towering a foot above her. He was dressed in a suit and looked good in it, but his face was wary.

'Come in,' said Harriet, preceding him into the caravan. 'Would you like a drink?'

'No, thanks. Has Gareth been hereabouts?' He lowered his long body on to a bench. Something about him was unmistakable Henry Hawksworth, perhaps the arrogance.

'If Gareth comes here I shall shoot him,' she said calmly. 'I've got a gun. You can tell him I said that.'

'Gareth and me don't speak.' He leaned back and let the silence develop.

At last Harriet said, 'What do you want from me? I thought you were squabbling with Gareth about the island.'

'I got a claim to it as good as his.'

'And mine is better than both,' said Harriet, sipping the drink she had poured herself.

'That as may be. You ain't getting anywhere though, are you?' He grinned at her with an attempt at cheer, but a tiny muscle twitched next to his eye.

Something's happened, thought Harriet. He's been forced out. 'You're going to have to tell me,' she said bluntly, and sat back to wait until he did.

Hatred made Jerome speak faster than usual, driven on by an emotion so powerful that it frightened Harriet to see it. That was the Hawksworth in him, such intensity of feeling, of purpose. They all had it in some degree.

'I left him alone in the big house,' said Jerome. 'I don't mind that, he can have the pictures, they ain't no good to me or my people. I weren't going to leave him his sister. She's safe with me, I take care of her. But he don't like that. He come one night and take her, and next thing I hear he's got her in some hospital.'

'What about Nathan, her child?' asked Harriet.

'He stays with me. My people see to him. Gareth don't want Madeline see, he just don't want me to have her. After she went we burned the house a little, but he put it out. Some of the pictures didn't look so good after that and it scared him. He started trying to get them off the island and I let him, I don't mind, I want him off the island. He's got enough of them now, he's got them safe. He don't really want Corusca, but he don't want me to get it. He's been to the authorities, telling tales. Says we do voodoo. Murder people. They going to send the police and make people say what he wants, he's set it up. He's going to do for me, Mrs. Hawksworth.'

Harriet watched him over the rim of her glass. 'Are you a bad man, Jerome?' she asked. 'That night at the fire – I remember all that.'

He tapped a long finger against his lips. 'That was a big, big magic. The people don't need that magic now.'

'What do they need?'

He breathed through his nose and stared at her darkly. 'Doctors. A hospital. Food to eat, clothes to wear. Corusca's poor, so poor. The people need the land, Harriet! I'll give it to them. I won't take it. That Gareth, he gives them nothing.'

'But I haven't got the island, it isn't mine,' she said, pretending innocence.

Jerome leaned forward. 'You come to the island. You be with me when the police come. We tell tales of old Hawksworth and what he did. Everyone knows about you, everyone believes you! You tell them how you trust me to take care of Corusca for you. How it grieves you to see the people suffering, because Gareth won't let go. How he has the collection, worth such a lot, and welcome to it. We're not greedy people, you and me. We tell how we're giving the land to the people.'

Harriet got up and washed her glass at the sink, suddenly annoyed. 'I won't let him have the collection. It's mine and I want it. Besides, if I give the land to the people, as you call them, what do I get? I don't have to do this for you, I don't get anything out of it.'

'You get something,' said Jerome. 'Beautiful island, Corusca. Beautiful house. If I rule that island you get the house, and after you can build a hotel. Not big, but very special. A special hotel on a very special island. That's what you can have.'

'I still want the collection.'

Jerome shrugged. 'You fight for it, girl, it ain't my war.'

They talked for a long time, about the island, about past times, about the future. At last Harriet went to bed and Jerome bedded down in one of the empty caravans. She lay and wondered if this was sensible. That island was tainted, nothing good ever came of it, and Jerome was the essence of the place. But if she didn't help him, Gareth would win. That was something she would never, ever permit.

Chapter Thirty-One

The trawler chugged and rolled in the choppy sea. Harriet leaned against the deckhouse, sickened by the smell of old fish, watching the dark smudge that was land swell on the horizon. She was jumpy with nerves, unwilling to remember the last time she had come here, yet haunted by thoughts of it. The day was cloudy, the wind changeable and jerky. She registered that automatically, only then realising that the wind was of no significance when you weren't sailing. To her surprise she had a sudden, sharp longing for a heeling deck, the quiet and the clean air of a sailing boat, she who had longed to be rid of the life.

The island was closer now. She could distinguish trees, protected from the sea by a white ribbon of sand. Above, shrouded in mist, rose the hills. It was hearbreakingly beautiful.

'She don't change. She always stay the same,' Jerome said.

'Is it evil?' she asked. 'I used to think so.'

'That wasn't the island. That was Hawksworth.'

They chugged smokily into the harbour. Harriet stared about her, remembering as if it were yesterday. A child stood watching them, a white boy. 'Hello, Nathan.' Harriet held out her hand, but he didn't approach her. He watched from blue eyes beneath a shaggy blond fringe, inexpertly cut with blunt shears. He wore men's shorts cut down, and a man's shirt minus the cuffs. She felt sudden guilt, though it wasn't her fault. The child had no-one to care for him.

Jerome took off his suit jacket and held it out, and Nathan ran to cradle it reverently in his arms. 'You been a good child?' asked Jerome, tilting the small chin.

'No.'

Jerome laughed and tousled his head.

Harriet was to stay in the big house. The thought appalled her, but if she truly thought she owned the place, then her husband's home was hers. There's nobody there, she told herself. No ghosts, no murderers. Victoria was born there, it wasn't all misery. And she stepped up into the wagon that was to take her home.

On the journey she felt again Corusca's charm. It would be a crime to drag this scented, tropical garden into the twentieth century, complete with concrete and motors and plastic. Here was Eden, and they had the chance to kill the snake. Why replace it with another kind of monster? Her mind drifted in the warm sunshine, visualising the small, palm-thatched hotel she would build, so discreet that from a distance nothing would be visible, not a beach umbrella or a neon sign anywhere. That would be its charm, it would be a jewel hidden in the island itself.

The wagon swung into the garden of the house. Harriet's hands clutched at her seat as she gazed about her. Everything overgrown, so like the first time. And the house – the marks of smoke blackened the walls, part of the roof had fallen in. Strewn from the windows was broken furniture, picture frames, charred curtains.

'Oh God,' she muttered to herself. 'How I hate this sort of mess.'

She went through the house from room to room, forcing herself to be unemotional. Jerome was right, Gareth had stripped it of the collection. Here and there hung a small and obscure picture, but on every wall were the tell-tale fade marks that spoke of paintings removed. Some of the furniture had gone too, the Louis Quinze, the tantalus taken from some ship hundreds of years before. She felt a sense of loss, though she had never thought them truly hers. But they belonged in the house. It was diminished by their departure.

The damage was mostly superficial, by smoke and some water. This house fights against destruction, she thought, they cannot defeat it. She reached out and shook a heavy velvet curtain, one that she had seen hung. It was dusty and moth-eaten at the hem, but the colour was as rich, the material as weighty, as when it had first come here. What lovely rooms they were, tall and spacious. A house like this was not for such as Gareth.

The next day, when she was barely settled, the police arrived. They came by launch, and as they landed someone started ringing the bell they usually reserved for summoning help when a fishing boat missed the harbour entrance and hit the reef. Harriet knew what it was, but when Nathan cycled fast up to the door, yelling, 'They're here, they're here. He says to be ready!' she wouldn't let the child go, holding on to him and saying 'Are there many of them? Is Gareth with them?'

'He sure is,' said Nathan, and spat emphatically.

'Stay here,' instructed Harriet. 'You're to stay with me. Jerome wants it like that.'

He eyed her rebelliously but when she went to change she was surprised to find him still there when she came down. 'You look good,' he said, and she nodded. It was advisable to be well-dressed when meeting strangers you wanted to impress and she had gone the whole way, in a drifting dress of white cotton jersey that wouldn't have looked out of place for afternoon tea at a Garden Party. 'Haven't you any shoes?' she asked the child. He shook his head. 'When I ask you about your shoes, say you got them wet.'

'Why?'

'Because I don't want them to think you haven't any. I'll buy you some, I promise.'

He shrugged again, clearly not concerned about shoes.

They waited. Parrots squabbled in the trees, unnaturally loud it seemed. Blood thundered in Harriet's ears, her heart beating so fast that it was a continuous rumble. She couldn't face Gareth, she knew she couldn't. Suddenly she picked up her skirts and began to run upstairs. The sound of wheels gave her pause.

'You can't go. They're here.' Nathan was watching her.

In the end you couldn't escape. She would finish that man, by God she would! When they entered she was poised on the stairs as if just descending.

There were six men, four in uniform. The other two were in tropical suits. She didn't look at them. One of them had to be Gareth. 'Why do you come storming into my house?' she asked gently. 'Is something wrong? I believe the knocker still works.'

'Like hell it's your house. I want you out Harriet, now! My lawyer's here to back me up. Tell them, Clive.'

The lawyer said nothing. With a supreme physical effort, Harriet turned her head and stared at Gareth. His hair was on end, his tie crooked. High colour stained his cheeks. 'My my,' she said, 'you do look a mess. I'm surprised they didn't try and lynch you the moment you came ashore.'

Gareth flushed and glared at her because Jerome had indeed prepared a reception committee that had erupted into apparently spontaneous abuse as soon as they saw him.

One of the policemen said, almost apologetically, 'If we could talk to you for a moment, ma'am? We've had a complaint from Mr. Hawksworth here and we have to investigate it.'

Harriet linked her fingers together. 'I never thought I would see the day when my husband's home would be squabbled over like this,' she said wearily. 'Very well, do come through. I'm afraid the house is in a terrible mess. Things have been taken, there's been a fire – I hardly know where to begin.' She led the way into the vast, impressive drawing room, its chandeliers still intact. Nathan stood and watched the procession then, as Gareth passed, threw a ripe tomato at him. It splashed against the man's trousers.

'You little bastard – '

'Nathan!' Harriet rushed to protect him. She felt distinct distaste for embracing him, but did so anyway. 'You mustn't do things like that, darling. I know how you feel but – you mustn't. Where are your shoes, dear?'

'I got them wet,' he said, completely dead-pan.

'Silly boy. Put them in the sunshine.'

'Can't I stay with you?'

This child will go far, thought Harriet wryly. 'Very well, dear,' she said sweetly, and hand in hand they went through to the drawing room.

Harriet and Nathan sat together, a touching study. Gareth didn't sit down at all, but paced about, making Harriet flinch every time he passed near her. 'Sit down, sir, please,' said the sergeant curtly. 'You're making the lady nervous.'

'Thank you, sergeant,' said Harriet in a low voice. 'He can be very violent.'

Gareth laughed shrilly.

The sergeant stated the case in a loud, flat, voice that made everything he said seem improbable. 'We are here to investigate serious charges made by Mr. Hawksworth, against you and a half-caste named Jerome, among others. He has specified certain practices, namely voodoo and drug-taking, and accuses the aforementioned Jerome of child murder. He says certain of the islanders will bear witness to this, and that he can conduct us to a major voodoo place of worship where human remains will be found.'

Harriet put her hand to her mouth. 'Well,' she said, 'are you sure there isn't anything else? Piracy on the high seas, slavery, brothel-keeping? People as depraved as we clearly are would surely not stop at a bit of murder.'

The sergeant coughed. 'I'm afraid we have to take these charges seriously, ma'am.'

Suddenly Nathan piped up, extending a finger towards Gareth and yelling: 'It's him! He does all the bad things, he took my mother away!'

'Be quiet, Nathan,' snapped Harriet.

The lawyer began to rummage in his briefcase. Gareth was biting his nails. Harriet sighed. 'It's like this,' she began, 'in my husband's young day, voodoo wasn't unusual on this island any more than any other. My husband was a very old man when he died, a great many things changed in his lifetime. But, obviously, Gareth heard the tales and remembered them. Now, when the people have chased him off the island, he wants revenge. That's all it is.'

The sergeant turned his hat in his hands. 'Are you saying voodoo isn't practised any more?'

'I'm sure it still holds sway up in the hills,' said Harriet. 'But in a very mild form – charms, love potions, that sort of thing. They might even run to murdering the odd chicken, but I assure you they would eat it afterwards. You see, my husband was a great man but he belonged to a past era. The island hasn't developed at all, it is terribly poor. You'll find dead babies all right, but they will have died of hunger and disease. That's what Jerome wants to tackle here, and I intend to help him.'

Again the sergeant turned his hat. 'And you deny any knowledge of drug taking?'

'Not at all. I'm quite sure Gareth has taken drugs. After all, his sister is even now in a dependency clinic. You'll understand I don't want to talk about these things here.' She gestured towards Nathan and the policeman nodded. There was a general feeling in the room that here was good sense, a decent, honourable, motherly woman.

'What a load of bullshit,' said Gareth slowly. 'Don't worry, sergeant, I'll find you the proof. I'll find you people who have been there, who will tell what they saw. That woman will do anything to get what she wants.'

The sergeant stood up. 'We will have to investigate, ma'am. We'll be here for a few days, looking around, talking to people.'

Harriet glanced quickly at Gareth, and as quickly away. 'If he's staying, I want a guard.'

The sergeant glanced from one to the other. 'I'll see what I can do.'

Harriet tried not to smirk.

Next day Jerome came to the house early. He was tense and wary, speaking in hushed tones in case he should be overheard by the policeman occupying himself by looking for things buried in the garden. 'They gone up to the hills. They gonna find things, we can't hide it all.'

'They won't find much,' whispered Harriet. 'Not in this climate. Anyway, you don't have to be responsible for it. Blame the hill people.'

'Someone will talk,' he said grimly.

'Haven't you seen to that? What about the bag?'

His eyes were very dark. 'I can't scare them enough no more, not with the police here.'

'Can't you?' She went to the window and looked out at the policeman, digging holes under the frangipani. The scent of the garden drifted in, so sweet, so sensual. She came back to Jerome and put her hands on his huge upper arms. 'Don't let Gareth win,' she said softly. 'He mustn't have any of this.'

Word came of finds in the hills and samples being sent to the mainland for analysis. The very air seemed thick and cloying, full of threats and lies and mystery. Nathan came and stood watching while Harriet scrubbed smokestains from the exquisite linenfold panelling in the library.

'They're digging by the rock,' he said suddenly.

Harriet stopped. She swallowed, and began again. 'Are they?'

'And they found Barnaby dead this morning.'

She dropped her brush with a clatter. She knew Barnaby, a man of about Jerome's age, gentle and nondescript. 'How did he die?'

Nathan shrugged. 'He was dead in his bed. Someone killed him. I guess he was going to tell.'

She got up and went to the child, taking him by the shoulders and shaking him. 'You – must – not – say – such – things! Perhaps it was a heart attack. Has anyone sent for Dr. Muller?'

Nathan shrugged. 'No-one has seen him since the police came. He hides all the time. He thinks he's going to die, too.'

She hurried downstairs and out to the ancient bicycle that was all the transport she had at her disposal. Quickly she mounted it and rode away, wincing as every squeak announced her departure to the policeman digging in the garden but no-one followed her. She rode breathlessly into town, aware that the day was growing dull, a thin haze of cloud obscuring the sun.

The street was deserted, there was no-one about. In the harbour a few boats tossed on a choppy swell, but no-one tended them. Dr. Muller's house was closed up and shuttered. She rode up to it and hammered on the door, knocking and knocking until at last a voice said feebly, 'Go away. I won't come out.'

'This is Harriet Hawksworth,' she said. 'Let me in at once, I must speak to you. If you don't let me in you will be in trouble, believe me.'

After a long pause there was the sound of bolts being drawn back. Harriet slipped through the door into a dark, hot room. It smelled of sweat.

He looked dirty and much older, a frightened man cowering away from the inevitable. 'I must get away,' he said, plucking at his lip. 'Now the police have come – I don't know what I should do. After all this time.'

'Have you seen the man who died, Barnaby?'

He shrugged. 'What is there to see? I don't care about that. They will come for me soon.'

Harriet wished she hadn't come. Muller had hitched his star to Henry Hawksworth, and then to his son Gareth, and now he was losing. He deserved to lose but it was horrible to watch. 'I thought you would talk to the police,' she said.

It wasn't sweat she could smell, but fear. 'Don't let them come for me,' he pleaded, catching her hand. 'Don't let them take me away.'

'I don't owe you a thing.' She pulled her hand free and wiped it down her skirt, pulling the door wide and running out into the dead quiet street.

All day the police searched in the hills. That night, with the wind wailing in the forest, a small procession trod unknown paths to a burial ground. Since the days of the pirates and before, dead men had lain silent on the hillsides. The police had not known Barnaby existed, they would not know that he had gone.

Towards midnight rain began to fall. It filled every hole and gulley. In that soil, in that heat, everything rotted back into the earth, and when the policemen went back up the mountain they could not even find the holes they had dug themselves. They asked in the villages and nobody said a word. Things had been bad, yes, when the old man was young. But these days things were better. If only we had a little more money, some help with the land, a hotel maybe. The island closed against the incomers.

The sergeant visited Harriet before he left. She and Nathan were spreading rugs out to air, now that the rain had stopped. She stood up, dusting her hands. 'Are you leaving us? I thought you'd stay much longer.'

'We've got to get back. I'll be making my report, of course.'

'May we know what will be in it?'

The sergeant grinned at her. He liked Harriet, she was about the most straightforward thing there was on this island. There was a feeling about the place – something about the way people looked at you. He'd been a policeman too long not to be able to sniff fear. But, well, it was an isolated place and these small communities were nervous of strangers. He could make excuses for them. 'There are samples to be analysed,' he said, 'but we didn't find too much. Your – er – stepson isn't too fond of you, is he?'

'Gareth? It's understandable. I have his inheritance. But if you got to know him a little better you'd see why.'

'Yeah. I get you.' The sergeant lingered a little, because she looked fresh and wholesome and she and the kid made a nice picture standing together. 'What's going to happen to the boy?' he asked. 'Going to send him to school, are you?'

'I haven't decided.'

Harriet watched him go, bouncing uncomfortably in the wagon as the horse picked its way along the track. Every time it rained the stones washed to the surface, and she would have to get some tarmac. She turned and gazed up at the house. Had she won it? Was this the last round or only the first? The legal wrangling could go on for years, but if she behaved as if it was hers, if she simply took it – who was to stop her? And, once she had established her home here, how could Gareth evict her? She thought of the apartment in New York, so cramped and cold. How Victoria would love to run along these beaches, splashing in these mild blue waves that looked so innocent in the sunshine. To live here always would be impossible, but to come back to Corusca after the rigours of city life would be bliss.

She turned again, and Nathan caught her eye. He was watching her, such a good-looking child. 'Dr. Muller shot himself last night,' he said.

Harriet felt her knees go suddenly weak. She sat down on the wet grass, and the child stared at her, expressionless. 'Sometimes I hate this place,' she whispered.

Chapter Thirty-Two

After Corusca, the Florida swamp seemed almost homely. Harriet felt an immense desire to get in touch again, to take up those threads she had left hanging while she was on the island.

Work had resumed on the Lake hotel while she was away, and the snags and problems were legion. Harriet was torn, she knew she should go to New York and see Leah and Victoria, she knew she should talk to Simone and Claud Thomas, yet she was needed here and no-one else would do. So she did what she could by telephone and sent effusive letters and cards to her daughter, once despatching a huge teddy bear that she knew would take up half Victoria's room. It didn't matter. Soon they wouldn't be in New York, soon they would be – where? Perhaps Corusca, perhaps elsewhere, she hadn't time to think of it now, when there was so much amiss with the hotel.

Big Tom came to see her one evening in her caravan. He looked strangely diminished when he was washed and in smart clothes, and seemed uneasy.

'Have a drink,' offered Harriet, wondering if this heralded another strike. She couldn't afford it, not at this juncture. The hotel had to be finished in three months, beyond that and the bank would lose its patience. Her credit with Mark Benjamin wouldn't stretch all the way to bankruptcy. She poured Tom a beer.

'I've been meaning to talk to you,' he began, leaning his massive elbows on the flimsy caravan table. Harriet heard it crack. 'There's something going on.'

'What sort of thing?'

'Well, I don't rightly know. While you was away I hung around some, keeping an eye on things. Seemed OK. Then when we started up again I began to notice. We do a job one day, two days later they check it and find a fault. So we do it again. Sometimes we do a job three and four times, and it ain't never right. Now, we didn't do that job wrong in the first place, no sir.'

'What sort of things?'

'I don't know. Concrete joints. Beams. Sometimes welded steel on those floating things that damned fool architect thought of. My thinking is that someone's coming round here at night and putting those things wrong.'

Harriet shivered. It sounded so horribly probable. 'Don't the men notice? I mean, they could have done it wrong, no-one's perfect.'

'They notice, course they do. But there's a lot of men here. Not often a man goes back on the job he did first time, it's someone else. At first I chased them on it, thinking it was bad work, but it ain't.'

Harriet got up and walked up and down her little strip of carpet. If only she had never started this hotel, if only she had stayed where she was safe. 'What do I do, Tom?' she asked. 'Do I call the police?'

'Nah.' He put his massive fist into the palm of his other hand. 'We'll see to it. You pay the extra time, OK?'

'You are a grasping bastard,' she said feelingly. 'And don't kill anyone. The publicity would be terrible.'

He stood up, grinning. 'Right on, Miz Hawksworth.'

The next night Harriet sat in her caravan, jumping with nerves. The men were out there somewhere, waiting. They had seen to it that during the day many jobs had been done which could easily be tampered with. If anyone was going to come they would come tonight.

The waiting was terrible. Two hours, three, and still only the trilling of night birds in the swamp, the bilious croaking of frogs and toads. She felt so confined she wanted to get out of the caravan, but if she did so the chances were she would be flattened by one of her own men. So she waited and waited.

Dawn was breaking. Harriet slumped uneasily, still in her clothes. There was a sudden yell, an Indian whoop, a chorus of voices like a pack of hunting hounds. Startled, she sat frozen, then leaped to the door, flinging it open and standing framed by the light. 'Who is it? Who have you got?' she shouted. The plastic wall of the caravan next to her head disintegrated. Pieces flew into her face. She fell back inside.

Big Tom came running, thundering through the door. 'Miz Hawksworth? You all right?'

She sat up, touching her face. 'I don't know. What was that?'

'We got one. Two others got away. One of them took a shot at you.'

Harriet stared at him in disbelief. 'Somebody shot at me? Somebody tried to kill me?'

'They sure did, ma'am.'

Some of the men were dragging their victim towards the caravan. Harriet felt sick, shocked and ill. When she looked into the bloodied face of Ed McIntyre something shifted in her head but she couldn't make the connection. 'What's he doing here?'

'It was him, ma'am. He was one of them. They'd use a man that knew about the place.'

'Yes – yes, I suppose so.' She stared at McIntyre, wondering what on earth she should do about him. 'I only fired you,' she said vaguely. 'I didn't mean – '

One of his eyes was closing. He mumbled through broken lips, 'What didn't you mean? You didn't think about what it would mean to me and you didn't care. The car's gone. We lost our house. My wife's talking about getting a divorce. You just blamed me for all the shit about this hotel.'

'Who put you up to it?'

He shrugged. 'I don't know and I don't care. I wish they had fucking shot you.'

She folded her arms around herself, as if in defence against his venom. He'd been bad at his job, she'd been right to sack him. But he was right, she hadn't given it any thought. It had been one of those things, one of the many things in a busy day. People were being sacked all over her organisation, it wasn't up to her to worry about each and every one, was it?

'Let him go,' she said unhappily. 'I don't want him here, take him away and let him go.'

'We could take him to the police,' said Tom.

'No, we couldn't. They'd call us vigilantes. And that's what we're going to be from now on. I want armed guards on this site night and day. See to it please, Tom.'

When she was alone she put her head into her hands and cried. People hated her, and it was so unfair when she was only trying to do her best. People hated her who did not even know her, they hated what she stood for and what she did. She felt so lonely suddenly. She longed for Victoria, and more than that she longed for Jake. He would understand. Her hand shaking, she picked up the telephone and booked a flight to New York.

A photographer caught her as she was walking through the airport, and she was too tired for smiles. Next day she appeared grim-faced under the heading: PROBLEMS FOR HAWKSWORTH – ARE THEY BUST? 'Harriet Hawksworth flew hastily back to New York yesterday to rescue her ailing company. Drained by the twin burdens of the new, disastrous Florida hotel and her massive legal bills as she fights to exclude her stepson from his inheritance, Harriet Hawksworth's business doesn't look good. Even her banker and "good friend" Mark Benjamin has expressed his concern. What does this grim expression tell us?'

Harriet didn't read it until late in the afternoon, and even then it didn't seem to matter much. Publicity was one thing, reality something very different. When she got to her apartment she had ached with weariness, was buoyed up only by the thought of seeing Victoria. There was a banner on the door saying 'Welcome home, Mummy', and a bunch of balloons tied to the handle.

She rang the bell, calling, 'Hello everyone! I'm home!' There was the sound of scuffling inside and Harriet wondered what sort of surprise they had for her. Then the door opened. Leah stood there, smiling nervously.

'Leah! How lovely to see you. Where is she then? Where's my little girl?'

Protruding from behind the sofa were a pair of well-shod feet. Harriet pounced on them, crying, 'I know where she's hiding!'

The feet kicked viciously. 'Go away! Go away, I don't like you. I don't want you here, go away!'

'But it's me, Mummy' said Harriet, her voice cracking with surprise and hurt.

Leah hurried across. 'I'm sorry, Mrs. Hawksworth, she's been a little fidgety lately. It's been a long time – '

'Not that long. I am her mother!' Determinedly Harriet dragged her daughter out. Furious grey eyes glared at her. 'I don't want you. I want Leah. Leah!' And she held out her arms to her nurse.

Harriet fought her desire to sack the woman. She wrestled with it for the best part of a week and by then was immersed in other problems. She hadn't realised how things were slipping in New York. Lunching with Mark Benjamin, she said shakily: 'You know I came back for a rest. Why didn't anyone tell me what was happening here?'

He shrugged and touched the back of her hand with his fork, a gesture of surprising intimacy in a public place. 'It's not so bad. If you get the hotel finished soon you'll be OK.'

'What about the law suit? I'm not letting up now. I've nearly beaten him.'

'I'm not so sure. When – if – it gets to court, if he gets the judgment then you are out. No matter if you've been living on that island for ten years, it won't matter to the judge.'

'It would take them another ten years to get me off,' she said sulkily.

'Maybe so.' His foot crossed the divide beneath the table and rubbed her calf. 'I've missed you like shit, Harriet.'

'Me too.' An automatic response, but was it true? When she thought about it, she hadn't missed him at all. Often, how often, she had thought, I wish Jake was here, I wish I could just talk to him about this, because he was on the same wavelength somehow. He didn't dote in the way Benjamin did. Had it irritated her before? It did now.

'I've got to go, Mark.' She rolled her napkin into a ball and tossed it on the table. 'Things to do.'

'Let's meet after hours. Tonight, or some day this week?'

'Darling, I'd love to, but I've got a few problems. Victoria's being difficult, I think it might be the nanny. You can't tell what happens when you're not there, can you? It might be anything.'

He wasn't all that interested in Harriet's childcare problems. His own wife brought his brood up herself and tended to bore him with tales of rashes and squabbles. He didn't need it from Harriet, too. He said brusquely, 'I think Leah's wonderful, and the child adores her!'

'Yes.'

Harriet was conscious of the most burning, vicious emotion she had ever experienced in her life. Pure, undiluted jealousy. Leah must go.

In the cab back to the office she tried to sort out her priorities. First, she must get in touch with Simone. It seemed she had been touring the hotels quite happily, but had suddenly dropped everything and rushed back to France. Projects hung in abeyance waiting for her, but she did not seem to be going to reappear. Why did people permit their personal lives to get in the way of business? thought Harriet angrily. It wasn't necessary. Then there was publicity. Once people thought you were failing it was a short step to failure. So, she must boost confidence, laugh off all the doom and gloom stories. The PR people would have to get on to it, arrange an interview with a tame reporter. If only that damned hotel was finished! Wasn't that the really important thing?

The cab stopped outside the office and she got out, signalling the commissionaire to pay. Her head was aching fit to burst. What on earth was she doing here at all when the one person in the world that was all hers didn't love her any more? It wasn't fair! Who was she doing it all for if not Victoria? Leah had stolen the child's affections, that was all there was to it. She should go as soon as Harriet could find someone else.

As soon as she stepped out of the lift she yelled: 'Maud! I want a new nanny right now.' She realised someone else was there and because she wasn't up to visitors grunted morosely and ignored him.

'I always said you shouldn't be allowed out on your own.'

Harriet spun on her heel. 'Jake! Oh Jake, Jake, I was never so glad to see anyone in my whole life!'

He caught her up and spun her round till her shoes fell off. 'You look bloody gorgeous!' They hugged, giggling with delight.

'Am I to contact the agencies right away?' enquired Maud in a thin voice. 'Oh, don't bother with that now. I'll talk to Jake about it. Jake always tells me what to do,' she said happily.

He held her at arm's length and said in amazement, 'You hate me telling you what to do! Giving you an order is like the scent of blood to a shark.'

'No, it's not!' She pouted at him, feeling all at once deliciously helpless. 'Just at the moment I really need your help.'

'Hmmm. Let's go to bed and talk about it.' He took her hand and began towing her, shoeless, to the lift. Harriet went scarlet, bubbling with protests. Maud picked up the shoes and handed them to her expressionlessly as she disappeared into the lift.

They were alone in the apartment. Jake's weight crushed Harriet, the bulk of his muscles pressed down on her. Everything about him seemed hard, tireless. He thrust at her as if he would go on for ever. Her mind turned in on itself. She was alone with intense, mounting pressure, building and building into a molten, liquid gold explosion.

His breath was hot on her cheek. She opened her eyes to find him watching her, his face slack with pleasure. She put her arms around him and held him close, reluctant to let him slip away. Why did she ever want more than this?

Later, Harriet made Eggs Benedict, at which she was rather good. So good in fact that she made them far too often. Jake watched her, wearing only his underpants.

'Why are you here?' she asked, trying to keep her voice light. Instead she sounded helplessly insecure.

'To see you.'

'Not just that, surely?' How lovely if it was just that.

''Course not. I'm building a boat for someone, we're discussing plans. And you'll never believe who it is – bloody Angus Derekson!'

Her mouth dropped open. 'You must be mad! If ever two people didn't get on it was you two.'

Jake considered. 'Things are a bit different nowadays. We're all older, I've got a few good things under my belt.'

'Like what?' She flipped the eggs expertly out of the pan.

'Oh, for Christ's sake! Don't you know I designed the winning boat in the last round the world race? Mine, my own work! The only one didn't get dismasted, have its hull stove in or have the whole crew seasick the entire trip. And it beat the fucking record!' He scowled at her, furious.

Harriet laughed at him. ''Course I knew. Never thought I'd hear you boast.'

He flushed. 'Well, I was rather pleased.'

'I did send you a telegram,' she commented. 'You didn't reply.'

'Oh, God, did you? I had stacks of them. Everybody I never wanted to speak to again congratulated me. Anyway, I was drunk for a week, the cottage got a bit messed up.'

'Oh, yes?' She whacked the plate down in front of him and he caught her hand.

'Oh, yes. And I didn't have to come here for the boat, I came to see you. I just added the boat to make it a full day. I didn't want to be twiddling my thumbs while you were conquering the world, or at least buying it.' He grimaced at the gadgets, pictures, chairs, posters and jars that crammed the little kitchen. It was Harriet's turn to flush.

Leah brought Victoria in around four o'clock. Harriet couldn't be natural, couldn't even look at the nanny. Jake chatted to her, asking how she had been, how her family were, all the things that Harriet didn't give a damn about. She brushed Victoria's hair rather pointedly, because it was tousled by the wind. The child grimaced and squirmed. 'Let Leah do it. Leah!'

'I'm doing it!' She could have cracked her with the brush.

Jake resolved the issue by making his handkerchief into a rabbit while Harriet did two plaits, largely because Leah always tied the child's hair with a ribbon. They didn't suit her. Victoria looked angular and rather plain.

'By the way, we're dining with Derekson and his wife,' said Jake casually.

'Suppose I've got another engagement?'

'Then suppose you cancel it? I'm only here four days, damn it.'

How he exasperated her! But oh, how delicious it was to have him here, turning a world which had seemed to threatening, so unpredictable, into a giant, never-serious game. He was so much more flexible than Harriet, bobbing along like a cork while she stood, fixed, and was battered. Which was why, of course, they didn't stick.

The Dereksons were waiting for them at one of those New York restaurants where people go to be seen with people. Harriet was flying all flags, in a tube of burgundy satin, boned to support her breasts and allow them almost to overflow. She wore diamond drop earrings, like miniature golf balls.

'Are those real?' asked Jake, peering at them as he tied his bow tie crooked.

'Yes, but I hire them. Don't tell anyone, though.' She straightened his tie.

'Just as long as you don't expect me to fight off any jewel thieves or muggers.' He reached into her dress and expertly scooped out her left breast, bending down to lick the nipple. Harriet felt dizzy. She never knew how much she missed sex until she had it again. It was like the first time, she was every bit as excited. But Jake stood up, posted her back into her dress and hitched up his trousers. 'We're late, that will have to wait till afterwards. Come on, love.'

She ached with frustration. If she needed proof that Jake slept around still, this was it. He didn't need it like she did.

Until she saw the Dereksons she couldn't remember what they looked like, but when she set eyes on them she couldn't imagine how she had forgotten. Derekson himself was a little older, a little more silver-haired, while Sheila's face, though mobile, now looked Chinese. She had drawn her hair back and fastened it into a bun with diamond hairclips. As Harriet approached they both began to stand, then Sheila Derekson sat down again quickly, as if she felt instinctively inferior but was denying it. A surge of power tingled in Harriet's veins. This was achievement, to strike fear into the hearts of those who used to see you as an object of pity. How sweet it was.

'Sheila! Angus!'

'Harriet! Jake!'

Smiles and enthusiasm overflowed. Derekson ordered champagne, clapping Jake on the shoulder two or three times as if to emphasise that they were friends once again. 'That was one bitch of a boat you checked out for me,' he said jovially. 'If I'd known then what you could do I'd have asked you to set up shop right there in Boston and build me a winner. One hell of a chance I lost.'

'I wouldn't have done it,' said Jake casually. 'I couldn't stay still long enough.'

'I hope you can now!' laughed Derekson. Nerves made him talk too loudly. Momentarily they all shared his nightmare of Jake building half a boat and then giving up.

Harriet chuckled. 'What happened to the *Real Sheila*?'

'Fetched up on a lee shore and sank,' said Derekson.

Insurance job, thought Harriet, surprising herself. Before she became involved with the Corporation such a thought would never have crossed her mind. 'How convenient,' she said wryly. 'What a good thing you can't sink a hotel, I might have been tempted.'

'From what I hear it is sinking,' said Derekson tactlessly.

'Don't believe all you hear. It's been a bastard but we're getting there.' She smiled and sipped her champagne.

Sheila Derekson heroically tried to join the conversation. 'I really never thought all those years ago that you'd become a tycoon, Harriet,' she began. 'These days I never open a paper without reading something about you.'

'And to think she started from nothing,' said Jake sardonically.

She wrinkled her nose at him. 'Don't be horrible. Where are you building the new boat, in Boston?'

'We can't tempt him,' declared Derekson. 'England or nowhere, that's the deal. He strikes a hard bargain. Guess there's no place like home.'

'Simply that I remember the *Real Sheila* too well,' said Jake. 'You were such an interfering sod, I figured the further away you were this time the better it would be for both of us.'

'I did not interfere!' Derekson flared up. 'You told me nothing and seemed to be ruining my boat. All I wanted was to know what was going on – '

'Angus – ' broke in his wife.

'I'm warning you, if you turn up at my yard I'll throw you out,' snapped Jake, gesturing with a fork.

'Jake!' cautioned Harriet.

The two men glared at each other, longing to resolve the old row, even if it meant the end of everything. 'I'm looking for a new nanny,' declared Harriet.

'Are you dear? A good one is so hard to find. Are you going to use an agency?' Harriet and Sheila hauled the party back to civility. When Jake began to listen to what was being said he broke in, saying, 'You can't get rid of Leah! She's marvellous.'

'Is she?' Harriet made a face.

'What's wrong with her? She's devoted to Victoria, you know she is.'

'That's rather it.' Harriet sipped her champagne and tried to sound reasonable but she wasn't being reasonable, she was being vindictive. 'Leah's not very keen on me. If Victoria forgot who I was it would suit Leah perfectly.'

'Rubbish! You're away too much. I wasn't going to say this now but since it's come up I will. You hardly see anything of the poor kid. If she forgets you it's because you're never there.'

'That isn't true!' Harriet was prepared to lie in her teeth to prevent him believing that. Guilt made her unnecessarily vehement. If she had to go away it wasn't because she wanted to, it was because she must.

'Oh look!' said Sheila Derekson. 'Isn't that Mark Benjamin? Look Harriet, he's waving at you.'

Harriet glanced across, flushing. She returned Benjamin's wave with a half-smile and a tiny flutter of fingers. Nonetheless he came across, dropping a kiss on to her bare shoulder.

'Harriet! Thought you were busy tonight.'

'As you can see, I am. Do you know Sheila and Angus Derekson? And this is Jake.'

'Jake?' He raised a quizzical eyebrow and Jake's teeth flashed in what was almost a snarl.

'Yeah. Is that your wife you've left looking miserable?'

Benjamin laughed. 'I'm sure she doesn't mind me talking to one of my most important customers. Have you known Harriet long?'

'Er – we have a mutual interest.' He grinned at Harriet and she laughed back. Benjamin's hand dropped on to her shoulder. 'What mutual interest?' he asked intently. 'A business relationship?'

'Your wife is looking sick as a parrot,' said Jake.

'Mark, dear, Jake is Victoria's father,' said Harriet. 'We sort of – ' She hesitated.

'Rub along,' said Jake, and everyone except Benjamin laughed uproariously.

He took grim-faced leave and went back to his table. Jake said, 'Really Harriet!' in falsetto tones, like a disapproving maiden aunt.

'I didn't ask him over,' she said defensively.

'That guy's got his divorce papers all drawn up. You should be bloody ashamed of yourself.'

She grimaced as he downed an oyster. Derekson said, 'The newspapers were full of it before she went to Florida.'

'He is a very nice man,' said Sheila, foreseeing yet another conflict. For some reason Harriet felt she should justify herself. 'It isn't my fault!' she said almost hysterically. 'I can't stay away from New York forever, Victoria's here and you've just been on at me about leaving her. I can't win, you're all criticising me!'

Jake reached out and took her hand, holding it very tight to calm her. 'OK love, OK. We'll talk about it later. I know it's hard. We all think you're a very clever girl.'

'Don't patronise me,' she snapped.

'Then stop parading your bloody lovers in front of me in restaurants.'

The evening teetered on the brink of complete disaster. Derekson mopped his brow with his handkerchief, mentally cursing the day he ever thought of asking Jake to build him a boat. But Jake's flash of jealousy had turned Harriet's mood to spring. She giggled and tweaked his tie. 'It's gone crooked again.' Her finger stroked his ear-lobe, because it was something they sometimes did in bed.

He relaxed visibly. 'Let's dance. Come on you two, let's all dance.'

So all four of them rushed on to the dancefloor, the Dereksons united in the face of the enemy, Jake and Harriet suddenly and inexplicably in love. They drank champagne, they danced some more, they were witty all the time they were eating. Jake told an extremely funny tale against himself, about a run-in while drunk with a poisonous spider who seemed equally helpless, and Sheila Derekson amazed them all by reciting at length an obscene poem. It was an absolutely wonderful evening.

Chapter Thirty-Three

Jake stared at the plans for so long that Harriet became nervous. Was there something she couldn't see? Something so fundamentally wrong that her hotel would collapse, sink, turn upside down and drown all the guests in the swamp? Again she went and topped up her glass.

'You're drinking too much.'

'No, I'm not. Anyway, you'd drink too much if you had my problems. Everyone's looked at those plans and no-one's come up with a decent answer. They all say it *could* work, this *may* be the solution, not "Here is the answer to your prayers, you are safe with me." I'm absolutely sick of it.'

He leaned back in the chair, squinting at the lines and projections through half-closed eyes. 'It's a bastard of a problem. They shouldn't have started till they'd cracked this one. It's not much use hoping the solution will present itself, it very rarely does.'

'They build nuclear power stations, don't they?' said Harriet morosely.

'What's that got to do with it?'

'They build them when they don't have a clue what to do with the waste. They hope the solution will come to them.'

'And it hasn't. Case proved.' He sat up and scrabbled for his pencil, where it had fallen down the side of his chair. 'Fear not, fair maiden, you are safe with me. I've got an idea.'

'Thank God for that.'

She watched attentively while he sketched something, changed a few things and sketched some more. Then he moved to the kitchen table and began work with pencil and ruler, making his usual professional job. Why hadn't she asked him before, she wondered? The connections between the central building and the floating pontoons had delayed the work more than anything else, even now the central building was nearly finished and the holes where the pontoons came in were inadequately blocked up with plywood and plastic.

'What are you doing?' She couldn't wait a minute longer.

'Look, the ends of the pontoons must be higher, right up to the level of the connection, and they must extend further back, like this. And they must be sealed here, in case of accidents. It shouldn't leak, but then neither should you sleep with married men.'

'You sleep with everyone,' snapped Harriet.

'Not denying it. The connection must be made with a staircase, leading down into the pontoon, and the staircase is on flexible joints like this. So, it moves up and down, all that changes is the angle of descent.'

'We'll have to raise the point at which the pontoons come in.'

'Only a couple of feet. It'll work, I'm sure of it. I'll talk to the architects to get the detailed drawings done. You realise my fee is astronomical?'

She put her arms round his neck. 'How much?'

'You don't sack Leah. And you spend more time with Victoria.'

'Hmmm. I don't know about Leah. OK, if you want.'

'I do want. She's my child too.'

Harriet let go of him and moved away.

He left before the end of the week. Harriet felt exhausted, more weary than ever in her life. Jake was such a drain on her emotions, upsetting the even tenor of her days and plunging her into excitement, or depression, or suddenly demanding that she should consider not just that she wanted to do something but why she wanted to do it. Harriet Hawksworth didn't answer to people for her actions any more. It was tiring, hiding things. The trouble at the hotel, the attempt to kill her, Gareth, the law suit. And now the problem of Madeline, niggling and unresolved.

Gareth had ceased to pay for his sister's upkeep. He had stopped the cheques at about the time Harriet went to Corusca, posing her with an obvious dilemma. The home was appealing to her for payment, and perhaps, as her husband's child, it was up to her to pay for Madeline. Yet she had no desire at all to be responsible for the girl, any more than her strange and difficult son.

As if she didn't have enough drains on her coffers! Bills poured in at every post, but somehow she couldn't make the connection between what she bought, or what she did and these seemingly arbitrary demands for money. Each purchase or project seemed so eminently reasonable that it would be foolish not to go through with it. She needed a car and a Ferrari suited her image, it was good for publicity. It wasn't the most up to date model so they were offering a good discount and immediate delivery. Why shouldn't she have it, she deserved some fun didn't she? So the Ferrari was purchased to tootle round in when her chauffeur was off duty, and when she was out driving she saw this marvellous riding stables where Victoria could keep a pony, and then of course there was riding kit – none of it seemed unreasonable at the time.

The sum total was horrifying. She had to have more money. If she could only get her hands on the collection she would have unlimited funds, but even Mr. Younger was beginning to be doubtful about her success. At their last meeting, when she had remained implacable, he burst out: 'Surely the man's entitled to something, Mrs. Hawksworth!'

'Nothing at all,' was the unforgiving reply. 'I want the collection.' And so the legal bills mounted, month by expensive month.

That was one problem that wasn't a problem: she was going after the collection whatever it cost. But other things needed some attention. She rang through to Maud, hardly able to summon the energy to press the button. 'I want to go and visit Miss Hawksworth in the clinic. Fix it for this afternoon, please.'

'Yes, Mrs. Hawksworth.'

The clinic was out of town, a large house surrounded by high white walls. It looked like an ambassador's house, discreetly fortified, whereas in fact all the precautions were to stop the inmates getting out. Here the wealthy and prestigious deposited their embarrassments, the retarded or deformed children, the alcoholic wives, the druggy teenagers. When Harriet rang the bell on the gate a man in uniform answered. He was wearing a gun.

But once inside menace was replaced by an atmosphere of smiling, bright-eyed lunacy. A man sat on a garden bench giggling helplessly to himself, a boy and a girl strolled past arm in arm, 'Hi,' they said, waving with the exaggerated gestures common to those who are stoned on something. People in clean uniforms moved briskly along, smiling, always smiling. It was as if everyone in the place had had a frontal lobotomy. Only being there made Harriet feel she was going mad.

The 'Executive Head' of the clinic was a blue-rinsed lady in her fifties. She greeted Harriet warmly, launching at once into the pep-talk that was clearly trotted out to everyone. 'In the pressured society that exists today is it any wonder that some fall by the wayside? The mark of true civilisation is to care for those weaker than ourselves with love and compassion, to shelter them from the harsh winds of the outside world. Here we give them that love, we give them that shelter. We don't ever hold back. Are you holding back, Mrs. Hawksworth? Can you put your hand on your heart and deny that?'

'Yes. No. Madeline isn't really my responsibility, Mrs. Willerby.' Under a gaze of such compassionate avarice Harriet felt very uncomfortable. 'She's been here a long time. Isn't it time she was cured?'

Mrs. Willerby sighed. 'Some of us will never be ready to face the outside world again,' she said sadly.

Harriet felt a stab of irritation. 'It is hardly fair to expect me to finance her here for the rest of her days,' she snapped. 'The woman's still in her twenties. I could be paying out for seventy years. I could be dead and still not have finished!'

'The Lord counts not his forgiveness,' said Mrs. Willerby, inclining her head to indicate prayer.

'I haven't got divine resources.'

They rose in mutual dislike to go and visit the patient. A child in a wheelchair nearly ran Harriet down, and was snapped at by Mrs. Willerby. Apart from the wheelchair he seemed fitter than Harriet herself. They stopped at a large, flower-filled dayroom overlooking the gardens.

'Madeline,' called Mrs. Willerby. A dark blonde head turned. Yes, thought Harriet, that could be Madeline – a pretty, slightly sulky face, the Hawksworth length and leanness. But instead of the tousled straw hair there was sleek, clean elegance, in place of the ragged beach clothes a pencil skirt and cashmere sweater.

'Hello, Harriet. How kind of you to come.'

'I'm so glad you remember me, Madeline.'

'How could I forget?' They shook hands formally. Harriet turned to Mrs. Willerby. 'Thank you so much. I should like to speak to Madeline alone for a little.'

'We don't like her to become agitated,' said Mrs. Willerby icily.

'I promise not to agitate her.'

They waited until she had left, speaking meaningfully to the watching nurse before she did so. The nurse moved a little closer. Madeline went back to her seat by the window, gesturing Harriet to an empty chair. 'The old bat hates us to talk to anyone. Thinks we'll split on her.'

'What about?'

'I don't know.' Madeline didn't appear interested in tale-telling. 'Why doesn't Gareth come any more? What's happening?'

'He's busy, I suppose.' She waited for Madeline to say something more, but instead the girl began to chew a fingernail, then caught herself and put her hands together in her lap. She gazed out of the window, staring at nothing.

'Don't you want to get out of here?' asked Harriet. 'Don't you want to know how Nathan is?'

Madeline shrugged. 'How is he?'

'He's fine – fine. Don't you miss him?'

A look of vague concern crossed her peaceful face. 'I don't know. It's hard to miss someone you don't remember too well. I think I've forgotten what he looks like. You do, in here, you forget.'

'But you can't like it in here, Madeline! It's almost a prison.'

'I thought that was what you wanted. I thought that was why I was here.'

There was a pause. Harriet said, 'I didn't put you here. It was Gareth.'

'He wouldn't do it.' Again Madeline gazed out at the people pacing the paths between the rose beds.

Harriet said in a low, rushed voice: 'You could come out if you wanted. I'm not making you stay here, you seem perfectly well to me. You could go back to Corusca, Jerome would take care of you. Wouldn't you like to do that?'

Madeline's face was a study in confusion. 'But I'm not allowed to leave, they say I'm not to. I thought – could I really go back? Go home?'

'Yes.' Harriet smoothed her palms together, suddenly nervous. Jerome would indeed take care of Madeline, he would take very good care. Harriet closed her eyes at the thought of the care Madeline had received from both her brothers. 'It might not be best to go to Corusca straight away,' she prevaricated. 'Perhaps Florida. I've a hotel that's nearly finished, you could stay there and work perhaps. You could have Nathan too.'

At last the girl's attention was hers. 'I would do anything you wanted,' she whispered, 'anything at all. Please take me away from here.'

On the drive home, with the Ferrari idling miserably at fifty, Harriet turned everything over in her mind. By the simple expedient of giving her a home and a job she had brought Madeline to her side, detached her from Gareth. The man was now isolated, standing alone against a woman seen to be caring tenderly for the family and its dependants. Which would be fine, except she had the feeling that she was losing her grip on one of them. She made a mental note to try again to get in touch with Simone. All her 'phone calls went unreturned; Simone was away, unavailable, resting. All her letters went unanswered. Last week, reluctantly, Harriet had instructed the auditors to make a special investigation of the refurbishment accounts, Simone's special trust. It was all she could think of to do.

A man tried to hustle her for money on the pavement outside the apartment. Harriet shook him off violently, hating him and New York in equal measure. It was time to find a new apartment, somewhere prestigious where she didn't have to run the gauntlet of people like that when she stepped from the garage to her own front door. The incident upset her out of all proportion to its magnitude. When she walked into the apartment she could have wept.

'Mrs. Hawksworth, ma'am.' Leah was looking anxious.

'I'm very tired, Leah, can't it wait?' Harriet went to pour herself a drink.

'It's Victoria, ma'am. She's had an accident.'

Harriet froze, the gin bottle half tilted. When she turned gin slopped on to the floor. 'What have you done to her? You've killed her, you bitch!'

'It's only a cut, Mrs. Hawksworth!' Leah was brushed aside as Harriet raced to her daughter's bedroom. Victoria was sitting up in bed, doing a jigsaw. Her right hand was encased in a huge white bandage.

'Darling, darling, it's all right, Mummy's here! What has naughty Leah done to you?'

'I cut myself. Leah didn't do it.'

Harriet spun round upon the nanny. 'How bad is it?'

'We had to have four stitches, ma'am. She fell in the park, and there was glass. The doctor he give her an injection too, it's quite all right, Mrs. Hawksworth.' The girl smiled tentatively. She had known for weeks that her position here was precarious. Had it not been for the very real love she had for her charge, she would have left long ago. Harriet's resentment was like a wall.

'I'll talk to you later,' said Harriet, and turned back to her daughter.

Leah went to sit shivering in her bedroom. Perhaps it wasn't such a bad thing, she told herself. A child should look to its mother first. The way it had been recently, with no time off and total responsibility, she was without any life of her own. The best thing would be to go back home, find herself a place where they had other children and other servants, so she had some company. She began to pack, though try as she would the tears fell. When Harriet knocked on the door and entered, Leah faced her puffy-eyed.

'I think I'd best be leaving, Mrs. Hawksworth,' she said softly.

Harriet, shamed out of the dismissal she had been about to utter, felt her anger die a death. 'I'm sorry, Leah,' she said tearfully. 'I really am. But I do think it would be best.'

* * *

Harriet dined with Mark Benjamin a few days later. It wasn't something that she had intended, but when he telephoned she was feeling so isolated and unhappy, so beset by problems the temptation had been too much. So they sat together once more in a quiet corner of a quiet restaurant, holding hands beneath the table.

'Did you see the rave article about the hotel?' Harriet asked.

Benjamin nodded. 'There's a lot of interest. Everyone's waiting for the opening.'

'I know, I know! I just hope people aren't disappointed. I haven't been able to get Simone to go near the place and it's all in the hands of a consultant no more than twenty-two years old, Mike Lawns. He seems to have caught on to my ideas, but – well, he really is original. I just wish Simone was handling it,' she tailed off unhappily.

'Going to go over and see her?' asked Benjamin, rubbing his knee against hers.

'Oh, no.' Harriet neither returned nor resisted the pressure. She didn't care whether she slept with him or not, but just now, when she felt so friendless, she needed his company. 'We'll have to have an opening shindig,' she sighed. The Florida Lake Hotel had caused her more anguish than anything in her life, excepting Jake.

'You could keep it small, no need to go overboard.'

But when had Harriet ever played safe? She pulled her hand out of his and linked her fingers together on the crisp tablecloth. Her eyes sparkled.

'Let's make it a great party, for a great hotel. I'm going to invite everyone I know, including you. I'll invite everyone I have ever known. It's going to be the best party since – since the world was made! No-one will ever forget it!'

Excitement illuminated her. She tilted her head and let her hair sweep across the bare skin of her back. This would be the moment in her life when everyone saw what she had achieved, when everyone took stock of what Harriet Hawksworth had become. She had conquered poverty, obscurity, even fear. She was going to stand before them all and be acclaimed!

Chapter Thirty-Four

Fireflies flickered in the darkness, passing over the quiet waters of the slow-running creek like messengers from another world. They glowed, bright as candles, then disappeared into the mist. In the evenings, in the twilight, there was magic abroad.

Harriet leaned on the verandah of her suite and breathed deep of the wet, dead-leaf odour she knew so well. Yesterday one of the bar staff hired for the opening party had been heard to say: 'What a shit-hole this is! What does the cow think she's doing putting a hotel here, for God's sake?' Harriet had sacked him on the spot. If no-one else could see the charm of this place, the charm of being different, what hope was there?

It was time to dress. There seemed to be a lull in activity, a strange quiet descending on the place, for there were no other guests dressing. No-one but herself was permitted to stay in the hotel until after tonight. Now that the evening was upon her she wished, how she wished, that she had chosen not the flamboyant green that had seemed right in New York, but something svelte and discreet in black. Suppose they didn't come, suppose they came but didn't like it? Suppose it was the biggest and most expensive flop in the history of the world?

She slipped out of her robe and stood before the huge looking glass that Mike Lawns had installed in her suite. It was French, curlicued in gold, and stretched to the ceiling. In it she was reflected mercilessly. Her breasts were beginning to sag. The fat, banished for so long, was edging on to her hips. It was time for a stiff diet and a month of rigorous exercise, but if she was thinner, fitter, more perfect, would she then be happy? Perhaps, in the end, you had to acknowledge that what you were seeking was not to be had.

The dress disguised everything, as it should when she had paid – oh, too much. Her bosom, forced upwards, overflowed in white abundance, causing her hairdresser to tremble as he brushed and combed. Her brown eyes watched him, reflecting the room's yellow light. They had agreed that on this one night Harriet should wear her hair piled regally on top of her head. The diamond earrings, hired once again, bounced gently against her neck. She looked very different, perhaps slightly hard. She instructed the hairdresser to pull down some tendrils to soften the look.

A knock sounded on the door. It was the new nanny, Margaret, leading a sulky Victoria by the hand. 'There now! Doesn't Mummy look wonderful?'

Victoria stared and said, 'That dress is rude.'

'Don't be silly, darling,' said Harriet. 'Anyway, you look gorgeous.'

Victoria was attired in white lace pantaloons beneath a white lace dress. Her black hair was held in a knot of flowers from which ringlets fell gloriously. She looked so perfect that one could almost eat her, thought Harriet, risking her own make-up by bending down to hug her. Victoria returned the embrace listlessly. 'Don't want to go to the party,' she said grumpily.

'Nonsense, darling. Daddy's coming.'

'But Nathan isn't!'

'No.'

Harriet's face stiffened. For herself she didn't mind Nathan, he was interestingly wild and undisciplined. As long as he kept out of her way and didn't do any damage, then he and his peculiar mother were welcome enough. All she did ask was that some attempt be made to send the boy to school rather than letting him chase alligators in the swamp all day, and that his mother should not parade naked in the corridors. But to see the mesmeric effect he had on Victoria – that was another matter entirely. Victoria worshipped him, she dogged his footsteps whenever she could. And God knows what that witch-child knew and might be telling her! As soon as the party was over Nathan was being sent away to school, Harriet was brooking no argument. In the meantime Victoria sulked.

Madeline wasn't nearly so disruptive. Sometimes she forgot where she was, which resulted in the wanderings, but generally speaking she was innocuous enough. She worked, spasmodically, ordering wines for the hotel chain, entirely under direction. Once or twice she got drunk and it had taken her a week to recover, but that was to be anticipated. After so long locked away from temptation, was it any wonder that she succumbed to it now? She seemed distant, one might think half-asleep, as if her life was nothing if she must forego the excitements of excess, degradation, the magical delusions that led, in the end, to insanity.

Strange wailings emanated from a giant raft moored out on the swamp. It was the orchestra, fifty strong, tuning up well clear of the terraces where the guests would dance. It occurred to Harriet that the musicians and catering staff might well outnumber the guests. She had estimated around two hundred people, but some had been too busy, others away on holiday, and some made excuses that meant they considered one party insufficient reason to trek to Florida. The agonies suffered by all hostesses before the party begins tore at her flesh. How she wished she had never thought of this!

Meanwhile, all over the state, people were getting ready to come to Harriet's party. Unbeknown to her even the people who had refused had thought better of it and decided to attend. Her office had been besieged throughout the day by people who hadn't been invited and wished to be. One enterprising tycoon hired out his private jet to would-be partygoers.

Somehow the Hawksworth mystique had triumphed. A local television station had broadcast an item about the hotel opening, and because it was Hawksworth it had been picked up and networked. The fireworks, the fashions, the food, all of it was suddenly news. Squads of reporters were preparing to saunter in and mingle with the guests, some from publications which, granted no hope of admission, were planning to paddle in via canoes. Everyone knew about the party, everyone wanted to go. But Harriet, watching the tables being laid with impossible amounts of food and drink, sat like a little girl at the top of one of the flights of steps Jake had designed and chewed her well-manicured nails.

Gradually, half an hour before time, people began to arrive. Out of the darkness came the drone of expensive motors bringing their charges along the newly made road. One of the security guards on permanent duty at the hotel these days came rushing up to Harriet. 'I'm sorry, ma'am, but we're going to need help. Them danged photographers is all over the place. Hundreds of them!'

'They'll probably go soon,' said Harriet, standing up and gloomily shaking her dress. 'They won't get in the way.'

The security guard wiped his sweating brow. 'Ma'am, the guests to your party are stacking up way back to the road fork. There's no way going to be enough space to park the cars and the ladies won't want to walk in the mud down the track! I aint never seen so much style. There's hundreds of them!'

Harriet reached out and held on to his arm. 'I didn't think anyone was going to come,' she said shakily.

The man laughed, suddenly indulgent. 'It looks to me like you've got one hell of a party!'

The sudden, heady taste of success galvanised Harriet into action. She clapped her hands, summoning the manager like the genie of the lamp.

'Andrew, we need men to park cars, lots of men. And we may run out of champagne, so arrange for more supplies from town if need be. They might have to come out by boat from the landing up the creek if the road's blocked. Oh yes, and send more men to the gate, they can't check all the tickets.'

'Yes, ma'am.' Even Andrew, hired for his imperturbability, looked rattled by news of the coming siege. He strode away, past the first guests walking along the broad terraces and exclaiming at the lights, the fountains, the glorious waterland scene that lay before them. The hotel rose up like a giant glass island out of a green and glassy sea. It might have risen up at just that moment conjured from the depths by the music drifting in from the night. It might have been made of spun sugar, so delicate and beautiful it seemed. And stepping towards them, smiling, serene, was the legendary Harriet Hawksworth.

Jake had been dubious when he heard about Harriet's party. He knew her well enough to know how important it was to her, but setting that aside he had no wish to go. Harriet in triumph was the Harriet he had least wish to know, but then, if he didn't go where would be her triumph? There is always one person in everyone's life who matters most, and he and Harriet, whatever their differences, came first with each other. He couldn't leave her alone at her own party and so, reluctantly, he came.

As for Simone, she was eager to attend, feverishly so. Months had passed since she had spoken to Harriet, and there had been only the most cursory attempts to break the silence. Why had Harriet not flown to Paris? Wasn't Simone worth even that to her? Week by week she had awaited the opportunity to confront Harriet with the catalogue of her woes and the justification of her actions, but until now nothing had presented itself. Tonight, in front of everyone, she would at last make her point.

Mark Benjamin, his wife at his side, also planned a confrontation. He was sure that Harriet would not deny him, would publicly acknowledge his place in her life. And, since they were civilised people, once that was seen and reported upon, the necessary adjustments would be made and he would become, at a stroke, one of the new men. Not for him the decline into greying obscurity, beset by teenage children and the standards of a past generation; he would take a new and brilliant wife to stand at his side. After the first sharp bitterness he and Patti would become friends once again. She might even thank him one day for releasing her in turn to a brighter future.

Just then she reached out and touched him nervously on the arm, because she knew what was in the air and was denying it. 'We will have a nice time won't we, Mark?' she asked, making yet another pointless request for reassurance.

At another time, in another place, he would have taken her hand. Instead he sat immobile. 'It should be most interesting,' he said coldly.

That night, too, someone else waited in nervous anticipation of what was to come. She sat in her cab, smoking an unaccustomed cigarette begged from the driver, wondering if she was out of her mind to be doing this. A lot of water had gone under the bridge since last they met, it was hard to believe Harriet would still be bitter. Look how far she had come, and all because of that one short week so long ago. Who knows, she might even be grateful. If she wasn't, well, it wouldn't be the first knock this week, this year, this lifetime. Natalie was getting used to them.

Out in the swamp still another uninvited guest was waiting, and he had waited longer than any other. He could have done it before, easily, but would that have held so much savour? Tonight, Harriet was celebrating victory. Gareth was preparing her defeat.

She watched Jake walking through the crowds, nodding here and there to people he knew. Jake always knew more people than you thought he did, just as he had more money, more talent and more acumen than he liked to pretend. The black hair was going grey at the temples but the smile was as wide, white and raffish as ever. Harriet was suddenly so proud of him. When he reached her, they hugged tightly.

'I didn't think anyone was going to come,' she whispered breathlessly.

'You knew I would. I might have got a drink, it's as dry as the desert.'

'They've had to get more glasses, we ran out. Who are these people, Jake? They all look so rich.'

'That's who they are then, rich people. Isn't that all that matters?'

'What do you mean?' She eyed him warily. But he wasn't going to burst her balloon, not at her own party. He picked up her glass of champagne and drank some, and it was at once refilled by the waiter detailed exclusively to Mrs. Hawksworth. Jake felt another flare of anger, but again he stamped on it and drank the champagne.

He had the feeling that tonight he was having his nose rubbed in it.

This was what Harriet had done by herself. If I had stuck with you, she seemed to be saying, I'd just be a dowdy housewife in a broken-down cottage, answering the 'phone for your damned business. Now look!

'Where's Victoria?' he asked, interrupting Harriet's conversation with two people newly arrived.

'What? In the green suite, I think. I'm sorry, Jake, I'm busy.' She turned again to her guests, leaving him to find the green suite for himself.

People, hundreds of people, dancing, drinking, gazing avidly at the food set out in fantastic profusion, waiting to be devoured. Every now and then a familiar face, but he avoided them, he didn't want to talk. The party mood wasn't for him tonight, which proved he was getting old. For once he would have preferred a quiet dinner, a glass of wine and a congenial companion, although if that was Harriet she would be taking messages and talking business half the night. He caught sight of someone in the throng – he stopped and stared.

'Natalie?'

She turned, her face anxious, strained. He couldn't help but see the lines, banished by her automatic smile. God, but she looked terrible, thin, old, tired. He tried not to let his eyes focus on her neck, crêpe skin over cords, slightly yellow.

'Jake!' She pushed her way through to him. 'I wondered if you'd be here. I wanted to talk to Harriet, but there are so many people.'

'Oh, yeah, you need a pass to talk to Harriet. Surely she didn't send you an invitation, did she?'

'Oh, no.' The grin was a faint reminder of Natalie's old sparkle. 'There's been a black market in tickets for weeks, I took advantage of it. I must speak to Harriet, Jake, I simply must!'

He glanced back at the throng filling the steps before Harriet. 'Not a chance for at least an hour or so. I'm going to see Victoria, want to come along? I'm told she's in the green suite, which I assume is that bilious symphony over there. I didn't know the smart people were into green walls, carpets, ceilings, and even furniture. Only green people permitted to set foot in it, I should think.'

Natalie gazed round at everything. 'It's good, you know. All the different shades, it's very clever.'

'I'm sure it will be that,' said Jake sourly. 'Harriet is so fucking clever I could strangle her.'

'Number one green person,' said Natalie, and laughed. Jake chuckled with her. 'No, Harriet buys what she wants. I don't think my dreams are up for sale.'

They walked on until they found Victoria, sitting in her drifts of lace and picking at the food her nanny thought suitable for her. 'Hello, honey' said Jake, picking her up and popping a kiss on her nose.

Victoria giggled and said 'Don't', then kissed his nose back. They played for a minute, kissing noses, until one or other of them looked like fracturing a skull.

'Enough for now,' said Jake. 'Where's Leah? Is she enjoying the party?'

The nanny looked discomfited and Victoria rather awkward. 'Well?' said Jake again.

'Mummy said I wasn't to say. She said she'd explain.'

'Explain what?' Jake turned very quickly to Margaret, who blushed and started to stammer. 'Has Leah been dismissed?' asked Jake very softly.

'Leah said she'd come and see me, but she hasn't! Daddy I want her SO MUCH! Go and get her for me, Daddy.'

Jake lifted his daughter onto his lap. 'Did Leah want to go, lovey? Did she say she did?'

Victoria sniffed. 'She said I was a big girl and didn't need her any more. But, Daddy, I do! Margaret doesn't know our games or anything. She doesn't know what to do when I'm sick. And Mummy was cross because I fell over and cut myself, she said it was Leah's fault. Look, they had to sew me up or my insides would have all come out.' She pointed to her hand where the scar still showed.

'Your insides don't come out, love, not through cuts,' said Jake vaguely.

He and Natalie stayed for a little longer, but the nanny was clearly uncomfortable. Just as they rose to go a fair-haired boy came into the room. Victoria jumped up and ran to him. 'Now we can play,' she said happily. 'This is Nathan.'

'Hello, Nathan' said Jake. 'Who are you?'

'Nathan,' said the child with blank insolence.

'He's Nathan Hawksworth,' said Victoria, as if they were both being tiresome. 'He lives here and he's my friend. Come on, Nathan, let's go and see the party.'

'Oh, no, you don't!' interrupted Jake, fielding her as she ran. 'Little girls shouldn't be at grown-up parties, they should be in bed.'

'Mrs. Hawksworth said for one night – ' said the nanny tentatively.

'In here only,' instructed Jake.

'What are you afraid of?' said the boy.

Jake stopped and stared at him. The child stared back, until at last his gaze fell. 'When you're with my daughter you play little children's games,' said Jake softly. 'Don't let them out of your sight, Margaret.'

'Strange kid,' said Natalie, walking back on the endless green carpet.

'Bit more than strange. He's come from that island, you know? God knows what he's seen. I can't have him associating with Victoria, I won't have it.'

Natalie grunted. Jake looked at her and saw that she was very pale. 'You OK?'

'Not feeling so good. Let's sit for a minute.'

They sank into a deep green sofa. Jake intercepted a waiter and relieved him of two glasses and a bottle of champagne. Natalie sipped, almost groaning with relief. She let her head fall back against the seat.

'What's wrong?' asked Jake.

She opened one eye. 'Cancer. Don't worry, I'm not dying – yet. Treatment makes you feel lousy.'

'That why you wanted to talk to Harriet? Money?'

She nodded. 'Not for the treatment, that's OK. One thing I never economised on was health insurance.' She wagged an admonitory finger, and the gesture seemed to exhaust her. Suddenly she said, 'Christ, Jake, I've made one hell of a mess of my life. Nobody needs to tell me it's my own fault, I know that. But when this thing came up I thought, What the shit point is there in surviving if all I've got is one stinking room and a shared bathroom? No job, no friends, no nothing. I thought of something Harriet once said. I guess it was a damn fool idea.' She laughed, almost tearfully.

'What did she say?'

'Stupid really. She said the one thing I might be good at would be running a brothel. I thought – you know, she's into some pretty shady things with that island, everybody knows they run drugs from it – I thought she might want to set me up. All I need is the house. I can get the girls, and they'd be well off! Class place, lots of protection. What do you think?'

Jake sighed. How to tell Natalie that her idea was terrible, that to appeal to Harriet was to ask for public humiliation? He couldn't tell her. 'Lot of hassle, running a brothel,' he commented. 'Why don't you open a shop?'

'What sort of shop?'

He shrugged. 'Gifts, perhaps. Sailing gear. How about sailing clothes? Women are always complaining if they do the job they're ugly, and if they're not ugly they don't do the job. It wouldn't get you arrested.'

'I still haven't got the money.' Natalie looked sadly down at her hands, turning her glass between fleshless fingers. Even her nails showed yellow beneath their polish.

Jake felt a rush of painful compassion. 'I'll give it to you,' he said softly. 'For old time's sake.'

Natalie's face crumpled into tears.

Simone was dancing with her husband. It was years since they had danced together, and Georges was only doing so now because no-one here spoke French and he couldn't spend the evening, as he usually did, in the midst of the exclusive circle of his friends. He was a small man, arrogantly French, and Simone adored him. She knew quite well that he had only accompanied her to America because his latest mistress had deserted him and there was currently no political scandal in the French government. Usually she hid behind her sophistication but tonight her delight in him, and his indifference, verged on the pathetic.

Wearied by endless hellos, Harriet was wandering about alone. People seemed to be in awe of her, she was almost a wallflower at her own party. Then she saw Simone and froze on the edge of the dancefloor, her mind whirling. Why on earth had she come? Picking up her skirts she swept on to the floor and caught Simone's arm. 'Simone! I must talk to you.'

'Madame, if you will excuse. We are dancing.'

Harriet looked down at the little man and said, 'You must be Georges Lalange. How do you do. May I introduce myself? Your hostess, Harriet Hawksworth.'

He inclined his head. 'My apologies. And now, if we may continue?'

'I want to talk to you, Simone,' said Harriet coldly.

'I will speak to her, Georges,' said Simone. 'She deserves to know what I think of her.'

'Thank you.' Harriet led the way up the steps from the dancefloor to a wicker sofa behind a palm. To her surprise not only Simone followed, but also Georges.

He lit a cigarette, and then as Simone clicked her fingers irritably, lit one for her. They were clearly both very angry. 'What is it that has upset you?' asked Harriet crisply. 'Didn't you embezzle enough to keep you happy? I could have prosecuted.'

'I was owed that money,' sneered Simone. 'What did you pay me? A pittance! You are a thief.'

'If you had wanted more you could have asked for it,' said Harriet. 'I should have been told if you were dissatisfied.'

'And when I needed more, did you give it! No, you told your bullyboy to pay me off, you made him treat me like a dirty beggar. I helped you because I wanted my inheritance. But see what has happened! Again and again we need money, and you buy the shares, cheaper and cheaper, until at last we will be paupers, with nothing! And you will have your hands on Paris couture! How happy that will make you.'

Harriet was bewildered. 'But – I don't have shares in your business. I haven't bought any.'

Georges leaned forward, wreathed in acrid smoke. 'We must sell. Our shares are not publicly traded. We telephone your office and at once the instruction is to buy. Who gives that instruction?'

'I don't know.'

Andrew, the hotel manager, leaned warily round the palm. 'Andrew! Please find Mr. Thomas for me,' instructed Harriet. 'We must get to the bottom of this.' She sat watching the pair before her while they waited. 'You think,' she said slowly, 'that I am trying to drive you out of business by keeping you short of cash. And that when you are desperate I buy your shares in a private transaction at rock bottom prices. That is so?'

'It is what happens.' Georges lit another cigarette. 'You pretend to care for Simone. It was only pretence. My wife is often foolish.' He let his eyes roam over Harriet, an obvious, appreciative stare. Simone looked away, blinking rapidly.

Claud Thomas came bustling round the palm, a presence of such stark ordinariness that Harriet felt soothed. He was redolent of order, offices, neat typed messages and clear instructions. 'Claud,' she said happily, 'Simone asserts that the Hawksworth Corporation has been buying shares in their couture business, at my instruction. I've explained to them that I have issued no such instruction. Will you confirm that?'

Thomas looked from one to the other. 'I'm sorry, Mrs. Hawksworth, I can't confirm it. While you were ill a transaction was made, with Madame Lalange's agreement, I understand. An instruction was lodged on the computer that this was one of the shares we were to purchase – as you know we hold instructions on a number of shares. When they come up, we buy if the price seems reasonable.'

'Who has been beating the price down?' asked Harriet tightly. 'Because someone has.'

'Do you want me to consult Jacobson, the investment manager?' asked Thomas. 'He is usually very close to all our dealings.'

Harriet felt sick. What more proof did she need that Hawksworth was bigger than she was, when investment managers she barely knew made deals she knew nothing about? 'I think it's all quite clear,' she said thinly. 'Thank you, Claud. Do go back and enjoy yourself, your wife must be wondering where you are. I hope she's having a good time.'

When he had gone the three of them sat in silence. 'I'm sorry,' said Harriet at last. 'I assure you, I didn't know.'

'I think it only fair to tell you that I am now supporting Gareth in his suit' said Simone. 'He tells me that he is about to appeal for control of the Corporation because of your extravagance and illegal dealings.'

'What illegal dealings?' Harriet's head came up.

Simone shrugged. 'Drug trafficking from Corusca. The authorities have a great deal of evidence. I imagine it is Jerome, but then you and he are together on that island, are you not?' The Frenchwoman looked tauntingly down her long thin nose.

But they had touched Harriet's most tender nerve. 'Just because of a minor confusion in the office you would go over to Gareth?' she said softly, her voice trembling with rage. 'You are a mercenary, unscrupulous cow, Simone, and your husband's no more than a lecherous yapping terrier! Look at him, leering at everything except you. There's Hawksworth in you all right – thieving, deceiving, lying bitch – but there's no Hawksworth pride. No wonder Henry left you out. He despised you!' She was on her feet and screaming. Faces appeared round the palm, Claud Thomas, people she didn't know.

Harriet pushed through them, out and down the steps. Mark Benjamin caught her arm. 'Harriet! Darling, what's happening?'

'Don't darling me,' she snarled. He tried to put his arm around her waist but she struck him off hard, in full view of the dancefloor. 'Don't paw me! I don't need it! Find someone else to boost your ego and make you feel young, I haven't got the time or the inclination!' And she rushed on, the green dress billowing, a magnificent, terrifying figure in an uncontrollable rage. She had to find Jake, she told herself, if she found Jake it would be all right.

She found him. Lounging on a sofa, his bow tie off and his shirt unbuttoned down to the thick, black hair on his chest. And next to him, unbelievably, like something out of a nightmare, was Natalie, her feet on his lap, her long thin arm outstretched to touch him. Something inside her clicked. She saw Natalie and Jake, Jake and Natalie, mating like animals, taking what was absolutely, totally hers. She reached out blindly for something to throw, anything, and her fingers closed on a bowl of salad brought from the buffet. With a sound like a growl she threw it into Natalie's laughing face.

Jake reached out to her. 'Harriet!'

She couldn't bear him to touch her. Dragging herself out of his grasp she ran through the hotel. Hide, get away, get out of here, whispered a small inner voice. The people were in her way. She had a sudden vision of herself, how distraught she must seem. She slowed, smiling mechanically, and turned, as if going somewhere, towards one of the bedroom complexes. Oh God, she had to get away from them all, to blessed privacy. One of the doors was slightly open and she almost fell into the room beyond.

There was hardly any light, except for one dim bulb above the bed. There were ten people in the room, yet no-one turned round as she entered. A thick, heavy scent filled the air, catching at Harriet's throat. Like Alice through the looking glass she had stepped into another world.

Two men lay on the floor together, kissing. On the bed was a woman, quite naked, and next to her a man wearing only a shirt. He was asleep, but the woman lay on her back, her eyes fixed and unblinking. Harriet realised it was Madeline. A woman in evening dress got up from the floor and staggered out into the corridor and as if the balance of the room had been changed by her departure, people started to move around. They had the slow, deliberate movements of the heavily drugged, as if walking in treacle. A fat man pulled himself on to the bed and straddled Madeline. He grunted, freeing himself from his clothes, and then settled inside her. He began slow, deliberate movements.

Harriet gagged. She put her hands up to her mouth, unable to take her eyes off Madeline's unmoving face. The girl's pupils were no more than pinpricks and her breath came at longer and longer intervals.

'Madeline,' whispered Harriet, and it sounded loud in the silent room. No-one took any notice. Then, as Harriet turned to go, a strange expression crossed the still face that watched her. Could it be triumph?

Harriet left the room, sick and swaying. She needed air, and she needed solitude. The exits to the terraces were thronged with people, but no-one knew the hotel as well as she did. She made for a service door, treading on her skirt and tearing it but caring not a jot. Crying to herself, she scrambled out on to the narrow walkway that ran the length of each pontoon, and clung to the flimsy guardrail. It was always the same: whenever she reached for victory, all she held was disaster. Simone she could tolerate, Benjamin she could understand, but for Jake to use this evening to humiliate her, this one special evening – she couldn't take it.

She wouldn't think of that, she would think of Madeline. Where was the point in trying to save that girl? She should have sent her back to Jerome, let him do what he liked with her. She didn't want to be saved. Madeline had escaped back into her own insanity.

I shall go mad too, thought Harriet. I need help. Why doesn't anyone help me? Why does no-one ever think of it? In the dark, she stared down at the water. Could you drown just by wanting to? It would be good to find peace, music was crashing against her brain, she longed to be free of it, and the light was painful, too bright and flickering. Her hand went up to shield her eyes, and she stared through her fingers at the glare. Light, licking up against the wooden boarding, dissolving the plastic shielding on the wall. A warm breath, like a dragon's kiss, wafted through the air towards her.

Harriet began to run and to scream. 'Fire!' she shrieked. 'Fire! Quickly, quickly, the hotel's burning!'

No-one heard her. The music was playing, the lights on the terraces failed to penetrate the gloom in which she stood. She turned again to the fire, and for a moment it seemed gentle and caressing, licking so sweetly at the structure on which it fed. And still she stood, watching it. Do something, screamed her mind, Think what to do!

She pulled open the service door again and ran back inside. A couple were staggering along, very drunk. She caught their arms and said urgently: 'There's a fire. Please go straight out to your car.' They stared at her bemusedly. 'There's a fire!' yelled Harriet, and thought, the alarm, if I ring that they'll realise. She dragged off her high-heeled shoe and battered one of the glass alarms with the steel tip. A klaxon began to sound, like an excited donkey. Harriet put her shoe back on and ran on, thinking Victoria, I must get to her.

People were looking puzzled. 'Fire. There's a fire. Please leave immediately,' Harriet kept repeating. And then there was Jake.

'What the hell's going on?'

She barely glanced at him. 'The hotel's on fire. Everyone must leave, right away. Get the fire brigade, would you?'

He caught her arm and stared at her. 'Is this your doing?'

'Don't be so bloody silly! I must get Victoria!' She pulled away, trying not to run. So many people. If they panicked, someone would be killed.

'What's happening, what is it?' they kept asking.

'A fire, a small fire. Please leave right away.' The half-smile, the calm manner, but where was Victoria?

She met the nanny, Margaret, standing bewildered in the corridor, her sleepy charge in her arms. 'Thank God.' Harriet swallowed and put her hands to her head, so that she could think calmly and sensibly what should be done.

The manager was at her elbow. 'Mrs. Hawksworth? What do we do?'

She glanced out of the window. One of the pontoons was blazing now, lighting up the lake. 'Margaret, take Victoria out by the service way. Show her please, Andrew. I must make an announcement.'

Picking up her skirts she pushed her way through the thronging and confused people. No-one seemed to want to get out. They were standing at the windows watching the burning pontoon as if it were fireworks. She couldn't get through the crowds, she would be too late! Pushing up a window she climbed out on to the narrow walkway and ran, slipping and sliding, to the terrace. She grabbed the cabaret microphone, praying that it would be on.

'Ladies and gentlemen,' she began. It wasn't loud enough. 'Turn this thing up!' she shouted, and after agonising seconds someone found the knob. Again she spoke into the microphone. 'Please, there is a very serious fire,' she began. 'It is spreading throughout the hotel. Everyone must leave right now, do not think you are safe. If you are by a window push it hard, into its cleaning position, and climb out. Do it now. If there is a walkway use that, but if there is none those who can swim should go out anyway and swim to the bank. Do it now.'

The people round her were grinning to each other, they didn't think it was that serious. It was only one pontoon wasn't it, everything else was safe? Then someone screamed. Flames were licking up on to the restaurant complex, taking hold with frightening rapidity.

'I knew it,' whispered Harriet.

Andrew was at her side. 'Your daughter's out,' he said quickly. 'But there are cars blocking the road, the fire service won't be able to get through.'

'Oh, God.' She looked round desperately. 'To hell with fighting it, let's get these people out! I'll clear the restaurant, you organise elsewhere.'

She had to struggle against a tide of people rushing out. 'Please, get out by the windows,' she kept saying to them. Their faces were blank. Stark terror seemed to have rendered them deaf to her advice. She pushed up window after window and grabbed the young and able, yelling, 'Get out there! There isn't room for everyone inside!'

For the first time she was aware of smoke, chemical tasting from the burning furnishings. The fire was roaring like a furnace, driving everyone before it. Harriet seized a cloth and put it over her nose. People died from smoke and fumes. In the restaurant people might be dying now. She pushed on because it was all her fault. If anyone died it would be on her hands.

An old man was wandering about, his glasses lost, his eyes streaming. He wouldn't get out in time. She dragged him to a window and made him sit outside on the narrow ledge. Thank God someone had

had the sense to use the musicians' raft to rescue the stranded. It was coming along now with almost a full cargo. Jake was punting it. When he saw her, he yelled, 'Harriet! Get on here, the whole lot's burning!'

She ignored him and went back into the building. A body was lying on the floor, she went on all fours and crawled towards it. The heat struck her. For the first time, there were flashes of fire in the thick air. It was a woman, unconscious, perhaps dead. Harriet put her arms around the torso and heaved, beyond the point at which she would normally have given up. She got the woman to the window but couldn't get her up. The air from outside was feeding the flames. At each open window the fire roared like a gigantic bellows.

Jake was still there, his punt dangerously crowded. He was struggling to hold it close by. When he saw Harriet he jumped across, cursing as his hands met the melting plastic of the window cladding. He hauled the woman through, dropping her down to the people on the raft. 'Now you,' He reached for Harriet.

'Too many people. I'll go along the ledge.' She evaded his hand and ran in stockinged feet along the outside of the building. One of the news photographers, risking life and limb for the picture of his career, snapped her. Green skirts held up, long slim legs racing, a cloth tied loosely round her neck and her face streaked with smoke, she was silhouetted against the blaze. No-one who saw the picture ever forgot it.

By the time the fire service arrived it was all too late. People milled about crying or filled with that strange euphoria which comes with escape from death. Some people almost seemed to think the fire had made the party. Fortunately there was no shortage of water and Harriet stood, for once helpless, as the fire was put out. After a while firemen with breathing gear went into the buildings and searched. Because Jake knew the plans he went with them, and because there was nothing else to do Harriet found her manager and organised coffee and snacks from an undamaged kitchen. She was dreading the next hour, knowing what must be found.

The restaurant complex was clear, largely because of Harriet. People had only been sight-seeing there as the food was being served on a buffet elsewhere, so it had not been crowded. But the bedrooms – how she dreaded their return from the blackened, twisted rooms. At last they emerged like spacemen with their air tanks and tubes, and the fire chief signalled for covered stretchers. I won't think of it, thought Harriet. I won't allow myself to think of it.

Someone came up to her and said, 'What a terrible thing to happen to your lovely hotel, Mrs. Hawksworth. How could it have started?'

'How indeed?' she said drily and turned away. Her eye lighted on Nathan, eating a sandwich and looking interested in what was going on. She swallowed. Signalling to her manager, she said, 'Andrew, I want Nathan taken into town right now, please. And I mean right now.' She wouldn't look at either of them.

There were six stretchers in all. After one brief glance she pretended they weren't there. The firemen came out, Jake came out, and she organised coffee and sandwiches. All at once everybody seemed to be crying, except her.

Jake said, 'What a bloody mess.'

She nodded. 'Some party.'

'People are dead, you know!' he flared. 'It's more than a spoiled party! Your hotel has killed people!'

She turned away quickly. That was not something she was going to think about now, there was only so much you could think about at one time and she just couldn't.

The fire chief came across. 'There'll be an investigation, ma'am.'

'Yes. I think it was deliberate. Perhaps your men would like to use one of the rooms to rest in, I'll arrange it.'

'That's kind, ma'am, we'd appreciate it. But I wonder if I could trouble you, ma'am – I believe we need your help in identifying the deceased.'

Jake watched as she crossed to the stretchers. They had died from smoke and fumes, which slightly lessened the horror. Harriet went from one long shape to the next, shaking her head. At the last, she stopped. From the very first moment she had seen the fire, she had known this was coming.

'Madeline Hawksworth,' she said clearly. 'My step-daughter.'

She came back to the group on the terrace, her face calm and expressionless. Jake wiped the sweat from his brow with a filthy hand. God, but he was tired. 'Don't you care at all?' he demanded. 'The girl's dead, doesn't that mean anything? Or is it all money now, and being famous, and knowing the best people? And because she's a Hawksworth, and not in the Harriet fan club, she doesn't count, any more than I do, or Victoria, or anyone at all!'

There was a crash and Harriet turned. The roof of the dining complex was collapsing in on itself. She put up her hands to her chest and pushed at her heart, as if to stifle what she felt. 'My hotel,' she said mournfully. 'I've lost my beautiful hotel.'

Jake's breath came in a long, exhausted sigh. 'God help you, Harriet Hawksworth,' he whispered. 'No-one else can.'

Part Two: Victoria

Chapter One

The staircase was lined from bottom to top with huge boards of polished mahogany, each bearing the names of girls who had achieved rank in every year since the school's foundation at the end of the last century. On the last board, newly painted, were some ten names. About halfway down was the name 'Victoria Hawksworth'. The young lady in question was viewing the board with displeasure.

'I thought I told you my name isn't Hawksworth, it's Jakes.'

'Victoria, dear, your mother likes you to be called Hawksworth. You know that.'

'My mother likes a lot of things, but that doesn't mean *I* have to like them. I'm my own person, Miss Wild! I know perfectly well I was only promoted because of my mother, I'm not stupid!'

'Victoria!' Miss Wild's soft and ladylike tones became steely. 'You know how much we dislike this immoderate language. It isn't fitting for a girl of your standing, or your intelligence. We will hear no more of it, please.'

The girl turned on her heel and flounced off, her whole manner one of defiance. Miss Wild sighed and clasped her hands together. Sometimes she really felt she was getting too old for girls and their tantrums, she longed for the uncomplicated brutality of a boys' school where at least you could beat them when they rebelled. Victoria Hawksworth would certainly benefit from a beating or two, and should have had them a great many years before. A spoiled brat, with the peculiar hallmarks of neglect so common to rich children. So much of everything, so little of what mattered.

She would have been surprised to learn that Victoria was of much the same opinion. Psychology was her latest passion and she lay for hours on her bed reading Jung and Freud, swallowing wholesale the doctrines in *Sanity, Madness and the Family* and then regurgitating them to her unfortunate room-mate, Carrie.

'I'm struggling to find myself,' she declared. 'I'm fighting to get away from my rich and dominating mother. I shan't be able to fulfil myself until I achieve dichotomy between my father's influence and my mother's, then I can be myself.'

'I thought you said your mother didn't take any notice of you,' said Carrie absently, filing her nails and reading at one and the same time.

'She doesn't. But she dominates by edict, she delegates people to do what she says. Did I tell you she nearly got sent to prison once? Miss Wild thinks she's oh so nice, she doesn't know she nearly got jailed for drug smuggling!'

'Bet she does,' said Carrie. 'I've known for years.'

'Have you?' Victoria was taken aback. 'Why didn't you tell me?'

'Figured you might be embarrassed about it. I would. I'm embarrassed about Gerard being gay, and he's only my cousin. Your mother's different.'

'I hope you don't invite him when I come to stay,' said Victoria darkly. 'I might catch Aids.'

'Exactly what were you intending to do with poor Gerard?' demanded Carrie, widening naughty eyes. 'I'd better warn him he isn't safe!'

Victoria blushed and threw a cushion at her.

The tale of her mother's narrow escape had emerged during Victoria's last Christmas holiday. They'd stayed in New York instead of going to Corusca, in the vast, silent apartment they had lived in for ten years or so.

Victoria languished in the dull, foggy days following Christmas. Her cousin Nathan was staying with them, which her mother didn't like at all. He had dropped out of school as soon as he could and bummed around in the Caribbean mostly. No-one knew why he had turned up on the doorstep in New York two days before Christmas, looking as tall and blond and handsome as ever. Harriet's instructions had been that Nathan and Victoria were not to sit in rooms alone together, and were to be accompanied when on walks. Needless to say they succeeded in shrugging off Margaret's increasingly laboured companionship on outings by the simple expedient of striding up the nearest hill.

'You'd think I was the criminal, not your loathsome mother,' said Nathan.

'What do you mean?' Victoria was fascinated and repelled by him at one and the same time. He had no innocence. When he talked to her she felt that he considered her a baby still, while he had been old forever.

'It was after the Florida Lake caught fire. The fire that killed my mother.'

His matter-of-factness shocked Victoria, who liked to pretend an equal indifference to parental claims. 'Does it make you sad to talk about it?' she asked gently.

'Nope. She was pretty well insane – used to talk to me about the monsters in her head. It was a deal more peaceful once she was gone.'

'But the hotel caught fire by accident! It wasn't my mother's fault.'

Nathan chewed his lip. 'Could have been. It was somebody's fault. Was said she needed money so badly the insurance looked like manna from heaven. But I don't think it was her, though if the whole place had gone up I would. She never does anything by halves.'

He reached out and took Victoria's gloved hand. She carefully withdrew it and put it in her pocket. 'I'm not a baby any more,' she said frostily. 'I don't do just what you tell me.'

'Isn't that disappointing?' said Nathan, and grinned at her.

'Tell me about my mother,' said Victoria. 'What was she arrested for?'

'Smuggling dope. They were landing it on Corusca and then taking it off in small boats. She claimed she didn't know a thing about it, but they found a ton of stuff in the big house. They got Jerome for it, and he was like king of the island. He said she wasn't in on it, which shows what a swell guy he is, and all sorts of character witnesses stood up and spoke about her courage in the fire, how hard she worked and all that. That was when Uncle Gareth nearly got control of the Corporation. She was fighting on all fronts for a while.'

'She sure hates Gareth,' said Victoria wonderingly.

'Sure does. You know those pictures she buys? They're from the old Hawksworth Collection, every time he sells one she tries to buy it even if it nearly cripples her. Thinks they're hers. Frightening, really, that sort of greed.'

Victoria discovered in herself a dislike of hearing someone else say what she so frequently uttered. 'She knows a lot about art,' she said defensively. 'I've learned a lot from her. We've got some good stuff, not all of it well-known. Sometimes she buys modern pieces.'

'Anyway she got let off,' said Nathan vaguely. 'Jake sort of held her together until she was through it.'

A satisfied smile spread over Victoria's face. 'He's really kind, my father. I can't understand how he got tangled up with her, can you? I mean, he could have had anyone.'

That Christmas seemed the time to find out the truth. Although it was a subject her mother was always reluctant to discuss, she asked about Jake.

'How did you get to know him?' she demanded, watching her mother make up at her dressing table. 'I should know. He's my father.'

Harriet paused in the act of applying eyebrow pencil. Her face became wary, as it always did when the topic of Jake came up. 'We were sort of thrown together. We were both in some trouble.'

'What sort of trouble?'

Harriet turned and wagged the pencil at her. 'None of your business. You've had a different life from me or your father. You wouldn't understand.'

'Of course I would,' flared Victoria. 'You just don't want me to find out how you trapped him! I bet you got pregnant to try and make him marry you!'

'Victoria!' Harriet was white, her cheeks flying twin red flags of colour. 'You don't know anything about it, and even if you did it isn't any of your business. It's private. Between him and me.'

'You're always foul to him.'

'He's not always been that sweet to me.'

'Yes, he has! I know all about the drug smuggling, I know everything about that. He helped you then, didn't he?'

Harriet's face seemed to crumple, as if losing internal support. Outwardly she remained quite still. 'Has Nathan been talking to you?'

'No,' lied her daughter. 'I found out by myself. So you're not as good as you should be, are you?'

'I had nothing to do with drugs,' said Harriet tightly. 'I wasn't convicted.'

'Only because Father got you off. He should have let you get sent to jail, then I could have gone to him and lived a proper life! You treat me like a criminal myself, I might as well be in prison!' Her hands balled into fists and she slammed them against the couch.

'Jake is not that wonderful,' said Harriet in a muffled voice. 'If he was so bloody wonderful we'd have stayed together, I wouldn't have had to – you don't know him, Victoria. You don't know how unreliable he can be. Oh, yes, he's there when you're desperate, you can count on him then. It's in the long, boring ordinary days that he's going to let you down. And *how* he lets you down!'

'Never your fault, I suppose?' retorted Victoria nastily.

'Don't talk to me like that! Jake isn't a saint, he just isn't. If we'd stayed together you know what sort of life you'd have had? Bumming around from boat to boat, squalid house to stinking yacht, no proper schooling. Jake always off on some new project, nothing settled, nothing permanent. If you stay home you stay there by yourself, he cannot sit still.'

'Not with you, he can't,' snarled Victoria.

Harriet snapped the top on her eyebrow pencil. 'No. Not with me.'

The girl had the sudden feeling that she was swimming out of her depth. In an attempt to regain her footing she said viciously, 'You're jealous! That's why you won't let me go and stay with him, you're so scared he'll steal me from you. You can't let go of anything, you want to hold on and hold on until you're a bony old skeleton! Well, you won't hold on to me. I hate you, Mother!'

'Victoria – ' But her daughter slammed out of the room. Past experience had taught Harriet the futility of reasoning with her. All you could do was wait until she calmed down.

Harriet wept shaken tears. The things she longed to say were the things she couldn't. Jake didn't want Victoria to visit him, the offers had been made but were always refused. The jibe about clinging hurt more. Couldn't the child see that her mother was trying to protect her, that when the time came she would indeed be set free? Harriet would never demand as her own mother had demanded. The child had been sent to boarding school to give her independence, friends, a different life, yet everything Harriet had done seemed to have been misunderstood.

Nevertheless Victoria had gone back to school with only the usual grumblings. When you thought of the problems and difficulties most parents seemed to have with their teenage children, Harriet supposed she wasn't doing so badly. Of course, it was a question of opportunity to a great extent. The nanny was retained as a chaperone, so Victoria never had the chance to take drugs or get pregnant or have a nervous breakdown. She moved from nunlike seclusion at school to careful supervision at home and would emerge in due course as a beautiful, brilliant, unsullied college student. Still, an environment of absolute femininity was perhaps not such a good thing. The solution might have been for Jake to be persuaded to take her occasionally, but he never would. He saw her briefly, two or three times a year, a glamorous matelot dispensing charm and heady masculinity. He was always travelling, and Victoria was at school or on Corusca for the summer.

Harriet thoughtfully smoothed the skin over her cheekbones. There would be time for everything when Victoria was old enough, mature enough, to understand men, her father, the world outside. Till then she would be kept safe.

The plan, so simple and logical when devised, seemed suddenly to have become a childish prank. When Victoria came to pack her bag she found there were so many things she simply could not leave, from her teddy bear to three pairs of shoes to a photograph of Jake, that in the end she could barely lift it high enough to balance it on the window sill.

'This is pretty stupid,' said Carrie in a sing-song voice.

'So you keep saying. I'll leave some of this stuff. Oh!' Victoria ran her hands through her hair despairingly. 'I need it all! I can't go all that way without my clothes.'

Carrie knelt down next to her and began ruthlessly discarding items of clothing. 'You don't need three nightdresses. How many pairs of panties are you taking, for Christ's sake? And surely you can leave your boots behind?'

'They go with my skirt,' said Victoria. 'Anyway, I do need all those things. It's a long journey, I've got to change.'

'How about learning to do the washing?' said Carrie caustically. She was at the school courtesy of a dead aunt's bequest, and returned home to very average surroundings. Victoria's cushioned existence inspired both envy and horror in her kindly breast.

'If I don't go soon the gates will be closed,' hissed Victoria, frantically stuffing clothing into the bag. She heaved it shut and then flung it on to the window sill.

'You really oughtn't to be doing this,' said Carrie, not expecting to be listened to.

'Remember, you were asleep when I left. And don't post the letter till tomorrow evening.' Victoria joined her bag on the window sill.

All at once she looked very young and frightened, a little girl dressed up in expensive clothes: designer jeans, cashmere sweater, leather jacket, hi-tech trainers. She wore too much make-up, but then at home she wasn't allowed to wear any.

'You look too rich,' said Carrie in a panic. 'Suppose you get kidnapped?'

'Then at long last something exciting will have happened to me! I can learn to shoot people.' She began to pick her way carefully down the slates, a feat performed many times but never with luggage.

When she reached the flat roof of the garage, Carrie groaned with relief. 'Don't do anything stupid' she hissed into the night.

'Love you forever, Carrie! 'Bye!' Victoria swung herself skilfully over the side of the roof and dropped down to the grass.

It was a long walk into town but she didn't dare thumb a lift. The young ladies' academy had its fair share of runaways, and the local people were used to them. You got handed back like a parcel before you'd been gone an hour. So Victoria slogged down the road, hiding behind trees when cars came by. It was very dark. She had never been out alone at night, except on Corusca, and there it was different. Her mother was all powerful on the island, and even if she did meet anyone they would be known to her and would only take her light-fishing if her mother said they could.

Victoria loved Corusca more than anywhere in the world and one of the biggest rows she had ever had with Harriet had been over the question of building a hotel near the big house. In the end nothing had been done, but Harriet was probably biding her time. She never gave up on anything.

The bag seemed to weigh twice as much as before, and was determined to strike her behind the knees at every step. She felt an unexpected longing for the warmth and dull security of her school bed. But the gates would be closed by now, she wouldn't be able to get in, so there was nothing for it but to press on.

Fortunately for Victoria, money was never a problem. From her earliest years she had been given more cash than she could spend, and now she had a charge card at several stores and her own bank account into which she poured the money she received as birthday presents. Her father never sent her money. He sent glamorous sailing gear which she never wore because her mother wouldn't let her go out in a blow, or else technical books on boat design. That was when he remembered. He didn't always. Anyway, getting a plane ticket had been a piece of cake, she had ordered it through her mother's usual travel company by the simple expedient of a telephone call.

'I'm going to visit my father in England, I haven't been before. Yes, I'm so excited. Mother says first-class, is that all right? That's very kind of you. Thank you. Thank you so much.' The ticket went on the Corporation's massive bill and by the time anyone queried it she would be long gone.

At last, the outskirts of town. Some boys were leaning against the wall outside a bar and they began to whistle and shout at her.

'Well, ain't you the pretty one?'

'Why don't you let me give you a hand with that heavy old bag?

Victoria ignored them until a long, stringy youth came and walked next to her, 'What's your name? Let me buy you a drink?'

She turned and blazed at him, her grey eyes startling. 'Go away. I don't want to talk to you so leave me alone.'

The boy recoiled, mostly because she was indeed so very pretty, and he was still scared of girls. Cat-calls followed her down the street.

The bus didn't go until one in the morning. Victoria sat huddled on a seat in the bus station, aware that one or two of the drivers were talking about her. After a while one of them, a middle-aged, fattish man, came and bent down to talk to her. 'What are you doing here, missie? Does your mother know you're here?'

'I'm going to her' lied Victoria. 'I've been staying with my father. He – they're divorced. They don't get on too well. I was going to go back at the end of the vacation because I'm missing school. He doesn't want me to go but he's working all day and he drinks – I thought I'd better go home. I promise I'll call him when I get there, but he'll know where I am anyway.'

'Is that the truth now? It isn't safe for a little girl like you out alone at night.'

'I'm seventeen! Almost.'

The driver nodded. He went back to the others and they spent a few moments discussing the shocking state of family life today. Someone brought Victoria a coffee and a sandwich and let her wait in the drivers' room till the bus came in.

Her schedule was calculated exactly. Airport at 6 a.m. for the 7 a.m. flight, before the school discovered she was missing, before her mother could be alerted and guess what was afoot. Weariness was something she had not taken into consideration. She was so tired she could hardly put one foot in front of the other, the world was seen through a mist. It would have been no surprise to anyone who knew her, because Victoria could sleep the clock round quite easily. She felt almost tearful. If her mother had walked into the airport lounge at that moment Victoria would have fallen into her arms with relief.

But everything went smoothly. Apparently girls her age took international flights on their own all the time. She went into the washroom and tried to wake herself up by splashing cold water on her face, and almost missed hearing her flight called. She ran to the gate, and the steward took time out to talk to her. 'No hurry, miss, we won't leave without you. Hawksworth. That wouldn't be Hawksworth Hotels, would it?'

He grinned at her, expecting her to deny it. 'That's right,' she said tensely. 'I'm going to see my father.'

'Is your mother seeing you off?' He looked eagerly about, because Harriet Hawksworth was famous.

'I've sent her home. It's embarrassing when people stare, and anyway she always cries. Don't tell anyone who I am, will you?'

'Not if you don't wish it, ma'am.' His manner had become markedly more respectful.

Victoria walked on to the plane and sat down. She'd done it! Everything swirled in a haze of weary unreality, she was sure that if she closed her eyes for a moment she would hear Carrie calling her to get dressed. Her eyes drifted shut. How good it would be if it was Carrie. Adventures were very frightening when they happened in real life. She didn't stir even when the stewardess came and fastened her seat belt.

Chapter Two

Jake's cottage didn't look at all as Victoria had imagined it. Somehow she had expected something a great deal less tumbledown. As it was the gate was broken and the front door was horrible frosted glass in the midst of fairly genuine age, and when it had been fitted they had cut back the white rendering and failed to replace it. The garden was a complete jungle, full of paint tins and wood shavings. Over the sad little place towered three vast sheds in gleaming aluminium and from them came the sound of radios, hammering, whistling and the screech of drills.

She tried the door of the cottage and found it open. Never in her life denied anything, Victoria was used to walking where it pleased her to go. Besides, by now her mother would have got in touch with Jake and told him she was coming, so she was certain to be expected. But the interior of the cottage showed no signs of being prepared for a guest. It smelled, of bodies and beer and dog.

The dog in question rose from his snooze before the dead ashes of many fires, that were spilling out on to the worn carpet, and began to bark. He was some sort of retriever, large-jawed and noisy. Victoria recoiled from him, because she wasn't used to pets. Her mother was casual with dogs and often said how much she would like one if they lived in a house, but Victoria was secretly scared of them.

'Go away, you horrid thing,' she exclaimed, trying to hide behind a filthy sofa with the stuffing coming out.

'Anything I can do for you?' A woman was standing in the doorway. She seemed to have just got out of bed. She had tousled blonde hair, a torn pink dressing gown and bare toes sporting chipped nail varnish.

'I was looking for my father,' said Victoria haughtily. 'Andrew Jakes. My name is Victoria Jakes.'

The woman lifted one eyebrow. 'Oh, yes. Your mother's been on the 'phone, half out of her mind worrying about you. I told her what I'm telling you, Jake isn't here.'

'But – where is he?' This eventuality had not once occurred to Victoria. She had not endured a journey of such length and difficulty for this to happen.

The woman shrugged. 'Buggered if I know. From what I hear in town he went off to talk to some bloke about a boat and ended up sailing with him.'

Victoria nodded eagerly. 'Yes, that sounds like the sort of thing he'd do, he's always very kind.'

'Kind? Jake? More like he got pissed and thought he had a chance of shagging the bloke's wife. The bastard never even left a message, just expects me to stay here, feed the dog and give him a flat on the back welcome when he gets home.'

Most of this escaped Victoria, but she did understand that the woman wasn't at all the sort of person who ought to be associated with her father.

'Does he know how you keep house while he's away?' she asked primly. 'I don't think he'll like the mess in here.'

The woman paused in the act of lighting a cigarette. 'Look here, Miss Prim and Bloody Proper, if Jake wants his house cleaned up he can bloody well pay for it. One attempt I made at smartening the place up and all the thanks I got was a thick ear. He's a pig in a bloody pigstye, he is, and I'm not staying here to be insulted. I've got a nice place of my own, and I was a fool to leave it. I'm off, and *you* can feed the bloody dog.'

'I shall tell him exactly what you said when he comes back,' said Victoria shrilly.

The woman gave a loud, coarse laugh. 'I shouldn't bother, sweetheart. I've told him myself often enough, he knows it by heart. You ought to ring your mother, she's very upset.'

When the woman had gone Victoria didn't know what she ought to do. She was very hungry but the fridge yielded only mouldy yoghurt, beer in cans and a piece of rock-hard cheese. Sleep also beckoned, but the frowsy smell of the beds put her off. The dog padded round after her, jaws gaping horribly. Victoria felt a wave of anger against her mother. Imagine living in luxury as she did while Jake struggled in poverty and squalor! How brave of him never to complain or ask for money. If it was the last thing she did she would force her mother to do something for Jake. He must spend all his money on those few trips to see her, and the infrequent presents were all he could afford. It made her weep to think of it.

Hunger finally drove her to the sheds. She knocked tentatively on one of the huge doors, where notices read 'No Admittance – that means bugger off whoever you are and go and annoy someone else'. When there was no cessation in the hammering and whistling she pushed the door and went in. A man seated at a vast, paper-covered desk roared, true to the notice, 'Can't you read? Bugger off!'

Victoria flinched but stepped resolutely forward. 'You mustn't speak to me like that. My father owns this business.'

The man threw down his pencil and stared at her. 'Victoria, It's got to be! Well, you're certainly prettier than your father. My name's Mac, by the way. I knew you when you were still in nappies.'

'How do you do?' said Victoria coldly. 'Can you tell me where my father is?'

'Not a bloody clue,' said Mac, and stood up.

Over the years he had become a little less taciturn, a lot more prosperous. He had a house in Cowes now, and an understanding with a wealthy widow, and they spent their evenings together rubbing their hands over their bank statements. Nowadays he made no secret of the fact that he thought Jake's lifestyle ludicrous, his business methods profligate and his profits amazing. 'The best thing for us to do is to take you to a hotel in Cowes,' he told Victoria. 'I've got my wee car outside – ' nowadays he ran a Mercedes ' – and you'll be a deal more comfortable elsewhere.'

'I can't leave the cottage,' said Victoria. 'This woman told me to feed the dog. There isn't anything to feed it with.'

'Oh, Christ.' Mac raised his eyes to heaven. 'I'll see to the dog, you just settle yourself somewhere decent. As soon as your dad turns up you can have a nice chat and go home to your mum. Harriet must be frantic.'

'Do you know my mother?' asked Victoria frostily.

'I do that, and there isn't a better woman alive.' Mac's opinion was slightly coloured by Harriet's wealth, which removed any lingering doubts he might have harboured about her.

'In that case I'll stay here.' Victoria walked round the desk and sat herself down in Mac's chair. He gaped at her.

Just then the door opened and Jake came in. The smell of whisky and seawater mingled in an unholy cocktail, he had three days' growth of beard and eyes like an insomniac bloodhound. Victoria rose, her smile stiffening on her lips. He didn't see her.

'Shitty weather,' he said. 'Everyone but me was sick. Not even I can screw someone who's throwing up, even if I could have stopped sailing the boat. Some party.'

'And you still couldn't manage to let us know what was happening,' said Mac sourly.

'I didn't think you'd miss me, you old bastard. Admit it, you can't wait to get rid of me.' He yawned capaciously and took off his oilskin jacket.

'Hello, Father.'

His head snapped back into position. 'Fuck me, Victoria! Oh God, no.'

It was too much for her. In her mind's eye she had imagined Jake throwing wide his arms, embracing her, perhaps even shedding the odd manly tear on her hair. 'I knew one day you would come to me,' he would whisper. 'Only I truly understand you.' The expression of undiluted horror on his face had not been anticipated. She got up and ran sobbing back to the house.

'Tell me this is a nightmare. Please make her go away,' said Jake, closing his eyes against the world.

'She's run away to her dear father,' said Mac with a hint of a laugh.

'Harriet's been 'phoning once an hour, so make sure you get back to her. Oh, and you're out of dog food.'

'Couldn't Deirdre stagger out and buy some? Oh God, I'd forgotten her. Deirdre!' He turned and raced out of the shed.

Victoria was hunched on a kitchen chair, sobbing prettily. 'You can stop that,' said Jake. 'Is Deirdre here? She was when I left.'

'She went when I came,' said Victoria, sniffing. 'She told me to feed the dog but there isn't any food!'

'What the hell do you think this is? I thought we couldn't have run out that quickly.' He unearthed a box of tins from underneath a pile of newspapers. The dog, envisaging sustenance, slavered over his feet. Jake expertly opened a tin and upended it on a plate that had held egg and chips.

'That's disgusting!' Victoria almost gagged.

Jake stared at her wearily. 'Oh, God,' he said again.

He made a cup of tea and they sat either side of the table drinking it. 'You've got to ring your mother,' he said.

Victoria's head came up. 'I don't want to speak to her ever again! Imagine letting you live like this!' Her gesture encompassed the grease-encrusted cooker, the dog, the half-empty coffee cup on the mantelpiece, the peeling wallpaper, everything.

'Suppose it is a bit of a shambles,' said Jake, looking at it with an attempt at objectivity. 'I'm not here all that often, and about twice a year a woman comes in and cleans up. She'll come in a week or two. But what's it got to do with Harriet?'

Victoria choked back sobs. 'You don't have to be brave,' she whispered. 'I know how independent you are.'

'Er – am I suffering from some terminal disease I don't know about?' asked Jake curiously.

'Of course not, you're just poor!' She uttered the word as if it were indeed a disease, and probably terminal at that.

Jake chuckled to himself. 'We all know who brought you up. Ring your mother, will you, and be quick about it. I've got one hell of a hangover and I don't like repeating myself.'

He sat waiting while Victoria dialled. At length she said, 'Hello, Mummy,' in frosty tones. 'It's me!'

Even at some distance from the 'phone Jake could hear Harriet's voice rising and falling hysterically, the weeping, the raging, the relief. He gestured to Victoria and took the 'phone.

'Harriet, shut up, will you, it's me. I'll put her on the first flight back, OK?'

'No!' yelled Victoria. 'I won't go.'

'You'll do as you're bloody told,' said Jake in an aside. 'By the way, Harriet, she thinks you're letting me live in poverty and squalor. She thinks you ought to give poor old Jake a hand-out now and then, isn't that sweet?'

Harriet didn't say anything for a moment, then she spoke levelly. 'Look, Jake, I don't think it's such a good idea to send her back right now, she's been very unsettled lately. You keep her for a bit. You can get to know each other.'

'Like hell we will! I am sending her straight back home and that's all there is to it!' He yelled too loudly and winced as his head pounded. He was in no condition for rowing.

'It will be good for both of you,' said Harriet decisively. 'Anyway you'll have to keep her because I've withdrawn her from school and I'm closing the house here while I go on an extended tour of the hotels. So there isn't anywhere else to go unless it's Corusca, and I believe Nathan's there at the moment.'

'Have you been allowing her to associate with that hellion? Is that what's behind all this?'

'Not at all,' said Harriet, and her voice broke. 'I wish you'd stop shouting at me, Jake. I've hardly had any sleep and I've been worried to death. It's time you did your share of worrying, I've had enough!'

He sighed. If Harriet felt bad he felt worse. 'You don't have to cry about it. All I'm saying is, she can't stay here.'

'Then you'd better sort something out,' said Harriet wearily. 'I don't want to talk any more.' She hung up on him.

Jake closed his eyes again. This was all more than he could cope with, especially with a hangover and no sleep and vague memories of arranging to meet Cassandra in her hotel tonight.

'We'd better get someone in to clean this up,' said Victoria distastefully. 'I'll pay for it.'

Jake opened his eyes. 'Victoria, dear,' he said grittily. 'Let me put you straight on one thing: I am not destitute. In fact, my accountant would like me to move to a tax haven, so I think we can assume I can afford the necessities of life.'

'Then – ?' She gestured to the squalor all around.

'It's like this because I can't be bothered changing it. It suits me. It's the way it's been since your mother left, though I admit she kept it a great deal cleaner.'

Victoria moved to pick up the 'phone. 'I'll call the cleaning company,' she said distastefully. 'Mother is always so bourgeois.'

Jake put his hand over the telephone. 'Er – I don't think so. If you want it clean, then you clean it. I'll help you. We can be bourgeois together.' He smiled at her, flashing hard white teeth in a tiger smile, an expression so different from any she had ever seen on his face that she was shocked.

'I'm not doing this!' She put her hands together as if to keep them from anything dirty.

Jake hauled himself to his feet. 'We'll springclean. You can start by stripping the beds, there's a washing machine in the shed out there. Get a move on.'

'No!' Victoria was good at saying no. At home and at school, when she said no in that tone everyone became distressed and tried to reason with her, placate her, offer her rewards if only she would comply with what was asked. Jake didn't do any of these things. He swung his arm back and clouted her hard, on the bottom.

She shrieked. 'You can't hit me!'

'I just have. And I'll do it again if I don't get some action.'

'You brute!'

'Too true, sweetheart. Move! Now!'

And Victoria moved, with a speed that would have amazed her games mistress who had spent terms trying to persuade her to do more than lanquidly drift round the basketball pitch, complaining about the cold and her fingernails.

By evening the cottage was only half-finished. Every feeble effort Victoria made enraged Jake further, so that he extended and extended the schedule of work until they were almost committed to taking the floors up to whitewash the joists. The curtains followed the sheets into the washing machine and promptly shrank. While they were flapping on the line Jake cleaned half the windows in the house, but Victoria couldn't seem to get her half clean and left them smeared. So he made her go up a ladder and do the outside ones, too, squealing with fright but too terrified of Jake to come down before the job was done.

They took up the sitting room carpet and washed the flags underneath, and afterwards Jake made Victoria oil them with some concoction used for decks. He had never done it before, but it seemed like a good idea. Then they shampooed the carpet together, spreading it out in the field and scrubbing it.

'This is ridiculous,' complained Victoria, her hair hanging in the suds as she scrubbed. 'A carpet this old should be thrown away, it's disgusting.'

'It has sentimental meaning for me,' said Jake bleakly. 'Your mother stood on this very carpet and threw things. Nothing else would ever be the same.'

'Did you make her work like this?' asked her daughter.

'Your mother was never so bleeding lazy,' snarled Jake. 'If you knew how hard she's worked for you, you might be a bit more grateful!'

All at once Victoria sat back on her heels on the soaking carpet. Her jeans were filthy, her nails broken, she was exhausted and starving and miserable. 'I want to go home!' she wailed, letting the tears cascade down her cheeks.

'Hard luck. You wanted to come, you put up with it.'

But he was being rather hard on her, he decided. It wasn't her fault that she had been brought up to expect flunkies to do the work. Besides his hangover was subsiding and the urge to kick everybody and everything was becoming a distant memory. 'Let's leave this to dry and get something to eat,' he said cheerfully.

'I thought I was going to be starved to death.'

He grinned at her, and he was the Jake she knew once again. 'You deserve it, but it would be a rum do if we all got what we deserved. We'll nip down to the pub and get something.'

'I can't go like this.' She began patting at her hair.

'If you don't, you will starve. Come on.'

Victoria cringed as they walked into the pub, filthy, bedraggled, Jake in trousers through at the knee and a jumper that a tramp would have discarded.

'Who's this then?' said the barmaid archly. 'Bit young for you, Jake!'

'My daughter. Pint please, Mabel, and Coca-Cola for Victoria. Chicken and chips twice.'

'Can't I see the menu?' Since the age of three Victoria had dined à la carte at the best restaurants.

'The only decent thing's chicken and chips, take my word for it. Oh, my God, Cassandra!' Jake was never one to pass up an assignation. He stuffed some money into Victoria's hands, saying, 'Look, you can eat mine, too. Play the machines or something, I'll be back in an hour or so.' He downed most of his beer, told her she could have the last inch, and left.

Mabel looked from the swinging door to Victoria's shocked face and said, 'Never mind dear. See much of him, do you?'

'No. I've never – he's never behaved like this before.'

Mabel patted her hand. 'Don't let it worry you, that's all. He's all right really, once you get used to him. Too much charm, he gets away with things. They always say your mother was the one to handle him, but even she got tired of the goings on, I suppose. Before my time that was.'

'What do you mean – goings on?'

Mabel shrugged. 'Well, what is it always with men? But you're too young to worry about things like that, and besides, with you here he might sober up a bit. He's been wilder than ever lately, we don't know what he'll do next.'

Victoria pondered this silently, sipping in turn at the Coca-Cola and the beer. When the food arrived she was ravenous and ate everything, even though the chips were undercooked and the chicken flabby. Two young men were playing snooker. As she finished her meal the taller one, quite good-looking, came and sat beside her.

'Hello. Mind if I share your table?'

'Not at all.' Victoria assumed the haughty expression habitual when boys spoke to her, because they made her feel so ill at ease.

'You're Jake's daughter, aren't you? Victoria?'

'Yes. How did you know?'

'Oh,' he grinned deprecatingly. 'I work at the yard.' He clearly expected her to congratulate him or something but she said, 'I suppose lots of people round here must.'

'No! It's a plum job, Jake won't take anybody. Look, why don't I buy you a drink?'

He bought her gin. Victoria had never drunk spirits before, although she had tasted the finest wines. Paul, as the boy was called, began to seem so clever and funny. She thought she hadn't enjoyed herself so much in all her life.

'Let's go out for a breath of air,' he suggested.

'That would be nice.' She wove her way to the door.

It was very dark outside, and rather cold. Victoria shivered and Paul said, 'It's warmer over here.' He drew her into the shadow of a doorway. His hands were on her sweater, moving about restlessly, and as she opened her mouth to object he kissed her. The sensation of a tongue probing her mouth like the head of a blind worm was so incredible that she was frozen into compliance. He tasted of beer, it was pleasant and frightening and revolting at one and the same time. Then his big, strong hand closed on her breast, the first hand that had ever touched her there. A shaft of feeling coursed through her body. She was suddenly aware of heat, in her belly, between her legs. She pulled away. 'Stop it.'

He was very excited. 'You shouldn't come here if you don't like it. You do like it, don't you?' He bent to kiss her again and she let him, but he was groping at her jeans now, rubbing her bottom, trying to reach between her legs. 'Don't!' She wriggled away, but he had her trapped in the doorway.

'Come on,' he breathed, crushing her against the wall, everything about him hard and threatening and eager.

'No! Leave me alone!'

'Victoria? What the hell are you doing there?'

Paul sprang away as Jake's square body loomed out of the darkness. 'Mabel said you'd left with someone. And look who it is!'

'He wouldn't leave me alone,' said Victoria tearfully.

'Wouldn't he now?' Jake turned to his horrified employee.

'She wanted to come, sir! She didn't say – I mean – Oh, Christ!'

Jake sighed wearily. This day was not turning out well for him. What should have been a comfortable, relaxed passing of the hours had been arduous, difficult, and was now embarrassing. How could he bawl out someone for doing what he had done a million times? What the hell did these girls expect when they came out in the dark with you – philosophy?

'Look, Paul, I'll talk to you in the morning. Victoria, get in the car.'

Jake drove an old, uncomfortable Land-Rover. Victoria sat hunched in the passenger seat, weeping a little.

'What did he do?' said Jake, ramming the car into gear.

'He was horrible,' said Victoria.

'How horrible?' Jake wasn't at all sure of the extent of Victoria's experience or knowledge. He vaguely imagined that all girls in America were probably sexually practised by about thirteen or so.

'He put his tongue in my mouth,' said Victoria, and burst into violent weeping.

Jake drove a little more, thinking hard. How he wished he had talked to Harriet all those times she had wanted to discuss Victoria, but their relationship had been so prickly and difficult. Somehow over the years it had seemed easier to forget emotion by being cursory with Harriet. He stopped the car and watched his daughter cry into a tissue.

'Been a bit of a hard day for you, hasn't it?' he said gently.

'It's been a horrible day.'

He touched her hair, though the gesture embarrassed him. Then he put his hands on the steering wheel and stared resolutely forward. 'You do know how babies are made, I suppose?' he began firmly.

'You don't have to tell me that,' said Victoria. 'Mummy did.'

'Oh, so it's Mummy now is it? Did she tell you everything? About how men feel about these things?'

'Just eggs and so on. Some of the girls at school have – you know.'

'Oh, yes, I know,' said Jake. Indeed he did, having spent the past couple of hours inserting himself into a lady who should have known better. He hadn't enjoyed it all that much, which was his usual judgment on such meetings. They seemed so uncaring, somehow.

'Look,' he began, 'men – most men – have an enormous sex drive. Especially when they're young they want more than anything else to – do it.' He felt incredibly hot and bothered. 'You do know what happens, don't you?'

'Mummy didn't say anything about tongues,' said Victoria morosely.

'Didn't you like that? It's quite fun actually, when you get used to it.'

'You didn't do that to Mummy did you?'

'Oh God.' Jake felt himself blushing from toes to hair, he was relieved it was dark. 'People do a lot of odd things before they actually – well, mate. But you should care about someone before you get involved in groping each other, it's not something to do lightly.' It occurred to him that he hadn't cared about anyone he'd screwed for years. Floundering his way out of deep water, he rushed on: 'You're a very pretty girl, Victoria. If you go out in the dark with a young man like Paul, whose whole purpose in life is getting his end – I mean, making love – then he's going to be pretty difficult if you won't go along with it.'

'He was horrible,' wept Victoria. 'He kept touching me.'

'Well, he would,' protested Jake. 'You shouldn't have gone if you didn't want him to!'

'I thought he might kiss me. I didn't think it would be – '

'Tongues,' said Jake resignedly. 'Grown-up games, lovey. Next-time just make sure you want to go, and that you know the bloke you're going with. Paul's OK actually, nice chap. Must have thought he'd struck gold.'

'I don't care if I never see him again as long as I live,' flared his daughter.

Jake took no notice of that. 'What I'm trying to say is – ' he began, and then wondered what exactly he was trying to say. 'The whole point of this is – ' he tried again. 'Oh, for Christ's sake! Whatever else you do, Victoria, keep your knickers on. I am not facing your mother and telling her you've lost your virginity, I haven't got that kind of courage. Is that quite clear?'

She was regarding him with horror. 'You are disgusting,' she whispered, and began to cry again.

Chapter Three

In the morning Jake and Victoria were extremely polite to each other. It occurred to Jake that he hadn't made a very good impression the previous day, and he was surprised to find that it concerned him. Here was his daughter, gently bred, inexperienced, and he had made her work like a slave, suffer the sexual urges of one of his workforce and sleep in a draughty bedroom with peeling wallpaper. So he put a cloth on the breakfast table, put a plate on it to cover the patch of mildew, and made toast.

Victoria ate with a strange expression on her face. 'Don't you ever eat proper food?' she asked eventually.

'What's wrong with it?' Jake had never been very concerned about eating, and lately had lost what interest he had.

'The bread's gone mouldy. I don't suppose it'll kill me, though.' She munched on resignedly.

'Look,' said Jake after a while, 'you can see I'm not cut out for this sort of thing. Wouldn't you rather go back to your mum? After all, what are you going to do around here? You can't drive, we're miles from town, and when you get there it's not all that brilliant. There's only sailing makes the place worth anything, and there isn't anyone for you to go out with.'

Sighing, Victoria said, 'I'm glad I didn't know what you were like. I used to think you were so wonderful.'

'Thanks a lot.' It was to be expected that she should be disillusioned but it hurt to be found so much below par. 'Let's 'phone, shall we?'

'She'll be in bed.'

'I don't suppose she'll mind being woken up to be told you're sorry you left and you realise how lucky you are.'

Jake made the call, and when Harriet answered, still half asleep, he was suddenly transported back to the times they had woken together and lay talking in the early morning dark. Unexpected longing choked him.

'Harriet?' he said huskily.

'Hello Jake. Is she OK?'

'Yes, she's fine but she wants to come home.'

'No she doesn't, you want to get rid of her. Anyway, she can't. I'm off in the morning.'

'Don't be difficult. All you've got to do is arrange to have her met at the airport.'

Still sleepy, Harriet said, 'But I'm not going to arrange it. It's your turn to cope. I'm doing other things.'

'Harriet, this is no time to argue, this is important. Here, speak to Victoria.'

Victoria took the telephone, saying breathlessly, 'Mummy? He made me do all the cleaning. And there's nothing to do and my room's horrible. I want to come home, I'm sorry I ran away. Shall I ring when I have my flight number?'

Harriet's voice suddenly sounded rather distant. 'I got your letter yesterday, the one you sent from school. I think you're probably right, I have made you live a sheltered life. So I'm sorry, darling, but I've made arrangements. I thought you wanted to be with your father.'

'But, Mummy, he's a pig!'

A chuckle came over the line. 'Do you think so, darling? And in your letter you said you'd be perfectly happy if only you lived there, instead of in beastly luxury with me. Besides, I'm sure you'll get used to him, and you're bound to find something to do.'

'The bathroom in this house is squalid,' declared Victoria, as if that clinched the matter.

'You'd better mention it to your father. Write to the office if you want to dear, they'll forward the mail. Have a nice time. 'Bye.'

Victoria glowered at her father. 'She won't have me back.'

'So I gather. Well.' He looked like a man who has found the Holy Grail and had it snatched away. There was nothing to do but get on with things. He said wearily, 'Perhaps this is the right thing for you. You'll have to help in the sheds, that's all.'

'Can't we at least get the house seen to?' raged Victoria. 'The lousy food, and the curtains, and the horrible brown stains in the bath!'

He sighed. 'I suppose I have let things go quite a bit. There's a firm in town could see to it. I'll drop you off there and you can arrange everything.'

'Me?' She looked flattered and appalled at one and the same time.

'Yeah. You're the one who wants three inch thick carpets and pink toilets.' He stamped out to work.

For a few days Victoria immersed herself in the delights of house renovation. She spent money like water, ordering a new front door, an entire fitted kitchen, wooden panelling for the sitting room, and a bath that bubbled in fair imitation of a jacuzzi. Fortunately Jake was listening when she innocently chattered about the jacuzzi, and managed to cancel most of her excesses when he went into the shop.

'She said she had permission,' said the salesman, very disappointed at the crashing of his hopes.

'Not that much permission,' said Jake. He was beginning to realise that you could not expect judgment from Victoria. She was sulking in the car.

'The kitchen wouldn't look good in plastic,' he reasoned to her unresponsive shoulder.

'It looks horrible now. My ideas would have looked lovely.'

'In a New York apartment, maybe, but not in a country cottage on a riverbank.'

He realised how old she was making him feel. It was all the early nights, his system wasn't used to it. Since he couldn't coax Victoria back into the showroom because she said he had made her look a fool, he went back in himself and ordered a new Aga, a sink unit, and two old oak dressers.

'Find them in some antique shop and mark them up,' he instructed. 'I don't want to be bothered looking. She can have her bathroom, but not that goddamned bath.'

One of the worst things about his predicament, he thought, was the abstinence. No casual seductions, no boozing, no unexplained absences. Harriet must be killing herself laughing, he told himself, settling down for another evening of Victoria reading a bit, sighing a lot and staring out of the window like a heifer marooned on a mud island.

'You might at least get a television,' she complained, as she did every night.

Jake felt his temper quivering against the bit. 'Why don't you knit?' he said tightly. 'I'm working.'

'I can't knit. Are you going to teach me?'

It suddenly occurred to him that she was as ready for a fight as he was. The shock of meeting himself in her took his anger away. He laughed. 'Let's go and have a meal somewhere. We can meet a few people.'

She lit up like a candle, the sulks disappearing in a wreath of smiles. My, but she's pretty, said Jake to himself. Tall and slim, with that white skin and black hair and clear, blue-grey eyes. She ran upstairs and put on a clean pair of jeans and a very tight T-shirt which displayed too obviously the absence of any bra.

'I'm not taking you out like that,' he declared.

'I promise to keep my coat on,' said Victoria, and flounced past him. He just couldn't face the effort of making her go up and change.

They went to a bar where Jake was sure of meeting some yachting cronies. True enough, a couple of charter men were ensconced at a corner table and one or two people from the clubs waved to him. The men at the table beckoned to him, and Jake went across, introducing them to Victoria.

'Victoria, this is Geoff Lewes, Jim Defarge. My daughter, Victoria.'

'Didn't know you had a daughter,' said Geoff. 'And such a pretty one.'

'Not often we see you in such attractive company,' added Jim.

Having paid lip-service to Victoria's presence they proceeded to take no notice of her at all, indulging in long, rambling and technical chat about slots and channels, differentials and centres of effort. After a while Victoria got up, went to the bar and pointedly ordered a prawn salad. She returned to the table, fished in Jake's pocket for the money and paid for it. Then she ate it, still ignored by the men. She took off her coat.

The comparative quiet of the bar was ruptured by a gang of boys entering, bringing with them cold air and exuberance. A look of haughty disinterest came over Victoria, replacing the rigid boredom of a moment before. It had not escaped her that one of the boys was Paul.

He saw her and the colour swept to his hair. She nodded stiffly, and with a nervous glance at Jake, who was taking no notice, Paul crossed over to her. 'Hello. I thought I might see you at the yard, but I haven't.'

'I've been busy.' Her long fingers twirled an empty glass.

'Like a drink?'

'That's quite all right, thank you.'

'It's no trouble, honest. Gin, wasn't it? Come over, I can introduce you to my mates.'

The invitation was marvellous, but she made a proper show of reluctance first. Then she sauntered across and was enveloped in the group of tall, raw-boned boys none of whom could understand how Paul had managed it. They were showing off for her and became raucous. The publican kept telling them to simmer down.

'Let's go for a drive,' suggested Paul. 'We've got two cars, we can all get in. Victoria can sit on my knee.'

'I'm supposed to be with my father,' she protested. 'Wait a minute, I'll ask.'

She went back to the table and slipped her coat over her shoulders. 'Dad, I'm just going for a drive. See you later, OK?'

Jake's attention was suddenly all hers. 'Oh Christ, love, I'd forgotten you. What do you want to do?' He scanned the group of boys, and Paul.

'I'll be off then,' said Victoria, making for the door. He couldn't call her back without humiliating her in front of everyone. He said nothing.

'I wouldn't have let my daughter go off like that,' said Geoff gloomily.

'You haven't got a daughter,' snarled Jake. 'All you've got are bloody lecherous swines of sons that want to seduce mine. God! Whatever happened to tea dances, and chaperones, and bleeding chastity belts!'

'My wife would never have let our Annie go off with a group of lads,' commented Jim. 'They picked her up at our house, and they said where they were going, and they had to have her back by ten-thirty strict. And look at her, married five years and two lovely kiddies.'

Jake couldn't get his mind back on the conversation that had fascinated him previously. He kept wondering if he should have made a scene and refused to let her go. If he should have insisted she wore something different. But it was his fault anyway because he had ignored her, and it had been almost deliberate. The conversation of a sixteen-year-old he found tolerable in fairly limited doses, he realised.

Normally he would have invited the men back for a nightcap after closing time, but tonight he wasn't in the mood. He drove alone back to the cottage and stood in the sitting room with the lights out and the curtains open watching for Victoria to come home. In the last few years they had made a makeshift road across the field direct to the house, though it collapsed in winter. At around one-thirty, when Jake was about to telephone the police and ask if there had been any fatal accidents that night, a car began driving at speed along the track, its headlights raking the sky. It screeched to a halt, and two people extricated themselves from the crush of bodies inside.

'Thank God,' muttered Jake fervently. 'Just as long as she isn't dead.'

All gratitude evaporated as the couple glued themselves together by the front door. Paul was breathing hard and every now and then Victoria laughed or said something softly. The gang in the car were cheering them on in sibilant whispers. Jake flung open the front door and switched on the light.

'What the hell do you think you're doing?' he heard himself

declaiming. 'Do you realise what time this is, Victoria? Paul? Get yourself in here, young lady, and straight to bed!' She scuttled past him and up the stairs.

'I'm sorry we're late, sir,' said Paul, struggling to regain his composure. 'I didn't know you were waiting up.'

'I wasn't waiting up,' lied Jake, aware that he should at least have got into pyjamas. Furious with everyone and everything, he slammed the door shut, only to hear an upstairs window being opened and Victoria calling: 'Night, Paul. Thanks.'

'See you tomorrow,' called Paul, and they proceeded to conduct an inane conversation through the window. Jake wrenched the door open again.

'Will you go bloody home!' he roared. 'I can do without balcony scenes!' When at last the car had roared away again, he poured himself a large scotch.

At breakfast Victoria looked happier than at any time since her arrival, Jake realised.

'Going to see much of Paul, are you?' he asked heartily.

'Don't know.' She gazed dreamily across the kitchen, looking at nothing.

Jake said, 'I think it's best if you don't go out with groups of boys. If he wants to take you out he's got to pick you up from here, say where he's taking you, and have you back by ten-thirty sharp.'

She opened her grey eyes wide. 'That is just stupid,' she said witheringly.

He gulped. 'Nothing stupid about it. It's reasonable. Sensible. Safe.'

'If you're worried about me getting pregnant, I promise I won't,' she declared. 'I know all about it.'

Jake was struck dumb for a second then he said huskily, 'Last time we talked you hadn't even kissed anyone! How come we're now into contraception?'

'Are you against sex outside marriage?' asked Victoria vaguely, crunching into her wholemeal toast. He had taken to having bread delivered, it seemed best.

'Yes,' said Jake wildly. 'Absolutely. No sex until you are married.'

'Like you and Mother?'

'Yes! No! Oh God, Victoria, if I'd known what trouble it was going to get me into I would never – it's best not to. Believe me, I know.'

'Paul says you have strings and strings of women,' said Victoria. 'The men see them going home, sated with passion.'

'I think they mean hung over,' said Jake bitterly.

From then on he felt he was fighting uphill. Victoria took to drifting in and out of the sheds, fetching and carrying things, taking telephone calls, always in skintight jeans, or shorts, or a cheesecloth dress she had bought in town. Productivity virtually collapsed when the sun came out and so did Victoria in a bikini. Mac demanded that Jake do something about her.

'We canna work with all the lads gawping at her! That poor wee Paul is going to go blind soon, I'll tell you. She's torturing him.'

'Thank God for that,' said Jake. 'I'll start worrying when he starts looking happy. Really, Mac, I have tried to talk to her, I keep on trying. She says it's sick to see evil in the human form. What is the world coming to if she can't take advantage of a little sunshine? She wants us to realise she would be overdressed for a nudist camp, which I have to admit is probably true. I just can't find out what that has to do with anything, somehow.'

'You'll have to ban her from the sheds. Someone's going to cut a finger off soon, and as for Paul, he'll never walk again! Girl her age trailing around like a – '

'Watch it' said Jake sharply. 'It's only her innocence that lets her do this sort of thing. I won't have you behaving as if – '

'She's behaving as if,' said Mac pointedly. 'You are the girl's father, Jake. For once in your life you have to take responsibility!'

But was he really responsible? After all, Victoria couldn't be watched night and day; she was only here now because Harriet had kept her on a leash so short the girl was nearly strangled. Everybody has to learn their own lessons, reasoned Jake. The more we repress her, the harder she fights. The time had come for Victoria to have an object lesson in restraint.

That night when Paul drove up at half-past ten and parked interminably in the shadows, Jake tried to pretend he hadn't noticed. Most nights he virtually flung the car door open and hauled Victoria inside, but this time he thought he would let her go a little further, let her realise just what sort of game she was playing. He couldn't always be there to stop her, she must see how difficult things might get. Nothing terrible could happen outside the front door, but she might end up shocked. He went resolutely upstairs, but sat on the edge of the bed worrying.

In the car, Victoria was dizzy with excitement. She had been riding the wave for days, watching the men watching her, hearing Paul's declarations of love and passion whenever he could get her alone. 'Just let me get close to you,' he was whispering. 'Just let me feel what you're like.'

Her breasts ached from the pressure of his hands, her mouth was puffy with kisses. She too longed to go on. When he was close to her she found her hips pressing into him, her legs spreading wide. Tonight she was wearing her cheesecloth dress in a deliberate act of enticement. His hands were on her thighs, groping at the elastic of her panties.

'If your dad comes now he'll kill me,' he was muttering. But he couldn't resist probing the soft, virgin wetness of the girl, putting his big craftsman's fingers into her. She was gyrating against him, her eyes closed, face ecstatic. They had to do it. He unzipped his trousers, his erection like iron, and then nothing could have stopped him.

Desperation made him harsh. He couldn't get in, he *had* to get in! The searing pain brought her to her senses. She opened her eyes and was aware of what was happening to her.

'No! I don't want to!'

Because she didn't, really, she only wanted the excitement. The man on top of her was a stranger, a brute, forcing himself into her body. Her flesh parted and she shrieked, was conscious of pain, pressure, volume inside her. Paul subsided, gasping, on to her.

She fell through the front door into the dark house. She was sobbing, it hurt to walk, her legs were wet with slime. Jake turned on the light. He faced his daughter, and there was no hiding what had happened.

'Oh God.'

He ran to the front door, but he was too late. He could hear the sound of a car being drive away very fast.

'I didn't know what he was going to do,' sobbed Victoria. 'I didn't know till he was doing it! He hurt me.' She sank down to the floor, her arms folded over her stomach.

Jake felt like crying. He crouched down next to her and cradled her in his arms. The smell of sex came to him, so familiar and now so terrible. Her innocence was gone before she was ready to lose it, because he had not protected her from herself.

'I might have a baby,' sobbed Victoria.

'I thought you knew all about that,' said Jake wearily. How he wished Harriet was there. It was so lonely being the only one responsible, and all these years he had let her be that. After a while he took his shivering daughter upstairs and put her to bed.

His first thought was to tear Paul limb from limb and hang the pieces from the telephone wires. But, pleasant as it would be, it was neither fair nor in Victoria's interest. The last thing she needed was for everyone to know what had happened. He had such a sense of failure. For the first time he experienced the awful judgment that a child's behaviour levels on its parents. Some, if not all, must be your fault because you did, or did not do, this or that thing. Jake's sins went back a very long way.

In a short and vicious interview the next morning, Paul received his cards. 'You leave at the end of the month, and I don't want anyone to know you're going,' said Jake. 'And that's to protect my daughter, not you. One word about this and you lose your front teeth, I promise you.'

'I want to marry her, sir,' said Paul.

'Don't be ridiculous. Anyone who can't restrain his carnal desires is not marrying my daughter.'

'What's going to happen to her, sir?'

Jake realised he thought Victoria was going to be sent to a nunnery. 'This isn't the middle ages,' he declared, wishing that it was, because then he could have disembowelled Paul as and when he liked. 'I shall take her with me to deliver the MX yacht. After that she's going back to school.'

Paul said desperately, 'You'll need an extra hand, sir. I do love Victoria. I know she hates me now, but if I had a chance – '

'The only way you would get on that yacht would be strapped head down next to the rudder,' said Jake with infinite weariness. 'It would give me great pleasure to see you drowning in six feet of water. Am I plain enough? You want me to explain further?'

When he had his office to himself once again, Jake leaned back in his chair and felt his head throbbing. Suppose she was pregnant? Harriet would never forgive him. But in the cold light of day he wondered if this had been inevitable. A girl with Victoria's looks, with no experience of boys at all, no experience even of going shopping by herself, rushing headlong after excitement. She had never denied herself anything, all the rules were imposed from outside. As long as she wasn't pregnant this was no tragedy, just a painful lesson in being human. He had intended that a lesson should be learned, but not this drastically.

At lunchtime he found Victoria dressed in a shapeless shirt of his over a skirt let down three inches. She wouldn't meet his eyes.

'Cheer up,' he declared. 'We're going to deliver a yacht next week, you me and Mac. It's going to the Caribbean, so I can drop you off with your mum at some time or another. But we'll make a trip of it and stop off on the way. You haven't seen Spain, have you? Thought we might put in for a few days.'

'I'd better not come,' she said dismally. 'You don't want to bother with someone like me. Just send me back by freighter or something.'

'Victoria,' said Jake grittily, 'this isn't the end of the world. It's – an experience, that's all. Everybody has to do it sometime.'

'I behaved horribly.' She was shedding miserable tears into the soup she was trying to eat.

He touched her hand. 'Shall I tell you something? You think you've behaved badly – well, you have. But people do behave badly, and afterwards they know better. Did your mother ever tell you why she and I broke up?'

'It was because she wanted the money,' said Victoria, lifting her head. 'She had to live in America and you wouldn't go.'

'No, that was after. What really finished us was that I had sex with her best friend. Harriet was ill, the friend was there, I did it. Your mother has never, ever forgiven me and I don't think she ever will. And I think perhaps she's right. It was unforgivable.'

Victoria stared at him. 'Poor Mummy.'

'Yeah, poor Mummy. But in the end poor all of us, because if I'd behaved better we could all have lived different lives.'

They ate their lunch in thoughtful silence. Victoria kept glancing at her father as if seeing him for the first time. Jake found it worrying. He kept remembering Harriet's face all those years ago, the shell she had thrown over herself and her pain. It had seemed then as if his life was at an end, as if nothing would ever make it bearable.

'Does she have lovers?' he asked suddenly. 'I know I shouldn't ask you that, it's probably one of the major "don'ts" in the book. She used to have a thing going with that banker.'

Victoria stared at him. 'I don't know. I don't think so. Sometimes men come round and bring her presents and take her to the theatre and things, but she always chases them off. She's not a warm person, you see.'

'She used to be. She was lovely, once.' Jake felt embarrassed, as if he had revealed more of himself than he had intended. 'Will you tell her about this?' he asked abruptly.

'No. Will you?'

'No.' They looked at each other. For the first time it seemed that they might be friends.

Chapter Four

Victoria had often sailed in dinghies, and had once spent a week aboard a motor-sailor when her mother accepted an invitation from a couple with a daughter about the same age. Harriet had hated it, and in a moment of rare honesty had told her daughter that if she had realised they were going to drive round and round in endless circles she would have suggested they spend the holiday watching the tumble drier in the comfort of their own home.

'Don't you like sailing?' Victoria had asked.

'Darling,' said Harriet, 'this isn't sailing.'

Until she went to sea with Jake, Victoria had never been able to confirm this. But from the moment he weighed anchor on the as yet unnamed MX, a medium sized racer with no concessions to comfort, she realised her mother had spoken the unvarnished truth. This plunging, spray-filled exhilaration was beyond imagination, satisfying some primeval urge to ride the elements. The wind was brisk, the sky gunmetal grey, and all but the hardiest were taking in reefs and heading for home. Jake's yacht lay hard over, carrying a lot of sail and flying over the waves. It was thrilling and terrifying and absolutely wonderful!

'OK, pudding?' he asked once. 'Be sick downwind, remember.'

'I'm not sick. I want to do something.'

He glanced at her. 'Take the wheel while I go for'rd. I want to check that the staysail isn't rubbing.'

For blissful moments she was in charge! But she let the boat drift off the wind and he shouted at her.

The weather forecast was fair, predicting a blowy night followed by a few days of relative calm. Unfortunately, for once the met office had got it wrong, and the depression they foresaw scuttling away south deepened markedly. By the morning it was clear that they were in for a storm, and already some yachts that had put to sea expecting a fair crossing were deciding to turn back. Some that in Jake's opinion should have turned back were battling on. They saw them, already struggling, willing to take a risk because they did not know how big the risk was.

'This is the sort of thing that gets people killed,' said Jake gloomily.

Mac chewed on a sandwich. 'Want to run for it?' They were both thinking of Victoria.

'No. Close in we'll be dodging all these weekend sailors too ill to steer.'

'Are we going to drown?' asked Victoria breathlessly.

Jake tried not to smile. It was very odd, but one of the hallmarks of the very young was the apparent casualness with which they contemplated death. They had most to lose, but were most prepared to lose it. The nearer you got to eternity, the less you fancied the trip.

'Sorry to disappoint you, but this thing is designed to withstand half a hurricane on weekdays and a whole one on Sundays. We won't go down, though other people might.'

Listening on the radio that night, it appeared that lifeboats were hopping in and out of port like rabbits out of their holes. Dismastings, a trawler damaged by a big sea when its gear became tangled on the bottom, a party of fishermen who should never have gone out in the first place and now rolled helplessly in a cruiser with a dead motor. Jake was less worried about the weather, more the many tankers and freighters that thronged these waters. In dirty weather a yacht showed up very badly on radar screens, and it might be that they wouldn't be looking anyway because they didn't expect one to be out. He and Mac took it turn and turn about on watch, sometimes sitting together in the shelter of the cockpit, looking out at the seas and talking now and then.

Victoria, wrapped cosily in her bunk, felt almost shy of them, because they were unafraid, and in their element, and enjoying themselves. Men were so different, she felt. In the world of women in which she lived they seemed almost unnecessary except to remove rubbish or climb ladders. Now, watching her father's calmness and competence, knowing herself safe in his care, she knew a sharp yearning for a different childhood where the two sides of life balanced each other and in turn taught her balance. She didn't know or understand men, and it worried her. They had power over her that she could only guess at. All at once she wanted her mother there, to ask 'Was it like this for you? Did you give them up because you couldn't handle them either?' Jake wasn't what she had thought him. He was both more and less. No wonder her mother had become so strong. For a man like that, as difficult as Victoria suspected he could be, you needed strength.

Jake decided to put in at a port on the north coast of Spain. The weather remained foul, and the Bay of Biscay was its usual unpleasant self, whipping up vicious storms unpredictably. They were eating erratically, and Victoria was starting to look greasy-haired and tired. When he realised it was only her period he was so relieved he broke out the rum, and sat in the cockpit thanking God.

'There's a boat over there,' she said.

Jake glanced at her. 'Put your lifeline on. I won't tell you again, I'll sling you overboard. Christ! That doesn't look so good, does it?' He hopped on to the foredeck to get a better view, but the little boat was so far down in the water that it was still hard to see. The mast stuck naked into the air, not a shred of sail was to be seen.

'Lying ahull,' said Mac, joining him. 'Could be abandoned.'

'Let's look her over.'

They pulled the MX round, a difficult manoeuvre with the wind gusting and shifting through several points of the compass. Victoria got her finger torn by wire and Jake yelled at her for stupidity. As they approached the other yacht, a short fat motor-sailor with a Dutch registration, Jake got out a megaphone and began yelling. Victoria shivered. There was something ghostly about the soaking and deserted deck of the little boat, but if she turned her eyes from it to the waves, rolling endlessly on as if from some infinite power source, she felt a horrible sense of unreality, as if there was no home or comfort or security, not even a damp little cabin into which she could retreat. It was the same cold sense of abandonment reported by men in space, she thought, watching the world below endlessly because they knew themselves so far from home and safety.

Jake saw her face and thought she looked sick. 'Go below and lie down,' he advised.

'I want to see if anyone's there.'

In a brilliant piece of seamanship considering the conditions, Jake brought the MX up on the port side of the motor-sailor and shouted again. After a minute there was a sudden flurry of movement, the hatch burst open and a man came on deck. He was short, fat and very frightened. He waved his arms frantically at Jake, shouting in Dutch and then English. Three more faces appeared, his wife and two small children.

'Shit,' said Jake. 'What a bloody bore.'

'Our motor has gone,' yelled the man. 'It does not work! The wind is too strong for our sails, please help us!'

'Where are you from?' bellowed Jake.

'Arcachon! We travel to Santander!'

Suddenly Mac started to swear violently and unfastened the parcel of rubber dinghy from its lashings. 'Bloody dangerous in this sea,' said Jake. 'We could call for help and stand by.'

'We'd be here twelve hours, and those kids have had enough. There's nothing wrong with the sodding boat. All they need is some sail.'

'What they need is their bottoms kicking. Children should never be on board in this weather.' Jake was angry and anxious at one and the same time. It was a terrible risk for Mac to go across, and not only for Mac. They were short-handed on the MX as it was. He had vaguely intended to pick up one or two extra crew in Lisbon.

'I'll get you a chart,' he said irritably. 'I suppose we shall all have to go to bloody Santander.'

Victoria said, 'We ought to leave them. It's not fair to expect us to help. They shouldn't have come out in the first place.'

Jake assumed, rightly, that the scared faces on the other boat had shaken Victoria but he hadn't time to humour her. 'Don't be stupid, please,' he said witheringly.

They threw a line to the little motor-sailor and the Dutchman and his wife hauled Mac and the dinghy across. Only when safely over the taffrail did Mac release his lifeline from the MX, and only then did Jake let out the breath he had been unaware he was holding.

'That didn't look very safe,' said Victoria.

'Could say that,' commented her father. 'I thought I was about to see my best friend drown, as it happens.'

They stood off for another half-hour while Mac calmed the hysterics of the family and sorted out sails. The motor-sailor began to look much less forlorn, and as her mainsail went up, the sun came out. 'That should cheer them up,' said Jake. 'Christ, will you look at that roll. No wonder they panicked. I bet the kids are being sick everywhere.'

'Do we have to stay next to them all the way into port?' asked Victoria.

'We can't go that slow, we'd have to sail in circles. No, we'll go on ahead and get someone to come out and tow them in. Those things aren't in the least manoeuverable when under sail. Oh, the excitement of being at sea, it all helps to enliven our dull little lives. Take the wheel, I think we can put the odd rag out to dry.' He went for'rd to break out more sail, thinking that if Victoria had looked tired as a passenger she was going to be exhausted as the crew.

To begin with she enjoyed the responsibility of being a valued crew member, instead of a passenger sometimes permitted to make a sandwich. As the hours wore on the novelty wore off, and she began to get bad-tempered. When once again Jake hauled her back on deck into the cold and the wet, just as she got more or less dry and comfortable, she turned and swore at him. 'Fuck off! I won't go.'

When she used that word at home it invariably caused an earthquake. Jake didn't turn a hair. 'Either you put your coat on and get up there,' he said reasonably 'or I haul you out without it. Nobody planned on making you work, but since you must you'd better be good-tempered.'

Victoria intended to put her coat on and go, but she thought she would send another shaft into her father's flesh first. 'Anyone with any sense would have brought more men,' she said waspishly. 'I think mother's right, you're not to be trusted.'

Jake didn't reply. Instead he caught her by the arm and propelled her through the hatch, giving her bottom a hefty boot to help her on her way. She fell into the cockpit, soaking her jumper in a puddle, and burst into tears. 'I didn't want to come anyway! I hate your horrid boat!'

'Belt up, will you?' said Jake wearily. 'If you're sorry you came then I am certainly sorry I brought you. Fool that I was, I thought you might show some of your better qualities under pressure. Perhaps these *are* your better qualities.'

Victoria seethed inwardly. I hate him, she told herself. He's a brute, I knew he was. When at last Jake let her go shivering down below once again, she turned and said bitingly, 'I'm so glad you weren't around when I was little. I didn't think I was, but I am.'

Jake swallowed the hurt. Later, when she had found some dry clothes, he said reasonably, 'I know I seem hard and I'm sorry. But it is important to sail this boat right, when things need doing they won't wait. You have to do as you're told.'

'You just like being rude to people,' she retorted. 'You didn't have to kick me.'

He sighed. 'I'm sorry I kicked you.'

'No, you're not.'

He wasn't going to beg her to forgive him. He almost felt like kicking her again.

They made port in the early hours of the morning. Victoria was white with exhaustion, and with what consciousness she had left brooded on how it was all Jake's fault. Tired as she was, she couldn't sleep. When her father came back on board after a consultation with the harbour-master, she sat up and said, 'I won't stay on this boat. I want to fly home, straight away.'

'If that's what you want.' Jake was too tired to argue about it. He pulled off his boots for the first time in many hours, and wriggled his toes luxuriously.

'Your feet smell,' said Victoria

He lost his temper. 'I daresay they do,' he said menacingly. 'And I'm sorry if it bothers you. I'm sorry the boat bothers you, and rescuing people. The next time I see someone in distress and I think you might be inconvenienced, I'll be sure to let them drown. After all, the fact that Mac's still out there struggling to get that boat home, and I've been sailing this thing almost single-handed because you were too precious to help, and the harbourmaster's even now getting ready to take a launch out to guide them in, and there's a woman on the quay whose husband's fishing boat has been missing since yesterday, none of that matters to you, does it? Just as long as Victoria's warm and comfortable and happy. Don't worry, you're not staying on this boat. I'm kicking you off first thing in the morning!'

He picked up his sea-boots to throw them at her. But she looked so young and tired and frightened. He put them down again and rolled into his bunk. Just at that moment he could bear no more of her.

Fraught nerves and jangled tempers were eased in the morning, when the Dutch boat made harbour, the missing fishing vessel was reported safe elsewhere, and Jake had had some sleep. He assumed, wrongly, that the hasty words of last night were as little regarded by Victoria as they were by him, born as he knew them to be out of weariness and anxiety. But although she drank her morning coffee and exclaimed at the lovely fresh bread as if she was quite happy, Victoria brooded. Jake was right, she was uncaring and self-centred and lazy. All she thought about was herself. Wherever she went she caused upset and disorder and pain. Her mother didn't want her any more, her father was tired of her, even Paul had let her go with merely an impassioned letter of repentance. She was unloved because she was unlovable, she decided.

Later that morning Jake took her across to the Dutch boat. Mac was still in residence, largely because he was enjoying being worshipped by the family. It was the first time they had taken their boat so far from home, but since it had withstood what they considered to be quite a bad storm last season, and their rolypoly children loved sailing, they had departed on a great adventure. Jake drank schnapps and listened to them reciting Mac's heroic qualities, how brave he was, how calm, how resourceful.

'He has taught us so much,' said the mother, beaming at him adoringly.

'Just make sure you dinna go to sea in such weather again,' said Mac tersely. One of the children began singing a sea shanty Mac had taught them, the schnapps fumes began to thicken, a tin of biscuits was passed round and Victoria began to cry.

Jake took her for a walk along the harbour wall. 'What's the matter?' he asked stolidly. He always seemed to be asking that question and the answers never got any better.

'I'm so unhappy,' she wept.

'I can see that. Look, I know I was hasty last night. I know I behave like Captain Bligh when we're sailing, your mother often used to complain about it. But, Victoria, you weren't behaving very well, sweetheart. I think you know that, don't you?'

'I know you hate me. I don't blame you for it.'

Jake wondered if it would be best if he drowned her, himself, or both of them. If they went on with this conversation he knew he would lose his temper and then they would be in a worse mess than ever. 'I don't hate you,' he said patiently. 'I just want you to behave like an adult, take some adult responsibility and think about someone else occasionally. Not often, just now and then.'

Victoria said nothing, trudging along with her hands in her pockets. A seagull dipped down and screeched at them. 'It's getting hot,' said Jake. 'Why don't we go into town for lunch?'

'I'm too old to be cheered up with an ice cream sundae,' she said miserably.

'How about half a bottle of wine?' coaxed Jake. 'Or rum, or whatever else it takes? I can't stand these sulks, Victoria, I think it only fair to warn you!'

She stopped and faced him, and her tragic expression was so lovely that he had to smile. 'I know you think I'm silly,' she said, 'but I'm going to leave the boat. I've decided to travel around Europe, to discover myself. I should see Venice before it sinks. I might learn to find happiness.'

Jake felt his jaw muscles go into spasm, and carefully tried to relax them. 'You are not bumming around Europe on your own. You are sixteen, and Venice isn't going to disappear before you're twenty-one, I can guarantee it. You would get into an awful lot of trouble.'

'I shall go, whether you like it or not.' She started to walk rapidly back to the boat.

The argument raged for most of the day. Secretly Jake was amazed that Victoria had the willpower to press on in the face of his forcibly expressed opposition, but as Mac said they were as stubborn as each other. In mid-afternoon she flung her fully packed bag on to the deck, Jake threw it below again, she pushed it up through the forward hatch and he dumped it overboard. Mac was left to fish it out while the two protagonists yelled at each other. Eventually Victoria lay sobbing below while Jake huddled on deck in a state of shock.

'I can't take it, Mac. I think I'd rather be dead,' he said hoarsely.

'She's certainly determined,' said Mac admiringly. 'I haven't seen you this upset since Harriet.'

'That isn't a coincidence. Look, am I being unreasonable? Like hell I'm being unreasonable, she's only sixteen!'

Mac eyed him gloomily. 'Seems to me she's hellbent on growing up. She's had no independence and she wants some. Give her some rope.'

'And let her hang herself? No thanks.'

Mac chewed on a biscuit from the Dutch boat. 'If we sent her back to Harriet now she wouldn't settle. Can't you compromise? Let her be an au pair girl or something.'

A wide smile of relief spread over Jake's taut features. 'What a brilliant idea. May your bowels never fail to open. Victoria! Get up here and find out what we've decided.'

Chapter Five

Jake had once built a boat for a man in Lisbon, a Portuguese aristocrat who divided his time between any of his three houses, who had six children and two wives, several titles he didn't use and a great deal of charm. Jake telephoned him from Santander, praying that he would be prepared to take Victoria as an au pair, or cook, or chimney-sweep or anything else that would get her off the boat and into the household.

Raoul Pereira was only too pleased to help his good friend Jake, and as it happened the call was fortuitous because he was only then thinking that he needed a new boat, not a racing yacht this time, more a family cruiser. Surely Jake would oblige?

With one telephone call Jake committed himself to building the only non-racing yacht of his career to date, abandoning without question one of the main principles by which he lived, which was that he wasn't interested in cruisers. It was worth it if only for the look on Victoria's face.

'Is he really grand? How old are his children? What will I do for clothes, will Mummy send them?' Jake mumbled vague replies. He was bracing himself for a frank talk on contraception.

The Pereiras had a palace outside Lisbon. It wasn't called a palace, but one look at the turrets and formal gardens, the flunkeys and gold-topped gates, and Victoria knew it was a palace. She was paralysed with fright, a totally new experience for her. From her earliest years she had been used to life on the top rung of the ladder, and suddenly she saw the rungs stretching away into the clouds and she staring up at them.

'I haven't any clothes,' she hissed to her father as the taxi delivered them to the door.

'I have told you a thousand times, I sent a cable to Harriet, she'll have done something. You might have fourteen trunks waiting for you for all I know, crammed with diamond-studded knickers.' He got irritably out of the car, not in the least soothed by the vista of smooth green lawns, gentle fountains and peacocks trailing their tails like Edwardian ladies in a huff.

The front door opened and Raoul Pereira appeared, arms outstretched in welcome. 'Jake, how good to see you my friend! And this is your so beautiful daughter, I am enchanted!'

Victoria's face lost its sulkiness. She stepped towards the tall, slim, distinctly foreign man like Bambi coming shyly out of the forest. Jake was torn between pride and amusement as all Harriet's training emerged in the polite handshake, the formal, structured phrases she recited so carefully. Raoul lifted her hand to his lips and she smiled in delight.

'You are so lovely. I am overcome,' he said softly.

'Stop trying to ensnare my daughter Raoul,' said Jake. 'Otherwise I build you a cruiser guaranteed to have everyone ill within the hour. That should dampen your enthusiasm.'

'You have no romance, you old bastard,' said Raoul, with the determined use of a swearword common to those who would like to be thought absolutely fluent in a language.

The Pereira family was gathering in the vast hall. It ranged from twin boys of six, through girls of twelve and fourteen, another girl of seventeen and an elder son, Jaime, who was absent. Teresa, the seventeen-year-old, saw Victoria and grinned widely. Victoria's face relaxed. She would have a friend. But even as she realised that they all spoke perfect English, with the exception of the two boys who didn't care, she was conscious of anxiety about her father. Suppose he didn't behave? Suppose he was as boorish here, in this magnificent house, as he was at home?

At dinner that evening Pereira's mother, the Condesa, presided. Pereira said smoothly that his wife was travelling. Jake talked to the Condesa, she was an acknowledged expert in wine and the family owned a wine-shipping company. He had met her twice before when staying to discuss the racing yacht. After a while she leaned across and said confidentially to him, 'Why does your daughter keep watching you? Does she think you will get drunk?'

He grinned. 'Probably. I must ask you Condesa to keep a special eye on her. She's had a very sheltered upbringing, she has no experience.'

The Condesa sighed. 'Girls are allowed too much freedom nowadays.'

'How true.' Jake took this as reassurance. He wasn't to know that the Pereira household was hoping against hope that Victoria would provide a stabilising influence for Teresa, who had been impossibly rebellious ever since Pereira's second wife had left. Raoul had been having an affair with the wife of a friend, a civilised arrangement disrupted when Teresa found them entwined in the summer pavilion. The subsequent upheaval had rocked the household to its foundations.

Jake found time for a chat with Victoria before he left. 'I've arranged for you to draw money from a bank in Lisbon,' he instructed. 'If you need more you have to tell me, you're not to get into debt. I expect you to manage, is that clear?'

'I don't see why I should have to learn to be frugal, unless it's some character-building exercise,' she said witheringly.

'You can spend it when you earn it, and not until,' said Jake, conscious of an overwhelming desire to be back on the boat with only the taciturn and thoroughly unemotional Mac for company. 'And you will remember what I told you? About judgment and restraint and – '

'French letters and pills,' finished Victoria in a bored voice. 'You're obsessed with sex, Dad, you really are.'

'Above all,' said Jake patiently, 'you are not to be a trouble to the family. But I know you won't,' he added insincerely. 'Have fun sweetheart.'

'I thought you'd banned it,' said Victoria, dropping her pretty chin into her hands.

Jake bent and kissed her on the nose. 'I used to do that to you when you were little. Look, I'm arranging to meet Harriet when I've delivered the boat, we'll have a talk about what's to happen to you. Until then be good!'

Victoria waved until his car was out of sight. Then she stood in the golden sunshine looking out to the land beyond the gardens, where the soil was baked yellow and the vines and olives lived in the dust. Even the air smelled different, of garlic and oil and fresh herbs growing. It was glorious.

Raoul Pereira came round the side of the house. He was wearing tight jeans and a shirt unbuttoned to the waist. 'Let me show you our horses,' he said, extending a hand to her.

Teresa came out of the house and stood beside Victoria. 'I will show her the horses,' she said coldly. Her father shrugged, smiled and walked past them into the house.

The girls walked round to the stables, past gardeners hoeing weeds and pruning climbers. 'He is a pig,' said Teresa, unconsciously echoing Victoria's description of her own father. 'He thinks of nothing but doing it to women. I saw him, you know, with our neighbour's wife, Cristine. He was right inside her, and she was squealing, and his hair was all on end. He looked disgusting, so thin and old.'

'Did you surprise them?' asked Victoria, wide-eyed.

'Oh, yes. But I knew it had been happening. He's been doing it all his life, with the maids and people. I saw him go to the pavilion and I followed, and there he was. Cristine has had to run away, her husband beat her so. He'll try and do it to you, I can tell.'

They reached the stable courtyard, immaculately swept and lined with tubs of flowers. On one side were lines of boxes, and over each door was the veined and lovely head of a thoroughbred.

'This is Douro – this is Porto – this is Ziana, my mare. She is very sensitive, only I can ride her.'

'I'm sure I could,' said Victoria. 'I've ridden a lot at home.'

Teresa's face was unreadable. 'Very well,' she said. 'Early tomorrow. We must ride early or it is too hot. After that – we shall go to Lisbon, shopping.'

'Can we do just what we like?' asked Victoria curiously. 'I thought your grandmother was in charge, that's what my father said.'

'She stays in bed till lunchtime, and then she sees her friends. She doesn't care what we do.'

In the morning Victoria put on the riding clothes her mother had sent, and emerged looking very English and proper in hard hat, jodphurs and black jacket. Teresa rode in jeans, swinging on to the gelding, Porto, with the ease of one who has ridden since they could walk. Victoria, who was much less experienced, was given a leg-up on to Ziana. Without a pause Teresa led the way out into the fields, and as soon as Ziana set foot on earth she was away. Victoria lost whip, stirrups and nerve. She screamed to be saved, then since there was no-one to save her, collected her wits and tried to stop the mare. To her surprise it was easy, because Ziana was immaculately schooled. Victoria got off and waited for Teresa to come up on Porto. 'You're right, I can't ride her,' she said ruefully. 'Let's change.'

That one incident made up to Teresa for the fact that Victoria was taller, prettier and somehow more lustrous than herself. Small but with great physical courage, Teresa could afford to let Victoria shine.

Freedom – it was something Victoria had never before experienced. The younger children were cared for by a nursery staff, but Teresa was beyond their control. So provided they kept out of the way of Raoul Pereira, no-one commented on their actions at all. If they wished to go into Lisbon they had only to make sure the chauffeur had no other commitments and they could go. There was a pool for them to swim in, horses for them to ride, they could spend hours dressing up in each other's clothes if they wished. They raided the attics for silks and laces of bygone days, and once appeared at dinner in lace mantillas and hoops, Teresa's short, brown figure slightly comic but Victoria stunning in black. Raoul Pereira gasped at the white bosom she revealed, but his daughter's fulminating gaze deterred him. Not so Jaime. Lately returned from visiting friends, he first saw Victoria that night, and never really recovered.

The girls lay in bed and giggled about Jaime's infatuation. 'Will you let him do it to you?' said Teresa. 'Will you let him climb on top of you and put his hands on you and – '

'Don't! I don't know. I might.'

'Would you?' Teresa sat up and switched on the light. 'Would you really?'

'I don't know.' Victoria tried to imagine it. He was so tall, and the hair that was mouse-brown on Teresa was golden-tinted in her brother. It was exciting to have men look at you as the Pereiras looked, to have them touch your hand as if even to do that thrilled them. Raoul was disgusting, as his daughter said. He liked to come and talk to her when she was sunbathing in her bikini, and once he had taken her suntan oil and smoothed it on to her legs, going higher and higher until she snatched the oil from him and pulled her knees up to her chin. 'Thank you, Mr. Pereira,' she said briskly.

'You excite me, Victoria,' he whispered, and blew her a kiss.

But Jaime was shyer, sweeter, less overt. He came riding with them and sometimes trailed round the shops in Lisbon, carrying their parcels with a mocking air that could not entirely hide his adoration. Victoria's thoughts went back to Paul in the car. It had all been so quick, so unpleasant. But women did enjoy it, and Teresa said Cristine had been ecstatic when Raoul was doing it to her. 'Like a trance, like a religious seeing a vision,' she said.

The girls couldn't see how that state was achieved. Victoria had told Teresa all about Paul and how much it had hurt, but it only served to make Teresa envious. She was determined to lose her virginity, to spite her father, to achieve adulthood and to catch up with Victoria. Sometimes the girls would sit at a café table and speculate on this or that man passing, and if he would do. At least, thought Victoria, I do know what it's like. But if that was all, what was all the fuss about?

The girls were becoming bored with the activities available to them. 'We ought to have a job,' said Teresa. 'We could work in a shop and try on all the clothes!' For her it was only day-dreaming, because the Pereira girls did not of course work in shops. But Victoria thought it a marvellous idea.

'We'll go and get jobs,' she declared. 'You will have to do most of the talking because my Portugeuse isn't very good yet. We'll have to get jobs together.'

So, off they went to Lisbon, leaving their chauffeur-driven car and wandering through the glossy streets. It is a smart city, with more chic than Madrid, slightly less than Paris, with a certain provincial air because it is not large. Teresa kept stopping to buy hot doughnuts or an ice-cream from street stalls. Victoria thought she would be fat when she was older. 'We are looking for jobs,' she told her, but to Teresa it was only a game. They tried two or three places but they looked with disbelief at the two girls in their expensive, restrained clothes that they had tried to make less restrained by the addition of scarves and belts and chains.

'Let us go and drink something,' said Teresa, already bored with the plan.

Born with greater determination, Victoria said, 'We'll try here' and dragged her friend into a hat shop.

It was a very expensive shop, designed to appeal to the mothers of brides rather than the brides themselves. The proprietor stepped silently out from his lair and prowled towards them, a hint of hostility in his manner since he could tell these were not customers. Teresa wasn't paying attention so Victoria, in halting Portuguese, explained what they required.

'You are American?' The man spoke in heavily accented English.

'English. I was brought up in America. My friend is Portuguese – '

'I am acquainted with Miss Pereira.' He inclined his head towards Teresa, who stopped giggling. If the man knew her family she should behave. 'Come.' He gestured Victoria towards a chair. She sat down, because he was insistent, saying, 'It was a job we wanted – perhaps I didn't explain – we don't want a hat.'

'You will try some.' He began selecting hats and putting them on Victoria's head, scooping her luxuriant hair up or back, making it into a bun, hiding it completely within the hat. Victoria gave up protesting, she even gave up making polite noises about the hats since he took no notice. Teresa stood by, trying to hide her smiles. At last the man stopped.

'My name is Joseph Montado. You will model for my ladies from four to half-past six on Mondays, Wednesdays and Fridays. I ask that you wear a plain dress in white or navy blue, and high heels. Your hair must be clean but unbound, I will arrange it to suit the hats we are to show.'

'But – what about Teresa?'

Senor Montado looked down his long nose, that had seen and despised more young girls than either of them could count. 'An interesting young woman, but too short to model. I am sure that she will make her mark elsewhere.'

The girls reeled out into the street. Teresa was affronted, and hid it beneath mockery. 'Modelling! For that old man, I swear he has a boyfriend. But of course you won't go.'

'Oh, yes I will,' said Victoria. 'The hats were lovely, especially the ones with veils. I've never worn hats before.'

'They are for fat old ladies.'

They went and sat at a café table, and drank coffee and brandy although neither of them had a head for spirits. Teresa gazed morosely out at the crowds. When two young men walked past once, and then twice, Victoria ignored them but Teresa smiled encouragingly. When they asked if they could sit down, Teresa answered yes while Victoria hissed at her in English: 'They're horrible! No!'

The young men sat down, one of them very dark, his forearms covered in thick black hair. He smelled faintly of sweat and his body was short and powerful. He lit a cigarette, which Victoria disliked, and stared assessingly at the girls. Victoria turned away. The other was quite sweet, very shy of her, and they made slow conversation. He corrected her grammar very carefully, and all the while Teresa and the dark, powerful man talked in rapid sentences.

Teresa stood up. 'We are going. Do you want to come?'

Victoria was taken by surprise. 'Where to? Where are you going?'

'An apartment. Come on, we're going now, it isn't far.'

Victoria looked wildly from Teresa to the man, he was holding her arm tightly, his thigh against hers. His arousal was almost tangible. 'You mustn't,' she said desperately. 'You don't know him. My father says you must never go with people you don't know.'

'Oh, baby Victoria,' mocked Teresa. 'I am going and you can come if you want to.'

Everything in her wanted to say no. But she could not leave Teresa alone with this man so she followed behind, her escort still with her, still making careful sentences about the weather. The apartment wasn't near, it was away from the centre in the midst of low-rise blocks where washing hung from pink or blue balconies, where old cars roared in narrow streets and women in black watched them pass, their faces creased and expressionless.

Victoria caught Teresa's arm. 'Let's go home.'

'No. You go if you want.'

But Victoria was lost and could not go. At last they went into a building, up narrow concrete stairs where the smell of garlic and oil and urine caught in the throat. They went in at a door and there was the sound of flies buzzing, and somewhere near a woman shouting angrily. It was a poor flat, the furniture cheap and battered, a picture of the Virgin Mary cut from a magazine and stuck on the wall, with a candle pinned at either side. The dark man started to kiss Teresa. His hands reached in to her bra for her fat breasts, large for such a small girl, and when he had them exposed he called to his friend to look at how good they were. Teresa laughed nervously and in a fit of bravado she held her blouse open and shook herself. Victoria rushed out on to the balcony, her escort at her heels, patting her shoulder consolingly.

In the room behind Teresa lay sprawled on the floor. She cried out suddenly, exultantly. After a moment Victoria turned. The man got to his feet, still huge, dripping, and forced himself back into his trousers. Then he went to the table and poured himself a glass of wine, drinking it in one gulp. Victoria ran out of the flat, down the stairs and into the street. She vomited into the gutter.

Later, Teresa came down. 'Are you all right?' she asked.

Victoria nodded. 'That man was horrible. You'll catch something.'

'I shall see him again on Wednesday' said Teresa contentedly. 'Such a man! Such power, such size! When you go to your modelling I shall go to my lover. Imagine, I have a lover! Wonderful!' She did a little dance and she smelled of the man, of his sweat. Victoria shuddered.

Chapter Six

Victoria observed herself critically in the huge looking glass. Her thick, black hair was parted in the centre and pulled back behind her ears into a bun, unobtrusively augmented with a hair piece. The look was severe and ageing, only suited to extreme youth. Against it the pallor of her skin, the sharpness of jaw and eyebrow, were thrown into relief. When she settled the wide, black velvet hat on her head and drew the folds of veil into a collar on her neck, the effect was stunning.

Senor Montado came into the room. 'That is good,' he said dispassionately. 'Remember for the white straw your hair must be unfastened.'

'I can't do it so quickly,' complained Victoria. 'It isn't possible.'

'It must be possible. I shall give you more money.'

'No amount of money will take hairpins out quickly,' she snapped. 'You mustn't rush me, I won't be rushed. It spoils everything to have it rushed at the end. If you rush me, I won't do it any more.'

Senor Montado for once gave her his attention. Since Victoria's fashion shows began, his sales had doubled, though whether they would remain at this inflated level remained to be seen. However wonderful the hats looked on Victoria's lovely head, they would scarcely achieve so much for their purchasers. But he was selling dreams, and even in the light of day dreams can retain their charm. His clientele was entranced by his 'Victoria' hats.

He changed the subject, which Victoria recognised as capitulation. 'Why do you work for me?' he asked. 'Is it not for money?'

'I don't need it. My parents are wealthy. But I like doing this, it's fun.'

'More fun than the games of Miss Pereira?'

Victoria shot him a startled glance. He was watching her, like an aged but not necessarily hostile lizard. She licked her lips, unsure of what she should tell him. Finally she said quietly, 'I'm sure she doesn't realise what she's doing. I mean, he could blackmail her or anything.'

Senor Montado inclined his head. 'I think you must say this to your friend. But we delay and my ladies are waiting. On, Victoria!'

In the evening Victoria and Teresa went walking in the gardens. Cicadas clattered in the dry grass and the breeze rustled the lavender bushes. Victoria closed her fingers on a bloom and took the warm scent on to her skin. She watched Teresa. 'Senor Montado knows,' she said. 'I suppose others do, too.'

Teresa swung round, furious. 'You have told them! You are no friend to me, I knew it!'

'You know I didn't tell.'

They were silent. Teresa said 'What shall I do if my father finds out?' She didn't expect an answer. Chastity, or at least discretion, was demanded of a Pereira girl. Even in this day and age it was assumed that Teresa would marry well, in her own class, and from that union bring forth children who would go on and do the same. After the children then she could dally a little, work, drink too much, eat too much, let herself go. If this was known of Teresa now, that future would be closed to her.

'Tell him you won't go and see him again,' said Victoria.

Teresa shook her head. 'I can't. He can be very angry, you don't know.'

Victoria could well imagine. The black-chested machismo of the man had frightened her from the first, he would trample on women and think it their due. 'He won't dare come here,' she said. 'He may not know who you are.'

Teresa's face twisted. 'He knows.'

On Wednesday Victoria went as usual to the hat shop but Teresa stayed at home. It was a hot afternoon. There was a letter from Harriet in Victoria's bag and she intended to read it in the car on the way home, savouring the phrases. As time went on she was missing her mother more and more, the prosaic, level-headed judgment and absolute control of Harriet. She never had doubts and uncertainties, she decided what should be done and did it unwaveringly. How Victoria envied her.

The show was good, with the usual smattering of men sitting on the gilt chairs watching her. They were husbands or sons or brothers of clients, and sometimes they sent their cards in to her, with messages scribbled in Portuguese that she could not read. Rather than ask anyone to tell her what they said she ignored them, and gained a reputation for hauteur.

She changed and brushed her hair, preparing to leave by the side door. A figure in the passage outside alarmed her, she could see a shape through the frosted glass. It was him! She went close to the window, peering through the edge where the glass was clearest. He was standing on the corner watching both entrances at once, she could not mistake that wide, powerful figure. Black hairs covered even the backs of his hands, curling over cheap rings. Victoria stepped away from the door and went cautiously out into the main shop, still thronged with customers. He saw her through the window and turned, watching her. Her bag slipped from her fingers and she followed it down, scrabbling for her comb, money, the letter from her mother, chasing an errant tampon that danced merrily across the floor. Someone bent down and retrieved it for her, handing it back with a murmur. It was a clean, male hand and Victoria, scarlet with embarrassment, did not look at the face.

'That man,' said her rescuer, 'He is bothering you?'

She looked up then. A thin, large-nosed face, about thirty, probably French. He wore a silk tie and immaculate cream suit. 'He knows my friend, she won't see him, she's scared. I don't – ' She looked up helplessly.

'I will escort you.'

He took her arm and led her out of the shop. Footsteps followed them. Victoria would have run but for the restraining hand. 'He is no-one. A mechanic, perhaps?'

'I don't know. Oh look, there's the car. I must go – thank you.' She pulled herself free and dashed to the waiting vehicle. Only when she was safe in the car did she look back. Two men, both watching her. She drew the blind.

Raoul Pereira was at home that evening. The family dined, as usual, in the vast gilded room, under chandeliers cleaned once a year when everyone was away. A light breeze from the open window caused the pendants to tinkle against one another like heavenly bells.

'And how is your mother, Victoria?' enquired Raoul. They all knew she had received a letter.

'Very well, I think. She's going on a trip round some islands. She wants a site for a new hotel.'

Raoul raised his eyebrows. 'An amazing woman, I shall be interested to know her.'

'How fortunate that she is so far away,' interjected Teresa caustically. Her father's mouth twisted a little.

There was the sound of a motorbike engine, coming quickly closer. The Condesa said, 'Raoul, you must ask the men not to come to the house on such things. It is intolerable.' But before she had finished the motor had died. There was the jangle of the front doorbell.

'A late caller' said Pereira, rising to his feet.

Teresa and Victoria exchanged alarmed glances. 'We'll go upstairs,' said Teresa, folding her napkin, but her father said, 'You will sit down, Teresa. Our meal is not yet complete.'

From the hall came raised voices, male voices, shouting in Portuguese. Pereira went out, shutting the door behind him. The girls sat immobile, their faces set in expressions of studied calm. The Condesa was demanding querulously that someone should replenish the ice in the bucket, because it was melting and would ruin a good white wine. Nobody moved.

Suddenly the door burst open. He was there, drunk, furious, in no way diminished by his surroundings. He saw Teresa, screamed and pointed. To her eternal credit, Teresa's expression never changed.

'Do you know this man?' she asked her father. 'Is he a friend of yours?'

The man lunged across the table, shattering priceless glasses, spilling fruit juice and soup over the linen cloth. He caught Teresa's wrist and she screamed, unable to break free, dragged half across the table by her captor. He put his fingers in her hair, turned her face up and spat.

Pereira hit him, other men rushed in to restrain him. Later the police came and took him away, and the doctor was summoned to see to the Condesa, weak with shock. At around one in the morning both girls were called to Pereira's study.

'I wish to know what has been going on,' he said quietly.

Neither girl spoke. Eventually Pereira said, 'He knows too much about you, Teresa. He has said things I would not have thought ever to hear a man say about my daughter. Mondays, Wednesdays, Fridays.'

'She was at the shop – with me,' said Victoria.

Pereira turned on her. 'I do not need your lies! I know who led her to this with her easy American morals, I know who to blame! He is a taxi-driver! A daughter of Pereira, sleeping with a man who drives taxis!'

'And Pereira himself sleeping with another man's wife,' said Teresa. 'What did you expect?'

And suddenly they were screaming at each other in Portuguese, Pereira was slapping Teresa's defiant little face, hitting her as if he would kill her. His hand rose and fell, rose and fell.

Victoria lifted up the table-lamp and struck him above the ear. The skin of his head split like a ripe tomato and blood leaped onto the floor. Nobody moved. All that could be heard was harsh breathing.

The next day the house was very quiet. The children kept to their nursery, Pereira and Teresa to their rooms. Victoria crept down the staircase like a thief, jumping when Jaime stepped into the hall in front of her.

'Are you going to shout at me, too?' she asked hysterically. Her face was dead-white with blotches round her eyes.

Jaime said, 'It wasn't your fault. My father blames you because he cannot blame himself. Come, drink something.' He took her into the breakfast room, where rows of untouched dishes lined the sideboard. He poured hot, reviving coffee and Victoria sipped.

'I must go,' she said eventually. 'But I can't get in touch with my parents, they're travelling. I don't know what to do.'

Jaime took her hand. 'You must marry me. I have decided.'

She stared at him in amazement. Jaime was someone she hardly knew, pleasant certainly, but less to her than Porto the horse. 'I'm not old enough to marry,' she said uncertainly. 'My father wouldn't let me, I'm sure of it.'

Jaime turned her hand upwards and kissed her wrist, a long, sensual, gesture. It tingled nerves all over her skin, startling her into awareness. 'You'll be like your father when you're his age,' she said shakily, and pulled her hand free.

'Not with you in my bed. Oh, Victoria, I dream of your body, I burn to sink myself down in your flesh!'

'You don't know me.' She turned her head away and her young, tender neck and lovely profile, so close and so available, acted on him like alcohol. He began stroking her neck, whispering to her.

'I know what I need to know. I love you so much, you're so beautiful! When we are married we shall live all alone in one of my father's cottages. I shall make love to you again and again, night and day – '

The vague attraction she had felt for the boy withered in the heat of his passion. Couldn't he see that she didn't want this? She needed a friend, not a lover, not a husband. 'My head aches,' she said petulantly, and pushed at him. At that moment Jaime seemed indisputably foreign, quite blind to her thoughts and feelings.

'Come to my room.' He was trying to caress her breasts and she fended him off with rising hysteria. Why wouldn't he be her friend?

'Let me go!' She pulled away and ran out of the room.

It wasn't her day for the shop but the thought of its cool, ordered peace tempted like water in a desert. Without even stopping to get her bag she ran to the garage and demanded that the snoozing chauffeur take her there. As they drove away she could hear Jaime's voice calling insistently: 'Victoria! Victoria!'

Senor Montado raised his eyebrows a full millimetre when he saw her. She would have liked to fall into his arms and sob, but knew how little he would appreciate such histrionics. So she sat herself down on one of the gilt chairs and suspiciously bright-eyed said, 'I think I need some advice.'

He pulled an ostrich feather into greater perfection on a flat pink hat, that looked good on Victoria but no-one else. There were problems in employing a model with a superb hat face, it raised impossible expectations. 'They are saying Pereira has been killed,' he commented. 'But one has become used to such sensationalism.'

'He's got a cut head, that's all. But he's broken Teresa's nose and knocked out two of her teeth. I don't know what's going to happen!'

Now she did begin to cry and Senor Montado hissed through his teeth. 'Please, Victoria! I cannot have this in my shop.'

She pulled herself together and sat upright, breathing through her nose. A gloriously tragic figure, she delighted Montado's theatrical tastes while revolting his commercial ones. 'Why do you not go home?' he asked bluntly.

'My parents are travelling, I can't get in touch. And my father didn't give me enough money for the flight home. They'll be so ashamed of me!'

'One feels they would be more ashamed to be the parents of Teresa Pereira,' commented Montado. 'But they of course are reaping their own harvest. Victoria, you must go to Paris.'

'Why?'

He shrugged expressively. 'Why not? Because the gentleman who escorted you yesterday has offered you a position in his salon. Hats, and possibly later, couture. He spoke to me and left his card.' Montado proffered an unusually large square of pasteboard, engraved in silver. She read: 'Jacques Parnasse, Couturier. Rue de Samisson, Paris.' On the reverse was scrawled: 'Permittez cette jeune fille entrer de salon de m'approcher.'

Victoria's thoughts whirled madly, and then fastened on the one thing of importance. 'I can't afford the flight.'

'And so? Take the train.'

Senor Montado watched without curiosity as she walked away. He neither knew nor cared whether she took the course he suggested. The depths of his disillusion were not to be plumbed by youth and innocence, nor even by his sense that in Victoria he saw promise that for once might be fulfilled.

She decided that it would be best to approach Raoul and ask for the money for the flight home. He wanted rid of her and she wanted to go, so he would certainly lend it to her. But she quailed at the thought of approaching him, knowing full well what he would say to her, and she had not taken Jaime into consideration.

Every bit as much as she, Jaime Pereira was used to his own way and he had decided to have Victoria. Her possession would fulfil every one of his needs: that of emulating, but also beating his father, of possessing a beautiful foreign woman, and the indulgence of passions that could not be expressed in casual sex. He wanted to be violently in love, and Victoria was foreign, she was lovely, and she was in need. He was in love with needing her, and could not believe that feelings of such intensity could burn alone. He told his father he meant to marry her, which only increased Raoul's view that Victoria was a serpent in the midst of his family.

When she returned from the shop Pereira was downstairs. his head bandaged, his olive skin pale with rage.

'I want you out of my home,' he snapped as soon as he saw her.

She hesitated, trying to find the words to ask for money. Suddenly Jaime came quickly in from the garden, smelling of horses and saddle-soap. He went to Victoria and put his arm round her shoulders, effectively shielding her from his father. 'Victoria must stay. I insist.'

'Please – ' She couldn't get free. Besides, no-one was interested in what she had to say. Pereira began striding round the room, and instinctively she cowered against Jaime.

'You are not master of this house,' snapped Pereira. 'You are foolishly infatuated with this evil girl, who has corrupted Teresa and ensnared you. I want rid of her!' He slammed his hand down on a delicate little table, and a porcelain flower vase fell and broke. 'She is breaking my home!' yelled Pereira, almost in tears. Water from the vase ran on to the carpet.

'I really do want to go – ' began Victoria, but Jaime hushed her.

'We are to marry,' he insisted. 'I love her. A man like you can't know what it means! She is innocent, and I shall worship her forever!' He pulled her to him, pressing hot kisses on to her hair.

Victoria thought, The world has gone mad, they're foreigners, I don't understand them. All she wanted was to go home. The argument went on without her, and at last Jaime pulled her from the room. 'My sweet, my love, my angel,' he whispered, pressing himself against her. 'Don't be frightened. I won't let him hurt you.'

'I can't – I don't want –' She couldn't say it to him. It was bad enough for Raoul to hate her, for Teresa to lie in a darkened room and sob, let alone for Jaime to turn against her. There wasn't anyone to be her friend. So she let him kiss her, let him fondle her breasts, as if it were a dream and not really happening. It wasn't unpleasant, but soon she pulled away and said she was going to have a bath.

Lying in the suds, listening to the menacing quiet that filled the house, she knew she had to run away. The longer she stayed the worse things would become, and since there was only the train to Paris, that she must take. She remembered, with nausea, the things Jake had said would happen if she travelled alone in Europe. Robbery was the least of them. Murder, kidnap, rape, all might occur on the journey, and when she got there, if she got there, suppose Jacques Parnasse had forgotten her or regretted his offer, or thought she should sleep with him instead? The optimism that was the product of a gentle and sheltered upbringing was becoming dented in the face of reality. Depressed and rather tearful, she packed a single holdall, dressed in jeans and a shirt, and crept out of the house. It was getting dark. This time she didn't use the chauffeur, but caught the bus on the dusty road outside.

As a child Victoria had loved travel, the painless transition from one place to another with all the attendant novelties of food and toys and companions. Only now did she realise what travel was really like. That it was tiring, and dirty, and worrying, and very uncomfortable. On the first night she had waited four hours for a train, sitting hunched against a pillar expecting at any moment that Jaime Pereira would come looking for her.

When she had decided she must be safe, she saw him, striding amongst the preoccupied crowds like a golden god, the stationmaster at his heels explaining that he couldn't say whether or not one girl had come or gone, it was a station, he was busy, perhaps Senor Pereira would like a glass of something?

Victoria slid away behind the pillar, looking desperately for a means of escape. A local train was preparing to leave, going she did not know where. Quickly she picked up her bag and changed platforms, hunching her shoulders to reduce her conspicuous height. She joined a carriage full of people. They moved their baskets to make room for her, folded up the parcels of food they were eating. Someone offered her a chunk of the unpleasant grey Portuguese bread and she took it, chewing until it was a glutinous lump in her mouth then forcing it down. The train pulled out.

For three days she went from train to train, everybody suggesting that she should go back to Lisbon and take a train from there, but she never would. Instead she was shunted from branch line to branch line, moving slowly upcountry, sickened by train washrooms and stale food, her limbs aching from always sleeping upright. Once, by chance, she travelled first class, and though the air conditioning froze her the toilet was clean. Never again, she thought desperately, would she despise comfort.

But the connecting train was late and full of soldiers, the carriage was hot and the only seat next to a man smelling of garlic. She would have liked to stand by the window in the corridor but her bag was on the luggage rack and she was frightened it would be stolen. In the end she stood in the corridor, but the soldiers stroked her bottom as they passed and made suggestions. She was on the train all night. The soldiers played transistor radios and stamped to the music, and when they passed through tunnels threw bottles at the walls. They exploded like bombs. At about two in the morning the train crossed the border into Spain. Everyone was made to get off and line up at the passport office, and the soldiers roared bullfight songs, babies howled and the wind blew hot and oily.

Eventually she reached Madrid. Half-conscious through lack of food and sleep, she found she had to travel from one station to another. Out in the real world, away from the tracks and carriages, the sun shone bright enough to hurt. She slumped at a café table and was given Coca-Cola and fish with rice. Her money was dwindling, she wasn't anywhere near Paris, and was still too near the Pereiras. The first-class train had cost five times as much as any other, and they charged more for food if you bought it from a vendor at a station. It was best, people had said, to shop before you got on the train. So she trailed round shops and put oranges, bread, biscuits and mineral water into a plastic bag. She caught sight of herself in a mirror next to a till: a dirty, white-faced gipsy. And suddenly, without warning, she was enjoying herself!

Everyone thought she was so helpless, so much in need of protection, and here she was, in Madrid, without her parents, without friends, without even a package tour nanny. Victoria Jakes, independent person, independent traveller.

There was a fountain splashing in the square behind her, and a café was playing flamenco music very loud. She tucked her money safely into the front of her jeans, picked up her bags and began to walk to the station.

Chapter Seven

Harriet was bored. She lay on the terrace and resisted the temptation to go inside for another rum punch, because lately she had been in one of her drinking phases. They came upon her now and then, interspersed with periods of restraint. Over the years she had learned that she drank when she was upset, or unhappy, or as in this case bored, and did not when life was kind to her.

She got up and put on her wrap, because sun gave you wrinkles and today she felt as if she had enough already. Why wasn't anything exciting going to happen? The hotel site had been selected, boringly suitable, on an island delighted to have such an exclusive development. Once she would have revelled in the challenge of a new hotel, but she had done it all before.

Even the court case failed to interest her just at present, and for once it was going well. The lawyers told her that Gareth had failed to file in time against her application for a share in the collection on behalf of Nathan. Taking up the cudgels for Nathan had been a masterstroke, she felt. As an orphan and a Hawksworth, if anyone was to have the pictures and if it couldn't be Harriet herself, then quite a case could be made for Nathan. Besides, it revealed genuine-seeming altruism in her and made Gareth look grasping if he rejected the claim. So now, barring unforeseen events, Nathan might actually get his hands on what vestige of the collection remained, which was certainly something to celebrate.

To her surprise she didn't really care any more. Much more interesting, but closed to her, was the life Victoria was leading in Lisbon. She decided to put through a call to the office. There might be a letter waiting.

'Oh, Mrs. Hawksworth!' It was Maud's voice, shrill with relief. 'We've been trying to reach you! We rang last night but one of your servants said you'd gone out fishing.'

'Yes, I had, I went on one of the light boats. Nobody said you'd telephoned – I must speak to them. Is something wrong, Maud?'

'It seems there's been some trouble with Victoria – a Mr. Pereira telephoned us, saying some strange things, and then a Mr. Jaime Pereira who seems to be some sort of relation – Mrs. Hawksworth, Victoria has run away!'

'Oh – my – God.' Harriet wished, how she wished, she had drunk that rum punch. The world swam around her. 'What happened? Do they have any idea where she is?'

'Well, this Jaime Pereira seems to think she's coming home but we've heard nothing and I've checked with the airlines and there's no record of her. It seems he thinks Victoria is going to marry him. Whereas Mr. Pereira, who I assume is his father, blames Victoria for his daughter's affair with a taxi-driver, and says she's seduced his son!'

Harriet giggled. So did Maud, though neither woman thought it funny. 'Where in God's name is Jake?' said Harriet shrilly. 'Why is he never anywhere I can get him when I need him?'

'But he's in Nassau, Mrs. Hawksworth. He left a message yesterday to say he'd be there a few days if anyone wanted to contact him. He's hoping to meet up with you, I believe.'

'Why didn't anyone tell me? Good God, can't even my own office realise when things are urgent?'

Her hands shook in her lap for minutes after she finished the call. Nassau, she had to get to Nassau. Her mind couldn't cope with the practicalities of getting there. Where was Victoria? Wandering in Europe with no-one to take care of her, she might be dead! How dare these Pereira people accuse her child! If they had caused harm to come to her, Harriet would tear them apart with her bare hands!

Anger provided fuel for her actions. She summoned David, her servant. He looked after the house on Corusca in a relaxed manner that in normal times she found soothing. Now she castigated him for being useless and inefficient, and though she saw that he was hurt she took nothing back. She demanded a boat, instantly. She would fly from one of the islands that possessed the airstrip she had never before wished to install on Corusca. All would be provided, because no-one gainsaid Mrs. Hawksworth when she used that tone of voice. A maid was sent to pack, but she took too long. Harriet pushed her out of the way and thrust bundles of clothes indiscriminately into cases.

As the boat took her from the island she looked back and wondered why it still seemed strange to her. Nowadays it was almost her own creation, the twentieth century introduced as gently as if to a tribe of Amazon Indians who had never seen a wheel. In the end there had been no hotel and would be none, because Corusca was Harriet's own retreat and sometimes she hated hotels. But there was a small hospital, and telephones, and the people in the hills could market their crops elsewhere. A gentle, low key prosperity was seeping into the darkest corners of the clapboard houses. The children received vitamins and free milk, their elders cheap health care and limited access to the world beyond.

But they remained timid and unadventurous. When an occasional sailor ventured there the doors closed against him and no-one spoke. Fear could not be banished in half a generation, there was still too much that was secret and special about the place. They were creatures used to the night, blinking in the day. Harriet looked back at Corusca's dark hills and thick forests, where the mist hung like cloth and unseen birds called. After all this time, she understood nothing of the island's mystery.

Jake stretched out his legs and gazed across the bay, marvelling that such perfection could exist on the same planet as rainy old England. To sit in the evening and sip a drink, watching the people walking by in the sunshine, it was a taste of heaven. Except that the boat was delivered, and round every corner was someone who couldn't afford one who wanted one just like it, when he didn't make production boats for God's sake, and Mac had flown straight back because he had work to do at the yard and, as usual, he couldn't get hold of Harriet.

He suddenly felt depressed. The feeling had been hanging around all day and he had fought it, but now it caught up with him, the old black dog. He'd visited Natalie that afternoon, in her badly-run shop that only kept going because he bought half the stuff and gave it to people. She was yellow and thin and burnt out.

'Terrible, isn't it?' she said to him. 'When you still want to make love but no-one wants to love you? Why are we so fucking lonely, Jake?'

It had offended him that she should think they were the same. The penalty of independence was, undoubtedly, loneliness, but wasn't it also its prize? He sipped his drink and brooded, on loneliness, happiness, none of it ever quite satisfying. Whatever he did, whatever his success, it was never right. Everything was set on a bed of shifting sand. The foundations of friendships, business, habit, were all shallow and weak. These last years he had managed to organise his instability in a way, had built it into the fabric of his life. In the end though, what was there to hope for? Everything had been tried and none of it suited.

A woman was running up the road, struggling against the hill. Her breasts swung against her silk top, her feet in their silly high heels teetered and slipped on the stones. Arousal surged through him. God, but that was something he would like to get on top of, a voluptuous woman all sticky with sweat – God! It was Harriet!

He leaped up and yelled to her. 'Harriet! Where the hell have you been?' She stopped, gasping, looking round to see where he was. He wanted to laugh. All these years, all these changes, and she was still Harriet, looking round nervously to find someone to talk to. Other people saw only the gloss, he saw Harriet.

He went down to her and took her in his arms, pressing those soft breasts against him, licking the sweat from her cheek. 'Oh, but I fancy you, lady.'

For a minute Harriet leaned into him, her breathing harsh. 'Victoria – she's run away!'

'What?' He jerked back and stared at her. Harriet started to cry.

'You've got to do something! They want her to marry a taxi-driver because their daughter's slept with him, and you said you hadn't given her any money so she's probably gone to work in a brothel and they've killed her and thrown her in a ditch!'

Jake opened and closed his mouth several times. Then he said, 'Oh God, I'm sorry, Harriet. I know it's my fault.'

She hung on to his arm, uttering dry sobs. 'It's my fault, really. I sheltered her too much. These days you've got to let them do dreadful things. She hated that school, but I wouldn't listen –'

Jake briefly squeezed her. 'You weren't to know. Whatever it was we should have done, we didn't. I need a drink.'

'So do I.'

They went back to Jake's table and ordered two drinks each. Harriet was feeling thoroughly pathetic and held on to Jake's hand, sniffing.

'What did you say had happened?' he asked at last.

'I don't know! I think it's the daughter that's involved with the taxi-driver, but it might be the son. You don't suppose she's pregnant, do you?'

'What, Victoria? She'd better not be. I talked for an hour and a half on contraception, with pictures. It was a scarring experience.'

'You didn't!'

'I did. And she asked if I knew so much how come she'd arrived out of wedlock.'

Harriet put her hand over her mouth. 'What did you say?'

'Like all reasonable men I told her not to be so bloody impertinent and I'd tell her when she was older. I'm sorry, Harriet, but I was a failure as a father. A complete failure.'

She sighed. 'Well, according to Victoria, I'm a washout as a mother. But I did try, Jake! I tried so hard.'

'She's turned out OK. She's more capable than you think.'

'Is she? I remember when she couldn't tie her laces. I have to remind myself how old she is sometimes.'

They finished one drink and started on the next. Harriet said, 'Do you remember the row we had?'

He grimaced. 'Which one?'

'The night of the fire.'

Jake grunted. Since that night, that row, he and Harriet hadn't been the same. The intimacy they were sharing this evening was laid over years of distance. But he didn't want to talk about it because tonight he felt vulnerable. He said quickly, 'It wasn't true. Or at least, if it was, it wasn't true for always. You know I was jealous, don't you? I wanted you to need me more than you did. I wanted you to want me to fuck you. But you didn't need me for that. Or for anything else much.'

She looked surprised. 'I don't need you for things. I just need you for you.'

He wanted to cry. Distractedly he looked about him, saying, 'I must ring that bastard Pereira. We shouldn't be sitting here getting drunk.'

'Are you staying here? We can 'phone from your room.'

So they got up and went to the room, and Jake hunted round for the number while Harriet lay on the bed.

He placed the call and replaced the receiver while they waited to be connected. Harriet began to do exercises, lying on her back and kicking her legs in the air. A sense of unreality pervaded everything, even the room seemed bathed in pink light. The world had stopped, and would take its time to start again. They were in still space, their senses heightened by anxiety, each needing some reassurance.

'I'm supposed to do these to stop everything sagging,' she confided. 'Am I sagging, Jake?'

He sat on the dressing table watching her. 'I don't know. Let's see your breasts.'

'Oh, those have sagged. One doctor said I should have them made smaller.'

She sat up and took off her top. The smell of sweat and drink and perfume drifted across, he couldn't believe how exciting it was. 'Take your bra off,' he said. 'I can't tell otherwise.'

Her breasts swung free. She leaned over the edge of the bed and peered at them hanging. 'Great fat things. What do you think?'

He squatted down next to the bed and she stared at him. If he lay down her nipples would be in easy reach of his mouth, so he lay down and started sucking thoughtfully.

She said 'Are you sagging, Jake? Do men sag?'

He took her breast from his mouth, saying, 'See for yourself.'

So she unfastened his zip and said 'No, you're not.'

'We can't tell how long it will last though,' he remarked. 'I mean, we are getting older all the time.'

'What had we better do then?' asked Harriet very softly. She eased herself out of her trousers, kicking them off like a swimmer slowly treading water. He swung rapidly on to the bed, pushing her on to her back with ungentle hands. 'Take some exercise,' he advised.

He wondered afterwards, why did they always pretend it didn't matter? Sophisticated people playing elegant games, hiding emotion with a laugh. When the 'phone rang he had forgotten that it was expected, and when an accented voice said 'Senor Pereira for you' he said 'Who?'

Harriet scrambled across the bed, putting her ear close to the receiver. A voice said, 'Jake? Is that you Jake?'

'It is, Raoul. What have you done with my daughter?'

'What have *I* done? *I*? Your daughter has destroyed my home, quite destroyed it! My son hates me, he refuses to live in my house. Victoria has brought shame upon us, she has corrupted Teresa, a girl of seventeen!'

'I should remind you that Victoria isn't even seventeen. Where has she gone, Raoul? I want to know.'

'How can I tell? A girl like that, taking a job in a shop, she has run away with some gigolo I don't doubt. We know what sort of people you are. I would die before my son married her!'

'Don't worry, I'd kill you all before the wedding. What job did she take?'

Pereira sighed wearily. The anger he had sustained for days was draining out of him. 'It was a hat shop. She modelled the designs. The man there told Jaime that she had gone to Paris but she had no money, Teresa says. Just the little she earned and some of her allowance. So she cannot have gone and Jaime has been to the mortuary and in the hills and he has asked at the bordellos – '

'The man hasn't looked anywhere himself,' said Harriet loudly, getting up and walking round the room. 'She's in Paris, she must be. Victoria always gets where she wants to go.'

'Shut up, Harriet! Look, Raoul, what happened to Teresa? Well, what's it got to do with Victoria if she went to bed with a taxi-driver? Did Victoria hire the cab? Good God, man, you're unhinged. Oh, and you can forget about your cruiser. I don't build boats for people who mislay my daughter.'

When he disconnected, Harriet said, 'This isn't funny. You must see that.'

Jake got up and poured them both another drink. 'Thank God Victoria wasn't having the affair with the taxi-driver! I wonder if she had one with the son.'

'The son of that man? I'd rather it was the taxi-driver. What do we do Jake?'

He shrugged. 'Go to Paris. If the Consulate hasn't heard of her, we're at least near enough to call the police.'

Harriet's eyes flooded with unexpected tears. 'Suppose she's dead?' she wailed. Jake felt the muscles in his back become hard as stones.

When Victoria ran her tongue over her teeth she felt a thick, furry deposit. She hadn't cleaned them in days because the train to Paris had no drinking water in the washroom. Despite the skull and crossbones symbol over the tap a woman in the carriage took her baby's bottle several times a day and filled it from there, ladling in milk powder from a dirty spoon. Wet nappies were removed from the child and hung across the window to dry without benefit of laundering. The whole carriage smelled of urine.

A Swedish man, tall, thin and academic, offered Victoria one of his many oranges. He only had oranges so periodically he traded them for other things. To Victoria they were a present because she was running out of food and indeed money. Everyone knew where everyone else was going, because days on the train together induced great intimacy. The Swede spoke six languages and was an archaeologist.

Victoria took the baby while its mother went to mix another bottle. The child stared up at her earnestly as if it were saying, 'I don't suppose you've got any idea what we're doing here?'

'Look at its face, it thinks we're all mad,' said Victoria, showing everyone.

'What indeed is sanity?' said the Swede carefully. 'Madness is a question of degree. We should not ask who is sane, but who is least mad? Sanity must be unknowing, and from that we deduce that the man who is least mad is he who knows least. Madness is therefore knowledge.'

'Quite,' said Victoria.

The train pulled into Paris later that day. Madness is knowledge, Victoria kept thinking. And I don't know anything about this place. So I'm still sane.

The bonds formed on the long journey dissolved the moment each of them stepped onto the platform. Every one of them looked scruffy and unkempt, while the people in the station seemed unnaturally clean. Victoria found herself looking for a familiar face, perhaps her mother or Jake. How was she to find the Rue de Samisson? What was she to do if Jacques Parnasse didn't want her?

She went to a bureau de change and changed every last coin into francs. The city howled around her, cars, buses, people, unconcerned and excluding. More than anything Victoria wanted to be at home and safe, with someone to tell her when to go to bed, when to get up, what to eat and what to wear. A gendarme gazed down his nose at her when she haltingly asked him the way, and told her to get a bus. She crept away humbly.

The thought of spending the night in this great city frightened her very much. She felt a rush of anger against her parents, because they weren't there to help when she needed them. Next week was her birthday and did they care? Not a bit of it. They were about their own concerns, with never a thought for the child they had brought into the world. They don't love me, she told herself. Jake certainly doesn't. As for her mother – it was hard to forget the obsessive care that had marked Victoria's childhood. But it had been impersonal care, she reminded herself. She didn't like me to love people, not even Leah. Thinking of Leah now almost made her cry, because their time together was bathed in memory in warmth and happiness. It occurred to her, for the first time, that it must have been daunting for Leah, left alone in New York, far from friends or family, with the exclusive care of one very small, very rich child. Yet Leah had never once allowed her problems to press upon her charge. And now Victoria must be as brave.

Rue de Samisson was a small, polished street off the main thoroughfare. Victoria found the door quite easily, but stood outside its understated elegance feeling dirty and shy. All that showed was a slit of display window with one hat and a glove, next to a brass and mahogany door. Gathering courage, she pushed open the door and stepped on to thick cream carpet, so unmarked by feet that one gained the impression that the people that entered here stepped from perfect home to chauffeur driven car to shop without ever getting their shoes dirty. Victoria's once upmarket trainers were now down-market scruffy. But how would Harriet behave here? She consciously lifted her shoulders and smiled kindly at the receptionist.

'M. Parnasse, s'il vous plait.' She held out the card, noticing that her fingernails were dirty.

The woman behind the desk, so highly lacquered it was hard to tell her age, took the card and turned it several times. She stared at

Victoria, and all the assumed confidence fell away. She stared back like a sulky child.

The receptionist picked up the telephone and rang upstairs, speaking so rapidly that Victoria could not understand. She wanted to sit down but the cream couch would come off badly in an encounter with her jeans, so she stood with her bags at her feet like a displaced hippy. There she was when Jacques Parnasse came in, very young, very tired, with that quality which caught the attention, a certain depth in stance or expression, the sense of emotion contained by her skin. 'Victoria.' The word was almost a caress. She tried to say her carefully rehearsed words but her throat closed on them. Her eyes filled and she burst into tears.

Chapter Eight

The hotel was luxurious, but then Harriet was accustomed to luxury. Gone were the days when every free bathrobe or antique bed delighted her. She expected them, as she expected service and efficiency and a large desk.

'Do you remember that place we stayed when we were kicked off the *Real Sheila*?' said Jake.

'Oh, yes.' She paused in the act of taking out her silver-backed brushes. They had been an extravagance she had allowed herself last Christmas. 'I hated it.'

'You always hated being poor.'

She looked about her, taking in the room, the view, the well-stocked drinks cupboard. She could have this anywhere in the world, just by commanding that it should be so. 'It doesn't matter so much as it used to,' she commented. 'Actually none of it matters when I don't know where Victoria is.'

Jake sat on the edge of the bed. 'What makes you happy?' he asked suddenly.

Harriet glanced at him, and as quickly away. 'What a strange question. Pictures, perhaps. Corusca. I don't know.' How to admit that she was almost never happy? She was merely not unhappy, and that had to be enough. 'We all know what makes you happy,' she said waspishly. 'Sex and bloody boats.'

Jake flung himself back on the bed and looked up at the ceiling. 'They're what I've got,' he said thoughtfully. 'I'm not sure they're what I want, though.'

Briskly she hung two coats up in the wardrobe. 'We all have to make do, that's one of life's little lessons. Whatever you have it is never quite right, it can't be.'

'You never used to be cynical.'

She said wistfully, thoughtfully, 'I never used to be a lot of things."

Jake said, 'I want to try again. You know that, don't you?'

'Yes.' She faced the wardrobe and said, 'It isn't any good. Just because we make it in bed, you think it can all be all right. But it wouldn't.'

She heard him sit up. 'Why not?'

Turning to face him she said simply, 'Because I can't give. It used to be you that held back, now it's me. I can't – love – like I should, and in the end we'd both be so hurt and we'd lose it all. So you see, we can't.'

He closed his eyes and she saw him swallow. 'I need help, Harriet,' he said harshly. 'I need you to help me. My life has gone sour on me and I don't know what to do.'

In a voice like breaking glass she said, 'I'm sorry. I can't.'

Victoria stretched and yawned, relishing the feel of clean cotton sheets. The morning traffic was growling in a rising crescendo, like lions about to be fed. But today she was safe from it all, she had escaped the pit and scrambled on to a ledge, high above the wild beasts prowling below. What a cell of a room this was, white bed, white walls, white rug on a polished floor.

Noises from the kitchen made her get up. She pulled on the robe Parnasse had lent her and went into the sitting-room, a vast empty space punctuated with white chairs, from which all else in the flat radiated. Parnasse was making coffee, clad only in a pair of minuscule briefs. Victoria perched herself on a kitchen chair that was so beautiful in design as to be barely functional, trying not to stare at him. A thin covering of grizzled fair hair grew all over him, like moss. The muscles in his belly were flat and hard, he had a perfect tan and his blue eyes seemed to twinkle. She found him heart-stoppingly attractive.

'You slept well?' Even his voice was delicious, she decided.

'Thank you. Wonderfully. But I haven't slept properly in days, you see, it was just so fantastic to lie down!'

'And now you are hungry.' He put coffee, croissants, butter and jam on the table and Victoria fell on everything, trying to retain the sophistication she thought was expected of her while feeding a very unsophisticated appetite. Parnasse sat opposite her and watched, smoking Camels. Victoria recalled that she disliked people who smoked while she ate, but in this instance she was prepared to make an exception. He was just so gorgeous.

'You are going to work for me?'

'Yes. Senor Montado said you wanted a hat model.'

'That is true. I also want a salon girl and I had thought you too fat, but I see you have lost weight on your journey.'

Victoria guiltily put down her croissant and jam. 'I haven't eaten anything in days,' she said mournfully. 'Not a proper meal, anyway.'

'I will watch your diet. You will stay here and work, it will be most convenient.'

Victoria swallowed. 'I don't think my mother would like that.'

'And what does work have to do with your mother? I do not know your mother, I am not employing your mother.'

'But – I ought to have a place of my own, perhaps. I know she'd think that.'

'This you cannot afford. You will stay with me and I will take care.' He got up and stood next to her, taking her thick hair in his hand and shaking her head as if she were a dog. Victoria's heart did a jig inside her. This man exuded sex like a perfume and oh, how she wanted it. Compared with him, Jaime Pereira was a child!

But he did no more. They took it in turns to use the bathroom and then went to the salon, Victoria wearing the blue dress she had used at the hat shop, Parnasse in one of his many beautiful suits. This time Victoria was swept past the receptionist and straight upstairs. A rattle of conversation ceased abruptly as they entered. She took in a large room, surrounded by gilt mirrors, chaises longue, couches, spindly Louis Quinze chairs. Huge arrangements of fresh flowers stood in a perfection that made them seem artificial.

'You do not come in here unless requested by the directrice or myself,' said Parnasse. 'Come, Victoria.' He swept her past the very correct and elegant lady who was the salon directrice, and into the workrooms. This was where affluence ended and drudgery began, on the long tables and sewing machines, in the cutting rooms and store cupboards. Rows of clothes hung swathed in perfect linen bags, made by women in chainstore navy blue who worked on dresses that cost more than their own annual pay. Irons hissed, electric fans buzzed. In the hat room a man was steaming felt on a model wooden head.

'Maurice, we will try the pink feather.'

Maurice put down his tiny steamiron and swore in French. He and Parnasse had a quickfire conversation, of which Victoria caught more than they intended.

'I'm not his girlfriend,' she said loudly. 'I'm here to work. I model hats.'

Maurice raised his eyebrows and Parnasse said, 'We do not need to tell Maurice everything, my dear.'

He was enjoying pretending they were sleeping together, Victoria decided. She wondered if she would be so embarrassed if it were true. They brought the pink hat, which had an unforgiving straight brim and a ridiculous feather. She swept her hair up into a bun and borrowed a pin from a dish Maurice proffered. Then she put on the hat.

'You see?' said Parnasse triumphantly. 'Victoria!'

He took her by the hand and paraded her everywhere, turning her this way and that calling, 'Voila! Victoria!' as if she were in a circus. Three or four girls, so tall and thin they could only be models, watched out of reptilian eyes. One of them, a striking woman with a long curved nose, turned her back pointedly.

'Who is that?' asked Victoria.

Parnasse smiled down at her. 'Nobody. Francine.'

The salon closed for two hours at lunchtime. Parnasse worked on, and Victoria was at a loose end. She went for a walk in the streets, staring at the delicious goods in shop windows, feeling badly dressed. In Paris you did not go by the rules, you made your own rules if you wished to look interesting. It was not enough to be dressed expensively, whatever your materials they must be assembled well. A girl walked past wearing flat boots and velvet trousers tucked into them, a belt over a thick jumper and huge earrings. Victoria determined to copy her, and then saw someone in cream tights, shoes, skirt and top, with a flame-red waistcoat and bag. She too looked fantastic, and equally worth imitating. Victoria's own sombre clothes seemed infinitely boring in comparison.

'You see, you do not fit in,' said a voice next to her. It was Francine. They walked together in uneasy companionship, the older woman tense and brittle with nerves. 'You are so young,' said Francine. 'But he likes them young.'

'I'm not having an affair with him.'

'But you will. And he will tire of you quickly, he always does.'

'Did he tire of you?' asked Victoria, lifting her chin. It seemed strange, challenging for the first time as one woman to another. Only a few months ago she was a child and would have deferred to this creature.

Francine laughed, as if it hurt her to do so. 'He was tired, I was tired, who knows. I tired of the endless girls. You think I will not mind, I do not care, I am the one he married. But in the end you despise him, and yourself. I am talking to you only because you are very young.'

Victoria was almost frightened of her. There was hatred in Francine's eyes, not of Victoria but of her youth. The stylish, intelligent girl that Parnasse married had become, in so short a time, a catwalk model of limited appeal, thin, bitter and lonely. No wonder Jacques doesn't love her, thought Victoria. Nobody could. And the thought of being somebody that no-one wanted struck her as being so sad. For a moment she was jolted beyond the self-absorption of her years.

She and Francine walked back to the salon together. Francine talked, in an endless wretched drone, about starving herself, and wrinkles, and the girl who killed herself because her hair began to fall out. 'It is no life,' she kept saying. 'A woman should have more than this.'

'Why don't you leave?' asked Victoria, and Francine fixed her with huge, miserable eyes. How could she go now, when she was past her best, when she knew nothing else, when to go would mean she could no longer torture herself over Jacques and know she was still alive?

In the afternoon they fitted Victoria with some of the dresses she was to show. It entailed standing until her legs shook, and when she complained they swore at her in French. Arms up, arms down, stand here, stand there, she is too full in the breast, too short in the leg, are you sure the man wants this girl? Victoria might have been a prize heifer going to market. Then they scraped her hair tight to her head and put hats on her, one after the other. And they sniffed.

Eventually Parnasse took her home. They walked through busy, end of day streets smelling of dust and petrol. Victoria was downcast.

'Don't sulk,' said Parnasse. 'I do not wish you to sulk.'

'I'm just tired.'

He walked too quickly for her, she had to run to keep up. The assumption that she would fit in with him clashed with her lifelong expectation of being considered, simply because she was herself. In any gathering Victoria thought herself special, because that was how she was always treated. Jake had given her a taste of humility but she hadn't liked it. She said 'I can't walk so fast. Please slow down.'

'I am in a hurry.'

'All right.' She ceased trying to keep pace with him. After a few strides he turned and came back to her.

'Victoria, what is the matter. Is it Francine?'

She looked up at him. He had a long, bulbous nose on a long, thin face. She tried to think of Paul's face and failed. What she remembered about Paul was a shocking end to pleasure, when he began pushing something unseen and huge into her body. She remembered Teresa after one of her afternoons, sitting trembling in the car, her eyes very bright. 'You don't know what it's like,' she whispered. 'He kept on and on, I thought I would die! At the end I screamed with joy, I actually screamed Victoria! I have never known pleasure like it.'

Victoria had loathed the taxi-driver, she hated the memory of Paul. Now she knew she did not like Jacques Parnasse. 'I'm hungry,' she said. Parnasse took her arm and made her keep up with him, fractionally slowing his stride. 'We will stay in and cook something.'

'No,' said Victoria. 'We'll go out.' So go out they did.

They came back to the flat at around eleven o'clock. At Victoria's insistence Parnasse had taken her round Paris, to the louche cafés where the artists and their hangers-on sat and drank wine, to the back-street taverns where old men drank absinthe. They had watched streetlights reflected in the Seine, the Eiffel tower looking like a depressingly small pile of scaffolding against the sky, the hump of Notre Dame brooding silently over the city and its bustle. Parnasse felt that he had paid for Victoria a dozen times over, never realising that Victoria knew her own worth. Besides, sitting on the doorstep waiting for them were Jake and Harriet.

A private detective had provided them with the address within six hours of being appointed, but during the evening the initial rush of euphoria had evaporated. Jake was restless, he had drunk too much in an effort to stem the grey tide that was threatening to engulf him. He sprawled on the step, a parody of relaxation, trying not to think of tomorrow. What was he to do, where was he to go? Two or three times Harriet had talked about her business, her mind clearly turning back to it even before they found Victoria. Why was it enough for her when it was not enough for him? Oh God, he thought to himself. Oh God, how can I tell Victoria what she should do with her life? What have I done?

Harriet stood up, shaking the creases out of her beautiful skirt. Parnasse hesitated, unsure what to make of them, a scruffy, thickly muscled man an improbable escort for a woman with such money and elegance.

Harriet held out her arms. 'Oh Victoria! Victoria!' She was crying and somehow that made Victoria cry, and they clung to each other, sobbing. Jake leaned on the doorpost and closed his eyes for a moment. He sighed, a long exhalation of relief. Then he fixed his clear grey gaze on Parnasse. 'Hello to you,' he said menacingly. 'Perhaps you'd like to explain what you are doing with my daughter?'

They went upstairs, Parnasse covering embarrassment with charm. Harriet wouldn't look at him, Jake was stony-faced. 'You are all right, darling?' asked Harriet again. 'I was so worried – and that man Pereira said such dreadful things and I'm sure you didn't really promise to marry that boy did you – '

'Don't witter, Harriet,' said Jake. 'What are you doing here, Vic? Why are you shacked up with this individual? He must be twice your age.'

'I suppose he must be,' said Victoria, looking regretfully at Parnasse. She hadn't intended to sleep with him tonight, and now of course she couldn't. She allowed herself a momentary longing for indulgence. 'He's been very kind,' she declared. 'I was going to move out anyway, when I got organised. We haven't made love, Mummy.'

'Victoria!' Harriet's cheeks flamed. Parnasse said quickly to Jake, 'You see, I have taken good care of her. She has a job at the salon, her own room, I have given her money. Victoria could have a great career as a model, I assure you.'

'How very kind' said Jake thinly.

'She can't be a model, she's got to come home,' said Harriet. 'I've bought her birthday candles.'

Victoria suddenly realised that her mother wasn't in control any more. In all her life she could never remember seeing her anything but calm, her emotions held so much in check that Victoria was never even aware of them. Yet here she was hiccupping with sobs and saying silly things. The see-saw of Victoria's confidence swung firmly down.

Jake crossed the room and put his arms around Harriet. That too was a new departure, Victoria couldn't remember them touching in years. Jake's face was rigid, his expression strange. Victoria wondered if he was ill. Parnasse said irritably, 'I have not the time to waste over the problems of one model.'

'Shut up,' said Jake fiercely, and Parnasse did. Harriet ducked her face into Jake's neck in an almost childlike gesture. He flinched.

Victoria said hastily, 'Why don't you two go back to the hotel and we'll talk in the morning? I'm quite safe here, honestly.' There was an unexplained longing to be rid of them. Her own problems were enough to concern her, those of her parents were simply embarrassing. Jake looked at her over Harriet's head.

'This is all your fault,' he said bitingly.

She twisted her hands. 'I'm sorry if it's upset you. Take her away, we can't talk like this.'

Jake's face was very grim. Victoria had the sudden feeling that he was desperate, as if confronting something he could not stand. He was as eager to go as she was to be rid of him, she was sure of it.

When they had gone Parnasse went to the kitchen and made coffee. He said, 'What will you do now, Victoria?'

Her face was very pale. She leaned against the wall, the curtain of her black hair like an inky shadow. 'I'll stay. Find a flat of my own, perhaps. I don't – I want to be free of my mother. Of both of them.'

'So.' He came close and tipped her chin. 'A grown-up girl, I see.'

'More grown-up than you think. I'm not a virgin, Jacques.'

He bent and kissed her. He tasted of cigarettes and the brandy he had drunk at the last café. The desire to sleep with him reared up quite suddenly, and as suddenly she thought of Francine. 'Not tonight,' she said, pulling away.

'Why not tonight? What is to stop us?'

But Victoria had grasped at a new and powerful truth. Sex was not apart from life, it could not be experienced separately. A great deal of pain would be spared if it were, but the act, the sensation, spread shock-waves out into marriages, jobs, homes, everything. Free love didn't exist, every act of love had a price tag. If she slept with Jacques Parnasse she would probably lose her job. The other girls, his past partners, would only then draw her into their group of discards. She did not want to be part of that group. Those who continued in this man's favour were those who did not share his bed – yet.

'Another night,' she said, and smiled at him. She wasn't a girl that smiled often. Like her father her habitual expression was one of challenge, a clear grey stare at the world. But when she did smile, it was infinitely seductive. For the first time in his life Parnasse wondered if he was making a fool of himself.

Jake sat on a bench with Harriet. The night air was cold, she was shivering uncontrollably. 'I told you she'd be all right,' he said.

'Yes. But she's different. She seems older.'

'We're all older.' He got to his feet and walked to the river, picking up a stone and throwing it hard at the glassy water. 'Bloody hell, Harriet, I hate you sometimes,' he said thickly.

'Don't start on me tonight.' She was shuddering, unfit for any onslaught.

'What night can I start? Or end, or anything? When you're back in your glossy office? At one of your endless glossy hotels? When is the time?'

She said with sudden perception, 'It isn't my fault you're lonely.'

'Of course it is.'

He pulled her to her feet and walked her briskly back to the hotel. It was very late, the people in the streets watched them warily, a gendarme in a cape pausing in his measured pacing to weigh them up.

'Gangster and sobbing victim,' said Jake loudly. 'Shortly after two in the morning a man with a wreck for a life dragged his long-time mistress back to a hotel bedroom. This woman has drained him over many years by demanding what he cannot provide and rejecting what he wants to give her.'

'I only wanted you to cuddle me,' she whispered. 'That wasn't so much.'

Jake said, 'It's all too much. Too bloody much.'

In their room, blessedly warm and quiet, he crumpled on to the bed. Harriet leaned across and took him in her arms. She cradled his head, thinking how Victoria would hate to see this. Everyone was so used to Jake's strength. You had to know him a very long time before you discovered his weaknesses.

He flew back to England the next day. Victoria, lunching with her mother, was unreasonably hurt.

'He should have said goodbye,' she insisted. 'There were things I wanted to tell him.'

Harriet, once again her calm self, said, 'He's not been very happy recently. Anyway, he's not too good at all this emotion. Neither of us are actually. In a lot of ways we're very alike.'

'No, you're not,' said Victoria emphatically. 'I used to think it was your fault you didn't stay together, but it wasn't that. You couldn't have been happy, you're much too different. He's dirty, untidy and promiscuous. And sort of – unreliable.'

'No, he isn't!' defended Harriet. 'He finds it hard to love people, that's all. He can't fit it into his life. He does what he wants and that's what he's always done. He never promises things he can't give. He's braver than I am. Much.'

Victoria said, 'You shouldn't see him. It isn't good for you.'

Harriet stared at her mutinously. She didn't know how to handle a moralising daughter, or perhaps a daughter of any kind. She pulled herself together. 'We haven't talked at all about you yet. What does that man want?'

Victoria looked at her speculatively from beneath heavy black brows. 'Well – what you might think, really. I'm not a schoolgirl any more, Mother.'

'Oh, dear.' Harriet looked as if she didn't know where to put herself.

Victoria said in a soothing voice. 'It's all right. I do know what I'm doing. And Paris is what I need right now, I think. If you help me find a flat and things, I shall be fine.'

'Darling, I can't leave you all alone in Europe, you're not seventeen till next week. Someone has to look after you.'

'I can look after myself. The way I see it is, I shall stay here and work for a while. It's real hard work being a model in a salon, with fittings and so on, and if a customer comes in and wants to see a dress that you wear then out you come and show it off. If I really made good I'd be a proper catwalk model to the big houses. Parnasse is only small beer, even if he doesn't like to admit it.'

'Like your Aunt Simone,' said Harriet thoughtfully. 'You like Simone, don't you, dear?'

'She's OK,' said Victoria. 'But you don't like her. Your face always goes stiff when you have to talk about her to anyone, and when you see her you smile too much.'

'Well,' said Harriet, grimacing, 'we had a terrible row some years ago. She threw in her lot with Gareth for a while because of something she thought I'd done. That took some forgiving.'

They each sipped at their coffee. Victoria wondered what her mother had done to upset Simone. It could be that Harriet was blameless, but then her mother always thought that about herself. It wasn't often true.

'I'll talk to her,' said Harriet. 'Will it be all right if I stay for your birthday, darling? I wanted to say – I mean – Jake and I talked. We agreed I'd been far too clinging, really. Smotherlove and all that. I don't really think you ought to be a model, but if you want to do it – Darling, wouldn't you rather go to college?'

All at once Victoria longed to go to college. She wanted to step right back into the warm coccoon she had only recently vacated. But she had declared herself an adult, had made a terrible nuisance of herself, and now was being given the freedom and responsibility she had asked for. What she had vaguely conceived to be an interlude had turned into mainstream life. She couldn't climb down.

'I can do other things later,' she said, smiling so widely that Harriet was immediately alarmed. 'I'll be fine. Just think how all my friends will envy me.'

Chapter Nine

The little house in the not very smart quarter told volumes about Simone. It was frilly where she was not, less expensive than she liked to pretend. Within the walls of her home she was the wife Georges wanted, soft and obedient, despite the fact that the wife he wanted was the one he strayed from. Harriet felt impatient with her. Why did she not let Georges see her for the strong woman she really was? If he did not love the real Simone he might at least respect her.

The two women sat in the drawing room and sipped wine. Harriet thought how fortunate it was that she had not seen Simone's home before she appointed her to oversee the hotel design. Simone looked at Harriet's expensive shoes and bag and thought how unfair it all was. But on the surface they maintained the calm pretence of friendship that had persisted since they made up the quarrel.

'Have you seen anything of Gareth?' asked Harriet stiffly.

'I would not tell you if I had,' said Simone. 'Really, Harriet, why do you still hate him so? You've won, it isn't necessary.'

'I lost,' said Harriet. 'He has the collection.'

Simone wrinkled her nose. 'Most of it sold, I hear. He would not have allowed Nathan's suit to go unchallenged if he was likely to achieve anything by it.'

'I suppose not,' said Harriet ruefully. She hadn't thought of that. Gareth saw the collection as money in the bank, he didn't desire it as she did. Those pictures represented for her the ultimate in achievement. If she possessed them she had at last taken the Hawksworths for everything they owed her. If she owned them she wouldn't hate any more. No more night-time terrors, no more starting if someone came up quickly behind her in the street.

'What is Gareth doing now?' she asked stiffly. 'Wasn't he in Japan?'

'China,' said Simone. 'He is travelling again, I believe. A letter last month from Hong Kong. One or two of our dresses were in an exhibition there, he saw them. He tells me he has applied to the court for a substitution of Coruscan assets for shares in the company.'

'He tried that before and got nowhere,' said Harriet crossly. 'The ownership of the island couldn't be determined, there weren't any documents. There's just the house and the land around it, and that's my marital home.'

'He tells me he has found the documents,' said Simone, lazily twirling her glass between her fingers. 'Behind a picture.'

In the silence Harriet could hear her heart thumping. 'They'll be forged. He's making it up.'

Simone gave a Gallic shrug. 'Perhaps. You did after all agree to that division, didn't you? But you won't have written anything down.'

'Naturally not.' That idiot letter, written in naivety so long ago! Harriet's people had sufficiently fudged the ownership issue at the last hearing to prevent the letter being used as evidence, but it was there, a weak link in her defences. If the case came to court again with the Coruscan title resolved the agreement might well be considered substantive.

With an effort Harriet turned her mind away from that most perturbing problem. She had lived with it for years and no doubt would for many more. 'What I wanted to ask you, Simone,' she began determinedly, 'was whether you would consider keeping an eye on Victoria?'

'Harriet, dear, I am so busy,' said Simone wearily. 'Another American trip soon since you want the LA Hawksworth reconditioned, my work at the salon, Georges – I haven't the time to run after a teenager. Although I admit I myself would not be happy with her in the care of Jacques Parnasse.' She raised her overplucked eyebrows in a meaningful grimace.

'She doesn't need a lot of care,' wheedled Harriet. 'Just somewhere to live, really. I wondered – '

Simone felt a stab of real anger, but concealed it with a smile. Not only did Harriet inveigle her way into their business, and had not relinquished the majority of her shares despite many hints, not only did she expect Simone to drop everything and rush off to LA to repair the damage done by a riot involving four ice-hockey teams and their supporters, but she also thought she could install her daughter in their home, just like that!

If only she was rich enough to cast it in her face. If only she could live again that day when Harriet had sat on the side of that hole in the floorboards. With what relish would Simone have pushed her through! But the salon was losing money once again, there were many empty seats at the last collection and would be more at this. Georges was despondent and when he was down he was expensive. She said, 'I don't know Harriet – perhaps some arrangement?'

After a little more talk and some discreet financial haggling, they went upstairs and looked at the befurbellowed room that was to be Victoria's. The girl would hate it, thought Harriet, but at least it was not within arm's length of Jacques Parnasse. She and Simone parted with insincere air-kissing in the direction of each other's cheeks.

Damn her, thought Simone, breathing the scent of expensive perfume and noting the gentle etching of lines around Harriet's eyes. She was far lovelier now than she had been as a girl. Assurance and grace had replaced all that jerky insecurity.

On occasion somebody, somewhere, fits into a mood, a moment, a collective train of thought so well that without apparent effort or ambition they are transported to fame. Harriet had known this in some measure when she became head of the Hawksworth Corporation, at a time when the world wanted glamorous women to prove that mystery and allure could live side by side with cold hard efficiency. Victoria, in Paris, fitted another mode. Pin-thin models of great height and no femininity were at one moment everything and at the next as tired as last week's lettuce. The clothes were softer, and they needed softer women to fill them. Who had the look? An influx of pale blondes and short redheads petered out in a matter of one or two months. And then – Victoria!

Someone saw her at Parnasse, then Simone needed a photograph of an outfit and she of all people was aware of style. The word, the picture, of a young girl with thick black hair, sensual and yet innocent, with breasts, a waist and the most creamy-white skin – in a week, everyone knew of her. She was too young to realise she was causing an unusual sensation, but Simone, totally Parisian, felt in her bones the tingle of cash registers. On one of Georges' rare nights in she lit candles, cooked fish and quail, and waited for him to ask his question.

'What have you to say to me, Simone?' Married so long, disillusioned so long, he knew when she was brewing something.

'Victoria.' The girl was out, again, with Jacques Parnasse. That was another thing to set the town talking, because Parnasse had never before fallen victim to any charm but his own. Yet the girl had him on a string. He was to be seen, embarrassed, at funfairs watching Victoria eat candyfloss. Harriet had implied that Simone should discourage the relationship, but with nothing said outright surely nothing need be done. Simone was conscious of a deep desire to have the girl pregnant or disgraced or something. Fortunately the desire for money over-rode such whims, as Harriet had known it would.

'We cannot use her in the salon,' said Georges grimly. 'We are not of the new style.'

'No.' Once again they were out of step, somehow. But if they took the quantum leap into the forefront of style they would lose their safe customers, the mature ladies who liked good suits. Under Simone's guidance they could have backed both horses, but Georges couldn't quite bring himself to bet on either.

'We must make deals,' she said. 'Not with Victoria, but a photographic agency. What about Henri Ciel? Victoria need never know we are receiving a dividend. And after all, if I control her career it will be justified.'

Georges sniffed. He liked Victoria, because she was polite to him and good to look at. He liked the clutter in the bathroom and the disturbance she caused in the smooth running of the house. Would it have been different if Simone had been able to bear children? Certainly it would. They would have moved on from this sterile occupation of limited space, would have expanded mutually. As it was, Simone watched him with nervous and vulnerable eyes, and tomorrow he would go out and amuse himself with his friends or his mistress. Why couldn't she take a lover? he wondered. There had been men in the past, one that he thought she might leave him for, though a barren woman wasn't much of a prize.

'She's a sweet girl,' he said, surprising himself.

'Spoiled, of course. Harriet has no discipline. So that's settled? You will speak to Henri?'

'As you wish my dear.' He got up from the table, leaning across to kiss Simone on the forehead. 'We must take care of her,' he added.

Simone looked up, a little bewildered. 'But of course, Georges.'

Simone felt uneasy. Gareth had arranged to meet her at an obscure restaurant, but still there was the chance that someone would see. Harriet had become so powerful in recent years, Simone could easily convince herself that she might have spies everywhere. Today she felt old and nervous. Why was Victoria so difficult, why did she not accept what was said to her? Instead she had taken an unreasoning dislike to Ciel, the agency head, declaring that he had sugar-candy taste and was not to be trusted. Worse, Georges laughed and agreed with her. And somehow she had persuaded that man Parnasse to organise her photographs, the head of an obscure house that had been nothing at a time when Simone had six full-time models . . . She paused and leaned against a wall for a moment. There was no point in becoming over-excited. Parnasse was moving up, she was sliding down. Damn Victoria!

Gareth was waiting at a corner table. As always, there was the slight chill on first meeting. It seemed to Simone that her half-brother was a man superficial to great depth, if that were possible. The knowable Gareth was spread out for all to see, vindictive, slightly cruel, rather witty on occasion. The unknowable Gareth lurked unseen. Simone realised that she had no idea how he spent his days. He had a motor cruiser, moored somewhere, he rented villas now and then. And of course he travelled, she thought to Pakistan and Bolivia, ostensibly trading in textiles.

'How are you?' She asked the question automatically, though in fact he looked prosperous and well. He sported a new, heavy gold ring studded with a triangle of diamonds. He was heavier, too, sporting quite a jowl nowadays. It served to give him an authority he had lacked in the past.

'You look tired, Simone.'

'I am tired. That brat comes in late! She goes everywhere with Parnasse, and leaves her clothes in piles for my maid to clear up. Every night a party. It would serve Harriet right if the girl got pregnant.'

'Harriet is never served right.' He sipped at his drink, whisky at midday.

'You drink too much,' said Simone.

They ate in spasmodic silence, Simone nervously chewing on tough chicken, Gareth risking the shellfish. 'The old man used to like prawns,' he said thoughtfully. 'I should have poisoned him. The mistakes we make in our youth! If I'd killed him when I meant to, everything would have been different.'

'You would have shut me out. I would have had nothing.'

He covered her hand with his own. 'You underestimate me, my dear. So does Harriet.'

Putting down her fork, Simone said, 'What do you want? Is it Victoria? She won't do as I ask, I've tried. It wouldn't worry me what happened to her. But then there's Harriet.'

'Don't worry about that. I'll instruct my bank to arrange a transfer, I've been doing pretty well lately.' Simone inclined her head, smiling. Inside she seethed. Why was she alone always short of funds? Other people, who deserved much less, always had more. Gareth said, 'Victoria is certainly lovely to look at. And everyone is looking, there's barely a magazine that hasn't featured her lately. Such innocent little breasts.' He smiled to himself, like a sultan interviewing for the harem. 'You must introduce us, Simone.'

The woman's head came up and she laughed, scornfully. 'If there is one thing Harriet has taught her daughter it is to beware of you! That hare won't run, I can assure you.'

'Don't be foolish, Simone. Introduce us.'

She watched him, her mouth half open. He thought how raddled she was looking. Harriet's fault, of course. Most things could be laid at Harriet's door, including, he hoped, her daughter's body.

Since Georges disliked Gareth intensely Simone chose an evening when he was out of town. He wasn't, of course, merely staying the night at his mistress's apartment, but the euphemism came in handy. Victoria flew in from the salon and changed quickly into black tights and high heeled shoes, a short blue cocktail dress in dark blue satin so tight that it outlined her belly and over it a black skating skirt like a pie frill. The ensemble was completed with huge electric blue earrings and a diamanté shawl across her cleavage. She looked amazing.

She came downstairs to exchange a brief word with Simone. Parnasse was due to collect her in twenty minutes or so, they were going to a reception at which Victoria would be photographed. Afterwards they might go to a club or a café, and Jacques would get drunk and tell her she was breaking his heart. The power she had over him excited her every bit as much as he did.

Gareth was sitting holding a drink, chatting comfortably with Simone. Victoria hesitated in the doorway, aware that he was in some way familiar, but unsure who he might be.

'Victoria, dear, this is my brother Gareth.'

She might as well have introdued Beelzebub himself. All through her childhood Victoria had been told that Gareth was evil, that he was stealing Harriet's money. Yet even as she froze in horror she looked at this ordinary man and knew it was ridiculous. Her mother always went overboard about things, and wills were notorious for polarising loyalties.

She extended her hand and said politely, 'How do you do? I'm so pleased to meet you after all this time.'

'And I you, my dear. Though I feel I know you, you're in every magazine I pick up! You are very beautiful, Victoria.'

'Thank you.' She sat down, her skirt high above her knees.

Gareth gazed at her in a fatherly way. 'It saddens me that your mother has never wanted to heal the rift between us,' he said. 'We're all getting older. My father died a very long time ago, this quarrel ought not to pass on down the generations. May we be friends, Victoria?'

'Er – I hope so.' She was somewhat taken aback. If her mother heard that she was friendly with Gareth she would be angry beyond belief, but it was not possible to say that now with Aunt Simone pouring drinks and this nice, ordinary man trying to make amends. 'I can't stay long,' she said quickly. 'Jacques will be calling for me.'

'Jacques Parnasse? I knew his wife. Does your mother know you go out with him, Victoria? He does seem rather old for you.'

He thought she was a child. Here it was again, everyone thinking she didn't know what she was doing. 'He's very nice,' she said stiffly. 'I like him.'

'I'm sure you do.' He was watching her consideringly. Suddenly he stood up. 'You look a little thin, my dear, a little tired. Eat more and sleep more, that's my advice. I must be going. I'm so glad I've been able to meet you.' He reached down and touched her cheek, his fingers surprisingly cold. Simone accompanied him to the door. There was a low murmur of voices and then he was gone.

Simone came back into the room and lit a cigarette, sending a restless spiral of smoke into the air. 'He's right, you don't look well. You should take something.'

'Like what? Vitamins?' Victoria might be burning the candle at both ends but she wasn't going to stop until it fell in two. She took a sip of her drink, a gin cocktail.

'You shouldn't drink, it is bad for your skin.'

'It keeps me awake,' snapped Victoria. 'I have to have something.'

'What is wrong with an early night?' demanded Simone, forcing a laugh. 'I know, I know, it is all so exciting. But, my dear, if you want to photograph well drink mineral water and take these. So much better for you. Believe me, I know. I tell all my girls.'

She held out a small tin box with an old-fashioned design of flowers on it, a cough-sweet box. Interested, Victoria took it.

The reception was large and prestigious. Victoria minced across the marble floor, unable to take large steps because of her tight skirt and teetering heels. She was reflected back at herself a thousand times by the mirrors lining the walls, and in them too she glimpsed the high, vaulted ceilings, celestial blue and white, supported by massive pillars decorated with flowers. Parnasse put his hand on her bottom. 'Why aren't you drinking?'

'I am.' She held up her glass of mineral water and toasted him. 'My aunt says I'm beginning to fade because of the drink. She's given me some pills to take.'

'What sort of pills?'

'I don't know. Vitamins.' She opened her bag and rattled the tin at him. Then she opened it and popped a pill into her mouth, washing it down with water. 'Now I shall bloom like an English rose.'

'If you were a rose I would creep into your heart like a bee and pierce you with my sting,' he said throatily. 'Oh, Victoria, you excite me.'

The reception lasted hours, but to Victoria it passed in a flash. She felt light and very happy. When Jacques put his hand on her arm tingles ran over her skin. An influential columnist put his arm around her and stroked her breast beneath her shawl and she let him. It was good to be touched, she had a great need of it. When they left she said, 'Let's go to the salon!'

He stared at her. 'Why? There is no-one there.'

'That's why I want to go.'

He opened the door with his own key and locked it again behind them. It was cold and quiet, yet Victoria felt a bubble of excitement deep within her. Jacques watched her speculatively. 'What do you want here, Victoria?'

They were in the showroom. She stood in the centre of the plush carpet and pulled off her shawl, holding it high above her head. 'I want you to thrill me,' she whispered. 'I'll do anything you want. But you must thrill me!'

She dropped her scarf to the floor where it glittered like fallen stars. One of her shoulder straps was slipping, so she pulled her arms roughly out of them and dragged the dress down to her waist. Parnasse took off his jacket and unloosened his tie. He was watching her out of hard eyes. Her nipples were taut as the stem of a plant, he crossed to her and took one between his fingers. She gasped and stood, wide-legged, her head hanging while he caressed her. He bent his head and took a mouthful of her free breast, and when she groaned he closed his teeth on her. She squealed and hung against him. He chuckled deep in his throat. Since she still straddled helplessly before him he reached under the skin-tight skirt.

Model-style, because it gave a better line, she was wearing pull-up stockings and nothing else. Her thighs were wet, held together by the skirt. Dragging it up to her waist he knelt in front of her, pushing his long nose between her legs. His tongue touched her, licked her. Colours flashed in her head, purple, emerald green. Why did I ever deny myself this? she thought in amazement, and then she was beyond thought, beyond everything except spreading tension. When her climax came the force of her convulsions crumpled her down on top of him.

She lay on the floor breathing hard. Blood roared in her ears, she was helpless and weak. He opened his trousers and got on top of her, forcing her knees apart. He couldn't hold himself. It was over in seconds.

Chapter Ten

Victoria was ill, her head ached, she thought she was dying. 'It was those pills,' she told Simone, 'they were bad for me.'

'Only because you drank before you took them.' Simone lit herself another cigarette, her third that morning. 'You were very late."

'Yes.'

She could hardly bear to think about the night before. She was deeply ashamed of herself, terrified that she might be pregnant. But, deep down, she felt a small flame of triumph. Amazing, delicious feelings! She wouldn't let Jacques do that again, it was too dangerous. How her head ached! 'Do you have an aspirin?' she asked Simone.

But her aunt went to Victoria's handbag, lying where she had let it fall the night before. She took a pill from the tin. 'One more won't hurt. And you have a photo session this morning, as well as the salon. I gave you these because I thought you were old enough to use them, but if you are too young I will take them away.'

'They made me ill,' the girl complained.

'You are ill through lack of sleep and bad food at that reception. Quickly, you are late.'

Obediently, Victoria swallowed down her pill.

The next few days were very strange. Caught up on a treadmill of salon, photographs and parties Victoria never seemed able to recover herself. Jacques was no help, for the affair was now on lines familiar to him. He had enjoyed her body once and now she should not deny him, he had the right to her at any time he pleased. So she took a pill to get her to work in the morning and there was Jacques, ignoring her until he could take her into his office and shut the door. The urge to resist had died in her. As she lay under him, the salon noises coming through the thin walls, a draught running along the carpet and chilling her, some part of her mind wondered what was happening. Why was she doing this? The pleasure of the first time did not come again, that heightened cascade of feeling. For the most part she felt numb.

When she went home she felt terrible, longing for sleep but unable to rest. Her skin jumped, the bare beginnings of thought seemed impossible. Simone said she had a chill and gave her some different pills, and for a day or so she felt better, though in some strange way separate from what was happening around her.

One day after work she went into the cloakroom, and sat on one of the hard upright chairs, her heart pounding. Francine was there, leaning against the mirror, crying and watching herself. Victoria knew she should talk to her. But she felt so breathless, and there was a feeling of fluttery panic, that could only be contained by silence. Francine rolled her face this way and that, and her mascara smudged on to the mirror and then on to her cheeks. It was as if the two women inhabited separate iron capsules of misery. After a while Victoria got up and went home.

In the morning, insulated by her morning pill, she could not understand the commotion. Police vans outside the salon, an ambulance arriving in a screech of tyres. She pushed her way up the stairs, intent on taking her coat off as usual, going to the fitting room and the hat room. The door to the cloakroom was open, but she had no curiosity. Then, passing it, she looked in upon the dead, mascara-coated face of Francine.

Alone in her bedroom Victoria painted her face. She took pot after pot of make-up and applied it, making great swirls of green and purple around her eyes, dotting her cheeks with doll-like colour, spreading lipstick from her lips to her nose, wide to her ears like the gashes on Francine's wrists. Death seemed to haunt her, it was a blessed isle to which she should retreat. After all, what was life but a nightmare of exhaustion and terror and wild, gargoyle faces staring at you out of the dark?

The door opened behind her. She looked round, expecting to see Simone, but it was Georges. He stared at her painted face and she stared back.

'Mon Dieu,' he said softly. 'What has happened to you?'

The room smelled stale. He wished he hadn't come back, it was only because he had left a drawing and the salon was chaos and he had desired a quiet cup of coffee at home. He moved into the room and Victoria's eyes watched him, the lifeless eyes of a doll.

Jake was in a meeting. They were discussing the new boat he had designed, a radical and totally risky departure from current thinking.

'Look at the worst case,' said Mac tightly. 'If it goes as wrong as it could, we'll be finished. We should build a half-size prototype.'

'We've already built three models,' snapped Jake. 'They don't perform like the real thing, and neither will anything except the real thing. For God's sake Mac, we have computer projections, lake tests, graphical projections – we didn't have any of those when we built the first one. And yet here you are shitting yourself over a bit of a risk.'

'We had nothing to lose when we started,' said Mac. 'You might not care about this place, Jake, but I do. Look at it. If this business goes down now it won't be just you that will suffer. There are men whose sons work here, whose daughters are in the office and the wives cooking in the canteen. You can't play ducks and drakes with families.'

Jake sighed and put his feet on the table. The other five men around it shifted uncomfortably, because Jake and Mac rarely had these disagreements in public and no-one knew how to behave. 'The illusion of security is just that, an illusion,' said Jake patiently. 'We are only as good as our last boat, and our last boat wasn't good enough. We made our name as a radical yard and if we aren't radical we aren't anything. This business wasn't just one leap in the dark, it's leap after leap after leap. The expertise in this yard is phenomenal. If we don't use it because we're too scared then we shouldn't be in boat building.'

'I am only saying – ' continued Mac, but then the 'phone shrilled.

Someone answered it and handed the receiver to Jake. 'A gentleman for you sir, French. Says it's urgent.'

Jake seized the receiver.

'Mr. Jakes? Georges Lalange here. Victoria is ill, you must come at once. I don't know what is the matter, I think drugs. She is in her room now, I can't get to her. No, no, I mean she does not understand me. A girl killed herself at the salon and there was a shock, but still – yes, the doctor is here, she will be taken to the hospital. We will expect you.'

Jake put the 'phone down and gazed at the men around him, surprised that they were still there. All he could think of was Harriet, which was ridiculous when Victoria was the one who was ill. What would she say about this boat? he found himself wondering stupidly. 'I've got to go to Paris. Victoria's ill.'

'That bloody girl,' said Mac, throwing his pencil on to the table. He stood up and looked after Jake's retreating figure. The other men round the table began to gather their papers. 'At least it's not Harriet,' said Mac despairingly. 'That he couldn't take. And he says *I'm* getting old.'

* * *

Jake found the hospital with difficulty, and it was that strange mixture of clinical efficiency and French disorder that the British can never understand. He didn't trust anyone there. He said to the doctor, 'She doesn't seem to know me. She looks blank. That is going to get better?'

The doctor sighed and spread his hands. 'Who can tell? She has been taking a powerful hallucinogen, we do not know what. Some pills were found in her room and the analysis is not straightforward. A sort of cocktail of drugs, cocaine-based we believe. There may be damage to the brain, however.'

'Brain damage? Are you out of your mind?'

'Regrettably sir, it may be your daughter who is out of hers.'

Jake went back and stared at Victoria. She lay in the bed, absolutely still, her grey eyes looking out vacantly at the world. Fear and rage rose up in him in equal amounts. He wanted to kill someone, anyone, but preferably whoever it was gave that poison to his girl. Georges caught at his arm, but at first Jake did not recognise him.

'Oh, it's you.' He blinked helplessly. 'What happened to her? Who did this?'

Georges' thin, bitter little face was drained of colour. 'I can tell you nothing,' he said softly.

Simone sat in her drawing room and smoked cigarette after cigarette. When Georges came in she stubbed out one half smoked and lit another. 'Well?'

'She may have brain damage.'

'Oh, my God.' Simone put her fingers to the bridge of her nose.

'It is the end, Simone. I tell you this so that I may hear the truth from you. The salon is finished, and so is this marriage. Was it your brother?'

Simone looked up at him, her mouth wide and slack. Her teeth were stained with lipstick. 'It wasn't me! I didn't know, I swear I did not! He said they were pills. Please Georges, don't be hasty, she'll get better!' She stubbed out the cigarette and tried to light another, but her hands were shaking.

'What did he pay you? Don't you know he peddles in drugs, don't you know that is how he lives? Of course you do. We have lived so long together and I never knew I had married an evil woman. Pah, I thought I was the one! With my little crimes, my little infidelities. I cannot bear you in my home. Get out, go away, take your filthy money. Out with you. Out!'

He seized her arm and propelled her towards the door. She was sobbing, pleading. 'No, Georges! I didn't think! I promise I didn't mean to hurt her. Please, Georges! Please!'

She stood in the street facing the closed door. Her fists banged against it, once, twice, three times. No-one came. She was conscious that people were watching her, the same people she had nodded to politely year after year, and here she was in the street with her blouse untucked and no bag or coat, and it coming on to rain. Georges would not let her in, and where could she go, what could she do? Stone cold sober, yet walking like a drunk, Simone blundered down the road.

The urge to blame someone was overwhelming. 'Was it my fault?' Jake asked, watching Georges' face intently. 'What went wrong? Was it Parnasse?'

'No, no – I don't know. He did nothing to help her. It was all so quick.'

Jake's frustration was choking him. Desperate for activity he went to see Parnasse, striding into his office without knocking. For a second, before he pulled down his mask of charm and concern, Parnasse showed fear. Jake said: 'Did you know?'

'My dear sir, how could I?' He spread his hands, affecting a posture of bafflement. Jake hit him hard, feeling the man's teeth break underneath his fist, watching his long nose slew sideways.

'I don't know what that's for,' said Jake breathlessly, 'but I'm sure you do.' Parnasse lay sprawled in a corner, his mouth pouring blood and ivory. Jake wished the sight was more satisfying.

He went out, past the shocked faces of people crammed in doorways. Someone, somewhere, applauded.

Victoria remained alive but senseless. Jake decided to wait a day before he told Harriet, then two days, three, four. He couldn't bear to tell her. A letter came from her to Victoria, Georges brought it to the hospital. Sitting in the corridor, Jake opened it and could almost hear Harriet speaking.

> 'Darling, it's your turn to write but since I don't suppose you will then I must! I saw you on the cover of *Elle*, you looked fantastic. I bought twenty copies and leave them lying around in my office so when anyone comes in they say "Who is this?" and I reply airily "My daughter, Victoria." It's lovely!
>
> 'Did you get the things I sent for your birthday? I don't suppose Simone made much of a fuss. I know she can be strange but she isn't as bad as she seems. But, darling, there is one thing I want to stress. I have heard that Gareth is in Europe. Please don't have anything to do with him at all, not for my sake because my quarrels aren't yours, but because he isn't a nice man. The word is that he's one of

the drug barons everyone reads about and nobody knows. He certainly travels a lot, and lately he has had an awful lot of money. I'm sure Simone wouldn't be so silly as to introduce you, she knows how I would view that, but if he does cross your path WALK THE OTHER WAY!

'It was lovely to talk to you on the 'phone the other day. Do write. Love, Mummy.'

Jake was suddenly sick with misery. 'Those bloody, bloody Hawksworths,' he whispered to himself. 'Oh God, Harriet, what am I going to say to you?' The letter was crumpled in his hand. Was it Gareth? Could it have been? Georges was walking towards him, maintaining a supercilious air that was in most part real. The man despised everyone but his inner circle. He probably despises me, thought Jake, but not Victoria. He cares about her.

They went without speaking to the canteen and bought two cups of filter coffee. They sat and waited for the liquid to trickle down, and Jake sighed wearily. 'Was it Gareth? Did Simone put him on to her?'

Georges didn't move but his fingers, resting on the thick twill of his suit trousers, trembled very slightly. 'Simone – denies it,' he said at length.

'I'd better talk to her then,' said Jake, trying to meet the Frenchman's eyes. Georges looked away and said quickly, 'I wish you to understand that I had no part in this. I owe loyalty to my wife, though I consider my marriage to be at an end. It was Gareth, I think, though I have not seen him in some years – a man of consummate evil, I believe.'

'You wife's not so charming either,' said Jake calmly. At one moment calm, the next absolute rage. He swept the table clear with one scythe of his arm, shouting: 'She was in your care, damn you! A sixteen-year-old girl, and that bitch poisoned her!'

'This will not help Victoria,' said Georges, taking out a spotless handkerchief and wiping drops of coffee from his suit. He gazed round at the watching people as if daring them to take an interest in him. If he wished for privacy he should have it.

'Where is Gareth?' asked Jake softly.

'I suggest you speak to Harriet. My wife always maintained that Harriet had a sixth sense where Gareth was concerned, or more likely a private detective agency.'

Jake stood up, his feet crunching on broken pottery and plastic filters. 'I could do with that coffee,' he said ruefully.

'It would not have been good.' Georges got up and walked out. Jake strolled slowly after him, reflecting that Georges was a brave man. He had been very frightened sitting there, and had managed to disguise it. Jake wished he was controlling himself half as well, and knew he was not.

The problem with business, reflected Harriet, was that some days were soporific with boredom and others wild with activity, and you never knew which was going to be which. Sometimes hell broke out when you had wound down to thinking about reorganising the desks downstairs, or contributing to the staff magazine, and the transition was mind-blowing. Today, for example, there had been four write-to-the-top complaint letters, all she suspected from people trying to cash in on her 'free night if not satisfied' offer, and very little else. Maud was considering having her varicose veins seen to in the lull. Harriet had been wrestling with herself as to whether or not she could pop over to see Jake or Victoria, although she was pretty sure neither wanted to see her. Victoria was busy, Jake was cross.

In the midst of this sleepy day there came the visitor. Reception had rung through in a panic to say that there was a gentleman downstairs who swore he knew Mrs. Hawksworth personally and should they call the police? Enquiries elicited that he was very tall, black, shabbily dressed and rather strange. Harriet went down in the elevator to peer surreptitiously at him through the palm fronds in the lobby, and there, looking about him with all the controlled dislike of a captured hawk, was Jerome.

She stepped forward slowly. The doorman, an elderly uniformed gentleman who thought they had a visiting assassin, declared nervously: 'Now you just go on upstairs, ma'am and we'll deal with this person.'

'That's all right,' said Harriet. 'I do know him. Hello, Jerome.'

'Harriet, we have to talk.' He had the prison look, short hair and an air of wariness. She led the way upstairs.

Seated behind her desk she said chattily, 'How good it is to see you again.'

'It is indeed. I've come for my island, Harriet.'

She blinked. Then she said carefully, 'Your island? I don't think it's anybody's. The house and the land around it is mine, and the rest – well, people live on it, farm it. The people own it.'

'And they are my people.'

She took a little time before replying. At length she said, 'There have been a lot of changes. There's a hospital and roads, the children have a proper school. I've done a lot for them.'

'Of course you did. I saved you so you could take care, I knew you would. And now I am back and it is mine. You were only ever the caretaker.'

'And what were you, king?'

Jerome put his head back and laughed. 'My, my, look at her. So very grand. All alone in this great big office. What happened to your man, Harriet? Couldn't you keep him?'

'No, I couldn't. But I run a good business and I look after the island. Times have changed, Jerome, there isn't room in the islands for an overlord in the old style. By all means come back, I can find something for you. But it isn't your island. It isn't anybody's.'

'Anybody's but yours,' he said softly. 'You think you know Corusca? You think you understand it? I tell you, lady, you don't know nothing!'

She got up and went to look out of the window, her office commanding not the panoramic view that went with vast overheads, but a low-rise outlook on to a small park. 'I have put so much into that place,' she said softly. 'The house is beautiful, quite beautiful. And I didn't build a hotel, I couldn't bring myself to do it, to spoil things. There's a helicopter to take people away if they're really ill, could you give them that? You'd just take them back to fear and suspicion and – and voodoo magic!'

'It ain't your garden, Harriet.'

She spun round on him. 'And it isn't your empire! Neither is it Gareth's, though he wants to get his greasy paws on it, too. It was left to me and I'm keeping it.'

'Why?'

She didn't know why. Except that Corusca was a place apart from the wrangles and disappointments that beset her elsewhere. When she was there she didn't have to know that she was alone in the world, that in all the years she had lived she had never managed to forge a single, unbreakable bond. Your children fought to escape from you. Your lovers left you in anger and acrimony. But on Corusca, that magical, remote isle full of sunshine and inky blackness, she lived in dreams.

Jerome left without saying where he was going. She tried to offer him money, to put him in his allotted place as receiver of her goodwill, but he looked at her and laughed. Oh God, she thought. Oh God, what now? And when she went home Nathan was there.

He was the last person she wanted to see. The housekeeper had let him in and he lounged on one of her pale satin sofas, sipping a drink and looking at the pictures round the walls.

'What the hell do you want?'

He stood up slowly. 'Hard day, Aunt Harriet?'

'Yes, and I bet you know why. You've seen him, haven't you? Whose side are you on, Nathan?'

He shrugged. 'My own. I put my bag in the spare room. Do I move it out again?'

She went and poured herself a drink, a large one. 'No, of course you don't. I'm sorry. I don't suppose you've heard from Victoria, have you?'

'No. She doesn't write to me. I wish she did.'

Harriet gave him a jaundiced stare. 'I don't. What are you doing at the moment anyway, crewing?'

He nodded. 'Some. But I brought some things for you to look at. Over there.' Four brown paper parcels stood against the wall behind a chair.

Harriet said, 'Those are pictures.'

'Yup. Gareth sent them to me. I thought you might like to see.'

Harriet went across and unwrapped each parcel. A slow chill went through her, spreading from her hands to her arms, to her body and at last to her heart. In each parcel were two or three pictures, in frames, and every one of them was slashed into ribbons. On the last, still just recognisable as Titian, there was a note. She pulled it out of the frame and read it.

'My dear Nathan – the remains of the collection, for old time's sake. I seem to be in funds and don't require them. Whilst preparing these for packing I had the good fortune to find the original papers endowing Josiah Hawksworth and his heirs with the island of Corusca, in perpetuity. Do impress upon your Aunt Harriet that if she wishes me to relinquish my claim then I am prepared to accept the Corporation in exchange. Otherwise I shall make do with the island, the choice is hers. Yours, Gareth.'

She found she was fighting tears. 'Why is all this happening to me?' she wept. 'I've worked so hard for so many years and I can never be safe! He's always getting at me, trying to take things away! And the pictures, the wonderful, wonderful, pictures!'

It was too much and she wept, stroking the tattered pieces of canvas as if she would put them back together, picking up each crumb of fractured oilpaint and carefully saving it. Nathan said, 'The island is Jerome's.'

Harriet's head came up. 'It's mine! I'm the only one that deserves it, I'm the only one who cares enough. For Jerome it's a magic kingdom, for Gareth a drug-running base. All I want is a decent life for the people there, nothing else.'

Nathan got up to pour himself another drink. 'The island's caught you as it does everyone. It's a great flypaper. Look how it's spoiled your life, and yet you still love it.'

'It hasn't spoiled anything,' said Harriet, distractedly piecing together some torn shreds of canvas that made up an arm and part of a chair.

'But you go back to it for comfort. You use it when you should use people.'

Harriet got up carefully and piled the pictures together. 'Do you want these? I'll send them to a restorer, they might be able to do something. Are you changing for dinner, because if you are will you make sure when you come down that you don't have any half-baked advice to hand out? I don't need someone as young as you to tell me where I've gone wrong, I can see that for myself!'

He went to the door. 'But you don't look, do you, Aunt Harriet?'

Over breakfast she poured coffee from a silver pot, the lace of her housecoat falling back from her wrist. Nathan said, 'Why don't you take more lovers?'

The stream of coffee stopped, and then poured again. 'Because one thing you don't get from lovers is love,' said Harriet stiffly. 'You don't know yet, but the richer you are the murkier the pool. Everybody wants something, nobody wants to give anything. And I don't like other women's husbands. OK, Nathan? Satisfied?'

He laughed and buttered himself some toast. 'Victoria doesn't understand you at all, which is foolish when you're so simple to understand.'

'I'm glad you think so. Personally I find Victoria incomprehensible. Are you sure you haven't heard from her? It's gone very quiet in Paris.'

'You'd know if anything was wrong,' said Nathan, biting into his toast.

Victoria sat on a chair, her hands folded neatly in her lap. 'Victoria,' said Jake loudly. 'Victoria!'

She turned very slowly and looked at him. 'Yes?'

He swallowed. 'I want you to stand up and walk round the room. Come on, do it.'

Obedient as a puppet, she got up and walked round the room, her legs slightly unco-ordinated.

'It is better than might have been hoped,' said Georges, trowelling cynicism over his emotions.

'It's bloody awful,' said Jake. 'Victoria, sit down. I've got to take her to her mother and I don't think I've got the courage.'

'Mummy?' Victoria's blank face moved slightly.

'Yes, Mummy,' said Jake. 'You want Mummy, don't you? I'll take you to Mummy?'

'Mummy,' repeated Victoria, like a record with the needle stuck.

They took a plane from Charles de Gaulle, Victoria in a large hat that hid her face. The sudden illness of the new young star had been reported extensively, but in the fast-moving fashion world they came and they went, cracking up under the strain of work and broken love affairs with depressing regularity. Still, Jake did not want to advertise that his beautiful daughter was turned, perhaps irrevocably, into a walking vegetable. Again and again he rehearsed how he was going to tell Harriet. He wished now he had written to her, but the thought of her opening a letter over breakfast and reading – what? What could he say that would not destroy her? Every day she was spared this was a day's reprieve.

He looked at Victoria's face, still and expressionless beside him. The loveliness was somehow diminished even in repose by the lack of a life within. Yet he couldn't persuade himself that the girl he knew was indeed gone. Sometimes, briefly, she looked at him and he saw her, staring out at him like someone in chains. He found that more harrowing than to have lost her altogether.

Chapter Eleven

In the past few years Jake had not visited Harriet's home. On the rare occasions he saw Victoria he had met her from school, or in the islands, because for a reason he was not prepared to analyse Harriet's home made him uncomfortable. Now, sitting in her elegant, understated drawing room, he knew how he must have frustrated her in the past. He had condemned a woman who loved beauty to live in a small, ugly house, without anything of merit, and yet she had done so without much complaint. Perhaps she should have complained, he thought suddenly. If she had held out for what she wanted, together, with me, she could have had it. But Harriet was uncompromising. With her it was this or that, no bargains, no middle ground.

Nathan said, 'We have to talk about this.'

Jake got up and went to the window, unreasonably angered that this boy should be taking the initiative. 'Nothing to talk about, certainly not with you. I don't know why Harriet puts up with you. When's she coming home?'

'Any time now, I think. You're not the only person who cares about Victoria.'

Jake turned on him. 'Don't kid me you care! You bloody Hawksworths are all the same. Me first, the rest nowhere.'

Nathan grinned, mouth wide beneath his shock of sun-bleached hair. 'I thought you majored in selfishness, Jake.'

There was a silence. 'Perhaps you're right,' said Jake. His gaze strayed to Victoria, sitting quietly, her hands in her lap. When Nathan first saw her his face changed, momentarily registering something Jake did not recognise. Pain? Understanding? In a second the look was gone and when Jake tried to begin an explanation he had said harshly, 'I know. I can see, don't tell me.' And he did seem to know.

The street was not visible from the window and the first they knew of Harriet was when she opened the front door. Jake closed his eyes. He couldn't do it, he couldn't tell her!

'Hello! Nathan?' called Harriet.

Nathan went into the hall. 'There's trouble,' he said quietly. 'Victoria's here, and she's ill.'

Harriet flew into the room. She saw Victoria seated so still on the sofa, saw her head turn slowly, the eyes take time to focus. 'Mummy?' said Victoria dreamily.

Harriet put her hands to her mouth. 'They've turned her into Madeline,' she whimpered. 'I can't bear it. It's Madeline!'

Jake said, 'It was drugs. She might get better, Harriet!'

She went to the sofa and put her arms round the girl, crying and rocking her to and fro, to and fro. 'What have they done to you?' she kept whispering. 'What have they done?'

Jake yelled at her: 'Why don't you say it? Why don't you blame me?'

'I don't care about you,' she snapped. 'Can't you see?'

He turned away quickly and banged against a display cabinet, he the least clumsy of men. It held a collection of tiny porcelain cups which fell against each other, tinkling like bells.

After a while Harriet said weakly, 'We must get doctors. Someone can cure her.'

'They didn't cure my mother,' said Nathan. Harriet looked across at him. She had the unmistakable conviction that he was suffering, which was odd when she never felt at all in tune with Nathan. He was a closed book to her. 'You don't have to stay,' she said. 'It's nothing to do with you.'

Nathan's eyes flared. 'You can't stop me caring,' he said softly.

'You keep your corrupt hands off her,' snapped Jake. 'For all I know you're in league with Gareth. What do you take? Do you get it from your uncle at cheap rates?'

'It isn't Nathan's fault,' said Harriet wearily. 'Where's the point in arguing?'

She took Victoria's limp hands in her own and tried to rub some life into them. The girl stared at her out of wide, unblinking eyes, so reminiscent of Madeline at her worst. In some strange way Harriet was totally unsurprised, it was as if she had known this was going to happen. Was that why she had held so tightly to the girl? Or was that merely justifying herself when she knew she had behaved foolishly in setting her free at sixteen?

Jake came across and tried to hold her but she struck him aside. This time her wound was too deep for comfort. He said nothing. When she looked up at him he was watching her with utter compassion.

'You don't have to feel sorry for me,' she said tightly.
'You let me feel what I want,' he said.

Medical opinion was varied. One doctor declared that the damage was substantial and they should not hope for further recovery. 'Be grateful she can look after herself,' he said bluntly. 'Think of the kids born worse than this can't feed themselves, can't go to the bathroom. She's not so bad.'

Others wanted to try electrical treatment, more drugs, flashing lights and buzzers. 'You've nothing to lose,' they said, and Jake and Harriet remembered the kids who couldn't feed themselves and declined.

And Nathan wouldn't go away. He stayed and endured all their coldness and barbed remarks, waiting until they were finally in despair. At last, over dinner one night when Victoria had to be reminded to take each and every mouthful of food, he said quietly, 'Why don't you let me take her to Corusca? I can cure her, I know it.'

Jake stared at him. 'What the shit do you want with her? Is it your idea of fun, a woman who can't resist you? Necrophilia for beginners, apply here.'

Harriet shuddered. 'Don't be disgusting, Jake.'

Nathan put his head against his knotted hands. He was breathing very quickly, as if under great strain. 'I know more about this than you. When I was small, my mother was like this. Worse, sometimes. Jerome cared for her most of the time, he was good to her. She used to get better. He gave her a special medicine, made of leaves. They're a poison in large quantities. It's a recognised drug but it would take forever to find out what. It has some effect on the brain. My mother didn't want to be better really, because then she had to remember things. The old man was so powerful he did what he liked. If he'd wanted to eat people he could have. You think I'm Gareth's son. I might have been, but I'm not. My father was Henry Hawksworth.'

Harriet said tightly, 'You don't know that. Your mother couldn't be trusted to tell the truth.'

Nathan shrugged. 'Jerome can. That was why Gareth shot the old man. A quarrel over my mother. I ought to be an idiot but I'm not. And what I know will make Victoria well.'

Jake burst out, 'If you think you're getting your filthy hands on her, to do with as you like, then you are fair and far out. Get out of this house.' He reached out and caught Nathan by the arms, forcing him up with the strength that always surprised, because he wasn't a big man.

Harriet grabbed him. 'Jake, no! If he can cure her then he must. Don't be stupid!'

Jake stared at her. 'You realise what you have here? You name it and he has seen it, Harriet. You want to put our daughter in the hands of someone who doesn't have any of the normal taboos the rest of us carry around, he comes from a world where anything goes so long as you can get away with it. We've been irresponsible enough with this girl. We don't have to throw her to the wolves, and a particularly inbred one at that.'

'There isn't anything else!' screamed Harriet. 'I don't like it either but we must!'

Jake let Nathan go. The boy's face was a white mask concealing what was within. 'I'd never hurt Victoria,' he said. 'I've never done anything to hurt either of you, but you judge me just the same.'

Jake sighed and emptied the last of the wine into his own and Nathan's glasses. 'Let me warn you, lad, your uncle Gareth is living on borrowed time right now. The moment you harm one hair of my daughter's head, whatever your motives, you will join him. I haven't got anything to lose and you have rather a lot.'

Nathan glanced across at Victoria, sitting gazing vacantly across the room. 'Have I?' he said.

Corusca was exquisite in the early morning light. The mist enshrouded it like muslin, softening the great crags and dimming the greens to gentleness. Nathan shinned up the mast with the casualness of a boy up a coconut palm, and Jake said ruefully, 'It used to be easy for me once. I wonder if I can still do it?'

Harriet wasn't listening. She was staring out at the island, dreaming to the hush of the wind in the sails. As always, without fail, when she came to Corusca she sloughed off her old life and stepped into a different existence. Had the island spoiled her or would she be nothing without it?

Nathan was looking for the wreck of a fishing boat that was close to the deep-water channel. Life wasn't easy for the fishermen hereabouts, the waters were always treacherous though they looked so kind. He shouted and waved to Jake, who nodded and swung the wheel over. The boat leaned sluggishly, she was hired and designed for idiots. A movement caught Harriet's eye. It was Victoria, standing up to look out at the island. Harriet's heart jumped erratically. What would she give, what wouldn't she give, to have Victoria well?

They moored at the new wooden fishing quay Harriet had paid for. The village was deceptively quiet, in the lull following the early landings from the boats before the shops began trading and the children went to school. She noticed one of the houses had tables outside for pots, another foray into commercialism. Perhaps it pleased her, she wasn't sure. David was there with the pony and trap. Harriet greeted him briefly. They travelled to the house in silence, with only the calls of the birds and the clop, clop, clop of the horse's hooves for company.

The heat multiplied as the day progressed. By lunchtime it was impossible to walk on the sand, and metal left in the sun could not be touched. They lunched desultorily, and the lethargy occasioned by the heat fought with Harriet's restlessness. They were here, they had come. What now?

Nathan said, 'I'll take her this afternoon.'

Jake said, 'I'm coming,' and Harriet added, 'So am I.'

'No. We agreed. I'm taking her alone.'

They stared at him, belligerent and challenging, two people quite unused to relinquishing the reins, who had never found anyone who could do things better than themselves. Harriet nodded abruptly, and got up.

She walked down to the beach, her hands sunk in the pockets of her dress. It was so hot, painfully hot. Where would he take her, what would he do? She ran back to the house and found Jake in the hall, kicking hard at a pillar, hard enough to hurt.

'It's so hot, he won't have taken her hat. She has to have a hat.'

'He took her hat. Oh God, Harriet, in all the things we've done is this the worst?'

She sat down on the stairs. 'Perhaps. I can't remember anything else except putting Mother in a home. Now I can put Victoria in, too.'

'Don't be stupid.' He sat down next to her and took her hand. 'For once let's face something together.'

She said tightly, 'I think I'm too frozen up. Leave me alone, Jake, please.'

After a minute he got up and went away.

Nathan held Victoria's hand and dragged her along the track. Since his boyhood, when it had been trodden into a narrow trail by many feet, it had become overgrown and difficult. Victoria's breathing sounded harsh. She was pulling on his hand, and suddenly he felt an impulse of cruelty. There was no-one to see him now. He dragged her to him and shook her, hard. 'Walk, damn you! Walk!'

She wore only a thin summer dress and a pair of pants. Her breasts jiggled against him and for a second he closed his eyes that were already stinging from the sweat. If they knew what he felt for this girl they would never have let her go, if they knew how hot he was for her. He had wanted her for as long as he could remember, lived for the times he could see her, walk with her. He opened his eyes and looked into her dead face. Taking her hand again he pulled her along the track.

They climbed through the heat of the day and on into the evening. Victoria was moaning with exhaustion, sometimes he almost carried her.

'Since when were you so pathetic?' he demanded. 'You used to half kill yourself before you'd let me win.'

The grey eyes looked up at him with that tantalising glimmer in their depths. 'I want Mummy,' she said.

Nathan pushed her on. 'You can't have Mummy. You can't have her till you wake up. Oh, Victoria, don't you want me?'

They were forcing their way through a spiky thicket. She screamed and wailed again, 'I want Mummy!'

'Go to hell,' he shouted, and fought his way past her, feeling the thorns cutting into his flesh. He reached down and hauled the girl on and through, watching the red lines appear on her bare arms and legs, rejoicing in her pain and her sobbing. They fell together on to a wide, flat rock. Nathan looked around at the plateau, devoid of trees or undergrowth, simply a grassy circle set on a mountainside within the forest. 'They're right, you know,' he whispered, holding Victoria in an iron grip. 'There's nothing I haven't seen.'

When he let her go she curled up into the foetal position, sucking her thumb. He said, 'You're not dead in there, you're hiding. There's nothing to hide from here, it's only me.'

Her eyes followed him, dark and unblinking. If the old Victoria was not there he had hurt and frightened a child.

Nathan stood up and cupped his hands round his mouth. He shouted 'Ho!' and the echo 'Ho! Ho! Ho!' came back to him out of the forest. A flock of bright birds rose up, screeching, and settled again after scant seconds. The sweat trickled into the corners of his mouth, salt as seawater.

A man stepped out of the undergrowth behind the great rock. Nathan went to greet him, stepping over the prone figure of Victoria.

'Hi. I thought you might have given us up.'

Jerome said, 'You have hurt her.'

'Only a little. She wouldn't walk.'

They went together to look down at the girl and she stared up at them, expressionless and unmoving. 'It breaks me up so see her like this,' said Nathan. 'It makes me angry.'

'You've seen it before,' commented Jerome. He bent down and looked at her, waving fingers in front of her eyes, lifting one of her hands and watching it fall again, the only voluntary movement a curling of the fingers. He seemed to find it interesting, but then he said, 'Remember, she is safe now, she is far away from us. I can bring her back, but if she don't want to come she'll not stay. I gave Madeline all that she wished, and I couldn't keep her. I loved that woman.'

Nathan shook his head, still watching Victoria. 'Nobody really loved her, not even me. My mother was a token. Whoever had her felt he had won. And the old man never wanted anything he had had before.'

Jerome crossed to him and put a long black arm around his shoulders. 'Come, man, don't dwell on the past! We make you a pretty girl to love, you can give her the world. You a tough boy, Nathan, you always was. The only one tougher is me.'

Nathan grimaced. 'You don't know Jake.'

'That man! Harriet got him by the nose, though she don't know it. Yeah, he's tough enough but he don't know Corusca! How I missed this beautiful island.' He spread his arms out wide in their sweat-soaked white shirt and strode around the grassy plateau, as if embracing the very air that wrapped the island round.

The sun was dipping behind the mountains. They roused Victoria and gave her water to drink, drawn from a spring that bubbled up under the rock. She was trembling as if ill. Jerome said, 'She must eat nothing. Take care she don't eat berries.'

They set off, climbing again through the forest on a trail only recently trodden down. Victoria was whimpering and hanging back. Again and again Nathan had to drag her forward, and he was not gentle. At last Jerome stopped.

They were before a tiny hut made of branches woven through each other and the surrounding trees. Brushwood filled the spaces in the walls and the floor was a soft bed of dried grass. The entrance was covered with a thin, woven cloth of the type used by the women of the island for wrapping fish. Nathan pushed Victoria into the hut, following close behind.

'Wait,' said Jerome. When he pulled down the door curtain the hut was a dark green cave, the dim light of the forest filtering unevenly through the weave of the cloth.

It grew quite dark. Victoria began to cry, whimpering 'Mummy' like a two year old. Nathan reached out and took her in his arms, but she did not respond. He rubbed himself against her, deliberately seeking arousal. He could have her now and she would not resist. He couldn't understand why he hesitated. All his sexual encounters had been without emotion, bored whores or good-time girls who hung about the sailing yachts to cook and crew and oblige the men by opening their legs when required. Sometimes a girl might seem to like him, but he never stopped to make certain. Feelings were locked away inside him, and this unhappiness, this tenderness he could not explain, had somehow seeped under the bolted door.

The grey eyes stared at him without comprehension and he stared back, just as mystified. He wanted her, how he wanted her, but not like this. He wanted her to love him. 'Why don't you kiss me?' he said. Although she was almost always absolutely obedient, she put her hands in her lap and turned her head away. Nathan hit her full on her black curly head.

Victoria shrieked and fell into the corner, her arms around her ears. Appalled at himself he went to her.

'Leave me alone,' she whispered, cowering down.

He took her arms and shook her. 'You know what I'm saying to you! Victoria, listen to me!'

The curtain drew aside and Jerome came into the hut. Nathan burst out: 'She knows what's going on. I can see from looking at her.'

Jerome lost none of his calm. 'Like I said, she's hiding. Leave her be, man.' He had gathered some plants in a small pot. Working slowly and deliberately he drew aside the curtain and built a small fire outside the door. Then he began stripping the leaves and the bark from the plants he had collected. He threw the parts he did not want on to the fire and they flared up, filling the air with a brief sharp odour. 'Bring her to the fire,' said Jerome, and Nathan went to Victoria. She resisted him, but when he forced her to sit before the flames she stretched out her hands and warmed them. The forest was cold at night, losing its heat quite suddenly.

Jerome worked in the bowl with a large round stone, mashing the material he had collected until it degenerated into fibres and a greasy liquid. He added water from a pot, then tipped the entire contents into a muslin bag. The liquid strained through slowly.

'Why did you add water?' asked Nathan. 'It only makes more to strain.'

'It won't run if it's too thick.' Jerome put his finger into the juice he had collected and tasted it. 'So long since I done this,' he commented.

'Just don't make her worse,' said Nathan.

At last, when almost all the liquid was in the bowl, Jerome made a space in the ashes at the side of the fire and carefully set the bowl to heat. It was very slow to boil and Nathan began to get impatient. 'If we put it further in it would be quicker,' he suggested.

'Has to be slow,' said Jerome. 'This ain't just medicine. This is magic!'

Nathan was all at once aware of where he was. The little hut, so green that it was part of the forest, the blackness all around him that hid night creatures and snakes. Jerome's face was illumined by the flames, his long legs bent like an insect's as he crouched over his concoction. Huge feathery moths singed their wings at the fire, when one brushed Victoria's cheek she threw her head up and gasped. They were very quiet. The liquid in the pot bubbled to thick scum.

Jerome pulled the pot out with quick fingers, turning it on the grass to cool it. Three times this way, four times that, it might have meant something or nothing. He went back into the hut and came out with a tiny wooden flask. Two drops from it were shaken into the bowl and at once the mixture turned deepest red. Food colouring, Nathan's sense told him. Magic, insisted his soul.

'Victoria. Drink.' Jerome squatted beside her and put his long, pink-palmed hand against her cheek. 'Drink,' he said again.

She stared at him almost pleadingly. He said, 'You ain't gonna do no good hiding. I don't promise you sweetness, I don't promise you joy. But I say this to you: pain and sorrow, they like wild dogs. They bite you, here, here, so bad. Then they run, off back to the forest. You know they still there – but they don't bite you every day. And the sun shines, and the fish taste good, and your man lie down with you in the afternoon. Ain't that worth a little bleeding now and then?'

He held the bowl to her lips. She sipped, as if expecting foulness, then she drank. Nathan let out his breath in a long sigh.

Jerome led her to the hut and laid her down on the grass bed. 'You sleep now,' he told her.

Nathan said, 'Won't you stay?'

Jerome stepped out of the circle of light around the fire, his eyes gleaming in the dark. 'I got things to see to. She'll come to in a while. If she like you, she'll stay with you. If she don't there ain't nothing I can do to help you, man.' He turned and went into the forest, swallowed up by the night as if stepping back into the world's primeval youth.

Nathan sat in the doorway of the hut and watched the shadows turn from black to darkest grey, and then to purple. The girl murmured in her sleep again, unhappily. She was increasingly restless and he didn't know what to do. Suddenly she cried out. He turned to see her, eyes wide open, terror marking her face.

'Victoria! It's all right, I'm here. It's me.'

'Oh God. Oh God, oh God.' She put her hands up and began to cry, the tears flooding out of her. Nathan took her in his arms and held her close, thigh to thigh, her breasts against his heart, her smooth cheek against the stubble of his beard. The force of her sobs shook them both.

He longed to get away from her, away from this grief that seemed to pass through to him, that he was breathing with every gasp of air. His breath was coming in dry gulps. He thought he would explode, he thought he was dying. The ball of heat in his chest thrust itself up and out of him, leaving in a wail of agony. For the first time he could ever remember, Nathan wept.

Victoria was as weak and ill as someone recovering from flu. Her head hurt and when Nathan moved the curtain across the door the light flooded in and stabbed her eyes. 'Why isn't there anything to eat?' she asked petulantly. 'I'm so hungry.'

He rummaged in his pockets and found a handful of stale peanuts that he had put there at some time. She ate them one by one. She said, 'I feel so tired. But if I sleep I think I might die. My skin's jumping.'

'I'll rub your arms,' offered Nathan, but she said quickly, 'No thank you. I'm too dirty, I smell.'

The sun was pouring down heat like golden rain. Victoria crawled out of the hut to relieve herself in the bushes. When she came back she lay down in the open and let the sun beat on her, boiling the poisons out. The sweat oozed out of her pores, soaking her thin dress and outlining the contours of a body grown desperately thin. After a while she got up and staggered to the hut. 'I wish I could wash,' she said miserably.

Wanting to touch her and aware that it would be wrong, Nathan said, 'Come to the waterfall. We can wash there.'

'What waterfall? There isn't one on Corusca.'

'There's more to Corusca than anyone knows. It's secret, but I'll take you there. Can you walk?'

She nodded, hugging her arms round herself like someone very sick.

They climbed up through the trees, and once or twice Victoria collapsed and lay gasping against the hillside, her mouth stretched wide as she struggled for air. Nathan said nothing, but waited for her to recover. They went on, through stretches that he barely remembered, travelling further than he had thought. At last they stood on the edge of a ravine, a thin channel cut through the mountainside. High up, where the ravine was deepest, a narrow stream cast itself down over the rock. Below was a black pool, the sides lined with moss and scarlet flowers.

Victoria swayed but did not reach out for Nathan to help her. 'We can't get down there.'

'There's a track. We walk along the bottom to the pool.'

She shrugged, almost despairing. There was a greenish tinge to her skin. Nathan led the way through the undergrowth and down a precipitous path. Now he had to help her, holding her hand and guiding her steps. Once she almost fell and she shrieked and clutched at him. He said, 'You see. I won't let you fall.'

When they reached the stream they struggled along its banks towards the pool. Somehow it had come to be very important that they should get there, although they could easily have washed anywhere. Victoria watched Nathan's back in front of her and remembered the taxi-driver's back as he thrust into Teresa. When he turned to help her she looked at his crotch and thought of Paul, and Jacques Parnasse, and her own hot longing that disgusted her calm self.

They came to the pool and she said, 'I'm so dirty.'

'So am I,' said Nathan. 'We can wash ourselves clean.'

From below the water fell in an erratic chute, churning half the pool into froth and filling the air with its roar. The scarlet flowers were continually soaked by the spray and little birds risked the fall and fed on the nectar in the flowers. Nathan took off his clothes. His penis was distended but not quite erect. Victoria took off her own clothes and dropped them into a dip in the rock where the spray collected. Nathan turned away so she could not see him, and she said, 'You needn't worry, I'm not shocked. I've slept with men.'

'You don't have to tell me,' he said.

'But I want to.' For a new beginning, there must be no old guilt. She stood quite still, her hair a black mat of curls, matched almost exactly by the shadow at the base of her belly. Nathan watched her, entranced and almost wary. She looked unreal.

Victoria said, 'The first was a boy, and he excited me so much. I didn't want him to do it though, and when he did it was like being split in two. The other was a Frenchman and I was drugged. The first time with him I was wild, I behaved so oddly. And he satisfied me. But after that – he used me like a piece of meat. I despised myself, Nathan. I hated myself.'

Because it was so much less than he had feared, he laughed and tossed the shock of blond hair out of his eyes. 'You're so like your mother sometimes, so unforgiving. You've got nothing to be ashamed of.'

He reached down into the pool and splashed the water into silver rain. He said wildly, 'Not even my mother loved me, I've never known love. Suppose that's because of the way I am? I think so sometimes, I think no-one who knows me will ever love me because of what I am. I used to think you loved me once. I used to steal your hair ribbons and keep them in a box. I've had a lot of girls, so many. That isn't making love.'

'Perhaps we ought never to try,' said Victoria. 'If it was just the same then everything would be pointless.'

They stepped gingerly into the freezing pool. The shock of cold water on her skin made Victoria shudder and forced her to breathe in short and painful gasps. As she got used to it she floated in water so green that it was a surprise to lift up an arm and see the drops fall in colourless splashes. She lay on her back to soak her hair, closed her eyes and sank below the surface, the wet hair like waterweed streaming upwards. Nathan swam under the water and took hold of her round the waist. They came up together and she was furious with him. 'Stop it! I can't swim so well, I'll drown!'

'I saved you, I can drown you,' said Nathan, holding her against him.

Her face became very still. 'Don't make me owe you things. It would spoil it if I was grateful.'

He let her go, very slowly. 'Don't hate me,' he said.

'I don't.'

'Victoria, don't hate me, I can't bear it!'

'I don't, I don't. But you're rushing me! I don't know who I am, I don't know who you are!'

He swam to the edge of the pool and drew himself out. 'All I know is, I love you,' he said simply.

She swam around watching him for a while. He sat on a rock, pulling the moss off in handfuls and throwing it into the pool. She thought, This is so like my mother. She never followed her instincts, she reasoned and planned her way to misery. The cold was eating its way into her bones and she swam to the side. Nathan did not reach down to her but sat there, shredding the moss. 'I am grateful,' said Victoria.

The sun was like a warm cloak wrapping itself around her. The little birds twittered amongst the flowers. 'You don't own me and you never will,' she added.

The Hawksworth fingers, Hawksworth through and through, continued their shredding.

'Nathan – ' She reached out and put her hand on his shoulder, her fingers still cold against sun-warmed skin. 'You're part of me. You always have been. As a child I worshipped you. When I was older it was different. I didn't want to get to know you too well. I always knew we were special, but I had to try some things, taste some life. I don't know if this is forever. But right now, what I feel for you is love.'

'I want forever,' he said, and at last his fingers were still.

'Perhaps it is,' whispered Victoria. She bent her head and kissed his brown shoulder, the long, sensual kiss of a grown woman.

On the cliff high above them, Jerome looked down. Two white bodies linked together in the unmistakable spreadeagling of love. He grinned to himself, and shook his head. 'So much fuss,' he said to himself. 'So much fuss.'

Chapter Twelve

The sea had a metallic tinge to it that day, and the air was hazy.

'Storm,' said Jake, and went to stare up at the green hills.

'They must come back.' Harriet stood closer to him than for days. 'If they don't, will you go and look for them?'

'Perhaps. I don't know.'

He went down to see to the hire boat moored in the harbour. Harriet watched him go, wondering what she ought to do or say. Just at the moment she hadn't the mental energy to do anything but worry about Victoria. Even rage had no place when set against anxiety. She felt maimed by worry, less than a whole person. And yet, and yet – sometimes it was hard to stand by yourself, and harder still to abandon the habit that had sustained you for so long. Vulnerability had never brought her anything but pain. She clung to her shell like a crab.

Jake had not returned when they walked down the track. Even at this distance she could see that Victoria was different, because she was walking as she used to do, long-legged and proud. The tears began to course down Harriet's cheeks. She began to wave and shout to them, and she saw them stop, hesitate and come on.

They met in the garden, and clung together. Nathan stood watching, his face closed and expressionless. When mother and daughter parted he reached out and took Victoria's hand. Harriet looked from one to the other. As if to make his point quite obvious, Nathan pulled Victoria in front of him, sliding his arms round her waist like shackles.

'Nothing for nothing,' said Harriet bitterly. 'An old Hawksworth custom.'

'Don't be silly,' said Victoria. 'It isn't like that at all. We love each other.'

'Do you indeed?' Even Harriet was surprised at the venom she injected into the words. She didn't dislike Nathan, she barely knew him, and for what he had done for Victoria she must surely be grateful. She pulled herself together and said, 'Anyway, we must open champagne. Oh, Victoria, it's so wonderful to see you look cross with me! Just like before!'

Jake came back when they were more than a little squiffy. Nathan was talking, his cheeks flushed with champagne and excitement. He kept touching Victoria, as if intent on establishing ownership. 'I've always known Victoria and I were meant for each other, I always knew it was right. She used to wear those sweet white dresses with the frills and I thought she was so pure and good. And I was the poor relation she kept candy for.'

'Hello,' said Jake huskily. They all turned and looked at him.

'Hello,' said Victoria. She blushed to the roots of her hair and looked away. 'I'm better.'

'Yes – yes.' Emotion threatened to choke him and he turned to go. Harriet jumped up and caught his arm. 'Don't be silly, don't go. Stay and be happy.'

He didn't want to join the party, he couldn't bear it. But Harriet held on to him and said, 'Please, Jake. You must. At least we can be a family when we celebrate.'

A thousand words rose in his throat but he swallowed them down. There were things that had to be said, had to be done, but now wasn't the time.

They opened more champagne and the party went on. Victoria and Nathan lounged on a sofa and petted each other, reaching a point at which Harriet became embarrassed. 'Do stop it,' she said jerkily. 'I hope you realise that whatever you feel now might not be real. It's an odd place, Corusca.'

'We love each other,' drawled Nathan, drawing a lazy hand over Victoria's breasts. 'We shall live here forever and have four children.'

'Forty-four,' said Victoria, pulling his head down towards her.

Suddenly, Jake couldn't tolerate any more. He had put up with Nathan thus far, and was going no further. He got up and stood over them. 'You'll get a basket of idiots,' he said viciously, intending to hurt and shock. 'Do you realise, Vic, that Nathan is about as scrambled a load of genes as you're likely to get? By his own admission he's the product of incest between his mother and her father, and the old man's second wife may well have been his half-sister, if the local gossip is anything to go by. I can see you're besotted with each other and that's fine – in himself he seems OK – although I have the feeling that even you don't know him very well. But you don't marry him, and you don't have children.'

Black silence. Harriet became aware that twigs and sand were beating a tattoo against the windows. 'It's blowing,' she said softly.

'Yes. They're forecasting big winds. Victoria, Nathan, you'd better go and get changed, and we'd all better sober up.' He stood over them, solid and uncompromising.

'It isn't my fault,' said Nathan thickly.

'Nobody said it was. If you love her, you'll see that I'm right. I'm sorry.'

Victoria whispered, 'I don't know what to do. I didn't know.'

Suddenly Nathan pushed her aside and lunged at Jake. 'You bastard! Why did you have to spoil things, the one good thing I've ever had? You don't know it would be wrong, but you want it to be!' He swung a wild punch and Jake, survivor of many a brawl, rocked back on his heels to avoid it and then hit him hard in the solar plexus. Nathan fell like a stone.

'Oh God, Jake, do you have to?' screamed Harriet. 'Why now? Why can't you ever do anything right?'

He turned on her furiously. 'Like what? Like let him get her pregnant? There isn't a right time, and the longer you leave it the worse it gets.'

Victoria was sitting with her arms around herself, rocking to and fro.

Nathan pushed himself up on hands and knees, then reached for her, saying, 'It'll be all right. We'll work something out.'

She stared at him, wide-eyed. 'But – if we couldn't have children!'

'Does that matter? Does it matter more than me?'

She wanted to say no, because he needed her to say it. But was Nathan enough? Would he fill up her life forever? Involuntarily she avoided his gaze. A howl began somewhere deep in Nathan's chest.

Jake said, 'Oh Christ, now he's going to bloody cry.'

'Don't be so cruel! You're always so cruel. Nathan hasn't done anything to you!' Harriet clutched at her hair, trying to still the thoughts that whirled in her head. 'Why, why, why do these things keep happening? It's all that bastard Gareth's fault, if it wasn't for him we'd be happy!'

'You cannot blame him for your own inadequacies,' snapped Jake. 'He doesn't make you this greedy. You can't let anyone have anything for themselves. For all I know his attack on Victoria was because of the way you behaved! Look at the way you went after the collection, as if you couldn't bear to let him have one single penny that might be yours. I tell you, Harriet, it has been sickening to watch.'

The injustice of it made her gasp. Was that how it had seemed from the outside? 'It wasn't like that at all,' she said feebly. 'It was his fault. He hurt me.'

'Several million dollars worth of hurt, it seems.'

Her head came up. 'Quite possibly! I don't know what sort of figure you put on rape, let alone the death of an unborn child, let alone all the children I might have had, could have had, WE could have had! How much is that worth, how much hate and misery and pain? One hell of a damn lot, I can tell you!'

Jake stared at her. He licked his lips. Finally he said, 'Why in God's name didn't you tell me?'

Ridiculously she began to cry. It annoyed her. 'I didn't want you to know. He made me feel – I felt so dirty. As if it was my fault. I didn't want you to know how dirty I was. The way it happened was – I thought I would pretend it hadn't happened. I was ill, and afterwards I was different.'

He nodded. 'Yes, you were different. Harder.'

'You could have stayed then,' she said miserably. 'I wanted you then.'

'You could have told me then. But you didn't.'

He felt immeasurably tired. Nathan's head was in Victoria's lap, she was patting his back in a futile attempt at comfort. Where had it all gone wrong? If you looked back along the years you might almost say the mistake was made on the day he and Harriet met. From that day to this they had been misunderstanding each other. How he wished they had done it differently.

The storm raged into the night. A palm tree came down and crashed into the conservatory, letting in the wind and the rain-lashed sea. Part of the roof blew off around dawn and the upstairs floors were a playground for the gale, howling and tearing, blowing out windows and ripping the curtains into shreds that fled into the lightening darkness. They huddled in a room downstairs, a cupboard pushed across the window and their feet lifted out of the water that ran across the floor.

Harriet dozed, aware that Jake did not. Nathan and Victoria lay together on a sofa, because when Victoria lay down Nathan followed and lay beside her. His misery was pathetic and unattractive. Eventually, when Victoria stirred, Harriet said to her, 'Let's go and look at the storm.' They left the room together and went to stand on the windswept landing, looking out at air filled with detritus travelling hectically to nowhere. Harriet said wearily, 'I can't face putting it back together again. I'm too tired.'

'I wish I was in New York,' said Victoria. 'I always feel I can cope with things there.'

'When you were little this was your favourite place.' She put her face dangerously near one of the remaining panes of glass, already creaking under the strain. Victoria pulled her away, saying, 'Don't. Mummy, what am I going to do?'

Harriet sighed. 'I don't know. What you want to do. I'm no judge. I've never felt so lonely and miserable in my life.'

'If you hadn't had me, would you have been happier?'

Her mother put an arm round her shoulders. 'Oh, no. You're worth all the pain, darling, truly you are. I wouldn't have missed a moment of it.'

'That's what I thought.' Victoria tapped a finger against her lips. 'I so hate to hurt Nathan. I really do love him. I just don't know if it's that much.'

'I can't tell you a thing about love,' said Harriet dispiritedly. 'The only thing I have learned for sure in this life is that in the end you have to make your own decisions and then live with the consequences.'

'But you always seem so sure!' exclaimed Victoria.

Harriet laughed. 'Me? Darling, you don't know me at all.'

In the morning Harriet went with Jake to the harbour. The wind was still strong, but the worst of the storm was ended. The people were picking up the pieces of their lives as they had done before and would do again, a thousand times. The hire boat was covered in mud thrown from somewhere, and a fence had landed on it. Jake threw the pieces of wood into the oily waters of the harbour.

'Nathan's in one hell of a state,' he said grimly. 'If we're not careful he'll be the next Hawksworth inmate of some loony bin.'

'Oh God, you don't think so, do you? I thought it was just young love. It hurts so much at that age.'

Jake grinned. 'Tell me when it stops.'

Harriet said nothing. She picked up a broom and began brushing the slime off the deck. 'I don't want to go on,' she said suddenly. 'But there's Gareth.'

Jake said, 'Are we OK talking about him?'

She shrugged. 'Long time ago.'

'I must have been so blind. So bloody stupid. I could kick myself black and blue. Oh, Harriet, I'm sorry.'

'There's nothing to be sorry about,' she said briskly. 'But he won't go away just because I'm being grown up about things. After this last effort, he scares me witless. I think we should tell the police.'

Jake thought for a moment. 'We can't prove a damn thing.'

'Couldn't we try?' She leaned on her broom wistfully. She was getting a little bit fatter, and he thought it suited her. She was like a full-blown rose. He said, 'Why don't we try really hard. Why don't we set it up?'

'Jake – we couldn't!'

He came and took her broom away, using it to send a cascade of mud into the sea. 'We not only can, but will. Now, where would he hate gaol most? It'll have to be the States, he might bribe his way out otherwise and that would be nasty. Yes, I think Gareth's going to have a short and healthy boat-trip.'

'I hope you know what you're doing,' gulped Harriet. 'Don't you end up in prison!'

He grunted noncommittally. Suddenly he looked up at her, his eyes brilliant in his brown face. 'Why did you never let me help you? Why were you always Miss Independence?'

After a moment she said, 'I couldn't let you help me. I would have got used to it. I never yet leaned on you but you didn't move.'

He let out his breath, slowly. 'And I never loved you but you threw it back in my face.'

Jake put to sea that night, and took Nathan with him. That night, too, Jerome came down from the mountains.

Mac sat in the casino and watched sourly as the pile of chips before him diminished. He was playing to lose and it was painful, though remarkably easy. He wondered at the stupidity of the people around him who apparently enjoyed this mindless game, who didn't care that they were regarded as prey by the silky men in evening suits. When he had got through the required five thousand he pushed himself back from the table, ignoring the croupier's offer of cards. She was pretty enough, but the professionalism showed through like steel.

The man near him, who had played the same table for three nights past, also pushed back his chair. 'You're having a bad run.'

'Aye. I should stick to trawling maybe.'

'Yes, I heard you had some boats.'

Over the past few days Mac had allowed it to be known that his trawler fleet, one of the biggest and most successful in Scotland, owed much of its prosperity to a disregard of fishing limits, quotas, and other people's nets. Mac ordered himself a drink, pointedly not offering the stranger anything. 'Are you the law?' he asked.

'What makes you say that?'

'The way you've been hanging around my shirt-tails. But you're a sight too flash maybe. What do you want?'

The man shrugged. 'Depends. Are you interested in doing some business?'

Wrinkling his rather pointed nose, Mac said, 'Oh aye, illegal business.'

'Does that bother you?'

'Not at a price.'

They left the casino together, Mac staying carefully in the light.

'You can trust me,' said his companion.

'Oh aye. Is it drugs?'

'I think we ought to discuss that somewhere private, don't you?' The man smiled, a rather oily smile.

'We'll go to my yacht.'

'That's hardly neutral ground.'

'It's as neutral as I want to be. Take it or leave it.'

Without acceptance as such, they walked together to the harbour, their feet ringing in the silence. The yacht was moored against one of the pontoons out in deep water, a prime and very expensive spot. She towered above the boats around her, beautiful and spectacular. Everyone had noticed her sailing into harbour, a thoroughbred through and through, every inch of her built for speed.

'She's a beautiful boat,' commented the man.

'Aye.' Mac looked around to see who was watching. It was a moonless night, the only light coming from boats or inadequate bulbs strung along the quays. A dog was wandering about, lifting its leg against bollards. Mac stepped smoothly and easily on to the boat. His companion followed awkwardly.

'In here,' said Mac, and stood aside to let him go into the cabin.

Jake and Nathan were sitting in the dark. Jake stuck out a leg and tripped the man conclusively, sending him crashing to the cabin sole. Then he switched on the light. 'Hello, Gareth,' he said softly. 'Remember me?'

'What in God's name – ' Gareth struggled up, blinking like an owl. 'This is ridiculous! What do you want?'

Jake looked at him thoughtfully. 'Difficult to say, really. What do you think, Nathan?'

Nathan reached out and straight-armed Gareth on the shoulder. 'We know what you did to Victoria,' he said softly.

'And to Madeline,' added Mac.

'And to Harriet,' said Jake.

Gareth looked from one to the other. Suddenly he lunged for the door, a fat man made desperate. Jake caught him and hit him twice, the blows sounding sodden against blubbery flesh.

Mac said, 'Easy man. Don't do it yet. Make him suffer.'

Gareth glared up at him. 'No trawler fleet? It doesn't matter, this yacht would do. I can make you a millionaire. Just a few packages, now and then. Don't you want to be rich?'

'I'm rich enough.' Mac went to the galley and cut himself a piece of cheese.

Nathan said 'How long to the tide?'

'An hour.' Jake squatted down beside Gareth. 'You really shouldn't have hurt Harriet, I think that was your biggest mistake. Still, you're going to have a lot of time to think about where you went wrong, and since we don't want you dashing off anywhere let's tie you up.' He picked up a reel of cord.

'It was years ago,' said Gareth. 'She enjoyed it!'

Jake hit him in the mouth, feeling the man's teeth shift against his fist. Nathan took the rope. While Gareth struggled they stripped him completely naked, revealing a white, hairless body. Bending his legs up behind him they tied ankles to wrists. He lay in a distorted circle, and began to sob.

'She took everything! She got what she deserved, they all did! Women are nothing, they don't count. They're to be used. Look what trouble they cause when they get powerful. They pretend they love you, but it's a trick to make them stronger. She was a whore, I had her all the time, she'd let anyone. Madeline was the same, she wouldn't leave me alone, it wasn't my fault! You don't understand what women are like. They're evil!'

The three men stood watching the ranting figure on the floor. Jake went to the cooker and began heating a skewer in the gas flame. Gareth started to scream and Jake said, 'Turn on the radio someone.'

Mac whispered, 'You canna! Have some sense, man.'

Nathan said, 'He must. It's only right.'

Turning off the flame Jake tossed the skewer into the sink and said to Nathan, 'I knew I was right about you. There isn't anything you wouldn't do.'

Nathan said, 'I'd never hurt Victoria.'

They put to sea in the early hours, heading for the Straits of Gibraltar. The winds were light and variable, but the yacht, honed to a nicety, skimmed onward. Mac said, 'I used to think you couldn't build for light airs but you're learning.'

Jake grunted. It was impossible to think about anything but the figure in the cabin, becoming more unhinged with every passing hour. They had dressed him and tied him to a bunk but he talked continually about his childhood, fantasies so terrible that in the end they gave him half a bottle of whisky and sent him to sleep.

'None of it's true,' said Nathan.

Jake said, 'Knowing the old man, it might have been.'

The weather worsened as they moved into the Atlantic. The boat picked up speed and the man in the cabin sat crying and whispering to himself behind the gag. Mac said suddenly, shedding oilskins like layers of thought, 'The poor creature ought to be locked away, where he canna hurt others or himself.'

'That's where he's going,' said Jake. 'I've arranged to pick up a cruiser and some dope in Nassau. Gareth's going to be left as a sitting duck for a coastguard patrol.'

'If we don't get nabbed first,' Mac complained.

Jake grinned. 'Don't worry, I've been careful.'

Nathan said suddenly, 'We ought to kill him. It's only right.'

'Don't be stupid, laddie!' Mac did not like Nathan.

'Look what he did to Victoria. The man's an animal!'

'Listen here,' said Jake softly. 'We are not into murder, torture or anything like that. Let's pretend we're decent, civilised people. We're setting him up to be caught doing what he's been doing for years.'

'But I want revenge,' said Nathan.

Jake snapped at him: 'If my daughter heard you now, she'd know that you and Gareth are more than a touch related. Just shut up and be sensible.'

Nathan was on watch that night. The wind was cold, and it was raining in a thin grey drizzle. Below, Jake and Mac slept while Gareth mumbled to himself.

Jake was woken by a scream. He shot into wakefulness, sitting up and cracking his head on the roof above his bunk. 'What was that? What's happening?' Mac was stumbling upright. Jake pushed past him and out into the grey of dawn.

Nathan was in the very act of propelling Gareth over the rail. The man's hands were tied, but his feet were scrabbling for a foothold on the deck.

'Nathan! For God's sake, no!' Jake leaped forward, and Nathan, realising he was about to be thwarted, gave a convulsive heave. Jake caught at the man's coat, but he couldn't hold him. The cloth slipped from his fingers and Gareth was floating in the sea. His mouth opened and closed.

'Help me!'

In a reflex action Jake flung a ring over the side, then remembered the man's hands were tied. In those waters, at that temperature, he wouldn't live above five minutes.

'I had to. For Victoria,' said Nathan.

Jake shouldered him aside. 'Shut up! Put her round and help me get the dinghy out. Quick!'

But Nathan wouldn't. Mac switched on the deck floodlight and swung the beam over the waves. 'He's gone. We'll no find him now.'

'We can damn well try.'

Between them Mac and Jake turned the boat and came back to the patch of sea where they thought Gareth had gone over. There was no sign of him. After a while they found the ring Jake had thrown to him, and they threw it on board. An hour, two hours, and they knew it was hopeless. Nathan made cocoa.

'Pleased with yourself, are you?' demanded Jake. 'Got what you wanted? I hope it makes you happy.'

The boy stared from under his shock of blond fringe. 'You don't understand. He was a Hawksworth. It was the only way.'

The rain came down again, harder than before. They made sail, taking the cold east wind and using it.

The house, that had stood so long against storms and attack, seemed to be giving up at last. A palm tree had fallen on to the conservatory. Harriet could not rouse herself to have it removed. She went and stood amidst the shattered glass, looking at the segmented bark of the tree and wondering what she ought to do. There was the sound of glass crunching underfoot. She looked up and saw Jerome.

'The island don't like you,' he said.

'It wouldn't like you any better,' she said drily. 'Are you going to help clear this up?'

'What for should I do that? I don't need this big house.'

Exhausted and drained, Harriet sank down on the palm tree trunk. 'Why do you do this to me?' she asked wearily. 'I'm doing a good job here, I love Corusca. You've helped me in the past and I'm grateful. But this is my island. I don't mind you living here, but it belongs to me.'

'I saved your daughter,' said Jerome. 'Nathan didn't know how.'

She nodded. Grimly, miserably, she hammered her fist on the trunk of the tree. Nothing ever came free, it all had to be paid for. Jerome had named his price and it was her own, beloved island.

'What will you do here?' she asked at last.

'The things you should have done. The hotel, the airstrip, the houses. This island's been your playground. The people here need work and good strong houses, so they can stand the storms.'

'I've done so much!' she objected. 'And I've kept it special, and secret.'

'You've done it your way. We'll do it ours.'

She wanted to fight him but had no strength to do it. Vaguely she thought, I owe him Corusca and if the debt isn't paid I shall suffer for it. Jerome claimed the island, Nathan wanted to claim Victoria. The island yes, she had to give it up, it was time, but Victoria would decide for herself what she should do.

Jerome walked away down the beach, and she watched him, dull resentment burning inside her. At last, when he was out of sight, she wandered round the house, taking note of all the changes she had made. Had she done it all wrong? Not meaning to do so was not enough.

Victoria came downstairs with three pieces of broken china in her hands. 'I always loved this. Leah used to keep pot pourri in it.'

'I was jealous of her,' said Harriet. 'You loved her more than me.'

'Not more. I loved her, though.'

'Have you thought about Nathan?' asked Harriet. It was the question she had avoided asking for days.

The girl nodded. 'I've thought. He can't manage without me, Mummy.'

'That's silly! He'd be upset of course, but he'd get over it. My God, I should know.'

'Really!' Victoria looked at her scornfully. 'You've never got over Jake, never. You've spent your whole life proving you can manage without him and hoping he'll come and stop you doing it.'

'I have not!' said Harriet. 'We collide and separate, like snooker balls.' She took the china from her daughter and tried to fit the pieces together. 'What do you want to do? Forgetting Nathan, what about modelling again? You were a tremendous success.'

Victoria considered. 'No. The end was so horrible. I don't think I'll ever go back to Paris.'

'Well, then, college? You still could, darling.'

Victoria shook her head. 'I think – if I had my choice – I'd like to run Hawksworth.'

'What do you mean? *I'm* running Hawksworth!'

'Of course you are. I only said I'd like to.'

Ruffled, Harriet put down the pieces of china. She went out of the house, walking quickly along the beach in the opposite direction to Jerome, her gait uneven because of the rubbish thrown up by the storm. A piece of a boat, a tin can, hundreds of dead crabs. Jerome could have it, the whole horrible island, because it had hurt her and was hurting her. She stopped and stared out at the sea. What was she left?

So had the island appeared the first time he saw it, a long shadow on the sea. On a whim, Jake put the wheel over and ordered shortened sail. They glided elegantly along the island's length, inching closer, mesmerised by the mountains fringed by white beaches, perfect symmetry in design.

'We'll anchor off from the house,' said Jake.

'Don't be so bloody stupid,' said Mac. 'We'll end up on the reef and this boat is worth a bob or two.'

'The wind's settled,' said Nathan. He stood on the foredeck, blond, intense, staring at the island.

Jake gave the wheel to Mac and went to talk to him. 'I want you to leave her alone,' he said bluntly. 'Don't make her share in your bad luck.'

Nathan closed his eyes tight, turning his face away.

They anchored off and swam to the shore. Mac stayed on the boat, watching them and swearing. The two men made it a race, pushing themselves as if their lives depended on it. By a supreme effort of will, Jake won. He stood on the sand, panting, while Nathan followed like a wet dog.

'You mean to take everything from me, and you want me to help you do it,' gasped Nathan.

Jake considered. 'That's about it,' he said at last. 'I think, if you really care for her as you say you do, as I think you do, you'll let her go.'

They walked in silence up to the house. Victoria came out, then Harriet. They came running down the beach.

'We saw the boat! And we haven't made the beds or anything,' cried Victoria. She was wearing a loose white dress that billowed around her. She ran to her father and hugged him. Nathan stood waiting, his hands by his sides, but when Jake released his daughter she stood still, linking her fingers in embarrassment.

Harriet said, 'Why don't you two go and talk?' To avoid the necessity for hugs and kisses, she picked up a green coconut and stood turning it in her fingers.

'Do you want to talk?' asked Nathan. He had thought Jake would do the talking but he said nothing.

Victoria nodded. 'Yes. I think we'd better.'

'Come along, Jake.' Harriet turned and bustled back into the house, still carrying the heavy nut. Jake followed slowly until they reached the dining room. Harriet put the coconut down hard on the gleaming polished table.

'What happened?' she asked jerkily. 'We haven't heard anything.'

'It didn't go as planned,' he said.

'Where is he then?' Her voice trembled. Try as she would, she was still terrified of Gareth.

'He drowned,' said Jake. 'Nathan drowned him.'

Into the silence Harriet croaked, 'Nathan? It was Nathan? Did he mean it?'

'He very much meant it. And – I don't know what to say to Victoria. If she's finished with him it doesn't matter, but if she isn't I think she should know. I want him to tell her himself.'

She let out her breath, very slowly, and sank into a dining chair. 'I'm glad he's gone,' she whispered.

'I wish you'd talked to me when it happened. It explains such a lot.'

She almost smiled. 'I couldn't. But I wish you'd known without me saying, that would have been best. I've made such a mess of everything.'

Jake sat on the table, muscled thighs wide apart. The scar from his broken leg still showed as a blue ridge, after all these years. 'Not everything. Thousands of people have cause to be grateful to you, thousands of people are prosperous because of you. I wish I could say as much.'

'You can,' said Harriet. Then she added, 'Almost.'

'Never give anything away, do you?' said Jake wryly.

Suddenly she said, 'Jerome's having the island actually. I'm giving it to him.'

The words took a little time to sink in. 'Thank God for that,' he said at last. 'I never could see what there was to like about this place. The people here shut you out somehow, have you noticed that?'

'Yes.' Harriet reached out and put her hand on Jake's leg, a firm and deliberate contact. 'What are you going to do?' she asked stiffly. 'Before, in France, when you were upset, I wanted to say – I wanted to help. But I couldn't. And you got by. And over Victoria, you wanted to help me and I wanted you to, but again – I couldn't. And I got by. But I wish it had been different.'

He picked up her hand and held it, light, almost impersonal contact.

'Well, that's the way it goes. By the way, I'm giving Mac the day to day running of the business. The yard's going to build a few ordinary bread and butter boats for a change, give themselves a base. The feeling is that it's too damned risky doing it my way all the time. Once you get big it's not your firm any more and you don't call the tune.'

'I know,' said Harriet ruefully. 'You told me that years ago and I didn't believe you. There comes a time when it's best to step aside and let other people see what they can do. It is hard, though.'

Jake looked at her oddly. She was wearing a plain cotton blouse, the rough island cotton that scratched, and a washed-out denim skirt. It was years since he had seen her anything other than elegant. 'You look about twenty-five,' he said suddenly. 'Younger than when I met you.'

She grinned. 'I got tired of being Mrs. Hawksworth. I've been her so long I'd forgotten to be me. Incidentally, you're not the only one out of a job. Hawksworth Inc. has a brand new head.'

'My God, you're not letting Victoria loose on it! They'll be bankrupt within a week!'

She pulled her hand free and stood up. 'Not Victoria, no. It's a Hawksworth company, it should belong to a Hawksworth. Nathan.'

Jake breathed in and out through his nose. Then he said, 'That's fair. More than fair. I didn't think you had it in you.'

'I think you have to stand on the edge of disaster to see what is really important,' she said softly. 'I nearly lost Victoria. That frightened me so much. But I realised it would frighten me a great deal more to lose you.'

'Don't be stupid,' he said roughly. 'We've been lost to each other for more years than we can count.'

Harriet's eyes were brilliant. 'Have we? I used to think that but I don't any more. Most people have threads that keep them together, lots and lots of them. We only seem to have had Victoria – but even she wasn't really a thread. We didn't need them. You matter to me, Jake, and you always have.'

He came across and hugged her. 'I know that. We got tangled up once and we've never got free, but what use is it? We can't get on together.'

'We only ever tried once, and we didn't try very hard,' said Harriet in a muffled voice.

There was a silence. Jake said, 'Every time I make this offer you say no.'

Harriet said, 'You just never make the right offer at the right time. It's always in the middle of things. Anyway, you've turned me down as often as I have you.'

Jake laughed. 'Who's counting? Look, I'm not sure I want to take up with an unemployed woman with a doubtful past.'

'And I've nowhere to live,' said Harriet, pushing her chin on to his chest. 'Victoria can have the New York apartment.'

'And I'm letting Mac have the cottage, he's wanted it for years. All I've got is a boat just at present.'

'Does it leak?' asked Harriet. 'I don't like it when they leak.'

Jake said cautiously, 'Not as yet. But we can take it a few places and see what happens, if you like.'

They went hand in hand on to the terrace and stood looking out at the yacht bobbing gently at anchor beyond the reef. Far down the beach two people walked, heads bent in conversation.

'I always thought I'd keep her safe,' said Harriet wildly. 'I didn't ever mean this to happen to her.'

Jake took her face between his hands. 'You can blame me as much as you. It should have been different, and somehow it wasn't. We can't change it now.'

She locked her arms tight around his waist. 'All our eggs are in one basket and the basket won't do as it's told. Her father's child, she is.'

'Her mother's daughter,' retorted Jake.

They walked down to the beach together, slowly making their way towards the distant figures. Jake said, 'I want her to find a nice bloke, a lawyer or something, and get married and have four kids and perhaps start a fashion shop.'

Harriet laughed at him. 'I wish we'd had four children. I wish I'd started a fashion shop.'

'So do I. And she'll do what she wants, I suppose.' He sighed ruefully. Then he said, 'I think it's time we got married, you know.'

Harriet swallowed. 'Well – we could. An end to all things Hawksworth.'

'And about time too,' said Jake. 'Will you leave me when I'm old and grey?'

Harriet scuffed at the pure white grains of sand. 'I wasn't thinking of leaving you ever.'

There was a shell on the beach in front of them. Still wet from the sea it gleamed as pink as an English spring dawn. She reached down and picked it up, thinking how strange it was that out of chaos, betrayal and despair there could still be hope. Perhaps for all of them there could be a new beginning.